THREE TO SHOW

THREE TO SHOW

A TRILOGY
by
Dick Francis

Harper & Row, Publishers
New York and Evanston

A JOAN KAHN–HARPER NOVEL OF SUSPENSE

This work consists of three books which were first published in England. *Dead Cert* appeared in 1962, followed by *Nerve* in 1964 and *Odds Against* in 1965.

THREE TO SHOW. Copyright © 1962, 1964, 1965, 1969 by Dick Francis. All rights reserved. Printed in the United States of America. No part of this book may be used or reproduced in any manner whatsoever without written permission except in the case of brief quotations embodied in critical articles and reviews. For information address Harper & Row, Publishers, Incorporated, 49 East 33rd Street, New York, N.Y. 10016. Published simultaneously in Canada by Fitzhenry & Whiteside Limited, Toronto.

CONTENTS

One DEAD CERT   1

Two NERVE   225

Three ODDS AGAINST   443

THREE TO SHOW

ONE

DEAD CERT

1

The mingled smells of hot horse and cold river mist filled my nostrils. I could hear only the swish and thud of galloping hooves and the occasional sharp click of horse-shoes striking against each other. Behind me, strung out, rode a group of men dressed like myself in white silk breeches and harlequin jerseys, and in front, his body vividly red and green against the pale curtain of fog, one solitary rider steadied his horse to jump the birch fence stretching blackly across his path.

All, in fact, was going as expected. Bill Davidson was about to win his ninety-seventh steeplechase. Admiral, his chestnut horse, was amply proving he was still the best hunter 'chaser in the kingdom, and I, as often before, had been admiring their combined back view for several minutes.

Ahead of me the powerful chestnut hindquarters bunched, tensed, sprang: Admiral cleared the fence with the effortlessness of the really great performer. And he'd gained another two lengths, I saw, as I followed him over. We were down at the far end of Maidenhead racecourse with more than half a mile to go to the winning post. I hadn't a hope of catching him.

The February fog was getting denser. It was now impossible to see much farther than from one fence to the next, and the silent surrounding whiteness seemed to shut us, an isolated string of riders, into a private lonely limbo. Speed was the only reality. Winning post, crowds, stands and stewards, left behind in the mist, lay again invisibly ahead, but on the long deserted mile and a half circuit it was quite difficult to believe they were really there.

It was an eerie, severed world in which anything might happen. And something did.

We rounded the first part of the bend at the bottom of the racecourse and straightened to jump the next fence. Bill was a good ten lengths in front of me and the other horses, and hadn't exerted himself. He seldom needed to.

The attendant at the next fence strolled across the course from the outside to the inside, patting the top of the birch as he went, and ducked under the rails. Bill glanced back over his shoulder and I saw the flash of his teeth as he smiled with satisfaction to see me so far behind. Then he turned his head towards the fence and measured his distance.

Admiral met the fence perfectly. He rose to it as if flight were not only for birds.

And he fell.

Aghast, I saw the flurry of chestnut legs threshing the air as the horse pitched over in a somersault. I had a glimpse of Bill's bright-clad figure hurtling head downwards from the highest point of his trajectory, and I heard the crash of Admiral landing upside down after him.

Automatically I swerved over to the right and kicked my horse into the fence. In mid-air, as I crossed it, I looked down at Bill. He lay loosely on the ground with one arm outstretched. His eyes were shut. Admiral had fallen solidly, back downwards, across Bill's unprotected abdomen, and he was rolling backwards and forwards in a frantic effort to stand up again.

I had a brief impression that something lay beneath them. Something incongruous, which ought not to be there. But I was going too fast to see properly.

As my horse pressed on away from the fence, I felt as sick as if I'd been kicked in the stomach myself. There had been a quality about that fall which put it straight into the killing class.

I looked over my shoulder. Admiral succeeded in getting to his feet and cantered off loose, and the attendant stepped forward and bent over Bill, who still lay motionless on the ground. I turned back to attend to the race. I had been left in front and I ought to stay there. At the side of the course a black-suited, white-sashed First-Aid man was running towards and past me. He had been standing at the fence I was now approaching, and was on his way to help Bill.

I booted my horse into the next three fences, but my heart was no longer in it, and when I emerged as the winner into the full view of the crowded stands, the mixed gasp and groan which greeted me seemed an apt enough welcome. I passed the winning post, patted my mount's neck, and looked at the stands. Most heads were still turned towards the last fence, searching in the impenetrable mist for Admiral, the odds-on certainty who had lost his first race for two years.

Even the pleasant middle-aged woman whose horse I was riding met me with the question "What happened to Admiral?"

"He fell," I said.

"How lucky," said Mrs. Mervyn, laughing happily.

She took hold of the bridle and led her horse into the winner's unsaddling enclosure. I slid off and undid the girth buckles with fingers clumsy from shock. She patted the horse and chattered on about how delighted she was to have won, and how unexpected it was, and how fortunate that Admiral had tripped up for a change, though a great pity in another way, of course.

I nodded and smiled at her and didn't answer, because what I would have said would have been savage and unkind. Let her enjoy her win, I thought. They come seldom enough. And Bill might, after all, be all right.

I tugged the saddle off the horse and, leaving a beaming Mrs. Mervyn receiving congratulations from all around, pressed through the crowd into the weighing room. I sat on the scales, was passed as correct, walked into the changing room, and put my gear down on the bench.

Clem, the racecourse valet who looked after my stuff, came over. He was a small elderly man, very spry and tidy, with a weather-beaten face and wrists whose tendons stood out like tight strung cords.

He picked up my saddle and ran his hand caressingly over the leather. It was a habit he had grown into, I imagined, from long years of caring for fine-grained skins. He stroked a saddle as another man would a pretty girl's cheek, savouring the suppleness, the bloom.

"Well done, sir," he said; but he didn't look overjoyed.

I didn't want to be congratulated. I said abruptly, "Admiral should have won."

"Did he fall?" asked Clem anxiously.

"Yes," I said. I couldn't understand it, thinking about it.

"Is Major Davidson all right sir?" asked Clem. He valeted Bill too and, I knew, looked upon him as a sort of minor god.

"I don't know," I said. But the hard saddle-tree had hit him plumb in the belly with the weight of a big horse falling at thirty miles an hour behind it. What chance has he got, poor beggar, I thought.

I shrugged my arms into my sheepskin coat and went along to the First-Aid room. Bill's wife, Scilla, was standing outside the door there, pale and shaking and doing her best not to be frightened. Her small neat figure was dressed gaily in scarlet, and a mink hat sat provocatively on top of her cloudy dark curls. They were clothes for success, not sorrow.

"Alan," she said, with relief, when she saw me. "The doctor's looking at him and asked me to wait here. What do you think? Is he bad?" She was pleading, and I hadn't much comfort to give her. I put my arm round her shoulders.

She asked me if I had seen Bill fall, and I told her he had dived on to his head and might be slightly concussed.

The door opened, and a tall slim well-groomed man came out. The doctor.

"Are you Mrs. Davidson?" he said to Scilla. She nodded.

"I'm afraid your husband will have to go along to the hospital," he said. "It wouldn't be sensible to send him home without an X-ray." He smiled reassuringly, and I felt some of the tension go out of Scilla's body.

"Can I go in and see him?" she said.

The doctor hesitated. "Yes," he said finally, "but he's almost unconscious. He had a bit of a bang on the head. Don't try to wake him."

When I started to follow Scilla into the First-Aid room the doctor put his hand on my arm to stop me.

"You're Mr. York, aren't you?" he asked. He had given me a regulation check after an easy fall I'd had the day before.

"Yes."

"Do you know these people well?"

"Yes. I live with them most of the time."

The doctor closed his lips tight, thinking. Then he said, "It's not good. The concussion's not much, but he's bleeding internally, possibly from a ruptured spleen. I've telephoned the hospital to take him in as an emergency case as soon as we can get him there."

As he spoke, one of the racecourse ambulances backed up towards us. The men jumped out, opened the rear doors, took out a big stretcher and carried it into the First-Aid room. The doctor went in after them. Soon they all reappeared with Bill on the stretcher. Scilla followed, the anxiety plain on her face, deep and well-founded.

Bill's firm brown humorous face now lolled flaccid, bluish-white, and covered with fine beads of sweat. He was gasping slightly through his open mouth, and his hands were restlessly pulling at the blanket which covered him. He was still wearing his green and red checked racing colours, the most ominous sign of all.

Scilla said to me, "I'm going with him in the ambulance. Can you come?"

"I've a ride in the last race," I said. "I'll come along to the hospital straight after that. Don't worry, he'll be all right." But I didn't believe it, and nor did she.

After they had gone I walked along beside the weighing room building and down through the car park until I came to the bank of the river. Swollen from recently melted snow, the Thames was flowing fast, sandy brown and grey with froths of white. The water swirled out of the mist a hundred yards to my right, churned round the bend where I stood and disappeared again into the fog. Troubled, confused, not seeing a clear course ahead. Just like me.

For there was something wrong about Bill's accident.

Back in Bulawayo where I got my schooling, the mathematics master spent hours (too many, I thought in my youth) teaching us to draw correct inferences from a few known facts. But deduction was his hobby as well as his job, and occasionally we had been able to side-track him from problems of geometry or algebra to those of Sherlock Holmes. He produced class after class of boys keenly observant of well worn toe-caps on charwomen and vicars and calluses on the finger tips of harpists; and the mathematics standard of the school was exceptionally high.

Now, thousands of miles and seven years away from the sunbaked schoolroom, standing in an English fog and growing very cold, I remembered my master and took out my facts, and had a look at them.

Known facts . . . Admiral, a superb jumper, had fallen abruptly in full flight for no apparent reason. The racecourse attendant had walked across the course behind the fence as Bill and I rode towards it, but this was not at all unusual. And as I had cleared the fence, and while I was looking down at Bill, somewhere on the edge of my vision there had been a dull damp gleam from something grey and metallic. I thought about these things for a long time.

The inference was there all right, but unbelievable. I had to find out if it was the correct one.

I went back into the weighing room to collect my kit and weigh out for the last race, but as I packed the flat lead pieces into my weight cloth to bring my weight up to that set by the handicapper, the loudspeakers were turned on and it was announced that owing to the thickening fog the last race had been abandoned.

There was a rush then in the changing room and the tea and fruit-cake disappeared at a quickened tempo. It was a long time since breakfast, and I stuffed a couple of beef sandwiches into my mouth while I changed. I arranged with Clem for my kit to go to Plumpton, where I was due to ride four days later, and set off on an uninviting walk. I wanted to have a close look at the place where Bill had fallen.

It is a long way on foot from the stands to the far end of Maidenhead racecourse, and by the time I got there my shoes, socks and trouser legs were wet through from the long sodden grass. It was very cold, very foggy. There was no one about.

I reached the fence, the harmless, softish, easy-to-jump fence, made of black birch twigs standing upright. Three feet thick at the bottom slanting to half that size at the top, four feet six inches tall, about ten yards wide. Ordinary, easy.

I looked carefully along the landing side of the fence. There was nothing unusual. Round I went to the take-off side. Nothing. I poked around the wing which guides the horses into the fence, the one on the inside of the course, the side Bill had been when he fell. Still nothing.

It was down underneath the wing on the outside of the course that I found what I was looking for. There it lay in the long grass, half hidden, beaded with drops of mist, coiled and deadly.

Wire.

There was a good deal of it, a pale silver grey, wound into a ring about a foot across, and weighted down with a piece of wood. One end of it led up the main side post of the wing and was fastened round it two feet above the level of the top of the birch. Fastened, I saw, very securely indeed. I could not untwist it with my fingers.

I went back to the inside wing and had a look at the post. Two feet above the fence there was a groove in the wood. This post had once been painted white, and the mark showed clearly.

It was clear to me that only one person could have fixed the wire in place. The attendant. The man whom I myself had seen walk across from one side of the course to the other. The man, I thought bitterly, whom I had left to *help* Bill.

In a three mile 'chase at Maidenhead one rode twice round the course. On the first circuit there had been no trouble at this fence. Nine horses had jumped it safely, with Admiral lying third and biding his time, and me riding alongside telling Bill I didn't think much of the English climate.

Second time round, Admiral was lengths out in front. As soon as the attendant had seen him land over the fence before this one, he must have walked over holding the free end of wire and wound it round the opposite post so that it stretched there taut in the air, almost invisible, two feet above the birch. At that height it would catch the high-leaping Admiral straight across the shoulders.

The callousness of it awoke a slow deep anger which, though I did not then know it, was to remain with me as a spur for many weeks to come.

Whether the horse had snapped the wire when he hit it, or pulled it off the post, I could not be sure. But as I could find no separate pieces, and the coil by the outer wing was all one length, I thought it likely that the falling horse had jerked the less secure end down with him. None of the seven horses following me had been brought down. Like me, they must have jumped clear over the remains of the trap.

Unless the attendant was a lunatic, which could by no means be ruled out, it was a deliberate attack on a particular horse and rider. Bill on Admiral had normally reached the front by this stage in a race, often having opened up a lead of twenty lengths, and his red and green colours, even on a misty day, were easy to see.

At this point, greatly disturbed, I began the walk back. It was already growing dark. I had been longer at the fence than I had realised, and when I at length reached the weighing room, intending to tell the Clerk of the Course about the wire, I found everyone except the caretaker had gone.

The caretaker, who was old and bad-tempered and incessantly sucked his teeth, told me he did not know where the Clerk of the Course could be found. He said the racecourse manager had driven off towards the town five minutes earlier. He did not know where the manager had been going, nor when he would be back; and with a grumbling tale that he had five separate stoves besides the central boiler to see to, and that the fog was bad for his bronchitis, the caretaker shuffled purposefully off towards the dim murky bulk of the grandstand.

Undecided, I watched him go. I ought, I knew, to tell someone in authority about the wire. But who? The Stewards who had been at the meeting were all on their way home, creeping wearily through the fog, unreachable. The manager had gone; the Clerk of the Course's office, I discovered, was locked. It would take me a long time to locate any of them, persuade them to return to the racecourse and get them to drive down the course over the rough ground in the dark; and after that there would be discussion, repetition, statements. It would be hours before I could get away.

Meanwhile Bill was fighting for his life in Maidenhead hospital, and I wanted profoundly to know if he were winning. Scilla faced racking hours of anxiety and I had promised to be with her as soon as I could. Already I had delayed too long. The wire, fog-bound and firmly twisted round the post, would keep until tomorrow, I thought; but Bill might not.

Bill's Jaguar was alone in the car park. I climbed in, switched on the side lights and the fog lights and drove off. I turned left at the gates, went gingerly along the road for two miles, turned left again over the river, twisted through Maidenhead's one way streets, and finally arrived at the hospital.

There was no sign of Scilla in the brightly lit busy hall. I asked the porter.

"Mrs. Davidson? Husband a jockey? That's right, she's down there in the waiting room. Fourth door on the left."

I found her. Her dark eyes looked enormous, shadowed with grey smudges beneath them. All other colour had gone from her sad strained face, and she had taken off her frivolous hat.

"How is he?" I asked.

"I don't know. They just tell me not to worry." She was very close to tears.

I sat down beside her and held her hand.

"You're a comfort, Alan," she said.

Presently the door opened and a fair young doctor came in, stethoscope dangling.

"Mrs. Davidson, I think . . ." he paused, "I think you should come and sit with your husband."

"How is he?"

"Not . . . very well. We are doing all we can." Turning to me he said, "Are you a relative?"

"A friend. I am going to drive Mrs. Davidson home."

"I see," he said. "Will you wait, or come back for her? Later this evening." There was meaning in his careful voice, his neutral words. I looked closely into his face, and I knew that Bill was dying.

"I'll wait."

"Good."

I waited for four hours, getting to know intimately the pattern of the curtains and the cracks in the brown linoleum. Mostly, I thought about wire.

At last a nurse came, serious, young, pretty.

"I am so sorry . . . Major Davidson is dead."

Mrs. Davidson would like me to go and see him, she said, if I would follow her. She took me down the long corridors, and into a white room, not very big, where Scilla sat beside the single bed.

Scilla looked up at me. She couldn't speak.

Bill lay there, grey and quiet, finished. The best friend a man could wish for.

2

Early next morning I drove Scilla, worn out from the vigil she had insisted on keeping all night beside Bill's body, and heavily drugged now with sedatives, home to the Cotswolds. The children came out and met her on the doorstep, their three faces solemn and round-eyed. Behind them stood Joan, the briskly competent girl who looked after them, and to whom I had telephoned the news the evening before.

There on the step Scilla sat down and wept. The children knelt and sat beside her, putting their arms round her, doing their best to comfort a grief they could only dimly understand.

Presently Scilla went upstairs to bed. I drew the curtains for her and tucked her in, and kissed her cheek. She was exhausted and very sleepy, and I hoped it would be many hours before she woke again.

I went along to my own room and changed my clothes. Downstairs I found Joan putting coffee, bacon and eggs and hot rolls for me on the kitchen table. I gave the children the chocolate bars I had bought for them the previous morning (how very long ago it seemed) and they sat with me, munching, while I ate my breakfast. Joan poured herself some coffee.

"Alan?" said William. He was five, the youngest, and he would never go on speaking until you said "Yes?" to show you were listening.

"Yes?" I said.

"What happened to Daddy?"

So I told them about it, all of it except the wire.

They were unusually silent for a while. Then Henry, just eight, asked calmly, "Is he going to be buried or burnt?"

Before I could answer, he and his elder sister Polly launched into a heated and astonishingly well-informed discussion about the respective merits of burial and cremation. I was horrified, but relieved too, and Joan, catching my eye, was hard put to it not to laugh.

The innocent toughness of their conversation started me on my way back to Maidenhead in a more cheerful frame of mind. I put Bill's big car in the garage and set off in my own little dark blue Lotus. The fog had completely gone, but I drove slowly (for me), working out what was best to do.

First I called at the hospital. I collected Bill's clothes, signed forms, made arrangements. There was to be a routine post mortem examination the next day.

It was Sunday. I drove to the racecourse, but the gates were locked. Back in the town the Clerk of the Course's office was shut and empty. I telephoned his home, but there was no answer.

After some hesitation I rang up the Senior Steward of the National Hunt Committee, going straight to the top steeplechase authority. Sir Creswell Stampe's butler said he would see if Sir Creswell was available. I said it was very important that I should speak with him. Presently he came on the line.

"I certainly hope what you have to say *is* very important, Mr. York. I am in the middle of luncheon with my guests."

"Have you heard, sir, that Major Davidson died yesterday evening?"

"Yes. I'm very sorry about it, very sorry indeed." He waited. I took a deep breath.

"His fall wasn't an accident," I said.

"What do you mean?"

"Major Davidson's horse was brought down by wire," I said.

I told him about my search at the fence, and what I had found there.

"You have let Mr. Dace know about this?" he asked. Mr. Dace was the Clerk of the Course.

I explained that I had been unable to find him.

"So you rang me. I see." He paused. "Well, Mr. York, if you are right, this is too serious to be dealt with entirely by the National Hunt Committee. I think you should inform the police in Maidenhead without delay. Let me know this evening, without fail, what is happening. I will try to get in touch with Mr. Dace."

I put down the receiver. The buck had been passed, I thought. I could imagine the Stampe roast beef congealing on the plate while Sir Creswell set the wires humming.

The police station in the deserted Sunday street was dark, dusty-looking and uninviting. I went in. There were three desks behind the counter, and at one of them sat a young constable reading a newspaper of the juicier sort. Keeping up with his crime, I reflected.

"Can I help you sir?" he said, getting up.

"Is there anyone else here?" I asked. "I mean, someone senior? It's about a . . . a death."

"Just a minute sir." He went out of a door at the back, and returned to say, "Will you come in here, please?"

He stood aside to let me into a little inner office, and shut the door behind me.

The man who rose to his feet was small for a policeman, thick-set, dark, and in his late thirties. He looked more of a fighter than a thinker, but I found later that his brain matched his physique. His desk was littered with papers and heavy looking law books. The gas fire had made a comfortable warm fug, and his ashtray was overflowing. He, too, was spending his Sunday afternoon reading up crime.

"Good afternoon. I am Inspector Lodge," he said. He gestured to a chair facing his desk, asking me to sit down. He sat down again himself, and began to shape his papers into neat piles.

"You have come about a death?" My own words, repeated, sounded foolish, but his tone was matter-of-fact.

"It's about a Major Davidson . . ." I began.

"Oh yes. We had a report. He died in the hospital last night after a fall at the races." He waited politely for me to go on.

"That fall was engineered," I said bluntly.

Inspector Lodge looked at me steadily, then drew a sheet of paper out of a drawer, unscrewed his fountain pen, and wrote, I could see, the date and the time. A methodical man.

"I think we had better start at the beginning," he said. "What is your name?"

"Alan York."

"Age?"

"Twenty-four."

"Address?"

I gave Davidsons' address, explaining whose it was, and that I lived there a good deal.

"Where is your own home?"

"In Southern Rhodesia," I said. "On a cattle station near a village called Induna, about fifteen miles from Bulawayo."

"And you are a professional jockey?"

"No, an amateur. I work in London three days or so a week."

"Occupation?"

"I represent my father in his London office."

"And your father's business?"

"The Bailey York Trading Company."

"What do you trade in?" asked Lodge.

"Copper, lead, cattle. Anything and everything. We're transporters mainly," I said.

He wrote it all down, in quick distinctive script.

"Now then," he put down the pen, "what is it all about?"

"I don't know what it's about," I said, "but this is what happened." I told him the whole thing. He listened without interrupting, then he said, "What made you even begin to suspect that this was not a normal fall?"

"Admiral is the safest jumper there is. He's surefooted, like a cat. He doesn't make mistakes."

But I could see from his politely surprised expression that he knew little, if anything, about steeplechasing, and thought that one horse was as likely to fall as another.

I tried again. "Admiral is brilliant over fences. He would never fall like that, going into an easy fence in his own time, not being pressed. He took off perfectly. I saw him. That fall was unnatural. It looked to me as though something had been used to bring him down. I thought it might be wire, and I went back to look, and it was. That's all."

"Hm. Was the horse likely to win?" asked Lodge.

"Certain," I said.

"And who did win?"

"I did," I said.

Lodge paused, and bit the end of his pen.

"How do the racecourse attendants get their jobs?" he asked.

"I don't really know. They are casual staff, taken on for the meeting, I think," I said.

"Why would a racecourse attendant wish to harm Major Davidson?" He said this naively, and I looked at him sharply.

"Do you think I have made it all up?" I asked.

"No." He sighed. "I suppose I don't. Perhaps I should have said, how difficult would it be for someone who wished to harm Major Davidson to get taken on as a racecourse attendant?"

"Easy," I said.

"We'll have to find out." He reflected. "It's a very chancy way to murder a man."

"Whoever planned it can't have meant to kill him," I said flatly.

"Why not?"

"Because it was so unlikely that he would die. I should think it was simply meant to stop him winning."

"Why was such a fall unlikely to result in death?" said Lodge. "It sounds highly dangerous to me."

I said: "It could have been meant to injure him, I suppose. Usually, when a horse is going fast and hits a fence hard when you're not expecting it, you get catapulted out of the saddle. You fly through the air and hit the ground way out in front of where your horse falls. That may do a lot of damage, but it doesn't often kill. But Bill Davidson wasn't flung off forwards. His toe may have stuck in his stirrup, though that's not very likely. Perhaps the wire caught round his leg and pulled him back. Anyway, he fell straight down and his horse crashed on top of him. Even then it was sheer bad luck that the saddle tree hit him in the stomach. You couldn't even hope to kill a man like that on purpose."

"I see. You seem to have given it some thought."

"Yes." The pattern of the hospital waiting room curtains, the brown linoleum, came back into my mind in association.

"Can you think of anyone who might wish to hurt Major Davidson?" asked Lodge.

"No," I said. "He was very well liked."

Lodge got up and stretched. "We'll go and have a look at your wire," he said. He put his head out into the big office. "Wright, go and see if Hawkins is there, and tell him I want a car if there's one available."

There was a car. Hawkins (I presumed) drove; I sat in the back with Lodge. The main gates of the racecourse were still locked, but there were ways and means, I found. A police key opened another, inconspicuous, gate in the wooden fence.

"In case of fire," said Lodge, seeing my sideways look.

There was no one about in the racecourse buildings: the manager was out. Hawkins drove over the course into the centre and headed down towards the farthest fence. We bumped a good deal on the uneven ground. The car drew up just short of the inside wing, and Lodge and I climbed out.

I led the way past the fence to the outer wing.

"The wire is over here," I said.

But I was wrong.

There was the post, the wing, the long grass, the birch fence. And no coil of wire.

"Are you sure this is the right fence?" said Lodge.

"Yes," I said. We stood looking at the course set out in front of us. We were at the very far end, the stands a blurred massive block in the distance. The fence by which we stood was alone on a short straight between two curves, and the nearest fence to us was three hundred yards to the left, round a shallow bend.

"You jump that fence," I said, pointing away to it. "Then there's quite a long run, as you can see, to this one." I patted the fence beside us. "Then twenty yards after we land over this one there is that sharpish left turn into the straight. The next fence is some way up the straight, to allow the horses to balance themselves properly after coming round the bend, before they have to jump. It's a good course."

"You couldn't have made a mistake in the mist?"

"No. This is the fence," I said.

Lodge sighed. "Well, we'll take a closer look."

But all there was to be seen was a shallow groove on the once white inner post, and a deeper groove on the outer post, where the wire had bitten into the wood. Both grooves needed looking for and would ordinarily have been unnoticed. Both were at the same level, six feet, six inches from the ground.

"Very inconclusive indeed," said Lodge.

We went back to Maidenhead in silence. Glum and feeling foolish, I knew now that even though I could reach no one in authority, I should have found someone, anyone, even the caretaker, the day before, to go back to the fence with me, after I had found the wire, to see it in its place. A witness who had seen wire fastened to a fence, even though it would have been dark and foggy, even though perhaps he could not swear at which fence he had seen it, would definitely have been better than no witness at all. I tried to console myself with the possibility that the attendant had been returning to the fence with his wire clippers at the same time that I was walking back to the stands, and that even if I had returned at once with a witness, it would already have been too late.

From Maidenhead police station I called Sir Creswell Stampe. I had parted him this time, he said, from his toasted muffins. The news that the wire had disappeared didn't please him either.

"You should have got someone else to see it at once. Photographed it. Removed it. We can't proceed without evidence. I can't think why you didn't have sense enough to act more quickly, either. You have been very irresponsible, Mr. York." And with these few kind words he put down his receiver.

Depressed, I drove home.

I put my head quietly round Scilla's door. Her room was dark, but I could hear her even breathing. She was still sound asleep.

Downstairs Joan and the children were sitting on the floor in front of the welcoming log fire playing poker. I had introduced them to the game one rainy day when the children were tired of snap and rummy and had been behaving very badly, quarrelling and shouting and raising tempers all round. Poker, the hitherto mysterious game of the cowboys in Westerns, had worked a miracle.

Henry developed in a few weeks into the sort of player you wouldn't sit down with twice without careful thought. His razor-sharp mathematical mind knew the odds to a fraction against any particular card turning up; his visual memory was formidable; and his air of slight bewilderment, calculated to be misleading, led many an unsuspecting adult straight into his traps. I admired Henry. He could out-bluff an angel.

Polly played well enough for me to be sure she would never lose continually in ordinary company, and even William knew a running flush from a full house.

They had been at it for some time. Henry's pile of poker chips was, as usual, three times as big as anyone else's.

Polly said, "Henry won all the chips a little while ago, so we had to share them out and start all over again."

Henry grinned. Cards were an open book to him and he couldn't help reading.

I took ten of Henry's chips and sat in with them. Joan dealt. She gave me a pair of fives and I drew another one. Henry discarded and drew two cards only, and looked satisfied.

The others threw in during the first two rounds. Then I boldly advanced two more chips to join the two on the table. "Raise you two, Henry," I said.

Henry glanced at me to make sure I was looking at him, then made a great show of indecision, drumming his fingers on the table and sighing. Knowing his habit of bluffing, I suspected he had a whopper of a hand and was scheming how to get me to disgorge the largest possible number of chips.

"Raise you one," he said at last.

I was just about to put another two chips firmly out, but I stopped and said, "Oh no you don't, Henry. Not this time," and I threw in my hand. I pushed the four chips across to him. "This time you get four, and no more."

"What did you have, Alan?" Polly turned my cards over, showing the three fives.

Henry grinned. He made no attempt to stop Polly looking at his cards too. He had a pair of Kings. Just one pair.

"Got you that time, Alan," he said happily.

William and Polly groaned heavily.

We played until I had won back my reputation and a respectable number of Henry's chips. Then it was the children's bedtime, and I went up to see Scilla.

She was awake, lying in the dark.

"Come in, Alan."

I went over and switched on the bedside light. The first shock was over. She looked calm, peaceful.

"Hungry?" I asked. She had not eaten since lunch the day before.

"Do you know, Alan, I am," she said as if surprised.

I went downstairs and with Joan rustled up some supper. I carried the tray up and ate with Scilla. Sitting propped up with pillows, alone in the big bed, she began to tell me about how she had met Bill, the things they had done together, the fun they had had. Her eyes shone with remembered happiness. She talked for a long time, all about Bill, and I did not stop her until her lips began to tremble. Then I told her about Henry and his pair of kings and she smiled and grew calm again.

I wanted very much to ask her whether Bill had been in any trouble or had been threatened in any way during the last few weeks, but it wasn't the right time to do it. So I got her to take another of the sedatives the hospital had given me for her, turned off her light, and said good night.

As I undressed in my own room the tiredness hit me. I had been awake for over forty hours, few of which could be called restful. I flopped into bed. It was one of those times when the act of falling asleep is a conscious, delicious luxury.

Half an hour later Joan shook me awake again. She was in her dressing-gown.

"Alan, wake up for goodness sake. I've been knocking on your door for ages."

"What's the matter?"

"You're wanted on the telephone. Personal call," she said.

"Oh no," I groaned. It felt like the middle of the night. I looked at my watch. Eleven o'clock.

I staggered downstairs, eyes bleary with sleep.

"Hello?"

"Mr. Alan York?"

"Yes."

"Hold on, please." Some clicks on the line. I yawned.

"Mr. York? I have a message for you from Inspector Lodge, Maidenhead police. He would like you to come here to the police station tomorrow afternoon, at four o'clock."

"I'll be there," I said. I rang off, went back to bed, and slept and slept.

Lodge was waiting for me. He rose, shook hands, pointed to a chair. I sat down. The desk was clear now of everything except a neat, quarto-sized folder placed squarely in front of him. Slightly behind me, at a small table in the corner, sat a constable in uniform, pencil in hand, shorthand notebook at the ready.

"I have some statements here," Lodge tapped the file, "which I will tell you about. Then I have some questions to ask." He opened the file and took out two sheets of paper clipped together.

"This is a statement from Mr. J. L. Dace, Clerk of the Course of Maidenhead racecourse. In it he says nine of the attendants, the men who stand by to make temporary repairs to the fences during the races, are regularly employed in that capacity. Three of them were new this meeting."

Lodge laid down this statement, and took out the next.

"This is a statement from George Watkins, one of the regular attendants. He says they draw lots among themselves to decide which fence each of them shall stand by. There are two at some fences. On Friday they drew lots as usual, but on Saturday one of the new men volunteered to go down to the farthest fence. None of them likes having to go right down there, Watkins says, because it is too far to walk back between races to 'have a bit' on a horse. So they were glad enough to let the stranger take that fence, and they drew lots for the rest."

"What did this attendant look like?" I asked.

"You saw him yourself," said Lodge.

"No, not really," I said. "All he was to me was a man. I didn't look at him. There's at least one attendant at every fence. I wouldn't know any of them again."

"Watkins says he thinks he'd know the man again, but he can't describe him. Ordinary, he says. Not tall, not short. Middle-aged, he thinks. Wore a cap, old grey suit, loose mackintosh."

"They all do," I said gloomily.

Lodge said, "He gave his name as Thomas Cook. Said he was out of work, had a job to go to next week and was filling in time. Very plausible, nothing odd about him at all, Watkins says. He spoke like a Londoner though, not with a Berkshire accent."

Lodge laid the paper down, and took out another.

"This is a statement from John Russell of the St. John Ambulance Brigade. He says he was standing beside the first fence in the straight watching the horses go round the bottom of the course. Because of the mist he says he could see only three fences: the one he was standing beside, the next fence up the straight, and the farthest fence, where Major Davidson fell. The fence before that, which was opposite him on the far side of the course, was an indistinct blur.

"He saw Major Davidson race out of the mist after he had jumped that fence. Then he saw him fall at the next. Major Davidson did not reappear, though his horse got up and galloped off riderless. Russell began to walk towards the fence where he had seen Major Davidson fall; then when you, Mr. York, passed him looking over your shoulder, he began to run. He found Major Davidson lying on the ground."

"Did he see the wire?" I asked eagerly.

"No. I asked him if he had seen anything at all unusual. I didn't mention wire specifically. He said there was nothing."

"Didn't he see the attendant roll up the wire while he was running towards him?"

"I asked him if he could see either Major Davidson or the attendant as he ran towards them. He says that owing to the sharp bend and the rails round it he could not see them until he was quite close. I gather he ran round the course instead of cutting across the corner through the long rough grass because it was too wet."

"I see," I said despondently. "And what was the attendant doing when he got there?"

"Standing beside Major Davidson looking down at him. He says the attendant looked frightened. This surprised Russell, because although he was knocked out Major Davidson did not appear to him to be badly injured. He waved his white flag, the next First-Aid man saw it and waved his, and the message was thus relayed through the fog all the way up the course to the ambulance."

"What did the attendant do then?"

"Nothing particular. He stayed beside the fence after the ambulance had taken Major Davidson away, and Russell says he was there until the abandonment of the last race was announced."

Clutching at straws, I said, "Did he go back with the other attendants and collect his pay?"

Lodge looked at me with interest. "No," he said, "he didn't."

He took out another paper.

"This is a statement from Peter Smith, head travelling lad for the Gregory stables, where Admiral is trained. He says that after Admiral got loose at Maidenhead he tried to jump a blackthorn hedge. He stuck in it and was caught beside it, scared and bleeding. There are cuts and scratches all over the horse's shoulders, chest and forelegs." He looked up. "If the wire left any mark on him at all, it is impossible to distinguish it now."

"You have been thorough," I said, "and quick."

"Yes. We were lucky, for once, to find everyone we wanted without delay."

There was only one paper left. Lodge picked it up, spoke slowly.

"This is the report of the post mortem on Major Davidson. Cause of death was multiple internal injuries. Liver and spleen were both ruptured."

He sat back in his chair and looked at his hands.

"Now, Mr. York, I have been directed to ask you some questions which . . ." his dark eyes came up to mine suddenly, ". . . which I do not think you will like. Just answer them." His half smile was friendly.

"Fire away," I said.

"Are you in love with Mrs. Davidson?"

I sat up straight, surprised.

"No," I said.

"But you live with her?"

"I live with the whole family," I said.

"Why?"

"I have no home in England. When I first got to know Bill Davidson he asked me to his house for a week-end. I liked it there, and I suppose they liked me. Anyway, they asked me often. Gradually the week-ends got longer and longer, until Bill and Scilla suggested I should make their house my headquarters. I spend a night or two every week in London."

"How long have you lived at the Davidsons'?" asked Lodge.

"About seven months."

"Were your relations with Major Davidson friendly?"

"Yes, very."

"And with Mrs. Davidson?"

"Yes."

"But you do not love her?"

"I am extremely fond of her. As an elder sister," I said, sitting tight on my anger. "She is ten years older than I am."

Lodge's expression said quite plainly that age had nothing to do with it. I was aware, just then, that the constable in the corner was writing down my replies.

I relaxed. I said, tranquilly, "She was very much in love with her husband, and he with her."

Lodge's mouth twitched at the corners. He looked, of all things, amused. Then he began again.

"I understand," he said, "that Major Davidson was the leading amateur steeplechase jockey in this country?"

"Yes."

"And you yourself finished second to him, a year ago, after your first season's racing in England?"

I stared at him. I said, "For someone who hardly knew steeplechasing existed twenty-four hours ago, you've wasted no time."

"Were you second to Major Davidson on the amateur riders' list last year? And were you not likely to be second to him again? Is it not also likely that now, in his absence, you will head the list?"

"Yes, yes, and I hope so," I said. The accusation was as plain as could be, but I was not going to rush unasked into protestations of my innocence. I waited. If he wanted the suggestion made that I had sought to injure or kill Bill in order to acquire either his wife or his racing prestige, or both, Lodge would have to make it himself.

But he didn't. A full minute ticked by, during which I sat still. Finally Lodge grinned.

"Well, I think that's all, then, Mr. York. The information you gave us yesterday and your answers today will be typed together as one statement, and I shall be glad if you will read and sign it."

The policeman with the notebook stood up and walked into the outer office. Lodge said, "The coroner's inquest on Major Davidson is to be held on Thursday. You will be needed as a witness; and Mrs. Davidson, too, for evidence of identification. We'll be getting in touch with her."

He asked me questions about steeplechasing, ordinary conversational questions, until the statement was ready. I read it carefully and signed it. It was accurate and perfectly fair. I could imagine these pages joining the others in Lodge's tidy file. How fat would it grow before he found the accidental murderer of Bill Davidson?

If he ever did.

He stood up and held out his hand, and I shook it. I liked him. I wondered who had "directed" him to find out if I might have arranged the crime I had myself reported.

3

I rode at Plumpton two days later.

The police had been very discreet in their enquiries, and Sir Creswell also, for there was no speculation in the weighing room about Bill's death. The grapevine was silent.

I plunged into the bustle of a normal racing day, the minor frustration of a lot of jockeys changing in the smallish space, the unprintable jokes, the laughter, the cluster of cold half-undressed men round the red-hot coke stove.

Clem gave me my clean breeches, some pants, a thin fawn underjersey, a fresh white stock for my neck, and a pair of nylon stockings. I stripped and put on the racing things. On top of the nylon stockings (laddered, as always) my soft, light, close fitting racing boots slid on easily. Clem handed me my racing colours, the thick woollen sweater of coffee and cream checks, and the brown satin cap. He tied my stock for me. I pulled on the jersey, and slid the cap on to my crash helmet, ready to put on later.

Clem said, "Only the one ride today, Sir?" He pulled two thick rubber bands from his large apron pocket and slipped them over my wrists. They were to anchor the sleeves of my jersey and prevent the wind blowing them up my arms.

"Yes," I said. "So far, anyway." I was always hopeful.

"Will you be wanting to borrow a light saddle? The weight's near your limit, I should think."

"No," I said, "I'd rather use my own saddle if I can. I'll get on the trial scales with that first, and see how much overweight I am."

"Right you are, sir."

I went over with Clem, picked up my six pound racing saddle

with its girths and stirrup leathers wound round it, and weighed myself with it, my crash helmet perched temporarily and insecurely on the back of my head. The total came to ten stone, nine pounds, which was four pounds more than the handicapper thought my horse deserved.

Clem took back the saddle, and I put my helmet on the bench again.

"I think I'll carry the overweight, Clem," I said.

"Right." He hurried off to attend to someone else.

I could have got down to the proper weight—just—by using a three pound "postage stamp" saddle and changing into silk colours and "paper" boots. But as I was riding my own horse I could please myself, and he was an angular animal whose ribs would probably have been rubbed raw by too small a saddle.

He, Forlorn Hope, my newest acquisition, was a strongly-built brown gelding only five years old. He looked as though he would develop into a 'chaser in a year or two, but meanwhile I was riding him in novice hurdle races to give him some sorely needed experience.

His unreliability as a jumper had made Scilla, the evening before, beg me not to ride him at Plumpton, a course full of snares for the unwary.

Unbearably strung up, and facing her loss for the first time without the help of drugs, she was angry and pleading by turns.

"Don't, Alan. Not a novice hurdle at Plumpton. You know your wretched Forlorn Hope isn't safe. You haven't got to do it, so why do you?"

"I like it."

"There never was a horse more aptly named," she said, miserably.

"He'll learn," I said. "But not if I don't give him the opportunity."

"Put someone else up. Please."

"There isn't any point in my having a horse if I don't ride it myself. That's really why I came to England at all, to race. You know that."

"You'll be killed, like Bill." She began to cry, helplessly, worn out. I tried to reason with her.

"No, I won't. If Bill had been killed in a motor crash you wouldn't expect me to stop driving a car. Steeplechasing's just as safe and unsafe as motoring." I paused, but she went on crying. "There are thousands more people killed on the roads than on the race-track," I said.

At this outrageous statement she recovered enough to point out acidly the difference in the number of people engaged in the two pursuits.

"Very few people are killed by steeplechasing," I tried again.

"Bill was . . ."

"Only about one a year, out of hundreds," I went on.

"Bill was the second since Christmas."

"Yes." I looked at her warily. There were still tears in her eyes.

"Scilla, was Bill in any sort of trouble recently?"

"Why ever do you ask?" She was astounded by my question.

"Was he?"

"Of course not."

"Not worried about anything?" I persisted.

"No. Did he seem worried to you?"

"No," I said. It was quite true. Until the moment of his fall Bill had been the same as I had always known him, cheerful, poised, reliable. He had had, and enjoyed, a pretty wife, three attractive children, a grey stone manor house, a considerable fortune and the best hunter 'chaser in England. A happy man. And rack my memory as I would, I could not recall the slightest ruffling of the pattern.

"Then why do you ask?" said Scilla, again.

I told her as gradually, as gently as I could, that Bill's fall had not been an ordinary accident. I told her about the wire and about Lodge's investigations.

She sat like stone, absolutely stunned.

"Oh no," she said. "Oh, no. Oh, no."

As I stood now outside the weighing room at Plumpton I could still see her stricken face. She had raised no more objections to my racing. What I had told her had driven every other thought out of her head.

A firm hand came down on my shoulder. I knew it well. It belonged to Pete Gregory, racehorse trainer, a burly man nearly six feet tall, running to fat, growing bald, but in his day, I had been told, the toughest man ever to put his foot in a racing stirrup.

"Hello, Alan me lad. I'm glad to see you're here. I've already declared you for your horse in the second race."

"How is he?" I asked.

"All right. A bit thin, still." Forlorn Hope had only been in his stable for a month. "I should give him an 'easy,' coming up the hill the first time, or he'll blow up before the finish. He needs more time before we can hope for much."

"O.K." I said.

"Come out and see what the going is like," said Pete. "I want to talk to you." He hitched the strap of his binoculars higher on his shoulder.

We walked down through the gate on to the course and dug our heels experimentally into the turf. They sank in an inch.

"Not bad, considering all the snow that melted into it a fortnight ago," I said.

"Nice and soft for you to fall on," said Pete with elementary humour.

We went up the rise to the nearest hurdle. The landing side had a little too much give in it, but we knew the ground at the other end of the course was better drained. It was all right.

Pete said abruptly, "Did you see Admiral fall at Maidenhead?" He had been in Ireland buying a horse when it happened and had only just returned.

"Yes. I was about ten lengths behind him," I said, looking down the course, concentrating on the hurdle track.

"Well?"

"Well, what?" I said.

"What happened? Why did he fall?" There was some sort of urgency in his voice, more than one would expect, even in the circumstances. I looked at him. His eyes were grey, unsmiling, intent. Moved by an instinct I didn't understand, I retreated into vagueness.

"He just fell," I said. "When I went over the fence he was on the ground with Bill underneath him."

"Did Admiral meet the fence all wrong, then?" he probed.

"Not as far as I could see. He must have hit the top of it." This was near enough to the truth.

"There wasn't . . . anything else?" Pete's eyes were fierce, as if they would look into my brain.

"What do you mean?" I avoided the direct answer.

"Nothing." His anxious expression relaxed. "If you didn't see anything..." We began to walk back. It troubled me that I hadn't told Pete the truth. He had been too searching, too aware. I was certain he was not the man to risk destroying a great horse like Admiral, let alone a friend, but why was he so relieved now he believed I had noticed nothing?

I had just decided to ask him to explain his attitude, and to tell him what had really happened, when he began to speak.

"Have you got a ride in the Amateur 'Chase, Alan?" He was back to normal, bluff and smiling.

"No, I haven't," I said. "Pete, look..."

But he interrupted, "I had a horse arrive in my yard five or six days ago, with an engagement in today's Amateur 'Chase. A chestnut. Good sort of animal, I should say. He seems to be fit enough —he's come from a small stable in the West country—and his new owner is very keen to run him. I tried to ring you this morning about it, but you'd already left."

"What's his name?" I asked, for all this preamble of Pete's was, I knew, his way of cajoling me into something I might not be too delighted to do.

"Heavens Above."

"Never heard of him. What's he done?" I asked.

"Well, not much. He's young, of course..."

I interrupted. "What *exactly* has he done?"

Pete sighed and gave in. "He's only had two runs, both down in Devon last autumn. He didn't fall, but—er—he got rid of his jockey both times. But he jumped well enough over my schooling fences this morning. I don't think you'd have any difficulty in getting him round safely, and that's the main thing at this stage."

"Pete, I don't like to say no, but..." I began.

"His owner is so hoping you'll ride him. It's her first horse, and it's running for the first time in her brand new colours. I brought her to the races with me. She's very excited. I said I'd ask you..."

"I don't think..." I tried again.

"Well at least meet her," said Pete.

"If I meet her, you know it'll be far more difficult for me to refuse to ride her horse."

Pete didn't deny it.

I went on, "I suppose she's another of your dear old ladies about to go into a nursing home from which she is unlikely to return, and wants a final thrill before she meets her fate?"

This was the sad tale which Pete had used not long before to inveigle me on to a bad horse against my better judgement. And I often saw the old lady at the races afterwards. The nursing home and her fate were still presumably awaiting her.

"This one is not," said Pete, "a dear old lady."

We came to a stop in the paddock, and Pete looked around him and beckoned to someone. Out of the corner of my eye I saw a woman begin to walk towards us. It was already, without unforgivable rudeness, too late to escape. I had time for one heart-felt oath in Pete's ear before I turned to be introduced to the new owner of the jockey-depositing Heavens Above.

"Miss Ellery-Penn, Alan York," said Pete.

I was lost before she spoke a word. The first thing I said was, "I'll be glad to ride your horse."

Pete was laughing openly at me.

She was beautiful. She had clear features, wonderful skin, smiling grey eyes, dark glossy hair falling almost to her shoulders. And she was used to the effect she had on men: but how could she help it?

Pete said, "Right, then. I'll declare you for the amateurs'—it's the fourth race. I'll give the colours to Clem." He went off towards the weighing room.

"I am so glad you agreed to ride my horse," the girl said. Her voice was low-pitched and unhurried. "He's a birthday present. Rather a problem one, don't you think? My Uncle George, who is a dear fellow but just the slightest bit off the beat, *advertised* in *The Times* for a racehorse. My aunt says he received fifty replies and bought this horse without seeing it because he liked the name. He said it would be more amusing for me to have a horse for my birthday than the conventional string of pearls."

"Your Uncle George sounds fascinating," I said.

"But just a little devastating to live with." She had a trick of lifting the last two or three words in a sentence so that they sounded like a question. As if she had added "Don't you agree?" to her remark.

"Do you in fact live with him?" I asked.

"Oh, yes. Parents divorced in the murky past. Scattered to the four winds, and all that."

"I'm sorry."

"Waste no sympathy. I can't remember either of them. They abandoned me on Uncle George's doorstep, figuratively speaking, at the tender age of two."

"Uncle George has done a good job," I said, looking at her with the frankest admiration.

She accepted this without gaucherie, almost as a matter of course.

"Aunt Deb, actually. She is faintly more on the ball than Uncle George. Absolute pets, the pair of them."

"Are they here today?" I asked.

"No, they aren't," said Miss Ellery-Penn. "Uncle George remarked that having given me a passport into a new world peopled entirely by brave and charming young men, it would defeat the object if my path were cluttered up with elderly relatives."

"I am getting fonder of Uncle George every minute," I said.

Miss Ellery-Penn gave me a heavenly smile which held no promises of any sort.

"Have you seen my horse? Isn't he a duck?" she said.

"I haven't seen him. I'm afraid I didn't know he existed until five minutes ago. How did Uncle George happen to send him to Pete Gregory? Did he pick the stable with a pin?"

She laughed. "No, I don't think so. He had the stable all planned. He said I could get a Major Davidson to ride for me if the horse went to Mr. Gregory's." She reflected, wrinkling her brow. "He was quite upset on Monday when he read in the paper that Major Davidson had been killed."

"Did he know him?" I asked idly, watching the delicious curves at the corners of her red mouth.

"No, I'm sure he didn't know him personally. Probably he knew his father. He seems to know most people's fathers. He just said 'Good God, Davidson's dead' in a shocked sort of way and went on eating his toast. But he didn't hear me or Aunt Deb until we had asked him four times for the marmalade!"

"And that was all?"

"Yes. Why do you ask?" said Miss Ellery-Penn, curiously.

"Oh, nothing special," I said. "Bill Davidson and I were good friends."

She nodded. "I see." She dismissed the subject. "Now what do I have to do in my new role of racehorse owner? I don't particularly want to make a frightful boob on my first day. Any comments and instructions from you will be welcome, Mr. York."

"My name is Alan," I said.

She gave me an appraising look. It told me plainer than words that although she was young she was already experienced at fending off unwelcome attentions and not being rushed into relationships she was not prepared for.

But finally she smiled, and said, "Mine is Kate." She bestowed her name like a gift; I was pleased to receive it.

"How much do you know about racing?" I asked.

"Not a thing. Never set foot on the Turf before today." She gave the capital letter its full value, ironically.

"Do you ride, yourself?"

"Positively not."

"Perhaps your Uncle George is fond of horses? Perhaps he hunts?" I suggested.

"Uncle George is the most un-addicted man to horses I have ever met. He says one end kicks and the other bites, and as for hunting, he says that he has cosier things to do than chase bushy tailed vermin in the gravest discomfort over waterlogged countryside in the depths of winter."

I laughed. "Perhaps he bets. Off the course?" I asked.

"Uncle George has been known to ask, on Cup Final day, what has won the Derby."

"Then why Heavens Above?"

"Wider horizons for me, Uncle George says. My education has been along the well-tramped lines of boarding school, finishing school and an over-chaperoned tour of Europe. I needed to get the smell of museums out of my nose, Uncle George said."

"So he gave you a racehorse for your twenty-first birthday," I stated matter-of-factly.

"Yes," she said: then she looked at me sharply. I grinned. I had jumped her defences, that time.

"There's nothing special for you to do as an owner," I said, "except go along to those stalls over there," I pointed, "before the fourth race, to see your horse being saddled up. Then you'll go into the parade ring with Pete, and stand around making intelligent remarks about the weather until I arrive and mount and go out for the race."

"What do I do if he wins?"

"Do you expect him to win?" I asked. I was not sure how much she really knew about her horse.

"Mr. Gregory says he won't."

I was relieved. I did not want her to be disappointed.

"We'll all know much more about him after the race. But if he should come in the first three, he will be unsaddled down there opposite the weighing room. Otherwise, you'll find us up here on the grass."

It was nearly time for the first race. I took the delectable Miss Ellery-Penn on to the stands and fulfilled Uncle George's design by introducing to her several brave and charming young men. I unfortunately realised that by the time I came back from riding in the novice hurdle, I should probably be an "also ran" in the race for Miss Ellery-Penn's attentions.

I watched her captivating a group of my friends. She was a vivid, vital person. It seemed to me that she had an inexhaustible inner fire battened down tight under hatches, and only the warmth from it was allowed to escape into the amused, slow voice. Kate was going to be potently attractive even in middle age, I thought inconsequently, and it crossed my mind that had Scilla possessed this springing vitality instead of her retiring, serene passiveness, Inspector Lodge's implications might not have been very far off the mark.

After we had watched the first race I left Kate deciding which of her new acquaintances should have the honour of taking her to coffee, and went off to weigh out for the novice hurdle. Looking back, I saw her setting off to the refreshment room with a trail of admirers, rather like a comet with a tail. A flashing, bewitching comet.

For the first time in my life I regretted that I was going to ride in a race.

4

In the changing room Sandy Mason stood with his hands on his hips and laid about him with his tongue. His red hair curled strongly, his legs, firmly planted with the feet apart, were as rigid as posts. From the top to toe he vibrated with life. He was a stocky man in his thirties, on the short side, very strong, with dark brown eyes fringed disconcertingly by pale, reddish lashes.

As a jockey, a professional, he was not among the top dozen, but he had had a good deal of success, mainly owing to his fighting spirit. Nothing ever frightened him. He would thrust his sometimes unwilling mounts into the smallest openings, even occasionally into openings which did not exist until he made them by sheer force. His aggressiveness in races had got him into hot water more than once with the Stewards, but he was not particularly unpopular with the other jockeys, owing to his irrepressible, infectious cheerfulness.

His sense of humour was as vigorous as the rest of him, and if I thought privately that some of his jokes were too unkindly practical or too revoltingly obscene, I appeared to be in a minority.

"Which of you sods has half-inched my balancing pole?" he roared in a voice which carried splendidly above the busy chatter to every corner of the room. To this enquiry into the whereabouts of his whip, he received no reply.

"Why don't you lot get up off your fannies and see if you're hatching it," he said to three or four jockeys who were sitting on a bench pulling on their boots. They looked up appreciatively and waited for the rest of the tirade. Sandy kept up a flow of invective without repeating himself until one of the valets produced the missing whip.

"Where did you find it?" demanded Sandy. "Who had it? I'll twist his bloody arm."

"It was on the floor under the bench, in your own place."

Sandy was never embarrassed by his mistakes. He roared with laughter and took the whip. "I'll forgive you all this time, then." He went out into the weighing room carrying his saddle and whacking the air with his whip as if to make sure it was as pliable as usual. He always used it a good deal in the course of a race.

As he passed me where I stood just inside the changing room door, his eyes lifted to mine with one of the darting, laughing glances which made him likeable in spite of his faults. I turned and watched him go over and sit on the scales, parking the whip on the table beside him. He said something I couldn't hear, and both the Clerk of the Scales and the Judge, who was sitting there learning the colours so that he could distinguish them at the finish, laughed as they checked him against their lists and passed him for the race.

There had been rumours, a while back, that Sandy had "stopped" a few horses and had been rewarded handsomely by bookmakers for the service. But nothing had been proved, and the official enquiry had lasted barely an hour. Those who had felt the rough edge of Sandy's practical jokes believed him capable of anything. Everyone else pointed out that stopping a horse was entirely out of character for one who had been in trouble for trying too ruthlessly to win.

Watching the free and easy way he handled the two racing officials, I could understand that in face of that friendly, open manner, the Stewards at the enquiry must have found it impossible, in the absence of solidly convincing evidence, to believe him guilty. The general opinion among the jockeys was that Sandy had "strangled" a couple at one stage, but not during the past few months.

"Stopping" a horse can be done by missing the start, setting off some lengths behind, and staying at the back. Then the crooked jockey can ride a fairly honest finish from the second last fence, when he is closely under the eyes of the crowd, secure in the knowledge that he has left his horse far too much to do and cannot possibly win. It is rare enough, because a jocky seen to do it regularly soon finds himself unemployed.

During my one and a half season's racing I had seen it happen only twice. It was the same man both times, a fair, round-faced youth called Joe Nantwich. On the second occasion, about two months ago, he had been lucky to escape with his licence, for he had been foolish enough to try it in a race where one of the jockeys was David Stampe, the tale-bearing younger son of the Senior Steward.

Joe, and, I was sure, Sandy too, had both gone to the lengths of deliberately holding back horses which, without their interference, would have been certain to win. They had, in fact, been guilty of criminal fraud. But was I so very much better, I wondered, as I tied on my helmet and took my saddle over to the scales? For I proposed to take Forlorn Hope sensibly over the hurdles, concentrating on getting round the course; and I had no intention of riding him all out in the faint possibility that he might finish in the first three. He was not properly fit, and too hard a race would do him great harm. Of course if by some unforeseen circumstances, such as a lot of falls among the other horses, I found myself placed with a winning chance, I intended to seize it. There is a world of difference between "stopping" and "not trying hard, but willing to win": but the result for disgruntled backers is the same. They lose their money.

I took my saddle out to the saddling boxes, where Pete was already waiting with Forlorn Hope. He saddled up, and Rupert, the tiny stable lad, led the horse out into the parade ring. Pete and I strolled in after him, discussing the other horses in the race. There was no sign of Kate.

When the time came I mounted and rode out on to the course. The familiar excitement was in my blood again. Not Bill's death nor Scilla's mourning, nor the thought of Kate making progress with someone else, could affect the gripping happiness I always felt when cantering down to the starting gate. The speed of racing, the quick decisions, the risks, these were what I badly needed to counteract the safeties of civilisation. One can be too secure. Adventure is good for the soul, especially for someone like me, whose father stopped counting after the fourth million.

And my father, with an understanding based on his own much wilder youth, had given me unconditionally a fast car and three good horses and turned me loose in a country five thousand miles from home. He said however, as he despatched me with his blessing, that he thought steeplechasing was rather mild for one who had been taken crocodile hunting on the Zambezi every year since he was ten. My father's annual month away from his trading empire usually meant for us a dash across the veldt and a plunge into the primeval forest, sometimes equipped with the absolute minimum of kit and no one but ourselves to carry it. And I, for whom the deep jungle was a familiar playground, found the challenge I needed in a tamed land, on friendly animals, in a sport hemmed all about with rules and regulations. It was very odd, when one came to consider it.

The starter called the roll to make sure everyone had arrived, while we circled round and checked the tightness of the girths. I found Joe Nantwich guiding his horse along beside me. He was wearing his usual unpleasant expression, half petulance, half swank.

"Are you going back to the Davidsons' after the races, Alan?" he asked. He always spoke to me with a familiarity I slightly resented, though I tried not to.

"Yes," I said. Then I thought of Kate. "I may not go at once, though."

"Will you give me a lift as far as Epsom?"

"I don't go that way," I said, very politely.

"But you go through Dorking. I could get a bus on from there if you don't want to go to Epsom. I came with someone who is going on to Kent, so I've got to find some transport home." He was persistent, and although I thought he could easily find someone going directly to Epsom if he tried hard enough, I agreed in the end to take him.

We lined up for the start. Joe was on one side of me and Sandy on the other, and from the looks they gave each other across me, there was no love lost between them. Sandy's smile was a nasty one: Joe's round baby face puckered up like a child trying not to cry. I imagined that Sandy had been puncturing Joe's inflated ego with one of those famous practical jokes, such as filling the feet of his racing boots with jam.

Then we were off, and I gave all my attention to getting Forlorn Hope round as neatly, quickly and safely as I could. He was still very green and inclined to waver as he met the clattering hurdles, but the basic spring was there. He was going so well that for over half of the race I lay in third place, staying slightly towards the outside, to give him a clear view of the obstacles. The last quarter mile coming up the hill was too much for him, though, and we finished sixth. I was satisfied; and Scilla would be reassured.

Sandy Mason finished ahead of me. Then Joe Nantwich's horse galloped past loose, reins dangling, and looking back to the far end of the course I saw the tiny figure of Joe himself trudging back to the stands. No doubt I would be hearing a stride by stride account of the calamity all the way to Dorking.

I unsaddled, went back to the weighing room, changed into Kate's brand new colours, got Clem to pack me a weight cloth with ten pounds of flat lead pieces, the weight I needed for the Amateur 'Chase, and went out to see what had become of Miss Ellery-Penn.

She was leaning on the parade ring rails, looking alternately at the horses and (with too much approval, I thought) at Dane Hillman, one of the brave and charming young men I had introduced to her.

"Mr. Hillman has been telling me," said Kate, "that that poor looking bag of bones over there—the one with his head down by his knees and those floppy ears—is the fastest horse in the race. Am I to believe it, or is the mickey being gently taken?"

"No mickey," I said. "That's the best horse. Not on looks, I grant you, but he's a certainty today, in this company."

Dane said, "Horses who go along with their heads down like that are nearly always good jumpers. They look where they're going."

"But I like this gorgeous creature coming round now," said Kate, looking at a bay with an arched neck and high head carriage. Most of his body was covered by a rug to keep out the February cold, but at the back his glossy rump swelled roundly.

"He's much too fat," said Dane. "He probably ate his head off during the snow and hasn't had enough exercise since. He'll blow up when he's asked to do anything."

Kate sighed. "Horses appear to be as full of paradoxes as G. K. Chesterton. The duds look good, and the good look duds."

"Not always," said Dane and I together.

"I shall be glad," said Dane, "to give you a prolonged course in racehorse recognition, Miss Ellery-Penn."

"I am a slow learner, Mr. Hillman."

"All the better," said Dane, cheerfully.

"Aren't you riding today, Dane?" I asked hopefully.

"In the last two, my lad. Don't worry, I shall be able to look after Miss Ellery-Penn for you while you ride her horse." He grinned.

"Are you a jockey too, Mr. Hillman?" asked Kate in a surprised voice.

"Yes," said Dane, and left it at that. He was the rising star of the profession, clearly heading straight to the top. Pete Gregory had first claim on him, which, apart from natural affinity, brought us together a good deal. Strangers often mistook us for each other. We were the same age, both dark, both of middle height and medium build. On horseback the difference was greater; he was a better jockey than I would ever be.

"I thought all jockeys were instantly recognisable as having come straight from Lilliput," said Kate, "but you two are quite a decent size." She had to look up to both of us, although she was tall enough herself.

We laughed. I said, "Steeplechasing jockeys are nearly all a decent size. It's easier to stick on over big fences if you have long legs to grip with."

"Several of the Flat chaps are as tall as us, too," said Dane. "But they are very skinny, of course."

"All my illusions are being shattered," said Kate.

Dane said, "I like your new horse, Alan. He'll make a good 'chaser next year."

"Are you riding your own horses today, too?" Kate asked Dane.

"No, I'm not. I haven't any," said Dane. "I'm a professional, so I'm not allowed to own racehorses."

"A professional?" Kate's eyebrows went up. She had clearly taken in the superlative tailoring of the suit under the short camel overcoat, the pleasant voice, the gentle manners. Another illusion was being shattered, I was amused to see.

"Yes. I ride for my life," said Dane, smiling. "Unlike Alan, I haven't a stinking rich father. But I get paid for doing what I like best in the world. It's a very satisfactory state of affairs."

Kate looked carefully from one to the other of us. "Perhaps in time I shall understand what makes you want to risk your elegant necks," she said.

"When you find out, please tell us," said Dane. "It's still a mystery to me."

We wandered back to the stands and watched the third race.

The poor looking horse won in a canter by twenty lengths. Kate's fancy was tailed-off after a mile and refused at the third last fence.

"Don't imagine that we always know what's going to win," said Dane. "Jockeys are bad tipsters. But that one was a cert, a dead cert."

A dead cert. The casual, everyday racing expression jabbed in my mind like a needle. Bill Davidson's attacker had relied on Admiral's being a certainty.

A dead cert. Dead...

Kate's horse, for a pig in a poke, was not as bad as I feared. At the second fence he put in a short one and screwed in mid-air. I came clear out of the saddle and landed back in it more by luck than judgement. This was obviously the trick which had rid Heavens Above of his former jockey, who now had all my sympathy. He did it again at the third open ditch, but the rest of our journey was uneventful. The horse even found an unsuspected turn of foot up the hill and, passing several tired animals, ran on into fourth place.

Kate was delighted.

"Bless Uncle George for a brainwave," she said. "I've never had such a happy day in my life."

"I thought you were coming off at the second, Alan," said Pete Gregory, as I undid the girth buckles.

"So did I," I said, feelingly. "It was sheer luck I didn't."

Pete watched the way Heavens Above was breathing: the ribs were moving in and out a good deal, but not labouring. He said, "He's remarkably fit, considering everything. I think we'll win a race or two with him before the end of the season."

"Can't we all go and celebrate with the odd magnum?" asked Kate. Her eyes were shining with excitement.

Pete laughed. "Wait till you have a winner, for the magnum," he said. "I'd like to have drunk a more modest toast to the future with you, though, but I've a runner in the next. Alan will take you, no doubt." He looked at me sideways, very amused still at my complete surrender to the charm of Miss Ellery-Penn.

"Will you wait for me, Kate?" I asked. "I have to go and weigh in now, because we were fourth. I'll change and be out as quickly as I can."

"I'll come down outside the weighing room," promised Kate, nodding.

I weighed in, gave my saddle to Clem, washed, and changed back into ordinary clothes. Kate was waiting outside the weighing room, looking at a group of girls standing near her chatting.

"Who are they?" asked Kate. "They have been here all the time I have, just doing nothing."

"Jockeys' wives, mostly," I said, grinning. "Waiting outside the weighing room is their chief occupation."

"And Jockeys' girl friends too, I suppose," said Kate, wryly.

"Yes," I said. "And I've just found out how nice it is to know there is someone waiting for you outside."

We went round to the bar, and settled for cups of coffee.

"Uncle George will be shattered to hear we drank to Heavens Above so non-alcoholically," said Kate. "Don't grain and grapes figure in your life?"

"Oh, yes, of course. But I've never got used to them at three o'clock in the afternoon. How about you?"

"Champers for breakfast is my passion," said Kate, with smiling eyes.

I asked her then if she would spend the evening with me, but she said she could not. Aunt Deb, it appeared, was having a dinner party, and Uncle George would be agog to hear how the birthday present had got on.

"Tomorrow, then?"

Kate hesitated and looked down at her glass. "I'm . . . er . . . I'm going out with Dane, tomorrow."

"Blast him," I said, exploding.

Kate positively giggled.

"Friday?" I suggested.

"That will be lovely," said Kate.

We went up on to the stands and watched Dane win the fifth race by a short head. Kate cheered him home uninhibitedly.

5

A battle was raging in the car park. I walked out of the gate to go home after the last race, and came to a dead stop. In the open space between the gate and the first rank of parked cars, at least twenty men were fighting, and fighting to hurt. Even at first glance there was a vicious quality about the strictly non-Queensberry type blows.

It was astounding. Scuffles between two or three men are common on racecourses, but a clash of this size and seriousness had to be caused by more than a disagreement over a bet.

I looked closer. There was no doubt about it. Some of the men were wearing brass knuckles. A length of bicycle chain swung briefly in the air. The two men nearest to me were lying on the ground, almost motionless, but rigid with exertion, as if locked in some strange native ritual. The fingers of one were clamped round the wrist of the other, whose hand held a knife with a sharp three-inch blade. Not long enough to be readily lethal, it was designed to rip and disfigure.

There seemed to be two fairly equally matched sides fighting each other, but one could not distinguish which was which. The man with the knife, who was slowly getting the worst of it, I saw to be little more than a boy; but most of the men were in their full strength. The only older-looking fighter was on his knees in the centre with his arms folded over his head, while the fight raged on around him.

They fought in uncanny silence. Only their heavy breathing and a few grunts were to be heard. The semi-circle of open-mouthed homeward-bound racegoers watching them was growing larger, but no one felt inclined to walk into the mêlée and try to stop it.

I found one of the newspaper sellers at my elbow.

"What's it all about?" I asked. Nothing much to do with racing escapes the newsboys.

"It's the taxi-drivers," he said. "There's two rival gangs of 'em, one lot from London and one lot from Brighton. There's usually trouble when they meet."

"Why?"

"Couldn't tell you, Mr. York. But this isn't the first time they've been at it."

I looked back at the struggling mob. One or two of them still had peaked caps on. Some pairs were rolling about on the ground, some were straining and heaving against the sides of the taxis. There were two rows of taxis parked there. All the drivers were fighting.

The fists and what they held in the way of ironmongery were doing a lot of damage. Two of the men were bent over, clasping their bellies in agony. There was blood on nearly all their faces, and the clothes of some of them had been torn off to the skin.

They fought on with appalling fury, taking no notice at all of the swelling crowd around them.

"They'll kill each other," said a girl standing next to me, watching the scene in a mixture of horror and fascination.

I glanced up over her head at the man standing on the other side of her, a big man well over six feet tall, with a deeply tanned skin. He was watching the fight with grim disapproval, his strong profile bleak, his eyes narrowed. I could not remember his name, though I had a feeling I ought to know it.

The crowd was growing uneasy, and began looking round for the police. The girl's remark was not idle. Any of the men might die, if they were unlucky, from the murderous chopping, gouging and slogging, which showed no signs of abating.

The fight had caused a traffic jam in the car park. A policeman came, took a look, and disappeared fast for reinforcements. He returned with four constables on foot and one on horseback, all armed with truncheons. They plunged into the battle, but it took them several minutes to stop it.

More police arrived. The taxi-drivers were dragged and herded into two groups. Both lots appeared to be equally battered, and neither side seemed to have won. The battlefield was strewn with caps and torn pieces of coats and shirts. Two shoes, one brown, one black, lay on their sides ten feet apart. Patches of blood stained the ground. The police began making a small pile of collected weapons.

The main excitement over, people began drifting away. The little knot of prospective customers for the taxis moved across to ask a policeman how long the drivers would be detained. The tall sunburned man who had been standing near me went over to join them.

One of the racing journalists paused beside me, scribbling busily in his notebook.

"Who is that very big man over there, John?" I asked him. He looked up and focused his eyes. He said, "His name's Tudor, I think. Owns a couple of horses. A newly arrived tycoon type. I don't know much about him. He doesn't look too pleased about the transport situation."

Tudor, in fact, looked heavily angry, his lower jaw jutting forward obstinately. I was still sure there was something about this man which I ought to remember, but I did not know what. He was not having any success with the policeman, who was shaking his head. The taxis remained empty and driverless.

"What's it all about?" I asked the journalist.

"Gang warfare, my spies tell me," he said cheerfully.

Five of the taxi-drivers were now lying flat out on the cold damp ground. One of them groaned steadily.

The journalist said, "Hospital and police station in about equal proportions, I should say. What a story!"

The man who was groaning rolled over and vomited.

"I'm going back to phone this lot through to the office," said the journalist. "Are you off home now?"

"I'm waiting for that wretched Joe Nantwich," I said. "I promised him a lift to Dorking, but I haven't seen a sign of him since the fourth race. It would be just like him to get a lift right home with someone else and forget to let me know."

"The last I saw of him, he was having a few unfriendly words with Sandy in the gents, and getting the worst of it."

"Those two really hate each other," I said.

"Do you know why?"

"No idea. Have you?" I asked.

"No," said the journalist. He smiled good-bye and went back into the racecourse towards the telephone.

Two ambulances drove up to collect the injured drivers. A policeman climbed into the back of each ambulance with them, and another sat in front beside the driver. With full loads the ambulances trundled slowly up the road to the main gates.

The remaining drivers began to shiver as the heat of battle died out of them and the raw February afternoon took over. They were stiff and bruised, but unrepentant. A man in one group stepped forward, gave the other group a sneer, and spat, insultingly, on the ground in their direction. His shirt was in ribbons and his face was swelling in lumps. The muscles of his forearm would have done credit to a blacksmith, and silky dark hair grew low on his forehead in a widow's peak. A dangerous looking man. A policeman touched his arm to bring him back into the group and he jumped round and snarled at him. Two more policemen began to close in, and the dark haired man subsided angrily.

I was just giving Joe up when he came out of the gate and hailed me with no apology for his lateness. But I was not the only person to notice his arrival.

The tall dark Mr. Tudor strode towards us.

"Nantwich, be so good as to give me a lift into Brighton, will you?" he said, authoritatively. "As you can see, the taxis are out of action, and I have an important appointment in Brighton in twenty minutes."

Joe looked at the taxi-drivers with vague eyes.

"What's happened?" he said.

"Never mind that now," said Tudor impatiently. "Where is your car?"

Joe looked at him blankly. His brain seemed to be working at half speed. He said, "Oh—er—it isn't here, sir. I've got a lift."

"With you?" said Tudor to me. I nodded. Joe, typically, had not introduced us.

"I'll be obliged if you will take me into Brighton," said Tudor, briskly. "I'll pay you the regular taxi fare."

He was forceful and in a hurry. It would have been difficult to refuse to do him a favour so small to me, so clearly important for him.

"I'll take you for nothing," I said, "but you'll find it a bit of a squeeze. I have a two-seater sports car."

"If it's too small for all of us, Nantwich can stay here and you can come back for him," said Tudor in a firm voice. Joe showed no surprise, but I thought that the dark Mr. Tudor was too practised at consulting no one's convenience but his own.

We skirted the groups of battered taxi-drivers, and threaded our way to my car. Tudor got in. He was so large that it was hopeless to try to wedge Joe in as well.

"I'll come back for you, Joe," I said, stifling my irritation. "Wait for me up on the main road."

I climbed into the car, nosed slowly out of the car park, up the racecourse road, and turned out towards Brighton. There was too much traffic for the Lotus to show off the power of the purring Climax engine, and going along at a steady forty gave me time to concentrate on my puzzling passenger.

Glancing down as I changed gear, I saw his hand resting on his knee, the fingers spread and tense. And suddenly I knew where I had seen him before. It was his hand, darkly tanned, with the faint blueish tint under the finger-nails, that I knew.

He had been standing in the bar at Sandown with his back towards me and his hand resting flat on the counter beside him, next to his glass. He had been talking to Bill; and I had waited there, behind him, not wanting to interrupt their conversation. Then Tudor finished his drink and left, and I had talked with Bill.

Now I glanced at his face.

"It's a great shame about Bill Davidson," I said.

The brown hand jumped slightly on his knee. He turned his head and looked at me while I drove.

"Yes, indeed it is." He spoke slowly. "I had been hoping he would ride a horse for me at Cheltenham."

"A great horseman," I said.

"Yes indeed."

"I was just behind him when he fell," I said, and on an impulse added, "There are a great many questions to be asked about it."

I felt Tudor's huge body shift beside me. I knew he was still looking at me, and I found his presence overpowering. "I suppose so," he said. He hesitated, but added nothing more. He looked at his watch.

"Take me to the Pavilion Plaza Hotel, if you please. I have to attend a business meeting there," he said.

"Is it near the Pavilion?" I asked.

"Fairly. I will direct you when we get there." His tone relegated me to the status of chauffeur.

We drove for some miles in silence. My passenger sat apparently deep in thought. When we reached Brighton he told me the way to the hotel.

"Thank you," he said, without warmth, as he lifted his bulk clumsily out of the low-slung car. He had an air of accepting considerable favours as merely his due, even when done him by complete strangers. He took two steps away from the car, then turned back and said, "What is your name?"

"Alan York," I said. "Good afternoon." I drove off without waiting for an answer. I could be brusque too. Glancing in the mirror I saw him standing on the pavement looking after me.

I went back to the racecourse.

Joe was waiting for me, sitting on the bank at the side of the road. He had some difficulty opening the car door, and he stumbled into his seat, muttering. He lurched over against me, and I discovered that Joe Nantwich was drunk.

The daylight was almost gone. I turned on the lights. I could think of pleasanter things to do than drive the twisty roads to Dorking with Joe breathing alcohol all over me. I sighed, and let in the clutch.

Joe was nursing a grievance. He would be. Everything which went wrong for Joe was someone else's fault, according to him. Barely twenty, he was a chronic grumbler. It was hard to know which was worse to put up with, his grousing or his bragging, and that he was treated with tolerance by the other jockeys said much for their good nature. Joe's saving grace was his undoubted ability as a jockey, but he had put that to bad use already by his "stopping" activities, and now he was threatening it altogether by getting drunk in the middle of the afternoon.

"I would have won that race," he whined.

"You're a fool, Joe," I said.

"No, honestly, Alan, I would have won that race. I had him placed just right. I had the others beat, I had 'em stone cold. Just right." He made sawing motions with his hands.

"You're a fool to drink so much at the races," I said.

DEAD CERT 47

"Eh?" He couldn't focus.

"Drink," I said. "You've had too much to drink."

"No, no, no, no . . ." The words came dribbling out, as if once he had started to speak it was too much effort to stop.

"Owners won't put you on their horses if they see you getting drunk," I said, feeling it was no business of mine, after all.

"I can win any race, drunk or not," said Joe.

"Not many owners would believe it."

"They know I'm good."

"So you are, but you won't be if you go on like this," I said.

"I can drink and I can ride and I can ride and I can drink. If I want to." He belched.

I let it pass. What Joe needed was a firm hand applied ten years ago. He looked all set now on the road to ruin and he wasn't going to thank anyone for directions off it.

He was whining again. "That bloody Mason . . ."

I didn't say anything. He tried again.

"That bloody Sandy, he tipped me off. He bloody well tipped me off over the bloody rails. I'd have won that race as easy as kiss your hand and he knew it and tipped me off over the bloody rails."

"Don't be silly, Joe."

"You can't say I wouldn't have won the race," said Joe argumentatively.

"And I can't say you would have won it," I said. "You fell at least a mile from home."

"I didn't fall. I'm telling you, aren't I? Sandy bloody Mason tipped me off over the rails."

"How?" I asked idly, concentrating on the road.

"He squeezed me against the rails. I shouted to him to give me more room. And do you know what he did? Do you know? He laughed. He bloody well laughed. Then he tipped me over. He stuck his knee into me and gave a heave and off I went over the bloody rails." His whining voice finished on a definite sob.

I looked at him. Two tears were rolling down his round cheeks. They glistened in the light from the dashboard, and fell with a tiny flash on to the furry collar of his sheepskin coat.

"Sandy wouldn't do a thing like that," I said mildly.

"Oh yes he would. He told me he'd get even with me. He said I'd be sorry. But I couldn't help it, Alan, I really couldn't." Two more tears rolled down.

I was out of my depth. I had no idea what he was talking about; but it began to look as though Sandy, if he had unseated him, had had his reasons.

Joe went on talking. "You're always decent to me, Alan, you're not like the others. You're my friend . . ." He put his hand heavily on my arm, pawing, leaning over towards me and giving me the benefit of the full force of his alcoholic breath. The delicate steering of the Lotus reacted to his sudden weight on my arm with a violent swerve towards the curb.

I shook him off. "For God's sake sit up, Joe, or you'll have us in the ditch," I said.

But he was too immersed in his own troubles to hear me. He pulled my arm again. There was a lay-by just ahead. I slowed, turned into it, and stopped the car.

"If you won't sit up and leave me alone you can get out and walk," I said, trying to get through to him with a rough tone.

But he was still on his own track, and weeping noisily now.

"You don't know what it's like to be in trouble," he sobbed. I resigned myself to listen. The quicker he got his resentments off his chest, I thought, the quicker he would relax and go to sleep.

"What trouble?" I said. I was not in the least interested.

"Alan, I'll tell you because you're a pal, a decent pal." He put his hand on my knee. I pushed it off.

Amid a fresh burst of tears Joe blurted, "I was supposed to stop a horse and I didn't, and Sandy lost a lot of money and said he'd get even with me and he's been following me around saying that for days and days and I knew he'd do something awful and he has." He paused for breath. "Lucky for me I hit a soft patch or I might have broken my neck. It wasn't funny. And that bloody Sandy," he choked on the name, "was laughing. I'll make him laugh on the other side of his bloody face."

This last sentence made me smile. Joe with his baby face, strong of body perhaps, but weak of character, was no match for the tough, forceful Sandy, more than ten years older and incalculably more self-assured. Joe's bragging, like his whining, sprang from feelings of insecurity. But the beginning of his outburst was something different.

"What horse did you not stop?" I asked, "and how did Sandy know you were supposed to be going to stop one?"

For a second I thought caution would silence him, but after the smallest hesitation he babbled on. The drink was still at the flood. So were the tears.

From the self-pitying, hiccuping, half incoherent voice I learned a sorry enough story. Shorn of blasphemy and reduced to essentials, it was this. Joe had been paid well for stopping horses on several occasions, two of which I had seen myself. But when David Stampe had told his father the Senior Steward about the last one, and Joe had nearly lost his licence, it gave him a steadying shock. The next time he was asked to stop a horse he said he would, but in the event, from understandable nerves, he had not done it thoroughly enough early in the race, and at the finish was faced with the plain knowledge that if he lost the race he would lose his licence as well. He won. This had happened ten days ago.

I was puzzled. "Is Sandy the only person who has harmed you?"

"He tipped me over the rails . . ." He was ready to start all over again.

I interrupted. "It wasn't Sandy, surely, who was paying you not to win?"

"No. I don't think so. I don't know," he snivelled.

"Do you mean you don't know who was paying you? Ever?"

"A man rang up and told me when he wanted me to stop one, and afterwards I got a packet full of money through the post."

"How many times have you done it?" I asked.

"Ten," said Joe, "all in the last six months." I stared at him.

"Often it was easy," said Joe defensively. "The ——s wouldn't have won anyway, even if I'd helped them."

"How much did you get for it?"

"A hundred. Twice it was two-fifty." Joe's tongue was still running away with him, and I believed him. It was big money, and anyone prepared to pay on that scale would surely want considerable revenge when Joe won against orders. But Sandy? I couldn't believe it.

"What did Sandy say to you after you won?" I asked.

Joe was still crying. "He said he'd backed the horse I beat and that he'd get even with me," said Joe. And it seemed that Sandy had done that.

"You didn't get your parcel of money, I suppose?"

"No," said Joe, sniffing.

"Haven't you any idea where they come from?" I asked.

"Some had London postmarks," said Joe. "I didn't take much notice." Too eager to count the contents to look closely at the wrappings, no doubt.

"Well," I said, "surely now that Sandy has had his little revenge, you are in the clear? Can't you possibly stop crying about it? It's all over. What are you in such a state about?"

For answer Joe took a paper from his jacket pocket and gave it to me.

"You might as well know it all. I don't know what to do. Help me, Alan. I'm frightened."

In the light from the dashboard I could see that this was true. And Joe was beginning to sober up.

I unfolded the paper and switched on the lights inside the car. It was a single sheet of thin, ordinary typing paper. In simple capital letters, written with a ball-point pen, were five words: BOLINGBROKE. YOU WILL BE PUNISHED.

"Bolingbroke is the horse you were supposed to stop and didn't?"

"Yes." The tears no longer welled in his eyes.

"When did you get this?" I asked.

"I found it in my pocket, today, when I put my jacket on after I'd changed. Just before the fifth race. It wasn't there when I took it off."

"And you spent the rest of the afternoon in the bar, in a blue funk, I suppose," I said.

"Yes . . . and I went back there while you took Mr. Tudor to Brighton. I didn't think anything was going to happen to me because of Bolingbroke, and I've been frightened ever since he won. And just as I was thinking it was all right Sandy pushed me over the rails and then I found this letter in my pocket. It isn't fair." The self-pity still whined in his voice.

I gave him back the paper.

"What am I to do?" said Joe.

I couldn't tell him, because I didn't know. He had got himself into a thorough mess, and he had good reason to be afraid. People who manipulated horses and jockeys to that extent were certain to play rough. The time lag of ten days between Bolingbroke's win and the arrival of the note could mean, I thought, that there was a cat-and-mouse, rather than a straightforward mentality at work. Which was little comfort to offer Joe.

Apart from some convulsive hiccups and sniffs, Joe seemed to have recovered from his tears, and the worst of the drunkenness was over. I switched off the inside lights, started the car up, and pulled back on to the road. As I had hoped, Joe soon went to sleep. He snored loudly.

Approaching Dorking, I woke him up. I had some questions to ask.

"Joe, who is that Mr. Tudor I took to Brighton? He knows you."

"He owns Bolingbroke," said Joe. "I often ride for him."

I was surprised. "Was he pleased when Bolingbroke won?" I asked.

"I suppose so. He wasn't there. He sent me ten-per-cent afterwards, though, and a letter thanking me. The usual thing."

"He hasn't been in racing long, has he?" I asked.

"Popped up about the same time you did," said Joe, with a distinct return to his old brash manner. "Both of you arrived with dark suntans in the middle of winter."

I had come by air from the burning African summer to the icy reception of October in England: but after eighteen months my skin was as pale as an Englishman's. Tudor's, on the other hand, remained dark.

Joe was sniggering. "You know why Mr. Clifford bloody Tudor lives at Brighton? It gives him an excuse to be sunburnt all the year round. Touch of the old tar, really."

After that I had no compunction in turning Joe out at the bus stop for Epsom. Unloading his troubles on to me seemed, for the present at least, to have restored his ego.

I drove back to the Cotswolds. At first I thought about Sandy Mason and wondered how he had got wind of Joe's intention to stop Bolingbroke.

But for the last hour of the journey I thought about Kate.

6

Scilla was lying asleep on the sofa with a rug over her legs and a half-full glass on a low table beside her. I picked up the glass and sniffed. Brandy. She usually drank gin and Campari. Brandy was for bad days only.

She opened her eyes. "Alan! I'm so glad you're back. What time is it?"

"Half past nine," I said.

"You must be starving," she said, pushing off the rug. "Why ever didn't you wake me? Dinner was ready hours ago."

"I've only just got here, and Joan is cooking now, so relax," I said.

We went in to eat. I sat in my usual place. Bill's chair, opposite Scilla, was empty. I made a mental note to move it back against the wall.

Half way through the steaks, Scilla said, breaking a long silence, "Two policemen came to see me today."

"Did they? About the inquest tomorrow?"

"No, it was about Bill." She pushed her plate away. "They asked me if he was in any trouble, as you did. They asked me the same questions in different ways for over half an hour. One of them suggested that if I was as fond of my husband as I said I was and on excellent terms with him, I ought to know if something was wrong in his life. They were rather nasty, really."

She was not looking at me. She kept her eyes down, regarding her half-eaten, congealing steak, and there was a slight embarrassment in her manner, which was unusual.

"I can imagine," I said, realising what was the matter. "They asked you, I suppose, to explain your relationship with me, and why I was still living in your house?"

She glanced up in surprise and evident relief. "Yes, they did. I didn't know how to tell you. It seems so ordinary to me that you should be here, yet I couldn't seem to make them understand that."

"I'll go tomorrow, Scilla," I said. "I'm not letting you in for any more gossip. If the police can think that you were cheating Bill with me, so can the village and the county. I've been exceedingly thoughtless, and I'm very very sorry." For I, too, had found it quite natural to stay on in Bill's house after his death.

"You will certainly not go tomorrow on my account, Alan," said Scilla with more resolution than I would have given her credit for. "I need you here. I shall do nothing but cry all the time if I don't have you to talk to, especially in the evenings. I can get through the days, with the children and the house to think about. But the nights . . ." And in her suddenly ravaged face I could read all the tearing, savage pain of a loss four days old.

"I don't care what anyone says," she said through starting tears, "I need you here. Please, please, don't go away."

"I'll stay," I said. "Don't worry. I'll stay as long as you want me to. But you must promise to tell me when you are ready for me to go."

She dried her eyes and raised a smile. "When I begin to worry about my reputation, you mean? I promise."

I had driven the better part of three hundred miles besides riding in two races, and I was tired. We went to our beds early, Scilla promising to take her sleeping pills.

But at two o'clock in the morning she opened my bedroom door. I woke at once. She came over and switched on my bedside light, and sat down on my bed.

She looked ridiculously young and defenceless. She was wearing a pale blue knee-length chiffon nightdress which flowed transparently about her slender body and fell like mist over the small round breasts.

I propped myself up on my elbow and ran my fingers through my hair.

"I can't sleep," she said.

"Did you take the pills?" I asked.

But I could answer my own question. Her eyes looked drugged, and in her right mind she would not have come into my room so revealingly undressed.

"Yes, I took them. They've made me a bit groggy, but I'm still awake. I took an extra one." Her voice was slurred and dopey. "Will you talk for a bit?" she said. "Then perhaps I'll feel more sleepy. When I'm on my own I just lie and think about Bill . . . Tell me more about Plumpton . . . You said you rode another horse . . . Tell me about it. Please . . ."

So I sat up in bed and wrapped my eiderdown round her shoulders, and told her about Kate's birthday present and Uncle George, thinking how often I had told Polly and Henry and William bedside stories to send them to sleep. But after a while I saw she was not listening, and presently the slow heavy tears were falling from her bent head on to her hands.

"You must think me a terrible fool to cry so much," she said, "but I just can't help it." She lay down weakly beside me, her head on my pillow. She took hold of my hand and closed her eyes. I looked down at her sweet, pretty face with the tears trickling past her ears into her cloudy dark hair, and gently kissed her forehead. Her body shook with two heavy sobs. I lay down and slid my arm under her neck. She turned towards me and clung to me, holding me fiercely, sobbing slowly with her deep terrible grief.

And at last, gradually, the sleeping pills did their job. She relaxed, breathing audibly, her hand twisted into the jacket of my pyjamas. She was lying half on top of my bedclothes, and the February night was cold. I tugged the sheet and blankets gently from underneath her with my free hand and spread them over her, and pulled the eiderdown up over our shoulders. I switched off the light and lay in the dark, gently cradling her until her breath grew soft and she was soundly asleep.

I smiled to think of Inspector Lodge's face if he could have seen us. And I reflected that I should not have been content to be so passive a bedfellow had I held Kate in my arms instead.

During the night Scilla twisted uneasily several times, murmuring jumbled words that made no sense, seeming to be calmed each time by my hand stroking her hair. Towards morning she was quiet. I got up, wrapped her in the eiderdown, and carried her back to her own bed. I knew that if she woke in my room, with the drugs worn off, she would be unnecessarily ashamed and upset.

She was still sleeping peacefully when I left her.

A few hours later, after a hurried breakfast, I drove her to Maidenhead to attend the inquest. She slept most of the way and did not refer to what had happened in the night. I was not sure she even remembered.

Lodge must have been waiting for us, for he met us as soon as we went in. He was carrying a sheaf of papers, and looked businesslike and solid. I introduced him to Scilla, and his eyes sharpened appreciatively at the sight of her pale prettiness. But what he said was a surprise.

"I'd like to apologise," he began, "for the rather unpleasant suggestions which have been put to you and Mr. York about each other." He turned to me. "We are now satisfied that you were in no way responsible for Major Davidson's death."

"That's big of you," I said lightly, but I was glad to hear it.

Lodge went on, "You can say what you like to the Coroner about the wire, of course, but I'd better warn you that he won't be too enthusiastic. He hates anything fancy, and you've no evidence. Don't worry if you don't agree with his verdict—I think it's sure to be accidental death—because inquests can always be reopened, if need be."

In view of this I was not disturbed when the Coroner, a heavily-moustached man of fifty, listened keenly enough to my account of Bill's fall, but dealt a little brusquely with my wire theory. Lodge testified that he had accompanied me to the racecourse to look for the wire I had reported, but that there had been none there.

The man who had been riding directly behind me when Bill fell was also called. He was an amateur rider who lived in Yorkshire, and he'd had to come a long way. He said, with an apologetic glance for me, that he had seen nothing suspicious at the fence, and that in his opinion it was a normal fall. Unexpected maybe, but not mysterious. He radiated common sense.

Had Mr. York, the Coroner enquired in a doubtful voice, mentioned the possible existence of wire to anyone at all on the day of the race? Mr. York had not.

The Coroner, summing up medical, police, and all other evidence, found that Major Davidson had died of injuries resulting from his horse having fallen in a steeplechase. He was not convinced, he said, that the fall was anything but an accident.

Owing to a mistake about the time, the local paper had failed to send a representative to the inquest, and from lack of detailed reporting the proceedings rated only small paragraphs in the evening and morning papers. The word "wire" was not mentioned. This omission did not worry me one way or the other, but Scilla was relieved. She said she could not yet stand questions from inquisitive friends, let alone reporters.

Bill's funeral was held quietly in the village on Friday morning, attended only by his family and close friends. Bearing one corner of his coffin on my shoulder and bidding my private good-byes, I knew for sure that I would not be satisfied until his death was avenged. I didn't know how it was to be done, and, strangely enough, I didn't feel any urgency about it. But in time, I promised him, in time, I'll do it.

Scilla's sister had come to the funeral and was to stay with her for two or three days; so, missing lunch out of deference to the light weight I was committed to ride at on the following day, I drove up to London to spend some long overdue hours in the office, arranging the details of insurance and customs duty on a series of shipments of copper.

The office staff were experts. My job was to discuss with Hughes, my second in command, the day-to-day affairs of the company, to make decisions and agree to plans made by Hughes, and to sign my name to endless documents and letters. It seldom took me more than three days a week. On Sunday it was my weekly task to write to my father. I had a feeling he skipped the filial introduction and the accounts of my racing, and fastened his sharp brain only on my report of the week's trade and my assessment of the future.

Those Sunday reports had been part of my life for ten years. School homework could wait, my father used to say. It was more important for me to know every detail about the kingdom I was to inherit; and to this end he made me study continually the papers he brought home from his office. By the time I left school I could appraise at a glance the significance of fluctuations in the world prices of raw materials, even if I had no idea when Charles I was beheaded.

On Friday evening I waited impatiently for Kate to join me for dinner. Unwrapped from the heavy overcoat and woolly boots she had worn at Plumpton, she was more ravishing than ever. She wore a glowing red dress, simple and devastating, and her dark hair fell smoothly to her shoulders. She seemed to be alight from within with her own brand of effervescence. The evening was fun and, to me at least, entirely satisfactory. We ate, we danced, we talked.

While we swayed lazily round the floor to some dreamy slow-tempo music, Kate introduced the only solemn note of the evening.

"I saw a bit about your friend's inquest in this morning's paper," she said.

I brushed my lips against her hair. It smelled sweet. "Accidental death," I murmured vaguely. "I don't think."

"Hm?" Kate looked up.

"I'll tell you about it one day, when I know the whole story," I said, enjoying the taut line of her neck as she tilted her face up to mine. It was strange, I thought, that it was possible to feel two strong emotions at once. Pleasure in surrendering to the seduction of the music with a dancing Kate balanced in my arms, and a tugging sympathy for Scilla trying to come to terms with her loneliness eighty miles away in the windy Cotswold hills.

"Tell me now," said Kate with interest. "If it wasn't accidental death, what was it?"

I hesitated. I didn't want too much reality pushing the evening's magic sideways.

"Come on, come on," she urged, smiling. "You can't stop there. I'll die of suspense."

So I told her about the wire. It shocked her enough to stop her dancing, and we stood flat-footed in the middle of the floor with the other couples flowing round and bumping into us.

"Dear heavens," she said, "how . . . how wicked."

She wanted me to explain why the inquest verdict had been what it was, and after I had told her that with the wire gone there was no evidence of anything else, she said, "I can't bear to think of anyone getting away with so disgusting a trick."

"Nor can I," I said, "and they won't, I promise you, if I can help it."

"That's good," she said seriously. She began to sway again to the music, and I took her in my arms and we drifted back into the dance. We didn't mention Bill again.

It seemed to me for long periods that evening as if my feet were not in proper contact with the floor, and the most extraordinary tremors constantly shook my knees. Kate seemed to notice nothing:

she was friendly, funny, brimming over with gaiety, and utterly unsentimental.

When at length I helped her into the chauffeur-driven car which Uncle George had sent up from Sussex to take her home, I had discovered how painful it is to love. I was excited, keyed up. And also anxious; for I was sure that she did not feel as intensely about me as I about her.

I already knew I wanted to marry Kate. The thought that she might not have me was a bitter one.

The next day I went to Kempton Park races. Outside the weighing room I ran into Dane. We talked about the going, the weather, Pete's latest plans for us, and the horses. Usual jockey stuff. Then Dane said, "You took Kate out last night?"

"Yes."

"Where did you go?"

"The River Club," I said. "Where did you take her?"

"Didn't she tell you?" asked Dane.

"She said to ask you."

"River Club," said Dane.

"Damn it," I said. But I had to laugh.

"Honours even," said Dane.

"Did she ask you down to stay with Uncle George?" I asked suspiciously.

"I'm going today, after the races," said Dane, smiling. "And you?"

"Next Saturday," I said gloomily. "You know, Dane, she's teasing us abominably."

"I can stand it," said Dane. He tapped me on the shoulder. "Don't look so miserable, it may never happen."

"That's what I'm afraid of," I sighed. He laughed and went into the weighing room.

It was an uneventful afternoon. I rode my big black mare in a novice 'chase and Dane beat me by two lengths. At the end of the day we walked out to the car park together.

"How is Mrs. Davidson bearing up?" Dane asked.

"Fairly well, considering the bottom has dropped out of her world."

"Jockeys' wives' nightmare come true."

"Yes," I said.

"It makes you pause a bit, before you ask a girl to put up with that sort of constant worry," said Dane, thoughtfully.

"Kate?" I asked. He looked round sharply and grinned.

"I suppose so. Do you mind?"

"Yes," I said, keeping my voice light. "I mind very much."

We came to his car first, and he put his race glasses and hat on the seat. His suitcase was in the back.

"So long, mate," he said. "I'll keep you posted."

I watched him drive off, answered his wave. I seldom felt envious of anybody, but at that moment I envied Dane sorely.

I climbed into the Lotus and pointed its low blue nose towards home.

It was on the road through Maidenhead Thicket that I saw the horse-box. It was parked in a lay-by on the near side, with tools scattered on the ground round it and the bonnet up. It was facing me as I approached, as if it had broken down on its way into Maidenhead. A man was walking a horse up and down in front of it.

The driver, standing by the bonnet scratching his head, saw me coming and gestured to me to stop. I pulled up beside him. He walked round to talk to me through the window, a middle-aged man, unremarkable, wearing a leather jacket.

"Do you know anything about engines, sir?" he asked.

"Not as much as you, I should think," I said, smiling. He had grease on his hands. If a horse-box driver couldn't find the fault in his own motor, it would be a long job for whoever did. "I'll take you back into Maidenhead, though, if you like. There's bound to be someone there who can help you."

"That's extremely kind of you, sir," he said, civilly. "Thank you very much. But—er—I'm in a bit of a difficulty." He looked into the car and saw my binoculars on the seat beside me. His face lightened up. "You don't possibly know anything about horses, sir?"

"A bit, yes," I said.

"Well, it's like this, sir. I've got these two horses going to the London docks. They're being exported. Well, that one's all right." He pointed to the horse walking up and down. "But the other one, he don't seem so good. Sweating hard, he's been, the last hour or so, and biting at his stomach. He keeps trying to lie down. Looks ill. The lad's in there with him now, and he's proper worried, I can tell you."

"It sounds as though it might be colic," I said. "If it is, he ought to be walking round, too. It's the only way to get him better. It's essential to keep them on the move when they've got colic."

The driver looked troubled. "It's a lot to ask, sir," he said, tentatively, "but would you have a look at him? Motors are my fancy, not horses, except to back 'em. And these lads are not too bright. I don't want a rocket from the boss for not looking after things properly."

"All right," I said, "I'll have a look. But I'm not a vet, you know, by a long way."

He smiled in a relieved fashion. "Thank you, sir. Anyway, you'll know if I've got to get a vet at once or not, I should think."

I parked the car in the lay-by behind the horse-box. The door at the back of the horse-box opened and a hand, the stable lad's, I supposed, reached out to help me up. He took me by the wrist.

He didn't leave go.

There were three men waiting for me inside the horse-box. And no horse, sick or otherwise. After a flurried ten seconds during which my eyes were still unused to the dim light, I ended up standing with my back to the end post of one of the partition walls.

The horse-box was divided into three stalls with two partition walls between them, and there was a space across the whole width of the box at the back, usually occupied by lads travelling with their horses.

Two of the men held my arms. They stood one each side of the partition and slightly behind me, and they had an uncomfortable leverage on my shoulders. The post of the partition was padded with matting, as it always is in racehorse boxes, to save the horses hurting themselves while they travel. The matting tickled my neck.

The driver stepped up into the box and shut the door. His manner, still incredibly deferential, held a hint of triumph. It was entitled to. He had set a neat trap.

"Very sorry to have to do this, sir," he said politely. It was macabre.

"If it's money you want," I said, "you're going to be unlucky. I don't bet much and I didn't have a good day at the races today. I'm afraid you've gone to a lot of trouble for a measly eight quid."

"We don't want your money, sir," he said. "Though as you're offering it we might as well take it, at that." And still smiling pleasantly he put his hand inside my jacket and took my wallet out of the inside pocket.

I kicked his shin as hard as I could, but was hampered because of my position against the post. As soon as they felt me move the two men behind me jerked my arms painfully backwards.

"I shouldn't do that, sir, if I was you," said the friendly driver, rubbing his leg. He opened my wallet and took out the money, which he folded carefully and stowed inside his leather coat. He peered at the other things in the wallet, then stepped towards me, and put it back in my pocket. He was smiling faintly.

I stood still.

"That's better," he said, approvingly.

"What's all this about?" I asked. I had some idea that they intended to ransom me to my distant millionaire parent. Along the lines of "Cable us ten thousand pounds or we post your son back to you in small pieces." That would mean that they knew all along who I was, and had not just stopped any random motorist in a likely-looking car to rob him.

"Surely you know, sir?" said the driver.

"I've no idea."

"I was asked to give you a message, Mr. York."

So he did know who I was. And he had not this minute discovered it from my wallet, which contained only money, stamps, and a cheque book in plain view. One or two things with my name on were in a flapped pocket, but he had not looked there.

"What makes you think my name is York?" I asked, trying a shot at outraged surprise. It was no good.

"Mr. Alan York, sir, was scheduled to drive along this road on his way from Kempton Park to the Cotswolds at approximately five fifteen p.m. on Saturday, February 27th, in a dark blue Lotus Elite, licence number KAB 890. I must thank you, sir, for making it easy for me to intercept you. You could go a month on the road without seeing another car like yours. I'd have had a job flagging you down if you'd been driving, say, a Ford or an Austin." His tone was still conversational.

"Get on with the message. I'm listening," I said.

"Deeds speak louder than words," said the driver, mildly.

He came close and unbuttoned my jacket, looking at me steadily with wide eyes, daring me to kick him. I didn't move. He untied my tie, opened the neck of my shirt. We looked into each other's eyes. I hoped mine were as expressionless as his. I let my arms go slack in the grip of the two men behind me, and felt them relax their hold slightly.

The driver stepped back and looked towards the fourth man, who had been leaning against the horse-box wall, silently. "He's all yours, Sonny. Deliver the message," he said.

Sonny was young, with sideboards. But I didn't look at his face, particularly. I looked at his hands.

He had a knife. The hilt lay in his palm, and his fingers were lightly curled round it, not gripping. The way a professional holds a knife.

There was nothing of the driver's mock deference in Sonny's manner. He was enjoying his work. He stood squarely in front of me and put the point of his short blade on my breastbone. It scarcely pricked, so light was his touch.

Oh bloody hell, I thought. My father would not be at all pleased to receive ransom messages reinforced by pleas from me for my own safety. I would never be able to live it down. And I was sure that this little melodrama was intended to soften me up into a suitably frightened state of mind. I sagged against the post, as if to shrink away from the knife. Sonny's grim mouth smiled thinly in a sneer.

Using the post as a springboard I thrust forwards and sideways as strongly as I knew how, bringing my knee up hard into Sonny's groin and tearing my arms out of the slackened grasp of the men behind me.

I leaped for the door and got it open. In the small area of the horse-box I had no chance, but I thought that if only I could get out into the thicket I might be able to deal with them. I had learned a nasty trick or two about fighting from my cousin, who lived in Kenya and had taken lessons from the Mau Mau.

But I didn't make it.

I tried to swing out with the door, but it was stiff and slow. The driver grabbed my ankle. I shook his hand off, but the vital second had gone. The two men who had held me clutched at my clothes. Through the open door I glimpsed the man who had been leading the horse up and down. He was looking enquiringly at the horse-box. I had forgotten about him.

I lashed out furiously with feet, fists, and elbows, but they were too much for me. I ended up where I began, against the matting-padded post with my arms pulled backwards. This time the two men were none too gentle. They slammed me back against the post hard and put their weight on my arms. I felt the wrench in my shoulders and down my chest to my stomach. I shut my teeth.

Sonny, clutching his abdomen, was half sitting, half kneeling in the corner. He watched with satisfaction.

"That hurt the bastard, Peaky," he said. "Do it again."

Peaky and his mate did it again.

Sonny laughed. Not a nice laugh.

A little more pressure and I should have some torn ligaments and a dislocated shoulder. There didn't seem to be much I could do about it.

The driver shut the horse-box door and picked the knife up from the floor, where it had fallen. He was not looking quite so calm as before. My fist had connected with his nose and blood was trickling out of it. But his temper was intact.

"Stop it. Stop it, Peaky," he said. "The boss said we weren't to hurt him. He made quite a point of it. You wouldn't want the boss to know you disobeyed him, would you?" There was a threat in his voice.

The tension on my arms slowly relaxed. Sonny's smile turned to a sullen scowl. It appeared I had the boss to thank for something, even if not much.

"Now, Mr. York," said the driver reproachfully, wiping his nose on a blue handkerchief, "all that was quite unnecessary. We only want to give you a message."

"I don't like listening with knives sticking into me," I said.

The driver sighed. "Yes, sir, I can see that was a mistake. It was meant for you to understand that the warning is serious, see. Take no notice of it, and you'll find you're in real trouble. I'm telling you, real trouble."

"What warning?" I said, mystified.

"You're to lay off asking questions about Major Davidson," he said.

"*What?*" I goggled at him. It was so unexpected. "I haven't been asking questions about Major Davidson," I said weakly.

"I don't know about that, I'm sure," said the driver, mopping away, "but that's the message, and you'd do well to take heed of it, sir. I'm telling you for your own good. The boss don't like people poking into his affairs."

"Who is the boss?" I asked.

"Now, sir, you know better than to ask questions like that. Sonny, go and tell Bert we've finished here. We'll load up the horse."

Sonny stood up with a groan and went over to the door, his hand still pressed to his groin. He yelled something out of the window.

"Stand still, Mr. York, and you'll come to no harm," said the driver, his politeness unimpaired. He mopped, and looked at his handkerchief to see if his nose was still bleeding. It was. I took his advice, and stood still. He opened the door and climbed down out of the horse-box. A little time passed during which Sonny and I exchanged glares and nobody said anything.

Then there was the noise of bolts and clips being undone, and the side of the horse-box which formed the ramp was lowered to the ground. The fifth man, Bert, led the horse up the ramp and fastened him into the nearest stall. The driver raised the ramp again and fastened it.

I used the brief period while what was left of the daylight flooded into the box, to twist my head round as far as I could and take a clear look at Peaky. I saw what I expected, but it only increased my bewilderment.

The driver climbed into the cab, shut the door, and started the engine.

Bert said, "Take him over to the door." I needed no urging. The horse-box began to move. Bert opened the door. Peaky and his pal let go of my arms and Bert gave me a push. I hit the ground just as the accelerating horse-box pulled out of the lay-by on to the deserted road. It was as well I had had a good deal of practice at falling off horses. Instinctively, I landed on my shoulder and rolled.

I sat on the ground and looked after the speeding horse-box. The number plate was mostly obscured by thick dust, but I had time to see the registration letters. They were APX.

The Lotus still stood in the lay-by. I picked myself up, dusted the worst off my suit, and walked over to it. I intended to follow the horse-box and see where it went. But the thorough driver had seen to it that I should not. The car would not start. Opening the bonnet to see how much damage had been done, I found that three of the four sparking plugs had been taken out. They lay in a neat row on the battery. It took me ten minutes to replace them, because my hands were trembling.

By then I had no hope of catching the horse-box or of finding anyone who had noticed its direction. I got back into the car and fastened the neck of my shirt. My tie was missing altogether.

I took out the A.A. book and looked up the registration letters PX. For what it was worth, the horse-box was originally registered in West Sussex. If the number plate were genuine, it might be possible to discover the present owner. For a quarter of an hour I sat and thought. Then I started the car, turned it, and drove back into Maidenhead.

The town was bright with lights, though nearly all the shops were shut. The door of the police station was open wide. I went in and asked for Inspector Lodge.

"He isn't in yet," said the policeman at the enquiry desk, glancing up at the clock. It was ten past six. "He'll be here any minute, if you care to wait, sir."

"He isn't in yet? Do you mean he is just starting work for the day?"

"Yes, sir. He's on late turn. Busy evening here, Saturdays." He grinned. "Dance halls, pubs, and car crashes." I smiled back, sat down on the bench and waited. After five minutes Lodge came in quickly, peeling off his coat.

"Evening, Small, what's new?" he said to the policeman at the enquiry desk.

"Gentleman here to see you, sir," said Small, gesturing to me. "He's only been waiting a few minutes."

Lodge turned round. I stood up. "Good evening," I said.

"Good evening, Mr. York." Lodge gave me a piercing look but showed no surprise at seeing me. His eyes fell to the neck of my shirt, and his eyebrows rose a fraction. But he said only, "What can I do for you?"

"Are you very busy?" I asked. "If you have time, I would like to tell you . . . how I lost my tie." In mid-sentence I flunked saying baldly that I had been manhandled. As it was, Small looked at me curiously, clearly thinking me mad to come into a police station to tell an inspector how I lost my tie.

But Lodge, whose perception was acute, said, "Come into my office, Mr. York." He led the way. He hung up his hat and coat on pegs and lit the gas fire, but its glowing bars couldn't make a cosy place of the austere, square, filing-cabineted little room.

Lodge sat behind his tidy desk, and I, as before, faced him. He offered me a cigarette and gave me a light. As the smoke went comfortingly down into my lungs, I was wondering where to begin.

I said, "Have you got any further with the Major Davidson business since the day before yesterday?"

"No, I'm afraid not. It no longer has any sort of priority with us. Yesterday we discussed it in conference and consulted your Senior Steward, Sir Creswell Stampe. In view of the verdict at the inquest, your story is considered, on the whole, to be the product of a youthful and overheated imagination. No one but you saw any wire. The grooves on the posts of the fence may or may not have been caused by wire, but there is no indication *when* they were made. I understand it is fairly common practice for groundsmen to raise a wire across a fence so that members of the riding public shall not try to jump it and make holes in the birch." He paused, then went on, "Sir Creswell says the view of the National Hunt Committee, several of whom he has talked to on the telephone, is that you made a mistake. If you saw any wire, they contend, it must have belonged to the groundsman."

"Have they asked him?" I said.

Lodge sighed. "The head groundsman says he didn't leave any wire on the course, but one of his staff is old and vague, and can't be sure that he didn't."

We looked at each other in glum silence.

"And what do you think, yourself?" I asked finally.

Lodge said, "I believe you saw the wire and that Major Davidson was brought down by it. There is one fact which I personally consider significant enough to justify this belief. It is that the attendant who gave his name as Thomas Cook did not collect the pay due to him for two days' work. In my experience there has to be a very good reason for a workman to ignore his pay packet." He smiled sardonically.

"I could give you another fact to prove that Major Davidson's fall was no accident," I said, "but you'll have to take my word for it again. No evidence."

"Go on."

"Someone has been to great pains to tell me not to ask awkward questions about it." I told him about the events in and around the horse-box, and added, "And how's that for the product of a youthful and overheated imagination?"

DEAD CERT 67

"When did all this happen?" asked Lodge.

"About an hour ago."

"And what were you doing between then and the time you arrived here?"

"Thinking," I said, stubbing out my cigarette.

"Oh," said Lodge. "Well, have you given any thought to the improbabilities in your story? My chief isn't going to like them when I make my report."

"Don't make it then," I said, smiling. "But I suppose the most glaring improbability is that five men, a horse, and a horse-box should all be employed to give a warning which might much more easily have been sent by post."

"That certainly indicates an organisation of unusual size," said Lodge, with a touch of irony.

"There are at least ten of them," I said. "One or two are probably in hospital, though."

Lodge sat up straighter.

"What do you mean? How do you know?"

"The five men who stopped me today are all taxi-drivers. Either from London or Brighton, but I don't know which. I saw them at Plumpton races three days ago, fighting a pitched battle against a rival gang."

"What?" Lodge exclaimed. Then he said, "Yes, I saw a paragraph about it in a newspaper. Do you recognise them positively?"

"Yes," I said. "Sonny had his knife out at Plumpton, too, but he was pinned down by a big heavy man, and didn't get much chance to use it. But I saw his face quite clearly. Peaky you couldn't mistake, with that dark widow's peak growing down his forehead. The other three were all rounded up into the same group at Plumpton. I was waiting to give someone a lift, and I had a long time to look at the taxi-drivers after the fight was over. Bert, the man with the horse, had a black eye today, and the man who held my right arm, whose name I don't know, he had some sticking plaster on his forehead. But why were they all free? The last I saw of them, they were bound for the cells, I thought, for disturbing the peace."

"They may be out on bail, or else they were let off with a fine. I don't know, without seeing a report," said Lodge. "Now why, in your opinion, were so many sent to warn you?"

"Rather flattering, sending five, when you come to think of it," I grinned. "Perhaps the taxi business is in the doldrums and they hadn't anything else to do. Or else it was, as the driver said, to ram the point home."

"Which brings me," said Lodge, "to another improbability. Why, if you were faced with a knife at your chest, did you throw yourself forward? Wasn't that asking for trouble?"

"I wouldn't have been so keen if he'd held the point a bit higher up; but it was against my breastbone. You'd need a hammer to get a knife through that. I reckoned that I'd knock it out of Sonny's hand rather than into me, and that's what happened."

"Didn't it cut you at all?"

"Not much," I said.

"Let's see," said Lodge, getting up and coming round the desk. I opened my shirt again. Between the second and third buttons there was a shallow cut an inch or so long in the skin over my breastbone. Some blood had clotted on the cut and there was a dried rusty trail down my chest where a few drops had run. My shirt was spotted here and there. Nothing. I hadn't felt it much.

Lodge sat down again. I buttoned my shirt.

"Now," he said, picking up his pen and biting the end of it. "What questions have you been asking about Major Davidson, and of whom have you asked them?"

"That is really what is most surprising about the whole affair," I said. "I've hardly asked anything of anybody. And I certainly haven't had any useful answers."

"But you must have touched a nerve somewhere," said Lodge. He took a sheet of paper out of the drawer. "Tell me the names of everyone with whom you have discussed the wire."

"With you," I said promptly. "And with Mrs. Davidson. And everyone at the inquest heard me say I'd found it."

"But I noticed that the inquest wasn't properly reported in the papers. There was no mention of wire in the press," he said. "And anyone seeing you at the inquest wouldn't have got the impression that you were hell-bent on unravelling the mystery. You took the verdict very calmly and not at all as if you disagreed with it."

"Thanks to your warning me in advance what to expect," I said.

Lodge's list looked short and unsatisfactory on the large sheet of paper.

"Anyone else?" he said.

"Oh . . . a friend . . . a Miss Ellery-Penn. I told her last night."

"Girl friend?" he asked bluntly. He wrote her down.

"Yes," I said.

"Anyone else?"

"No."

"Why not?" he asked, pushing the paper away.

"I reckoned you and Sir Creswell needed a clear field. I thought I might mess things up for you if I asked too many questions. Put people on their guard, ready with their answers—that sort of thing. But it seems, from what you've said about dropping your enquiries, that I might as well have gone ahead." I spoke a little bitterly.

Lodge looked at me carefully. "You resent being considered youthful and hot-headed," he said.

"Twenty-four isn't young," I said. "I seem to remember England once had a Prime Minister of that age. He didn't do so badly."

"That's irrelevant, and you know it," he said.

I grinned.

Lodge said, "What do you propose to do now?"

"Go home," I said, looking at my watch.

"No, I meant about Major Davidson."

"Ask as many questions as I can think of," I said promptly.

"In spite of the warning?"

"Because of it," I said. "The very fact that five men were sent to warn me off means that there is a good deal to find out. Bill Davidson was a good friend, you know. I can't tamely let whoever caused his death get away with it." I thought a moment. "First, I'll find out who owns the taxis which Peaky and Co. drive."

"Well, unofficially, I wish you luck," said Lodge. "But be careful."

"Sure," I said, standing up.

Lodge came to the street door of the police station and shook hands. "Let me know how you get on," he said.

"Yes, I will."

He raised his hand in a friendly gesture, and went in. I resumed my interrupted journey to the Cotswolds. My wrenched shoulders were aching abominably, but as long as I concentrated on Bill's accident I could forget them.

It struck me that both the accident and the affair of the horse-box should give some clue to the mind which had hatched them.

It was reasonable to assume it was the same mind. Both events were elaborate, where some simpler plan would have been effective, and the word "devious" drifted into my thoughts and I dredged around in my memory chasing its echo. Finally I traced it to Joe Nantwich and the threatening letter that had reached him ten days late, but decided that Joe's troubles had nothing to do with Bill's.

Both the attack on Bill and the warning to me had been, I was certain, more violent in the event than in the plan. Bill had died partly by bad luck; and I would have been less roughly handled had I not tried to escape. I came to the conclusion that I was looking for someone with a fanciful imagination, someone prepared to be brutal up to a point, and whose little squibs, because of their complicated nature, were apt to go off with bigger bangs than were intended.

And it was comforting to realise that my adversary was not a man of superhuman intelligence. He could make mistakes. His biggest so far, I thought, was to go to great lengths to deliver an unnecessary warning whose sole effect was to stir me to greater action.

For two days I did nothing. There was no harm in giving the impression that the warning was being taken to heart.

I played poker with the children and lost to Henry because half my mind was occupied with his father's affairs.

Henry said, "You aren't thinking what you're doing, Alan," in a mock sorrowful tone as he rooked me of ten chips with two pairs.

"I expect he's in love," said Polly, turning on me an assessing female eye. There was that, too.

"Pooh," said Henry. He dealt the cards.

"What's in love?" said William, who was playing tiddly-winks with his chips, to Henry's annoyance.

"Soppy stuff," said Henry. "Kissing, and all that slush."

"Mummy's in love with me," said William, a cuddly child.

"Don't be silly," said Polly loftily, from her eleven years. "In love means weddings and brides and confetti and things."

"Well, Alan," said Henry, in a scornful voice, "you'd better get out of love quick or you won't have any chips left."

William picked up his hand. His eyes and mouth opened wide. This meant he had at least two aces. They were the only cards he ever raised on. I saw Henry give him a flick of a glance, then look back at his own hand. He discarded three and took three more, and at his turn, he pushed away his cards. I turned them over. Two queens and two tens. Henry was a realist. He knew when to give in. And William, bouncing up and down with excitement, won only four chips with three aces and a pair of fives.

Not for the first time I wondered at the quirks of heredity. Bill had been a friendly, genuine man of many solid virtues. Scilla, matching him, was compassionate and loving. Neither was at all intellectually gifted; yet they had endowed their elder son with a piercing, exceptional intelligence.

And how could I guess, as I cut the cards for Polly and helped William straighten up his leaning tower of chips, that Henry already held in his sharp eight-year-old brain the key to the puzzle of his father's death.

He didn't know it himself.

7

The Cheltenham National Hunt Festival meeting started on Tuesday, March 2nd.

Three days of superlative racing lay ahead, and the finest 'chasers in the world crowded into the racecourse stables. Ferries from Ireland brought them across by boat and plane load; dark horses from the bogs whose supernatural turn of foot was foretold in thick mysterious brogue, and golden geldings who had already taken prizes and cups galore across the Irish Sea.

Horse-boxes from Scotland, from Kent, from Devon, from everywhere, converged on Gloucestershire. Inside, they carried Grand National winners, champion hurdlers, all-conquering handicappers, splendid hunters: the aristocrats among jumpers.

With four big races in the three days reserved for them alone, every amateur jockey in the country who could beg, borrow or buy a mount hurried to the course. A ride at Cheltenham was an honour: a win at Cheltenham an experience never to be forgotten. The amateur jockeys embraced the Festival with passionate fervour.

But one amateur jockey, Alan York, felt none of this passionate fervour as he drove into the car park. I could not explain it to myself, but for once the hum of the gathering crowd, the expectant faces, the sunshine of the cold invigorating March morning, even the prospect of riding three good horses at the meeting, stirred me not at all.

Outside the main gate I sought out the newspaper seller I had spoken to at Plumpton. He was a short, tubby little Cockney with a large moustache and a cheerful temperament. He saw me coming, and held out a paper.

"Morning, Mr. York," he said. "Do you fancy your horse today?"

"You might have a bit on," I said, "but not your shirt. There's the Irishman to be reckoned with."

"You'll do him, all right."

"Well, I hope so." I waited while he sold a newspaper to an elderly man with enormous race glasses. Then I said, "Do you remember the taxi-drivers fighting at Plumpton?"

"Couldn't hardly forget it, could I?" He beamed.

"You told me one lot came from London and one from Brighton."

"Yes, that's right."

"Which lot were which?" I said. He looked mystified. I said, "Which lot came from London and which came from Brighton?"

"Oh, I see." He sold a paper to two middle-aged ladies wearing thick tweeds and ribbed woollen stockings, and gave them change. Then he turned back to me.

"Which lot was which, like? Hm . . . I see 'em often enough, you know, but they ain't a friendly lot. They don't talk to you. Not like the private chauffeurs, see? I'd know the Brighton lot if I could see 'em, though. Know 'em by sight, see?" He broke off to yell "Midday Special" at the top of his lungs, and as a result sold three more papers. I waited patiently.

"How do you recognise them?" I asked.

"By their faces, o'course." He thought it a foolish question.

"Yes, but which faces? Can you describe them?"

"Oh, I see. There's all sorts."

"Can't you describe just one of them?" I asked.

He narrowed his eyes, thinking, and tugged his moustache. "One of 'em. Well, there's one nasty looking chap with sort of slitty eyes. I wouldn't like a ride in his taxi. You'd know him by his hair, I reckon. It grows nearly down to his eyebrows. Rum looking cove. What do you want him for?"

"I don't want him," I said. "I just want to know where he comes from."

"Brighton, that's it." He beamed at me. "There's another one I see sometimes, too. A young ted with sideboards, always cleaning his nails with a knife."

"Thanks a lot," I said. I gave him a pound note and his beam grew wider. He tucked it into an inside pocket.

"Best of luck, sir," he said. I left him, with "Midday Special" ringing in my ears, and went in to the weighing room, pondering on the information that my captors with the horse-box came from Brighton. Whoever had sent them could not have imagined that I had seen them before, and could find them again.

Preoccupied, I suddenly realised that Pete Gregory was talking to me. ". . . Had a puncture on the way, but they've got here safely, that's the main thing. Are you listening, Alan?"

"Yes, Pete. Sorry. I was thinking."

"Glad to hear you can," said Pete with a fat laugh. Tough and shrewd though he was, his sense of humour had never grown up. Schoolboy insults passed as the highest form of wit for him; but one got used to it.

"How is Palindrome?" I asked. My best horse.

"He's fine. I was just telling you, they had a puncture . . ." He broke off, exasperated. He hated having to repeat things. "Oh well . . . do you want to go over to the stables and have a look at him?"

"Yes, please," I said.

We walked down to the stables. Pete had to come with me because of the tight security rules. Even owners could not visit their horses without the trainer to vouch for them, and stable boys had passes with their photographs on, to show at the stable gate. It was all designed to prevent the doping or "nobbling" of horses.

In his box I patted my beautiful 'chaser, an eight-year-old bay with black points, and gave him a lump of sugar. Pete clicked his tongue disapprovingly and said, "Not before the race," like a nanny who had caught her charge being given sweets before lunch. I grinned. Pete had a phobia on the subject.

"Sugar will give him more energy," I said, giving Palindrome another lump and making a fuss of him. "He looks well."

"He ought to win if you judge it right," said Pete. "Keep your eyes on that Irishman, Barney. He'll try to slip you all with a sudden burst as you go into the water so that he can start up the hill six lengths in front. I've seen him do it time and again. He gets everyone else chasing him like mad up the hill using up all the reserves they need for the finish. Now, either you burst with him, and go up the hill at his pace and no faster, or, if you lose him, take it easy up the hill and pile on the pressure when you're coming down again. Clear?"

"As glass," I said. Whatever one might think of Pete's jokes, his advice on how to ride races was invaluable, and I owed a great deal to it.

I gave Palindrome a final pat, and we went out into the yard. Owing to the security system, it was the quietest place on the racecourse.

"Pete, was Bill in any trouble, do you know?" I said, plunging in abruptly.

He finished shutting the door of Palindrome's box, and turned round slowly, and stood looking at me vaguely for so long that I began to wonder if he had heard my question.

But at last he said, "That's a big word, trouble. Something happened . . ."

"What?" I said, as he lapsed into silence again.

But instead of answering, he said, "Why should you think there was any . . . trouble?"

I told him about the wire. He listened with a calm, unsurprised expression, but his grey eyes were bleak.

He said, "Why haven't we all heard about it before?"

"I told Sir Creswell Stampe and the police a week ago," I said, "but with the wire gone they've nothing tangible to go on, and they're dropping it."

"But you're not?" said Pete. "Can't say I blame you. I can't help you much, though. There's only one thing . . . Bill told me he'd had a telephone call which made him laugh. But I didn't listen properly to what he said—I was thinking about my horses, you know how it is. It was something about Admiral falling. He thought it was a huge joke and I didn't go into it with him to find out what I'd missed. I didn't think it was important. When Bill was killed I did wonder if there could possibly be anything odd about it, but I asked you, and you said you hadn't noticed anything . . ." His voice trailed off.

"Yes, I'm sorry," I said. Then I asked, "How long before his accident did Bill tell you about the telephone call?"

"The last time I spoke to him," Pete said. "It was on the Friday morning, just before I flew to Ireland. I rang him to say that all was ready for Admiral's race at Maidenhead the next day."

We began to walk back to the weighing room. On an impulse I said, "Pete, do you ever use the Brighton taxis?" He lived and trained on the Sussex Downs.

"Not often," he said. "Why?"

"There are one or two taxi-drivers there I'd like to have a few words with," I said, not adding that I'd prefer to have the words with them one at a time in a deserted back alley.

"There are several taxi lines in Brighton, as far as I know," he said. "If you want to find one particular driver, why don't you try the railway station? That's where I've usually taken a taxi from. They line up there in droves for the London trains." His attention drifted off as an Irish horse passed us on its way into the paddock for the first race.

"That's Connemara Pal or I'm a Dutchman," said Pete enviously. "I took one of my owners over and tried to buy him, last August, but they wanted eight thousand for him. He was tucked away in a broken down hut behind some pig-styes, so my owner wouldn't pay that price. And now look at him. He won the Leopardstown novice 'chase on Boxing Day by twenty lengths and wouldn't have blown a candle out afterwards. Best young horse we'll see this year." Pete's mind was firmly back in its familiar groove, and we talked about the Irish raid until we were back in the weighing room.

I sought out Clem, who was very busy, and checked with him that my kit was all right, and that he knew the weight I was due to carry on Palindrome.

Kate had told me she was not coming to Cheltenham, so I went in search of the next best thing: news of her.

Dane's peg and section of bench were in the smaller of the two changing rooms, and he was sitting only one place away from the roaring stove, a sure sign of his rise in the jockeys' world. Champions get the warmest places by unwritten right. Beginners shiver beside the draughty doors.

He was clad in his shirt and pants, and was pulling on his nylon stockings. There was a hole in each foot and both his big toes were sticking comically out of them. He had long narrow feet, and long, narrow delicately strong hands to match.

"It's all very well for you to laugh," said Dane, pulling the tops of the stockings over his knees. "They don't seem to make nylons for size eleven shoes . . ."

"Get Walter to get you some stretching ones," I suggested. "Have you a busy day?"

"Three, including the Champion Hurdle," said Dane. "Pete has entered half the stable here." He grinned at me. "I might just find time to tell you about the Penn household, though, if that's what you're after. Shall I start with Uncle George, or Aunt Deb, or . . ." He broke off to pull on his silk breeches and his riding boots. His valet, Walter, gave him his under-jersey and some particularly vile pink and orange colours. Whoever had chosen them had paid no regard to their effect against a manly complexion. ". . . Or do you want to hear about Kate?" finished Dane, covering up the sickening jersey with a windproof jacket.

The changing room was filling up, packed with the extra Irish jockeys who had come over for the meeting and were in high spirits and robust voice. Dane and I went out into the crowded weighing room, where at least one could hear oneself speak.

"Uncle George," he said, "is a gem. And I'm not going to spoil him for you by telling you about him. Aunt Deb is the Honourable Mrs. Penn to you and me, mate, and Aunt Deb to Kate alone. She has a chilly sort of charm that lets you know she would be downright rude if she were not so well bred. She disapproved of me, for a start. I think she disapproves on principle of everything to do with racing, including Heavens Above and Uncle George's idea of a birthday present."

"Go on," I urged, anxious for him to come to the most interesting part of the chronicle before someone else buttonholed him.

"Ah yes. Kate. Gorgeous, heavenly Kate. Strictly, you know, her name is Kate Ellery, not Penn at all. Uncle George added the hyphen and the Penn to her name when he took her in. He said it would be easier for her to have the same surname as him—save a lot of explanations. I suppose it does," said Dane, musingly, knowing full well how he was tantalising me. He relented, and grinned. "She sent you her love."

I felt a warm glow inside. The Cheltenham Festival meeting suddenly seemed not a bad place to be, after all.

"Thanks," I said, trying not to smile fatuously and scarcely succeeding. Dane looked at me speculatively; but I changed the subject back to racing, and presently I asked him if he had ever heard Bill Davidson spoken of in connection with any sort of odd happenings.

"No, I never did," he said positively. I told him about the wire. His reaction was typical.

"Poor Bill," he said with anger. "Poor old Bill. What a bloody shame."

"So if you hear anything which might have even the faintest significance..."

"I'll pass it on to you," he promised.

At that moment Joe Nantwich walked straight into Dane as if he hadn't seen him. He stopped without apology, took a step back, and then went on his way to the changing room. His eyes were wide, unfocused, staring.

"He's drunk," said Dane, incredulously. "His breath smells like a distillery."

"He has his troubles," I said.

"He'll have more still before the afternoon's much older. Just wait till one of the Stewards catches that alcoholic blast."

Joe reappeared at our side. It was true that one could smell his approach a good yard away. Without preamble he spoke directly to me.

"I've had another one." He took a paper out of his pocket. It had been screwed up and straightened out again, so that it was wrinkled in a hundred fine lines, but its ball-pointed message was still abundantly clear.

"BOLINGBROKE. THIS WEEK," it said.

"When did you get it?" I asked.

"It was here when I arrived, waiting for me in the letter rack."

"You've tanked up pretty quickly, then," I said.

"I'm not drunk," said Joe indignantly. "I only had a couple of quick ones in the bar opposite the weighing room."

Dane and I raised our eyebrows in unison. The bar opposite the weighing room had no front wall, and anyone drinking there was in full view of every trainer, owner and Steward who walked out of the weighing room. There might be a surer way for a jockey to commit professional suicide than to have "a couple of quick ones" at that bar before the first race, but I couldn't think of it off-hand. Joe hiccuped.

"Double quick ones, I imagine," said Dane with a smile, taking the paper out of my hand and reading it. "What does it mean, Bolingbroke this week? Why are you so steamed up about it?"

Joe snatched the paper away and stuffed it back into his pocket. He seemed for the first time to be aware that Dane was listening.

"It's none of your business," he said rudely.

I felt a great impulse to assure him it was none of mine either. But he turned back to me and said, "What shall I do?" in a voice full of whining self-pity.

"Are you riding today?" I asked.

"I'm in the fourth and the last. Those bloody amateurs have got two races all to themselves today. A bit thick, isn't it, leaving us only four races to earn our living in? Why don't the fat-arsed gentlemen riders stick to the point-to-points where they belong? That's all they're —— well fit for," he added, alliteratively.

There was a small silence. Dane laughed. Joe was after all not too drunk to realise he was riding his hobby horse in front of the wrong man. He said weakly, in his smarmiest voice, "Well, Alan, of course I didn't mean you personally . . ."

"If you still want my advice, in view of your opinion of amateur jockeys," I said, keeping a straight face, "you should drink three cups of strong black coffee and stay out of sight as long as you can."

"I mean, what shall I do about this note?" Joe had a thicker skin than a coach-hide cabin trunk.

"Pay it no attention at all," I said. "I should think that whoever wrote it is playing with you. Perhaps he knows you like to drown your sorrows in whisky and is relying on you to destroy yourself without his having to do anything but send you frightening letters. A neat, bloodless, and effective revenge."

The sullen pout on Joe's babyish face slowly changed into a mulish determination which was only slightly less repellent.

"No one's going to do that to me," he said, with an aggressiveness which I guessed would diminish with the alcohol level in his blood. We weaved off out of the weighing-room door, presumably in search of black coffee. Before Dane could ask me what was going on, he received a hearty slap on the back from Sandy Mason, who was staring after Joe with dislike.

"What's up with that stupid little clot?" he asked, but he didn't wait for an answer. He said, "Look, Dane, be a pal and gen me up on this horse of Gregory's I'm riding in the first. I've never seen it before, as far as I know. It seems the owner likes my red hair or something." Sandy's infectious laugh made several people look round with answering smiles.

"Sure," said Dane. They launched into a technical discussion and I turned away from them. But Dane touched my arm.

He said, "Is it all right for me to tell people, say Sandy for instance, about the wire and Bill?"

"Yes, do. You might strike oil with someone I wouldn't have thought of asking about it. But be careful." I thought of telling him about the warning in the horse-box, but it was a long story and it seemed enough to say, "Remember that you're stirring up people who can kill, even if by mistake."

He looked startled. "Yes, you're right. I'll be careful."

We turned back to Sandy together.

"What are you two so solemn about? Has someone swiped that luscious brunette you're both so keen on?" he said.

"It's about Bill Davidson," said Dane, disregarding this.

"What about him?"

"The fall that killed him was caused by some wire being strung across the top of the fence. Alan saw it."

Sandy looked aghast. "Alan saw it," he repeated, and then, as the full meaning of what Dane had said sank in, "but that's murder."

I pointed out the reasons for supposing that murder had not been intended. Sandy's brown eyes stared at me unwinkingly until I had finished.

"I guess you're right," he said. "What are you going to do about it?"

"He's trying to find out what is behind it all," said Dane. "We thought you might be able to help. Have you heard anything that might explain it? People tell you things, you know."

Sandy ran his strong brown hands through his unruly red hair, and rubbed the nape of his neck. This brain massage produced no great thoughts, however. "Yes, but mostly they tell me about their girl friends or their bets or such like. Not Major Davidson though. We weren't exactly on a bosom pals basis, because he thought I strangled a horse belonging to a friend of his. Well," said Sandy with an engaging grin, "maybe I did, at that. Anyway, we had words, as they say, a few months ago."

"See if your bookmaker friends have heard any whispers, then," said Dane. "They usually have their ears usefully to the ground."

"O.K.," said Sandy. "I'll pass the news along and see what happens. Now come on, we haven't much time before the first and I want to know what this sod of a horse is going to do." And as Dane hesitated, he said, "Come on, you don't have to wrap it up. Gregory only asks me to ride for him when it's such a stinker that he daren't ask any sensible man to get up on it."

"It's a mare," said Dane, "with a beastly habit of galloping into the bottoms of fences as if they weren't there. She usually ends up in the open ditch."

"Well thanks," said Sandy, apparently undaunted by this news. "I'll tan her hide for her and she'll soon change her ways. See you later, then." He went into the changing room.

Dane looked after him. "The horse isn't foaled that could frighten that blighter Sandy," he said with admiration.

"Nothing wrong with his nerve," I agreed. "But why ever is Pete running an animal like that here, of all places?"

"The owner fancies having a runner at Cheltenham. You know how it is. Snob value, and so on," he said indulgently.

We were being jostled continually, as we talked, by the throng of trainers and owners. We went outside. Dane was immediately appropriated by a pair of racing journalists who wanted his views on his mount in the Gold Cup, two days distant.

The afternoon wore on. The racing began. With the fine sunny day and the holiday mood of the crowd, the excitement was almost crackling in the air.

Sandy got the mare over the first open ditch but disappeared into the next. He came back with a broad smile, cursing hard.

Joe reappeared after the second race, looking less drunk but more frightened. I avoided him shamelessly.

Dane, riding like a demon, won the Champion Hurdle by a head. Pete, patting his horse and sharing with the owner the congratulations of the great crowd round the unsaddling enclosure, was so delighted he could hardly speak. Large and red-faced, he stood there with his hat pushed back showing his baldness, trying to look as if this sort of thing happened every day, when it was in fact the most important winner he had trained.

He was so overcome that he forgot, as we stood some time later in the parade ring before the amateur's race, to make his customary joke about Palindrome going backwards as well as forwards. And when I, following his advice to the letter, stuck like a shadow to the

Irishman when he tried to slip the field, lay a scant length behind him all the way to the last fence, and passed him with a satisfying spurt fifty yards from the winning post, Pete said his day was complete.

I could have hugged him, I was so elated. Although I had won several races back in Rhodesia and about thirty since I had been in England, this was my first win at Cheltenham. I felt as high as if I had already drunk the champagne which waited unopened in the changing room, the customary crateful of celebration for Champion Hurdle day. Palindrome was, in my eyes, the most beautiful, most intelligent, most perfect horse in the world. I walked on air to the scales to weigh in, and changed into my ordinary clothes, and had still not returned to earth when I went outside again. The gloom I had arrived in seemed a thousand years ago. I was so happy I could have turned cartwheels like a child. Such total, unqualified fulfillment comes rarely enough: and unexpectedly, I wished that my father were there to share it.

The problem of Bill had receded like a dot in the distance, and it was only because I had earlier planned to do it that I directed my airy steps down to the horse-box parking ground.

It was packed. About twenty horses ran in each race that day, and almost every horse-box available must have been pressed into service to bring them. I sauntered along the rows, humming light-heartedly, looking at the number plates with half an eye and less attention.

And there it was.

APX 708.

My happiness burst like a bubble.

There was no doubt it was the same horse-box. Regulation wooden Jennings design. Elderly, with dull and battered varnish. No name of owner or trainer painted anywhere on the doors or bodywork.

There was no one in the driver's cab. I walked round to the back, opened the door, and climbed in.

The horse-box was empty except for a bucket, a hay net and a rug, the normal travelling kit for racehorses. The floor was strewn with straw, whereas three days earlier it had been swept clean.

The rug, I thought, might give me a clue as to where the box had come from. Most trainers and some owners have their initials embroidered or sewn in tape in large letters on the corners of their horse rugs. If there were initials on this one, it would be easy.

I picked it up. It was pale fawn with a dark brown binding. I found the initials. I stood there as if turned to stone. Plainly in view, embroidered in dark brown silk, were the letters A.Y.

It was my own rug.

Pete, when I ran him to earth, looked in no mood to answer any questions needing much thought. He leaned back against the weighing-room wall with a glass of champagne in one hand and a cigar in the other, surrounded by a pack of friends similarly equipped. From their rosy smiling faces I gathered the celebration had already been going on for some time.

Dane thrust a glass into my hand.

"Where have you been? Well done on Palindrome. Have some bubbly. The owner's paying, God bless him." His eyes were alight with that fantastic, top-of-the-world elation that I had so lately felt myself. It began to creep back into me too. It was, after all, a great day. Mysteries could wait.

I drank a sip of champagne and said, "Well done yourself, you old son-of-a-gun. And here's to the Gold Cup."

"No such luck," said Dane, "I haven't much chance in that." And from his laughing face I gathered he didn't care, either. We emptied our glasses. "I'll get another bottle," he said, diving into the noisy, crowded changing room.

Looking around I saw Joe Nantwich backed up into a nearby corner by the enormous Mr. Tudor. The big man was doing the talking, forcefully, his dark face almost merging with the shadows. Joe, still dressed in racing colours, listened very unhappily.

Dane came back with the bubbles fizzing out of a newly-opened bottle and filled our glasses. He followed my gaze.

"I don't know whether Joe was sober or not, but didn't he make a hash of the last race?" he said.

"I didn't see it."

"Brother, you sure missed something. He didn't try a yard. His horse damned nearly stopped altogether at the hurdle over on the far side, and it was second favourite, too. What you see now," he gestured with the bottle, "is, I should think, our Joe getting the well deserved sack."

"That man owns Bolingbroke," I said.

"Yes, that's right. Same colours. What a fool Joe is. Owners with five or six goodish horses don't grow on bushes any more."

Clifford Tudor had nearly done. As he turned away from Joe in our direction we heard the tail end of his remarks.

". . . think you can make a fool of me and get away with it. The Stewards can warn you off altogether, as far as I'm concerned."

He strode past us, giving me a nod of recognition, which surprised me, and went out.

Joe leaned against the wall for support. His face was pallid and sweating. He looked ill. He took a few unsteady steps towards us and spoke without caution, as if he had forgotten that Stewards and members of the National Hunt Committee might easily overhear.

"I had a phone call this morning. The same voice as always. He just said, 'Don't win the sixth race' and rang off before I could say anything. And then that note saying 'Bolingbroke, this week' . . . I don't understand it . . . and I didn't win the race and now that bloody wog says he'll get another jockey . . . and the Stewards have started an enquiry about my riding . . . and I feel sick."

"Have some champagne," said Dane, encouragingly.

"Don't be so bloody helpful," said Joe, clutching his stomach and departing towards the changing room.

"What the hell's going on?" said Dane.

"I don't know," I said, perplexed and more interested in Joe's troubles than I had been before. The phone call was inconsistent, I thought, with the notes. One ordered business as usual, the other promised revenge. "I wonder if Joe always tells the truth," I said.

"Highly unlikely," said Dane, dismissing it.

One of the Stewards came and reminded us that even after the Champion Hurdle, drinking in the weighing room itself was frowned on, and would we please drift along into the changing room. Dane did that, but I finished my drink and went outside.

Pete, still attended by a posse of friends, had decided that it was time to go home. The friends were unwilling. The racecourse bars, they were saying, were still open.

I walked purposefully up to Pete, and he made me his excuse for breaking away. We went towards the gates.

"Whew, what a day!" said Pete, mopping his brow with a white handkerchief and throwing away the stub of his cigar.

"A wonderful day," I agreed, looking at him carefully.

"You can take that anxious look off your face, Alan, my lad. I'm as sober as a judge and I'm driving myself home."

"Good. In that case you'll have no difficulty in answering one small question for me?"

"Shoot."

"In what horse-box did Palindrome come to Cheltenham?" I said.

"Eh? I hired one. I had five runners here today. The hurdler, the mare and the black gelding came in my own box. I had to hire one for Palindrome and the novice Dane rode in the first."

"Where did you hire it from?"

"What's the matter?" asked Pete. "I know it's a bit old, and it had a puncture on the way, as I told you, but it didn't do him any harm. Can't have done, or he wouldn't have won."

"No, it's nothing like that," I said. "I just want to know where that horse-box comes from."

"It's not worth buying, if that's what you're after. Too old by half."

"Pete, I don't want to buy it. Just tell me where it comes from."

"The firm I usually hire a box from, Littlepeths of Steyning." He frowned. "Wait a minute. At first they said all their boxes were booked up; then they said they could get me a box if I didn't mind an old one."

"Who drove it here?" I asked.

"Oh, one of their usual drivers. He was swearing a bit at having to drive such an old hen coop. He said the firm had got two good horse-boxes out of action in Cheltenham week and he took a poor view of the administration."

"Do you know him well?"

"Not exactly well. He often drives the hired boxes, that's all. He's always grousing about something. Now, what is all this in aid of?"

"It may have something to do with Bill's death," I said, "but I'm not sure what. Can you find out where the box really comes from? Ask the hire firm? And don't mention me, if you don't mind."

"Is it important?" asked Pete.

"Yes, it is."

"I'll ring 'em tomorrow morning, then," he said.

As soon as he saw me the next day, Pete said, "I asked about that horse-box. It belongs to a farmer near Steyning. I've got his name and address here." He tucked two fingers into his breast pocket, brought out a slip of paper, and gave it to me. "The farmer uses the box to take his hunters around, and his children's show jumpers in the summer. He sometimes lets the hire firm use it, if he's not needing it. Is that what you wanted?"

"Yes, thank you very much," I said. I put the paper in my wallet.

By the end of the Festival meeting I had repeated the story of the wire to at least ten more people, in the hope that someone might know why it had been put there. The tale spread fast round the racecourse.

I told fat Lew Panake, the well-dressed bookmaker who took my occasional bets. He promised to "sound out the boys" and let me know.

I told Calvin Bone, a professional punter, whose nose for the smell of dirty work was as unerring as a bloodhound's.

I told a sly little tout who made his living passing on stray pieces of information to anyone who would pay for them.

I told the newspaper seller, who tugged his moustache and ignored a customer.

I told a racing journalist who could scent a doping scandal five furlongs away.

I told an army friend of Bill's; I told Clem in the weighing room; I told Pete Gregory's head travelling lad.

From all this busy sowing of the wind I learned absolutely nothing. And I would still, I supposed, have to reap the whirlwind.

8

On Saturday morning as I sat with Scilla and the children and Joan round the large kitchen table having a solidly domestic breakfast, the telephone rang.

Scilla went to answer it, but came back saying, "It's for you, Alan. He wouldn't give his name."

I went into the drawing-room and picked up the receiver. The March sun streamed through the windows on to a big bowl of red and yellow striped crocuses which stood on the telephone table. I said, "Alan York speaking."

"Mr. York, I gave you a warning a week ago today. You have chosen to ignore it."

I felt the hairs rising on my neck. My scalp itched. It was a soft voice with a husky, whispering note to it, not savage or forceful, but almost mildly conversational.

I didn't answer. The voice said, "Mr. York? Are you still there?"

"Yes."

"Mr. York, I am not a violent man. Indeed, I dislike violence. I go out of my way to avoid it, Mr. York. But sometimes it is thrust upon me, sometimes it is the only way to achieve results. Do you understand me, Mr. York?"

"Yes," I said.

"If I were a violent man, Mr. York, I would have sent you a rougher warning last week. And I'm giving you another chance, to show you how reluctant I am to harm you. Just mind your own business and stop asking foolish questions. That's all. Just stop asking questions, and nothing will happen to you." There was a pause, then the soft voice went on, with a shade, a first tinge of menace, "Of course, if

I find that violence is absolutely necessary, I always get someone else to apply it. So that I don't have to watch. So that it is not too painful to me. You do understand me, I hope, Mr. York?"

"Yes," I said again. I thought of Sonny, his vicious grin, and his knife.

"Good, then that's all. I do so hope you will be sensible. Good morning, Mr. York." There was a click as he broke the connection.

I jiggled the telephone rest to recall the operator. When she answered I asked if she could tell me where the call had come from.

"One moment, please," she said. She suffered from enlarged adenoids. She came back. "It was routed through London," she said, "but I can't trace it beyond there. So sorry."

"Never mind. Thank you very much," I said.

"Pleasure, I'm sure," said the adenoids.

I put down the receiver and went back to my breakfast.

"Who was that?" asked Henry, spreading marmalade thickly on his toast.

"Man about a dog," I said.

"Or in other words," said Polly, "ask no questions and you'll be told no thumping lies."

Henry made a face at her and bit deeply into his toast. The marmalade oozed out of one corner of his mouth. He licked it.

"Henry always wants to know who's ringing up," said William.

"Yes, darling," said Scilla absently, rubbing some egg off his jersey. "I wish you would lean over your plate when you eat, William." She kissed the top of his blond head.

I passed my cup to Joan for more coffee.

Henry said, "Will you take us out to tea in Cheltenham, Alan? Can we have some of those squelchy cream things like last time, and ice-cream sodas with straws, and some peanuts for coming home?"

"Oh, yes," said William, blissfully.

"I'd love to," I said, "but I can't, today. We'll do it next week, perhaps." The day of my visit to Kate's house had come at last. I was to stay there for two nights, and I planned to put in a day at the office on Monday.

Seeing the children's disappointed faces I explained, "Today I'm going to stay with a friend. I won't be back until Monday evening."

"What a bore," said Henry.

The Lotus ate up the miles between the Cotswolds and Sussex with the deep purr of a contented cat. I covered the fifty miles of good road from Cirencester to Newbury in fifty-three minutes, not because I was in a great hurry, but out of sheer pleasure in driving my car at the speed it was designed for. And I was going towards Kate. Eventually.

Newbury slowed me to a crawl, to a halt. Then I zipped briefly down the Basingstoke road, past the American air base at Greenham Common, and from the twisty village of Kingsclere onwards drove at a sedate pace which seldom rose over sixty.

Kate lived about four miles from Burgess Hill, in Sussex.

I arrived in Burgess Hill at twenty-past one, found my way to the railway station, and parked in a corner, tucked away behind a large shooting brake. I went into the station and bought a return ticket to Brighton. I didn't care to reconnoitre in Brighton by car: the Lotus had already identified me into one mess, and I hesitated to show my hand by taking it where it could be spotted by a cruising taxi driven by Peaky, Sonny, Bert or the rest.

The journey took sixteen minutes. On the train I asked myself, for at least the hundredth time, what chance remark of mine had landed me in the horse-box hornets' nest. Whom had I alarmed by not only revealing that I knew about the wire, but more especially by saying that I intended to find out who had put it there? I could think of only two possible answers; and one of them I didn't like a bit.

I remembered saying to Clifford Tudor on the way from Plumpton to Brighton that a lot of questions would have to be answered about Bill's death; which was as good as telling him straight out that I knew the fall hadn't been an accident, and that I meant to do something about it.

And I had made the same thing quite clear to Kate. To Kate. To Kate. To Kate. The wheels of the train took up the refrain and mocked me.

Well, I hadn't sworn her to secrecy, and I hadn't seen any need to. She could have passed on what I had said to the whole of England, for all I knew. But she hadn't had much time. It had been after midnight when she left me in London, and the horse-box had been waiting for me seventeen hours later.

The train slowed into Brighton station. I walked up the platform and through the gate in a cluster of fellow passengers, but hung back as we came through the booking hall and out towards the forecourt. There were about twelve taxis parked there, their drivers standing outside them, surveying the outpouring passengers for custom. I looked at all the drivers carefully, face by face.

They were all strangers. None of them had been at Plumpton.

Not unduly discouraged, I found a convenient corner with a clear view of arriving taxis and settled myself to wait, resolutely ignoring the cold draught blowing down my neck. Taxis came and went like busy bees, bringing passengers, taking them away. The trains from London attracted them like honey.

Gradually a pattern emerged. There were four distinct groups of them. One group had a broad green line painted down the wings, with the name Green Band on the doors. A second group had yellow shields on the doors, with small letters in black on the shields. A third group were bright cobalt blue all over. Into the fourth group I put the indeterminate taxis which did not belong to the other lines.

I waited for nearly two hours, growing stiffer and stiffer, and receiving more and more curious looks from the station staff. I looked at my watch. The last train I could catch and still arrive at Kate's at the right time was due to leave in six minutes. I had begun to straighten up and massage my cold neck, ready to go and board it, when at last my patience was rewarded.

Empty taxis began to arrive and form a waiting line, which I now knew meant that another London train was due. The drivers got out of their cars and clustered in little groups, talking. Three dusty black taxis arrived in minor convoy and pulled up at the end of the line. They had faded yellow shields painted on the doors. The drivers got out.

One of them was the polite driver of the horse-box. A sensible, solid citizen, he looked. Middle-aged, unremarkable, calm. I did not know the others.

I had three minutes left. The black letters were tantalisingly small on the yellow shields. I couldn't get close enough to read them without the polite driver seeing me, and I had not time to wait until he had gone. I went over to the ticket office, hovered impatiently while a woman argued about half fares for her teen-age child, and asked a simple question.

"What is the name of the taxis with yellow shields on the doors?" The young man in the office gave me an uninterested glance.

"Marconicars, sir. Radio cabs, they are."

"Thank you," I said, and sprinted for the platform.

Kate lived in a superbly proportioned Queen Anne house which generations of gothic-ruin-minded Victorians had left miraculously unspoilt. Its graceful symmetry, its creamy gravelled drive, its tidy lawns already mown in early spring, its air of solid serenity, all spoke of a social and financial security of such long standing that it was to be taken entirely for granted.

Inside, the house was charming, with just a saving touch of shabbiness about the furnishings, as if, though rich, the inhabitants saw no need to be either ostentatious or extravagant.

Kate met me at the door and took my arm, and walked me across the hall.

"Aunt Deb is waiting to give you tea," she said. "Tea is a bit of a ritual with Aunt Deb. You will be in her good graces for being punctual, thank goodness. She is very Edwardian, you'll find. The times have moved without her in many ways." She sounded anxious and apologetic, which meant to me that she loved her aunt protectively, and wished me to make allowances. I squeezed her arm reassuringly, and said, "Don't worry."

Kate opened one of the white panelled doors and we went into the drawing-room. It was a pleasant room, wood panelled and painted white, with a dark plum-coloured carpet, good Persian rugs, and flower patterned curtains. On a sofa at right angles to a glowing log fire sat a woman of about seventy. Beside her stood a low round table bearing a silver tray with Crown Derby cups and saucers and a Georgian silver teapot and cream jug. A dark brown dachshund lay asleep at her feet.

Kate walked across the room and said with some formality, "Aunt Deb, may I introduce Alan York?"

Aunt Deb extended to me her hand, palm downwards. I shook it, feeling that in her younger days it would have been kissed.

"I am delighted to meet you, Mr. York," said Aunt Deb. And I saw exactly what Dane meant about her chilly, well-bred manner. She had no warmth, no genuine welcome in her voice. She was still, for all her years, or even perhaps because of them, exceedingly good looking. Straight eyebrows, perfect nose, clearly outlined mouth. Grey hair cut and dressed by a first-class man. A slim, firm body, straight back, elegant legs crossed at the ankles. A fine silk shirt under a casual tweed suit, hand-made shoes of soft leather. She had everything. Everything except the inner fire which would make Kate at that age worth six of Aunt Deb.

She poured me some tea, and Kate handed it to me. There were pâté sandwiches and a home-made Madeira cake, and although tea was usually a meal I avoided if possible, I found my jinks in Brighton and no lunch had made me hungry. I ate and drank, and Aunt Deb talked.

"Kate tells me you are a jockey, Mr. York." She said it as if it were as dubious as a criminal record. "Of course I am sure you must find it very amusing, but when I was a gel it was not considered an acceptable occupation in acquaintances. But this is Kate's home, and she may ask whoever she likes here, as she knows."

I said mildly, "Surely Aubrey Hastings and Geoffrey Bennett were both jockeys and acceptable when you were—er—younger?"

She raised her eyebrows, surprised. "But they were gentlemen," she said.

I looked at Kate. She had stuffed the back of her hand against her mouth, but her eyes were laughing.

"Yes," I said to Aunt Deb, with a straight face. "That makes a difference, of course."

"You may realise then," she said, looking at me a little less frigidly, "that I do not altogether approve of my niece's new interests. It is one thing to own a racehorse, but quite another to make personal friends of the jockeys one employs to ride it. I am very fond of my niece. I do not wish her to make an undesirable . . . alliance. She is perhaps too young, and has led too sheltered a life, to understand what is acceptable and what is not. But I am sure you do, Mr. York?"

Kate, blushing painfully, said "Aunt Deb!" This was apparently worse than she was prepared for.

"I understand you very well, Mrs. Penn," I said, politely.

"Good," she said. "In that case, I hope you will have an enjoyable stay with us. May I give you some more tea?"

Having firmly pointed out to me my place and having received what she took to be my acknowledgement of it, she was prepared to be a gracious hostess. She had the calm authority of one whose wishes had been law from the nursery. She began to talk pleasantly enough about the weather and her garden, and how the sunshine was bringing on the daffodils.

Then the door opened and a man came in. I stood up.

Kate said, "Uncle George, this is Alan York."

He looked ten years younger than his wife. He had thick well-groomed grey hair and a scrubbed pink complexion with a fresh-from-the-bathroom moistness about it, and when he shook hands his palm was soft and moist also.

Aunt Deb said, without disapproval in her voice, "George, Mr. York is one of Kate's jockey friends."

He nodded. "Yes, Kate told me you were coming. Glad to have you here."

He watched Aunt Deb pour him a cup of tea, and took it from her, giving her a smile of remarkable fondness.

He was too fat for his height, but it was not a bloated-belly fatness. It was spread all over him as though he were padded. The total effect was of a jolly rotundity. He had the vaguely good-natured expression so often found on fat people, a certain bland, almost foolish, looseness of the facial muscles. And yet his fat-lidded eyes, appraising me over the rim of the teacup as he drank, were shrewd and unsmiling. He reminded me of so many businessmen I had met in my work, the slap-you-on-the-back, come-and-play-golf men who would ladle out the Krug '49 and caviar with one hand while they tried to take over your contracts with the other.

He put down his cup and smiled, and the impression faded.

"I am very interested to meet you, Mr. York," he said, sitting down and gesturing to me to do the same. He looked me over carefully, inch by inch, while he asked me what I thought of Heavens Above. We discussed the horse's possibilities with Kate, which meant that I did most of the talking, as Kate knew little more than she had at Plumpton, and Uncle George's total information about racing seemed to be confined to Midday Sun's having won the Derby in 1937.

"He remembers it because of Mad Dogs and Englishmen," said Kate. "He hums it all the time. I don't think he knows the name of a single other horse."

"Oh, yes I do," protested Uncle George. "Bucephalus, Pegasus and Black Bess."

I laughed. "Then why did you give a racehorse to your niece?" I asked.

Uncle George opened his mouth and shut it again. He blinked. Then he said, "I thought she should meet more people. She has no young company here with us, and I believe we may have given her too sheltered an upbringing."

Aunt Deb, who had been bored into silence by the subject of horses, returned to the conversation at this point.

"Nonsense," she said briskly. "She has been brought up as I was, which is the right way. Gels are given too much freedom nowadays, with the result that they lose their heads and elope with fortune hunters or men-about-town of unsavoury background. Gels need strictness and guidance if they are to behave as ladies, and make suitable, well-connected marriages."

She at least had the grace to avoid looking directly at me while she spoke. She leaned over and patted the sleeping dachshund instead.

Uncle George changed the subject with an almost audible jolt, and asked me where I lived.

"Southern Rhodesia," I said.

"Indeed?" said Aunt Deb. "How interesting. Do your parents plan to settle there permanently?" It was a delicate, practised, social probe.

"They were both born there," I answered.

"And will they be coming to visit you in England?" asked Uncle George.

"My mother died when I was ten. My father might come some time if he is not too busy."

"Too busy doing what?" asked Uncle George interestedly.

"He's a trader," I said, giving my usual usefully noncommittal answer to this question. "Trader" could cover anything from a rag-and-bone man to what he actually was, the head of the biggest general trading concern in the Federation. Both Uncle George and Aunt Deb looked unsatisfied by this reply, but I did not add to it. It would have embarrassed and angered Aunt Deb to have had my pedigree and prospects laid out before her after her little lecture on jockeys, and in any case for Dane's sake I could not do it. He had faced Aunt Deb's social snobbery without any of the defences I could muster if I wanted to, and I certainly felt myself no better man than he.

I made instead a remark admiring an arrangement of rose prints on the white panelled walls, which pleased Aunt Deb but brought forth a sardonic glance from Uncle George.

"We keep our ancestors in the dining-room," he said.

Kate stood up. "I'll show Alan where he's sleeping, and so on," she said.

"Did you come by car?" Uncle George asked. I nodded. He said to Kate, "Then ask Culbertson to put Mr. York's car in the garage, will you, my dear?"

"Yes, Uncle George," said Kate, smiling at him.

As we crossed the hall again for me to fetch my suitcase from the car, Kate said, "Uncle George's chauffeur's name is not really Culbertson. It's Higgins, or something like that. Uncle George began to call him Culbertson because he plays bridge, and soon we all did it. Culbertson seems quite resigned to it now. Trust Uncle George," said Kate, laughing, "to have a chauffeur who plays bridge."

"Does Uncle George play bridge?"

"No, he doesn't like cards, or games of any sort. He says there are too many rules to them. He says he doesn't like learning rules and he can't be bothered to keep them. I should think bridge with all those conventions would drive him dotty. Aunt Deb can play quite respectably, but she doesn't make a thing of it."

I lifted my suitcase out of the car, and we turned back.

Kate said, "Why didn't you tell Aunt Deb you were an amateur rider and rich, and so on?"

"Why didn't you?" I asked. "Before I came."

She was taken aback. "I . . . I . . . because . . ." She could not bring out the truthful answer, so I said it for her.

"Because of Dane?"

"Yes, because of Dane." She looked uncomfortable.

"That's quite all right by me," I said lightly. "And I like you for it." I kissed her cheek, and she laughed and turned away from me, and ran up the stairs in relief.

After luncheon—Aunt Deb gave the word three syllables—on Sunday I was given permission to take Kate out for a drive.

In the morning Aunt Deb had been to church with Kate and me in attendance. The church was a mile distant from the house, and

Culbertson drove us there in a well polished Daimler. I, by Aunt Deb's decree, sat beside him. She and Kate went in the back.

While we stood in the drive waiting for Aunt Deb to come out of the house, Kate explained that Uncle George never went to church.

"He spends most of his time in his study. That's the little room next to the breakfast room," she said. "He talks to all his friends on the telephone for hours, and he's writing a treatise or a monograph or something about Red Indians, I think, and he only comes out for meals and things like that."

"Rather dull for your Aunt," I said, admiring the way the March sunlight lay along the perfect line of her jaw and lit red glints in her dark eyelashes.

"Oh, he takes her up to Town once a week. She has her hair done, and he looks things up in the library of the British Museum. Then they have a jolly lunch at the Ritz or somewhere stuffy like that, and go to a matinee or an exhibition in the afternoon. A thoroughly debauched programme," said Kate, with a dazzling smile.

After lunch, Uncle George invited me into his study to see what he called his "trophies." These were a collection of objects belonging to various primitive or barbaric peoples, and, as far as I could judge, would have done credit to any small museum.

Ranks of weapons, together with some jewellery, pots and ritual objects were labelled and mounted on shelves inside glass cases which lined three walls of the room. Among others, there were pieces from Central Africa and the Polynesian Islands, from the Viking age of Norway and from the Maoris of New Zealand. Uncle George's interest covered the globe.

"I study one people at a time," he explained. "It gives me something to do since I retired, and I find it enthralling. Did you know that in the Fiji Islands the men used to fatten women like cattle and eat them?"

His eyes gleamed, and I had a suspicion that part of the pleasure he derived from primitive peoples lay in contemplation of their primitive violences. Perhaps he needed a mental antidote to those lunches at the Ritz, and the matinees.

I said, "Which people are you studying now? Kate said something about Red Indians . . . ?"

He seemed pleased that I was taking an interest in his hobby.

"Yes. I am doing a survey of all the ancient peoples of the Americas, and the North American Indians were my last subject. Their case is over here."

He showed me over to one corner. The collection of feathers, beads, knives and arrows looked almost ridiculously like those in Western films, but I had no doubt that these were genuine. And in the centre hung a hank of black hair with a withered lump of matter dangling from it, and underneath was gummed the laconic label, "Scalp."

I turned round, and surprised Uncle George watching me with a look of secret enjoyment. He let his gaze slide past me to the case.

"Oh, yes," he said. "The scalp's a real one. It's only about a hundred years old."

"Interesting," I said noncommittally.

"I spent a year on the North American Indians because there are so many different tribes," he went on. "But I've moved on to Central America now. Next I'll do the South Americans, the Incas and the Fuegians and so on. I'm not a scholar, of course, and I don't do any field work, but I do write articles sometimes for various publications. At the moment I am engaged on a series about Indians for the *Boys' Stupendous Weekly*." His fat cheeks shook as he laughed silently at what appeared to be an immense private joke. Then he straightened his lips and the pink folds of flesh grew still, and he began to drift back towards the door.

I followed him, and paused by his big, carved, black oak desk which stood squarely in front of the window. On it, besides two telephones and a silver pen tray, lay several cardboard folders with pale blue stick-on labels marked Arapaho, Cherokee, Sioux, Navajo and Mohawk.

Separated from these was another folder marked Mayas, and I idly stretched out my hand to open it, because I had never heard of such a tribe. Uncle George's plump fingers came down firmly on the folder, holding it shut.

"I have only just started on this nation," he said apologetically. "And there's nothing worth looking at yet."

"I've never heard of that tribe," I said.

"They were Central American Indians, not North," he said pleasantly. "They were astronomers and mathematicians, you know. Very civilised. I am finding them fascinating. They discovered that rubber bounced, and they made balls of it long before it was known in Europe. At the moment I am looking into their wars. I am trying to find out what they did with their prisoners of war. Several of their frescoes show prisoners begging for mercy." He paused, his eyes fixed on me, assessing me. "Would you like to help me correlate the references I have so far collected?" he said.

"Well . . . er . . . er . . ." I began.

Uncle George's jowls shook again. "I didn't suppose you would," he said. "You'd rather take Kate for a drive, no doubt."

As I had been wondering how Aunt Deb would react to a similar suggestion, this was a gift. So three o'clock found Kate and me walking round to the big garage behind the house, with Aunt Deb's grudging consent to our being absent at tea-time.

"You remember me telling you, a week ago, while we were dancing, about the way Bill Davidson died?" I said casually, while I helped Kate open the garage doors.

"How could I forget?"

"Did you by any chance mention it to anyone the next morning? There wasn't any reason why you shouldn't . . . but I'd like very much to know if you did."

She wrinkled her nose. "I can't really remember, but I don't think so. Only Aunt Deb and Uncle George, of course, at breakfast. I can't think of anyone else. I didn't think there was any secret about it, though." Her voice rose at the end into a question.

"There wasn't," I said, reassuringly, fastening back the door. "What did Uncle George do before he retired and took up anthropology?"

"Retired?" she said. "Oh, that's only one of his jokes. He retired when he was about thirty, I think, as soon as he inherited a whacking great private income from his father. For decades he and Aunt Deb used to set off round the world every three years or so, collecting all those gruesome relics he was showing you in the study. What did you think of them?"

I couldn't help a look of distaste, and she laughed and said, "That's what I think too, but I'd never let him suspect it. He's so devoted to them all."

The garage was a converted barn. There was plenty of room for the four cars standing in it in a row. The Daimler, a new cream coloured convertible, my Lotus, and after a gap, the social outcast, an old black eight-horse-power saloon. All of them, including mine, were spotless. Culbertson was conscientious.

"We use that old car for shopping in the village and so on," said Kate. "This gorgeous cream job is mine. Uncle George gave it to me a year ago when I came home from Switzerland. Isn't it absolutely rapturous?" She stroked it with love.

"Can we go out in yours, instead of mine?" I asked. "I would like that very much, if you wouldn't mind."

She was pleased. She let down the roof and tied a blue silk scarf over her head, and drove us out of the garage into the sunlight, down the drive, and on to the road towards the village.

"Where shall we go?" she said.

"I'd like to go to Steyning," I said.

"That's an odd sort of place to choose," she said. "How about the sea?"

"I want to call on a farmer in Washington, near Steyning, to ask him about his horse-box," I said. And I told her how some men in a horse-box had rather forcefully told me not to ask questions about Bill's death.

"It was a horse-box belonging to this farmer at Washington," I finished. "I want to ask him who hired it from him last Saturday."

"Good heavens," said Kate. "What a lark." And she drove a little faster. I sat sideways and enjoyed the sight of her. The beautiful profile, the blue scarf whipped by the wind, with one escaping wisp of hair blowing on her forehead, the cherry-red curving mouth. She could twist your heart.

It was ten miles to Washington. We went into the village and stopped, and I asked some children on their way home from Sunday school where farmer Lawson lived.

"Up by there," said the tallest girl, pointing.

"Up by there" turned out to be a prosperous workmanlike farm with a yellow old farmhouse and a large new Dutch barn rising behind it. Kate drove into the yard and stopped, and we walked round through a garden gate to the front of the house. Sunday afternoon was not a good time to call on a farmer, who was probably enjoying his one carefree nap of the week, but it couldn't be helped.

We rang the door bell, and after a long pause the door opened. A youngish good-looking man holding a newspaper looked at us enquiringly.

"Could I speak to Mr. Lawson, please?" I said.

"I'm Lawson," he said. He yawned.

"This is your farm?" I asked.

"Yes. What can I do for you?" He yawned again.

I said I understood he had a horse-box for hire. He rubbed his nose with his thumb while he looked us over. Then he said, "It's very old, and it depends when you want it."

"Could we see it, do you think?" I asked.

"Yes," he said. "Hang on, a moment." He went indoors and we heard his voice calling out and a girl's voice answering him. Then he came back without the newspaper.

"It's round here," he said, leading the way. The horse-box stood out in the open, sheltered only by the hay piled in the Dutch barn. APX 708. My old friend.

I told Lawson then that I didn't really want to hire his box, but I wanted to know who had hired it eight days ago. And because he thought this question decidedly queer and was showing signs of hustling us off at once, I told him why I wanted to know.

"It can't have been my box," he said at once.

"It was," I said.

"I didn't hire it to anyone, eight days ago. It was standing right here all day."

"It was in Maidenhead," I said, obstinately.

He looked at me for a full half minute. Then he said, "If you are right, it was taken without me knowing about it. I and my family were all away last week-end. We were in London."

"How many people would know you were away?" I asked.

He laughed. "About twelve million, I should think. We were on one of those family quiz shows on television on Friday night. My wife, my eldest son, my daughter and I. The younger boy wasn't allowed on because he's only ten. He was furious about it. My wife said on the programme that we were all going to the Zoo on Saturday and to the Tower of London on Sunday, and we weren't going home until Monday."

I sighed. "And how soon before you went up to the quiz show did you know about it?"

"A couple of weeks. It was all in the local papers, that we were going. I was a bit annoyed about it, really. It doesn't do to let every tramp in the neighbourhood know you'll be away. Of course, there are my cowmen about, but it's not the same."

"Could you ask them if they saw anyone borrow your box?"

"I suppose I could. It's almost milking time, they'll be in soon. But I can't help thinking you've mistaken the number plate."

"Have you a middleweight thoroughbred bay hunter, then," I said, "with a white star on his forehead, one lop ear, and a straggly tail?"

His scepticism vanished abruptly. "Yes, I have," he said. "He's in the stable over there."

We went and had a look at him. It was the horse Bert had been leading up and down, all right.

"Surely your men would have missed him when they went to give him his evening feed?" I said.

"My brother—he lives a mile away—borrows him whenever he wants. The men would just assume he'd got him. I'll ask the cowmen."

"Will you ask them at the same time if they found a necktie in the box?" I said. "I lost one there, and I'm rather attached to it. I'd give ten bob to have it back."

"I'll ask them," said Lawson. "Come into the house while you wait." He took us through the back door, along a stone-flagged hall into a comfortably battered sitting-room, and left us. The voices of his wife and children and clatter of teacups could be heard in the distance. A half-finished jig-saw puzzle was scattered on a table; some toy railway lines snaked round the floor.

At length Lawson came back. "I'm very sorry," he said, "the cowmen thought my brother had the horse and none of them noticed the box had gone. They said they didn't find your tie, either. They're as blind as bats unless it's something of theirs that's missing."

I thanked him all the same for his trouble, and he asked me to let him know, if I found out, who had taken his box.

Kate and I drove off towards the sea.

She said, "Not a very productive bit of sleuthing, do you think? Anyone in the world could have borrowed the horse-box."

"It must have been someone who knew it was there," I pointed out. "I expect it was because it was so available that they got the idea of using it at all. If they hadn't known it would be easy to borrow, they'd have delivered their message some other way. I dare say one of those cowmen knows more than he's telling. Probably took a quiet tenner to turn a blind eye, and threw in the horse for local colour. Naturally he wouldn't confess it in a hurry to Lawson this afternoon."

"Well, never mind," said Kate lightheartedly. "Perhaps it's just as well Farmer Lawson had nothing to do with it. It would have been rather shattering if he had turned out to be the head of the gang. You would probably have been bopped behind the ear with a gun butt and dumped in a bag of cement out at sea and I would have been tied up on the railway lines in the path of oncoming diesels."

I laughed. "If I'd thought he could have possibly been the leader of the gang I wouldn't have taken you there."

She glanced at me. "You be careful," she said, "or you'll grow into a cosseting old dear like Uncle George. He's never let Aunt Deb within arm's length of discomfort, let alone danger. I think that's why she's so out of touch with modern life."

"You don't think danger should be avoided, then?" I asked.

"Of course not. I mean, if there's something you've got to do, then to hell with the danger." She gave an airy wave with her right hand to illustrate this carefree point of view, and a car's horn sounded vigorously just behind us. A man swept past glaring at Kate for her unintentional signal. She laughed.

She swung the car down to the sea in Worthing, and drove eastwards along the coast road. The smell of salt and seaweed was strong and refreshing. We passed the acres of new bungalows outside Worthing, the docks and the power stations of Shoreham, Southwick and Portslade, the sedate façades of Hove, and came at length to the long promenade at Brighton. Kate turned deftly into a square in the town, and stopped the car.

"Let's go down by the sea," she said. "I love it."

We walked across the road, down some steps, and staggered across the bank of shingle on to the sand. Kate took her shoes off and poured out a stream of little stones. The sun shone warmly and the tide was out. We walked slowly along the beach for about a mile, jumping over the breakwaters, and then turned and went back. It was a heavenly afternoon.

As we strolled hand in hand up the road towards Kate's car, I saw for the first time that she had parked it only a hundred yards from the Pavilion Plaza Hotel, where I had driven Clifford Tudor from Plumpton ten days earlier.

And talk of the devil, I thought. There he was. The big man was standing on the steps of the hotel, talking to the uniformed doorman. Even at a distance there was no mistaking that size, that dark skin, that important carriage of the head. I watched him idly.

Just before we arrived at Kate's car a taxi came up from behind us, passed us, and drew up outside the Pavilion Plaza. It was a black taxi with a yellow shield on the door, and this time it was close enough for me to read the name: Marconicars. I looked quickly at the driver and saw his profile as he went past. He had a large nose and a receding chin, and I had never seen him before.

Clifford Tudor said a few last words to the doorman, strode across the pavement, and got straight into the taxi without pausing to tell the driver where he wanted to go. The taxi drove off without delay.

"What are you staring at?" said Kate, as we stood beside her car.

"Nothing much," I said. "I'll tell you about it if you'd like some tea in the Pavilion Plaza Hotel."

"That's a dull dump," she said. "Aunt Deb approves of it."

"More sleuthing," I said.

"All right, then. Got your magnifying glass and bloodhound handy?"

We went into the hotel. Kate said she would go and tidy her hair. While she was gone I asked the young girl in the reception desk if she knew where I could find Clifford Tudor. She fluttered her eyelashes at me and I grinned encouragingly back.

"You've just missed him, I'm afraid," she said. "He's gone back to his flat."

"Does he come here often?" I asked.

She looked at me in surprise. "I thought you knew. He's on the board of governors. One of the chief shareholders. In fact," she added with remarkable frankness, "he very nearly owns this place and has more say in running it than the manager." It was clear from her voice and manner that she thoroughly approved of Mr. Tudor.

"Has he got a car?" I asked.

This was a very odd question, but she prattled on without hesitation. "Yes, he's got a lovely big car with a long bonnet and lots of chromium. Real classy. But he doesn't use it, of course. Mostly it's taxis for him. Why, just this minute I rang for one of those radio cabs for him. Real useful, they are. You just ring their office and they radio a message to the taxi that's nearest here and in no time at all it's pulling up outside. All the guests use them . . ."

"Mavis!"

The talkative girl stopped dead and looked round guiltily. A severe girl in her late twenties had come into the reception desk.

"Thank you for relieving me, Mavis. You may go now," she said.

Mavis gave me a flirting smile and disappeared.

"Now, sir, can I help you?" She was polite enough, but not the type to gossip about her employers.

"Er—can we have afternoon tea here?" I asked.

She glanced at the clock. "It's a little late for tea, but go along into the lounge and the waiter will attend to you."

Kate eyed the resulting fishpaste sandwiches with disfavour. "This is one of the hazards of detecting, I suppose," she said, taking a tentative bite. "What did you find out about what?"

I said I was not altogether sure, but that I was interested in anything that had even the remotest connection with the yellow shield taxis or with Bill Davidson, and Clifford Tudor was connected in the most commonplace way with both.

"Nothing in it, I shouldn't think," said Kate, finishing the sandwich but refusing another.

I sighed. "I don't think so, either," I said.

"What next, then?"

"If I could find out who owns the yellow shield taxis . . ."

"Let's ring them up and ask," said Kate, standing up. She led the way to the telephone and looked up the number in the directory.

"I'll do it," she said. "I'll say I have a complaint to make and I want to write directly to the owner about it."

She got through to the taxi office and gave a tremendous performance, demanding the names and addresses of the owners, managers and the company's solicitors. Finally, she put down the receiver and looked at me disgustedly.

"They wouldn't tell me a single thing," she said. "He was a really patient man, I must say. He didn't get ruffled when I was really quite rude to him. But all he would say was, "Please write to us with the details of your complaint and we will look into it fully." He said it was not the company's policy to disclose the names of its owners and he had no authority to do it. He wouldn't budge an inch."

"Never mind. It was a darned good try. I didn't really think they would tell you. But it gives me an idea . . ."

I rang up the Maidenhead police station and asked for Inspector Lodge. He was off duty, I was told. Would I care to leave a message? I would.

I said, "This is Alan York speaking. Will you please ask Inspector Lodge if he can find out who owns or controls the Marconicar radio taxi cabs in Brighton? He will know what it is about."

The voice in Maidenhead said he would give Inspector Lodge the message in the morning, but could not undertake to confirm that Inspector Lodge would institute the requested enquiries. Nice official jargon. I thanked him and rang off.

Kate was standing close to me in the telephone box. She was wearing a delicate flowery scent, so faint that it was little more than a quiver in the air. I kissed her, gently. Her lips were soft and dry and sweet. She put her hands on my shoulders, and looked into my eyes, and smiled. I kissed her again.

A man opened the door of the telephone box. He laughed when he saw us. "I'm so sorry . . . I want to telephone . . ." We stepped out of the box in confusion.

I looked at my watch. It was nearly half-past six.

"What time does Aunt Deb expect us back?" I asked.

"Dinner is at eight. We've got until then," said Kate. "Let's walk through the Lanes and look at the antique shops."

We went slowly down the back pathways of Brighton, pausing before each brightly lit window to admire the contents. And stopping, too, in one or two corners in the growing dusk, to continue where we had left off in the telephone box. Kate's kisses were sweet and virginal. She was unpractised in love, and though her body trembled once or twice in my arms, there was no passion, no hunger in her response.

At the end of one of the Lanes, while we were discussing whether to go any further, some lights were suddenly switched on behind us. We turned round. The licensee of the Blue Duck was opening his doors for the evening. It looked a cosy place.

"How about a snifter before we go back?" I suggested.

"Lovely," said Kate. And in this casual inconsequential way we made the most decisive move in our afternoon's sleuthing.

We went into the Blue Duck.

9

The bar was covered with a big sheet of gleaming copper. The beer handles shone. The glasses sparkled. It was a clean, friendly little room with warm lighting and original oils of fishing villages round the walls.

Kate and I leaned on the bar and discussed sherries with the innkeeper. He was a military-looking man of about fifty with a bristly moustache waxed at the ends. I put him down as a retired sergeant-major. But he knew his stuff, and the sherry he recommended to us was excellent. We were his first customers, and we stood chatting to him. He had the friendly manner of all good innkeepers, but underlying this I saw a definite wariness. It was like the nostril cocked for danger in a springbok; uneasy, even when all appeared safe. But I didn't pay much attention, for his troubles, I thought erroneously, had nothing to do with me.

Another man and a girl came in, and Kate and I turned to take our drinks over to one of the small scattered tables. As we did so she stumbled, knocked her glass against the edge of the bar and broke it. A jagged edge cut her hand, and it began to bleed freely.

The innkeeper called his wife, a thin, small woman with bleached hair. She saw the blood welling out of Kate's hand, and exclaimed with concern, "Come and put it under the cold tap. That'll stop the bleeding. Mind you don't get it on your nice coat."

She opened a hatch in the bar to let us through, and led us into her kitchen, which was as spotless as the bar. On a table at one side were slices of bread, butter, cooked meats and chopped salads. We had interrupted the innkeeper's wife in making sandwiches for the evening's customers. She went across to the sink, turned on the tap, and beckoned to Kate to put her hand in the running water. I stood just inside the kitchen door looking round me.

"I'm so sorry to be giving you all this trouble," said Kate, as the blood dripped into the sink. "It really isn't a very bad cut. There just seems to be an awful lot of gore coming out of it."

"It's no trouble at all, dear," said the innkeeper's wife. "I'll find you a bandage." She opened a dresser drawer to look for one, giving Kate a reassuring smile.

I started to walk over from the doorway to take a closer look at the damage. Instantly there was a deadly menacing snarl, and a black alsatian dog emerged from a box beside the refrigerator. His yellow eyes were fixed on me, his mouth was slightly open with the top lip drawn back, and the razor-sharp teeth were parted. There was a collar round his neck, but he was not chained up. Another snarl rumbled deep in his throat.

I stood stock still in the centre of the kitchen.

The innkeeper's wife took a heavy stick from beside the dresser and went over to the dog. She seemed flustered.

"Lie down, Prince. Lie down." She pointed with the stick to the box. The dog, after a second's hesitation, stepped back into it and sat erect, still looking at me with the utmost hostility. I didn't move.

"I'm very sorry, sir. He doesn't like strange men. He's a very good guard dog, you see. He won't hurt you now, not while I'm here." And she laid the stick on the dresser, and went over to Kate with cotton wool, disinfectant, and a bandage.

I took a step towards Kate. Muscles rippled along the dog's back, but he stayed in his box. I finished the journey to the sink. The bleeding had almost stopped, and, as Kate said, it was not a bad cut. The innkeeper's wife dabbed it with cotton wool soaked in disinfectant, dried it, and wound on a length of white gauze bandage.

I leaned against the draining board, looking at the dog and the heavy stick, and remembering the underlying edginess of the innkeeper. They added up to just one thing.

Protection.

Protection against what? Protection against Protection, said my brain, dutifully, in a refrain. Someone had been trying the Protection racket on mine host. Pay up or we smash up your pub . . . or you . . . or your wife. But this particular innkeeper, whether or not I was right about his sergeant-major past, looked tough enough to defy that sort of bullying. The collectors of Protection had been met, or were to be met, by an authentically lethal alsatian. They were likely to need protection themselves.

The innkeeper put his head round the door.

"All right?" he said.

"It's fine, thank you very much," said Kate.

"I've been admiring your dog," I said.

The innkeeper took a step into the room. Prince turned his head away from me for the first time and looked at his master.

"He's a fine fellow," he agreed.

Suddenly out of nowhere there floated into my mind a peach of an idea. There could not, after all, be too many gangs in Brighton, and I had wondered several times why a taxi line should employ thugs and fight pitched battles. So I said, with a regrettable lack of caution, "Marconicars."

The innkeeper's professionally friendly smile vanished, and he suddenly looked at me with appalling, vivid hate. He picked the heavy stick off the dresser and raised it to hit me. The dog was out of his box in one fluid stride, crouching ready to spring, with his ears flat and his teeth bared. I had struck oil with a vengeance.

Kate came to the rescue. She stepped to my side and said, without the slightest trace of alarm, "For heaven's sake don't hit him too hard because Aunt Deb is expecting us for roast lamb and the odd potato within half an hour or so and she is very strict about us being back on the dot."

This surprising drivel made the innkeeper hesitate long enough for me to say, "I don't belong to the Marconicars. I'm against them. Do be a good chap and put that stick down, and tell Prince his fangs are not required."

The innkeeper lowered the stick, but he left Prince where he was, on guard four feet in front of me.

Kate said to me, "Whatever have we walked into?" The bandage was trailing from her hand, and the blood was beginning to ooze through. She wound up the rest of the bandage unconcernedly and tucked in the end.

"Protection, I think?" I said to the innkeeper. "It was just a wild guess, about the taxis. I'd worked out why you need such an effective guard dog, and I've been thinking about taxi-drivers for days. The two things just clicked, that's all."

"Some of the Marconicar taxi-drivers beat him up a bit a week ago," said Kate conversationally to the innkeeper's wife. "So you can't expect him to be quite sane on the subject."

The innkeeper gave us both a long look. Then he went to his dog and put his hand round its neck and fondled it under its chin. The wicked yellow eyes closed, the lips relaxed over the sharp teeth, and the dog leaned against his master's leg in devotion. The innkeeper patted its rump, and sent it back to its box.

"A good dog, Prince," he said, with a touch of irony. "Well now, we can't leave the bar unattended. Sue, dear, will you look after the customers while I talk to these young people?"

"There's the sandwiches not made yet," protested Sue.

"I'll do them," said Kate, cheerfully. "And let's hope I don't bleed into them too much." She picked up a knife and began to butter the slices of bread. The innkeeper and his wife looked less able to deal with Kate than with the taxi-drivers; but after hesitating a moment, the wife went out to the bar.

"Now, sir," said the innkeeper.

I outlined for him the story of Bill's death and my close contact with the taxi-drivers in the horse-box. I said, "If I can find out who's at the back of Marconicars, I'll probably have the man who arranged Major Davidson's accident."

"Yes, I see that," he said. "I hope you have more luck than I've had. Trying to find out who owns Marconicars is like running head on into a brick wall. Dead end. I'll tell you all I can, though. The more people sniping at them, the sooner they'll be liquidated." He leaned over and picked up two sandwiches. He gave one to me, and bit into the other.

"Don't forget to leave room for the roast lamb," said Kate, seeing me eating. She looked at her watch. "Oh, dear, we'll be terribly late for dinner and I hate to make Aunt Deb cross." But she went on placidly with her buttering.

"I bought the Blue Duck eighteen months ago," said the innkeeper. "When I got out into civvy street."

"Sergeant-major?" I murmured.

"Regimental," he said, with justifiable pride. "Thomkins, my name is. Well, I bought the Blue Duck with my savings and my retirement pay, and dead cheap it was too. Too cheap. I should have known there'd be a catch. We hadn't been here more than three weeks, and taking good money too, when this chap comes in one night and says as bold as brass that if we didn't pay up like the last landlord it'd be just too bad for us. And he picked up six glasses off the bar and smashed them. He said he wanted fifty quid a week. Well, I ask you, fifty quid! No wonder the last landlord wanted to get out. I was told afterwards he'd been trying to sell the place for months, but all the locals found out they would be buying trouble and left it alone for some muggins like me straight out of the army and still wet behind the ears to come along and jump in with my big feet."

Innkeeper Thomkins chewed on his sandwich while he thought.

"Well, then, I told him to eff off. And he came back the next night with about five others and smashed the place to bits. They knocked me out with one of my own bottles and locked my wife in the heads. Then they smashed all the bottles in the bar and all the glasses, and all the chairs. When I came round I was lying on the floor in the mess, and they were standing over me in a ring. They said that was just a taste. If I didn't cough up the fifty quid a week they'd be back to smash every bottle in the store-room and all the wine in the cellar. After that, they said, it would be my wife."

His face was furious, as he relived it.

"What happened?" I asked.

"Well, my God, after the Germans and the Japs I wasn't giving in meekly to some little runts at the English sea-side. I paid up for a couple of months to give myself a bit of breathing space, but fifty quid takes a bit of finding, on top of overheads and taxes. It's a good little business, see, but at that rate I wasn't going to be left with much more than my pension. It wasn't on."

"Did you tell the police?" I asked.

A curious look of shame came into Thomkins' face. "No," he said hesitantly, "not then I didn't. I didn't know then where the men had come from, see, and they'd threatened God knows what if I went to the police. Anyway, it's not good army tactics to re-engage an enemy who has defeated you once, unless you've got reinforcements. That's when I started to think about a dog. And I did go to the police later," he finished, a little defensively.

"Surely the police can close the Marconicar taxi line if it's being used for systematic crime," I said.

"Well, you'd think so," he said, "but it isn't like that. It's a real taxi service, you know. A big one. Most of the drivers are on the up and up and don't even know what's going on. I told a couple of them once that they were a front for the protection racket and they refused to believe me. The crooked ones look so plausible, see? Just like the others. They drive a taxi up to your door at closing time, say, all innocent like, and walk in and ask quietly for the money; and as like as not they'll pick up a customer in the pub and drive him home for the normal fare as respectable as you please."

"Couldn't you have a policeman in plain clothes sitting at the bar ready to arrest the taxi driver when he came to collect the money?" suggested Kate.

The innkeeper said bitterly, "It wouldn't do no good, miss. It isn't only that they come in on different days, at different times, so that a copper might have to wait a fortnight to catch one, but there aren't any grounds for arrest. They've got an I.O.U. with my signature on it for fifty pounds, and if there was any trouble with the police, all they'd have to do would be show it, and they couldn't be touched. The police'll help all right if you can give them something they can use in court, but when it's just one man's word against another, they can't do much."

"A pity you signed the I.O.U.," I sighed.

"I didn't," he said, indignantly, "but it looks like my signature, even to me. I tried to grab it once, but the chap who showed it to me said it wouldn't matter if I tore it up, they'd soon make out another one. They must have had my signature on a letter or something, and copied it. Easy enough to do."

"You do pay them, then," I said, rather disappointed.

"Not on your nellie, I don't," said the innkeeper, his moustache bristling. "I haven't paid them a sou for a year or more. Not since I got Prince. He chewed four of them up in a month, and that discouraged them, I can tell you. But they're still around all the time. Sue and I daren't go out much, and we always go together and take Prince with us. I've had burglar alarm bells put on all the doors and windows and they go off with an awful clatter if anyone tries to break in while we're out or asleep. It's no way to live, sir. It's getting on Sue's nerves."

"What a dismal story," said Kate, licking chutney off her fingers. "Surely you can't go on like that for ever?"

"Oh, no, miss, we're beating them now. It isn't only us, see, that they got money from. They had a regular round. Ten or eleven pubs like ours—free houses. And a lot of little shops, tobacconists, souvenir shops, that sort of thing, and six or seven little cafés. None of the big places. They only pick on businesses run by the people who own them, like us. When I cottoned to that I went round to every place I thought they might be putting the screws on and asked the owners straight out if they were paying protection. It took me weeks, it's such a big area. The ones that were paying were all dead scared, of course, and wouldn't talk, but I knew who they were, just by the way they clammed up. I told them we ought to stop paying and fight. But a lot of them have kids and they wouldn't risk it, and you can't blame them."

"What did you do?" asked Kate, enthralled.

"I got Prince. A year old, he was then. I'd done a bit of dog handling in the army, and I trained Prince to be a proper fighter."

"You did, indeed," I said, looking at the dog who now lay peacefully in his box with his chin on his paws.

"I took him round and showed him to some of the other victims of the protection racket," Thomkins went on, "and told them that if they'd get dogs too we'd chase off the taxi-drivers. Some of them didn't realise the taxis were mixed up in it. They were too scared to open their eyes. Anyway, in the end a lot of them did get dogs and I helped to train them, but it's difficult, the dog's only got to obey one master, see, and I had to get them to obey someone else, not me. Still, they weren't too bad. Not as good as Prince, of course."

"Of course," said Kate.

The innkeeper looked at her suspiciously, but she was demurely piling sandwiches on to a plate.

"Go on," I said.

"In the end I got some of the people with children to join in too. They bought alsatians or bull terriers, and we arranged a system for taking all the kiddies to school by car. Those regular walks to school laid them wide open to trouble, see? I hired a judo expert and his car to do nothing but ferry the children and their mothers about. We all club together to pay him. He's expensive, of course, but nothing approaching the protection money."

"How splendid," said Kate warmly.

"We're beating them all right, but it isn't all plain sailing yet. They smashed up the Cockleshell Café a fortnight ago, just round the corner from here. But we've got a system to deal with that, too, now. Several of us went round to help clear up the mess, and we all put something into the hat to pay for new tables and chairs. They've got an alsatian bitch at that café, and she'd come into season and they'd locked her in a bedroom. I ask you! Dogs are best," said the innkeeper, seriously.

Kate gave a snort of delight.

"Have the taxi-drivers attacked any of you personally, or has it always been your property?" I asked.

"Apart from being hit on the head with my own bottle, you mean?" The innkeeper pulled up his sleeve and showed us one end of a scar on his forearm. "That's about seven inches long. Three of them jumped me one evening when I went out to post a letter. It was just after Prince had sent one of their fellows off, and silly like, I went out without him. It was only a step to the pillar box, see? A mistake though. They made a mess of me, but I got a good look at them. They told me I'd get the same again if I went to the police. But I rang the boys in blue right up, and told them the lot. It was a blond young brute who slashed my arm and my evidence got him six months," he said with satisfaction. "After that I was careful not to move a step without Prince, and they've never got near enough to have another go at me."

"How about the other victims?" I asked.

"Same as me," he said. "Three or four of them were beaten up and slashed with knives. After I'd got them dogs I persuaded some of them to tell the police. They'd had the worst of it by then, I thought, but they were still scared of giving evidence in court. The gang have never actually killed anyone, as far as I know. It wouldn't be sense, any how, would it? A man can't pay up if he's dead."

"No," I said, thoughtfully. "I suppose he can't. They might reckon that one death would bring everyone else to heel, though."

"You needn't think I haven't that in my mind all the time," he said sombrely. "But there's a deal of difference between six months for assault and a life sentence or a hanging, and I expect that's what has stopped 'em. This isn't Chicago after all, though you'd wonder sometimes."

I said, "I suppose if they can't get money from their old victims, the gang try "protecting" people who don't know about your systems and your dogs . . ."

The innkeeper interrupted, "We've got a system for that, too. We put an advertisement in the Brighton paper every week telling anyone who has been threatened with Protection to write to a Box number and they will get help. It works a treat, I can tell you."

Kate and I looked at him with genuine admiration.

"They should have made you a general," I said, "not a sergeant-major."

"I've planned a few incidents in my time," he said modestly. "Those young lieutenants in the war, straight out of civvy street and rushed through an officer course, they were glad enough now and then for a suggestion from a regular." He stirred, "Well, how about a drink now?"

But Kate and I thanked him and excused ourselves, as it was already eight o'clock. Thomkins and I promised to let each other know how we fared in battle, and we parted on the best of terms. But I didn't attempt to pat Prince.

Aunt Deb sat in the drawing-room tapping her foot. Kate apologised very prettily for our lateness, and Aunt Deb thawed. She and Kate were clearly deeply attached to each other.

During dinner it was to Uncle George that Kate addressed most of the account of our afternoon's adventures. She told him amusingly and lightly about the wandering horse-box and made a rude joke about the Pavilion Plaza's paste sandwiches, which drew a mild reproof from Aunt Deb to the effect that the Pavilion Plaza was the most hospitable of the Brighton hotels. I gave a fleeting thought to the flighty Mavis, whom I had suspected, perhaps unjustly, of dispensing her own brand of hospitality on the upper floors.

"And then we had a drink in a darling little pub called the Blue Duck," said Kate, leaving out the telephone box and our walk through the Lanes. "I cut my hand there—" she held it out complete with bandage, "—but not very badly of course, and we went into the kitchen to wash the blood off, and that's what made us late. They had the most terrifying alsatian there that I'd ever seen in my life. He snarled a couple of times at Alan and made him shiver in his shoes like a jelly . . ." she paused to eat a mouthful of roast lamb.

"Do you not care for dogs, Mr. York?" said Aunt Deb, with a touch of disdain. She was devoted to her dachshund.

"It depends," I said.

Kate said, "You don't exactly fall in love with Prince. I expect they call him Prince because he's black. The Black Prince. Anyway, he's useful if any dog is. If I told you two dears what the man who keeps the Blue Duck told Alan and me about the skulduggery that goes on in respectable little old Brighton, you wouldn't sleep sound in your beds."

"Then please don't tell us, Kate dear," said Aunt Deb. "I have enough trouble with insomnia as it is."

I looked at Uncle George to see how he liked being deprived of the end of the story, and saw him push his half-filled plate away with a gesture of revulsion, as if he were suddenly about to vomit.

He noticed I was watching, and with a wry smile said, "Indigestion, I'm afraid. Another of the boring nuisances of old age. We're a couple of old crocks now, you know."

He tried to raise a chuckle, but it was a poor affair. There was a tinge of grey in the pink cheeks, and fine beads of sweat had appeared on the already moist-looking skin. Something was deeply wrong in Uncle George's world.

Aunt Deb looked very concerned about it, and as sheltering her from unpleasant realities was for him so old and ingrained a habit, he made a great effort to rally his resources. He took a sip of water and blotted his mouth on his napkin, and I saw the tremor in his chubby hands. But there was steel in the man under all that fat, and he cleared his throat and spoke normally enough.

He said, "It quite slipped my mind, Kate my dear, but while you were out Gregory rang up to talk to you about Heavens Above. I asked him how the horse was doing and he said it had something wrong with its leg and won't be able to run on Thursday at Bristol as you planned."

Kate looked disappointed. "Is he lame?" she asked.

Uncle George said, "I could swear Gregory said the horse had thrown out a splint. He hadn't broken any bones though, had he? Most peculiar." He was mystified, and so, I saw, was Kate.

"Horses' leg bones sometimes grow knobs all of a sudden, and that is what a splint is," I said. "The leg is hot and tender while the splint is forming, but it usually lasts only two or three weeks. Heavens Above will be sound again after that."

"What a pest," said Kate. "I was so looking forward to Thursday. Will you be going to Bristol, Alan, now that my horse isn't running?"

"Yes," I said. "I'm riding Palindrome there. Do try and come,

Kate, it would be lovely to see you." I spoke enthusiastically, which made Aunt Deb straighten her back and bend on me a look of renewed disapproval.

"It is not good for a young gel's reputation for her to be seen too often in the company of jockeys," she said.

At eleven o'clock, when Uncle George had locked the study door on his collection of trophies, and when Aunt Deb had swallowed her nightly quota of sleeping pills, Kate and I went out of the house to put her car away in the garage. We had left it in the drive in our haste before dinner.

The lights of the house, muted by curtains, took the blackness out of the night, so that I could still see Kate's face as she walked beside me.

I opened the car door for her, but she paused before stepping in.

"They're getting old," she said, in a sad voice, "and I don't know what I'd do without them."

"They'll live for years yet," I said.

"I hope so . . . Aunt Deb looks very tired sometimes, and Uncle George used to have so much more bounce. I think he's worried about something now . . . and I'm afraid it's Aunt Deb's heart, thought they haven't said . . . They'd never tell me if there was anything wrong with them." She shivered.

I put my arms round her and kissed her. She smiled.

"You're a kind person, Alan."

I didn't feel kind. I wanted to throw her in the car and drive off with her at once to some wild and lonely hollow on the Downs for a purpose of which the cave men would thoroughly have approved. It was an effort for me to hold her lightly, and yet essential.

"I love you, Kate," I said, and I controlled even my breathing.

"No," she said. "Don't say it. Please don't say it." She traced my eyebrows with her finger. The dim light was reflected in her eyes as she looked at me, her body leaning gently against mine, her head held back.

"Why not?"

"Because I don't know . . . I'm not sure . . . I've liked you kissing me and I like being with you. But love is so big a word. It's too important. I'm . . . I'm not . . . ready . . ."

And there it was. Kate the beautiful, the brave, the friendly, was also Kate the unawakened. She was not aware yet of the fire that I perceived in her at every turn. It had been battened down from childhood by her Edwardian aunt, and how to release it without shocking her was a puzzle.

"Love's easy to learn," I said. "It's like taking a risk. You set your mind on it and refuse to be afraid, and in no time you feel terrifically exhilarated and all your inhibitions fly out of the window."

"And you're left holding the baby," said Kate, keeping her feet on the ground.

"We could get married first," I said, smiling at her.

"No. Dear Alan. No. Not yet." Then she said, almost in a whisper, "I'm so sorry."

She got into the car and drove slowly round to the barn garage. I followed behind the car and helped her shut the big garage doors, and walked back with her to the house. On the doorstep she paused and squeezed my hand, and gave me a soft, brief, sisterly kiss.

I didn't want it.

I didn't feel at all like a brother.

10

On Tuesday it began to rain, cold slanting rain which lashed at the opening daffodils and covered the flowers with splashed up mud. The children went to school in shining black capes with sou'westers pulled down to their eyes and gum boots up to their knees. All that could be seen of William was his cherubic mouth with milk stains at the corners.

Scilla and I spent the day sorting out Bill's clothes and personal belongings. She was far more composed than I would have expected, and seemed to have won through to an acceptance that he was gone and that life must be lived without him. Neither of us had mentioned, since it happened, the night she had spent in my bed, and I had become convinced that when she woke the next morning she had had no memory of it. Grief and drugs had played tricks with her mind.

We sorted Bill's things into piles. The biggest section was to be saved for Henry and William, and into this pile Scilla put not only cuff links and studs and two gold watches, but dinner jackets and a morning suit and grey top hat. I teased her about it.

"It isn't silly," she said. "Henry will be needing them in ten years, if not before. He'll be very glad to have them." And she added a hacking jacket and two new white silk shirts.

"We might just as well put everything back into the cupboards and wait for Henry and William to grow," I said.

"That's not a bad idea," said Scilla, bequeathing to the little boys their father's best riding breeches and his warmly-lined white mackintosh.

We finished the clothes, went downstairs to the cosy study, and turned our attention to Bill's papers. His desk was full of them. He clearly hated to throw away old bills and letters, and in the bottom drawer we found a bundle of letters that Scilla had written to him before their marriage. She sat on the window seat reading them nostalgically while I sorted out the rest.

Bill had been methodical. The bills were clipped together in chronological order, and the letters were in boxes and files. There were some miscellaneous collections in the pigeon holes, and a pile of old, empty, used envelopes with day-to-day notes on the backs. They were reminders to himself, mostly, with messages like "Tell Simpson to mend fence in five acre field," and "Polly's birthday Tuesday." I looked through them quickly, hovering them over the heap bound for the wastepaper basket.

I stopped suddenly. On one of them, in Bill's loopy sprawling handwriting, was the name Clifford Tudor, and underneath, a telephone number and an address in Brighton.

"Do you know anyone called Clifford Tudor?" I asked Scilla.

"Never heard of him," she said without looking up.

If Tudor had asked Bill to ride for him, as he had told me when I drove him from Plumpton to Brighton, it was perfectly natural for Bill to have his name and address. I turned the envelope over. It had come from a local tradesman, whose name was printed on the top left hand corner, and the postmark was date-stamped January, which meant that Bill had only recently acquired Tudor's address.

I put the envelope in my pocket and went on sorting. After the old envelopes I started on the pigeon holes. There were old photographs and some pages the children had drawn and written on with straggly letters in their babyhood, address books, luggage labels, a birthday card, school reports, and various notebooks of different shapes and sizes.

"You'd better look through these, Scilla," I said.

"You look," she said, glancing up from her letters with a smile. "You can tell me what's what, and I'll look at them presently."

Bill had had no secrets. The notebooks mainly contained his day-to-day expenses, jotted down to help his accountant at the annual reckoning. They went back some years. I found the latest, and leafed through it.

School fees, hay for the horses, a new garden hose, a repair to the Jaguar's head-lamp in Bristol, a present for Scilla, a bet on Admiral, a donation to charity. And that was the end. After that came the blank pages which were not going to be filled up.

I looked again at the last entries. A bet on Admiral. Ten pounds to win, Bill had written. And the date was the day of his death. Whatever had been said to Bill about Admiral's falling, he had taken it as a joke and had backed himself to win in spite of it. I would dearly have liked to know what the "joke" had been. He had told Pete, whose mind was with the horses. He had not told Scilla, nor any of his friends as far as I could find out. Possibly he had thought it so unimportant that after he spoke to Pete it had wholly slipped his mind.

I stacked up the notebooks and began on the last pigeon hole full of oddments. Among them were fifteen or twenty of the betting tickets issued by bookmakers at race meetings. As evidence of bets lost, they are usually torn up or thrown away by disappointed punters, not carefully preserved in a tidy desk.

"Why did Bill keep these betting tickets?" I asked Scilla.

"Henry had a craze for them not long ago, don't you remember?" she said. "And after it wore off Bill still brought some home for him. I think he kept them in case William wanted to play bookmakers in his turn."

I did remember. I had backed a lot of horses for halfpennies with Henry the bookmaker, the little shark. They never won.

The extra tickets Bill had saved for him were from several different bookmakers. It was part of Bill's pleasure at the races to walk among the bookmakers' stands in Tattersall's and put his actual cash on at the best odds, instead of betting on credit with a bookmaker on the rails.

"Do you want to keep them for William still?" I asked.

"May as well," said Scilla.

I put them back in the desk, and finished the job. It was late in the afternoon. We went into the drawing-room, stoked up the fire, and settled into armchairs.

She said, "Alan, I want to give you something which belonged to Bill. Now, don't say anything until I've finished. I've been wondering what you'd like best, and I'm sure I've chosen right."

She looked from me to the fire and held her hands out to warm them.

She said, "You are to have Admiral."

"No." I was definite.

"Why not?" She looked up, sounding disappointed.

"Dearest Scilla, it's far too much," I said. "I thought you meant something like a cigarette case, a keepsake. You can't possibly give me Admiral. He's worth thousands. You must sell him, or run him in your name if you want to keep him, but you can't give him to me. It wouldn't be fair to you or the children for me to have him."

"He might be worth thousands if I sold him—but I couldn't sell him, you know. I couldn't bear to do that. He meant so much to Bill. How could I sell him as soon as Bill's back was turned? And if I keep him and run him, I'll have to pay the bills, which might not be easy for a while with death duties hanging over me. If I give him to you, he's in hands Bill would approve of, and you can pay for his keep. I've thought it all out, so you're not to argue. Admiral is yours."

She meant it.

"Then let me lease him from you," I said.

"No, he's a gift. From Bill to you, if you like."

And on those terms I gave in, and thanked her as best I could.

The following morning, early, I drove to Pete Gregory's stables in Sussex to jump my green young Forlorn Hope over the schooling hurdles. A drizzling rain was falling as I arrived, and only because I had come so far did we bother to take the horses out. It was not a very satisfactory session, with Forlorn Hope slipping on the wet grass as we approached the first hurdle and not taking on the others with any spirit after that.

We gave it up and went down to Pete's house. I told him Admiral was to be mine and that I would be riding him.

He said, "He's in the Foxhunters' at Liverpool, did you know?"

"So he is!" I exclaimed delightedly. I had not yet ridden round the Grand National course, and the sudden prospect of doing it a fortnight later was exciting.

"You want to have a go?"

"Yes, indeed," I said.

We talked over the plans for my other horses, Pete telling me Palindrome was in fine fettle after his Cheltenham race and a certainty for the following day at Bristol. We went out to look at him and the others, and I inspected the splint which Heavens Above was throwing out. His leg was tender, but it would right itself in time.

When I left Pete's I went back to Brighton, parking the Lotus and taking a train as before. I walked out of Brighton station with a brief glance at the three taxis standing there (no yellow shields) and walked briskly in the direction of the headquarters of the Marconicars as listed in the telephone directory.

I had no particular plan, but I was sure the core of the mystery was in Brighton, and if I wanted to discover it, I would have to dig around on the spot. My feelers on the racecourse had still brought me nothing but a husky warning on the telephone.

The Marconicars offices were on the ground floor of a converted Regency terrace house. I went straight into the narrow hall.

The stairs rose on the right, and on the left were two doors, with a third, marked Private, facing me at the far end of the passage. A neat board on the door nearest the entrance said "Enquiries." I went in.

It had once been an elegant room and even the office equipment could not entirely spoil its proportions. There were two girls sitting at desks with typewriters in front of them, and through the half-open folded dividing doors I could see into an inner office where a third girl sat in front of a switchboard. She was speaking into a microphone.

"Yes, madam, a taxi will call for you in three minutes," she said. "Thank you." She had a pleasant high voice of excellent carrying quality.

The two girls in the outer office looked at me expectantly. They wore tight sweaters and large quantities of mascara. I spoke to the one nearest the door.

"Er . . . I'm enquiring about booking some taxis . . . for a wedding. My sister's," I added, improvising and inventing the sister I never had. "Is that possible?"

"Oh, yes, I think so," she said. "I'll ask the manager. He usually deals with big bookings."

I said, "I'm only asking for an estimate . . . on behalf of my sister. She has asked me to try all the firms, to find out which will be most —er—reasonable. I can't give you a definite booking until I've consulted her again."

"I see," she said. "Well, I'll ask Mr. Fielder to see you." She went out, down the passage, and through the door marked Private.

While I waited I grinned at the other girl, who patted her hair, and I listened to the girl at switchboard.

"Just a minute, sir. I'll see if there's a taxi in your area," she was saying. She flipped a switch and said, "Come in, any car in Hove two. Come in, any car in Hove two."

There was a silence and then a man's voice said out of the radio receiving set, "It looks as though there's no one in Hove two, Marigold. I could get there in five minutes. I've just dropped a fare in Langbury Place."

"Right, Jim." She gave him the address, flipped the switch again, and spoke into the telephone. "A taxi will be with you in five minutes, sir. I am sorry for the delay, we have no cars available who can reach you faster than that. Thank you, sir." As soon as she had finished speaking the telephone rang again. She said, "Marconicars. Can I help you?"

Down the hall came the clip clop of high heels on linoleum, and the girl came back from Mr. Fielder. She said, "The manager can see you now, sir."

"Thank you," I said. I went down the hall and through the open door at the end.

The man who rose to greet me and shake hands was a heavy, well-tailored, urbane man in his middle forties. He wore spectacles with heavy black frames, had smooth black hair and hard blue eyes. He seemed a man of too strong a personality to be sitting in the back office of a taxi firm, too high-powered an executive for the range of his job.

I felt my heart jump absurdly, and I had a moment's panic in which I feared he knew who I was and what I was trying to do. But his gaze was calm and businesslike, and he said only, "I understand you wish to make a block booking for a wedding."

"Yes," I said, and launched into fictitious details. He made notes, added up some figures, wrote out an estimate, and held it out to me. I took it. His writing was strong and black. It fitted him.

"Thank you," I said. "I'll give this to my sister, and let you know."

As I went out of his door and shut it behind me, I looked back at him. He was sitting behind his desk staring at me through his glasses with unwinking blue eyes. I could read nothing in his face.

I went back into the front office and said, "I've got the estimate I wanted. Thank you for your help." I turned to go, and had a second thought. "By the way, do you know where I can find Mr. Clifford Tudor?" I asked.

The girls, showing no surprise at my enquiry, said they did not know.

"Marigold might find out for you," said one of them. "I'll ask her."

Marigold, finishing her call, agreed to help. She pressed the switch. "All cars. Did anyone pick up Mr. Tudor today? Come in please."

A man's voice said, "I took him to the station this morning, Marigold. He caught the London train."

"Thanks, Mike," said Marigold.

"She knows all their voices," said one of the girls, admiringly. "They never have to tell her the number of their car."

"Do you all know Mr. Tudor well?" I asked.

"Never seen him," said one girl, and the others shook their heads in agreement.

"He's one of our regulars. He takes a car whenever he wants one, and we book it here. The driver tells Marigold where he's taking him. Mr. Tudor has a monthly account, and we make it up and send it to him."

"Suppose the driver takes Mr. Tudor from place to place and fails to report it to Marigold?" I asked conversationally.

"He wouldn't be so silly. The drivers get commission on regulars. Instead of tips, do you see? We put ten per cent on the bills to save the regulars having to tip the drivers every five minutes."

"A good idea," I said. "Do you have many regulars?"

"Dozens," said one of the girls. "But Mr. Tudor is about our best client."

"And how many taxis are there?" I asked.

"Thirty-one. Some of them will be in the garage for servicing, of course, and sometimes in the winter we only have half of them on the road. There's a lot of competition from the other firms."

"Who actually owns the Marconicars?" I asked casually.

They said they didn't know and couldn't care less.

"Not Mr. Fielder?" I asked.

"Oh, no," said Marigold. "I don't think so. There's a Chairman, I believe, but we've never seen him. Mr. Fielder can't be all that high up, because he sometimes takes over from me in the evenings and at week-ends. Though another girl comes in to relieve me on my days off, of course."

They suddenly all seemed to realise that this had nothing to do with my sister's wedding. It was time to go, and I went.

I stood outside on the pavement wondering what to do next. There was a café opposite, across the broad street, and it was nearly lunch-time. I went over and into the café, which smelled of cabbage, and because I had arrived before the rush there was a table free by the window. Through the chaste net curtains of the Olde Oake Café I had a clear view of the Marconicar office. For what it was worth.

A stout girl with wispy hair pushed a typed menu card in front of me. I looked at it, depressed. English home cooking at its very plainest. Tomato soup, choice of fried cod, sausages in batter, or steak and kidney pie, with suet pudding and custard to follow. It was all designed with no regard for an amateur rider's weight. I asked for coffee. The girl said firmly I couldn't have coffee by itself at lunch-time, they needed the tables. I offered to pay for the full lunch if I could just have the coffee, and to this she agreed, clearly thinking me highly eccentric.

The coffee, when it came, was surprisingly strong and good. I was getting the first of the brew, I reflected, idly watching the Marconicar front door. No one interesting went in or out.

On the storey above the Marconicars a big red neon sign flashed on and off, showing little more than a flicker in the daylight. I glanced up at it. Across the full width of the narrow building was the name L. C. PERTH. The taxi office had "Marconicars" written in bright yellow on black along the top of its big window, and looking up I saw that the top storey was decorated with a large blue board bearing in white letters the information "Jenkins, Wholesale Hats."

The total effect was colourful indeed, but hardly what the Regency architect had had in mind. I had a mental picture of him turning in his grave so often that he made knots in his winding sheet, and I suppose I smiled, for a voice suddenly said, "Vandalism, isn't it?"

A middle-aged woman had sat down at my table, unnoticed by me as I gazed out of the window. She had a mournful horsey face with no make-up, a hideous brown hat which added years to her age, and an earnest look in her eyes. The café was filling up, and I could no longer have a table to myself.

"It's startling, certainly," I agreed.

"It ought not to be allowed. All these old houses in this district have been carved up and turned into offices, and it's really disgraceful how they look now. I belong to the Architectural Preservation Group," she confided solemnly, "and we're getting out a petition to stop people desecrating beautiful buildings with horrible advertisements."

"Are you having success?" I asked.

She looked depressed. "Not very much, I'm afraid. People just don't seem to care as they should. Would you believe it, half the people in Brighton don't know what a Regency house looks like, when they're surrounded by them all the time? Look at that row over there, with all those boards and signs. And that neon," her voice quivered with emotion, "is the last straw. It's only been there a few months. We've petitioned to make them take it down, but they won't."

"That's very discouraging," I said, watching the Marconicar door. The two typists came out and went chattering up the road, followed by two more girls whom I supposed to have come down from the upper floors.

My table companion chatted on between spoonfuls of tomato soup. "We can't get any satisfaction from Perth's at all because no one in authority there will meet us, and the men in the office say they can't take the sign down because it doesn't belong to them, but they won't tell us who it does belong to so that we can petition him in person." I found I sympathised with Perth's invisible ruler in his disinclination to meet the Architectural Preservation Group on the warpath. "It was bad enough before, when they had their name just painted on the windows, but neon . . ." Words failed her, at last.

Marigold left for lunch. Four men followed her. No one arrived.

I drank my coffee, parted from the middle-aged lady without regret, and gave it up for the day. I took the train back to my car and drove up to London. After a long afternoon in the office, I started for home at the tail end of the rush-hour traffic. In the hold-ups at crossings and roundabouts I began, as a change from Bill's mystery, to tackle Joe Nantwich's.

I pondered his "stopping" activities, his feud with Sandy Mason, his disgrace with Tudor, his obscure threatening notes. I thought about the internal workings of the weighing room, where only valets, jockeys and officials are allowed in the changing rooms, and trainers and owners are confined to the weighing room itself, while the press and the public may not enter at all.

If the "Bolingbroke, this week" note was to be believed, Joe would already have received his punishment, because "this week" was already last week. Yet I came to the conclusion that I would see him alive and well at Bristol on the following day, even if not in the best of spirits. For, by the time I reached home, I knew I could tell him who had written the notes, though I wasn't sure I was going to.

Sleep produces the answers to puzzles in the most amazing way. I went to bed on Wednesday night thinking I had spent a more or less fruitless morning in Brighton. But I woke on Thursday morning with a name in my mind and the knowledge that I had seen it before, and where. I went downstairs in my dressing-gown to Bill's desk, and took out the betting tickets he had saved for Henry. I shuffled through them, and found what I wanted. Three of them bore the name L. C. PERTH.

I turned them over. On their backs Bill had pencilled the name of a horse, the amount of his bet, and the date. He was always methodical. I took all the tickets up to my room, and looked up the races in the form book. I remembered many casual snatches of conversation. And a lot of things became clear to me.

But not enough, not enough.

11

It poured with rain at Bristol, a cold, steady unrelenting wetness which took most of the pleasure out of racing.

Kate sent a message that she was not coming because of the weather, which sounded unlike her, and I wondered what sort of pressure Aunt Deb had used to keep her at home.

The main gossip in the weighing room concerned Joe Nantwich. The Stewards had held an enquiry into his behaviour during the last race on Champion Hurdle day, and had, in the official phrase, "severely cautioned him as to his future riding." It was generally considered that he was very lucky indeed to have got off so lightly, in view of his past record.

Joe himself was almost as cocky as ever. From a distance his round pink face showed no traces of the fear or drunkenness which had made a sodden mess of him at Cheltenham. Yet I was told that he had spent the preceding Friday and Saturday and most of Sunday in the Turkish baths, scared out of his wits. He had drunk himself silly and sweated it off alternately during the whole of that time, confiding to the attendants in tears that he was safe with them, and refusing to get dressed and go home.

The authority for this story, and one who gave it its full flavour, was Sandy, who had happened, he said, to go into the Turkish baths on Sunday morning to lose a few pounds for Monday's racing.

I found Joe reading the notices. He was whistling through his teeth.

"Well, Joe," I said, "what makes you so cheerful?"

"Everything." He smirked. At close quarters I could see the fine lines round his mouth and the slightly bloodshot eyes, but his experiences had left no other signs of strain. "I didn't get suspended by the Stewards. And I got paid for losing that race."

"You what?" I exclaimed.

"I got paid. You know, I told you. The packet of money. It came this morning. A hundred quid." I stared at him. "Well, I did what I was told, didn't I?" he said aggrievedly.

"I suppose you did," I agreed, weakly.

"And another thing, those threatening notes. I fooled them you know. I stayed in the Turkish baths all over the week-end, and they couldn't harm me there. I got off scot free," said Joe, triumphantly, as if "this week" could not be altered to "next week." He did not realise either that he had already taken his punishment, that there are other agonies than physical ones. He had suffered a week of acute anxiety, followed by three days of paralysing fear, and he thought he had got off scot free.

"I'm glad you think so," I said, mildly. "Joe, answer me a question. The man who rings you up to tell you what horse not to win on, what does his voice sound like?"

"You couldn't tell who it is, not by listening to him. It might be anybody. It's a soft voice, and sort of fuzzy. Almost a whisper, sometimes, as if he were afraid of being overheard. But what does it matter?" said Joe. "As long as he delivers the lolly he can croak like a frog for all I care."

"Do you mean you'll stop another horse, if he asks you to?" I said.

"I might do. Or I might not," said Joe, belatedly deciding that he had been speaking much too freely. With a sly, sidelong look at me he edged away into the changing room. His resilience was fantastic.

Pete and Dane were discussing the day's plans not far away, and I went over to them. Pete was cursing the weather and saying it would play merry hell with the going, but that Palindrome, all the same, should be able to act on it.

"Go to the front at half way, and nothing else will be able to come to you. They're a poor lot. As far as I can see, you're a dead cert."

"That's good," I said, automatically, and then remembered with a mental wince that Admiral had been a dead cert at Maidenhead.

Dane asked me if I had enjoyed my stay with Kate and did not look too overjoyed by my enthusiastic answer.

"Curses on your head, pal, if you have cut me out with Kate." He said it in a mock ferocious voice, but I had an uncomfortable feeling that he meant it. Could a friendship survive between two men who were in love with the same girl? Suddenly at that moment, I didn't know; for I saw in Dane's familiar handsome face a passing flash of enmity. It was as disconcerting as a rock turning to quicksand. And I went rather thoughtfully into the changing room to find Sandy.

He was standing by the window, gazing through the curtain of rain which streamed down the glass. He changed into colours for the first race, and was looking out towards the parade ring, where two miserable looking horses were being led round by dripping, mackintoshed stable lads.

"We'll need windscreen wipers on our goggles in this little lot," he remarked, with unabashed good spirits. "Anyone for a mud bath? Blimey, it's enough to discourage ducks."

"How did you enjoy your Turkish bath on Sunday?" I asked, smiling.

"Oh, you heard about that, did you?"

"I think everyone has heard about it," I said.

"Good. Serve the little bastard right," said Sandy, grinning hugely.

"How did you know where to find him?" I asked.

"Asked his mother . . ." Sandy broke off in the middle of the word and his eyes widened.

"Yes," I said. "You sent him those threatening Bolingbroke notes."

"And what," said Sandy, with good humour, "makes you think so?"

"You like practical jokes, and you dislike Joe," I said. "The first note he received was put into his jacket while it hung in the changing room at Plumpton, so it had to be a jockey or a valet or an official who did it. It couldn't have been a bookmaker or a trainer or an owner or any member of the public. So I began to think that perhaps the person who planted the note in Joe's pocket was not the person who was paying him to stop horses. That person has, strangely enough, exacted no revenge at all. But I asked myself who else would be interested in tormenting Joe, and I came to you. You knew before the race that Joe was not supposed to win on Bolingbroke. When he won you told him you'd lost a lot of money, and you'd get even with him. And I guess you have. You even tracked him down to enjoy seeing him suffer."

"Revenge is sweet, and all that. Well, it's a fair cop," said Sandy. "Though how you know such a lot beats me."

"Joe told me most of it," I said.

"What a blabbermouth. That tongue of Joe's will get him into a right mess one of these days."

"Yes, it will," I said, thinking of the incautious way Joe had spoken of his "stopping" and its rewards.

"Did you tell him I had sent him those notes?" asked Sandy, with his first show of anxiety.

"No, I didn't. It would only stir up more trouble," I said.

"Thanks for that, anyway."

"And in reward for that small service, Sandy," I said, "will you tell me how you knew in advance that Bolingbroke was not supposed to win?"

He grinned widely, rocking gently on his heels, but he didn't answer.

"Go on," I said. "It isn't much to ask, and it might even give me a lead to that other mystery, about Bill Davidson."

Sandy shook his head. "It won't help you any," he said. "Joe told me himself."

"What?" I exclaimed.

"He told me himself. In the washroom when we were changing before the race. You know how he can't help swanking? He wanted to show off, and I was handy, and besides, he knew I'd stopped a horse or two in my time."

"What did he say?" I asked.

"He said if I wanted a lesson in how to choke a horse I'd better watch him on Bolingbroke. Well, a nod's as good as a wink to Sandy Mason. I got a punter to put fifty quid on Leica, which I reckoned was bound to win with Bolingbroke not trying. And look what happened. The little sod lost his nerve and beat Leica by two lengths. I could have throttled him. Fifty quid's a ruddy fortune, mate, as far as I'm concerned."

"Why did you wait as long as ten days before you gave him that first note?" I asked.

"I didn't think of it until then," he said, frankly. "But it was a damn good revenge, wasn't it? He nearly got his licence suspended at Cheltenham, and he sweated his guts out for three days at the week-end, all in the screaming heeby-jeebies worked up by yours truly." Sandy beamed. "You should have seen him in the Turkish baths. A sodden, whining, clutching wreck. In tears, and begging me to keep him safe. Me! What a laugh. I was nearly sick, trying not to laugh. A cracking good revenge, that was."

"And you put him over the rails at Plumpton, too," I said.

"I never did," said Sandy, indignantly. "Did he tell you that? He's a bloody liar. He fell off, I saw him. I've a good mind to frighten him again." His red hair bristled and his brown eyes sparkled. Then he relaxed. "Oh, well . . . I'll think of something, sometime. There's no rush. I'll make his life uncomfortable—ants in his pants, worms in his boots, that sort of thing. Harmless," and Sandy began to laugh. Then he said, "As you're such a roaring success as a private eye, how are you getting on with that other business?"

"Not fast enough," I said. "But I know a lot more than I did at this time last week, so I haven't lost hope. You haven't heard anything useful?" He shook his head.

"Not a squeak anywhere. You're not giving it up, then?"

"No," I said.

"Well, the best of British luck," said Sandy, grinning.

An official poked his head round the door. "Jockeys out, please," he said. It was nearly time for the first race.

Sandy put his helmet on and tied the strings. Then he took out his false teeth, the two centre incisors of the upper jaw, wrapped them in a handkerchief and tucked them into the pocket of the coat hanging on his peg. He, like most jockeys, never rode races wearing false teeth, for fear of losing them, or even swallowing them if he fell. He gave me a gap-toothed grin, sketched a farewell salute, and dived out into the rain.

It was still raining an hour later when I went out to ride Palindrome. Pete was waiting for me in the parade ring, the water dripping off the brim of his hat in a steady stream.

"Isn't this a God-awful day?" he said. "I'm glad it's you that's got to strip off and get soaked, and not me. I had a bellyful when I was riding. I hope you're good at swimming."

"Why?" I asked, mystified.

"If you are, you'll know how to keep your eyes open under water." I suspected another of Pete's rather feeble jokes, but he was serious. He pointed to the goggles slung round my neck. "You won't need those, for a start. With all the mud that's being kicked up today, they'd be covered before you'd gone a furlong."

"I'll leave them down, then," I said.

"Take them off. They'll only get in your way," he said.

So I took them off, and as I turned my head to ease the elastic over the back of my helmet, I caught a glimpse of a man walking along outside the parade ring. There were few people standing about owing to the rain, and I had a clear view of him.

It was Bert, the man in charge of the horse in the lay-by on Maidenhead Thicket. One of the Marconicar drivers.

He was not looking at me, but the sight of him was as unpleasant as an electric shock. He was a long way from base. He might have travelled the hundred and forty miles solely to enjoy an afternoon's racing in the rain. Or he might not.

I looked at Palindrome, plodding slowly round the parade ring in his waterproof rug.

A dead cert.

I shivered.

I knew I had made some progress towards my quarry, the man who had caused Bill's death, even though he himself was as unknown to me as ever. I had disregarded his two emphatic warnings and I feared I had left a broad enough trail for him to be well aware of my pursuit. Bert would not be at Bristol alone, I thought, and I could guess that a third deterrent message was on its way.

There are times when one could do without an intuition, and this was one of them. Palindrome, the dead cert. What had been done once would be tried again, and somewhere out on the rain-swept racecourse another strand of wire could be waiting. For no logical reason, I was certain of it.

It was too late to withdraw from the race. Palindrome was an odds-on favourite, and clearly in the best of health; he showed no lameness, no broken blood-vessels, none of the permitted excuses for a last minute cancellation. And if I myself were suddenly taken ill and couldn't ride, another jockey would be quickly found to take my place. I couldn't send someone out in my colours to take a fall designed for me.

If I refused point-blank, without explanation, to let Palindrome run in the race, my permit to ride would be withdrawn, and that would be the end of my steeplechasing.

If I said to the Stewards, "Someone is going to bring Palindrome down with wire," they might possibly send an official round the course to inspect the fences: but he wouldn't find anything. I was quite sure that if a wire were rigged, it would be, as in Bill's case, a last minute job.

If I rode in the race, but kept Palindrome reined in behind other horses the whole way, the wire might not be rigged at all. But my heart sank as I regarded the faces of the jockeys who had already ridden, and remembered in what state they had come back from their previous races. Mud was splashed on their faces like thick khaki chicken-pox, and their jerseys were soaked and muddied to such an extent that their colours were almost unrecognisable from a few steps away, let alone the distance from one fence to the next. My own coffee and cream colours would be particularly indistinct. A man waiting with wire would not be able to tell for certain which horse was in front, but he would expect me and act accordingly.

I looked at the other jockeys in the parade ring, now reluctantly taking off their raincoats and mounting their horses. There were about ten of them. They were men who had taught me a lot, and accepted me as one of themselves, and given me a companionship I enjoyed almost as much as the racing itself. If I let one of them crash in my place, I couldn't face them again.

It was no good. I'd have to ride Palindrome out in front and hope for the best. I remembered Kate saying, "If there's something you've got to do, then to hell with the danger."

To hell with the danger. After all, I could fall any day, without the aid of wire. If I fell today, with it, that would be just too bad. But it couldn't be helped. And I might be wrong; there might be no wire at all.

Pete said, "What's the matter? You look as if you'd seen a ghost."

"I'm all right," I said, taking off my coat. Palindrome was standing beside me, and I patted him, admiring his splendid intelligent head. My chief worry from then on was that he, at least, should come out of the next ten minutes unscathed.

I swung up on to his back and looked down at Pete, and said, "If . . . if Palindrome falls in this race, please will you ring up Inspector Lodge at Maidenhead police station, and tell him about it?"

"What on earth . . . ?"

"Promise," I said.

"All right. But I don't understand. You could tell him yourself, if you want to, and anyway, you won't fall."

"No, perhaps not," I said.

"I'll meet you in the winner's enclosure," he said, slapping Palindrome's rump as we moved off.

The rain was blowing into our faces as we lined up for the start in front of the stands, with two circuits of the course to complete. The tapes went up, and we were off.

Two or three horses jumped the first fence ahead of me, but after that I took Palindrome to the front, and stayed there. He was at his best, galloping and jumping with the smooth flow of a top class 'chaser. On any other day, the feel of this power beneath me would have pleased me beyond words. As it was, I scarcely noticed it.

Remembering Bill's fall, I was watching for an attendant to walk across behind a fence as the horses approached it. He would be uncoiling the wire, raising it, fixing it . . . I planned when I saw that to try to persuade Palindrome to take off too soon before the fence, so that he would hit the wire solidly with his chest when he was already past the height of his spread. That way, I hoped he might break or pull down the wire and still stay on his feet; and if we fell, it should not be in a shattering somersault like Admiral's. But it is easier to plan than to do, and I doubted whether a natural jumper like Palindrome *could* be persuaded to take off one short stride too soon.

We completed the first circuit without incident, squelching on the sodden turf. About a mile from home, on the far side of the course, I heard hoofbeats close behind, and looked over my shoulder. Most of the field were bunched up some way back, but two of them were chasing me with determination and they were almost up to Palindrome's quarters.

I shook him up and he responded immediately, and we widened the gap from our pursuers to about five lengths.

No attendant walked across the course.

I didn't see any wire.

But Palindrome hit it, just the same.

It wouldn't have been too bad a fall but for the horses behind me. I felt the heavy jerk on Palindrome's legs as we rose over the last fence on the far side of the course, and I shot off like a bullet, hitting the ground with my shoulder several yards ahead. Before I had stopped rolling the other horses were jumping the fence. They would have avoided a man on the ground if they possibly could, but in this case, I was told afterwards, they had to swerve round

Palindrome, who was struggling to get up, and found me straight in their path.

The galloping hooves thudded into my body. One of the horses kicked my head and my helmet split so drastically that it fell off. There were six seconds of bludgeoning, battering chaos, in which I could neither think nor move, but only feel.

When it was all over I lay on the wet ground, limp and growing numb, unable to get up, unable even to stir. I was lying on my back with my feet towards the fence. The rain fell on my face and trickled through my hair, and the drops felt so heavy on my eyelids that opening them was like lifting a weight. Through a slit, from under my rain-beaded lashes, I could see a man at the fence.

He wasn't coming to help me. He was very quickly coiling up a length of wire, starting on the outside of the course and working inwards. When he reached the inner post he put his hand in his raincoat pocket, drew out a tool, and clipped the wire where it was fastened eighteen inches above the fence. This time, he had not forgotten his wire cutters. He finished his job, hooked the coil over his arm, and turned towards me.

I knew him.

He was the driver of the horse-box.

The colour was going out of everything. The world looked grey to me, like an under-exposed film. The green grass was grey, the box driver's face was grey . . .

Then I saw that there was another man at the fence, and he was walking towards me. I knew him, too, and he was not a taxi-driver. I was so glad to find I had some help against the box driver that I could have wept with relief. I tried to tell him to look at the wire, so that this time there should be a witness. But the words could get no farther than my brain. My throat and tongue refused to form them.

He came over and stood beside me, and stooped down. I tried to smile and say hello, but not a muscle twitched. He straightened up.

He said, over his shoulder, to the box driver, "He's been knocked out." He turned back to me.

He said, "You nosey bastard," and he kicked me. I heard the ribs crack, and I felt the hot stab in my side. "Perhaps that'll teach you to mind your own business." He kicked me again. My grey world grew darker. I was nearly unconscious, but even in that dire moment some part of my mind went on working, and I knew why the attendant had not walked across with the wire. He had not needed to. He and his accomplice had stood on opposite sides of the course and had raised it between them.

I saw the foot drawn back a third time. It seemed hours, in my disjointed brain, until it came towards my eyes, growing bigger and bigger until it was all that I could see.

He kicked my face, and I went out like a light.

12

Hearing came back first. It came back suddenly, as if someone had pressed a switch. At one moment no messages of any sort were getting through the swirling, distorted dreams which seemed to have been going on inside my head for a very long time, and in the next I was lying in still blackness, with every sound sharp and distinct in my ears.

A woman's voice said, "He's still unconscious."

I wanted to tell her it was not true, but could not.

The sounds went on; swishing, rustling, clattering, the murmur of distant voices, the thump and rattle of water in pipes of ancient plumbing. I listened, but without much interest.

After a while I knew I was lying on my back. My limbs, when I became aware of them, were as heavy as lead and ached persistently, and ton weights rested on my eyelids.

I wondered where I was. Then I wondered who I was. I could remember nothing at all. This seemed too much to deal with, so I went to sleep.

The next time I woke up the weights were gone from my eyes. I opened them, and found I was lying in a dim light in a room whose fuzzy lines slowly grew clear. There was a wash-basin in one corner, a table with a white cloth on it, an easy chair with wooden arms, a window to my right, a door straight ahead. A bare, functional room.

The door opened and a nurse came in. She looked at me in pleased surprise and smiled. She had nice teeth.

"Hello there," she said. "So you've come back at last. How do you feel?"

"Fine," I said, but it came out as a whisper, and in any case it wasn't strictly true.

"Are you comfortable?" she asked, holding my wrist for the pulse.

"No," I said, giving up the pretence.

"I'll go and tell Dr. Mitcham you've woken up, and I expect he will come and see you. Will you be all right for a few minutes?" She wrote something on a board which lay on the table, gave me another bright smile, and swished out of the door.

So I was in hospital. But I still had no idea what had happened. Had I, I wondered, been run over by a steam roller? Or a herd of elephants?

Dr. Mitcham, when he came, would solve only half the mystery.

"Why am I here?" I asked, in a croaky whisper.

"You fell off a horse," he said.

"Who am I?"

At this question he tapped his teeth with the end of his pencil and looked at me steadily for some seconds. He was a blunt-featured young man with fluffy, already receding, fair hair, and bright intelligent pale blue eyes.

"I'd rather you remember that for yourself. You will, soon, I'm sure. Don't worry about it. Don't worry about anything. Just relax, and your memory will come back. Not all at once, don't expect that, but little by little you'll remember everything, except perhaps the fall itself."

"What is wrong with me, exactly?" I asked.

"Concussion is what has affected your memory. As to the rest of you," he surveyed me from head to foot, "you have a broken collar-bone, four cracked ribs and multiple contusions."

"Nothing serious, thank goodness," I croaked.

He opened his mouth and gasped, and then began to laugh. He said, "No, nothing serious. You lot are all the same. Quite mad."

"Which lot?" I said.

"Never mind, you'll remember soon," he said. "Just go to sleep for a while, if you can, and you'll probably understand a great deal more when you wake up."

I took his advice, closed my eyes and drifted to sleep. I dreamed of a husky voice which came from the centre of a bowl of red and yellow crocuses, whispering menacing things until I wanted to scream and run away, and then I realised it was my own voice whispering, and the crocuses faded into a vision of deep green forests with scarlet birds darting in the shadows. Then I thought I was very high up, looking to the ground, and I was leaning farther and farther forward until I fell, and this time what I said made perfect sense.

"I fell out of the tree." I knew it had happened in my boyhood.

There was an exclamation beside me. I opened my eyes. At the foot of the bed stood Dr. Mitcham.

"What tree?" he said.

"In the forest," I said. "I hit my head, and when I woke my father was kneeling beside me."

There was an exclamation again at my right hand. I rolled my head over to look.

He sat there, sunburnt, fit, distinguished, and at forty-six looking still a young man.

"Hi, there," I said.

"Do you know who this is?" asked Dr. Mitcham.

"My father."

"And what is your name?"

"Alan York," I said at once, and my memory bounded back. I could remember everything up to the morning I was going to Bristol races. I remembered setting off, but what happened after that was still a blank.

"How did you get here?" I asked my father.

"I flew over. Mrs. Davidson rang me up to tell me you had had a fall and were in hospital. I thought I'd better take a look."

"How long . . ." I began, slowly.

"How long were you unconscious?" said Dr. Mitcham. "This is Sunday morning. Two and a half days. Not too bad, considering the crack you had. I kept your crash-helmet for you to see." He opened a locker and took out the shell which had undoubtedly saved my life. It was nearly in two pieces.

"I'll need a new one," I said.

"Quite mad. You're all quite mad," said Dr. Mitcham.

This time I knew what he meant. I grinned, but it was a lopsided affair, because I discovered that half my face was swollen as well as stiff and sore. I began to put up my left hand to explore the damage, but I changed my mind before I had raised it six inches, owing to the sudden pain which the movement caused in my shoulder. In spite of the tight bandages which arched my shoulders backwards, I heard and felt the broken ends of collar-bone grate together.

As if they had been waiting for a signal, every dull separate ache in my battered body sprang to vicious, throbbing life. I drew in a deep breath, and the broken ribs sharply rebelled against it. It was a bad moment.

I shut my eyes. My father said anxiously, "Is he all right?" and Dr. Mitcham answered, "Yes, don't worry. I rather think his breakages have caught up with him. I'll give him something to ease it, shortly."

"I'll be out of bed tomorrow," I said. "I've been bruised before, and I've broken my collar-bone before. It doesn't last long." But I added ruefully to myself that *while* it lasted it was highly unpleasant.

"You will certainly not get up tomorrow," said Dr. Mitcham's voice. "You'll stay where you are for a week, to give that concussion a chance."

"I can't stay in bed for a week," I protested. "I shouldn't have the strength of a flea when I got up, and I'm going to ride Admiral at Liverpool."

"When is that?" asked Dr. Mitcham suspiciously.

"March twenty-fourth," I said.

There was a short silence while they worked it out.

"That's only a week on Thursday," said my father.

"You can put it right out of your head," said Dr. Mitcham severely.

"Promise me," said my father.

I opened my eyes and looked at him, and when I saw the anxiety in his face I understood for the first time in my life how much I meant to him. I was his only child, and for ten years, after my mother died, he had reared me himself, not delegating the job to a succession of housekeepers, boarding schools and tutors as many a rich man would have done, but spending time playing with me and teaching me, and making sure I learned in my teens how to live happily and usefully under the burden of extreme wealth. He himself had taught me how to face all kinds of danger, yet I realised that it must seem to him that if I insisted on taking my first tilt at Liverpool when I was precariously unfit, I was risking more than I had any right to do.

"I promise," I said. "I won't ride at Liverpool this month. But I'm going on racing afterwards."

"All right. It's a deal." He relaxed, smiling, and stood up. "I'll come again this afternoon."

"Where are you staying? Where are we now?" I asked.

"This is Bristol Hospital, and I'm staying with Mrs. Davidson," he said.

I said, "Did I get this lot at Bristol races? With Palindrome?" My father nodded. "How is he? Was he hurt? What sort of fall did he have?"

"No, he wasn't hurt," he said. "He's back in Gregory's stables. No one saw how or why he fell because it was raining so hard. Gregory said you had a premonition you were going to fall, and he asked me to tell you he had done what you wanted."

"I don't remember anything about it, and I don't know what it was I wanted him to do," I sighed. "It's very irritating."

Dr. Mitcham and my father went away and left me puzzling over the gap in my memory. I had an illusive feeling that I had known for a few seconds a fact of paramount significance, but grope as I would, my conscious life ended on the road to Bristol races and began again in Bristol Hospital.

The rest of the day passed slowly and miserably, with each small movement I made setting up a chorus of protest in every crushed muscle and nerve. I had been kicked by horses before, but never in so many places all at once, and I knew, though I couldn't see it, that my skin must be covered with large angry crimson patches which had spread and were turning black and finally yellow as the blood underneath congealed and dispersed. My face, I knew, must be giving the same rainbow performance, and I undoubtedly had two lovely black eyes.

The pills Dr. Mitcham had sent via the nurse with pretty teeth made less difference than I would have liked, so I lay with my eyes shut and pretended I was floating on the sea in the sunshine, with my grating bones and throbbing head cushioned by a gentle swell. I filled in the scene with sea-gulls and white clouds and children splashing in the shallows, and it worked well each time until I moved again.

Late in the evening my headache grew worse and I slid in and out of weird troubled dreams in which I imagined that my limbs had been torn off by heavy weights, and I woke soaked in sweat to wiggle my toes and fingers in an agony of fear that they were missing. But no sooner had the feel of them against the sheets sent relief flooding over me than I was drifting away into the same nightmare all over again. The cycle of short awakenings and long dreams went on and on, until I was no longer sure what was real and what was not.

So shattering was the night passed in this fashion that when Dr. Mitcham came into my room in the morning I implored him to show me that my hands and feet were in fact still attached to me. Without a word he stripped back the bedclothes, grasped my feet firmly, and lifted them a few inches so that I could see them. I raised my hands and looked at them, and laced my fingertips together over my stomach; and felt a complete idiot to have been so terrified over nothing.

"There's no need to be embarrassed," said Mitcham. "You can't expect your brain to be in perfect working order when you've been unconscious for so long. I promise you that you have no injuries you don't know about. No internal damage, no bits missing. You'll be as good as new in three weeks." His steady pale blue eyes were reliable. "Only," he added, "you'll have a scar on your face. We stitched up a cut over your left cheekbone."

As I had not been exactly handsome before, this news did not disturb me. I thanked him for his forbearance, and he pulled the sheet and blankets over me again. His blunt face suddenly lit up with a mischievous smile, and he said, "Yesterday *you* told *me* there was nothing seriously wrong with you and you'd be out of bed today, if I remember correctly."

"Blast you," I said weakly. "I'll be out of bed tomorrow."

In the end it was Thursday before I made it on to my feet, and I went home to Scilla's on Saturday morning feeling more tottery than I cared to admit, but in good spirits nevertheless. My father, who was still there but planning to leave early the next week, came to fetch me.

Scilla and Polly clicked their tongues and made sympathetic remarks as I levered myself out of the Jaguar at one quarter my usual speed and walked carefully up the front steps. But young Henry, giving me a sweeping, comprehensive glance which took in my black and yellow face and the long newly healed cut across one cheek, greeted me with, "And how's the horrible monster from outer space?"

"Go and boil your head," I said, and Henry grinned delightedly.

At seven o'clock in the evening, just after the children had gone upstairs to bed, Kate rang up. Scilla and my father decided to bring some wine up from the cellar, and left me alone in the drawing-room to talk to her.

"How are the cracks?" she asked.

"Knitting nicely," I said. "Thank you for your letter, and for the flowers."

"The flowers were Uncle George's idea," she said. "I said it was too much like a funeral, sending you flowers, and he thought that was so funny that he nearly choked. It didn't seem all that funny to me, actually, when I knew from Mrs. Davidson that it very nearly was your funeral."

"It was nowhere near that," I said. "Scilla was exaggerating. And whether it was your idea or Uncle George's, thank you anyway for the flowers."

"Lilies, I expect I should have sent, not tulips," Kate teased.

"You can send lilies next time," I said, taking pleasure in hearing her slow attractive voice.

"Good heavens, is there going to be a next time?"

"Bound to be," I said cheerfully.

"Well all right," said Kate, "I'll place a standing order with Interflora, for lilies."

"I love you, Kate," I said.

"I must say," she said happily, "it's nice hearing people say that."

"People? Who else has said it? And when?" I asked, fearing the worst.

"Well," she said, after a tiny pause, "Dane, as a matter of fact."

"Oh."

"Don't be so jealous," she said. "And Dane's just as bad as you. He glowers like a thunderstorm if he hears your name. You're both being childish."

"Yes ma'am," I said. "When will I see you again?"

We fixed a luncheon date in London, and before she rang off I told her again that I loved her. I was about to put down my own receiver, when I heard the most unexpected sound on the telephone.

A giggle. A quickly suppressed, but definite giggle.

I knew she had disconnected; but I said into the dead mouthpiece in front of me, "Hang on a minute, Kate, I—er—want to read you something . . . in the paper. Just a minute while I get it." I put my receiver down on the table, went carefully out of the drawing-room, up the stairs, and into Scilla's bedroom.

There stood the culprits, grouped in a guilty huddle round the extension telephone. Henry, with the receiver pressed to his ear; Polly, her head close against his; and William, looking earnestly up at them with his mouth open. They were all in pyjamas and dressing-gowns.

"And just what do you think you're doing?" I asked, with a severe expression.

"Oh golly," said Henry, dropping the receiver on to the bed as if it were suddenly too hot to hold.

"Alan!" said Polly, blushing deeply.

"How long have you been listening?" I demanded.

"Actually, right from the beginning," said Polly shamefacedly.

"Henry always listens," said William, proud of his brother.

"Shut up," said Henry.

"You little beasts," I said.

William looked hurt. He said again, "But Henry always listens. He listens to everyone. He's checking up, and that's good, isn't it? Henry checks up all the time, don't you, Henry?"

"Shut up, William," said Henry, getting red and furious.

"So Henry checks up, does he?" I said, frowning crossly at him. Henry stared back, caught out, but apparently unrepentant.

I advanced towards them, but the homily on the sacredness of privacy that I was about to deliver suddenly flew out of my mind. I stopped and thought.

"Henry, how long have you been listening to people on the telephone?" I asked mildly.

He looked at me warily. Finally he said, "Quite some time."

"Days? Weeks? Months?"

"Ages," said Polly, taking heart again as I no longer seemed angry with them.

"Did you ever listen to your father?" I asked.

"Yes, often," said Henry.

I paused, studying this tough, intelligent little boy. He was only eight, but if he knew the answers to what I was going to ask him, he would understand their significance and be appalled by his knowledge all his life. But I pressed on.

"Did you by any chance ever hear him talking to a man with a voice like this?" I asked. Then I made my voice husky and whispering, and said, "Am I speaking to Major Davidson?"

"Yes," said Henry without hesitation.

"When was that?" I asked, trying to show nothing of the excitement I felt. I was sure now that he had listened in to the telephone call which Bill had mentioned as a joke to Pete, who had not taken in what he said.

"It was that voice the last time I listened to Daddy," said Henry, matter-of-factly.

"Do you remember what the voice said?" I forced myself to speak slowly, gently.

"Oh yes, it was a joke. It was two days before he was killed," said Henry, without distress. "Just when we were going to bed, like now. The phone rang and I scooted in here and listened as usual. That man with the funny voice was saying, 'Are you going to ride Admiral on Saturday, Major Davidson?' and Daddy said he was." Henry paused. I waited, willing him to remember.

He screwed up his eyes in concentration and went on. "Then the man with the funny voice said, 'You are not to win on Admiral, Major Davidson.' Daddy just laughed, and the man said, 'I'll pay you five hundred pounds if you promise not to win.' And Daddy said, 'Go to hell,' and I nearly snorted because he was always telling me not to say that. Then the whispery man said he didn't want Daddy to win, and that Admiral would fall if Daddy didn't agree not to win, and Daddy said, 'You must be mad.' And then he put down the telephone, and I ran back to my room in case he should come up and find me listening."

"Did you say anything to your father about it?" I asked.

"No," said Henry frankly. "That's the big snag about listening. You have to be awfully careful not to know too much."

"Yes, I can see that," I said, trying not to smile.

Then I saw the flicker in Henry's eyes as the meaning of what he had heard grew clearer to him. He said jerkily, "It wasn't a joke after all, was it?"

"No, it wasn't," I said.

"But that man didn't make Admiral fall, did he? He couldn't . . . could he? Could he?" said Henry desperately, wanting me to reassure him. His eyes were stretched wide open, and he was beginning to realise that he had listened to the man who had caused his father's death. Although he would have to know one day about the strand of wire, I didn't think I ought to tell him at that moment.

"I don't really know. I don't expect so," I lied calmly. But Henry's wide eyes stared blindly at me as if he were looking at some inward horror.

"What's the matter?" said Polly. "I don't understand why Henry is so upset. Just because someone told Daddy they didn't want him to win is no reason for Henry to go off in a fit."

"Does he always remember so clearly what people say?" I asked Polly. "It's a month ago, now, since your father died."

"I expect Daddy and that man said a lot of things that Henry has forgotten," said Polly judiciously, "but he doesn't make things up." And I knew this was true. He was a truthful child.

He said stonily, "I don't see how he could have done it."

I was glad at least that Henry was dealing with his revelation practically and not emotionally. Perhaps I had not done him too much harm, after all, in making him understand what he had heard and disregarded.

"Come along to bed and don't worry about it, Henry," I said, holding out my hand to him. He took it, and uncharacteristically held on to it all the way along the landing and into his bedroom.

13

While I was dressing myself at tortoise pace the following morning the front door bell rang downstairs, and presently Joan came up to say that an Inspector Lodge would like to see me, please.

"Tell him I'll be down as soon as possible," I said, struggling to get my shirt on over the thick bracing bandage round my shoulders. I did up most of the buttons, but decided I didn't need a tie.

The strapping round my ribs felt tight and itched horribly, my head ached, large areas of flesh were black still and tender, I had slept badly, and I was altogether in a foul mood. The three aspirins I had swallowed in place of breakfast had not come up to scratch.

I picked up my socks, tried to bend to put them on with my one useful arm, found how far away my feet had become, and flung them across the room in a temper. The day before, in the hospital, the nurse with nice teeth had helped me to dress. Today perverseness stopped me asking my father to come and do it for me.

The sight of my smudgy, yellow, unshaven face in the looking-glass made matters no better. Henry's "horrible monster from outer space" was not so far off the mark. I longed to scratch the livid scar on my cheek, to relieve its irritation.

I plugged in my electric razor and took off the worst, brushed my hair sketchily, thrust my bare feet into slippers, put one arm into my hacking jacket and swung it over the other shoulder, and shuffled gingerly downstairs.

Lodge's face when he saw me was a picture.

"If you laugh at me I'll knock your block off. Next week," I said.

"I'm not laughing," said Lodge, his nostrils twitching madly as he tried to keep a straight face.

"It's not funny," I said emphatically.

"No."

I scowled at him.

My father said, glancing at me from behind his Sunday newspaper in the depths of an armchair by the fire, "You sound to me as if you need a stiff brandy."

"It's only half past ten," I said crossly.

"Emergencies can happen at any time of the day," said my father, standing up, "and this would appear to be a grave one." He opened the corner cupboard where Scilla kept a few bottles and glasses, poured out a third of a tumbler full of brandy, and splashed some soda into it. I complained that it was too strong, too early, and unnecessary.

My father handed me the glass. "Drink it and shut up," he said.

Furious, I took a large mouthful. It was strong and fiery, and bit into my throat. I rolled the second mouthful round my teeth so that the scarcely diluted spirit tingled on my gums, and when I swallowed I could feel it slide warmly down to my empty stomach.

"Did you have any breakfast?" asked my father.

"No," I said.

I took another, smaller gulp. The brandy worked fast. My bad temper began draining away, and in a minute or two I felt reasonably sane. Lodge and my father were looking at me intently as though I were a laboratory animal responding to an experiment.

"Oh very well then," I admitted grudgingly, "I feel better." I took a cigarette from the silver box on the table and lit it, and noticed the sun was shining.

"Good." My father sat down again.

It appeared that he and Lodge had introduced themselves while they waited for me, and Lodge had told him, among other things, about my adventures in the horse-box outside Maidenhead, a detail I had omitted from my letters. This I considered to be treachery of the basest sort, and said so; and I told them how Kate and I had tracked down the horse-box, and that that particular line of enquiry was a dead end.

I took my cigarette and glass across the room and sat on the window seat in the sun. Scilla was in the garden, cutting flowers. I waved to her.

Lodge, dressed today not in uniform but in grey flannels, fine wool shirt and sports jacket, opened his briefcase, which lay on the table, and pulled out some papers. He sat down beside the table and spread them out.

He said, "Mr. Gregory rang me up at the station on the morning after your fall at Bristol to tell me about it."

"Why on earth did he do that?" I asked.

"You asked him to," said Lodge. He hesitated, and went on, "I understand from your father that your memory is affected."

"Yes. Most bits of that day at Bristol have come back now, but I still can't remember going out of the weighing room to ride Palindrome, or the race or the fall, or anything." My last mental picture was of Sandy walking out into the rain. "Why did I ask Pete to tell you I fell?"

"You asked him before the race. You apparently thought you were likely to fall. So, unofficially, I checked up on that crash of yours." He smiled suddenly. "You've accounted for all my free time lately, and today is really my day off. Why I bother with you I really don't know!" But I guessed that he was as addicted to detecting as an alcoholic to drink. He couldn't help doing it.

He went on, "I went down to Gregory's stables and took a look at Palindrome. He had a distinct narrow wound across his front on those two pads of flesh . . ."

"Chest," I murmured.

". . . Chest, then; and I'll give you one guess at what cut him."

"Oh, no," I said, guessing, but not believing it.

"I checked up on the attendants at the fences," he said. "One of them was new and unknown to the others. He gave his name as Thomas Butler and an address which doesn't exist, and he volunteered to stand at the farthest fence from the stands, where you fell. His offer was readily accepted because of the rain and the distance of the fence from the bookmakers. The same story as at Maidenhead. Except that this time Butler collected his earnings in the normal way. Then I got the Clerk of the Course to let me inspect the fence, and I found a groove on each post six feet, six inches from the ground."

There was a short silence.

"Well, well, well," I said blankly. "It looks as though I was luckier than Bill."

"I wish you could remember something about it . . . anything. What made you suspect you would fall?" asked Lodge.

"I don't know."

"It was something that happened while you were in the parade ring waiting to mount." He leaned forward, his dark eyes fixed intently on my face, willing my sluggish memory to come to life. But I remembered nothing, and I still felt weary from head to foot. Concentration was altogether too much of an effort.

I looked out into the peaceful spring garden. Scilla held an armful of forsythia, golden yellow against her blue dress.

"I can't remember," I said flatly. "Perhaps it'll come back when my head stops aching."

Lodge sighed and sat back in his hard chair.

"I suppose," he said, a little bitterly, "that you do at least remember sending me a message from Brighton, asking me to do your investigating for you?"

"Yes, I do," I said. "How did you get on?"

"Not very well. No one seems to know who actually owns the Marconicar taxi line. It was taken over just after the war by a business man named Clifford Tudor . . ."

"What?" I said in astonishment.

"Clifford Tudor, respectable Brighton resident, British subject. Do you know him?"

"Yes," I said. "He owns several racehorses."

Lodge sorted out a paper from his briefcase. "Clifford Tudor, born Khroupista Thasos, in Trikkala, Greece. Naturalised nineteen thirty-nine, when he was twenty-five. He started life as a cook, but owing to natural business ability, he acquired his own restaurant that same year. He sold it for a large profit after the war, went to Brighton, and bought for next to nothing an old taxi business that had wilted from wartime restrictions and lack of petrol. Four years ago he sold the taxis, again at a profit, and put his money into the Pavilion Plaza Hotel. He is unmarried."

I leaned my head back against the window and waited for these details to mean something significant, but all that happened was that my inability to think increased.

Lodge went on. "The taxi line was bought from Tudor by nominees, and that's where the fog begins. There have been so many transfers of ownership from company to company, mostly through nominees who can't be traced, that no one can discover who is the actual present owner. All business matters are settled by a Mr.

Fielder, the manager. He says he consults with a person he calls "the Chairman" by telephone, but that "the Chairman" rings him up every morning, and never the other way round. He says the Chairman's name is Claud Thiveridge, but he doesn't know his address or telephone number."

"It sounds very fishy to me," said my father.

"It is," said Lodge. "There is no Claud Thiveridge on the electoral register, or in any other official list, including the telephone accounts department, in the whole of Kent, Surrey or Sussex. The operators in the telephone exchange are sure the office doesn't receive a long distance call regularly every morning, yet the morning call has been standard office routine for the last four years. As this means that the call must be a local one, it seems fairly certain that Claud Thiveridge is not the gentleman's real name."

He rubbed the palm of his hand round the back of his neck and looked at me steadily. "You know a lot more than you've told me, amnesia or not," he said. "Spill the beans, there's a good chap."

"You haven't told me what the Brighton police think of the Marconicars," I said.

Lodge hesitated. "Well, they were a little touchy on the subject, I would say. It seems they have had several complaints, but not much evidence that will stand up in court. What I have just told you is the result of their enquiries over the last few years."

"They would not seem," said my father dryly, "to have made spectacular progress. Come on, Alan, tell us what's going on."

Lodge turned his head towards him in surprise. My father smiled.

"My son is Sherlock Holmes reincarnated, didn't you know?" he said. "After he went to England I had to employ a detective to do the work he used to do in connection with frauds and swindles. As one of my head clerks put it, Mr. Alan has an unerring instinct for smelling out crooks."

"Mr. Alan's unerring instinct is no longer functioning," I said gloomily. Clouds were building up near the sun, and Scilla's back disappeared through the macrocarpa hedge by the kitchen door.

"Don't be infuriating, Alan," said my father. "Elucidate."

"Oh, all right." I stubbed out my cigarette, began to scratch my cheek, and dragged my fingers away from the scar with a strong effort of will. It went on itching.

"There's a lot I don't know," I said, "but the general gist appears to be this. The Marconicars have been in the protection racket for the last four years, intimidating small concerns like cafés and free house pubs. About a year ago, owing to the strongmindedness of one particular publican, mine host of the Blue Duck, business in the protection line began to get unexpectedly rough for the protectors. He set alsatians on them, in fact." I told my fascinated father and an aghast Lodge what Kate and I had learned in the Blue Duck's kitchen, carefully watched by the yellow eyed Prince.

"Ex-Regimental Sergeant-Major Thomkins made such serious inroads into the illicit profits of Marconicars," I continued, "that as a racket it was more or less defunct. The legitimate side hasn't been doing too well during the winter either, according to the typists who work in the office. There are too many taxis in Brighton for the number of fares at this time of year, I should think. Anyway, it seems to me that the Marconicar boss—the Chairman, your mysterious Claud Thiveridge—set about mending his fortunes by branching out into another form of crime. He bought, I think, the shaky bookmaking business on the floor above the Marconicars, in the same building."

I could almost smell the cabbage in the Olde Oake Café as I remembered it. "An earnest lady told me the bookmakers had been taken over by a new firm about six months ago, but that its name was still the same. L. C. PERTH, written in neon. She was very wrought up about them sticking such a garish sign on an architectural gem, and she and her old buildings society, whose name I forget, had tried to reason with the new owners to take down what they had just put up. Only they couldn't find out who the new owner was. It's too much of a coincidence to have two businesses, both shady, one above the other, both with invisible and untraceable owners. They must be owned by the same person."

"It doesn't follow, and I don't see the point," said my father.

"You will in a minute," I said. "Bill died because he wouldn't stop his horse winning a race. I know his death wasn't necessarily intended, but force was used against him. He was told not to win by a husky-voiced man on the telephone. Henry, Bill's elder son, he's eight—" I explained to Lodge, "has a habit of listening on the extension upstairs, and he heard every word. Two days before Bill died, Henry says, the voice offered him five hundred pounds to stop his horse winning, and when Bill laughed at this, the voice told him he wouldn't win because his horse would fall."

I paused, but neither Lodge nor my father said anything. Swallowing the last of the brandy, I went on. "There is a jockey called Joe Nantwich who during the last six months, ever since L. C. Perth changed hands, has regularly accepted a hundred pounds, sometimes more, to stop a horse winning. Joe gets his instructions by telephone from a husky-voiced man he has never met."

Lodge stirred on his hard, self-chosen chair.

I went on. "I, as you know, was set upon by the Marconicar drivers, and a few days later the man with the husky voice rang me up and told me to take heed of the warning I had been given in the horse-box. One doesn't have to be Sherlock Holmes to see that the crooked racing and the Marconicar protection racket were being run by the same man." I stopped.

"Finish it off, then," said my father impatiently.

"The only person who would offer a jockey a large sum to lose a race is a crooked bookmaker. If he *knows* a well fancied horse is not going to win, he can accept any amount of money on that horse without risk."

"Enlarge," said Lodge.

"Normally bookmakers try to balance their books so that whichever horse wins they come out on the winning side," I said. "If too many people want to back one horse, they accept the bets, but they back the horse themselves with another bookmaker; then if that horse wins, they collect their winnings from the second bookmaker, and pay it out to their customers. It's a universal system known as 'laying off.' Now suppose you were a crooked bookmaker and Joe Nantwich is to ride a fancied horse. You tip Joe the wink to lose. Then however much is betted with you on that horse, you do no laying off, because you know you won't have to pay out."

"I would have thought that a hundred pounds would have been more than it was worth," said Lodge, "since bookmakers normally make a profit anyway."

"Your friend wasn't satisfied with the legitimate gains from the taxis," my father pointed out.

I sighed, and shifted my stiff shoulders against the frame of the window.

"There's a bit more to it, of course," I said. "If a bookmaker knows he hasn't got to pay out on a certain horse, he can offer better odds on it. Not enough to be suspicious, but just enough to attract a lot of extra custom. A point better than anyone else would go to—say eleven to four, when the next best offer was five to two. The money would roll in, don't you think?"

I stood up and went towards the door, saying, "I'll show you something."

The stairs seemed steeper than usual. I went up to my room and fetched the racing form book and the little bunch of bookmakers' tickets, and shuffled back to the drawing-room. I laid the tickets out on the table in front of Lodge, and my father came over to have a look.

"These," I explained, "are some tickets Bill kept for his children to play with. Three of them, as you see, were issued by L. C. Perth, and all the others are from different firms, no two alike. Bill was a methodical man. On the backs of all the tickets he wrote the date, the details of his bet, and the name of the horse he'd put his money on. He used to search around in Tattersall's for the best odds and bet in cash, instead of betting on credit with Tote Investors or one of the bookmakers on the rails—those," I added for Lodge's benefit, as I could see the question forming on his lips, "are bookmakers who stand along the railing between Tattersall's and the Club enclosures, writing down bets made by Club members and other people known to them. They send out weekly accounts, win or lose. Bill didn't bet in large amounts, and he thought credit betting wasn't exciting enough."

Lodge turned over the three Perth tickets.

Bill's loopy writing was clear and unmistakable. I picked up the first ticket, and read aloud, "'Peripatetic. November 7th. Ten pounds staked at eleven to ten.' So he stood to win eleven pounds for his money." I opened the detailed form book and turned to November 7.

"Peripatetic," I said, "lost the two mile hurdle at Sandown that day by four lengths. He was ridden by Joe Nantwich. The starting price was eleven to ten on—that is, you have to stake eleven pounds to win ten—and had earlier been as low as eleven to eight on. L. C. Perth must have done a roaring trade at eleven to ten against."

I picked up the second card and read, "Sackbut. October 10th.

Five pounds staked at six to one." I opened the form book for that day. "Sackbut was unplaced at Newbury and Joe Nantwich rode it. The best price generally offered was five to one, and the starting price was seven to two."

I put the Sackbut ticket back on the table, and read the third card where it lay. "Malabar. December 2nd. Eight pounds staked at fifteen to eight." I laid the form book beside it, opened at December 2nd. "Malabar finished fourth at Birmingham. Joe Nantwich rode him. The starting price was six to four."

Lodge and my father silently checked the book with the ticket.

"I looked up all the other cards as well," I said. "Of course, as Bill still had the tickets, all the horses lost; but on only one of them did he get better odds than you'd expect. Joe didn't ride it, and I don't think it's significant, because it was an outsider at a hundred to six."

"I wish the racing fraternity would use only whole numbers and halves," said Lodge plaintively.

"Haven't you heard," I asked, "about the keen gambler who taught his baby son to count? One, six-to-four, two . . ."

Lodge laughed, his dark eyes crinkling at the corners. "I'll have to write down these figures on the Perth tickets alongside the form book information, and get it straightened out in my mind," he said, unscrewing his pen and settling to the task.

My father sat down beside him and watched the tell-tale list grow. I went back to the window seat and waited.

Presently Lodge said, "I can see why your father misses you as a fraud spotter." He put his pen back in his pocket.

I smiled and said, "If you want to read a really blatant fraud, you should look up the Irish racing in that form book. It's fantastic."

"Not today. This is quite enough to be going on with," said Lodge, rubbing his hand over his face and pinching his nose between thumb and forefinger.

"All that remains, as far as I'm concerned, is for you to tell us who is organising the whole thing," said my father with a touch of mockery, which from long understanding I interpreted as approval.

"That, dear Pa, I fear I cannot do," I said.

But Lodge said seriously, "Could it be anyone you know on the racecourse? It must be someone connected with racing. How about Perth, the bookmaker?"

"It could be. I don't know him. His name won't actually be Perth of course. That name was sold with the business. I'll have a bet on with him next time I go racing and see what happens," I said.

"You will do no such thing," said my father emphatically, and I felt too listless to argue.

"How about a jockey, or a trainer, or an owner?" asked Lodge.

"You'd better include the Stewards and the National Hunt Committee," I said, ironically. "They were almost the first to know I had discovered the wire and was looking into it. The man we are after knew very early on that I was inquisitive. I didn't tell many people I suspected more than an accident, or ask many pointed questions, before that affair in the horse-box."

"People you know . . ." said Lodge, musingly. "How about Gregory?"

"No," I said.

"Why not? He lives near Brighton, near enough for the Marconicar morning telephone call."

"He wouldn't risk hurting Bill or Admiral," I said.

"How can you be sure?" asked Lodge. "People aren't always what they seem, and murderers are often fond of animals, until they get in the way. One chap I saw at the assizes lately killed a nightwatchman and showed no remorse at all. But when evidence was given that the nightwatchman's dog had had his head bashed in too, the accused burst into tears and said he was sorry."

"Pathetic," I said. "But no dice. It isn't Pete."

"Faith or evidence?" persisted Lodge.

"Faith," I said grudgingly, because I was quite sure.

"Jockeys?" suggested Lodge, leaving it.

"None of them strikes me as being the type we're looking for," I said, "and I think you're overlooking the fact that racing came second on the programme and may even have been adopted solely because a shaky bookmaking business existed on the floor above the Marconicars. I mean, that in itself may have turned the boss of Marconicars towards racing."

"You may be right," admitted Lodge.

My father said, "It's just possible that the man who originally owned Marconicars decided to launch out into crime, and faked a sale to cover his tracks."

"Clifford Tudor, nee Thasos, do you mean?" asked Lodge with interest. My father nodded, and Lodge said to me, "How about it?"

"Tudor pops up all over the place," I said. "He knew Bill, and Bill had his address noted down on a scrap of paper." I put my hand into my jacket pocket. The old envelope was still there. I drew it out and looked at it again. "Tudor told me he had asked Bill to ride a horse for him."

"When did he tell you that?" asked Lodge.

"I gave him a lift from Plumpton races into Brighton, four days after Bill died. We talked about him on the way."

"Anything else?" asked Lodge.

"Well . . . Tudor's horses have been ridden—up until lately—by our corrupted friend Joe Nantwich. It was on Tudor's horse Bolingbroke that Joe won once when he had been instructed to lose . . . but at Cheltenham he threw away a race on a horse of Tudor's, and Tudor was very angry about it."

"Camouflage," suggested my father.

But I rested my aching head against the window, and said, "I don't think Tudor can possibly be the crook we're looking for."

"Why not?" asked Lodge. "He has the organising ability, he lives in Brighton, he owned the taxis, he employs Joe Nantwich, and he knew Major Davidson. He seems the best proposition so far."

"No," I said tiredly. "The best lead we've had is the taxis. If I hadn't recognised that the men who stopped me in the horse-box were also taxi-drivers, I'd never have found out anything at all. Whoever put them on to me can't possibly have imagined I would know them, or he wouldn't have done it. But if there's one person who knew I would recognise him, it's Clifford Tudor. He was standing near me while the taxi-drivers fought, and he knew I'd had time to look at them after the police had herded them into two groups."

"I don't rule him out altogether, even so," said Lodge, gathering his papers together and putting them back into his briefcase. "Criminals often make the stupidest mistakes."

I said, "If we ever do find your Claud Thiveridge, I think he will turn out to be someone I've never met and never heard of. A complete stranger. It's far more likely."

I wanted to believe it.

I did not want to have to face another possibility, one that I shied away from so uncomfortably that I could not bring myself even to lay it open for Lodge's inspection.

Who, besides Tudor, knew before the horse-box incident that I wanted Bill's death avenged? Kate. And to whom had she passed this on? To Uncle George. Uncle George, who, I suspected, housed a lean and hungry soul in his fat body, behind his fatuous expression.

Uncle George, out of the blue, had bought a horse for his niece. Why? To widen her interests, he had said. But through her, I thought, he would learn much of what went on at the races.

And Uncle George had sent Heavens Above to be trained in the stable which housed Bill's horse. Was it a coincidence . . . or the beginning of a scheme which Bill's unexpected death had cut short?

It was nebulous, unconvincing. It was based only on supposition, not on facts, and bolstered only by memory of the shock on Uncle George's face when Kate told him we had been to the Blue Duck—shock which he had called indigestion. And perhaps it had been indigestion, after all.

And all those primitive weapons in his study, the ritual objects and the scalp . . . were they the playthings of a man who relished violence? Or who loathed it? Or did both at the same time?

Scilla came into the drawing-room, carrying a copper bowl filled with forsythia and daffodils. She put it on the low table near me, and the spring sun suddenly shone on the golden flowers, so that they seemed like a burst of light, reflecting their colour upwards on to her face as she bent over them, tweaking them into order.

She gave me a sharp glance, and turned round to the others. "Alan looks very tired," she said. "What have you been doing?"

"Talking," I said, smiling at her.

"You'll find yourself back in hospital if you're not careful," she scolded mildly, and without pausing offered mid-morning coffee to Lodge and my father.

I was glad for the interruption, because I had not wished to discuss with them what was to be done next in pursuit of Mr. Claud Thiveridge. Every small advance I had made in his direction had brought its retribution, it was true; yet in each of his parries I had found a clue. My faulty memory was still cheating me of the information I had paid for with the drubbing at Bristol, but it did not deter me from wanting to see the business through.

I would get closer to Thiveridge. He would hit out again, and in doing it show me the next step towards him, like the flash of a gunshot in the dark revealing the hiding place of a sniper.

14

Joe Nantwich found the sniper first.

Eight days after Lodge's visit I drove down to West Sussex races, having put in a short morning at the office. My bruises had faded and gone; the ribs and collar-bone were mended and in perfect working order, and even my stubborn headache was losing its grip. I whistled my way into the changing room and presented to Clem my brand new crash-helmet, bought that morning from Bates of Jermyn Street for three guineas.

The weighing room was empty, and distant oohs and ahs proclaimed that the first race was in progress. Clem, who was tidying up the changing room after the tornado of getting a large number of jockeys out of their ordinary clothes, into racing colours, past the scales and out to the parade ring, greeted me warmly and shook hands.

"Glad to see you back, sir," he said, taking the helmet. With a ball-point pen he wrote my name on a piece of adhesive tape and stuck it on to the shiny shell. "Let's hope you won't be needing another new one of these in a hurry." He pressed his thumb firmly on to the adhesive tape.

"I'm starting again tomorrow, Clem," I said. "Can you bring my gear? Big saddle. There's no weight problem, I'm riding Admiral."

"Top flipping weight," said Clem, resignedly. "And a lot of lead, which Admiral isn't used to. Major Davidson hardly ever needed any." Clem gave me an assessing sideways look and added, "You've lost three or four pounds, I shouldn't wonder."

"All the better," I said cheerfully, turning to the door.

"Oh, just a minute, sir," said Clem. "Joe Nantwich asked me to let you know, if you came, that he has something to tell you."

"Oh, yes?" I said.

"He was asking for you on Saturday at Liverpool, but I told him you'd probably be coming here, as Mr. Gregory mentioned last week that you'd be riding Admiral tomorrow," said Clem, absent-mindedly picking up a saddle and smoothing his hand over the leather.

"Did Joe say what it was he wanted to tell me?" I asked.

"Yes, he wants to show you a bit of brown wrapping paper with something written on it. He said you'd be interested to see it, though I can't think why—the word I saw looked like something to do with chickens. He had the paper out in the changing room at Liverpool, and folded it up flat on the bench into a neat shape, and tucked it into the inside pocket of his jacket. Giggling over it, he was. He'd had a drink or two I reckon, but then most people had, it was after the National. He said what was written on the paper was double dutch to him, but it might be a clue, you never knew. I asked him a clue to what? But he wouldn't say, and anyway, I was too busy to bother with him much."

"I'll see him, and find out what it's all about," I said. "Has he still got the paper with him, do you know?"

"Yes, he has. He patted his pocket just now when he asked me if you were here, and I heard the paper crackle."

"Thanks, Clem," I said.

I went outside. The race was over, the winner was being led towards the unsaddling enclosure in front of the weighing room, and down from the stands streamed the hundreds of chattering racegoers. I stood near the weighing-room door, waiting for Joe and catching up with the latest gossip. Liverpool, I learned, had been disappointing, fabulous, bloody, a dead loss and the tops, according to who told it. I had not been there. I had been too busy getting intensive treatment on my shoulder muscles to help my strength back.

Sandy clapped me soundly on the back as he passed, remarking that it was "Bloody good to see your old physog on the horizon again, even if you do look like an understudy for Scarface." He went on, "Have you seen Joe? The little drip's been squealing for you."

"So I hear," I said. "I'm waiting for him now."

A couple of press men asked me my riding plans, and made note about Admiral for their morning edition. Sir Creswell Stampe noticed my existence with a nod of his distinguished head and the characteristic puffing up of his top lip which passed with him for a smile.

My content at being back in my favourite environment was somewhat marred by the sight of Dane strolling across the grass, talking intently to a slender, heart-catchingly beautiful girl at his side. Her face was turned intimately towards his, and she was laughing. It was Kate.

When they saw me they quickened their steps and approached me smiling, a striking pair evenly matched in grace and dark good looks.

Kate, who had got used to my battered face over lunch some days earlier, greeted me with a brisk "Hi, there," from which all undertones of love and longing were regrettably absent. She put her hand on my arm and asked me to walk down the course with her and Dane to watch the next race from beside the water jump.

I glanced at Dane. His smile was faint, and his dark eyes looked at me inscrutably, without welcome. My own muscles had tensed uncontrollably when I saw him and Kate together; so now I knew exactly how he felt about me.

It was as much unease over the low ebb of our friendship as desire to chase Claud Thiveridge which made me say, "I can't come at this instant. I must find Joe Nantwich first. How about later on . . . if you'd like to walk down again?"

"All right, Alan," she said. "Or maybe we could have tea together?" She turned away with Dane and said, "See you later," over her shoulder with a mischievous grin, in which I read her mockery of the jealousy she could arouse in me.

Watching them go, I forgot to look out for Joe, and went in to search for him through the weighing and changing rooms again. He wasn't there.

Pete towered over me as I returned to my post outside the door and greeted me like a long lost friend. His hat tipped back on his big head, his broad shoulders spreading apart the lapels of his coat, he gazed with good humour at my face, and said, "They've made a good job of sewing you up, you know. You were a very gory sight indeed last time I saw you. I suppose you still can't remember what happened?"

"No," I said, regretfully. "Sometimes I think . . . but I can't get hold of it . . ."

"Perhaps it's just as well," he said comfortingly, hitching the strap of his race glasses higher on to his shoulder and preparing to go into the weighing room.

"Pete," I said, "have you seen Joe anywhere? I think he's been asking for me."

"Yes," he said. "He was looking for you at Liverpool, too. He was very keen to show you something, an address I think, written on some brown paper."

"Did you see it?" I asked.

"Yes, as a matter of fact I did, but he annoys me and I didn't pay much attention. Chichester, I think the place was."

"Do you know where Joe is now?" I asked. "I've been waiting for him for some time, but there isn't a sign of him."

Pete's thin lips showed contempt. "Yes, I saw the little brute going into the bar, about ten minutes ago."

"Already!" I exclaimed.

"Drunken little sod," he said dispassionately. "I wouldn't put him up on one of my horses if he was the last jockey on earth."

"Which bar?" I pressed.

"Eh? Oh, the one at the back of Tattersall's, next to the Tote. He and another man went in with that dark fellow he rides for . . . Tudor, isn't that his name?"

I gaped at him. "But Tudor finished with Joe at Cheltenham . . . and very emphatically, too."

Pete shrugged. "Tudor went into the bar with Joe and the other chap a few steps behind him. Maybe it was only coincidence."

"Thanks, anyway," I said.

It was only a hundred yards round one corner to the bar where Joe had gone. It was a long wooden hut backing on to the high fence which divided the racecourse from the road. I wasted no time, but nonetheless when I stepped into the building and threaded my way through the overcoated, beer-drinking customers, I found that Joe was no longer there. Nor was Clifford Tudor.

I went outside again. The time for the second race was drawing near, and long impatient queues waited at the Tote next door to the bar, eyes flickering between racecards and wrist watches, money clutched ready in hopeful hands. The customers from the bar poured out, hurrying past me. Men were running across the grass towards the stands, coat-tails flapping. Bells rang loudly in the Tote building, and the queues squirmed with the compulsion to push their money through the little windows before the shutters came down.

I hovered indecisively. There was no sign of Joe in all this activity, and I decided to go up to the jockeys' box in the stands and look for him there. I put my head into the bar for a final check, but it was now empty except for three ageing young ladies mopping up the beer-slopped counter.

It was only because I was moving so slowly that I found Joe at all.

Owing to the curve of the road behind them, the Tote and bar buildings did not stand in a perfectly straight line. The gap between the two was narrow at the front, barely eighteen inches across; but it widened farther back until, by the high fence itself, the Tote and bar walls were four or five feet apart.

I glanced into this narrow area as I passed. And there was Joe. Only I did not know it was Joe until I got close to him.

At first I saw only a man lying on the ground in the corner made by the boundary fence and the end wall of the Tote, and thinking he might be ill, or faint, or even plain drunk, went in to see if he needed help.

He lay in shadow, but something about his shape and rag-doll relaxedness struck me with shocking recognition as I took the five or six strides across to him.

He was alive, but only just. Bright red frothy blood trickled from his nose and the corner of his mouth, and a pool of it lay under his cheek on the weedy gravel. His round young face still wore, incredibly, a look of sulky petulance, as if he did not realise that what had happened to him was more than a temporary inconvenience.

Joe had a knife in his body. Its thick black handle protruded incongruously from his yellow and white checked shirt, slanting downwards from underneath his breastbone. A small patch of blood stained the cloth round it, a mild enough indication of the damage the blade was doing inside.

His eyes were open, but vague and already glazing.

I said, urgently, "Joe!"

His eyes came round to mine and I saw them sharpen into focus and recognise me. A muscle moved in his cheek and his lips opened. He made a great effort to speak.

The scarlet blood suddenly spilled in a gush from his nostrils and welled up in a sticky, bottomless pool in his open mouth. He gave a single choking sound that was almost indecently faint, and over his immature face spread a look of profound astonishment. Then his flesh blanched and his eyes rolled up, and Joe was gone. For several seconds after he died his expression said clearly, "It's not fair." The skin settled in this crisis into the lines most accustomed to it in life.

Fighting nausea at the sweet smell of his blood, I shut the eyes with my fingers, and sat back on my heels, looking at him helplessly.

I knew it was useless, but after a moment or two I opened his coat and felt in his pockets for the brown paper he had wanted to show me. It was not there, and his death would not have made sense if it had been. The brown paper was, I thought, the wrapping from Joe's last payment for stopping a horse. It had to be. With something about it which he thought would disclose who had sent it. A postmark? An address? Something to do with chickens, Clem had said; and Pete said it was Chichester. Neither of these held any significance at all for me. According to Clem it meant nothing to Joe either, and he was simply going to show it to me because he had said he would.

He had always been too talkative for his own good. Not quick or quiet. Prudently and privately he could have telephoned to tell me his discovery as soon as he made it. But instead he had flourished the paper at Liverpool. Someone had taken drastic steps to make sure he did not show it to me.

"Poor, silly blabbermouth," I said softly, to his still body.

I got to my feet, and went back to the narrow entrance of the little area. There was no one about. The voice of the commentator boomed over the loudspeakers that the horses were approaching the second open ditch, which meant that the race was already half over and that I would have to hurry.

I ran the last fifty yards to the Clerk of the Course's office and thrust open the door. A nondescript, grey-haired man in glasses, sitting at a desk, looked up, startled, his pen in mid-air and the paper he was writing on pressed under the palm of his hand. He was the Clerk of the Course's secretary.

"Mr. Rollo isn't here?" I asked unnecessarily, glancing round the otherwise empty office.

"He's watching the race. Can I help you?" A dry voice, a dry manner. Not the sort of man one would choose to announce a murder to. But it had to be done. Suppressing all urgency from my voice I told him plainly and quietly that Joe Nantwich was lying dead between the Tote and the bar with a knife through his lungs. I suggested that he send for a canvas screen to put across the gap between the two buildings, as when the crowds began to stream towards the bar and the paying-out Tote windows after the race, someone would be certain to see him. The ground round his body would be well trodden over. Clues, if there were any, would be lost.

The eyes behind the spectacles grew round and disbelieving.

"It's not a joke," I said desperately. "The race is nearly over. Tell the police then. I'll find a screen." He still did not move. I could have shaken him, but I could not spare the time. "Hurry," I urged. But his hand had still not gone out to his telephone when I shut the door.

The ambulance room was attached to the end of the weighing-room building. I went in in a hurry, to find two motherly St. John's nurses drinking tea. I spoke to the younger one, a middle-aged soul of ample proportions.

"Put that down and come with me quickly," I said, hoping she would not argue. I picked up a stretcher which was standing against the wall, and as she put her cup down slowly, I added, "Bring a blanket. There's a man hurt. Please hurry."

The call to duty got my nurse moving without demur, and picking up a blanket she followed me across the paddock, though at under half speed.

The commentator's voice rose slightly as he described the race from the last fence, and crisply into the silence when the cheers died away came another voice announcing the winner. I reached the gap by the Tote building as he spoke the names of the second and third horses.

The first stalwart punters began to drift back towards the bar. I looked in at Joe. He had not been disturbed.

I set the stretcher up on end on its handles, to make a sort of screen across the gap. The nurse came up to me, breathing audibly. I took the blanket from her and hung it over the stretcher so that no one could see into the area at all.

"Listen," I said, trying to speak slowly. "There is a man between these two buildings. He is dead, not hurt. He has been killed with a knife. I am going to make sure that the police are coming, and I want you to stand here holding the stretcher up like this. Don't let anyone past you until I come back with a policeman. Do you understand?"

She did not answer. She twisted the stretcher a little so that she could peer through the gap. She took a long look. Then, drawing up her considerable bosom and with the light of battle in her eyes, she said firmly, "No one shall go in, I'll see to that."

I hurried back to the Clerk of the Course's office. Mr. Rollo was there himself this time, and after I had told him what had happened things at last began to move.

It is always difficult to find a place to be alone at the races. After I had taken a policeman along to where Joe lay, and seen the routine bustle begin, I needed a pause to think. I had had an idea while I crouched beside Joe's body, but it was not one to be acted upon headlong.

People thronged everywhere in the paddock and the racecourse buildings, and to get away from them I walked out on to the course and over the rough grass in the centre until the stands were some way behind. Distance, I hoped, would give me a sense of proportion as well as solitude.

I thought about Bill and Scilla, and also about what I owed to my father, now back in Rhodesia. I thought about the terrorised pub-keepers in Brighton and the bloody face of Joe Nantwich.

It was no use pretending that Joe's murder had not made a great deal of difference to the situation, for until now I had blithely pursued Mr. Claud Thiveridge in the belief that though he might arrange for people to be beaten up, he did not purposely kill. Now the boundary was crossed. The next killing would come easier, and the next easier still. The plucky, dog-owning rebels against protection were in greater danger than before, and I was probably responsible.

Joe had shown his brown paper to several people, and no one, including apparently himself, had immediately seen the meaning of what was written on it. Yet he had been killed before he could show it to me. To me, then, the words would have told their tale. Perhaps to me alone.

I watched the rising wind blowing the grass in flattening ripples across the course, and heard the distant voices of the bookmakers as they shouted the odds for the next race.

The question to be answered was simple. Was I, or was I not, going on with the chase. I'm no hero. I did not want to end up dead. And there was no doubt that the idea I had had beside Joe's body was as safe as a stick of dynamite in a bonfire.

The horses for the third race came out and cantered down to the start. Idly I watched them. The race was run: the horses returned to the paddock: and still I stood in the centre of the course, dithering on top of my mental fence.

At last I walked back to the paddock. The jockeys were already out in the parade ring for the fourth race, and as I reached the weighing room one of the racecourse officials grabbed my arm, saying the police had been looking everywhere for me. They wanted me to make a statement, he said, and I would find them in the Clerk of the Course's office.

I went along there, and opened the door.

Mr. Rollo, spare and short, leaned against the window wearing a worried frown. His grey-haired bespectacled secretary still sat at his desk, his mouth slightly open as if even yet he had not grasped the reality of what had happened.

The police inspector, who introduced himself as Wakefield, had established himself at Mr. Rollo's table, and was attended by three constables, one of them armed with shorthand notebook and pencil. The racecourse doctor was sitting on a chair by the wall, and a man I did not know stood near him.

Wakefield was displeased with me for what he called my irresponsibility in disappearing for over half an hour at such a time. Big and thick, he dominated the room. Authority exuded from his short upspringing grey hair, his narrow eyes, his strong stubby fingers. A policeman to put the fear of God into evildoers. His baleful glare suggested that at the moment I should be included in this category.

"If you're quite ready, Mr. York," he began sarcastically, "we'll take your statement."

I looked round the crowded little office, and said, "I prefer to make my statement to you alone."

The inspector growled and erupted and argued; but finally everyone left except Wakefield, myself, and the notebook constable, to whom I agreed as a compromise. I told Wakefield exactly what had happened. The whole truth, and nothing but the truth.

Then I went back to the weighing room, and to every one of the dozens who clustered round asking for an eye-witness account, I said I had found Joe alive. Yes, I agreed steadily, he had spoken to me before he died. What did he say? Well, it was only two or three words, and I preferred not to discuss it at present, if they did not mind. I added that I had not actually mentioned it to the police yet, but of course I would if I thought it would be important. And I put on a puzzled, thoughtful expression, hoping I looked as if I had a key in my hand and was on the point of finding the right lock to put it in.

I took Kate to tea, and Pete, catching sight of us, came over to join us. To them, too, I told the same story, feeling ashamed, but not caring to risk their broadcasting the truth, that Joe had died without uttering a syllable.

Shortly before the sixth race I left the meeting. The last thing I saw, as I glanced back from the gate, was Wakefield and Clifford Tudor standing outside the door of the Clerk of the Course's office, shaking hands. Tudor, who had been with Joe so soon before his death, had apparently been "assisting the police with their investigations." Satisfactorily, it seemed.

I went through the car park to the Lotus, started up, and drove out towards the west, and along the straight secondary roads of the South Downs I opened up the engine and sent the little car along at over a hundred. No Marconicars, I thought with satisfaction, could compete with that. But to make quite certain I was not being followed I stopped once at a vantage point on top of a rise, and studied the road behind me with race glasses. It was deserted. There was nothing on my tail.

About thirty miles from the racecourse I stopped at an undistinguished roadhouse and booked a room for the night. I insisted also on a lock-up garage for the car. It was too far from Brighton to be within the normal reach of the Marconicars, but I was taking no chances. I wanted to be invisible. It is one thing to stick your neck out; but quite another to go to sleep in full view of the axe.

After a dull dinner I went to my room and wrote a letter to my father. A difficult one. I told him about Joe's death, and that I was trying to use it to entice Mr. Thiveridge out of his lair. I asked him, as lightly as I could, to forgive me. I am, I wrote, only hunting another crocodile.

I finished the letter, sealed it, went early to bed, and lay awake for a long time before I slept.

On the way back to the racecourse in the morning I stopped at a post office and air-mailed my letter. I also acquired four shillings-worth of pennies, which I stacked into a paper-wrapped roll. I took the spare pair of socks out of my overnight case and slid the roll of pennies down into the foot of one of them, knotting them there securely. I swung my little cosh experimentally on to the palm of my hand. It was heavy enough, I thought, to knock a man out. I put it in my trouser pocket and finished the journey to the course.

I asked a constable on duty in the paddock where I could find Inspector Wakefield if I wanted him. The constable said that Wakefield was at the station, he thought, and was not coming to the course that afternoon, although he had been there in the morning. I thanked him, and went into the weighing room, and asked several people in a loud voice to tell me if they saw Inspector Wakefield about, as I wanted to have a word with him about what Joe had said to me before he died.

The awareness of danger, though I had brought it on myself, had a noticeable effect on my nerves. The wrought-up, quickened pulse I always felt to some extent when cantering down to the start of a race was unduly magnified, so that I could hear my own heart beating. Every noise seemed louder, every chance remark more significant, every light brighter. But I was not so much afraid as excited.

I was careful only about what I turned my back to, having no intention of being attacked from behind. It was more likely, I thought, that someone would try to cajole me into an out of the way place as they must have done with Joe, because most of the racecourse was too public for murder.

A knife in the ribs seemed what I should be most wary of. Effective in Joe's case, it had the advantages—to its wielder—of being silent and accurate. Moreover the weapon was left with the body, so that there was no subsequent difficulty in getting rid of it. The black handle protruding from Joe had had the familiar knobbed shape of the sort of French steel cooking knife on sale in any hardware shop. Too common to be a clue of any kind, I suspected, and easy to replace with another to stick into the guts of a second victim. If anyone tried that I intended to be ready. My fingers closed comfortably on the pennies in my pocket.

I hoped to be able to deliver an attacker (unconscious from a four-shilling bump behind the ear) to Inspector Wakefield, to be charged with attempted murder. I had great faith that Wakefield's bulldog personality would shake information out of the toughest criminal in those circumstances, and that with reasonable luck a firm clue to Thiveridge's identity might disclose itself. It was too much to hope that Thiveridge would appear himself. I believed his husky avowal to me on the telephone that he hated personal violence and ordered others to do his dirty work for him, out of his squeamish sight.

I changed, and weighed on the trial scales, and chatted, and went about my ordinary business, and waited.

Nothing happened.

No one asked me to step into dim corners to discuss private business. No one showed any particular interest in what Joe was supposed to have told me before he died. Naturally his murder was still the chief topic of conversation, but it lost ground as the day wore on, and the living horses became more interesting to the inmates of the weighing room than the dead jockey.

Admiral was to run in the fifth race. By the time the fourth was over my nerves had calmed down and my tense readiness had evaporated. I had expected action before this. I had been at the meeting for nearly three hours, a man with essential information inviting to have his mouth permanently shut, and no move had been made against me.

It crossed my mind, not for the first time, that cause and effect in the Thiveridge organisation never followed closely on each other. Joe's death happened two whole days after he showed his brown paper at Liverpool. The warning to me on the telephone was delivered two days after I had spread at Cheltenham the news of the wire which had killed Bill. The horse-box affair had taken at least a day to arrange. The Bristol wire was rigged to bring me down two days after my excursion into the Marconicar office.

I had begun to suspect that the whole organisation was still geared to the telephone call Thiveridge made every morning to Fielder, and that Fielder had no other way of getting urgent messages to his "Chairman," or of receiving instructions from him. Presumably Thiveridge still felt the delay in his news service was a lesser evil than providing an address or telephone number at which he could be reached and perhaps discovered.

Depressed, I was coming to believe that my carefully acted lies had not at all reached the ears for which they were meant, and felt that offering myself as bait to a predator who did not know he should be hunting me was a bit idiotic.

Trying to shake off this deflation, I went out to the parade ring to join Pete and mount Admiral. Bill's horse, now mine, looked as splendid as ever. With his intelligent head, deep chest, straight hocks, and good bone below the knee, he was a perfect example of what a top class steeplechaser should be.

"Even though he hasn't been on a racecourse since that ghastly day at Maidenhead, he's at the top of his form," said Pete, admiring him beside me. "You can't lose the race, so go along quietly for a while, getting used to him. You'll find he has plenty in reserve. You'll never get to the bottom of him. Bill used to take him to the front early on, as you know, but you don't need to. He's got a terrific turn of foot from the last."

"I'll do as you say," I said.

Pete gave me a leg-up. "Admiral's odds-on, again," he said. "If you make a mess of this race the crowd'll murder you. So will I." He grinned.

"I'll try to stay alive," I said, grinning back cheerfully.

Admiral was as superb to ride as he looked. He put himself right before every fence, making his spring at exactly the right moment and needing no help from the saddle. He had the low, flowing galloping stride of the really fast mover, and from the first fence onward I found racing on his back an almost ecstatic pleasure. Following Pete's advice I went round the whole course without forcing the pace, but riding into the last fence alongside two others, I gave Admiral a kick in the ribs and shook up the reins. He took off from just inside the wings and landed as far out on the other side, gaining two lengths in the air and shedding the other two horses like dead leaves. We came home alone, easy winners, to warm cheers from the stands.

In the winner's unsaddling enclosure, where I dismounted and undid the girths, Admiral behaved as if he had only been out for an exercise gallop, his belly hardly moving as he breathed. I patted his glossy chestnut neck, noticed that he was hardly sweating at all, and asked Pete, "What on earth can he do if he really tries?"

"The National, no less," said Pete, rocking back on his heels, and tipping his hat off his face, as he collected his due congratulations from all around.

I grinned, pulled the saddle off over my arm, and went into the weighing room to weigh-in and change. The familiar joy of winning flushed through my limbs, as warming as a hot bath, and I could have done hand-springs down the changing room if I hadn't known it was the horse to whom all credit was due, not the jockey.

Pete called to me to hurry up and we'd have a celebration drink together, so I changed quickly and went outside to join him. He steered me towards the bar next to the Tote building, and we stopped at the gap, looking in to where Joe had died. There was a shoulder-high wooden fence across the entrance now, to keep sensation seekers out. A rusty brown stain on the gravel was all that was left of Joe.

"A terrible thing, that," Pete said, as we stepped into the bar. "What did he say to you before he died?"

"I'll tell you sometime," I said idly. "But just now I'm more interested in where Admiral runs next." And over our drinks we talked solely about horses.

Returning to the weighing room we found two men in belted raincoats waiting for us near the door. They wore trilby hats and large shoes, and gave off that indefinable aura of solid menace which characterises many plain-clothes policemen.

One of them put his hand inside his coat, drew out a folded warrant and flipped it in my direction.

"Mr. York?"

"Yes."

"Inspector Wakefield's compliments, and will you come down to the police station to help his enquiries, please." The "please" he tacked on as an afterthought.

"Very well," I said, and asked Pete to see Clem about my kit.

"Sure," he said.

I walked with the two men across to the gate and through the car park.

"I'll get my car and follow you to the station," I said.

"There's a police car waiting for us in the road, sir," said the larger of the two. "Inspector Wakefield did say to bring you in it, and if you don't mind, sir, I'd rather do as the Inspector says."

I grinned. If Inspector Wakefield were my boss I'd do as he said, too. "All right," I agreed.

Ahead of us the sleek black Wolseley was parked outside the gate, with a uniformed driver standing beside it and another man in a peaked cap in the front passenger's seat.

Away towards my right, in front of the ranks of parked horse-boxes, several of the runners from Admiral's race were being led up and down to get the stiffness out of their limbs before they were loaded up for the journey home. Admiral was among them, with Victor, his lad, walking proudly at his head.

I was telling the man on my right, the smaller of the two, that there was my horse and wasn't he a beauty, when I got a shock which knocked the breath out of me as thoroughly as a kick in the stomach.

To cover myself I dropped my race glasses on to the turf and bent slowly to pick them up, my escort stopping a pace ahead of me to wait. I grasped the strap and slung it over my shoulder, straightening and looking back at the same time to where we had come from. Forty yards of grass separated us from the last row of cars. There was no one about except some distant people going home. I looked at my watch. The last race was just about to begin.

I turned round unhurriedly, letting my eyes travel blankly past the man on my right and on towards Admiral, now going away from me. As usual after a race, he was belted into a rug to avoid cooling down too quickly, and he still wore his bridle. Victor would change that for a head collar when he put him in the horse-box.

Victor's great drawback was his slow wits. Endowed with an instinctive feeling for horses and an inborn skill in looking after them, he had never risen above "doing his two" in forty years of stable life, and never would. I would have to do without much help from him.

"Victor," I shouted, and when he turned round I signalled to him to bring Admiral over.

"I just want to make sure the horse's legs are all right," I explained to the two men. They nodded and waited beside me, the larger one shifting from foot to foot.

I did not dare to take a third look, and in any case I knew I was not mistaken.

The man on my right was wearing the tie I had lost in the horse-box on Maidenhead Thicket.

It was made from a piece of silk which had been specially woven and given to me on my twenty-first birthday by a textile manufacturer who wanted to do business with my father. I had two other ties like it, and a scarf, and the pattern of small red and gold steamships interlaced with the letter Y on a dark green background was unique.

How likely was it that a junior C.I.D. officer should have come honestly by my tie, I asked myself urgently. Farmer Lawson had not found it, and none of his men admitted to having seen it. It was too much of a coincidence to be innocent that it should reappear round the throat of a man who was asking me to step into a car and go for a ride with him.

Here was the attack I had been waiting for, and I had damn nearly walked meekly into the trap. Getting out of it, when it was so nearly sprung, was not going to be easy. The "police" car was parked across the gateway barely twenty paces ahead, with the driver standing by the bonnet and looking in our direction. The menacing aura of my two tough escorts now revealed itself to be something a great deal more sinister than a manner assumed to deal with crooks. One of them, perhaps, had killed Joe.

If I gave the slightest sign of doubting them, I was sure the three of them would hustle me into the car and drive off in a cloud of dust, leaving only Victor to report doubtfully what he had seen. And that, as far as I was concerned, would be that. It was to be one of those rides from which the passenger did not return.

My plan to present Wakefield with an attempted murderer was no good. One, I could have managed. But not three, and another sitting in the car.

When Victor was within fifteen paces of me I let the strap of my race glasses slip from my shoulder, down my arm and into my hand. Abruptly, with all my strength, I swung the glasses like a scythe round the legs of the larger man and overbalanced him, tripped the smaller man with the one elementary judo throw I knew, and sprinted for Admiral.

The five seconds it took them to recover from the unexpected assault were enough. As they started after me with set faces I leaped on to Admiral's back, picked up the reins which lay loosely on his neck, and turned him round sharply out of Victor's grasp.

The third man was running towards me from the car. I kicked Admiral into a canter in two strides, swerving round the advancing chauffeur, and set him towards the hedge which formed the boundary of the car park. He cleared it powerfully, landing on the grass verge of the road a few yards in front of the black car. The fourth man had the door open and was scrambling out. I looked back quickly.

Victor was standing stock-still with his mouth open. The three men were all running towards the gate with purposeful strides. They had nearly reached it. I had barely time to hope they were not carrying guns, since I presented a large and close target, when I saw the sun glint on something bright in the hand of the man who was wearing my tie. It hardly seemed the moment to stop and discover whether the glint came from a black-handled chef's knife: but I nearly found out the hard way, because he drew back his arm and threw it at me. I flung myself flat on the horse's neck and it missed, and I heard it clatter on to the road beyond.

I urged Admiral straight across the road, ignoring the squeal of brakes from a speeding lorry, and jumped him into the field opposite. The land sloped upwards, so that when I reined-in about half-way up it and turned round to see what was happening, the road and the car park were spread out below like a map.

The men were making no attempt to follow. They had moved the Wolseley away from the gate and were now drawing to a halt some yards further along on the verge. It looked as if all four were inside the car.

Victor still stood in the car park, scratching his head as he looked up towards me. I could imagine his bewilderment. I wondered how long it would be before he went to tell Pete what had happened.

Once the last race was over the car park would be buzzing with people, and cars would pour out of the now unobstructed gateway.

I thought that then I would be able to return safely to the racecourse without being abducted.

At this point another black car drew up behind the Wolseley, and then another, and several others, until a line of eight or more stretched along the side of the road. There was something rather horribly familiar about the newcomers.

They were Marconicars.

15

All the drivers climbed out of the taxis and walked along towards the Wolseley. With its low expensive lines and its efficient-looking aerial on top, it still looked every inch a police car; but the reinforcements it had called up dispelled any last doubts it was possible to have about the nature of the "C.I.D. officers."

The men stood in a dark group on the road, and I sat on Admiral half-way up the field watching them. They seemed to be in no hurry, but having seen their armoury of bicycle chains, knives, and assorted knuckledusters when they fought the London gang at Plumpton, and with Joe's fate constantly in mind, I had no doubt what would happen if I let them catch me.

I was in a good position. They could not drive the taxis up the field because there was no gate into it from the road, nor could they hope to reach me on foot, and I was still confident that when the race crowd flocked out I could evade the enemy and return to the course.

Two things quickly happened to change the picture.

First, the men began looking and pointing towards the side of the field I was in. Turning my head to the right I saw a car driving downhill on the farther side of the hedge, and realised that there was a road there. Twisting round, I now took note for the first time that a large house with out-buildings and gardens spread extensively across the skyline.

Three of the taxis detached themselves from the line and drove round into the road on my right, stopping at intervals along it. I now had taxi drivers to the right and ahead, and the big house at my back, but I was still not unduly dismayed.

Then yet another Marconicar came dashing up and stopped with a jerk in front of the Wolseley. A stocky man swung open the door and raised himself out of the driver's seat. He strode across the road to the hedge, and stood there pointing up at me with his arm extended. I was still wondering why when I heard the low whine of a bullet passing at the level of my feet. There was no sound of a shot.

As I turned Admiral to gallop off across the field, a bullet hit the ground with a phut in front of me. Either the range was too far for accurate shooting with a gun fitted with a silencer, or . . . I began to sweat . . . the marksman was aiming deliberately low, not at me but at Admiral.

It was only an eight or ten acre field, nothing like big enough for safety. I used precious moments to pull the horse up and take a look at the ragged sprawling hedge on the far side of the field. It was threaded half-way up with barbed wire. Over my shoulder I could see the man with the gun running along the road parallel to the course I had just taken. He would soon be within range again.

I took Admiral back a little way, faced him towards the hedge and urged him to jump. He cleared the whole thing, wire and all, without bending so much as a twig. We landed in another field, this time occupied by a herd of cows but again small and much too open to the road. Also, I discovered, trotting along the top boundary, that barbed wire had been laid lavishly in three strong strands all round it. All pastures have a gate, however, and I came to it in the farthest corner. I opened it, guided Admiral through into the next field, and shut it behind me.

This field was fenced with posts and wire only, and it was the extent of the barbed wire which decided me then to put as much space as I could between me and my pursuers in the shortest possible time. If I let the taxi-drivers follow me slowly from field to field I might find myself in a corner that even Admiral could not jump out of.

I was glad the sun was shining, for at least I could tell in which direction I was going. Since I was already headed towards the east, and because it seemed sensible to have a definite destination to aim for, I decided to take Admiral back to his own stable in Pete's yard.

I reckoned I had about twelve miles to cover, and I racked my brains to remember what the country was like in between. I knew the patchwork farmland which I was then grappling with gave way at some point ahead to Forestry Commission plantations. Then there would be a short distance of bare downland before I reached the hollow and the small village where Pete trained. Of the roads which crossed this area I had but the vaguest idea, and on any of them I could be spotted by a cruising Marconicar.

With this thought uncomfortably in mind, I found another by-road ahead. I let myself out on to it through a gate, and was trotting down it, looking for an opening in the neglected growth on the other side, when a squat black car swept round a distant bend and sped uphill towards me. Without giving Admiral a good chance to sight himself I turned him sharply towards the overgrown hedge and kicked his ribs.

It was too high for him, and too unexpected, but he did his best. He leaped straight into the tangle of sagging wire and beech saplings, crashed his way heavily through, and scrambled up almost from his knees on to the higher ground of the next field. It had been ploughed and planted with mangolds and made heavy going, but I urged him into a canter, hearing behind me the screech of brakes forcefully applied. A glance showed me the driver thrusting through the hole Admiral had made, but he did not try to chase me and I realised thankfully that he was not the man with the gun.

All the same, he had his radio. My whereabouts would be known to all the Marconicars within a minute.

I put another field between us and the taxi before pulling up and dismounting to see what damage Admiral had done himself. To my relief there were only a few scratches and one jagged cut on his stifle from which a thread of blood was trickling. I left it to congeal.

Patting his neck and marvelling at how he retained his calm sensible nature in very upsetting circumstances, I grasped the leather roller he wore round his middle, and sprang up again on to his back. The rug he was wearing now gaped in a right-angled tear on one side, but I decided not to take it off as it gave more purchase for my legs than riding him completely bare-back.

Three or four fields farther on the arable land began to give way to bracken, and ahead lay the large enclosures of the Forestry Commission.

The trees, mostly conifers, were being grown in large orderly expanses with rough tracks between each section. These acted both as convenient roadways for the foresters and as breaks in case of fire. They occurred about one in each half-mile, and were crossed at intervals by tracks leading in the opposite direction.

I wanted to set a course towards the south-east, but by consulting my watch and the sun in conjunction, found that the tracks ran from almost due north to south, and from east to west. Fretting at the extra mileage this was going to cost me, I steered Admiral into an eastbound track, took the next turning right to the south, then the next left to the east, and so on, crabwise across the forest.

The sections of trees were of varying ages and stages of growth, and turning again to the south, I found the area on my left was planted with trees only two feet high. This did not specially alarm me until I saw, a hundred yards to my left, a red and white motor coach speeding along apparently through the middle of the plantation.

I pulled Admiral up. Looking carefully I could see the posts and the high wire fence which formed the boundary between the little trees and the road beyond. If I turned east at the next track according to schedule, I would be facing straight down to the road.

The far side of the road looked similar to the section I was in: regular rows of conifers, put there by careful design.

At some point, I knew, I would have to cross a road of some sort. If I retreated back into the part of the forest I had crossed and took no risks, I would have to stay there all night. All the same, I thought, as I cantered Admiral along the southbound track and turned into the east one, I could have wished for more cover just at that moment.

Ahead of me the wire gates to the road were open, but before going through them I stopped and took a look at the other side of the road. Not all the plantations were surrounded by high mesh wire like the one I was in, and opposite only three strands of plain wire threaded through concrete posts barred the way.

The road had to be crossed quickly because where I was I felt as sheltered as a cock pheasant on a snow field. The heads in all the passing cars turned curiously towards me. But I saw nothing which looked like a Marconicar, and waiting only for a gap in the traffic, I clicked my tongue and set Admiral towards the wire fence opposite. His hooves clattered loudly on the tarmac, drummed on the firm verge, and he lifted into the air like a bird. There was no track straight ahead, only some fairly sparsely growing tall pines, and as

Admiral landed I reined him in to a gentle trot before beginning to thread a way through them.

Coming eventually to another track I checked again with my watch and the sun to make sure it was still running from east to west, which it was, and set off along it at a good pace. The going underfoot was perfect, dry and springy with loam and pine needles, and Admiral, though he had completed a three mile race and covered several miles of an unorthodox cross-country course, showed no signs of flagging.

We made two more turns and the sky began to cloud over, dulling the brilliant spring afternoon; but it was not the fading of beauty which bothered me so much as the fact that you cannot use a wrist watch as a compass unless the sun is shining. I would have to be careful not to get lost.

Just ahead, to my right, a small grass-grown hill rose sharply to its little rounded summit, the conifer forest flowing round its edges like sea round a rock. I had now left the bigger trees and was cantering through sections of young feathery pines only slightly taller than the top of my head, and I could see the hill quite clearly. A man, a black distant silhouetted man, was standing on the top, waving his arms.

I did not connect him with myself at all because I thought I had slipped my pursuers, so that what happened next had the full shock of a totally unexpected disaster.

From a track to the right, which I had not yet reached and could not see, a sleek black shape rolled out across my path and stopped, blocking the whole width of the track. It was the Wolseley.

The young pines on each side of me were too thick and low growing to be penetrated. I flung a look over my shoulder. A squat black Marconicar was bumping up the track behind me.

I was so close to the Wolseley that I could see one of the men looking out of the rear window with a gloating grin on his face, and I decided then that even if I broke Admiral's neck and my own in trying to escape, it would be a great deal better than tamely giving in.

There was scarcely a pause between the arrival of the Wolseley and my legs squeezing tight into Admiral's sides.

I had no reason to suppose he would do it. A horse can dare just so much and no more. He had had a hard day already. He might be the best hunter-'chaser in England, but ... The thoughts flickered through my brain in a second and were gone. I concentrated wholly, desperately, on getting Admiral to jump.

He scarcely faltered. He put in a short stride and a long one, gathered the immense power of his hind-quarters beneath him, and thrust himself into the air. Undeterred even by the opening doors and the threatening shouts of the men scrambling out of the Wolseley, he jumped clear over its gleaming black bonnet. He did not even scratch the paint.

I nearly came off when we landed. Admiral stumbled, and I slipped off the rug round on to his shoulder, clinging literally for dear life to the leather roller with one hand and Admiral's plaited mane with the other. The reins hung down, swaying perilously near his galloping feet, and I was afraid he would put his foot through them and trip. I still had one leg half across his rump, and, bumping heavily against his side, I hauled myself inch by inch on to his back. A warning twinge in my shoulder told me my newly-mended collar-bone could not be relied upon for too much of this, but leaning along his neck and holding on with all my strength, I reached the reins, gathered them up, and finally succeeded in reducing Admiral to a less headlong pace.

When I got my breath back I looked to see if the Wolseley was following, but it was so far behind that I was not sure whether it was moving or not. I could not spare time to stop and find out.

I realised that I had underestimated the Marconicars, and that it was only thanks to Admiral's splendid courage that I was still free. They had had an advantage in knowing the lie of the land, and had used the little hill as a spotting point. I suspected that its summit commanded quite a large area, and that as soon as I had entered the younger pines I had been seen.

I was forced to admit that they had guessed which direction I would take and had circled round in front of me. And that being so, they probably knew I had been making for Pete's stable. If I went on I should find them in my way again, with perhaps as little warning and less chance of escape.

I had left the hill behind me, and turned right again on the next track, seeing in the distance a section of taller trees. The horse cantered along tirelessly, but he could not keep it up for ever. I had to reach shelter as quickly as I could, out of sight of the man still standing on the hill-top, and out of the danger of being ambushed on another of the straight and suddenly uninviting tracks. Once we were hidden in the big trees, I promised Admiral, he should have a rest.

The light was dim under the tall pines. They had been allowed to grow close together to encourage their bare trunks to height, and the crowns of foliage far above were matted together like a roof, shutting out most of the daylight. I was glad for the obscurity. I slowed Admiral to a walk and dismounted as we entered the trees, and we went quietly and deeply into them. It was like walking through a forest of telegraph poles. Which of course, I thought fleetingly, perhaps they were destined to be.

The forest felt like home, even though it was different from those I was schooled in. It was very quiet, very dark. No birds at all. No animals. The horse and I went steadily on, silent on the thick pine needles, relying on instinct to keep us on a straight course.

I did not find our situation particularly encouraging. Whichever way I went in this extensive plantation I would have to come to a road in the end, and within three or four square miles the Marconicars knew exactly where I was. They had only to stand round the forest like hounds waiting for the fox to break cover, then it would be view tally-ho over the radio intercoms and the hunt would be on again.

There was a track ahead. A narrow one. I tied the reins round a tree and went forward alone. Standing still on the edge of the track and giving, I hoped, a good imitation of a tree trunk in my tweed suit, I slowly turned my head both ways. The daylight was much stronger on the track owing to the gap in the trees overhead, and I could see quite clearly for several hundred yards. There was no one in sight.

I went back for Admiral, made a final check, and led him across the track. There was no alarm. We walked steadily on. Admiral had begun to sweat long ago and had worked up a lather after our dash away from the Wolseley, damping large patches of the rug. Now that he was cooling down it was not good for him to keep it on, but I hadn't a dry one to give him. I decided that a damp rug was better than no rug, and trudged on.

Eventually I began to hear the hum of traffic and the occasional toot of a horn, and as soon as I could see the road in the distance I tied Admiral to a tree and went on alone again.

The end of the plantation was marked by a fence made of only two strands of stout wire, looking as if it were designed mainly to prevent picnickers driving their cars farther in than the verge. I chose a tree as near to the fence as I could get, dropped down on to my belly behind it, and wriggled forward until I could look along the road. There was only sporadic traffic on it.

On the far side of the road there were no plantations, and no fence either. It was unorganised woodland, a mixture of trees, rhododendrons and briars. Perfect cover, if I could reach it.

A heavy lorry ground past five feet from my nose, emitting a choking cloud of diesel fumes. I put my face down into the pine needles and coughed. Two saloon cars sped by in the other direction, one trying to pass the other, followed by a single-decker country bus full of carefree people taking home their Tuesday afternoon's shopping. A pair of schoolgirls in green uniform cycled past without noticing me, and when their high twittering voices had faded into the distance and the road was empty, I put my hands under my chest to heave myself up and go back for Admiral.

At that moment two Marconicars came into sight round a bend. I dropped my face down again and lay absolutely still. They drove past my head slowly, and though I did not look at them, I guessed they must be staring keenly into the forest. I hoped wholeheartedly that I had left Admiral far enough back to be invisible, and that he would not make a noise.

The Marconicars swerved across the road and pulled up on the opposite verge barely twenty-five yards away. The drivers got out of the taxis and slammed the doors. I risked a glance at them. They were lighting cigarettes, leaning casually against the taxis, and chatting. I could hear the mumble of their voices, but not what they were saying.

They had not seen me, or Admiral. Yet. But they seemed to be in no hurry to move on. I glanced at my watch. It was six o'clock. An hour and a half since I had jumped off the racecourse. More important, there was only one hour of full daylight left. When it grew dark my mobility on Admiral would end and we should have to spend the night in the forest, as I could not get him to jump a fence if he could not see it.

There was a sudden clattering noise from one of the taxis. A driver put his hand through the window and brought out a hand microphone attached to a cord. He spoke into it distinctly, and this time I could make out what he said.

"Yeah, we got the road covered. No, he ain't crossed it yet." There was some more clattering on the taxi radio, and the driver answered, "Yeah, I'm sure. I'll let you know the second we see him." He put the microphone back in the taxi.

I began to get the glimmerings of an idea of how to use the manhunt I had caused.

But first things first, I thought; and slowly I started to slither backwards through the trees, pressing close to the ground and keeping my face down. I had left Admiral a good way inside the forest, and I was now certain that the taxi drivers could not see him. It was uncomfortable travelling on my stomach, but I knew if I stood up the drivers would see me moving among the bare tree trunks. When finally I got to my feet my suit was a filthy peat brown, clogged with prickling pine needles. I brushed off the dirt as best I could, went over to Admiral and untied his reins.

Out in the daylight on the road I could still catch glimpses, between the tree trunks, of the two taxis and their drivers, but knowing that they could not see me, I set off towards the west, keeping parallel with the road and at some distance from it. It was, I judged, a little more than a quarter of a mile before I saw another Marconicar parked at the side of the road. I turned back and, as I went along, began to collect an armful of small dead branches. About half-way between the parked taxis, where they were all out of my sight, I took Admiral right up to the wire fence to give him a look at it. Although extremely simple in construction, it was difficult to see in the shade of the trees. I set the dead branches up on end in a row to make it appear more solid; then jumped on to Admiral's back, and, taking him back a few paces, faced him towards the fence and waited for a heavy vehicle to come along. In still air the sound of hooves on tarmacadam would carry clearly, and I did not want the taxi drivers round the nearby bends to hear me crossing the road. The longer they believed I was still in the pine forest, the better. But how long the taxis would *remain* parked I did not know, and the palms of my hands grew damp with tension.

A motor bike sped past, and I stayed still with an effort; but then, obligingly, a big van loaded with empty milk bottles came rattling round the bend on my right. It could not have been better. As it went past me I trotted Admiral forward. He made nothing of the dead-wood patch of fence, popped over on to the grass verge, took three loping strides over the tarmac, and in an instant was safely in the scrub on the far side. The milk lorry rattled out of sight.

I pulled up behind the first big rhododendron, dismounted, and peered round it.

I had not been a second too soon. One of the Marconicars was rolling slowly along in the wake of the milk lorry, and the driver's head was turned towards the forest I had left.

If one driver believed me still there, they all did. I walked Admiral away from the road until it was safe to mount, then jumped on to his back and broke him into a slow trot. The ground now was unevenly moulded into little hillocks and hollows and overgrown with brambles, small conifers and the brown remains of last year's bracken, so I let the horse pick his own footing to a great extent while I worked out what I was going to do. After a little way he slowed to a walk and I left him to it, because if his limbs felt as heavy and tired as mine he was entitled to crawl.

As nearly as I could judge I travelled west, back the way I had come. If there is one thing you can be sure of in England, it is that a straight line in any direction will bring you to a road without much delay, and I had covered perhaps a mile when I came to the next one. Without going too close I followed it to the north.

I was hunting a prey myself, now. A taxi, detached from the herd.

Admiral was picking his way silently across a bare patch of leaf-moulded earth when I suddenly heard the now familiar clatter of a Marconicar radio, and the answering voice of its driver. I pulled up in two strides, dismounted, and tied Admiral to a nearby young tree. Then I climbed up into the branches.

Some way ahead I saw a white four-fingered signpost, and beside it stood a Marconicar, of which only the roof and the top half of the windows were visible. The rest was hidden from me by the rhododendrons, trees, and undergrowth which crowded the ground ahead. My old friend the pine forest rose in a dark green blur away to the right.

I climbed down from the tree and felt in my pocket for the roll of pennies. I also found two lumps of sugar, which I fed to Admiral.

He blew down his nostrils and nuzzled my hand, and I patted his neck gently and blessed Scilla for giving him to me.

With so much good cover it was easy enough to approach the cross-roads without being seen, but when, from the inside of an old rhododendron I at length had a clear view of the taxi, the driver was not in it. He was a youngish sallow-faced man in a bright blue suit, and he was standing bareheaded in the middle of the cross-roads with his feet well apart, jingling some coins in his pocket. He inspected all four directions, saw nothing, and yawned.

The radio clattered again, but the driver took no notice. I had intended to creep up to his taxi and knock him out before he could broadcast that I was there; but now I waited, and cursed him, and he stood still and blew his nose.

Suddenly he began to walk purposefully in my direction.

For an instant I thought he had seen me, but he had not. He wheeled round a large patch of brambles close in front of me, turned his back towards my hiding place, and began to relieve himself. It seemed hardly fair to attack a man at such a moment, and I know I was smiling as I stepped out of the rhododendron, but it was an opportunity not to be missed. I took three quick steps and swung, and the sock-wrapped roll of pennies connected solidly with the back of his head. He collapsed without a sound.

I put my wrists under his shoulders and dragged him back to where I had left Admiral. Working as quickly as I could I ripped all the brown binding off the edge of the horse rug and tested it for strength. It seemed strong enough. Fishing my penknife out of my trouser pocket I cut the binding into four pieces and tied together the driver's ankles and knees with two of them. Then I dragged him closer to the tree and tied his wrists behind him. The fourth piece of binding knotted him securely to the trunk.

I patted his pockets. His only weapon was a spiked metal knuckle-duster, which I transferred to my own jacket. He began to wake up. His gaze wandered fuzzily from me to Admiral and back again, and then his mouth opened with a gasp as he realised who I was.

He was not a big man in stature, nor, I now discovered, in courage. The sight of the horse looming so close above him seemed to worry him more than his trussed condition or the bump on the head.

"He'll tread on me," he yelled, fright drawing back his lips to show a nicotine-stained set of cheap artificial teeth.

"He's very particular what he walks on," I said.

"Take him away. Take him away," he shouted. Admiral began to move restlessly at the noise.

"Be quiet and he won't harm you," I said sharply to the driver, but he took no notice and shouted again. I stuffed my handkerchief unceremoniously into his mouth until his eyes bulged.

"Now shut up," I said. "If you keep quiet he won't harm you. If you screech you'll frighten him and he might lash out at you. Do you understand?"

He nodded. I took out the handkerchief, and he began to swear vindictively, but fairly quietly.

I soothed Admiral and lengthened his tether so that he could get his head down to a patch of grass. He began munching peacefully.

"What is your name?" I asked the taxi driver.

He spat and said nothing.

I asked him again, and he said, "What the ruddy hell has it got to do with you?"

I needed particularly to know his name and I was in a hurry.

With no feelings of compunction I took hold of Admiral's reins and turned him round so that the driver had a good close view of a massive pair of hind quarters. My captive's new found truculence vanished in a flash. He opened his mouth to yell.

"Don't," I said. "Remember he'll kick you if you make a noise. Now, what is your name?"

"John Smith."

"Try again," I said, backing Admiral a pace nearer.

The taxi-driver gave in completely, his mouth trembling and sweat breaking out on his forehead.

"Blake." He stumbled on the word.

"First name?"

"Corny. It's a nickname, sort of." His eyes flickered fearfully between me and Admiral's hind legs.

I asked him several questions about the working of the radio, keeping the horse handy. When I had learned all I wanted I untied the reins from the tree and fastened them to a sapling a few feet away, so that when it grew dark the horse would not accidentally tred on the taxi-driver.

Before leaving them I gave Blake a final warning. "Don't start yelling for help. For one thing there's no one to hear you, and for another, you'll upset the horse. He's a thoroughbred, which means nervous, from your point of view. If you frighten him by yelling he's strong enough to break his reins and lash out at you. Shut up and he'll stay tied up. Get it?" I knew if Admiral broke his reins he would not stop to attack the man, but luckily, Blake did not. He nodded, his body sagging with fear and frustration.

"I won't forget you're here," I said. "You won't have to stay here all night. Not that I care about you, but the horse needs to be in a stable."

Admiral had his head down to the grass. I gave his rump a pat, made sure the knots were still tight on the demoralised driver, and picked my way quickly through the bushes to the taxi.

The signpost was important, for I would have to come back and find it in the dark in miles of haphazard woodland. I wrote down all the names and mileages on all of its four arms, just to make sure. Then I got into the taxi and sat in the driver's seat.

Inside the taxi one could hear the radio as a voice and not as a clatter. The receiver was permanently tuned in so that each driver could hear all messages and replies going from taxis to base and base to taxis.

A man was saying, "Sid, here. No sign of him. I've got a good mile and a half of the road in view from up here, nearly the whole side of that wood he's in. I'll swear he hasn't got across here. The traffic's too thick for him to do it quickly. I'm sure to see him if he tries it." Sid's voice came out of the radio small and tinny, like a voice on the telephone, and he spoke casually, as if he were looking for a lost dog.

While he spoke I started the engine, sorted out the gears, and drove off along the road going south. The daylight was just beginning to fade. Half an hour of twilight, I calculated, and perhaps another ten minutes of dusk. I put my foot down on the accelerator.

There was a short silence on the radio. Then someone said, "He has got to be found before dark."

Even though I had been half-hoping, half-expecting it, the husky timbre-less whisper made me jerk in my seat. I gripped the steering wheel tightly and the muscles round my eyes contracted. The voice was so close it seemed suddenly as if the danger it spelled for me were close as well, and I had to reassure myself by looking out sideways at the deserted heathland, and backwards in the driving mirror at the empty road astern.

"We're doing our best, sir," said a quiet voice, respectfully. "I've been driving up and down this ruddy road for nearly an hour. Two miles up and two miles back. All the parked cars in my section are still in position."

"How many of you have guns?" said the whisper.

"Four altogether, sir. We could do with more, to be sure of him."

There was a pause. Then the husky voice said, "I have one here, but you haven't time to come in for it. You'll have to manage with what you've got."

"Yes, sir."

"Pay attention, all drivers. Aim for the horse. Shoot the horse. The man is not to be found with bullets in him. Do you understand?"

There was a chorus of assent.

"Fletcher, repeat your orders."

The polite taxi-driver said, "As soon as we spot him either in the trees or breaking cover, we shoot, aiming for the horse. Call up all drivers, chase and catch the man. We are to—er—restrain him as necessary, place him in one of the taxis, and wait for your instructions."

Half-way through this recital of plans for my disposal, I recognised his voice. The polite tone, in the first instance, gave him away. I had heard it on the Maidenhead road, luring me with its false respectability into a waiting trap: he was the driver of the horse-box. Fletcher. I made a note of it.

Suddenly, as if someone had pressed a switch, a light flooded into my brain and I remembered the fence at Bristol. I remembered the pouring rain on my face and the greyness of everything, and now clearly I remembered the horse-box driver cutting the wire down from the fence, rolling it up, and hanging it over his arm.

There was something else, too . . . but before I could pin it down I came to a halt sign at a main road. I turned left from my empty by-road into a stream of traffic, and began to look for a sign post which would tell me how far away I was from Brighton. After half a mile I found one. Eleven miles. Say, twenty minutes to my destination.

I thought back to the Bristol fence, but the shade had come down again in my memory, and now I was not even sure that any gaps in it remained. My fingers wandered of their own accord to the scar on my cheek and traced along it gently, but it was a gesture I had caught myself in once or twice before, and I attached no importance to it. Besides, the immediate future needed all my thought.

All the way to Brighton I listened to the husky voice. Its tone grew both more urgent and more violent. I found it weird at first to eavesdrop on a man-hunt of which I was myself the quarry, but after a few minutes I got used to it and paid it less and less attention, and this could have been a catastrophic mistake.

"Have you anything to report, twenty-three?" said the husky whisper. There was no reply on the radio. I was only half aware of it. More sharply the voice said, "Twenty-three. Blake, have you anything to report?"

I came back to the present with a jerk. I picked up the microphone, clicked over the switch, and said "No" in as bored and nasal a tone as I could muster.

"Answer more quickly next time," said the husky voice severely. He was apparently checking that all the outlying taxis were still in position, for he went on to ask three more drivers whether they had anything to report. I thanked heaven, as I switched off the microphone, that I had not had to impersonate Blake's voice for more than one second, for any attempt at conversation would have found me out. As it was, I listened more intently than before to the exchanges on the radio.

The whispering voice began to acquire tone and characteristics as I became more familiar with it, until it formed a pattern of phrasing and emphasis which tantalised me at first because I could not remember its origin.

Then I knew. I knew for sure, at last.

You can start on a plan that you think touches the limit of what you can do; and then you have to do much, much more. Once more into the breach . . . only the breach had got bigger. Stiffen the sinews, summon up the blood . . . and bend up every spirit to his full height. There was no one like Bill Shakespeare for bounding things in a nutshell.

I drove into the outskirts of Brighton very thoughtfully indeed.

16

A taxi-driver asking the way to the main police station would be enough to arouse suspicion in a moron. I parked the taxi in a side street and hurried round the corner to ask directions in the nearest shop.

It was a tobacconist's, and busy, so I buttonholed one of the customers, an elderly man with watery eyes and a cloth cap. He told me the way quite clearly, though with frequent sniffs.

"You in trouble, mate?" he enquired inquisitively, eyeing my dirty, dishevelled appearance as I thanked him.

"Lost my dog," I said, smiling, pulling out the most unexciting reason I could think of for wanting the police.

The watery-eyed man lost interest. I walked quickly back to the taxi and found two small boys listening open-mouthed to the radio. I got into the taxi, winked at them, and said, "It's a thrilling story on children's hour, isn't it?" Their little faces cleared and they grinned.

I drove off. The husky voice was saying, ". . . at all costs. I don't care how you do it. He must not get away. If you can't catch him alive you must kill him. No bullets, though."

"It would be more certain if you would let us shoot him, sir," said the polite voice of Fletcher.

Real children's hour stuff. I smiled a little sourly.

Following the watery-eyed man's instructions I found the police station without trouble. Lights shone inside it as I drove past. The daylight was going quickly.

I circled the police station until I found a quiet side turning a hundred yards away. There I stopped, close to the curb. I turned on the side-lights and shut the windows. The radio was still chattering, and the man with the husky voice could no longer keep his fury in control. For a last moment I listened to him conceding, now that time was running out, to Fletcher's plea that they should be allowed to shoot me on sight. Then with a grimace I got out of the taxi, shut the door, and walked away from it.

The Marconicars office, I reckoned, was not more than half a mile off. I half-walked, half-ran towards it, looking, as I went, for a telephone. The street lamps were suddenly turned on, the bulbs glowing palely in the fading light.

The red telephone box outside a sub-post office was lit up inside, too, and although my reason told me I was in no danger, instinct would have made me stay in darkness. The whispering voice had done my nerves no good.

Though I knew I was still out of sight of the Marconicar office, I went into the telephone box with a conscious effort. I asked enquiries for the number of the Maidenhead police station, and without delay was put through to the desk sergeant. Inspector Lodge, he told me, had left an hour earlier, but after some urging he parted with Lodge's home number. I thanked him and rang off.

Fumbling with haste, I fed more coins into the machine, and gave the operator the new number. It rang and rang. My heart sank, for if I couldn't get hold of Lodge quickly I did not stand nearly so good a chance of cleaning up the Marconicars the way I wanted. But at last a voice answered. A woman's.

"Inspector Lodge? Just a minute, I'll see if I can find him."

A pause. And, finally, Lodge's voice.

"Mr. York?"

I explained briefly what had happened. I said, "I've left the taxi in Melton Close, a hundred yards back from the main police station here. I want you to ring the Brighton police and get them to send someone responsible to fetch it in. Tell them to listen carefully to the radio in the taxi. Our friend with the husky voice is speaking on it, inciting all the drivers to kill me. That should settle the Marconicars once and for all, I should think. One of the drivers out looking for me is called Fletcher. He's the one who drove the horse-box at Maidenhead, and he also rigged that wire for me at Bristol. I've remembered about it. It's likely he did the same for Bill Davidson, don't you think?"

"Yes, I do. Where are you now?" asked Lodge.

"In a 'phone box," I said.

"Well, go back to the taxi and wait there while I telephone the Brighton police. I don't really understand why you didn't go straight to them and explain it at first hand yourself."

"I thought it would have more weight, coming from you. And anyway . . ." I broke off, realising just in time that I could not tell Lodge what I was going to do next. I said instead, "Don't tell the Brighton police to expect me back at the taxi. I've a few 'phone calls to make . . . er . . . I must tell Scilla I'll be late, and things like that. But you won't waste any time, will you? Mr. Claud Thiveridge won't go on talking for ever, especially after it gets dark."

"I'll ring at once," promised Lodge, disconnecting. I put down the receiver and pushed out into the street.

I went on my way, totting up the time I could count on before Lodge sent the Brighton police to the Marconicar office. He had to ring them up and give them a fairly lengthy account of what was going on. Then they had to find the taxi, listen to the radio, and make a shorthand record of what they heard, to be used as proof a court would accept that the whole organisation was illegal. Very shortly after that they would come chasing round to apprehend the owner of the voice. Ten minutes altogether perhaps, if they hustled; perhaps a quarter of an hour.

When the Marconicar office was in sight I stayed close to the buildings so that I should not be seen from the Marconicar window. The street was nearly empty, and across the road the Olde Oake Café had closed its doors for the night. Through the glass I could see the plump waitress tiredly piling the old oak chairs on to the old oak tables.

A small black car was parked by the curb ahead. I glanced at it cursorily, and then with sudden recognition. I stopped. I purposely had not told Lodge whose face I had attached to the husky voice, though I knew I ought to have done. The sight of his car, parked flagrantly barely twenty yards from the Marconicar door, gave me a chance to square things with my conscience. I lifted the bonnet, unclipped the distributor lid, and took off the rocker arm, which I put in my pocket. Whatever happened now, there would be no quick getaway for Mr. Thiveridge.

There were no lights on in the Marconicar office, nor in any of the floors above. The neon sign, L. C. PERTH, was flashing steadily on and off at two second intervals, wasting its message on the empty road. The only gambler in sight, I reflected, was myself.

Reaching the Marconicar window I bent double below the sill and edged past as close to the wall as I could press. The street door was closed, but opened readily at a touch. I stepped very quietly into the hall, leaving the door open behind me. The silence in the house was tensely oppressive, and for a cowardly instant I was tempted to go out into the street again and wait like a sensible citizen for the police.

Stepping cautiously I went down the hall and pressed my ear to the door of Fielder's room. I could hear nothing. I opened the door gently and looked in. The room was tidy and empty. Next I tried the door on my left, which led into the back office where Marigold by day presided over her radio switchboard.

Through the thick door I could hear nothing, but when I opened it an inch a faint hum reached my ears. There was no one in the office. I went quietly in.

The hum was coming from the radio equipment. A small red brightly glowing circle in the control panel indicated that it was switched on, and through a crack in the casing the tiny light of a valve shone blue-white. The microphone lay casually on its side on its ledge.

For a sickening moment I thought that my bird had flown during the time it had taken me to ring Lodge and travel the half mile from the taxi; then I remembered the car outside, and at the same time, looking for wires leading out of the radio, saw a narrow plastic-covered cable running up the far wall and into the ceiling.

Praying that the stairs in the old house would not creak, I went up them lightly and quickly, and pressed my ear to the panels of the door of the main office of L. C. Perth. There were some large painted capital letters beside my nose. I squinted across at them while I listened. They said PLEASE ENTER.

Owing to the solidity of the regency door I could hear only a fierce hissing sound, but by this time the whisper was so familiar to me that an inch of mahogany could not disguise it.

He was there.

The hair on the back of my neck began to itch.

I judged it must have been seven or eight minutes since I spoke to Lodge. As I had to give the Brighton police time to find the taxi and record something of what they would hear on its radio, I could not risk interrupting the husky voice too soon. But neither did I intend to hover where I was until the police arrived. I made myself count one hundred slowly, and it seemed the longest three minutes of my life. Then I rubbed the palm of my hand on my trousers, and gingerly took hold of the ornate glass doorknob.

It turned silently and I eased the door open a few inches. It made no noise at all. I could see straight into the unlit room.

He was sitting at a desk with his back turned squarely towards me, and he seemed to be looking out into the street. The neon sign flashed off and on outside the window, illuminating the whole of the room and lighting up his dusky outline with a red glow. Red reflections winked on chromium ashtrays and slid along the metal edges of filing cabinets. A row of black telephones, ranked like an army on a long desk, threw curious angular shadows on the wall.

At close quarters the husky whisper lost some of its disembodied menace, even though what it was saying was now almost hysterically violent.

The open door can have stirred no current of air, for the man at the desk went on talking into his microphone, completely unaware that I was standing behind him.

"Kill him," he said. "Kill him. He's in that wood somewhere. He's an animal. Hunt him. Turn your cars towards the wood and put the headlights on. You'd better start beating through the trees. Fletcher, organise it. I want York dead, and quickly. Shoot him down. Smash him."

The man paused and drew in so sharp a breath that it gagged in his throat. His hand stretched out for a glass of water, and he drank.

Fletcher's voice came tinnily into the room through an extension loud-speaker on the desk. "We haven't seen a sign of him since he went into the wood. I think he might have got past us."

The man at the desk shook with fury. He began to whisper again with a rough burring rasp.

"If he escapes, you'll pay for it. You'll pay, I tell you. I want him dead. I want him smashed. You can do what you like with him. Use those chains to good purpose, and the spiked knuckles. Tear him to pieces. If he lives it will be the end for all of us, remember that."

The whisper rose in tone to a thin sound like a strangled shriek. "Rip his guts out . . . smash . . . destroy . . ."

He went on for some time elaborating on the way I should be killed, until it was clear that his mind was very nearly unhinged.

Abruptly I had heard enough. I opened the door wide, and put my hand on the light switch, and pressed it down. The room was suddenly brilliantly flooded with light.

The man at the desk whirled round and gaped at me.

"Good evening, Uncle George," I said softly.

17

His eyes scorched with hate. The vacuous expression was torn away, the hidden personality now out in the open and as mean and savage as any crocodile. He was still Kate's amusing Uncle George in corpulent outline and country-gentleman tweeds, the Uncle George who had written for boys' magazines and taken his wife to matinees, but the face was the one which had had a knife stuck into Joe Nantwich and had urged a bloodthirsty mob to tear me to bits.

His hand snaked out across the desk and came up with a gun. It was a heavy, old-fashioned pistol, cumbersome, but deadly enough, and it was pointing straight at my chest. I resolutely looked at Uncle George's eyes, and not at the black hole in the barrel. I took a step towards him.

Then it came, the instant on which I had gambled my safety. *Uncle George hesitated.*

I saw the flicker, the drawing back. For all his sin, for all the horror he had spread into the lives of others, he had never himself committed an act of violence. When he had delivered his threatening warning to me on the telephone on the very morning that I went to stay in his house, he had told me that he hated even to watch violence; and in spite of, or perhaps because of, his vicarious pleasure in the brutalities of primitive nations, I believed him. He was the sort of man, I thought, who liked to contemplate atrocities he could never inflict himself. And now, in spite of the fury he felt against me, he couldn't immediately, face to face, shoot me down.

I gave him no time to screw himself up. One fast stride and I had my hand on his wrist. He was trying to stand up. Too late he found the power to kill and squeezed the trigger; but the bullet smashed harmlessly into the wall. I bent his arm outwards with force, and twisted the gun out of his grasp. His muscles were soft and without strength, and he didn't know how to fight.

I flung him back hard into his chair, knocking the wind out of him, and then I reached over and switched off his microphone. I wasn't anxious that either the police or the taxi drivers should overhear what I was going to say.

There was a crackle as I brushed against his coat. I pulled it open. A folded piece of brown paper protruded from an inner pocket, and I tugged it out and spread it open on the desk. He was gasping for breath and didn't try to stop me. I read what was on it.

Joe's address.

I turned it over. In one corner on the other side, scribbled carelessly as if someone were not sure of the spelling and had used the nearest piece of paper to try them out on, were the words:

    Chichen Itza
    Chitchen Itsa
    Chitsen

Not chickens, not Chichester. Chichen Itza. I had the vaguest memory of having heard it before. It was the name of an emperor I thought; and it meant nothing to me, nothing. Yet Joe had died for it.

I left the paper on the desk, and hoped that the police would find it useful.

The hysteria had drained out of Uncle George. He looked suddenly ill and old, now that his day was done. I could summon no compassion for him, all the same: but then it was not regard for Kate's uncle that had brought me into the Marconicar office, but love for Kate herself.

"The police will be here in less than a minute," I said, speaking slowly and distinctly. He shifted in his seat and made a sharp helpless gesture with his pudgy hands. I went on, "They have been listening in to what you have been saying on the radio."

Uncle George's eyes widened. "Twenty-three," he said, with a remnant of anger. "Twenty-three hasn't answered my last few calls."

I nodded. I said, "You will be charged with incitement to murder. Gaol for life, at least." I paused. "Think," I said with emphasis. "Think of your wife. You did it all for her, didn't you, so that she could go on living in the luxury she was used to?" I was guessing, but I felt sure it was true, and he didn't deny it.

"You have shielded her from reality too long," I said. "What will it do to her, if you are arrested and tried, and maybe hanged?"

Or to Kate either, I added hopelessly to myself.

Uncle George listened and stared at me, and slowly his gaze fell to the pistol I still held in my hand.

"It's quicker," I said.

There was a short silence.

Very faintly in the distance I heard an alarm bell. Uncle George heard it too. He looked up. He hated me still, but he had come to the end of the line, and he knew it.

"The police," I said. The bell grew perceptibly louder.

I took the three steps across to the door, turned, and tossed the gun back into Uncle George's lap. As his stubby fingers fumbled and clutched it I went through the door, closed it, and ran down the stairs. The front door was still open. I hurried through that and pulled it shut behind me. The police alarm bells were no longer ringing.

In the shadow of the building I slipped along into the dark porch of the next-door house; and I was only just in time. Two police cars slowed, crawled, and halted in front of the Marconicar building.

Over in the Olde Oake Café the lights were out. The plump waitress had gone home.

There had been no sound from upstairs. I shivered, struck by the horrifying thought that Uncle George, having already screwed himself once to pull the trigger, might just possibly shoot a policeman instead of himself. With the gun I had so thoughtfully given back to him.

As the doors of the police cars slammed open and the black figures poured out I took the first step towards them to warn them that their quarry was armed. But Uncle George's devotion to Aunt Deb's interests remained steadfast after all. I thought that the single crashing shot in the room behind the neon sign was the best thing he had ever done for her sake.

I waited for a few minutes in my dark doorway, and while I stood there a small crowd began to collect on the pavement, drawn by the noise of the shots and the presence of the police cars. I slipped unhurriedly among them, and after a little while walked quietly away.

Round two or three turnings I found a telephone box and stepped inside, feeling in my pocket for coins. The calls to Lodge had taken all my small change, and for a moment I looked blankly at the threepenny piece and two halfpennies which were all I could dredge from my trouser pocket. Then I remembered my cosh. I untied the sock, tipped some of the pennies out on to my hand, pushed four of them into the slot, and asked the operator for Pete's number.

He answered at the second ring.

He said, "Thank God you've rung. Where the hell have you been?"

"Touring Sussex."

"And where's Admiral?"

"Well . . . I left him tied to a tree somewhere in the heathland," I said.

Pete began to splutter, but I interrupted him.

"Can you send the horse-box to collect him? Get the driver to come down to Brighton and pick me up on the sea-front, near the main pier. And Pete . . . have you got a decent map of Sussex?"

"A map? Are you mad? Don't you know where you left him? Have you really just tied the best hunter 'chaser in the country to a tree and forgotten where?" He sounded exasperated.

"I'll find him easily if you send a map. Don't be too long, will you? I'll tell you all about it later. It's a bit complicated."

I put down the receiver, and after some thought, rang up the Blue Duck. Ex-Regimental Sergeant-Major Thomkins answered the 'phone himself.

"The enemy is routed, sergeant-major," I said. "The Marconicars are out of business."

"A lot of people will be thankful to hear it," said the strong deep voice, with a good deal of warmth.

I went on, "However, the mopping up operations are still in progress. Would you be interested in taking charge of a prisoner and delivering him to the police?"

"I would indeed," he said.

"Meet me down at the main pier, then, at the double, and I'll gen you up."

"I'm on my way," said the sergeant-major.

He joined me by the sea wall soon after I got there myself. It was quite dark by then, and the lights along the front barely lit the ghostly grey lines of the breaking waves.

We had not long to wait for the horse-box, and when it came, Pete himself poked his big bald head out of the passenger seat and called to me. He, I and the sergeant-major got into the back and sat on a couple of straw bales, and as we swayed to the movement of the box on its way west I told them all that had happened since the day Bill died at Maidenhead. All, that is, up to my last conversation with Lodge. Of my visit to the Marconicar office and the true identity of Claud Thiveridge, I said nothing. I didn't know how English law viewed the crime of inciting to suicide, and for various reasons had decided to tell no one about it.

Parts of the story Pete already knew, and part Thomkins knew, but I had to go over the whole thing for them both to get it clear from first to last.

The horse-box driver had been given my note of the all-important sign post, and by comparing it with the map Pete had brought, he drove us back to it in remarkably short time.

Both Admiral and Corny Blake were still attached to their various trees, and we led one and frog-marched the other into the horse-box. Admiral was overjoyed to see us, but Blake's emotions seemed slightly mixed, especially when he recognised Thomkins. It appeared that it was Blake who had bashed the sergeant-major on the head with one of his own bottles.

With a grin I fished Blake's brass knuckleduster out of my pocket and handed it to Thomkins. "The prisoner's armoury," I said.

Thomkins tossed the wicked-looking weapon in his hand and tried it on for size, and Blake gave one agonised look at it and rolled off his bale of straw in a dead faint.

"We had better go round by West Sussex racecourse, if you don't mind," I said. "My car is still in the car park there; I hope."

It was there, all alone in the big field, the rising moon glinting on its low dark shape. I stepped down into the road, shook hands with Thomkins and Pete, wished them luck, and watched the red tail lights of the horse-box until they disappeared into the darkness.

Then I went over and started my car, turned my back firmly on what was doubtless my duty—the answering of interminable questions in Brighton police station—and with a purring roar set off for the Cotswolds.

Driven by an irresistible curiosity, I made a detour along the coast to Portsmouth, taking a chance that the public library would still be open there; and it was. In the reference department I hefted out a volume of an encyclopaedia and looked up Chichen Itza. The first spelling on the paper was the right one.

Chichen Itza, I found, was not an emperor; it was a capital city. It was the ancient Yucatan capital of the Mayas, an Indian nation who had flourished in Central America fifteen hundred years ago.

I stared at the page until the words faded into a blur.

What happened next was partly, I suppose, delayed reaction from the abysmal fear I felt when I looked into the barrel of Uncle George's gun; and partly it was hunger and a wave of deathly tiredness, and the sudden letting up of the stresses of the past weeks. My hands, my whole body began to shake. I braced my foot against the leg of the table I was sitting at and gripped the big book hard to stop it. It went on for minutes, until I could have cried with weakness, but gradually the spasm lessened, and the tension went out of my muscles, and I was just plain cold.

Chichen Itza. I stood up stiffly and closed the book and put it back on the shelf, and went soberly out to the car. I had set a better trap than I knew, pretending to be on the point of understanding what Joe might have said before he died.

I remembered clearly the study lined with glass cases. I could see the heavy carved oak desk, the folders devoted to Indian tribes, and the one separate folder clearly marked "Mayas." Uncle George had told me too much about the Mayas: and he'd known that Chichen Itza would lead me conclusively to him.

18

What I had not managed to do for Kate by loving her, I had done by tearing her world apart.

She stood in front of me, rigidly controlling herself, with a look of such acrid unrelenting hatred that I tasted my misery literally as a bitterness in the mouth. The banked fires were burning fiercely at last. There was a new depth and maturity in her face, as if in two weeks she had become wholly a woman. It made her more desirable than ever.

The inquest and enquiry into the life and death of George Penn had been adjourned twice, and had just ended; and police, witnesses, and Kate and I were standing in the hall of the Brighton court building, preparing to leave.

The verdict of temporary insanity was merciful, but there had been no hiding from news-scenting journalists the extent of Uncle George's criminal activities, and L. C. Perth and Marconicars had been front page news, on and off, for a fortnight.

My getting Uncle George to kill himself had been no help after all to Aunt Deb. It had been impossible to keep the truth from her, and shock and distress had brought on a series of heart attacks, of which the fourth was fatal. But for Kate, though she knew nothing about it, it was still the best thing. She had had to face the knowledge of his guilt, but not his trial and punishment.

But my letters of condolence had been unanswered. My telephone calls had regularly found her "out." And now I saw why. She blamed me alone for the sorrows which had come to her.

"I loathe you," she said implacably. "You nauseate me. You wormed your way into our house and accepted everything we gave you . . ." I thought of those gentle kisses, and so, from the extra flash in her eyes, did Kate . . . "and all you have done in return is to hound a poor old man to his death, and kill a defenceless old woman as a result. I have no Uncle and no Aunt. I have no one anywhere at all. I have no one." She spoke in anguish. "Why did you do it? Why couldn't you leave them alone? Why did you have to destroy my home? You knew how much I loved them. I can't bear to look at you, I loathe you so much . . ."

I swallowed, and tried to work some saliva into my dry mouth. I said, "Do you remember the children who had to be driven to school by a judo expert to keep them safe?"

But Kate stared blackly back as if she hadn't heard. "You are the most beastly person I have ever known, and although you have made it impossible for me to forget you, I shall never think of you without . . . without . . ." Her throat moved convulsively as if she were going to be sick. She turned away abruptly and walked unsteadily out through the big main door into the street.

The flash of camera bulbs met her and caught her unawares, and I saw her throw up her arm in a forlorn attempt to hide her face. The vulnerability and the loneliness in the droop of her shoulders cried out for comfort, and I, who most wanted to give it, was the only person she wouldn't accept it from. I watched her walk quickly through the questioning newspapermen and get into the hired car which was waiting for her.

It drove off. I stared after it, numbly.

Presently I became aware that Lodge was standing at my elbow and had been talking for some seconds. I hadn't heard a word he said, and he appeared to be waiting for a reply.

"I beg your pardon," I said. "What did you say?"

Lodge glanced out through the door where Kate had gone and sighed. "It wasn't very important . . . Look, she'll see things more reasonably in a little while, when she begins to think straight again. I heard a good deal of what she said . . . but you aren't to blame because her uncle took to crime."

"If I had known . . ." I stopped, on the verge of adding the giveaway words "for sure": "If I had known that George Penn was Claud Thiveridge, I would have done things differently."

"Things worked out well for the Penns, I think," said Lodge. "A quick end has its mercies."

His tone was loaded with meaning, and I knew that he half guessed what part I had played in Uncle George's death. He had several times earlier remarked that my disappearance from Brighton at the moment of success was out of character, and had shown polite scepticism over my excuse that I was growing anxious about my horse. He had mentioned pointedly that the Brighton police, listening in the Marconicar taxi to Uncle George's ravings, had heard a faint murmur (indistinguishable) in the background, a single shot, and nothing more. They had not been able to account for this, apart from later finding the microphone switched off and a bullet in the wall, and had come to the conclusion that Uncle George had been testing the old pistol to see if it were in working order. The shot had, however, brought them in haste to the Marconicar building, where they had arrived just in time to hear him shoot himself.

"You may be right," I said non-committally to Lodge. His eyelids flickered, and he smiled and changed the subject.

"The Marconicar drivers come up in court again this week. You'll be there to give evidence, I suppose," he said.

"Yes," I agreed, not liking the prospect.

All the drivers who had been looking for me had been alarmed by the shot and the silence on their radios. Some had begun to drive back to Brighton, some had made for London, and one or two had left their taxis and started out on foot. But all had quickly been rounded up, as following the rather vague directions I had phoned to Lodge, the police had begun making road blocks round them while they were still listening to Uncle George. Now the drivers faced charges ranging from intimidation and grevious bodily harm to murder itself.

Records discovered in Uncle George's study, inside a folder marked with gory humour "Notes on Human Sacrifices," made it clear that Joe Nantwich had indeed been knifed by the man who had been wearing my tie.

And Uncle George's motives were now clear too. Keeping up old standards of luxury had been too much for his income after the war, and instead of making Aunt Deb face reality, or facing it himself, he had gradually spent most of his capital. With almost the last of it he had bought Marconicars and launched into crime. He had directed everything through Fielder and had apparently never seen with his own eyes the brutal results of his orders. I doubted whether his misdeeds had seemed either more or less real to him than the primitive barbarities he spent his time studying.

The police had found neat lists, in files going back four years, of the money he had collected from the little terrorised businesses; and occasionally against the name of a café or a shop or a pub, Lodge told me, was written the single word, "Persuaded."

The racing record was shorter and contained lists of sums of money which the police did not know the purpose of; but one sheet headed "Joe Nantwich" was clear enough. It was a list of dates and amounts, of which the smallest was one hundred pounds. And underneath was drawn a thick line, with the words: "Account closed" printed in Uncle George's neat handwriting.

With Kate gone, the press men had drifted away. Their fun was over.

"Are you ready to go?" I asked Lodge. I had picked him up in Maidenhead on my way down. He nodded, and we went out to my car.

I drive fastest when I'm happy. That day I had no trouble at all in keeping within the speed limit through all the twisty Sussex villages; and Lodge endured my gloomy silence without comment half the way back to Maidenhead.

Finally he said, "Miss Ellery-Penn was very useful to her uncle. Everything you did in pursuing him went straight back to him through her. No wonder he was so well informed about your movements."

I had lived with this thought for a long time now; but hearing someone else speak it aloud had a most extraordinary effect. A tingle ran up my spine and set my brain suddenly alive, as if an alarm bell were ringing in my subconscious.

We were running through scrub and heathland. I slowed, swung the car off the road on to the peaty verge, and stopped. Lodge looked at me questioningly.

"What you said . . . I want to think," I said.

He waited a while in silence, and then said, "What's worrying you? The case is over. There are no more mysteries."

I shook my head. "There's someone else," I said.

"What do you mean?"

"There's someone else we don't know about. Someone in Uncle George's confidence." In spite of everything, I still thought of him as Uncle George.

Lodge said, "Fielder, the manager, was rounded up. So were all the L. C. Perth operators, though they have been freed again. Only two of the clerks had any idea of what was going on, one who went to the race tracks and one in the office. They received their instructions through Fielder about which horses to accept unlimited money on."

"Joe was stopping horses for months before Uncle George gave Heavens Above to Kate, and she had never been racing before that. Someone else who goes racing must have been working for Uncle George," I said with conviction.

"Penn would need only the morning paper and a form book for choosing a horse to stop. He wouldn't need to go to the races himself. He didn't need an accomplice at the races apart from his bookmaker—Perth. You're imagining things."

"Uncle George didn't know enough about horses," I said.

"So he made out," said Lodge sceptically.

"Kate told me that for as long as she remembers he was a dead loss on the subject. He started the Marconicar Protection racket only four years ago, and the racing racket less than a year ago. Before that he had no reason to pretend. Therefore his ignorance of horses was genuine."

"I'll give you that," he said. "But I don't see that it proves anything."

"He *must* have had a contact on the racecourse. How else did he manage to pick on the one jockey who could most easily be corrupted?" I said.

"Perhaps he tried several, until he found a taker," suggested Lodge.

"No. Everyone would have talked about it, if he had."

"He tried Major Davidson," said Lodge. "That looks like a very bad mistake from your mythical adviser."

"Yes," I conceded. I changed to another tack. "There have been one or two things which have been relayed recently to Uncle George which Kate herself didn't know. How do you explain that?"

"What things?"

"Joe's bit of brown wrapping paper, for instance. He told everyone in the weighing room at Liverpool about it. Kate wasn't at the meeting. But two days later, on Uncle George's instructions, Joe was killed and the paper taken away from him."

Lodge pondered. "Someone might have rung her up on the Sunday and mentioned it in passing."

I thought fleetingly of Dane. I said, "Even then, it was surely not interesting enough for her to have told Uncle George."

"You never know," he said.

I started up and drove on in silence for some miles. I was loath to produce for his scepticism the most deep rooted of my reasons for believing an enemy still existed: the near-certainty that in the concussed gap in my memory I already knew who it was.

When at last I tentatively told him this, he treated it more seriously than I had expected. After some minutes of thought he pierced and appalled me by saying, "Perhaps your subconscious won't let you remember who this enemy of yours is *because you like him.*"

I dropped Lodge at Maidenhead and went on to the Cotswolds.

Entering the old stone house with the children noisily tumbling through the hall on their way to tea was like stepping into a sane world again. Scilla was coming down the stairs with her arms full of Polly's summer dresses: I went over and met her on the bottom step and kissed her cheek.

"Joan and I will have to lengthen all these," she said, nodding at the dresses. "Polly's growing at a rate of knots."

I followed her into the drawing-room and we sat down on the hearthrug in front of a newly-lit fire.

"Is it all over?" asked Scilla, pushing the dresses off her lap on to the floor.

"Yes, I think so." Too much was all over.

I told her about the inquest and the verdict. I said, "It was only because of Bill that George Penn was ever found out. Bill didn't die for nothing."

She didn't answer for a long time, and I saw the yellow flames glinting on the unshed tears in her eyes. Then she sniffed and shook her head as if to free herself from the past, and said, "Let's go and have tea with the children."

Polly wanted me to mend a puncture on her bicycle. Henry said he'd worked out some gambits in chess and would I play against him after tea. William gave me a sticky kiss and pressed an aged fruit drop into my palm as a present. I was home again.

19

The almost unbearable belief that I had lost Kate grew very little easier as the days passed. I couldn't get her out of my mind. When I woke in the morning the ache rushed in to spoil the day: when I slept I dreamed continually that she was running away down a long dark tunnel. I thought it unlikely I would ever see her again, and tried to make myself be sensible about it.

Then, a week after the inquest on Uncle George, I went to ride at Banbury races, and Kate was there. She was dressed in dark navy blue and there were big grey hollows round her eyes. Her face was pale and calm, and her expression didn't change when she saw me. She was waiting outside the weighing room, and spoke to me as soon as I drew near.

"Alan, I think I should apologise for what I said to you the other day." The words were clearly an effort.

"It's all right," I said.

"No . . . it's not. I thought about what you said . . . about those children going to school with the judo expert . . . and I realise Uncle George had got to be stopped." She paused. "It was not your fault Aunt Deb died. I'm sorry I said it was." She let out a breath as if she had performed an intolerable duty.

"Did you come all the way here especially to say that?" I asked.

"Yes. It has been worrying me that I was so unjust."

"My dear precious Kate," I said, the gloom of the past week beginning to vanish like morning mist, "I would have given anything for it not to have been Uncle George, believe me." I looked at her closely. "You look very hungry. Have you had anything to eat today?"

"No," she said, in a small voice.

"You must have some lunch," I said, and giving her no chance to refuse, took her arm and walked her briskly to the luncheon-room. There I watched her eat, pecking at first but soon with ravenous appetite, until some colour came back into her cheeks and a faint echo of her old gaiety to her manner.

She was well into her second helping of hot game pie when she said in a friendly tone, "I wish you'd eat something too."

I said, "I'm riding."

"Yes I know, I saw in the paper. Forlorn Hope, isn't it?" she asked between forkfuls.

"Yes," I said.

"You will be careful, won't you? He's not a very good jumper, Pete says."

I looked at her with delighted astonishment, and she blushed deeply.

"Kate!" I said.

"Well . . . I thought you'd never forgive me for being so abysmally beastly. I've spent the most vile week of my life regretting every word I said. But at least it brought me to my senses about you. I tried to tell myself I'd be delighted never to see you again and instead I got more and more miserable. I . . . I didn't think you'd come back for a second dose, after the way you looked at Brighton. So I thought if I wanted you to know I was sorry I'd have to come and tell you, and then I could see how . . . how you reacted."

"How did you expect me to react?"

"I thought you'd be rather toffee-nosed and cool, and I wouldn't have blamed you." She stuffed an inelegant amount of pie-crust into her mouth.

"Will you marry me, then, Kate?" I asked.

She said, "Yes" indistinctly with her mouth full and went on uninterruptedly cutting up her food. I waited patiently while she finished the pie and made good time with a stack of cheese and biscuits.

"When did you eat last?" I asked, as she eventually put down her napkin.

"Can't remember." She looked across at me with a new joy in her face and the old sadness beneath it, and I knew from that and from her remark about Forlorn Hope—the first concern she had ever shown for my safety—that she had indeed grown up.

I said, "I want to kiss you."

"Racecourses were not designed for the convenience of newly-affianced lovers," she said. "How about a horse-box?"

"We've only got ten minutes," I said. "I'm riding in the second race."

We borrowed Pete's horse-box without more ado. I took her in my arms, and found this time on Kate's lips a satisfactorily unsisterly response.

The ten minutes fled in a second, and the races wouldn't wait. We walked back, and I went into the weighing room and changed into colours, leaving Kate, who looked a bit dazed and said she felt it, sitting on a bench in the sun.

It was the first time I had been racing since Uncle George's inquest. I glanced uneasily round the changing room at the well-known faces, refusing to believe that any was the go-between who had brought death to Joe. Perhaps Lodge was right, and I didn't want to find out. I had liked Uncle George himself, once. Did I shrink from seeing the façade stripped from another friend to reveal the crocodile underneath?

Clem handed me my lead packed weight cloth. I looked at his patient wrinkled face, and thought, "Not you, not you."

It was a sort of treachery to reflect that Clem heard all that went on and that no event of any significance ever escaped his ears. "The oracle," some of the lads called him . . .

A hearty thump on the back cut off my speculations.

"Wotcher, me old cock sparrow, how's the sleuthing business?" bellowed Sandy, pausing and balancing his saddle on one knee while he looped up the girths. "How's Sherlock these days?"

"Retired," I said, grinning.

"No, really? After such grade A results?"

"I'll stick to steeplechasing, I think. It's less risky."

Sandy's friendly gaze strayed to the scar on my cheek.

"You're welcome to your little illusions, chum," he said. "You'll change your mind when you've broken as many bones as I have." He wound the girths round the saddle, tucked in the buckles, and with his helmet pushed far back on his head and his cheerful voice drawing heads round like a magnet, made his way out to the scales.

From across the changing room I had a good view of Dane's back solidly and deliberately turned towards me. Talking to someone by the gate, he had unfortunately seen Kate and me returning from the horse-box parking ground. He had had a good look at our radiant faces before we knew he was there, and he didn't need to have things spelled out for him. He had congratulated Kate in two clipped sentences, but to me he had still spoken not a word.

I went past his unyielding back and out to the paddock. He followed. Pete trained both the horses we were riding, and we both had to join him.

Pete jumped in with both feet.

"Alan, Kate's told me your news. Well done."

He received a fierce glower from Dane, and hastily began to assess the race. He was talking about Dane's mount, and my attention wandered.

There, ten yards away, stood the craggy Clifford Tudor, opulently rolling a cigar round his mouth and laying down the law to his trainer and jockey. Odd, I thought, how often I had come across that man. I watched him make heavy chopping motions with his dark hands to emphasise his points, and caught the young jockey, Joe's substitute, wrinkling his forehead in acute anxiety.

My gaze slid beyond him to where Sir Creswell Stampe was superintending the raising of his unamiable son David into the saddle, before going to take his judicial position in the Stewards' box. Beyond him again were other groups of owners and trainers planning their plans, hoping their hopes, giving their jockeys instructions (and counter-instructions) and calculating their last minute bets.

So many people I knew. So many people I liked. Which of them . . . which of them was not what he seemed?

Pete gave me a leg up on to Forlorn Hope's narrow back, and I waved to Kate, who was standing by the parade ring rails, and cantered down towards the start.

On the way Dane came past briskly, turning his head in my direction as he drew level. With cold eyes he said, "Blast you," giving both words equal punch, and shook up his horse to get away from me and give me no chance to reply. I let him go. Either he would get over it or he wouldn't; and in either case there wasn't much I could do about it.

There were eleven runners in the race. We circled round while the starter's assistant tightened girths and the starter himself called the roll. Sandy asked his permission to dismount in order to straighten his saddle, which had slipped forwards on the way down to the gate. The starter nodded, looking at his wristwatch and telling Sandy not to be too long. This particular starter hated to start his races late and grew fidgety over every minor delay.

Sandy unbuckled the girths, pulled his saddle straight, and tightened it up again. I was watching him instead of concentrating wholly on Forlorn Hope, so that what happened was entirely my own fault.

An attendant flapped open under my horse's nose the white flag which it was his job to wave aloft, to signal to the stands that the horses were about to start. My green young hurdler took fright, reared up like a circus horse, twisted sideways, and threw me off. I hit the ground almost flat on my back, winding myself, and I saw Forlorn Hope kick up his heels and depart at a smart pace up the course.

For a few seconds I lay there trying to get my breath back, and Sandy walked over with his hand outstretched to help me up, laughing and making some rude remark about my sudden descent.

The most extraordinary dizziness suddenly swept over me, and my senses began to play fantastic tricks. Lying in the spring sun, I felt rain on my face. Winded but unhurt, my body was momentarily invaded by shocking pain. In my whirling brain it seemed as if past and present had become confused, and that two completely different events were somehow happening at the same time.

I stared up into Sandy's face. There was the familiar wide gap-toothed grin, the false incisors removed for safety; there were the laughing brown eyes with the reddish lashes and the bold devil-may-care expression. The sunshine bathed his face in light. And what I saw as well was the same face looming towards me in pouring rain, with cruel eyes and a grim mouth. I heard a voice say, "You nosey bastard, perhaps that'll teach you to mind your own business;" and I threw up my hand to shield my cheek against the kick which was coming. . . .

My sight cleared and steadied, and Sandy and I were looking straight into each other's eyes as if a battle were being fought there. He dropped the hand outstretched to help me, and the friendliness went out of his face with the completeness of an actor shedding a role when the play is over.

I found my palm was still pressed against my cheek. I let it drop away, but the gesture had told its tale. I had remembered what had happened by the fence at Bristol, and Sandy knew it.

Strength returned to my limbs, and I stood up. The starter, consulting his watch in barely concealed annoyance, asked if I was all right. I replied that I was, and apologised for holding up the race. Some way down the course someone had caught Forlorn Hope, and as I watched he was turned round to be led back to the starting gate.

Sandy, showing no haste to remount, stood his ground in front of me.

"You can't prove a thing," he said, characteristically taking the bull by the horns. "No one can connect me with Penn."

"Fletcher," I said at once.

"He'll keep his mouth shut," said Sandy, with conviction. "He's my cousin."

Uncle George's racing venture, I now saw, had not been inspired solely by the availability of a shaky bookmaking business. The existence of an easily-recruited ally on the racecourse might have been the very factor which decided him, in the first place, to buy L. C. Perth.

I mentally reviewed the rest of the gang.

"How about Fielder?" I suggested after a short pause.

"I'm a voice on the phone to him. A voice called Smith. He doesn't know me from Adam," said Sandy.

Temporarily, I gave up. I said, "What did you do it for?"

"Money. What else?" he said scornfully, clearly thinking the question foolish.

"Why didn't you stop the horses yourself? Why let Joe collect the big fat fees for losing?"

Sandy seemed perfectly willing to explain. "I did stop a couple myself. The Stewards had me in over the second one, and I got off by the skin of my bloody teeth. I saw the red light, mate. I tipped the boss to try that little bastard Joe instead. Let him lose his licence, not me, I told him. But mind you, I was on to a bloody good percentage every time he strangled one."

"Which made you all the more angry when he won against orders on Bolingbroke," I said.

"That's right."

"Then Joe didn't tell you in the washroom he was going to pull Bolingbroke. You knew already."

"Proper little Sherlock," mocked Sandy.

"And you did put him over the rails at Plumpton, I suppose?"

"He bloody well deserved it. He lost me fifty quid on Leica as well as my bonus from the boss."

"Did he deserve to die, as well?" I asked bitterly.

The man leading Forlorn Hope back was now only a hundred yards away.

"The stupid little sod couldn't keep his mouth shut," said Sandy violently. "Waving that brown paper at Liverpool and yelling for you. I saw what was written on it, and told Fielder, that's all. I didn't know what it meant, but it was a ton to a tanner the boss wouldn't like it. Joe was asking for it."

"And after he'd got it, you rang Fielder and told him the job had been bungled, and Joe had lived long enough to talk to me?"

"Yes," said Sandy morosely. "I heard you telling every bloody body in the weighing room."

I couldn't resist it. I said, "I was lying. Joe died without saying a word."

As the full significance of this slowly dawned on him, his jaw dropped, and I saw him waver in some secret inner place as if an axe had hacked into the roots of his colossal self-confidence. He turned on his heel, strode across to where the starter's assistant held his horse, and swung abruptly into the saddle.

I went to meet Forlorn Hope, thanked the man who had brought him back, and remounted. The starter's patience had run out.

"Get into line, please," he said, and the circling horses began to straighten out across the course. I came up from behind and took a place alongside Sandy. I had one more question to ask.

"Tell me," I said, "why on earth did you get Penn to try to bribe Major Davidson? You must have known he wouldn't have stopped Admiral winning for all the money in the world."

"It was the boss's idea, not mine," said Sandy roughly. "I warned Fielder to tell him it wouldn't work, but the boss knew bee-all about horses and was pig-headed besides. Fielder said he wouldn't listen, because he thought if he fixed a cert it would be worth a fortune. He made a packet out of it, all right. He thought up the wire himself. And I'd be a ruddy sight better off if the wire had killed you too," he added, with a sudden spurt of venom.

The starter's hand swept down on the lever. The tape flew up, and, five minutes late, the horses bounded forward towards the first hurdle.

I don't know exactly when Sandy decided to put me over the rails. Perhaps the thought of all the money he would not be getting overwhelmed him, and perhaps I had brought it on myself by recalling that he had done it to Joe when Joe, as he saw it, had cheated him.

In any case, as we approached the second hurdle, he swerved his horse towards me. We were both in the group just behind the leaders, and I was on the inside, with the rails on my left.

I glanced at Sandy's face. His slitted eyes were concentrated on the jump ahead, but with every stride his horse drew nearer to mine. He wasn't leaving me much room, I thought.

Only just in time did I realise that he intended to leave me no room at all. He was aiming to crowd my horse so closely that I would be thrust into the six foot high wing leading up to the hurdles. A crash through the wings, I had been told, was one of the most dangerous of all falls. The time had clearly come for rapid evasive action if I were not to find this out for myself.

I literally hauled on the reins. Forlorn Hope lost impetus dramatically, and as soon as the quarters of Sandy's horse were past his shoulder I pulled his head unceremoniously to the right. It was only just in time. The hurdles were beneath his feet before he had time to see them, and he knocked one flat with his forelegs. The horse following us, going faster, bumped hard into the back of him, and the jockey yelled at me to mind what I was doing.

Forlorn Hope was too much of a novice to stand this sort of thing, and I decided that if I were not to ruin his nerve for good, I would have to keep him out of Sandy's way for the rest of the race.

But Sandy was not content with that. Along the straight in front of the stands he gradually worked himself back to my side. He was a better jockey than I and his horse was more experienced. When I tried to go faster, he kept pace, and when I slowed down, he slowed too. I could not shake him off. In front of the crowds, apart from keeping pace with me, he rode fairly enough; but round the next bend lay the long curved leg out into the comparatively deserted country, and what he might do there I hated to think.

I did consider pulling up and dropping out of the race altogether, but that seemed an even more ignominious defeat than being put over the rails.

As the field swept round the bend in a bunch, Sandy tried again. He closed his horse tight up against mine and very slightly behind. On my left I was jammed against Dane. He glanced across and shouted, "Get over, Sandy. Give us some room."

Sandy did not answer. Instead I felt his knee slide along under my thigh until it was pressing fiercely on my hamstrings. Then he gave a sudden violent jerk forwards and upwards with his whole leg.

My foot flew out of the stirrup and I lost my balance completely. I swayed wildly over to the left, my head tipping down beside my horse's neck, my fingers clutching frantically at his mane. I looked down and saw the blur of hooves pounding tight-packed round the bend, and I struggled to prevent myself slipping off among them. But all my weight was too far forward, and the jolt of the horse's galloping stride tended to tip me farther forward still. I knew that in a few seconds I would be off.

It was Dane who saved me. He put his hand on my side and literally pushed me back into my saddle.

"Thanks," I gasped, feeling with my right foot for the dangling stirrup.

Not far round the bend lay the next flight of hurdles, and I fought to get myself and the horse properly balanced before we met it. As we came round the bend the sun had shone straight into our faces, but swinging out towards the country it lay on our right. Glancing to see if Sandy was still beside me I caught the sunshine full in the eyes and was for a second dazzled. He was there. He appeared to me as a black silhouette against the sun.

I remembered then that on such bright days on this course the sun shone straight into the eyes of the crowds on the stands also, and that it was difficult for them to distinguish what was happening on the far side of the course. Whatever Sandy did, he could be fairly sure the Stewards would not be able to see.

I gained a yard or two on Sandy and Dane at the next hurdle, but over my shoulder I could hear Sandy clicking with his tongue to hurry his horse, and in a few more strides he was beside me again. His shadow lay across my horse's withers.

Suddenly he swung his arm; and had I not been so acutely ready he would have had me. He swung his right arm round his body in a chop at my face, slashing with his riding whip. I ducked in a reflex, without actually seeing the whip at all. The heavy blow landed across my helmet just above the peak, and knocked it clean off my head. It bounced away on the turf.

I felt, rather than saw, Sandy draw back his arm for another try. I slipped my own whip and the reins into my left hand, and when he struck, threw up my right. More by luck than design my fingers fastened on the stick and I gripped and twisted and pulled with the strength of desperation.

I had him half out of his saddle and I almost exulted; but at the vital moment he let go of his stick and regained his balance. Rebounding, his horse swerved away from me, leaving a gap, and I looked hopefully over my shoulder for one of the other runners to come up between us. But most of them had gone on in front, and there was no one close. I threw Sandy's stick away.

The next hurdle lay ahead. I kept well away from the rails and tried to steady Forlorn Hope so that he should have a fair chance at it, but I was all too aware that Sandy was beginning to close on me again with a burst of extra speed.

My horse jumped the hurdle in reasonable style. Sandy kicked his horse into a tremendous leap, and as he landed he pulled straight across in front of me.

Forlorn Hope crashed into the rails.

By some miracle he did not fall. He bounced off, staggered, faltered, and galloped on. My leg, which had been crushed just below the knee between his body and the rails, was completely numb. I looked down at it: it appeared to be doing its job all right, even though I no longer seemed to be connected to it. My silk breeches were ripped open across the knee, and in my new extremely expensive made-to-measure racing boots flapped a large triangular tear.

Illogically, this made me very angry.

Sandy was some lengths ahead and had not so far managed to pull back again. Dane came up on my right, and I was glad to see him there.

He yelled, "What the hell's going on? What the blazes does Sandy think he's playing at?"

"He's not playing," I shouted. "He wants to get me off."

"Why?" yelled Dane.

"He was working for George Penn. He was making a lot of money.

Now he isn't. He blames me," I shouted in snatches, the wind picking the words out of my mouth and blowing them back over my shoulder.

"With reason," shouted Dane.

"Yes," I agreed. I glanced at him, but now it was he who was outlined against the sun, and I could not see his expression clearly. If he felt badly enough about Kate to carry on where Sandy had for the moment left off, I should have no chance at all. He could ride rings round me, and Sandy, too.

We raced in silence towards the next hurdle, the last on the far side. Sandy was gradually slowing to wait for me.

Then Dane said, "Alan?"

"Yes?" I shouted back.

"Do you want to give Sandy some of his own medicine?"

"Yes." I suddenly had no reservations. It was a terrible thing to do, and if the Stewards saw me I'd lose my permit; but I had taken just about enough from Uncle George's assorted strong-arm boys.

Dane shouted, "I'll go up on his outside. You come outside me. Then I'll get away and leave him between you and the rails. O.K.?"

I nodded. I tried to foresee the future. If I unseated Sandy he would not dare to complain to the Stewards; and I, as he said, could give no tangible evidence against him to the police. There could be an uneasy truce between us. And fall for fall, the score would be equal.

"Come on, then," Dane shouted.

He kicked his horse and began to take his place on Sandy's right. I pulled away from the rails and urged Forlorn Hope to the outside. There was nearly a mile to go to the finish, and as no one had yet begun to put on the pressure the field was still fairly closely bunched just ahead of us. There was no one behind. After the hurdle lay the long oval bend leading round into the straight. If either Sandy or I were to get the other off, it would have to be done on the bend; once we were round into the straight the Stewards would have too clear a view of our behaviour.

Dane jumped the hurdle alongside Sandy with me not far behind. As soon as I was level with them both, Dane shook up his horse and sped clear away from us, leaving me, as he had promised, with Sandy between me and the rails.

I swung Forlorn Hope over roughly on to Sandy's horse, bumping him against the rails. Sandy yelled and lashed out with his fist. I hit his arm sharply with my stick.

I had got to unseat him without hurting his horse. I was being unfair enough already to the owner in trying to lose him the race by dislodging his jockey: if I could not do it without damaging the horse, I must not do it at all.

Shifting the reins into my right hand, I planted my left abruptly on Sandy's body just behind his armpit, and shoved. But I was too far away to get enough force behind it. He swayed in his saddle, but kept his balance. He began to swear at me.

We were on the crown of the bend. It had to be now or never. I pushed Sandy's horse harder against the rails. He yelled again. His leg, I knew, must be being crushed, pounded, even torn by the white-painted wood. With my own leg numb from the same treatment, I had no sympathy for him. Then his foot crashed into one of the uprights with an audible snap.

He screamed.

I gritted my teeth, shot out my arm, and pushed him with all my might. I knew if he had not gone then I would not have had the resolution to try again. But he began to topple, slowly, it seemed, at first, and then with an accelerating rush, as if he had been sucked away by a slipstream.

I caught a final glimpse of his face, eyes staring widely, mouth twisted with agony, as he fell into the long grass on the other side of the rails. Then I was round the bend into the straight, bruised, breathless, tattered and helmetless, but still on board.

Sandy's loose horse, relieved of his weight, spurted forward through the other runners.

Dane saw him, and turned round in his saddle and grinned at me, and jerked up his thumb.

TWO

NERVE

1

Art Mathews shot himself, loudly and messily, in the center of the parade ring at Dunstable races.

I was standing only six feet away from him, but he did it so quickly that had it been only six inches I would not have had time to stop him.

He had walked out of the changing room ahead of me, his narrow shoulders hunched inside the khaki jerkin he had put on over his racing colors, and his head down on his chest as if he were deep in thought. I noticed him stumble slightly down the two steps from the weighing room to the path; and when someone spoke to him on the short walk to the parade ring, he gave absolutely no sign of having heard. But it was just another walk from the weighing room to the parade ring, just another race like a hundred others. There was nothing to suggest that when he had stood talking for two or three minutes with the owner and the trainer of the horse he was due to ride, he would take off his jerkin, produce from under it as he dropped it to the ground a large automatic pistol, place the barrel against his temple, and squeeze the trigger.

Unhesitating. No pause for a final weighing up. No good-bys. The casualness of his movement was as shocking as its effect.

He hadn't even shut his eyes, and they were still open as he fell forward to the ground, his face hitting the grass with an audible thud and his helmet rolling off. The bullet had passed straight through his skull, and the exit wound lay open to the sky, a tangled, bloody mess of skin and hair and brain, with splinters of bone sticking out.

The crack of the gunshot echoed round the paddock, amplified by the high back wall of the stands. Heads turned searchingly and the busy buzz and hum of conversation from the three-deep railside racegoers grew hushed and finally silent as they took in the appalling, unbelievable, indisputable fact that what remained of Art Mathews lay face downward on the bright green turf.

Mr. John Brewar, the owner of Art's prospective mount, stood with his middle-aged mouth stretched open in a soundless oval, his eyes glazed with surprise. His plump, well-preserved wife toppled to the ground in the graceless sprawl of a genuine faint, and Corin Kellar, the trainer for whom both Art and I had been about to ride, went down on one knee and shook Art by the shoulder, as if he could still awaken one whose head was half blown away.

The sun shone brightly. The blue and orange silk on Art's back gleamed: his white breeches were spotless, and his racing boots had been polished into a clean, soft shine. I thought inconsequentially that he would have been glad that—from the neck down at least—he looked as immaculate as ever.

The two Stewards hurried over and stood stock-still, staring at Art's head. Horror dragged down their jaws and narrowed their eyes. It was part of their responsibility at a meeting to stand in the parade ring while the horses were led round before each race, so that they should be both witnesses and adjudicators if anything irregular should occur. Nothing as irregular as a public suicide of a top-notch steeplechase jockey had ever, I imagined, required their attention before.

The elder of them, Lord Tirrold, a tall, thin man with an executive mind, bent over Art for a closer inspection. I saw the muscles bunch along his jaw, and he looked up at me across Art's body and said quietly, "Finn . . . fetch a rug."

I walked twenty steps down the parade ring to where one of the horses due to run in the race stood in a little group with his owner, trainer and jockey. Without a word the trainer took the rug off the horse and held it out to me.

"Mathews?" he said incredulously.

I nodded unhappily and thanked him for the rug, and went back with it.

The other Steward, a sour-tempered hulk named Ballerton, was, I was meanly pleased to see, losing his cherished dignity by vomiting up his lunch.

Mr. Brewar pulled down his unconscious wife's rucked-up skirt and began anxiously to feel her pulse. Corin Kellar kept passing his hand over his face from forehead to chin, still down on one knee beside his jockey. His face was colorless, his hand shaking. He was taking it badly.

I handed one end of the rug to Lord Tirrold and we opened it out and spread it gently over the dead man. Lord Tirrold stood for a moment looking down at the motionless brown shape, then glanced round at the little silent groups of the people who had runners in the race. He went over and spoke to one or two, and presently the stable lads led all the horses out from the parade ring and back to the saddling boxes.

I stood looking down at Corin Kellar and his distress, which I thought he thoroughly deserved. I wondered how it felt to know one had driven a man to kill himself.

There was a click, and a voice announced over the loudspeaker system that owing to a serious accident in the parade ring the last two races would be abandoned. Tomorrow's meeting would be held as planned, it said, and would everyone please go home. As far as the growing crowd of racegoers round the ring was concerned, this might never have been said, for they remained glued to the rails with all eyes on the concealing rug. Nothing rivets human attention as hungrily as a bloody disaster, I thought tolerantly, picking up Art's helmet and whip from the grass.

Poor Art. Poor badgered, beleaguered Art, rubbing out his misery with a scrap of lead.

I turned away from his body and walked thoughtfully back to the weighing room.

While we changed back from riding kit into our normal clothes, the atmosphere down our end of the changing room was one of irreverence covering shock. Art, occupying by general consent the position of elder statesman among jockeys, though he was not actually at thirty-five by any means the eldest, had been much deferred to and respected. Distant in manner sometimes, withdrawn even, but an honest man and a good jockey. His one noticeable weakness, at which we usually smiled indulgently, was his conviction that a lost race was always due to some deficiency in his horse or its training and never to a mistake on his part. We all knew perfectly well that Art was no exception to the rule that every jockey misjudges things once in a while, but he would never admit a fault, and he could put up a persuasive defense every time if called to account.

"Thank the Lord," said Tick-Tock Ingersoll, stripping off his blue-and-black checked jersey, "that Art was considerate enough to let us all weigh out for the race before bumping himself off." Tick-Tock's face emerged from the woolly folds with a wide grin which faded comically when no one laughed.

"Well," he said, dropping his jersey absent-mindedly in a heap on the floor. "If he'd done it an hour ago we'd all have been ten quid out of pocket."

He was right. Our fees for each race were technically earned once we had sat on the scales and been checked out as carrying the correct weight, and they would be automatically paid whether we ran the race or not.

"In that case," said Peter Cloony, "we should put half of it into a fund for his widow." He was a small, quiet young man prone to overemotional, quickly roused and quickly spent bouts of pity both for others and for himself.

"Not ruddy likely," said Tick-Tock, who disliked him openly. "Ten quid's ten quid to me, and Mrs. Art's rolling in it. And snooty with it. Catch me giving her the time of day, you'll be lucky."

"It's a mark of respect," said Peter obstinately, looking round at us with rather damp large eyes and carefully refraining from returning young Tick-Tock's belligerent glare.

I sympathized with Tick-Tock. I needed the money, too. Besides, Mrs. Art had treated me, along with all the other rank-and-file jockeys, with her own particular arctic brand of coolness. Giving her a fiver in Art's memory wouldn't thaw her. Pale, straw-haired, light-eyed, she was the original ice maiden, I thought.

"Mrs. Art doesn't need our money," I said. "Remember how she bought herself a mink coat last winter and used it as a hedge against all of us who didn't measure up to her standards? She hardly knows two of us by name. Let's just buy Art a wreath, and perhaps a useful memorial, something he would have appreciated, like some hot showers in the washroom here."

Tick-Tock's angular young face registered delight. Peter Cloony bent on me a look of sorrowful reproof. But from the others came nods of agreement.

Grant Oldfield said violently, "He probably shot himself because that whey-faced bitch short-changed him in bed."

There was a curious little silence. A year ago, I reflected, a year ago we might have laughed. But a year ago Grant Oldfield would have said the same thing amusingly and perhaps vulgarly, but not with this ugly, unsmiling venom.

I was aware, we all were, that he didn't know or care a jot about the private practices of Art's marriage; but in the past months Grant had seemed more and more to be consumed by some inner rage, and lately he could scarcely make the most commonplace remark without in some way giving vent to it. It was caused, we thought, by the fact that he was going down the ladder again without ever having got to the top. He had always been ambitious and ruthless in character, and had developed a riding style to match. But at the vital point when he had attracted public attention with a string of successes and had begun to ride regularly for James Axminster, one of the very top trainers, something had happened to spoil it. He had lost the Axminster job, and other trainers booked him less and less. The race we had not run was his only engagement that day.

Grant was a dark, hairy, thickset man of thirty, with high cheekbones and a wide-nostriled nose bent permanently out of shape. I endured a great deal more of his company than I would have liked because my peg in the changing room at nearly all race courses was next to his, since both our kits were looked after by the same racecourse valet. He borrowed my things freely without asking first or thanking afterward and, if he had broken something, denied he had used it. When I first met him I had been amused by his pawky humor but two years later, by the day Art died, I was heartily sick of his thunderous moods, his roughness, and his vile temper.

Once or twice in the six weeks since the new season had begun I had found him standing with his head thrust forward looking round him in bewilderment, like a bull played out by a matador. A bull exhausted by fighting a piece of cloth, a bull baffled and broken, all his magnificent strength wasted on something he could not pin down with his horns. At such times I could pity Grant all right, but at all others I kept out of his way as much as I could.

Peter Cloony, paying him no attention as usual, indicated the peg on which Art's everyday clothes hung, and said, "What do you think we had better do with these?"

We all looked at them, the well-cut tweed suit neatly arranged on a hanger, with the small grip which contained his folded shirt and underclothes standing on the bench beneath. His almost obsessive tidiness was so familiar to us that it aroused no comment, but now that he was dead I was struck afresh by it. All the others hung up their jackets by the loop at the back of the neck, hooked their braces onto the pegs, and piled their other clothes into the tops of their trousers. Only Art had insisted on a hanger, and had provided his valet with one to bring for him.

Before we had got any further than an obscene suggestion from Grant, a race-course official threaded his way down the changing room, spotted me, and shouted, "Finn, the Stewards want you."

"Now?" I said, standing in shirt and underpants.

"At once." He grinned.

"All right." I finished dressing quickly, brushed my hair, walked through the weighing room, and knocked on the Stewards' door. They said to come in, and in I went.

All three Stewards were there, also the clerk of the course and Corin Kellar. They were sitting in uncomfortable-looking, straight-backed chairs around a large, oblong table.

Lord Tirrold said, "Come along in and close the door."

I did as he said.

He went on: "I know you were near Mathews when he . . . er . . . shot himself. Did you actually see him do it? I mean, did you see him take the pistol out and aim it, or did you look at him when you heard the shot?"

"I saw him take out the pistol and aim it, sir," I said.

"Very well. In that case the police may wish to take a statement from you; please do not leave the weighing-room building until they have seen you. We are waiting now for the inspector to come back from the first-aid room."

He nodded to dismiss me, but when I had my hand on the door-knob he said, "Finn . . . do you know of any reason why Mathews should have wished to end his life?"

I hesitated a fraction too long before I turned round, so that a plain "No" would have been unconvincing. I looked at Corin Kellar, who was busy studying his fingernails.

"Mr. Kellar might know," I said noncommittally.

The Stewards exchanged glances. Mr. Ballerton, still pallid from his bout of sickness by Art's body, made a pushing-away gesture with his hand, and said, "You're not asking us to believe that Mathews killed himself merely because Kellar was dissatisfied with his riding?" He turned to the other Stewards. "Really," he added forcefully, "if these jockeys get so big for their boots that they can't take a little well-earned criticism, it is time they looked about for other employment. But to suggest that Mathews killed himself because of a few hard words is irresponsible mischief."

At that point I remembered that Ballerton himself owned a horse which Corin Kellar trained. "Dissatisfied with his riding"—the colorless phrase he had used to describe the recent series of acrimonious post-race arguments between Art and the trainer suddenly seemed to me a deliberate attempt at oiling troubled waters. You know why Art killed himself, I thought: you helped to cause it, and you won't admit it.

I shifted my gaze back to Lord Tirrold and found him regarding me with speculation.

"That will be all, Finn," he said.

"Yes, sir," I said.

I went out and this time they did not call me back, but before I had crossed the weighing room the door opened again and shut and I heard Corin's voice behind me.

"Rob."

I turned round and waited for him.

"Thanks very much," he said sarcastically, "for tossing that little bomb into my lap."

"You had told them already," I said.

"Yes, and just as well."

He still looked shocked, his thin face deeply lined with worry. He was an exceptionally clever trainer, but a nervous, undependable man who offered you lifelong friendship one day and cut you dead the next. Just then, it appeared, he needed reassurance.

He said, "Surely you and the other jockeys don't believe Art killed himself because . . . er . . . I had decided to employ him less? He must have had another reason."

"Today was supposed to be his last as your jockey in any case, wasn't it?" I said.

He hesitated and then nodded, surprised at my knowing what had not been published. I didn't tell him that I had bumped into Art in the car park the evening before, and that Art, bitterly despairing and smarting from a corroding sense of injustice, had lowered the customary guard on his tongue enough to tell me that his job with Kellar was finished.

I said only, "He killed himself because you gave him the sack, and he did it in front of you to cause you the maximum amount of remorse. And that, if you want my opinion, is that."

"But people don't kill themselves because they've lost their jobs," he said, with a tinge of exasperation.

"Not if they're normal, no," I agreed.

"Every jockey knows he'll have to retire sometime. And Art was getting too old . . . he must have been mad."

"Yes, I suppose so," I said.

I left him standing there, trying to convince himself that he was in no way responsible for Art's death.

Back in the changing room the discussion on what to do with Art's clothes had been ended by his valet's taking charge of them, and Grant Oldfield, I was glad to find, had finished dressing and gone home. Most of the other jockeys had gone also, and the valets were busy tidying up the chaos they had left behind, sorting dirty white breeches into kit bags, and piling helmets, boots, whips and other gear into large wicker hampers. It had been a dry sunny day and for once there was no mud to wash off.

As I watched the quick, neat way they flipped the things into the baskets, ready to take the dirty ones home, clean them and return them laundered and polished on the following day, I reflected that possibly they did deserve the very large fees we had to pay them for the service. I knew I would loathe, after a day of traveling and of dressing jockeys, to have to face those hampers and bags when I reached home; take out the grubby piles and set to work. Ugh.

I had often seen Art paying his valet, counting through a wad of notes. At the height of the season it always amounted to over twenty pounds each week. My own valet, Young Mike (in his middle forties), twitched my helmet up from the bench and smiled at me as he went by. He earned more than most of the dozen or so jockeys he regularly looked after, and decidedly more than I did. But all the same . . . ugh!

Tick-Tock, whistling the latest hit tune between his teeth, sat on the bench and pulled on a pair of very fancy yellow socks. On top of those went smooth, slim-toed shoes reaching up to the ankle bone. He shook down the slender legs of his dark tweed trousers (no turnups) and feeling my gaze upon him looked up and grinned at me across the room.

He said, "Look your fill on the 'Tailor and Cutter's dream boy.'"

"My father in his time," I said blandly, "was a Twelve Best Dressed man."

"My grandfather had vicuna linings in his raincoats."

"My mother," I said, dredging for it, "has a Pucci shirt."

"Mine," he said carefully, "cooks in hers."

At this infantile exchange we regarded each other with high good humor. Five minutes of Tick-Tock's company were as cheering as rum punch in a snowstorm, and some of his happy-go-lucky enjoyment of living always rubbed off onto the next man. Let Art die of shame, let the murk spread in Grant Oldfield's soul; surely nothing could be really wrong in the racing world, I thought, while young Ingersoll ticked so gaily.

He waved his hand at me, adjusted his Tyrolean trilby, said, "See you tomorrow," and was gone.

But all the same there *was* something wrong in the racing world. Very wrong. I didn't know what; I could see only the symptoms, and see them all the more clearly, perhaps, since I had been only two years in the game. Between trainers and jockeys there seemed to be an all-round edginess, sudden outbursts of rancor, and an ebbing and flowing undercurrent of resentment and distrust. There was more to it, I thought, than the usual jungle beneath the surface of any fiercely competitive business, more to it than the equivalent of gray-flannel-suit maneuvering in the world of jodhpurs and hacking jackets; but Tick-Tock, to whom alone I had in any way suggested my misgivings, had brushed the whole thing aside.

"You must be on the wrong wavelength, pal," he said. "Look around you. Those are smiles you can see, boy. Smiles. It's an okay life by me."

The last few pieces of kit were disappearing into the hampers and some of the lids were already down. I drank a second cup of sugarless tea, lukewarm, and eyed the moist-looking pieces of fruit cake. As usual it took a good deal of resolution not to eat one. Being constantly hungry was the one thing I did not enjoy about race riding, and September was always a bad time of the year, with the remains of the summer's fat still having to be starved off. I sighed, averted my eyes from the cake, and tried to console myself that in another month my appetite would have shrunk back to its winter level.

Young Mike shouted down the room from the doorway through which he had been staggering with a hamper, "Rob, there's a copper here to see you."

I put down the cup and went out into the weighing room. A middle-aged, undistinguished-looking policeman in a peaked cap was waiting for me with a notebook in his hand.

"Robert Finn?" he asked.

"Yes," I said.

"I understand from Lord Tirrold that you saw Arthur Mathews put the pistol against his temple and pull the trigger?"

"Yes," I agreed.

He made a note; then he said, "It's a very straightforward case of suicide. There won't be any need for more than one witness at the inquest, apart from the doctor, and that will probably be Mr. Kellar. I don't think we will need to trouble you any further." He smiled briefly, shut the notebook, and put it in his pocket.

"That's all?" I asked rather blankly.

"Yes, that's all. When a man kills himself as publicly as this there's no question of accident or homicide. The only thing for the coroner to decide is the wording of his verdict."

"Unsound mind and so on?" I said.

"Yes," he said. "Thank you for waiting, though it was your Steward's idea, not mine. Good afternoon, then." He nodded at me, turned, and walked across toward the Stewards' room.

I collected my hat and binoculars and walked down to the racecourse station. The train was already waiting and full, and the only seat I could find was in a compartment packed with bookmakers' clerks playing cards on a suitcase balanced across their knees. They invited me to join them, and between Luton and St. Pancras I fear I repaid their kindness by winning from them the cost of the journey.

2

The flat in Kensington was empty. There were a few letters from the day's second post in the wire basket on the inner side of the door, and I fished them out and walked through into the sitting room, sorting out the two which were addressed to me.

As usual, the place looked as if it had lately received the attentions of a minor tornado. My mother's grand piano lay inches deep in piano scores, several of which had cascaded to the floor. Two music stands leaned at a drunken angle against the wall with a violin bow hooked onto one of them. The violin itself was propped up in an armchair, with its case open on the floor beside it. A cello and another music stand rested side by side like lovers along the length of the sofa. An oboe and two clarinets lay on a table beside another untidy pile of music, and round the room and on all the bedroom chairs which filled most of the floor space lay a profusion of white silk handkerchiefs, rosin, coffee cups and batons.

Running a practiced eye over the chaos I diagnosed the recent presence of my parents, two uncles and a cousin. As they never traveled far without their instruments, it was safe to predict that the whole circus was within walking distance and would return in a very short while. I had, I was thankful to realize, struck the interval.

I threaded a path to the window and looked out. No sign of returning Finns. The flat was at the top of a house two or three streets back from Hyde Park, and across the rooftops I could see the evening sunlight striking on the green dome of the Albert Hall. The Royal Institute of Music, where one of my uncles taught, rose in a solid dark mass beside it. The large airy apartment which was the headquarters of the Finn family was held by my father to be an economy, as it was within walking distance of where so many of them from time to time worked.

I was the odd one out. The talents with which both my parents' families had been lavishly endowed had not descended to me. This had become painfully clear to them when at the age of four I had failed to distinguish between the notes of an oboe and a cor anglais. To the uninitiated there may not seem to be much difference, but my father happened to be an oboist of international reputation, against whom other oboists were measured. Also, high musical talent, if it exists, is apparent in a child from an extremely early age, earlier than any other form of inborn ability, and at three years (when Mozart began composing) concertos and symphonies made less impression on me than the noise of the men emptying the dustbins.

By the time I was five my shattered parents had reluctantly faced the fact that the child they had bred by mistake (I had caused an important American tour to be canceled) was unmusical. Unmusical, that is, in their pure sense. I was not tone-deaf and soaring flights of melody had drawn from me childish tears, but I never had, and still have not, their complete understanding, intellectual, emotional, technical and spiritual, of the effect of putting certain sounds in certain orders.

My mother never being one to do things by halves, I had henceforth been shuffled off from London between schoolterms to a succession of long holidays on farms, ostensibly for my health, but in reality, I knew later, to free my parents for the complicated and lengthy concert tours in which they were engaged. I grew up into a sort of truce with them, in which it was tacitly agreed that as they had not intended to have a child in the first place, and as he had proved to be less than a (musical) credit to them in the second, the less we saw of each other the better.

They disapproved of my venture into jockeyship for no other reason than that racing had nothing to do with music. It was no use my pointing out that the one thing I had learned on the various holiday farms was how to ride (for I was enough my father's son for farming itself to bore me stiff) and that my present occupation was directly due to their actions in the past. To what they did not want to hear my acute-eared parents were sublimely deaf.

There was still no sign of them down in the street, nor of the uncle who lived with us who played the cello, nor of the visiting uncle and cousin, violin and clarinet.

I opened my two letters. The first informed me that my income tax returns were overdue. I slit the second envelope with a smiling and complacent anticipation of enjoyment, which just shows how often life can get up and slap you when you least expect it. In a familiar childish hand the letter said:

Dearest Rob,

I am afraid this may come as a surprise to you, but I am getting married. He is Sir Morton Henge, who you may have heard of, and he is very sweet and kind and no cracks from you about him being old enough to be my father, etc. I don't think I had better ask you to the reception, do you? Morton doesn't know about you and you will be a great dear not to let on to anybody about us, if you don't mind. I shall never forget you, dearest Rob, and all the sweet times we had together. Thank you for everything, and good-by.

Your loving Paulina

Sir Morton Henge, middle-aged widower and canning tycoon. Well, well. I wondered sardonically how his serious-minded son, whom I knew slightly, would enjoy the prospect of a cuddly twenty-year-old model girl for a stepmother. But being in a lopsided way able to laugh at Paulina's catch made it no less of a blow.

In the eighteen months since I had first met her she had progressed from mousy-haired obscurity to a blonde blossoming on the cover of at least one glossy magazine a week. In the past month her radiant eyes had smiled at me (and eight million other men) from a cigarette advertisement in every underground station in London. I had known that it was inevitable that one day she would forsake me if she struck gold in her profession, and our whole relationship had from the start been based on that assumption; but a future without her happy inanity and her generous love-making seemed all of a sudden more bleak than I had expected.

I went through to my bedroom and, putting down Paulina's letter on the chest of drawers, caught sight of myself in the oval mirror on the wall above it. That is the face, I thought, that she has been pleased to see beside her on her pillow, but which was no match for a title and a canning fortune. Looking objectively at my reflection I noted the black hair, black eyebrows and lashes, brown eyes

. . . not a distinguished face, nor handsome; too thin perhaps. Not bad, not good. Just a face.

I turned away and looked around the little sloping-ceilinged room which had been converted for me from a lumber room when I came home from my travels. There was very little in it; a bed, the chest of drawers, an armchair, and a bedside table with a lamp on it. One picture, an impressionist sketch of racing horses, hung on the wall facing my bed. There were no other ornaments, few books, no clutter. In six years of wandering round the world I had become so used to living with a minimum of possessions that, although I had now occupied this little room on and off for two years, I had amassed nothing to put into it.

A clothes cupboard had been built for me across one end of the room. I opened the door and tried to look at its contents as Paulina must have looked, the twice she had been there. One good dark-gray suit, one evening jacket with black trousers, one hacking jacket, two pairs of gray slacks, and a pair of jodhpurs. I took off the suit I was wearing and hung it at the end of the meager row, a tweed mixture of browns. They were enough for me, those clothes. They covered every situation. Sir Morton Henge probably counted his suits in dozens and had a manservant to look after them. I shrugged my shoulders. There was no profit in this melancholy stocktaking. Paulina was gone, and that was that.

Picking up a pair of black sneakers I shut the cupboard door and changed into jeans and an old checked shirt. That done, I contemplated the desert of time between then and the next day's racing. The trouble with me was that steeplechasing had got into my blood like a drug addiction, so that all the normal pleasures of life, and even Paulina herself, had become merely ways of passing as quickly as possible the hours away from it.

My stomach gave an extra twist, which I would like to have believed was due to romantic desolation at my blasted love life but which I knew very well was only the result of not having eaten for twenty-three hours. Admitting wryly that being jettisoned had not spoiled my appetite, I made for the kitchen. Before I reached it, however, the front door of the flat banged open and in trooped my parents, uncles and cousin.

"Hello, darling," said my mother, presenting a smooth sweet-smelling cheek for a kiss. It was her usual greeting to everyone from impresarios to back-row chorus singers, and when applied to me still utterly lacked any maternal quality. She was not a motherly person in any way. Tall, slender, and immensely chic in a style that looked casual but was the result of much thought and expenditure, she was becoming more and more a "presence" as she approached fifty. As a woman I knew her to be passionate and temperamental; as an artist to be a first-class imterpretive vehicle for the genius of Haydn, whose piano concertos she poured out with magical, meticulous, ecstatic precision. I had seen hardened music critics leave her performances with tears in their eyes. So I had never expected a broad motherly bosom to comfort my childish woes, nor a sock-darning, cakemaking mum to come home to.

My father, who treated me always with polite friendliness, said as a form of greeting, "Did you have a good day?" He always asked. I usually answered briefly yes or no, knowing that he was not really interested.

I said, "I saw a man kill himself. No, it wasn't a good day."

Five heads swiveled toward me.

My mother said, "Darling, what do you mean?"

"A jockey shot himself at the races. He was only six feet away from me. It was a mess." All five of them stood looking at me with their mouths open. I wished I hadn't told them, for it seemed even more horrible in memory than it had done at the time.

But they were unaffected. The cello uncle shut his mouth with a snap, shrugged, and went on into the sitting room, saying over his shoulder, "Well, if you will go in for these peculiar pursuits . . ."

My mother followed him with her eyes. There was a bass twang as he picked up his instrument from the sofa, and as if drawn by an irresistible magnet the others drifted after him. Only my cousin stayed long enough to spare Art a thought, then he too went back to his clarinet.

I listened to them retuning and setting up the music stands. They began to play a jigging piece for strings and woodwind that I particularly disliked. The flat was suddenly intolerable. I went out and down into the street and began to walk.

There was only one place to go if I wanted a certain kind of peace, and I didn't care to go there too often for fear of wearing out my welcome. But it was a full month since I had seen my cousin Joanna, and I needed some more of her company. Need. That was the only word for it.

She opened the door with her usual air of good-humored invitation.

"Well, hello," she said, smiling. I followed her into the big converted mews garage which served her as sitting room, bedroom and rehearsal room all in one. Half of the roof was a sloping skylight, through which the remains of the evening sun still shone. The size and comparative bareness of the room gave it unusual acoustic qualities; if one spoke ordinarily, it was like any other room; if one sang, as Joanna did, there was a satisfying illusion of distance and some good amplification from the concrete walls.

Joanna's voice was deep and clear and resonant. When she liked, in singing dramatic passages, she could color it with the suggestion of graininess, a very effective hint of a crack in the bell. She could have made a fortune as a blues singer; but having been born a true classical Finn, so commercial a use of her talent was out of the question. Instead she preferred songs which to me were unmelodic and unrewarding, though she seemed to be amassing a fair-sized reputation with them among people who enjoyed that sort of thing.

She had greeted me in a pair of jeans as old as my own and a black sweater streaked here and there with paint. On an easel stood a half-finished portrait of a man, with some brushes and paints on a table beside it.

"I'm trying my hand at oils," she said, picking up a brush and making a tentative dab at the picture, "but it's not going very well, damn it."

"Stick to charcoal, then," I said. She had drawn with flowing lines the racing horses which hung in my bedroom, short on anatomy but full of life and movement.

"I'll finish this, at least," she said.

I stood and watched her. She squeezed out some carmine.

Without looking at me she said, "What's the matter?"

I didn't answer. She paused with her brushes in the air and turned and regarded me calmly for some seconds.

"There's some steak in the kitchen," she said.

A mind reader, my cousin Joanna. I grinned at her and went out into the long narrow lean-to where she both took her bath and did her cooking. It was rump steak, thick and dark. I grilled it with a couple of tomatoes and made some French dressing for a lettuce I found already prepared in a wooden bowl. When the steak was done I divided it onto two plates and took the whole lot back to Joanna. It smelled wonderful.

She put down her brush and came to eat, wiping her hands on the seat of her pants.

"I'll say one thing for you, Rob, you cook a mean steak," she said, after her first mouthful.

"Thanks for nothing," I said, with my mouth full.

We ate every scrap. I finished first, and sat back and watched her. She had a fascinating face, full of strength and character, with straight dark eyebrows and, that night, no lipstick. She had tucked her short wavy hair in a no-nonsense style behind her ears, but on top it still curled forward onto her forehead in an untidy fringe.

My cousin Joanna was the reason I was still a bachelor, if one can be said to need a reason at twenty-six years of age. She was three months older than I, which had given her an advantage over me all our lives, and this was a pity, since I had been in love with her from the cradle. I had several times asked her to marry me, but she always said no. First cousins, she explained firmly, were too closely related. Besides which, she added, I didn't stir her blood.

Two other men, however, had done that for her. Both were musicians. And each of them in his turn in a most friendly way had told me how greatly having Joanna for a lover had deepened their appreciation of living, given new impetus to their musical inspiration, opened new vistas, and so on and so on. They were both rather intense brooding men with undeniably handsome faces, and I didn't like hearing what they had to say. On the first occasion, when I was eighteen, I departed in speed and grief to foreign lands, and somehow had not returned for six years. On the second occasion I went straight to a wild party, got thoroughly drunk for the first and only time in my life, and woke up in Paulina's bed. Both adventures had turned out to be satisfying and educational. But they had not cured me of Joanna.

She pushed away her empty plate and said, "Now, what's the matter?"

I told her about Art. She listened seriously and when I had finished she said, "The poor man. And his poor wife . . . Why did he do it, do you know?"

"I think it was because he lost his job," I said. "Art was such a perfectionist in everything. He was too proud . . . He would never admit he had done anything wrong in a race . . . And I think he simply couldn't face everyone's knowing he'd been given the sack. But the odd thing is, Joanna, that he looked as good as ever to me. I know he was thirty-five, but that's not really old for a jockey, and although it was obvious that he and Corin Kellar, the trainer who retained him, were always having rows when their horses didn't win, he hadn't lost any of his style. Someone else would have employed him, even if not one of the top stables like Corin's."

"And there you have it, I should think," she said. "Death was preferable to decline."

"Yes, it looks like it."

"I hope that when your time comes to retire you will do it less drastically," she said. I smiled, and she added, "And just what will you do when you retire?"

"Retire? I have only just started," I said.

"And in fourteen years' time you'll be a second-rate, battered, bitter forty, too old to make anything of your life and with nothing to live on but horsy memories that no one wants to listen to." She sounded quite annoyed at the prospect.

"You, on the other hand," I said, "will be a fat, middle-aged, contralto's understudy, scared stiff of losing your looks and aware that those precious vocal cords are growing less flexible every year."

She laughed. "How gloomy. But I see your point. From now on I'll try not to disapprove of your job because it lacks a future."

"But you'll go on disapproving for other reasons?"

"Certainly. It's basically frivolous, unproductive escapist, and it encourages people to waste time and money on inessentials."

"Like music," I said.

She glared at me. "For that you shall do the washing up," she said, getting to her feet and putting the plates together.

While I did my penance for the worst heresy possible in the Finn family, she went back to her portrait, but it was nearly dusk, and when I brought in a peace offering of some freshly made coffee she gave it up for the day.

"Is your television set working?" I asked, handing her a cup.

"Yes, I think so."

"Do you mind if we have it on for a quarter of an hour?"

"Who's playing?" she asked automatically.

I sighed. "No one. It's a racing program."

"Oh, very well. If you must." But she smiled.

I switched on, and we saw the end of a variety show. I enjoyed the songs of the last performer, a vivacious blonde, but Joanna, technique minded, said her breath control creaked. A batch of advertisements followed, and then the fluttering, urgent opening bars of "The Galloping Major," accompanied by speeded-up superimposed views of horses racing, announced the weekly fifteen minutes of "Turf Talk."

The well-known good-looking face of Maurice Kemp-Lore came on the screen, smiling and casual. He began in his easy charming way to introduce his guest of the evening, a prominent bookmaker, and his topic of the evening, the mathematics involved in making a book.

"But first," he said, "I would like to pay a tribute to the steeplechase jockey, Art Mathews, who died today by his own hand at Dunstable races. Many of you have watched him ride . . . I expect nearly all of you have seen televised races in which he has appeared . . . and you will feel with me a great sense of shock that such a long and successful career should end in a tragedy of this sort. Although never actually champion jockey, Art was acknowledged to be one of the six best steeplechase riders in the country, and his upright incorruptible character has been a splendid example to young jockeys just starting in the game."

Joanna lifted an eyebrow at me, and Maurice Kemp-Lore, neatly finishing off Art's glowing obituary, reintroduced the bookmaker, who gave a clear and fascinating demonstration of how to come out on the winning side. His talk, illustrated with films and animated charts, described the minute-by-minute decisions made daily in a big London starting price office, and was well up to the high standard of all the Kemp-Lore programs.

Kemp-Lore thanked him and rounded off the quarter of an hour with a review of the following week's racing, not tipping particular animals to win but giving snippets of information about people and horses on the basis that there would be more interest in the outcome of a race if the public already knew something of the background of the contestants. His anecdotes were always interesting or amusing, and I had heard him called the despair of racing journalists since he so often beat them to a good story.

He said finally, "See you all next week at the same time," and "The Galloping Major" faded him out.

I switched off the set. Joanna said, "Do you watch that every week?"

"Yes, if I can," I said. "It's a racing must. It's so full of things one ought not to miss, and quite often his guest is someone I've met."

"Mr. Kemp-Lore knows his onions, then?" she said.

"He does indeed," I said. "He was brought up to it. His father rode a Grand National winner back in the thirties and is now a big noise on the National Hunt Committee; which," I went on, seeing her blank look, "is the ruling body of steeplechasing."

"Oh. And has Mr. Kemp-Lore ridden any Grand National winners himself?" she asked.

"No," I said. "I don't think he rides much at all. Horses give him asthma, or something like that. I'm not sure. I only know him by sight. He is often at the races but I have never spoken to him."

Joanna's interest in racing, never very strong, subsided entirely at this point, and for an hour or so we gossiped amicably and aimlessly about how the world wagged.

The doorbell rang. She went to answer it and came back followed by the man whose portrait she was attempting, the second of her two blood stirrers, still stirring away. He put his arm possessively round her waist and kissed her. He nodded to me.

"How did the concert go?" she asked. He played a first violin in the London Symphony Orchestra.

"So-so," he said. "The Mozart B Flat went all right, except that some fool in the audience started clapping after the slow movement and ruined the transition to the allegro."

My cousin made sympathetic noises. I stood up. I did not enjoy seeing them so cozily together.

"Going?" asked Joanna, detaching herself.

"Yes."

"Good night, Rob," he said, yawning. He took off his black tie and loosened the neck of his shirt.

I said politely, "Good night, Brian." And may you rot, I thought.

Joanna came with me to the door and opened it, and I stepped out into the dark cobbled mews and turned to say good-by. She was silhouetted against the warm light in the studio room where Brian, I could see, was sitting down and taking off his shoes.

I said flatly, "Thank you for the steak . . . and the television."

"Come again," she said.

"Yes. Well, good night."

"Good night," she said, and then in an afterthought added, "How is Paulina?"

"She is going to marry," I said, "Sir Morton Henge."

I am not sure what I expected in the way of sympathy, but I should have known.

Joanna laughed.

3

Two weeks after Art died I stayed a night in Peter Cloony's house.

It was the first Cheltenham meeting of the season, and having no car I went down as usual on the race train, carrying some overnight things in a small suitcase. I had been engaged for two races at the meeting, one on each day, and I intended to find a back-street pub whose charges would make the smallest possible dent in my pocket. But Peter, seeing the case, asked me if I was fixed up for the night, and offered me a bed. It was kind of him, for we were not particularly close friends, and I thanked him and accepted.

From my point of view it was an unexciting day. My one ride, a novice hurdler revoltingly called Neddikins, had no chance of winning. His past form was a sorry record of falls and unfinished races. Tailed-off and pulled-up figured largely. I wondered why on earth the owner bothered with the wretched animal, but at the same time rehearsed in advance some complimentary things to say about it. I had long ago discovered that owners hated to be told their horses were useless and often would not again employ a jockey who spoke too much unpalatable truth. It was wiser not to answer the typical question, "What do you think we should do with beautiful Neddikins next?" with an unequivocal "Shoot it."

By working hard from start to finish I managed to wake Neddikins up slightly, so that although we finished plainly last, we were not exactly tailed off. A triumph, I considered it, to have got round at all, and to my surprise this was also the opinion of his trainer, who clapped me on the shoulder and offered me another novice hurdler on the following day.

Neddikins was the first horse I rode for James Axminster, and I knew I had been asked because he had not wanted to risk injury to his usual jockey. A good many rides of that sort came my way, but I was glad to have them. I reckoned if I could gain enough experience on bad horses when nothing much was expected of me, it would stand me in a good stead if ever I found myself on better ones.

At the end of the afternoon I joined Peter and we drove off in his sedate family sedan. He lived in a small village, scarcely more than a hamlet, in a hollow in the Cotswold Hills about twenty miles from Cheltenham. We turned off the main road into a narrow secondary road bordered on each side by thick hedges. It seemed to stretch interminably across bare farmland, but eventually, turning a corner, it came to the edge of the plateau and one could see a whole village spread out in the small valley below.

Peter pointed. "That bungalow down there is where I live. The one with the white windows."

I followed his finger. I had time to see a neatly fenced little garden round a new-looking house before a curve in the road hid it from view. We slid down the hill, rounded several blind corners with a good deal of necessary horn blowing, and at the beginning of the village curled into an even smaller lane and drew up outside Peter's home. It was modern, brick built, and freshly attractive, with neatly edged flower beds and shaved squares of lawn.

Peter's wife opened the white front door and came down the path to meet us. She was, I saw, very soon to have a child. She herself looked hardly old enough to have left school. She spoke shyly.

"Do come in," she said, shaking my hand. "Peter telephoned to say you were coming, and everything is ready."

I followed her into the bungalow. It was extremely neat and clean and smelled of furniture polish. All the floors were covered with mottled soft-blue linoleum, with a few terra-cotta rugs scattered about. Peter's wife, she told me during the evening, had made the rugs herself.

In the sitting room there was only a sofa, a television set, and a dining table with four chairs. The bareness of the room was to some extent disguised by one wall being almost completely covered in photographs. They had been framed by Peter himself and were edged in passe-partout in several different bright colors, so that the effect was gay and cheerful. Peter showed them to me while his wife cooked the dinner.

They were clearly devoted to each other. It showed in every glance, every word, every touch. They seemed very well matched; good-natured, quickly moved to sympathy, sensitive, and with not a vestige of a sense of humor between them.

"How long have you two been married?" I asked, biting into a wedge of cheese.

Peter said, "Nine months," and his wife blushed beguilingly.

We cleared away the dishes and washed them, and spent the evening watching television and talking about racing. When we went to bed they apologized for the state of my bedroom.

"We haven't furnished it properly yet," said Peter's wife, looking at me with anxious eyes.

"I'll be very comfortable indeed," I said. "You are so kind to have had me at all." She smiled happily.

The bedroom contained a bed and a chair only. There was the blue linoleum on the floor, with a terra-cotta rug. A small mirror on the wall, some thin rust-colored curtains at the window, and a hook and two hangers on the back of the door to serve as a wardrobe. I slept well.

In the morning, after breakfast, Peter did a lot of household jobs while his wife showed me round the small garden. She seemed to know every flower and growing vegetable individually. The plants were cherished as thoroughly as the house.

"Peter does most of my housework just now," she said, looking fondly back to the house. "The baby is due in six days. He says I mustn't strain myself."

"He is a most considerate husband," I said.

"The best in the world," she said fervently.

It was because Peter insisted at the last minute on driving down to the village shop to fetch a loaf of bread to save his wife the walk that we started out for Cheltenham later than we had intended.

We wound up the twisty hill too fast for prudence, but nothing luckily was on its way down. At least, it seemed to be lucky until we had streaked across the farmland and were slowing down to approach the turn into the main road. That was when we first saw the tank carrier. It was slewed across the road diagonally, completely blocking the way.

Peter's urgent tooting on the horn produced one soldier, who ambled over to the car and spoke soothingly.

"I'm very sorry, sir, but we were looking for the road to Timberley."

"You turned too soon. It's the next road on the right," said Peter impatiently.

"Yes, I know," said the soldier. "We realized we had turned too soon, and my mate tried to back out again, but he made a right mess of it, and we've hit the hedge on the other side. As a matter of fact," he said casually, "we're ruddy well stuck. My mate's just hitched a lorry to go and ring up our HQ about it."

We both got out of the car to have a look, but it was true. The great unwieldy trailer tank carrier was solidly jammed across the mouth of the narrow lane, and the driver had gone.

Pale and grim, Peter climbed back into his seat with me beside him. He had to reverse for a quarter of a mile before we came to a gateway he could turn the car in; then we backtracked down the long bend-ridden hill, raced through the village and out onto the road on the far side. It led south, away from Cheltenham, and we had to make a long detour to get back to the right direction. Altogether the tank carrier added at least twelve miles to our journey.

Several times Peter said, "I'll be late," in a despairing tone of voice. He was, I knew, due to ride in the first race, and the trainer for whom he rode liked him to report to him in the weighing room an hour earlier. Trainers had to state the name of the jockey who would be riding their horse at least three quarters of an hour before the event; if they took a chance and declared a jockey who had not arrived, and then he did not arrive at all, however good the reason, the trainer was in trouble with the Stewards. Peter rode for a man who never took this risk. If his jockey was not there an hour before the race, he found a substitute; and since Peter was his jockey, the rule was a good one, because he was by nature a last-minute rusher who left no time margin for things to go wrong.

We reached the race course just forty-three minutes before the first race. Peter sprinted from the car park, but he had some way to go and we both knew that he wouldn't do it. As I followed him more slowly and walked across the big expanse of tarmac toward the weighing room I heard the click of the loudspeakers being turned on, and the announcer began to recite the runners and riders of the first race. P. Cloony was not among them.

I found him in the changing room, sitting on the bench with his head in his hands.

"He didn't wait," he said miserably. "He didn't wait. I knew he wouldn't. I knew it. He's put Ingersoll up instead."

I looked across the room to where Tick-Tock was pulling his boots up over his nylon stockings. He already wore the scarlet jersey which should have been Peter's. He caught my eye and grimaced and shook his head in sympathy; but it was not his fault he had been given the ride, and he had no need to be too apologetic.

The worst of it was that Tick-Tock won. I was standing beside Peter on the jockeys' stand when the scarlet colors skated past the winning post, and he made a choking sound as if he were about to burst into tears. He managed not to, but there was a certain dampness about his eyes and his face had changed to a bloodless, grayish white.

"Never mind," I said awkwardly, embarrassed for him. "It's not the end of the world."

It had been unfortunate that we had arrived so late, but the trainer he rode for was a reasonable man, if impatient, and there was no question of his not engaging him in future. Peter did in fact ride for him again that same afternoon, but the horse ran less well than was expected, and pulled up lame. My last glimpse of him showed a face still dragged down in lines of disappointment, and he was boring everyone in the weighing room by harping on the tank carrier over and over again.

For myself, things went slightly better. The novice chaser fell at the water jump, but went down slowly and I suffered nothing but grass stains on my breeches.

The young hurdler I was to ride for James Axminster in the last race on the card had as vile a reputation as his stablemate of the previous day and I had made completing the race my sole target. But for some reason the wayward animal and I got on very well together from the start, and to my surprise, an emotion shared by every single person present, we came over the last hurdle in second place and passed the leading horse on the uphill stretch to the winning post. The odds-on favorite finished fourth. It was my second win of the season, and my first ever at Cheltenham: and it was greeted with dead silence.

I found myself trying to explain it away to James Axminster in the winner's unsaddling enclosure.

"I'm very sorry, sir," I said. "I couldn't help it." I knew he hadn't had a penny on it, and the owner had not even bothered to come to see the horse run.

He looked at me broodingly without answering, and I thought that there was one trainer who would not employ me again in a hurry. Sometimes it is as bad to win unexpectedly as to lose on a certainty.

I unbuckled the girths, pulled the saddle off over my arm, and stood waiting for the storm to break.

"Well, go along and weigh in," he said abruptly. "And when you're dressed I want to talk to you."

When I came out of the changing room he was standing just inside the weighing-room door talking to Lord Tirrold, whose horses he trained. They stopped talking and turned toward me as I went over to them, but I could not see their expressions clearly as they had their backs to the light.

James Axminster said, "What stable do you ride for most?"

I said, "I ride mainly for farmers who train their own horses. I haven't a steady job with a public trainer, but I have ridden for several when they have asked me. Mr. Kellar has put me up a few times." And that, I thought a little wryly, is the true picture of the smallness of the impression I had made in the racing world.

"I have heard one or two trainers say," said Lord Tirrold, speaking directly to Axminster, "that for their really bad horses they can always get Finn."

Axminster grinned back at him. "Just what I did today, and look at the result! How am I going to convince the owner it was as much a surprise to me as it will be to him when he hears about it? I've told him often that the horse is pretty useless." He turned to me. "You have made me look a proper fool, you know."

"I'm sorry, sir," I said again, and meant it.

"Don't look so glum about it. I'll give you another chance; several, in fact. There's a slow old plug you can ride for me on Saturday, if you're not booked already for that race, and two or three others next week. After that . . . we'll see."

"Thank you," I said dazedly. "Thank you very much."

It was as if he had thrust a gold brick into my hands when I had expected a scorpion: if I acquitted myself at all well on his horses, he might use me regularly as a second-string jockey. That would be, for me, a giant step up.

He smiled a warm, almost mischievous smile which crinkled the skin round his eyes and said, "Geranium in the handicap chase at Hereford on Saturday, then. Are you free?"

"Yes," I said.

"And you can do the weight? Ten stone?"

"Yes," I said. I'd need to lose another three pounds in the two days, but starvation had never seemed so attractive.

"Very well. I'll see you there."

"Yes, sir," I said.

He and Lord Tirrold turned away and went out of the weighing room together, and I heard them laugh. I watched them go, the thin angular Lord Tirrold and the even taller trainer, a pair who had between them won almost every important event in the National Hunt calendar.

James Axminster was a big man in every sense. Six-foot-four and solidly bulky, he moved and spoke and made decisions with easy assurance. He had a big face with a prominent nose and a square-looking heavy lower jaw. When he smiled his lower teeth showed in front of the upper ones, and they were good strong teeth, evenly set and unusually white.

His stable was one of the six largest in the country: his jockey, Pip Pankhurst, had been champion for the past two seasons; and his horses, about sixty of them, included some of the best alive. To have been offered a toe hold in this setup was almost as frightening as it was miraculous. If I messed up this chance, I thought, I might as well follow Art into oblivion.

I spent most of the next day running round Hyde Park in three sweaters and a wind cheater and resisting the temptation to drink pints of water to replace what I had sweated off. Some of the other jockeys used dehydrating pills to rid their bodies of fluid (which weighs more than fat and is easier to shift) but I had found, the only time I took some, that they left me feeling almost too weak to ride.

At about six o'clock I boiled three eggs and ate them without salt or bread, and then removed myself hurriedly, for my mother was entertaining some friends at dinner, and the girl who came to cook for us on these occasions was beginning to fill the kitchen with demoralizingly savory smells. I decided to go to the pictures to take my mind off my stomach; but it wasn't a great success as I chose the film somewhat carelessly and found myself watching three men staggering on their parched way through a blazing desert sharing out their rations into ever-dwindling morsels.

After that I went to the Turkish baths in Jermyn Street and spent the whole night there, sweating gently all evening and again when I woke in the morning. Then I went back to the flat and ate three more boiled eggs, which I no longer cared for very much, and at last made my way to Hereford.

The needle quivered when I sat on the scales with the lightest possible saddle and thin boots. It swung up over the ten-stone mark and pendulumed down and finally settled a hairsbreadth on the right side.

"Ten stone," said the clerk of the scales in a surprised voice. "What have you been doing? Sandpapering it off?"

"More or less." I grinned.

In the parade ring James Axminster looked at the number boards where the weights the horses carried were recorded, if they differed from those printed in the race cards. He turned back to me.

"No overweight?" he asked.

"No, sir," I said matter-of-factly, as if it were the easiest thing in the world.

"Hm." He beckoned the lad who was leading round the slow old plug I was to ride and said, "You'll have to kick this old mare along a bit. She's lazy. A good jumper, but that's about all."

I was used to kicking lazy horses. I kicked, and the mare jumped: and we finished third.

"Hm," said Axminster again as I unbuckled the girths. I took my saddle and weighed in—half a pound lighter—and changed into the colors of the other horse I had been engaged to ride that afternoon, and when I walked out into the weighing room, Axminster was waiting for me. He had a paper in his hand. He gave it to me without a word.

It was a list of five horses running in various races during the following week. Against each horse's name he had put the weight it had to carry and the race it was to run in. I read through them.

"Well?" he said. "Can you ride them?"

"I can ride four of them," I said. "But I'm already booked for that novice chase on Wednesday."

"Is it important? Can you get off?" he asked.

I would dearly have liked to say yes. The paper I held was an invitation to my personal paradise, and there was always the chance that if I refused one of his mounts, the man who got it might corner all the future ones.

"I . . . no," I said, "I ought not to. It's for the farmer who gave me my first few rides . . ."

Axminster smiled faintly, the lower teeth showing in front. "Very well. Ride the other four."

I said, "Thank you, sir. I'd be glad to." He turned away, and I folded up the precious list and put it in my pocket.

My other ride later that afternoon was for Corin Kellar. Since Art's death he had employed several different jockeys and moaned to them about the inconvenience of not having a first-class man always on call. As it was his treatment of Art that had driven a first-class man to leave him in the most drastic possible way, Tick-Tock and I considered him a case for psychiatry; but both of us were glad enough to ride his horses, and Tick-Tock had ridden more of them than anyone else.

"If Corin asks you," I said as we collected our saddles and helmets ready to weigh out for the race, "will you accept Art's job?"

"If he asks me, yes," said Tick-Tock. "He won't harass *me* into the hereafter." He looked up slantwise from under his rakishly tilted eyebrows, the thin-lipped, wide mouth stretched in a carefree grin. A vivid, almost aggressive sanity molded the angular planes of his face, and for a moment he seemed to me more than ever to have been born too soon. He was what I pictured twenty-first-century man should be—intensely alive, curiously innocent, with no taint of apathy or anger or greed. He made me feel old. He was nineteen.

We went out together to the parade ring.

"Paste on a toothy leer," he said. "The eye of the world has swiveled our way."

I glanced up. From its drafty platform a television camera swung its square snout toward us as it followed the progress of a gray horse round the ring. It tracked briefly over us and moved on.

"I'd forgotten we were on the air," I said indifferently.

"Oh, yes," said Tick-Tock, "and the great man himself is here somewhere too, the one and only M. Kemp-Lore no less. Puff pastry, that man is."

"How do you mean?" I asked.

"A quick riser. And full of hot air. But rich, man, and tasty. A good crisp flavor, nice and crunchy."

I laughed. We joined Corin and he began to give us both our instructions for the race. Tick-Tock's mount was a good one, but I was as usual riding a horse of whom little was expected, and quite rightly, as it turned out. We trailed in a long way behind, and I saw from the numbers going up in the frame that Corin's other horse had won.

Corin and Tick-Tock and the horse's owner were conducting a mutual admiration session in the winner's enclosure when I walked back to the weighing room with my saddle, but Corin caught me by the arm as I went past and asked me to come straight out again, when I had dumped my saddle and helmet, to tell him how the horse had run.

When I rejoined him he was talking to a man who had his back toward me. I hovered, not wanting to interrupt, but Corin saw me and beckoned, and I walked across to them. The man turned round. He was in his early thirties, I judged. Of average height and slim build, with good features and light hair. It never ceases to be disconcerting, meeting for the first time in the flesh a man whose face is as familiar to you as a brother's. It was Maurice Kemp-Lore.

Television is unflattering to everybody. It fattens the body and flattens the personality, so that to sparkle from the small screen an entertainer must be positively incandescent in real life, and Kemp-Lore was no exception. The charm which came over gradually in his program was instantly compelling when one met him. Intensely blue eyes looked at me from a firm, sun-tanned face; his handshake was quick and strong; his smile, infectious and warm, indicated his delight in meeting me. But it was a professional delight, and even as I responded to him I recognized that the effect he had on me was calculated. His stock in trade. All good interviewers know how to give people confidence so that they expand and flower, and Kemp-Lore was a master of his art. Dull men had shone as wits on his program, taciturn men chattered, bigoted men thought again.

"I see you were last in the race," he said. "Bad luck."

"Bad horse," said Corin, put into smiling good humor by his presence.

"I've been waiting for some time to do a program on—if you'll forgive me—an unsuccessful jockey." His smile took the sting out of his words. "Or at least, a jockey who is not yet successful. Perhaps that would be a fairer way of putting it?" His blue eyes twinkled. "Would you consider coming on my program and telling viewers what sort of life you lead? I have in mind your financial position, your reliance on chance rides, insecurity—that sort of thing. Just to give the public the reverse side of the coin. They know all about big retainers, and fat presents, and jockeys who win important races. I want to show them how a jockey who seldom wins even unimportant races manages to live. A jockey on the fringe." He smiled his warm smile. "Will you do it?"

"Yes," I said, "certainly. But I'm not really typical. I—"

He interrupted me. "Don't tell me anything now," he said. "I know enough about your career to find you suitable for what I have in mind, but I always prefer not to know the answers to my specific questions until we are actually on the air. It makes the whole thing more spontaneous. I have found that if I rehearse with my subject what we are going to say, the program comes over stiffly and unconvincingly. Instead, I will send you a list of the sort of questions I will be asking, and you can think out your replies. Okay?"

"Yes," I said. "All right."

"Good. Next Friday then. The program goes out at nine o'clock. Get to the studios by seven-thirty, will you? That gives time for seeing to lighting, makeup, and so on, and perhaps for a drink beforehand. Here is a card which will tell you how to get there." He produced a card which had UNIVERSAL TELECAST printed in large capitals on one side and a simplified map of Willesden on the other.

"Oh, and by the way, there will be a fee, of course, and your expenses." He smiled sympathetically, letting me know that he knew that that was good news.

"Thank you." I smiled back. "I'll be there."

He spoke a word to Corin and strolled away. I turned to Corin and caught on his face, as he watched the retreating figure of Kemp-Lore, the same expression that I saw so often on hangers-on round my parents. The smug, fawning smirk which meant I am on speaking terms with a famous person, clever me. It would have been more impressive, I thought, if like most other trainers he had taken knowing the illustrious Kemp-Lore entirely for granted.

"I know Maurice quite well," said Corin aloud, in a self-satisfied voice. "He asked my advice about whether you'd be any good as his —er—unsuccessful jockey, and I told him to go ahead."

"Thanks," I said, as he waited for it.

"Yes, a grand fellow, Maurice. Good family, you know. His father won the National—an amateur of course—and his sister is the best lady point-to-point rider there has been for years. Poor old Maurice, though, he hardly rides at all. Doesn't even hunt. Horses give him the most ghastly asthma, you know. He's very cut up about it. Still, he'd never have taken to broadcasting if he'd been able to race, so perhaps it's all for the best."

"I dare say," I said. I was still in lightweight silk colors and breeches and the afternoon was growing cool. I dragged the conversation back to the horse I had just come last on, got the post-mortem over, and eventually went back to the weighing room to change.

The jockeys had already gone out for the last race, but several others were standing about in various stages of undress, gossiping and putting on their street clothes. As I went down the room I saw Grant Oldfield standing by my peg, holding a paper in his hand, and on drawing nearer I was annoyed to find that it was the list of horses James Axminster had given me. Grant had been going through my pockets.

My protest was never uttered. Without a word, without any warning, Grant swung his fist and punched me heavily on the nose.

4

The amount of blood which resulted would have done credit to a clinicful of donors. It splashed in a scarlet stain down the front of my pale-green silk shirt and made big uneven blotches on the white breeches. There were large spots of it on the bench and on the floor and it was all over my hands where I had tried to wipe it out of my mouth.

"For God's sake, lay him down on his back," said one of the valets, hurrying over. His advice was almost unnecessary, since I was already lying down, mostly on the floor but half propped up by the leg of the bench. It was where that one blow, catching me off balance, had felled me.

Grant stood at my feet, looking down as if surprised to have caused so much mess. I could have laughed if I had not been so busy swallowing what seemed like cupfuls of my own blood.

Young Mike thrust a saddle under my shoulders and pushed my head backward over it. A second later he was piling a cold, wet towel across the bridge of my nose; and gradually the breath-clogging bleeding lessened and stopped.

"You'd better stay there for a bit," said Mike. "I'll go and get one of the first-aid men to see to you."

"Don't bother," I said. "Please don't bother, it's all right now."

He came back irresolutely from the door and stood by my head. He looked upside down to me, as my eyes were level with his ankles.

"What the hell did you do that for?" he said to Grant.

I wanted to hear his answer too, but Grant did not reply. He scowled down at me, then turned on his heel and pushed his way out of the changing room against the incoming tide of the jockeys returning from the last race. The list of Axminster horses fluttered to the floor in his wake. Mike picked it up and put it into my outstretched hand.

Tick-Tock dumped his saddle on the bench, tipped back his helmet, and put his hands on his hips.

"What have we here? A bloodbath?" he said.

"Nosebleed," I said.

"You don't say."

The others began crowding round and I decided I'd been lying down long enough. I lifted the towel off my face and stood up gingerly. All was well. The fountains had dried up.

"Grant socked him one," said one of the jockeys who had been there all the time.

"Why?"

"Ask me another," I said. "Or ask Grant."

"You ought to report it to the Stewards."

"It's not worth it," I said.

I cleaned myself up and changed, and walked down to the station with Tick-Tock.

"You must know why he hit you," he said. "Or was it merely target practice?"

I handed him Axminster's list. He read it and gave it back.

"Yes, I see. Hatred, envy and jealousy. You're stepping into the shoes he couldn't fill himself. He had his chance there, and he muffed it."

"What happened?" I asked. "Why did Axminster drop him?"

"I don't honestly know," Tick-Tock said. "You'd better ask Grant and find out what mistakes not to make." He grinned. "Your nose looks like a vulgar seaside postcard."

"It's good enough for the goggle box," I said. I told him about Maurice Kemp-Lore's invitation.

"My dear sir," he said, sweeping off his Tyrolean hat and making me a mocking bow, "I am impressed."

"You're a fool," I said, grinning.

"Thank God."

We went our ways, Tick-Tock to his digs in Berkshire and I to Kensington. The flat was empty, the usual state of affairs on Saturday evenings, a busy night for concerts. I took half the ice cubes from the refrigerator, wrapped them in a plastic bag and a tea towel, and lay down on the bed with the ice bag balanced on my forehead. My nose felt like a jelly. Grant's fist had had the power of severe mental disturbance behind it.

I shut my eyes and thought about them, Grant and Art; two disintegrated people. One had been driven to violence against himself, and the other had turned violent against the world. Poor things, I thought rather too complacently, they were not stable enough to deal with whatever had undermined them: and I remembered that easy pity, later on.

On the following Wednesday Peter Cloony came to the races bubbling over with happiness. The baby was a boy, his wife was fine, everything was rosy. He slapped us all on the back and told us we didn't know what we were missing. The horse he rode that afternoon started favorite and ran badly, but it didn't damp his spirits.

The next day he was due to ride in the first race, and he was late. We knew before he arrived that he had missed his chance, because five minutes before the deadline for declaring jockeys his trainer had sent an official into the changing room to find out if he was there, and he wasn't.

I was standing outside the weighing room when Peter finally came, forty minutes before the first race. He was running over the grass, anxiety clear on his face even from a distance. His trainer detached himself from the group of people he had been talking to and intercepted him. Fragments of angry remarks floated across to me.

"Is this your idea of an hour before the first? . . . I've had to get another jockey . . . very stupid of you . . . second time in a week . . . irresponsible . . . not the way to go on if you want to keep your job with me." He stalked away.

Peter brushed past me, white, trembling and looking sick, and when I went back into the changing room a short time later he was sitting on a bench with his head in his hands.

"What happened this time?" I asked. "Is your wife all right? And the baby?" I thought he must have been so busy attending to them that he had forgotten to watch the clock.

"They're fine," he said miserably. "My mother-in-law is staying with us to look after them. I wasn't late setting out . . . only five minutes or so . . . but—" he stood up and gazed at me with his large, moist-looking eyes "—you'll never believe it, but there was something else stuck across the lane, and I had to go miles round again, even farther than last time . . ." His voice trailed off as I looked at him in disbelief.

"Not another tank carrier?" I asked incredulously.

"No, a car. An old car, one of those heavy old Jaguars. It had its nose in the hedge and one front wheel in the ditch, and it was jammed tight, right across the lane."

"You couldn't have helped its driver push it straight again?" I asked.

"There wasn't any driver. No one at all. And the car doors were locked, and the hand brake was full on, and he'd left the thing in gear. The stinking bastard." Peter seldom used such strong language. "Another man had driven up the hill behind me and we both tried to shift the Jag, but it was absolutely hopeless. We had to reverse again for miles, and he had to go first, and he wouldn't hurry a yard . . . he had a new car and he was afraid of scratching it."

"It's very bad luck," I said inadequately.

"Bad luck!" he repeated explosively, apparently near to tears. "It's more than bad luck, it's—it's awful. I can't afford . . . I need the money." He stopped talking and swallowed several times, and sniffed. "We've got a big mortgage to pay off," he said, "and I didn't know babies could cost so much. And my wife had to stop working, which we hadn't reckoned on . . . we didn't mean to have a baby so soon."

I remembered vividly the new little bungalow with its cheap blue linoleum, its homemade terra-cotta rugs, its bare, bare furnishings. And he had a car to run and now a child to keep. I saw that the loss of a ten-guinea riding fee was a calamity.

He had not been booked for any other ride that afternoon, and he spent the whole day mooching about the weighing room so as to be under the eye of any trainers looking hurriedly for a jockey. He wore a desperate, hunted look all the time, and I knew that that alone would have discouraged me had I been a trainer. He left, unemployed and disconsolate, just before the fifth race, having done himself no good at all in the eyes of every trainer at the meeting.

I watched him trailing off to the car park as I walked down from the weighing room to the parade ring for my own one and only ride of the day, and I felt a surge of irritation against him. Why couldn't he pretend a little, make light of his misfortune, shrug it off? And why above all didn't he leave himself a margin for error on his journeys, when unprompt arrivals cost him so much? A punctured tire, a windscreen shattered by a flying stone, anything might make him late. It didn't have to be as unforeseeable as a tank carrier or a locked Jaguar wedged immovably across his path. And what a dismal coincidence, I reflected, that it should have happened twice in a week.

James Axminster smiled his disconcerting, heavy-jawed smile in the parade ring and introduced me to the owner of the horse I was to ride. He shook hands and we made the usual desultory pre-race conversation. The middle-aged handicap hurdler plodding sleepily round the ring was the third Axminster horse I had ridden during the week, and I had already grown to appreciate the sleekness and slickness of his organization. His horses were well schooled and beautifully turned out, and there was nothing makeshift or second best in any of his equipment. Success and prosperity spoke from every brightly initialed horse rug, every top quality bridle, every brush, bandage and bucket that came to the meetings.

In the two earlier races that week I had been riding the stable's second string while Pip Pankhurst took his usual place on the better horses. Thursday's handicap hurdle, however, was all my own because Pip could not do the weight.

"Anything under 10 stone 6, and it's yours," he told me cheerfully, when he found I was riding some of his stable's horses. "Anything under 10.6 is hardly worth riding, anyway."

By eating and drinking very little I had managed to keep my riding weight down to 10 stone for a whole week. This meant a body weight of 9 stone 8, which was a strain at my height, but with Pip in that ungrudging frame of mind it was well worth it.

James Axminster said, "At the fourth hurdle, you want to be somewhere in the middle. About three from home, providing they're not too strung out, you want to lie about fourth. He takes some time to get into top gear, so start him moving going into the second last. Keep him going, try to come up to the leader at the last and see how much you can gain in the air there. This horse is a great jumper, but has no finishing speed. Very one-paced. See what you can do, anyway."

He had not given me such detailed instructions before, and it was the first time he had mentioned anything about what to do at the last obstacle. I felt a deep quiver of excitement in my stomach. At last I was about to ride a horse whose trainer would not be thoroughly surprised if he won.

I followed my instructions to the letter, and coming into the last hurdle level with two other horses I kicked my old mount with all the determination I could muster. He responded with a zipping leap which sped him clean past the other horses in mid-air and landed us a good two lengths clear of them. I heard the clatter of the hurdles as the others rapped them, and basely hoped they had made stumbling, time-wasting landings. It was true that the old hurdler could not quicken. I got him balanced and ran him straight to the winning post, using my whip hardly at all and concentrating mainly on sitting still and not disturbing him. He held on gamely, and still had half a length in hand when we passed the post. It was a gorgeous moment.

"Well done," said Axminster matter-of-factly. Winners were nothing out of the ordinary to him. I unbuckled the girths and slid the saddle off over my arm, and patted the hurdler's sweating neck.

The owner was delighted. "Well done, well done," he said to the horse, Axminster and me indiscriminately. "I never thought he'd pull it off, James, even though I took your advice and backed him."

I looked quickly at Axminster. His piercingly blue eyes regarded me quizzically.

"Do you want the job?" he asked. "Second to Pip, regular?"

I nodded and dragged in a deep breath, and said, "Yes." It sounded like a croak.

The hurdler's owner laughed. "It's Finn's lucky week. John Ballerton tells me Maurice is interviewing him on his television program tomorrow evening."

"Really?" Axminster said. "I'll try and watch it."

I went to weigh in and change, and when I came out Axminster gave me another list of horses, four of them, which he wanted me to ride the following week.

"From now on," he said, "I don't want you to accept any rides without finding out first if I need you. All right?"

"Yes, sir," I said, trying not to show too much of the idiotic delight I was feeling. But he knew. He was too old a hand not to. His eyes glimmered with understanding and friendliness and promise.

I telephoned to Joanna. "How about dinner? I want to celebrate."
"What?" she asked economically.
"A winner. A new job. All's right with the world," I said.
"You sound as if you've been celebrating already."
"No," I said. "Any drunkenness you can hear in my voice is due to being hit on the head by good luck."
She laughed. "All right then. Where?"
"Hennibert's," I said. It was a small restaurant in St. James's Street with a standard of cooking to match its address, and prices to match both.
"Oh, yes," said Joanna. "Shall I come in my golden coach?"
"I mean it," I said. "I've earned forty pounds this week. I want to spend some of it. And besides, I'm hungry."
"You won't get a table," she said.
"It's booked."
"I'm sold," she said. "I'll be there at eight."

She came in a taxi, a compliment to me as she was a girl who liked walking. She wore a dress I had not seen before, a slender straight affair made of a firm, deep-blue material which moved with a faint shimmer when the light fell on it. Her springy dark hair curved neatly down onto the nape of her neck, and the slanting outward tapering lines she had drawn on her eyelids made her black eyes look bigger and deep-set and mysterious. Every male head turned to look at her as we walked down the room; yet she was not pretty, not eye-catchingly glamorous, not even notably well dressed. She looked . . . I surprised myself with the word . . . intelligent.

We ate avocados with French dressing and boeuf Stroganov with spinach, and late-crop strawberries and cream, and a mushroom and bacon and prune savory. For me, after so many bird-sized meals, it was a feast. We took a long time eating and drank a bottle of wine, and sat over our coffee talking with the ease of a friendship that stretched back to childhood. Most of the time, after so much practice, I could keep my more uncousinly feelings for Joanna well concealed from her; and it was necessary to conceal them because I knew from past experience that if I even approached the subject of love she would begin to fidget and avoid my eyes, and would very soon find a good reason for leaving. If I wanted to enjoy her company, it had to be on her terms.

She seemed genuinely pleased about the James Axminster job. Even though racing didn't interest her, she saw clearly what it meant to me.

"It's like the day the musical director at the Handel Society picked me out of the choir to sing my first recitative. I felt like a pouter pigeon and so full of air that I thought I would need guy ropes to keep my feet on the ground."

"Heady stuff," I agreed. My first elation had settled down to a warm cozy glow of satisfaction. I did not remember ever having felt so content.

I told her about the television program.

"Tomorrow?" she said. "Good, I think I'll be free to watch you. You don't do things by halves, do you?"

I grinned. "This is just the start," I said. I almost believed it.

We walked all the way back to Joanna's studio. It was a clear crisp night, with the stars blazing coldly in the black sky. Depth upon depth of infinity. We stopped in the dark mews outside Joanna's door and looked up.

"They put things into proportion, don't they?" she said.

"Yes." I wondered what it was that she needed to see in proportion. I looked at her. It was a mistake. The uptilted face with starlight reflected in the shadowy eyes, the dark hair tousled again by our walk, the strong line of throat, the jut of breasts close to my arm, they swept me ruthlessly into the turmoil I had been suppressing all evening.

"Thank you for coming," I said abruptly. "Good night, Joanna."

She said, surprised, "Wouldn't you like some more coffee . . . or something?"

Or something. Yes.

I said, "I couldn't eat or drink another thing. Anyway . . . there's Brian . . ."

"Brian's in Manchester, on tour," she said. But it was a statement of fact, not an invitation.

"Oh. Well, all the same, I think I'd better get some sleep," I said.

"All right, then." She was undisturbed. "A lovely dinner, Rob. Thank you." She put her hand for a moment on my shoulder in a friendly fashion and smiled good night. She put the key in her door and opened it and waved briefly to me as I turned and started back down the mews. She shut her door. I swore violently, aloud. It wasn't much relief. I looked up at the sky. The stars went on whizzing round in their courses, uncaring and cold.

5

They gave me what in the Finn family was known as F.I.P. treatment at the Universal Telecast Studios. Fairly Important Person. It meant being met by someone well enough up in the hierarchy of the organization for it to be clear that trouble was being taken, but not so high that he needed to be supported by lieutenants.

My mother was a connoisseur of all the shades between V.I.P. and F.I.P. and invariably noticed every detail of the pains or lack of them taken to make her feel comfortable. Her awareness had rubbed off on to me at a very early age and the whole gambit caused me a lot of quiet amusement when I grew up. Years of being a U.I.P. (Unimportant Person) had only sharpened my appreciation.

I went through the swinging glass doors into the large echoing entrance hall and asked the girl at the reception desk where I should go. She smiled kindly. Would I sit down, she said, gesturing to a nearby sofa. I sat. She spoke into the telephone: "Mr. Finn is here, Gordon."

Within ten seconds a burly young man with freckles and a rising-young-executive navy-blue pin-striped suit advanced briskly from one of the corridors.

"Mr. Finn?" he said expansively, holding out a hand protruding from a snowy gold-linked shirt cuff.

"Yes," I said, standing up and shaking hands.

"Glad to have you here. I am Gordon Kildare, Associate Producer. Maurice is up in the studio running over the last-minute details, so I suggest we go along and have a drink and a sandwich first." He led the way down the corridor he had come from and we turned in through an open door into a small impersonal reception room. On the table stood bottles and glasses and four plates of fat, freshly cut and appetizing-looking sandwiches.

"What will you have?" he asked hospitably, his hands hovering over the bottles.

"Nothing, thank you," I said.

He was not put out. "Perhaps afterward, then?" He poured some whisky into a glass, added soda and raised it to me, smiling. "Good luck," he said. "Is this your first time on television?"

I nodded.

"The great thing is to be natural." He picked up a sandwich with a pink filling and took a squelchy bite.

The door opened and two more men came in. Introduced to me as Dan something and Paul something, they were a shade less carefully dressed than Gordon Kildare, to whom they deferred. They too dug into the sandwiches and filled their glasses, and wished me luck and told me to be natural.

Maurice Kemp-Lore strode briskly in with a couple of sports-jacketed assistants in tow.

"My dear chap," he greeted me, shaking me warmly by the hand. "Glad to see you're here in good time. Has Gordon been looking after you? That's right. Now, what are you drinking?"

"Nothing just now," I said.

"Oh? Oh, well, never mind. Perhaps afterward? You got the list of questions all right?"

I nodded.

"Have you thought out some answers?"

"Yes," I said.

"Good, good. That's fine," he said.

Gordon handed him a well-filled glass and offered him the sandwiches. The assistants helped themselves. It dawned on me that the refreshments provided for the entertainment of visitors probably served all of them as their main evening meal.

Kemp-Lore looked at his watch. "Our other guest is cutting it rather fine." As he spoke the telephone rang. Gordon answered it, listened briefly, said, "He's here, Maurice," and opened the door.

Kemp-Lore went out first, followed by Gordon and either Dan or Paul, who looked very much alike. It was a more impressive welcoming committee than had been accorded me; I smiled to think of what my mother would have said.

A sports-jacketed assistant offered me sandwiches.

"No?" he said. "Oh, well, a lot of people feel like that beforehand. You'll be very hungry afterward." He put two sandwiches carefully together and stretched open his mouth to bite them.

The voice of Kemp-Lore could be heard coming back along the corridor talking with someone who spoke in a harsh voice with a nasal twang. I wondered idly who the other guest would be and whether I knew him. At the doorway Kemp-Lore stood respectfully back to let his guest precede him into the room. My spirits sank. Paunch and horn rims well to the fore, Mr. John Ballerton allowed himself to be ushered in.

Kemp-Lore introduced all the television men to him. "And Rob Finn, of course, you know?" he said.

Ballerton nodded coldly in my direction without meeting my eyes. Evidently it still rankled with him that I had seen him sicking up beside Art's body. Perhaps he knew that I had not kept it a secret from the other jockeys.

"It's time we went up to the studio, I think," Kemp-Lore said, looking inquiringly at Gordon, who nodded.

We all filed out into the corridor, and as I passed the table I noticed the sandwich plates now held nothing but crumbs and a few straggly pieces of cress.

The smallish studio held a chaotic-looking tangle of cameras trailing their thick cables over the floor. At one side there was a shallow carpet-covered platform on which stood three low chairs and a coffee table. A tray with three cups, cream jug and sugar bowl shared the table with three empty balloon brandy glasses, a silver cigarette box, and two large glass ashtrays.

Kemp-Lore took Ballerton and me toward this arrangement.

"We want to look as informal as possible," he said pleasantly. "As if we had just had dinner and were talking over coffee and brandy and cigars."

He asked Ballerton to sit in the left-hand chair and me in the right, and then took his place between us. Set in front and slightly to one side stood a monitor set with a blank screen; and in a semicircle a battery of cameras converged their menacing black lenses in our direction.

Gordon and his assistants spent some time checking their lights, which dazed us with a dazzling intensity for a few moments, and then tested for sound while the three of us made stilted conversation over the empty cups. When he was satisfied, Gordon came over to us.

"You all need makeup," he said. "Maurice, you'll see to yours as usual? Then Mr. Ballerton and Mr. Finn, I'll show you where to go, if you will follow me?"

He led us to a small room off one corner of the studio. There were two girls there in pink coveralls and bright smiles.

"It won't take long," they said, smoothing colored cream into our skins. "Just a little darkener under the eyes . . . that's right. Now powder . . ." They patted the powder on with pads of cotton wool, carefully flicking off the excess. "That's all."

I looked in the mirror. The makeup softened and blurred both the outlines of the face and the texture of the skin. I didn't much care for it.

"You'd look ill on television without it," the girls assured us. "You need makeup to look natural and healthy."

Ballerton frowned and complained as one of them powdered the bald patch on his head. The girl insisted politely. "It'll shine too much otherwise, you see," she said, and went on patting his head with the cotton wool.

He caught me grinning at him and it clearly made him furious, raising a dark flush under the sun-tone makeup. There was no question of his ever sharing a rueful joke at his own expense, and I should have known it. I sighed to myself. This made twice that I had seen him at what he considered a disadvantage, and though I had not meant at all to antagonize him, it seemed that I had made a thorough job of it.

We went back into the studio and Kemp-Lore beckoned to us to take our place in the chairs on the platform.

"I'll just run through the order of the program," he said, "so that you will know what to expect. After the introductory music I am going to talk to you first, John, along the lines we discussed. After that, Rob will tell us what his sort of life entails. We have some film of a race you rode in, Rob, which we are using as an illustration, and I plan to fit that in fairly near the beginning of our talk. It will be thrown on to that screen over there." He pointed.

"For the last few minutes, John will have a chance to comment on what you have said and we might have a final word or two from you. We'll see how it goes. Now, the great thing is to talk naturally. I've explained that too much rehearsal spoils the spontaneity of a program like this, but it means that a lot of the success of the next quarter of an hour depends on you. I'm sure you will both do splendidly." He finished his pep talk with a cheerful grin, and I did in fact feel confidence flowing into me from him.

One of the sports-jacketed assistants stepped onto the shallow platform with a coffee-pot in one hand and a brandy bottle in the other. He poured hot black coffee into the three cups, and put the pot down on the tray. Then he uncorked the brandy and wetted the bottom of the balloon glasses.

"No expense spared," he said cheerfully. He produced three cigars from the breast pocket of the sports jacket and offered them to us. Ballerton accepted one and sniffed it and rolled it between his fingers, curving his bad-tempered mouth into what passed with him for a smile.

"Two minutes," shouted a voice.

The spotlights flashed on, dazzling as before, blacking out everything in the studio. For a moment the monitor set showed a close-up of the coffee cups: then it went dark and the next picture on it was an animated cartoon advertising petrol. It was tuned now to what was actually being transmitted.

"Thirty seconds. Quiet please. Quiet please," Gordon said.

A hush fell over the whole area. I glanced at the monitor set in front of us. It was busy with a silent advertisement for soap flakes. Dimly seen beyond the lights, Gordon stood with his hand raised. There was dead silence. Steam rose gently from the three coffee cups. Everyone waited. Kemp-Lore beside me arranged his features in the well-known smile, looking straight ahead at the round black lens of the camera. The smile stayed in position for ten seconds without wavering.

On the monitor set the superimposed horses galloped and faded. Gordon's hand swept down briskly. The camera in front of Kemp-Lore developed a shining red eye and he began to speak, pleasantly, intimately, straight into a million sitting rooms.

"Good evening . . . tonight I am going to introduce you to two people who are both deeply involved with National Hunt racing, but who look at it, so to speak, from opposite poles. First, here is Mr. John Ballerton . . ." He gave him a good build-up but overdid the importance. There were about forty-nine other members of the National Hunt Committee (including Kemp-Lore's own father) all at least as active and devoted as the fat man now basking in praise.

Skillfully guided by Kemp-Lore, he talked about his duties as one of the three Stewards at a race meeting. It involved, he said, hearing both sides if there was an objection to a winner and awarding the race justly to the more deserving, and, yes, summoning jockeys and trainers for minor infringements of the rules and fining them a fiver or a tenner a time.

I watched him on the monitor set. I had to admit he looked a solid, sober, responsible citizen with right on his side. The aggressive horn rims gave him, on the screen, a definite air of authority; also for the occasion his habitually sour expression had given way to a rather persuasive geniality. No one watching the performance Kemp-Lore coaxed out of him would have suspected him to be the bigoted, pompous bully we knew on the race course. I understood at last how he had come to be voted on to the National Hunt Committee.

Before I expected it, Kemp-Lore was turning round to me. I swallowed convulsively. He smiled at the camera.

"And now," he said with the air of one producing a treat, "here is Rob Finn. This is a young steeplechase jockey just scratching the surface of his career. Few of you will have heard of him. He has won no big races, nor ridden any well-known horses, and that is why I have invited him here tonight to meet you, to give us all a glimpse of what it is like to try to break into a highly competitive sport."

The red light was burning on the camera pointing at me. I smiled at it faintly. My tongue stuck to the roof of my mouth.

"First," he went on, "here is a piece of film which shows Finn in action. He is the rider with the white cap, fourth from last."

We watched on the monitor set. I was all too easy to pick out. It was one of the first races I ever rode in, and my inexperience showed sorely. During the few seconds the film lasted the white cap lost two places, and as an illustration of an unsuccessful jockey it could not have been bettered.

The film faded out and Kemp-Lore said, smiling, "How did you set about starting to be a jockey, once you had decided on it?"

I said, "I knew three farmers who owned and trained their own horses, and I asked them to let me try my hand in a race."

"And did they?"

"Yes, in the end," I agreed. I could have added, "After I had promised to return the riding fees and not even ask for expenses"; but the method I had used to persuade a string of farmers to give me rides was strictly against the rules.

"Usually," Kemp-Lore said, turning toward the camera, which immediately glowed with its red eye, "jumping jockeys either start as amateur steeplechase riders or as apprentices on the flat, but I understand that you did neither of these things, Rob?"

"No," I said. "I started too old to be an apprentice and I couldn't be an amateur because I had earned my living riding horses."

"As a stable lad?" He put it in the form of a question but from his intonation he clearly expected me to say yes. It was, after all, by far the commonest background of jockeys riding as few races as I had been doing.

"No," I said.

He was waiting for me to go on, his eyebrows a fraction raised in a tinge of surprise mingled with what looked like the beginning of apprehension. Well, I thought in amusement, you wouldn't listen when I said I was hardly typical, so if my answers are not what you expect, it's entirely your own fault.

I said, "I was away from England for some years, wandering round the world, you know. Mainly in Australia and South America. Most of the time I got jobs as a stockman, but I spent a year in New South Wales working as a hand in a traveling rodeo. Ten seconds on the bucking bronc; that sort of thing." I grinned.

"Oh." The eyebrows rose another fraction, and there was a perceptible pause before he said, "How very interesting." He sounded as if he meant it. He went on: "I wish we had more time to hear about your experiences, but I want to give viewers a picture of the economics of a jockey in your position . . . trying to make a living on a race or two a week. Now, your fee is ten guineas a time, that's right? . . ."

He took me at some length through my finances, which didn't sound too good when dissected into traveling expenses, valets' fees, replacement of kit and so on. It emerged quite clearly that my net income over the past two years was less than I could have earned driving a delivery van, and that my future prospects were not demonstrably much better. I could almost feel the thought clicking into the viewers' heads that I was a fool.

Kemp-Lore turned deferentially to Ballerton. "John, have you any comment to make on what we have been hearing from Rob?"

A trace of purely malicious pleasure crept into Ballerton's man-of-authority smile.

"All these young jockeys complain too much," he stated in his harsh voice, ignoring the fact that I had not complained at all. "If they aren't very good at their job they shouldn't expect to be highly paid. Race-horse owners don't want to waste their money and their horses' chances by putting up jockeys in whom they have no confidence. I speak as an owner myself, of course."

"Eh . . . of course," said Kemp-Lore. "But surely every jockey has to make a start? And there must always be large numbers of jockeys who never quite reach the top grade, but who have a living to make, and families to support."

"They'd be better off in a factory, earning a fair wage on a production line," said Ballerton, with heavy, reasonable-sounding humor. "If they can't endure the fact that they are unsuccessful without sniveling about how poor they are, they ought to get out of racing altogether. Not many of them do," he added with an unkind chuckle, "because they like wearing those bright silks. People turn to look at them as they go by, and it flatters their little egos."

There was a gasp somewhere out in the dark studio at this ungentlemanly blow below the belt, and I saw out of the corner of my eye that the red spot on the camera pointing at me was glowing. What expression it had initially caught on my face I did not know, but I raised a smile for Mr. Ballerton then, as sweet and cheerful and forgiving a smile as ever turned the other cheek. It was made easier by the certain knowledge that wearing bright shirts was if anything an embarrassment to me, not a gratification.

Kemp-Lore's head switched to me. "And what do you say to that, Rob?"

I spoke truthfully, vehemently, and straight from the heart. "Give me a horse and a race to ride it in, and I don't care if I wear silks or . . . or . . . pajamas. I don't care if there's anyone watching or not. I don't care if I don't earn much money, or if I break my bones, or if I have to starve to keep my weight down. All I care about is racing . . . racing . . . and winning, if I can."

There was a small silence.

"I can't explain it," I said.

Both of them were staring at me. John Ballerton looked as if a squashed wasp had revived and stung him, and his earlier animosity settled and deepened into a scowl. And Kemp-Lore? There was an expression in his face that I could not read at all. There were only a few empty seconds before he turned smoothly back to his camera and slid the familiar smile into place, but I felt irrationally that something important had taken place in them. I found it oddly disturbing not to have the slightest clue to what it was.

Kemp-Lore launched into his usual review of the following week's racing, and was very soon closing the program with the customary words: "See you all next week at the same time."

The image on the monitor faded on Kemp-Lore's smile and changed to another soap advertisement. The hot spotlight flicked off and my eyes began to get used to not being dazzled.

Gordon strode up beaming. "A very good program. It came over well. Just what they like, an argument with an edge to it. Well done, well done, Mr. Ballerton, Mr. Finn. Splendid." He shook us both by the hand.

Kemp-Lore stood up and stretched and grinned around at us all. "Well, John. Well, Rob. Thank you both very much." He bent down, picked up my brandy glass and handed it to me. "Drink it," he said, "you deserve it." He smiled warmly. He crackled with released tension.

I smiled back and drank the brandy, and reflected again how superlative he was at his job. By encouraging Ballerton to needle me he had drawn from me, for the ears of a few million strangers, a more soul-baring statement than I would ever have made privately to a close friend.

A good deal of backslapping followed, and more plates of sandwiches were dealt with downstairs in the reception room before I left the television building and went back to Kensington. In view of the approval which had been generously, if undeservedly, heaped upon Ballerton and me after the show, I wondered why it was that I felt more apprehensive than I had before it started.

6

Three weeks and a day after the broadcast, Pip Pankhurst broke his leg. His horse, falling with him and on him at the last hurdle of the second race on a dreary, drizzly mid-November Saturday afternoon, made a thorough job of putting the champion jockey out of action for the bulk of the steeplechasing season.

The first-aid men beside the hurdle were slow to move him into the ambulance for the good reason that a sharp arrow of shinbone was sticking out at a crazy angle through a tear in the thin leather racing boot; and they finally managed to lift him onto a stretcher, one of them told me later, only because Pip slid off into a dead faint.

From the stands I saw only the white flag waving, the ambulance creeping down over the bumpy ground, and the flat, ominously unmoving figure of Pip on the ground. It would be untrue to say that I went down the stairs to the weighing room with a calm heart. However sincere my pity for his plight might be, the faint chance that I might take his place in the following race was playing hop, skip, and jump with my pulse.

It was the big race of the day, the big race of the week, a three-mile chase with a substantial prize put up by a firm of brewers. It had attracted a good number of top horses and had been well discussed on the sports pages of all the day's papers. Pip's mount, which belonged to Lord Tirrold, was the rising star of the Axminster stable; a stringy six-year-old brown gelding with nothing much to recommend him at first sight; but intelligent, fast, and a battler. He had all the qualities of a world beater, and his best years lay ahead. At present he was still reckoned "promising." He was called Template.

Stifling hope is a hopeless business. As I went into the weighing room I saw James Axminster talking to Pip's close friend, another leading jockey. The jockey shook his head, and across the room I watched his lips say, "No, I can't."

Axminster turned slowly round looking at faces. I stood still and waited. Gradually his head came round and he saw me. He looked at me steadily, pondering, unsmiling. Then his eyes went past me and focused on someone to my left. He came to a decision and walked briskly past me.

Well, what did I expect? I had ridden for him for only four weeks. Three winners. A dozen also-rans. During the past fortnight I had taken digs in the village near his stable and ridden out at exercise on his horses every morning; but I was still the new boy, the unknown, unsuccessful jockey of the television program. I began to walk disconsolately over to the changing-room door.

"Rob," he said in my ear. "Lord Tirrold says you can ride his horse. You'd better tell Pip's valet; he has the colors."

I half turned toward them. They stood together, the two tall men, looking at me appraisingly, knowing they were giving me the chance of a lifetime, but not sure that I was up to it.

"Yes, sir," I said, and went on into the changing room, queerly steadied by having believed that I had been passed over.

I rode better than I had ever done before, but that was probably because Template was the best horse I had ever ridden. He was smooth and steely, and his rocketing spring over the first fence had me gasping; but I was ready for it at the second, and exulted in it at the third; and by the fourth I knew I had entered a new dimension of racing.

Neither Axminster nor Lord Tirrold had given me any orders in the paddock on how to shape the race. They had been too concerned about Pip, whom they had just briefly visited. The sight of his shattered leg had left them upset and preoccupied.

Axminster said only, "Do the best you can, Rob," and Lord Tirrold, unusually tactless for so diplomatic a man, said gloomily, "I put a hundred on Template this morning. Oh, well, it's too late to cancel it, I suppose." Then seeing my rueful amusement he added, "I beg your pardon, Rob. I'm sure you'll do splendidly." But he did not sound convinced.

As the pattern of the race shifted and changed, I concentrated solely on keeping Template lying in about fourth position in the field of twelve runners. To be farther back meant leaving him a lot to do at the end, and to be farther forward meant that one could not see how well or how badly everyone else was going. Template jumped himself into third place at the second-last fence, and was still not under pressure. Coming toward the last I brought him to the outside, to give him a clear view, and urged him on. His stride immediately quickened. He took off so far in front of the fence that for a heartbreaking second I was sure he would land squarely on top of it, but I had underestimated his power. He landed yards out on the far side, collecting himself without faltering and surging ahead toward the winning post.

One of the two horses close in front had been passed in mid-air over the fence. There remained only a chestnut to be beaten. Only. Only the favorite, the choice of the critics, the public and the press. No disgrace, I fleetingly thought, to be beaten only by him.

I dug my knees into Template's sides and gave him two taps with the whip down his shoulder. He needed only this signal, I found, to put every ounce into getting to the front. He stretched his neck out and flattened his stride, and I knelt on his withers and squeezed him and moved with his rhythm, and kept my whip still for fear of disturbing him. He put his head in front of the chestnut's five strides from the winning post, and kept it there.

I was almost too exhausted to unbuckle the saddle. There was a cheer as we went into the unsaddling enclosure, and a lot of smiling faces, and some complimentary things were said, but I felt too weak and breathless to enjoy them. No race had ever before taken so much out of me. Nor given me so much, either.

Surprisingly Lord Tirrold and Axminster were almost subdued.

"That was all right, then," said Axminster, the lower teeth glimmering in a smile.

"He's a wonderful horse," I said fervently.

"Yes," said Lord Tirrold, "he is." He patted the dark sweating neck.

Axminster said, "Don't hang about then, Rob. Go and weigh in. You haven't any time to waste. You're riding in the next race. And the one after."

I stared at him.

"Well, what did you expect?" he said. "Pip's obviously going to be unfit for months. I took you on to ride second to him, and you will stand in for him until he comes back."

Tick-Tock said, "Some people would climb out of a septic tank smelling of lavender."
He was waiting for me to change at the end of the afternoon.
"Six weeks ago you were scrounging rides. Then you get yourself on television as a failure and make it obvious you aren't one. Sunday newspapers write columns about you and your version of the creed gets a splash in the *Times* as well. Now you do the understudy-into-star routine, and all that jazz. And properly, too. Three winners in one afternoon. What a nerve."
I grinned at him. "What goes up must come down. You can pick up the pieces later on."
I tied my tie and brushed my hair, and looked in the mirror at the fatuous smile I could not remove from my face. Days like this don't happen very often, I thought.
"Let's go and see Pip," I said abruptly, turning round.
"Okay," he agreed.
We asked the first-aid men where Pip had been taken, and as they were leaving in any case they gave us a lift to the hospital in the ambulance. It was not until they told us that we realized how seriously the leg was broken.
We saw Pip for only a few moments. He lay in a cubicle in the Casualty Department, a cradle over his leg and blankets up to his chin. A brisk nurse told us he was going to the operating theater within minutes, and not to disturb the patient, as he had been given his pre-med. "But you can say hello," she said, "as you've come."
Hello was just about all we did say. Pip looked terribly pale and his eyes were fuzzy, but he said weakly, "Who won the big race?"
"Template," I said, almost apologetically.
"You?"
I nodded. He smiled faintly. "You'll ride the lot now, then?"
"I'll keep them warm for you," I said. "You won't be long."
"Three bloody months." He shut his eyes. "Three bloody months."
The nurse came back with a stretcher trolley and two khaki-overalled porters, and asked us to leave. We waited outside in the hall, and saw them trundle Pip off toward the open lift.

"He'll be four months at least, with a leg like that," said Tick-Tock. "He might just be ready for Cheltenham in March. Just in time to take back all the horses and do you out of a chance in the Champion Hurdle and the Gold Cup."

"It can't be helped," I said. "It's only fair. And anything can happen before then."

I think Axminster had trouble persuading some of his owners that I was capable of taking Pip's place, because I didn't ride all of the stable's horses, not at first. But gradually as the weeks went by and I seemed to make no unforgivable bloomers, fewer and fewer other jockeys were engaged. I became used to seeing my name continually in the number boards, to riding three or four races a day, to going back to my digs contentedly tired in body and mind, and waking the next morning with energy and eagerness. In some ways, I even became used to winning. It was no longer a rarity for me to be led into the first's enclosure, or to talk to delighted owners, or to see my picture in the sporting papers.

I began earning a good deal of money, but I spent very little of it. There was always the knowledge, hovering in the background, that my prosperity was temporary. Pip's leg was mending.

Tick-Tock and I decided, however, to share the cost of buying a car. It was a secondhand cream-colored Mini-Cooper which did forty miles to the gallon on a long run and could shift along at a steady seventy on the flat, and a friend of Tick-Tock's who kept a garage had recommended it to him as a bargain.

"All we want now are some leopard-skin seat covers and a couple of blondes in the back," said Tick-Tock, as we dusted the small vehicle parked outside my digs, "and we'll look like one of those 'gracious living' advertisements in the *Tatler*." He lifted up the bonnet and took at least his tenth look at the engine. "A beautiful job of design," he said fondly.

Gracious living, good design or not, the little car smoothed our paths considerably, and within a fortnight I could not imagine how we had ever managed without it. Tick-Tock kept it where he lived, seven miles away, near the stable he rode for, and came to collect me whenever Axminster himself was not taking me to meetings in his own car. Race trains came and went without any further support from either of us, as we whizzed homeward through the black December afternoons in our cozy box on wheels.

While the gods heaped good fortune on my head, others fared badly.

Grant had offered neither explanation nor apology for hitting me on the nose. He had not, in fact, spoken one word to me since that day, but as at the same time he had also stopped borrowing my kit, I was not sure that I minded. He withdrew more and more into himself. The inner volcano of violence showed itself only in the stiffness of his body and the tightness of his lips, which seemed always to be compressed in fury. He loathed to be touched, even accidentally, and would swing round threateningly if anyone bumped into him in the changing room. With my peg at most meetings still next to his I had knocked into him several times, for however hard I tried it was impossible in those cramped quarters not to, and the glare he gave me each time was frankly murderous.

It was not only to me that he had stopped speaking. He no longer said much at all. The trainers and owners who still employed him could get him neither to discuss a race beforehand nor explain what had happened afterward. He listened to his orders in silence and left the trainer to draw his own conclusions through his race glasses about how the horse had run. When he did speak, his remarks were laden with such a burden of obscenity that even the hardened inmates of the changing room shifted uncomfortably.

Oddly enough Grant's riding skill had not degenerated with his character. He rode the same rough, tough race as always; but he had, we knew, begun to let out his anger onto his mounts, and twice during November he was called before the Stewards for "excessive use of the whip." The horses in question had each come in from their races with raw red weals on their flanks.

The Oldfield volcano erupted, as far as I was concerned, one cold afternoon in the jockeys' and trainers' car park at Warwick. I was late leaving the meeting as I had won the last race and been taken off to the bar afterward by the elated owner, one of my farmer friends. Tick-Tock had gone to a different meeting, and I had the car. By the time I got there the park was empty except for the Mini-Cooper and another car which was standing almost next to it, and two or three cars farther on down the row.

I went toward the Mini still smiling to myself with the pleasure of this latest win, and I did not see Grant until I was quite close to him. I was approaching the cars from behind, with Grant's on the right of mine. His near hind wheel lay on the grass, surrounded by a collection of implements spilling out of a holdall tool bag. A jack held up the bare axle of his black saloon and he was kneeling beside it with the spare wheel in his hand.

He saw me coming and he saw me smiling, and he thought I was laughing at him for having a puncture. I could actually see the uncontrollable fury rise in his face. He got to his feet and stood rigid, his thickset body hunched with belligerence, the strong shoulders bunching under his coat, his arms hanging down. Then he bent forward and from among the mess of tools picked up a tire lever. He swished it through the air, his eyes on me.

"I'll help you with your puncture, if you like," I said mildly.

For answer he took a step sideways, swung his arm in a sort of backward chop, and smashed the tire lever through the back window of the Mini-Cooper. The glass crashed and tinkled into the car, leaving only a fringe of jagged peaks round the frame.

Tick-Tock and I had had the car barely three weeks. My own anger rose quick and hot and I took a step toward Grant to save my most precious possession from further damage. He turned to face me squarely and lifted the tire lever again.

"Put it down," I said reasonably, standing still. We were now about four feet apart. He told me to do something which is biologically impossible.

"Don't be an ass, Grant," I said. "Put that thing down and let's get on with changing your tire."

"You . . . ," he said, "you took my job."

"No," I said. It was pointless to add more, not least because if he was going to try to hit me I wanted to have all my concentration focused on what he was doing, not on what I was saying.

His eyes were red-rimmed above the high cheekbones. The big nostrils flared open like black pits. With his wild face, his bursting anger, and the upheld quivering tire lever, he was a pretty frightening sight.

He slashed forward and downward at my head.

I think that at that moment he must have been truly insane, for had the blow connected he would surely have killed me, and he couldn't have hoped to get away with it with his car standing there with the wheel off. He was beyond thought.

I saw his arm go up a fraction before it came down, and it gave me time to duck sideways. The lever whistled past my right ear. His arm returned in a backhand, again aiming at my head. I ducked again underneath it, and this time, as his arm swung wide and his body lay open to me, I stepped close and hit him hard with my fist just below his breastbone. He grunted as the wind rushed out of his lungs, and the arm with the tire lever dropped, and his head came forward. I took a half pace to the right and hit him on the side of the neck with the edge of my hand.

He went down on his hands and knees, and then weakly sprawled on the grass. I took the tire lever from his slack fingers and put it with all the other tools into the holdall, and shut the whole thing into the boot of his car.

It was getting very cold and the early dusk was turning colors to black and gray. I squatted beside Grant. He was hovering on the edge of consciousness, breathing heavily and moaning slightly.

I said conversationally, close to his ear, "Grant, why did you get the sack from Axminster?"

He mumbled something I could not hear. I repeated my question. He said nothing. I sighed and stood up. It had been only a faint chance, after all.

Then he said distinctly, "He said I passed on the message."

"What message?"

"Passed on the message," he said, less clearly. I bent down and asked him again, "What message?" His lips moved but he said nothing more.

I decided that in spite of everything I could not just drive off and leave him lying there in the cold. I took out the tools again, and sorting out the brace, put the spare wheel on and tightened up the nuts. Then I pumped up the tire, let the jack down and slung it with the punctured wheel into the boot on top of the tools.

Grant was still not properly conscious. I knew I hadn't hit him hard enough to account for such a long semiwaking state, and it occurred to me that perhaps his disturbed brain was finding this a helpful way to dodge reality. I bent down and shook his shoulder and called his name. He opened his eyes. For a split second it seemed as though the old Grant smiled out of them, and then the resentment and bitterness flooded back as he remembered what had happened. I helped him sit up, and propped him against his car. He looked desperately tired, utterly worn out.

"O God," he said. "O God." It sounded like a true prayer, and it came from lips which usually blasphemed without thought.

"If you went to see a psychiatrist," I said gently, "you could get some help."

He didn't answer; but neither did he resist when I helped him into the passenger seat of the Mini-Cooper. He was in no state to drive his own car, and there was no one else about to look after him. I asked him where he lived, and he told me. His car was safe enough where it was, and I remarked that he could fetch it on the following day. He made no reply.

Luckily he lived only thirty miles away, and I drew up where he told me, outside a semidetached, featureless house on the outskirts of a small country town. There were no lights in the windows.

"Isn't your wife in?" I asked.

"She left me," he said absently. Then his jaw tensed and he said, "Mind your own —— business." He jerked the door open, climbed out and slammed it noisily. He shouted, "Take your bloody do-gooding off and —— it. I don't want your help, you ——."

He appeared to be back to his usual frame of mind, which was a pity, but there didn't seem to be any point in staying to hear more so I let in the clutch and drove off: but I had gone only half a mile down the road when I reluctantly came to the conclusion that he shouldn't be left alone in an empty house.

I was at that point in the center of the little town whose brightly lit shops were closing their doors for the day, and I stopped and asked an elderly woman with a shopping basket where I could find a doctor. She directed me to a large house in a quiet side street, and I parked outside and rang the doorbell.

A pretty girl appeared and said, "Surgery at six," and began to close the door again.

"If the doctor is in, please let me speak to him," I said quickly, "it's not a case for the surgery."

"Well, all right," she said and went away. Children's voices sounded noisily somewhere in the house. Presently a youngish, chubby, capable-looking man appeared, munching at a piece of cream-filled cake and wearing the resigned, inquiring expression of a doctor called to duty during his free time.

"Are you by any chance Grant Oldfield's doctor?" I asked. If he wasn't, I thought, he could tell me where else to go.

But he said at once, "Yes, I am. Has he had another fall?"

"Not exactly," I said, "but could you please come and take a look at him?"

"Now?"

"Yes, please," I said. "He . . . er . . . he was knocked out at the races."

"Half a mo," he said and went back into the house, reappearing with his medical bag and another piece of cake. "Can you run me down there? Save me getting my car out again for those few yards."

We went out to the Mini-Cooper and as soon as he sat in it he made a remark about the broken back window, not unreasonably, since gusts of December wind blowing through it were freezing our necks. I told him that Grant had smashed it, and explained how I had come to bring him home.

He listened in silence, licking the cream as it oozed out of the sides of the cake. Then he said, "Why did he attack you?"

"He seems to believe I took his job."

"And did you?"

"No," I said. "He lost it months before it was offered to me."

"Are you a jockey too, then?" he asked, looking at me curiously, and I nodded and told him my name. He said his was Parnell. I started the car and drove the few hundred yards back to Grant's house. It was still in complete darkness.

"I left him here not ten minutes ago," I said as we went up the path to the front door. The small front garden was ragged and uncared for, with rotting dead leaves and mournful grass-grown flower beds dimly visible in the light from the street lamp. We rang the bell. It sounded shrilly in the house, but produced no other results. We rang again. The doctor finished his cake and licked his fingers.

There was a faint rustle in the darkness of the patch of garden. The doctor unclipped from his breast pocket the pen-shaped torch he normally used for peering into eyes and down throats, and directed its tiny beam round the bordering privet hedge. It revealed first some pathetic rosebushes choked with last summer's unmown grass;

but in the corner where the hedge dividing the garden from the next-door one met the hedge bordering the road, the pinpoint of light steadied on the hunched shape of a man.

We went over to him. He was sitting on the ground, huddling back into the hedge, with his knees drawn up to his chin and his head resting on his folded arms.

"Come along, old chap," said the doctor encouragingly, and half helped, half pulled him to his feet. He felt in Grant's pockets, found a bunch of keys, and handed them to me. I went over and unlocked the front door and turned on the lights in the hall. The doctor guided Grant through the hall and into the first room we came to, which happened to be a dining room. Everything in it was covered with a thick layer of dust.

Grant collapsed in a heap on a dining-room chair and laid his head down on the dirty table. The doctor examined him, feeling his pulse, lifting up his eyelid and running both hands round the thick neck and the base of the skull. Grant moved irritably when Parnell's fingers touched the place where I had hit him and he said crossly, "Go away, go away."

Parnell stepped back a pace and sucked his teeth. "There's nothing physically wrong with him as far as I can see, except for what is going to be a stiff neck. We'd better get him into bed and I'll give him something to keep him quiet, and in the morning I'll arrange for him to see someone who can sort out his troubles for him. You'd better give me a ring during the evening if there's any change in his condition."

"I?" I said. "I'm not saying here all evening . . ."

"Oh, yes, I think so, don't you?" he said cheerfully, his eyes shining sardonically in his round face. "Who else? All night too, if you don't mind. After all, you hit him."

"Yes, but," I protested, "that's not what's the matter with him."

"Never mind. You cared enough to bring him home and to fetch me. Be a good chap and finish the job. I do really think someone ought to stay here all night . . . someone strong enough to deal with him in a crisis. It's not a job for elderly female relatives, even if we could rake one up so late in the day."

Put like that, it was difficult to refuse. We took Grant upstairs, balancing his thickset body between us as he stumbled up the treads. His bedroom was filthy. Dirty tangled sheets and blankets were piled in heaps on the unmade bed, dust lay thick on every surface, and soiled clothes were scattered over the floor and hung sordidly over chairs. The whole room smelled of sour sweat.

"We'd better put him somewhere else," I said, switching on lights and opening all the other doors on the small landing. One door led into a bathroom whose squalor defied description. Another opened onto a linen cupboard which still contained a few sheets in a neat pile, and the last revealed an empty bedroom with bright pink rosebuds on the walls. Grant stood blinking on the landing while I fetched some sheets and made up the bed for him. There were no clean pajamas. Dr. Parnell undressed Grant as far as his underpants and socks and made him get into the fresh bed. Then he went downstairs and returned with a glass of water, wearing so disgusted an expression that I knew without being told what state the kitchen must be in.

Opening his case, he shook two capsules onto his hand and told Grant to swallow them, which he docilely did. Grant at this time seemed to be sleepwalking; he was only a shell, his personality a blank. It was disturbing but, on the other hand, it made the business of putting him to bed much easier than it might have been.

Parnell looked at his watch. "I'm late for surgery," he said as Grant lay back on his pillow and shut his eyes. "Those pills ought to keep him quiet for a bit. Give him two more when he wakes up." He handed me a small bottle. "You know where to find me if you want me," he added with a callous grin. "Have a good night."

I spent a miserable evening and dined off a pint of milk I found on the back doorstep. Nothing else in the stinking kitchen was any longer edible. There were no books and no radio, and to pass the hours I made an effort to clean up some of the mess, but what that dreadful house really needed was a breezy spring day, lashings of disinfectant, and an army of strong-minded charwomen.

Several times I went softly in to see how Grant was doing, but he slept peacefully, flat on his back, until midnight. I found him then with his eyes open, but when I went close to him there was no recognition in them. He was still in a withdrawn blank state and he obediently, without a word, swallowed the capsules when I offered them to him. I waited until his eyes had closed again, then I locked his door and went downstairs and eventually fell uneasily asleep myself, wrapped in a traveling rug on a too-short sofa. There was no sound from Grant all night, and when I went up to him at six in the morning he was still sleeping quietly.

Dr. Parnell at least had the decency to release me at an early hour, arriving with a middle-aged male nurse at 7:30 in the freezing dawn. He had also brought a basket packed by his wife, containing eggs, bacon, bread, milk and coffee, and from his medical bag he produced a powerful battery razor.

"All modern conveniences," he said cheerfully, his round face beaming.

So I went back to the races washed, shaved and fed. But, thinking of the husk of a man I left behind me, not in a happy frame of mind.

7

"The trouble is, there's such a shortage of jockeys just now," said James Axminster.

We were on our way to Sandown, discussing whom he should engage to ride for him in the following week when he would be sending horses to two different places on the same day.

"You'd almost think there was a hoodoo on the whole tribe," he said, expertly swinging his large car between a wobbly girl cyclist and an oncoming furniture van. "Art shot himself, Pip's broken his leg, Grant's had a breakdown. Two or three others are out with more ordinary things like busted collarbones, and at least four quite useful chaps took that wretched Ballerton's misguided advice and are now churning out car bodies on assembly lines. There's Peter Cloony . . . but I've heard he's very unreliable and might not turn up in time; and Danny Higgs bets too much, they say, and Ingersoll doesn't always try, so I've been told . . ."

He slowed down while a mother pushed a perambulator and three small children untidily across the road in front of us, and went on talking. "Every time I think I've found a good up-and-coming jockey I seem to hear something to his disadvantage. With you, it was that film, the one they showed on that television program. It was shocking, wasn't it? I watched it and thought, My God, what have I done, asking this clod to ride for me, how ever will I explain it away to the owners?" He grinned. "I was on the point of ringing them all up and assuring them you'd not be on their horses after all. Luckily for you I remembered the way you had already ridden for me and I watched the rest of the program first, and when it had finished I had changed my mind. I had even begun to think I had perhaps struck oil in annexing you. Nothing that has happened since," he glanced at me sideways, smiling, "has led me to alter that opinion."

I smiled back. In the weeks since Pip broke his leg I had come to know him well, and liked him better with every day that passed. Not only was he a superb craftsman at his job and a tireless worker, but he was reliable in other ways. He was never moody; one did not have to approach him circumspectly every time to see if he was in a good or a bad humor because he was always the same, neither boisterous nor irritable, just reasonable and receptive. He said directly what he thought, so that one never had to search for innuendoes or suspect hidden sarcasm, and it made any relationship with him stable and free from worry. He was, on the other hand, in many ways thoroughly selfish. Unless it was a strictly business matter, his own comfort and convenience came first, second and third, and he would do a favor for someone else only if it caused him absolutely no personal sacrifice of time or effort. Even this was often a blessing to his stable lads, since it was typical of him, if the occasion arose, to give them a generous traveling allowance out of his own pocket to visit their homes, rather than go five miles out of his way to drop them on their doorsteps.

He had seemed from the first to be as satisfied with my company as I was with his, and had quite soon told me to drop the "sir" and stick to "James." Later the same week as he drove us back from Birmingham races, we passed some brightly lit posters advertising a concert which was to be held there that evening.

"Conductor, Sir Trelawny Finn," he read aloud, the enormous lettering catching his eye. "No relation, I suppose," he said jokingly.

"Well, yes, as a matter of fact, he's my uncle," I said.

There was a dead silence. Then he said, "And Caspar Finn?"

"My father." A pause.

"Anyone else?"

"Dame Olivia Cottin is my mother," I said matter-of-factly.

"Good God!" he said explosively.

I grinned.

"You keep it very quiet," he said.

"It's really the other way round," I said cheerfully. "They like to keep me quiet. A jockey in the family is a disgrace to them, you see. It embarrasses them. They don't like the connection to be noticed."

"All the same," he said thoughtfully, "it explains quite a lot about you that I had begun to wonder about. Where you got that air of confidence from . . . and why you've said so little about yourself."

I said, smiling, "I'd be very glad . . . James . . . if you'd not let my parentage loose in the weighing room, as a favor to them."

He had said he would not, and he had kept his word, but he had accepted me more firmly as a friend from then on. So when he ran through the reported shortcomings of Peter Cloony, Danny Higgs and Tick-Tock, it was with some confidence that I said, "You seem to have heard a great many rumors. Do you know all these things for a fact?"

"For a fact?" he repeated, surprised. "Well, Peter Cloony definitely missed two races a few weeks back because he was late. That's a fact."

I told him about Peter's atrocious luck in twice finding a vehicle stuck across the mouth of the narrow lane from his village to the main road. "As far as I know," I said, "he hasn't been late since then. His reputation for lateness seems to be built mainly on those two days."

"I've heard several times that he can't be trusted to turn up," said James obstinately.

"Who from?" I asked curiously.

"Oh, I don't know. Corin Kellar, for one. And of course Johnson, who employs him. Ballerton too, though it's against my better judgment to pay too much attention to what he says. It's common knowledge though."

"How about Danny Higgs, then?" I said. Danny was an irrepressible Cockney, tiny in size but ferociously brave.

"He bets too heavily," James said positively.

"Who says so?" I asked. I knew Danny broke the regulations by backing horses, but from what he said in the changing room, it was only in amounts of five or ten pounds, which would cause few trainers to look askance at him.

"Who says? I . . . er . . . Corin," he finished lamely. "Corin, come to think of it, has told me so several times. He says he never puts him up because of it."

"And Tick-Tock?" I said. "Who says Ingersoll doesn't always try?"

He didn't answer at once. Then he said, "Why shouldn't I believe what Corin says? He has no ax to grind. He's an excellent trainer, but he depends as we all do on securing good jockeys. He certainly wouldn't deny himself the use of people like Cloony and Higgs if he didn't have a good reason."

I thought for a few moments, and then said, "I know it's really none of my business, but would you mind very much telling me why you dropped Grant Oldfield? He told me himself that it was something to do with a message, but he wouldn't explain what." I refrained from mentioning that he had been semiconscious at the time.

"A message? Oh, yes, he passed on the message, I couldn't have that."

I still looked mystified. Axminster squeezed through the traffic lights on the amber and glanced sideways at me.

"The message," he said impatiently, "you know, the news. He was passing on the news. If we had a fancied runner, he would tip off a professional backer. The owner of the horse didn't get good odds to his money because the professional was there before him and spoiled the market. Three of my owners were very angry about it—no fun for them having to take two or three to one when they had expected sixes or sevens. So Grant had to go. It was a pity; he was a strong jockey, just what I needed."

"How did you discover that it was Grant passing on the information?"

"Maurice Kemp-Lore found out while he was working on one of those programs of his. Something to do with how professional backers work, I think it was, and he found out about Grant more or less by accident. He told me very apologetically, and just said it would be wiser not to let Grant know too much. But you can't work properly with a jockey and keep secrets from him, it's a hopeless setup."

"What did Grant say when you sacked him?" I asked.

"He denied the whole thing very indignantly. But of course he would. No jockey would ever confess to selling information if he wanted another trainer to take him on."

"Did you talk to the professional backer in question?" I asked.

"Yes, I did, as a matter of fact," he said. "I didn't want to believe it, you see. But it was open and shut. I had to press him a bit, because it didn't reflect well on him, but Lubbock, the professional, did admit that Grant had been tipping off over the telephone, and that he had been paying him ever since he had started to ride for me."

It seemed conclusive enough, but I had an elusive feeling that I had missed something somewhere.

I changed the subject. "Going back to Art," I said, "why was he always having rows with Corin?"

"I don't really know," James said reflectively. "I heard Corin say once or twice that Art didn't ride to orders. Perhaps it was that." He neatly passed two slow lorries on a traffic circle, and glanced at me again. "What are you getting at?"

"It seems to me sometimes that there is too much of a pattern," I said. "Too many jockeys are affected by rumors. You said yourself that there seems to be a hoodoo on the whole tribe."

"I didn't mean it seriously," he protested. "You're imagining things. And as for rumors, what rumor made Art kill himself, or broke Pip's leg, or made Grant sell information? Rumor didn't make Cloony late either."

"Danny Higgs doesn't bet heavily," I said, feeling I was fighting a rearguard action, "and Ingersoll rides as honestly as anyone."

"You can't know about Higgs," he pointed out; "and Ingersoll, let me remind you, was called in before the Stewards last week for easing his mount out of third place. John Ballerton owned the horse and he was very annoyed about it, he told me so himself."

I sighed. Tick-Tock's version was that, since Corin had told him not to overwork the horse, which was not fully fit, he had decided that he ought not to drive the horse too hard just for the sake of finishing third. Better to save the horse's energy for winning next time, he had thought, adopting a view commonly held and acted on by at least half the jockeys and trainers engaged in the sport; but owners and members of the public who had backed the horse for a place were liable to disagree. After the inquiry, changing with the wind as usual, Corin had been heard condemning Tick-Tock for his action.

"I may be quite wrong about it all," I said slowly, "I hope so. Only . . ."

"Only?" he prompted as I paused.

"Only," I finished lightly, "if you ever hear any rumors about me, will you remember what I think . . . and make utterly sure they're true before you believe them?"

"All right," he said, humoring me. "I think it's nonsense, but all right, I'll agree to that." He drove in silence for a while, and then said with an impatient shake of his big head, "No one stands to gain anything by trying to ruin jockeys. It's nonsense. Pointless."

"I know," I said. "Pointless."

We changed the subject.

Christmas came, and during the week before it, when there was no racing, I spent several days in Kensington. My parents greeted me with their usual friendly detachment and left me to my own devices. They were both preoccupied with crowded Christmas schedules, and my mother also spent each morning working at her piano on a new concerto which was to have its first performance in the new year. She started daily at seven punctually, and played, with short interruptions for coffee and thought, until twelve-thirty. I awoke as so often during my life to the sound of warming-up chromatics and wrist-loosening arpeggios, and lay lazily in bed listening to her pick her way phrase by phrase through a dissonant modern score, repeating and repeating each section until she was satisfied she knew it, until the notes flowed easily in their intended order.

I could picture her exactly, dressed for work in a cashmere sweater and ski pants, sitting upright on her special stool, with her head thrust forward as if to hear more from the piano than the notes themselves. She was digging the bones out of the piece, and I knew better than to interrupt her. Digging the bones, the essence, the composer's ultimate intention: and when she had these things firmly in her mind she would begin the process of clothing them with her own interpretation, sharpening the contrasts of mood and tone, until the finished conception emerged clear and shining and memorable.

My mother might not have been a comforting refuge in my childhood nor take much loving interest in me now I was a man, but she had by her example shown me many qualities to admire and value. Professionalism, for instance; a tough-minded singleness of purpose; a refusal to be content with a low standard when a higher one could be achieved merely by working. I had become self-reliant young and thoroughly as a result of her rejection of motherhood, and because I saw the grind behind the gloss of her public performances I grew up not expecting life's plums to be tossed into my lap without any effort from me. What mother could teach her son more?

Joanna's time was tangled inextricably with several performances in different places of the Christmas Oratorio. I managed to hook her only for one chilly morning's walk in the Park, which was not a success from my point of view since Handel easily shoved me into second place for her attention. She hummed bits of the Oratorio continuously from the Albert Gate to the Serpentine, and from the Serpentine to Bayswater Road. There I put her into a taxi and gave her a Christmasy lunch at the Savoy, where she appeared to restrain herself with difficulty from bursting into full song, as the acoustics in the entrance hall appealed to her. I couldn't decide whether or not she was being irritating on purpose, and if she was, why.

She was definitely a great deal less serene than usual, and there was a sort of brittleness in her manner which I didn't like and couldn't understand, until when we were halfway through some excellent mince pies it belatedly occurred to me that she might be unhappy. Unhappiness was not a state I had seen her in before, so I couldn't be sure. I waited until the coffee came, and then said casually, "What's up, Joanna?"

She looked at me, then she looked round the room, then at me again, then at her coffee.

Finally she said, "Brian wants me to marry him."

It wasn't what I expected, and it hurt. I found myself looking down at my own coffee; black and bitter, very appropriate, I thought.

"I don't know what to do," she said. "I was content as we were. Now I'm unsettled. Brian keeps talking about 'living in sin' and 'regularizing the position.' He goes to church a lot now, and he can't reconcile our relationship with his religion. I never thought of it as sinful, just as enjoyable and fruitful and . . . and comfortable. He is talking about buying a house and settling down, and sees me as the complete housewife, cleaning, mending, cooking, and so on. I'm not that sort of person. The thought appalls me. If I marry him, I know I'll be miserable . . ." Her voice trailed off.

"And if you don't marry him?" I asked.

"I'll be miserable then, too, because he refuses to go on as we are. We're not easy together any more. We nearly have rows. He says it's irresponsible and childish not to want to marry at my age, and I say I'll gladly marry him if we live as we do now, with him coming and going from the studio when he likes, and me free to work and come and go as I please too. But he doesn't want that. He wants to be respectable and conventional and . . . and stuffy." The last word came out explosively, steeped in contempt. There was a pause while she stirred her coffee vigorously. There was no sugar in it. I watched the nervous gesture, the long strong fingers with the pink varnished nails gripping the spoon too hard.

"How much do you love him?" I asked painfully.

"I don't know," she said unhappily. "I don't know any more what love is." She looked straight across the little table. "If it means that I want to spend my life attending to his creature comforts, then I don't love him. If it means being happy in bed, then I do."

She saw the movement in my face, and she said abruptly, "Oh, hell, Rob, I'm sorry. It's so long since you said anything . . . I thought you didn't still—"

"Never mind," I said. "It can't be helped."

"What . . . what do you think I should do?" she said after a pause, still fiddling with the coffee spoon.

"It's quite clear," I said positively, "that you should not marry Brian if you can't bear the prospect of the life he intends to lead. It wouldn't work for either of you."

"So?" she said in a small voice.

But I shook my head. The rest she would have to resolve for herself. No advice I could give her would be unbiased, and she must have known it.

She left presently to go to a rehearsal, and I paid the bill and wandered out into the festive streets. I bought some presents for my family on the way, walking slowly back to the flat. The sort of marriage which Joanna had offered Brian, and which he spurned, was what I most wanted in the world. Why, I wondered disconsolately, was life so ruddy unfair.

On Boxing Day Template won the King Chase, one of the ten top races of the year. It put him conclusively into the star class, and it didn't do me any harm either.

The race had been televised, and afterward, as was his custom, Maurice Kemp-Lore interviewed me as the winning jockey before the camera. Toward the end of the brief talk he invited me to say hello directly to Pip, who, he explained to viewers, was watching at home. I had seen Pip only a week or two earlier and had discussed big-race tactics with him, but I obligingly greeted him and said I hoped his leg was mending well. Kemp-Lore smilingly added, "We all wish you a speedy recovery, Pip," and the interview was over.

On the following day the sporting press was complimentary about the race, and a number of trainers I had not yet ridden for offered me mounts. I began to feel at last as though I were being accepted as a jockey in my own right, and not principally as a substitute for Pip. It even seemed likely that when Pip returned to his job I would not fade back into the wilderness, for two of the new trainers said they would put me up on their horses as often as I was free.

I had, of course, my share of falls during this period, for however fortunate I was I couldn't beat the law of averages: but no damage was done except for a few bruises here and there, and none of them was bad enough to stop me riding.

The worst fall from the spectators' point of view happened one Saturday afternoon in January, when the hurdler I was riding tripped over the flight of hurdles nearest to the grandstand and flung me off onto my head. I woke up dizzily as the first-aid men lifted me into the ambulance on a stretcher, and for a moment or two could not remember where I was.

James's face, looming over me as they carried me into the first-aid room, brought me back to earth with a click, and I asked him if his horse was all right.

"Yes," he said. "How about you?"

"Nothing broken," I assured him, having explored my limbs rather drunkenly during the short trip back in the ambulance.

"He rolled on you," he said.

"I'm not surprised." I grinned up at him. "I feel a bit squashed, come to think of it."

I lay for a while on a bed in the first-aid room, but there was nothing wrong with me that a good sleep wouldn't cure, and at the end of the afternoon I went back to Berkshire with James as expected.

"Are you all right?" he asked once, on the way.

"Yes," I said cheerfully. "Fine." Actually I felt dizzy now and then, and also shivery and unsettled, but concealing one's true state of health from trainers was an occupational habit, and I knew I would be fit again to ride on Monday.

The only person who was openly annoyed at the run of good luck I had had was John Ballerton, and I had caught him several times in the parade ring staring tight-lipped at me, with a patent and most unstewardly animosity.

Since the day of our joint broadcast we had exchanged the fewest possible words, but I had heard from Corin, who repeated it to me with sly relish, that Ballerton had said loudly to him and Maurice Kemp-Lore in the members' bar at Kempton, "Finn isn't worth all the fuss that's being made of him. He'll come down just as quickly as he's gone up, you'll see. And I for one won't weep about it."

In view of this it was astonishing that on the day after my fall I should be offered a ride on one of his horses. At first I refused to take Corin seriously. His telephone call woke me on the Sunday morning, and I was inclined to think the concussion had returned.

"If it were a choice between me and a sack of potatoes," I said sleepily, "he'd choose the potatoes."

"No, seriously, Rob, he wants you to ride Shantytown at Dunstable tomorrow." Corin's voice held no trace of humor. "I must say, I don't really understand why, as he's been so set against you before. But he was quite definite on the telephone, not five minutes ago. Perhaps it's an olive branch."

And perhaps not, I thought. My first instinct was to refuse to ride the horse, but I couldn't think of a reasonable excuse, as Corin had found out I was free for the race before he told me whose the horse was. A point-blank excuseless refusal was, while possible, a senseless course. It would give Ballerton a genuine grievance against me, and if he sincerely wanted to smooth over his hostility, which I doubted, I should only deepen it by spurning his offer.

Shantytown was no Template. Far, far from it. His uncertain temper and unreliable jumping were described to me in unreassuring terms by Tick-Tock on the way to Dunstable the following morning.

"A right one," he said, putting his foot down on the Mini-Cooper's accelerator. "A knacker's delight. Dog meat on the hoof."

"His form's not bad," I protested mildly, having looked it up the previous day.

"Hmph. Any time he's won or been placed it's because he's dragged his jockey's arms out of the sockets by a blast-off start and kept right on going. Hang on and hope, that's how to ride him when he's in that mood. His mouth is as hard as Gibraltar. In fact I cannot," finished Tick-Tock with satiric formality, "I cannot instantly recall any horse who is less receptive of his jockey's ideas."

There was no bitterness in his voice, but we were both aware that a few weeks ago riding Shantytown would have been his doubtful pleasure, not mine. Since his parade before the Stewards for not pushing his horse all out into third place, he had been ignored by Corin Kellar. It was the sort of injustice typical of Corin, to sack a man who ran into trouble looking after his interests, and it had done nothing to lay the unfair rumor that Tick-Tock was a habitual nontrier.

Apart from abruptly lessening the number of races he rode in, the rumor had had little effect on Tick-Tock himself. He shrugged his shoulders, and with a determined look on his angular young face stated, "They'll change their minds again in time. I'll mash every horse I ride into a pulp. I'll do my nut on every hopeless hack. No one henceforth will see me finish eighth when by bashing the beast I could be sixth."

I had smiled to hear these fighting words from one whose chief asset was his lightness of touch, but was relieved, too, that he was intact in spirits. No suicides, no mental breakdowns for him.

Shantytown, when it came to the race, was not what I had been led to expect. The damp raw January afternoon had drawn only a small crowd of stalwarts to watch a second-class program at a minor meeting, and as I watched the big chestnut plod round the parade ring I thought how well he matched the circumstances. Uninspiring.

But far from pulling my arms out of their sockets Shantytown seemed to me to be in danger of falling asleep. The start caught him flat-footed, so little interest was he taking in it, and I had to boot him into the first fence. He rose to it fairly well, but was slow in his recovery, and it was the same at every jump. It was puzzling, after what Tick-Tock had said, but horses do have their off days for no discernible reason, and I could only suppose that this was one of them.

We trailed round the entire three miles in the rear of the field, and finished ingloriously last. All my efforts to get him to quicken up the straight met with no response. Shantytown hadn't taken hold of his bit from the beginning, and at the end he seemed to be dead beat.

A hostile reception met us on our return. John Ballerton, with whom I had exchanged coldly polite "Good afternoons" in the parade ring before the race, now glowered like a July thunderstorm. Corin, standing on one leg and wearing an anxious, placatory expression, was obviously going to use me as the scapegoat for the horse's failure, to save his face as its trainer. That was always one of the hazards to be run in riding Corin's horses.

"What the hell do you think you were doing?" Ballerton said aggressively, as I slid off to the ground and began to unbuckle the saddle girths.

"I'm sorry, sir," I said. "He wouldn't go any faster."

"Don't talk such bloody rubbish," he said, "he always goes faster than that. I've never seen a more disgusting display of incompetence. You couldn't ride in a cart with a pig net over it. If you ask me, the horse wasn't given a chance. You missed the start and couldn't be bothered to make it up."

"I did say," said Corin to me reproachfully, "not to let him run away with you, and to keep tucked in behind for the first two miles. But I do think you carried my orders a bit too far—"

"A bit too far!" interrupted Ballerton furiously. "Were you afraid to let him go, or something? If you can't manage to ride a decent race on a horse which pulls, why the hell do you try to? Why not say straight out that you can't? Save us all a lot of time and money."

I said, "The horse didn't pull. There was no life in him."

"Kellar," Ballerton was nearly shouting, "is my horse a puller, or is he not?"

"He is," said Corin, not meeting my eyes.

"And you told me he was fit. On his toes."

"Yes," said Corin. "I thought he'd win."

They looked at me accusingly. Corin must have known that the horse had run listlessly because he had seen the race with experienced eyes, but he was not going to admit it. If I had to ride often for Corin, I thought wryly, I would soon have as many rows with him as Art had had.

Ballerton narrowed his eyes and said to me, "I asked you to ride Shantytown against my better judgment and only because Maurice Kemp-Lore insisted I had been misjudging you and that you were really a reliable man who would ride a genuine race. Well, I'm going to tell him he is wrong. Very wrong. You'll never ride another horse of mine, I promise you that."

He turned on his heel and stalked off, followed by Corin. My chief feeling, as I went back to the weighing room, was of irritation that I hadn't relied on instinct and refused to ride for him in the first place.

By the end of the afternoon the puzzlement I had felt over Shantytown's dead running had changed to a vague uneasiness, for neither of the other two horses I rode afterward did anything like as well as had been expected. Both were well backed, and both finished nearly last, and although their owners were a great deal nicer about it than Ballerton had been, their disappointment was obvious.

On the following day, still at Dunstable, the run of flops continued. I had been booked for three horses, and they all ran badly. I spent the whole depressing afternoon apologetically explaining to owner after owner that I had not been able to make their horses go faster. The third horse, in fact, went so badly that I had to pull him up halfway round. He was a slow jumper on the best of days, but on that particular one he took so long putting himself right and so long starting off again when he landed that the rest of the field was a whole fence ahead by the time we had gone a mile. It was hopeless. When I reined him in he slowed from a reluctant gallop to a walk in a couple of strides, sure sign of a very tired horse. I thought, as he was trained by a farmer-owner who might not know better, that he must have been given too stiff a training gallop on the previous day, but the farmer said he was sure he had not.

Runs of bad luck are commoner in racing than good ones, and the fact that six of my mounts in a row had made a showing far below their usual capabilities would not have attracted much notice had it not been for John Ballerton.

I changed into street clothes after the fifth race and strolled out of the weighing room to find him standing close by with a small circle of cronies. All the heads turned toward me with that sideways assessing look which meant they had been talking about me, and Ballerton said something forceful to them, of which the word "disgrace" floated across clearly.

Jockeys being as accustomed as politicians to abuse, I gave no sign of having heard what had obviously been intended for my ears, and walked casually off to the stands to watch the last race: but I did wonder how long and how maliciously Ballerton would hold Shantytown's failure against me and what effect his complaints would have on the number of horses I was asked to ride. He was not a man to keep his grudges to himself, and as a National Hunt Committee member he was not without influence either.

Up on the stands Maurice Kemp-Lore came across to talk to me. We had met briefly on race courses several times now and were on superficially friendly terms, but in spite of his charm, or perhaps because it sometimes seemed too polished, I felt his friendship came strictly into the professional, "might be useful" category. I did not believe that he liked me for my own sake.

He smiled vividly, the charm turned on to full wattage, his slim figure radiating health and confidence and his blue eyes achieving the near impossible of twinkling on a gray January afternoon. I smiled back automatically: one couldn't help it. All his impressive success stemmed from instantaneous, irresistible feeling of well-being he inspired in whomever he talked to, and there was no one from the Senior Steward down who did not enjoy his company, even if, like me, one suspected his unfailing motive was the gathering of material for his program.

"What bad luck, Rob," he said cheerfully. "I hear the good word I put in for you with John Ballerton has gone awry."

"You can say that again," I agreed. "But thanks for trying, anyway."

The blue eyes glimmered. "Anything to help," he said.

I could hear distinctly a faint high-pitched wheeze as he drew breath into his lungs, and I realized it was the first time I had encountered him in an asthmatic attack. I was vaguely sorry for him.

The horses for the sixth race cantered past, going down to the start.

"Are James's plans fixed for the Midwinter Cup?" he asked casually, his eyes on the horses. I smiled. But he had his job to do, I supposed, and there was no harm in telling him.

"Template runs, all being well," I said.

"And you ride him?"

"Yes," I agreed.

"How is Pip getting along?" he asked, wheezing quietly.

"They think his leg is mending well, but he is still in plaster," I said. "It comes off next week, I believe, and he might be ready for Cheltenham, but of course he won't be fit for the Midwinter."

The race in question was a richly endowed new event at Ascot, introduced to provide a high spot in mid-February, and nicely timed to give three full weeks for recovery and retuning before the Cheltenham Gold Cup. It lay almost a month ahead, on that day at Dunstable, and I was looking forward to it particularly as it seemed possible that it would be my last chance on Template. Pip would do his very best to be fit to ride him in the Gold Cup, and so would I have done in his place.

"What chance do you give Template in the Midwinter?" Maurice asked, watching the start through his race glasses.

"Oh, I hope he'll win," I said, grinning. "You can quote me."

"I probably will," he agreed, grinning back. We watched the race together, and such was the effect of his personality that I left Dunstable quite cheerfully, the dismal two days' results temporarily forgotten.

8

It was a false security. My charmed run of good luck had ended with a vengeance, and Dunstable proved to be only the fringe of the whirlpool. During the next two weeks I rode seventeen horses. Fifteen of them finished in the rear of the field, and in only two cases was this a fair result.

I couldn't understand it. As far as I knew there was no difference in my riding, and it was unbelievable that my mounts should all lose their form simultaneously. I began to worry about it, and that didn't help, as I could feel my confidence oozing away as each disturbing and embarrassing day passed.

There was one gray mare I particularly liked riding because of the speed of her reactions: she often seemed to know what I intended to do a split second before I gave her signals, rather as if she had sized up the situation as quickly as I had and was already taking independent action. She was sweet tempered and silken mouthed, and jumped magnificently. I liked her owner too, a short jolly farmer with a thick Norfolk accent, and while we watched her walk round the parade ring before her race he commiserated with me on my bad luck and said, "Never mind, lad. The mare will put you right. She'll not fail you. You'll do all right on her, never fear."

I went out smiling to the race because I too believed I would do all right on her. But that week she might have been another horse. Same color, same size, same pretty head. But no zip. It was like driving a car with four flat tires.

The jolly farmer looked less jolly and more pensive when I brought her back.

"She's not been last ever before, lad," he said reproachfully.

We looked her over, but there was nothing wrong with her that we could see, and she wasn't even blowing very hard.

"I could get her heart tested, I suppose," the farmer said doubtfully. "Are you sure you gave her her head, lad?"

"Yes," I said. "But she had no enthusiasm at all today."

The farmer shook his head, doleful and puzzled.

One of the horses I rode belonged to a tall sharp-faced woman who knew a great deal about racing and had no sympathy with bunglers. She laid straight into me with her tongue after I had eased her ultraexpensive new gelding from last into second-last place only feet from the winning post.

"I suppose you realize," she said in a loud, hard voice, unashamedly listened to by a large group of racegoers, "that in the last five minutes you had succeeded both in halving the value of my horse and in making me look a fool for having paid a fortune for him."

I apologized. I suggested possibly that her animal needed a little time.

"Time?" she repeated angrily. "For what? For you to wake up? You speak as if it were my judgment that is at fault, not yours. You lay far too far out of your ground. You should have taken closer order from the beginning." Her acid lecture went on and on and on, and I looked at the fine head of her glossy high-bred black gelding and admitted to myself that he was probably a great deal better than he had appeared.

One Wednesday was the big day for a ten-year-old schoolboy with sparkly brown eyes and a conspiratorial grin. His wealthy eccentric grandmother, having discovered that there was no minimum age laid down for race-horse owners, had given Hugo a colossal chestnut steeplechaser twice his height, and was considerate enough to foot the training bills as well.

I had become firm friends with Hugo. Knowing that I saw his horse most mornings at James's, he used to send me tiny parcels containing lumps of sugar filched from the dining table at his prep school, which I conscientiously passed on to their intended destination: and I used to write back to Hugo, giving him quite detailed accounts of how his giant pet was progressing.

On that Wednesday Hugo had not only begged a day off from school to see his horse run, but had brought three friends with him.

The four of them stood with me and James in the parade ring, Hugo's mother being the rare sort who liked her son to enjoy his limelight alone. As I had walked down from the weighing room she had smiled broadly to me from her station on the rails.

The four little boys were earnest and excited, and James and I had great fun with them before the race, treating them with seriousness and as man to man, which they obviously appreciated. This time, I promised myself, this time, for Hugo, I will win. I must.

But the big chestnut jumped very clumsily that day. On the far side of nearly every fence he ducked his head, and once, to prevent myself being hauled over in a somersault, I had to stretch forward down his neck with one hand only, letting go of the reins entirely with the other. The free arm, swinging up sideways, helped to bring my weight far enough back to keep me in the saddle, but the gesture known as "calling a cab" was not going to earn me any bonus points with James, who had denounced it often as the style of "bad, tired, scared or unfit amateurs."

Hugo's little face was pink when I dismounted, and the three friends glumly shuffled their feet behind him. With them as witnesses there would be no chance of Hugo's smoothing over the disaster with the rest of his schoolmates.

"I'm very sorry, Hugo," I said sincerely, apologizing for everything —myself, the horse, the race, and the miserliness of fate.

He answered with a stoicism which would have been a lesson to many of his seniors. "I expect it was an off day," he said kindly. "And anyway, someone always has to be last. That's what Daddy said when I came bottom in history." He looked at the chestnut forgivingly, and said to me, "I expect he's keen really, don't you?"

"Yes," I agreed. "Keen, very."

"Well," said Hugo, turning bravely to the friends, "that's that, then. We might as well have tea."

Failures like these were too numerous to escape anyone's attention, but as the days passed I noticed a change in the way people spoke to me. One or two, and Corin in particular, showed something like contempt. Others looked uncomfortable, others sympathetic, others pitying. Heads turned toward me wherever I went, and I could almost feel the wave of gossip I left in my wake. I didn't know exactly what they were saying, so I asked Tick-Tock.

"Pay no attention," he said. "Ride a couple of winners and they'll be throwing the laurel wreaths again, and backpedaling on everything they're saying now. It's bad-patchville, chum, that's all."

And that was all I could get out of him.

One Thursday evening James Axminster telephoned to my digs and asked me to go up to his house. I walked up in the dark, rather miserably wondering whether he, like two other trainers that day, was going to find an excuse for putting someone else up on his horses. I couldn't blame him. Owners could make it impossible for him to continue with a jockey so thoroughly in the doldrums.

James called me into his office, a square room joining his house to the stable yard. Its walls were covered with racing photographs, bookshelves, a long row of racing colors on clothes hangers, and filing cabinets. A huge roll-top desk stood in front of the window, which looked out onto the yard. There were three broken-springed armchairs with faded chintz covers, a decrepit Turkish carpet on the floor, and a red-hot coal fire in the grate. I had spent a good many hours there in the past three months, discussing past performances and future plans.

James waited for me and stood aside to let me go in first. He followed me in and shut the door, and faced me almost aggressively across the familiar room.

"I hear," he said without preamble, "that you have lost your nerve."

The room was very still. The fire crackled slightly. A horse in a nearby loose box banged the floor with his hoof. I stared at James, and he stared straight back, gravely.

I didn't answer. The silence lengthened. It was not a surprise. I had guessed what was being said about me when Tick-Tock had refused to tell me what it was.

"No one is to blame for losing his nerve," James said noncommittally. "But a trainer cannot continue to employ someone to whom it has happened."

I still said nothing.

He waited for a few seconds, and then went on: "You have been showing the classic symptoms . . . trailing round nearly last, pulling up for no clear reason, never going fast enough to keep warm, and calling a cab. Keeping at the back out of trouble, that's what you've been doing."

I thought about it, rather numbly.

"A few weeks ago," he said, "I promised you that if I heard any rumors about you I would make sure they were true before I believed them. Do you remember?"

I nodded.

"I heard this rumor last Saturday," he said. "Several people sympathized with me because my jockey had lost his nerve. I didn't believe it. I have watched you closely ever since."

I waited dumbly for the ax. During the week I had been last five times out of seven.

He walked abruptly over to an armchair by the fire and sat down heavily.

Irritably he said, "Oh, sit down, Rob. Don't just stand there like a stricken ox, saying nothing."

I sat down and looked at the fire.

"I expected you to deny it," he said in a tired voice. "Is it true, then?"

"No," I said.

"Is that all you've got to say? It isn't enough. What has happened to you? You owe me an explanation."

I owed him much more than an explanation.

"I can't explain," I said despairingly. "Every horse I've ridden in the past three weeks seems to have had its feet dipped in treacle. The difference is in the horses . . . I am the same." It sounded futile and incredible, even to me.

"You have certainly lost your touch," he said slowly. "Perhaps Ballerton is right—"

"Ballerton?" I said sharply.

"He's always said you were not as good as you were made out to be, and that I'd pushed you on too fast . . . given you a top job when you weren't ready for it. Today he has been going round smugly saying, 'I told you so.' He can't leave the subject alone, he's so pleased."

"I'm sorry, James," I said.

"Are you ill, or something?" he asked exasperatedly.

"No," I said.

"They say the fall you had three weeks ago was what frightened you—the day you got knocked out and your horse rolled on you. But you were all right going home, weren't you? I remember you being a bit sore, but you didn't seem in the least scared of falling again."

"I didn't give that fall another thought," I said.

"Then why, Rob, why?"

But I shook my head. I didn't know why.

He stood up and opened a cupboard which contained bottles and glasses, poured out two whiskies, and handed one to me.

"I can't convince myself yet that you've lost your nerve," he said. "Remembering the way you rode Template on Boxing Day, only a month ago, it seems impossible. No one could change as fundamentally in so short a time. Before I took you on, wasn't it your stock in trade to ride all the rough and dangerous horses that trainers didn't want to risk their best jockeys on? That's why I first engaged you, I remember it clearly. And all those years you spent in wherever it was as a stockman, and that spell in a rodeo . . . you aren't the sort of man to lose his nerve suddenly and for nothing, and especially not when you're in the middle of a most spectacularly successful season."

I smiled for almost the first time that day, realizing how deeply I wanted him not to lose faith in me.

I said, "I feel as if I'm fighting a fog. I tried everything I knew today to get those horses to go faster, but they were all half dead. Or I was. I don't know . . . it's a pretty ghastly mess."

"I'm afraid it is," he said gloomily. "And I'm having owner trouble about it, as you can imagine. All the original doubters are doubting again. I can't reassure them . . . it's like a Stock Exchange crash: catching. And you're the bad stock that's being jettisoned."

"What rides can I still expect?" I said.

He sighed. "I don't exactly know. You can have all the Broome runners because he's on a cruise in the Mediterranean and won't hear the rumors for a while. And my two as well; they both run next week. For the rest, we'll have to wait and see."

I could hardly bring myself to say it, but I had to know.

"How about Template?" I asked.

He looked at me steadily. "I haven't heard from George Tirrold," he said. "I think he will agree that he can't chuck you out after you've won so many races for him. He is not easily stampeded, there's that to hope for, and it was he who drew my attention to you in the first place. Unless something worse happens," he finished judiciously, "I think you can still count on riding Template in the

Midwinter a week on Saturday. But if you bring him in last in that . . . it will be the end."

I stood up and drained the whisky.

"I'll win that race," I said; "whatever the cost, I'll win it."

We went silently together to the races the following day, but when we arrived I discovered that two of my three prospective mounts were mine no longer. I had been, in the expressive phrase, jocked off. The owners, the trainer in question brusquely explained, thought they would have no chance of winning if they put me up as planned. Very sorry and all that, he said, but no dice.

I stood on the stands and watched both the horses run well: one of them won, and the other finished a close third. I ignored as best I could the speculative, sideways glances from all the other jockeys, trainers and press men standing near me. If they wanted to see how I was taking it, that was their affair: just as it was mine if I wanted to conceal from them the inescapable bitterness of these two results.

I went out to ride James's runner in the fourth race absolutely determined to win. The horse was capable of it on his day, and I knew him to be a competent jumper and a willing battler in a close finish.

We came last.

All the way round I could barely keep him in touch with the rest of the field. In the end he cantered slowly past the winning post with his head down in tiredness, and mine down too, in defeat and humiliation. I felt ill.

It was an effort to go back and face the music. I felt more like driving the Mini-Cooper at top speed into a nice solid tree.

The freckle-faced lad who looked after the horse deliberately did not glance at me when he took hold of the reins in the paddock. He usually greeted me with a beaming smile. I slid off the horse. The owner and James stood there, their faces blank. No one said anything. There was nothing to say. Finally, without a word, the owner shrugged his shoulders and turned on his heel, and walked off.

I took my saddle off the horse and the lad led him away.

James said, "It can't go on, Rob."

I knew it.

He said, "I'm sorry. I'm very sorry. I'll have to get someone else to ride my horses tomorrow."

I nodded.

He gave me a searching look in which puzzlement and doubt were tinged for the first time with pity. I found it unbearable.

"I think I'll go to Kensington tonight after the races," I said, trying to speak evenly. "Instead of coming back with you."

"Very well," he said, obviously relieved at not having to face an embarrassing return journey. "I really am sorry, Rob."

"Yes," I said. "I know."

I took my saddle back to the weighing room, acutely aware of the glances that followed me. The conversation in the changing room died into an embarrassed silence when I walked in. I went over to my peg, put the saddle on the bench, and began to take off my colors. I looked at the circle of faces turned toward me, reading on some curiosity, on some hostility, on some sympathy, and on one or two pleasure. No contempt; they would leave that to people who didn't ride, to the people who didn't know at first hand how formidable a big fence can look to a jockey on a bad horse. In the changing room there was too much consciousness in their minds of "there but for the grace of God go I" for them to feel contempt.

They began to talk again, but not much to me. I guessed they didn't know what to say. Nor did I.

I felt neither more nor less courageous than I had done all my life. It was surely impossible, I thought confusedly, to be subconsciously afraid, to keep out of trouble, and yet think one was as willing as ever to accept risks. Three weeks earlier I would have laughed at the idea. But the shattering fact remained that none of the twenty-eight horses I had ridden since I had been knocked out in that fall had made any show at all. They were trained by several different trainers and owned by different owners; all they had had in common was me. There were too many of them for it to be coincidence, especially as those I had been removed from had done well.

Round and round in a jumble went the profitless thoughts, the hopeless statistics, the feeling that the sky had fallen. I put on my street clothes and brushed my hair, and was surprised to see in the mirror that I looked the same as usual.

I went to the steps outside the weighing room and heard the normal chatter which my presence had muffled in the changing room break out cheerfully again as soon as I was gone. No one outside seemed very anxious to talk to me, either; no one, that is, except a weedy little ferret of a man, who worked, I knew, for one of the minor sporting papers.

He was standing with John Ballerton, but when he caught sight of me he came directly over.

"Oh, Finn," he said, taking a notebook and pencil out of his pocket and looking at me with a sly, malicious smile. "May I have a list of the horses you are riding tomorrow? And next week?"

I looked across at Ballerton. There was a smirk of triumph on his heavy face. I took a great grip on my rising temper and spoke mildly to the reporter.

"Ask Mr. Axminster," I said. He looked disappointed, but he didn't know how close he had come to feeling my fist in his face. I had just enough sense to know that letting fly at him would be the worst thing I could do.

I strode away from him, seething with rage; but the day had not done with me even yet. Corin, crossing my path purposefully, stopped me and said, "I suppose you've seen this?" He held out a copy of the paper for which the ferrety little man wrote.

"No," I said. "And I don't want to."

Corin smiled thinly, enjoying himself. "I think you ought to sue them. Everyone thinks so. You'll have to sue them when you've read it. You can't ignore it, or everyone will think—"

"Everyone can think what they damn well please," I said roughly, trying to walk on.

"Read it," insisted Corin, thrusting the paper in front of my eyes. "Everyone else has."

It needed only half a glance to see the headline. There was no missing it. In bold type it said NERVE LOST.

Against my will I began to read:

Nerve, depending on how it takes you, is either fear overcome by an effort of will, or a total lack of imagination. If you ride steeplechasing it doesn't matter which sort you have, as long as you have one of them.

Does anyone understand why one man is brave and another is not? Or why a person can be brave at one time and cowardly at another?

Maybe it is all a matter of hormones! Maybe a bang on the head can destroy the chemical makeup which produces courage. Who knows? Who knows?

The crumbling of a jumping jockey's nerve is a pathetic sight, as every recent racegoer will realize. But while one may extend sympathy to a man for a state which he cannot help, one must at the same time ask whether he is doing the right thing if he continues to seek and accept rides in races.

The public deserves a fair run for its money. If a jockey can't give it to them because he is afraid of hurting himself, he is taking fees under false pretenses.

But it is only a matter of time, of course, before owners and trainers withdraw their custom from such a man, and by forcing him into retirement protect the betting public from wasting any more of its money.

And a good thing too!

I gave the paper back to Corin and tried to lessen the clamped tension of my jaw muscles.

"I can't sue them," I said. "They don't mention my name."

He didn't look surprised, and I realized sharply that he had known it all along. He had wanted only the pleasure of watching me read, and there was still about his eyes a remnant of a very nasty smile.

"What did I ever do to you, Corin," I asked, "to make you feel the way you do?"

He looked taken aback, and said weakly, "Er . . . nothing . . ."

"Then I'm sorry for you," I said stonily. "I'm sorry for your spiteful, mean, cowardly little soul."

"Cowardly!" he exclaimed, stung and flushing. "Who are you to call anyone else cowardly? That's a laugh, that really is. Just wait till they hear this. Just wait till I tell—"

But I didn't wait. I had had far, far more than enough. I went back to Kensington in as deep and terrible a mood of despair as I ever hope to have to live through.

There was no one in the flat, and for once it was spotlessly tidy. The family, I concluded, were away. The kitchen confirmed it. There was no food or milk in the refrigerator, no bread in the bin, no fruit in the basket.

Back in the silent sitting room I took a nearly full whisky bottle out of the cupboard and lay down full length on the sofa. I uncorked the bottle and took two large gulps. The neat spirit bit into my gums and scorched down to my empty stomach. I put the cork in the bottle and the bottle on the floor beside me. What is the point of getting drunk, I thought. I'd only feel worse in the morning. I could stay drunk for several days perhaps, but it wouldn't do any good in the end. Nothing would do any good. Everything was finished. Everything was busted and gone.

I spent a long time looking at my hands. Hands. The touch they had for horses had earned me my living all my adult life. They looked the same as always. They were the same, I thought desperately. Nerves and muscles, strength and sensitivity, nothing was changed. But the memory of the last twenty-eight horses I had ridden denied it: heavy, cumbersome and unresponsive.

I knew no other skill but riding, nor had ever wanted any. I felt more than whole on horseback: I felt extended. Four extra limbs and a second brain. More speed, more strength, more courage . . . I winced at the word . . . and quicker reactions. A saddle was to me as the sea to a fish, natural and easy. Home. And a racing saddle? I drew in a breath, shivering. For a racing saddle, I thought bleakly, I am not sufficient.

It wasn't enough, after all, to *want* to race as well as anybody; one had to have the talent and the staying power as well, and I was face to face with the conviction that I was not good enough, that I was never going to be good enough, to take firm hold of the position which had been so nearly in my grasp. I had thought myself capable of seizing the incredible opportunity I had been given. The mess I had made of it, the weak degrading retreat from the brink of success, was tearing to shreds all I had known or believed about myself.

I picked up the whisky bottle and held it on my chest. It was all the company I had, and it offered sleep at least. But I suppose old habits cling hard: I held the bottle to my chest like a life jacket to a drowning man and I knew I wouldn't pull the cork out again. Not for a while. Not that night, anyway.

And what of the future? I could return during the next week and race on one or two of James's horses, if he would still let me, and perhaps even on Template in the Midwinter. But I no longer either expected or hoped to do well, and I could feel myself shrink at the prospect of going back to a race course to face all those stares and insults again. Better to start a new life at once, perhaps. But a new life doing what?

It couldn't be the old life. Being a stockman might have suited me at twenty, but it was not what I would want at thirty, nor at forty, nor at fifty. And whatever I did, wherever I went now, I would drag around with me the knowledge that I had totally failed at what I had tried hardest to do.

After a long time I stood up and put the bottle back in the cupboard.

It was then a good twenty-six hours since I had eaten, and despite everything my stomach was beginning its squeezing routine. On a second inspection the kitchen revealed only some assorted tins of escargots, cheese straws, and marrons glacés; so I went out and along the streets until I came to a decent-looking pub where I was sure I was not known by sight. I didn't want to have to talk.

I ordered ham sandwiches and a glass of beer, but when the food came the thick new white bread stuck tastelessly in my mouth and my throat kept closing convulsively against all attempts to swallow. This can't go on, I thought. I've got to eat. If I can't get drunk and I can't have Joanna and I can't . . . I can't be a jockey any more . . . at least I can eat now as much as I like, without worrying about gaining a pound or two . . . but after ten minutes' trying I had swallowed only two mouthfuls, and I couldn't manage another bite.

The fact that it was Friday had meant nothing to me all evening, and the approach of nine o'clock went unnoticed. But just when I had pushed away the sandwiches and was eyeing the beer with the beginnings of nausea, someone turned up the volume of the television set which stood at one end of the bar, and the opening bars of "The Galloping Major" suddenly blared out across the tinkling glasses and the buzzing voices. A large bunch of devotees who had settled themselves with full pint pots in front of the set made shooshing noises to those nearest to them, and by the time Maurice Kemp-Lore's tidy features materialized there was a more or less attentive audience to receive him. My little glass-topped table was as far as it could be from the door, so that it was more because leaving meant weaving my way through the sprawling silent crowd than from a positive desire to watch that I stayed where I was.

"Good evening," Maurice said, the spellbinding smile in place. "This evening we are going to talk about handicapping, and I have here to meet you two well-informed men who look at weights and measures from opposing angles. The first is Mr. Charles Jenkinson, who has been an official handicapper for several years." Mr. Jenkinson's self-conscious face appeared briefly on the screen. "And the other is the well-known trainer, Corin Kellar." Corin's thin face glowed with satisfaction. We'll never hear the last of this, I thought: and then with a stab remembered that I wouldn't be there to hear any of it.

"Mr. Jenkinson," said Maurice, "will explain how he builds a handicap. And Mr. Kellar will tell you how he tries to avoid having his horses defeated by their weights. The battle between handicappers and trainers is none the less fierce for being conducted in gentlemanly and largely uncomplaining reticence, and perhaps tonight you will capture a whiff of that unrelenting struggle." He smiled engagingly. "A handicapper's pinnacle of success is for every single runner in a race to pass the winning post in a straight line abreast—a multiple dead-heat—since it is his aim to give each horse an exactly equal chance. It never actually happens, but handicappers dream about it in their softer moments." He grinned sideways in a friendly fashion toward his guest, and when Mr. Jenkinson appeared on the screen one could almost see the self-confidence begin to flow in him as he started to talk about his job.

I listened with only half my mind, the rest being submerged in persistent misery, and Corin had been speaking for some moments before I paid much attention to him. He was being of necessity less than frank, since the bald truth would have lost him his license very smartly. In practice he felt no qualms at all when giving his jockey orders to start at the back and stay there, but in theory, I was sardonically amused to see, he was righteously on the side of the angels.

"Horses from my stable are always doing their best to win," he said, lying without a tremor.

"But surely you don't insist on them being ridden hard at the end when they've no chance at all?" said Maurice reasonably.

"As hard as necessary, yes," Corin asserted. "I hate to see jockeys easing up too soon, even if they are beaten. I dismissed a jockey a short while ago for not riding hard enough at the end. He could have come third if he had ridden the horse out . . ." His voice droned on, pious and petulant, and I thought of Tick-Tock, thrown to the Stewards for obeying his orders too conscientiously and now having trouble getting other trainers to trust him. I thought of Art, nagged and contradicted and driven to death; and the active dislike I already felt for Corin Kellar sharpened in that dim pub corner into hatred.

Maurice dragged him back to handicapping and finally wrung from him a grudging admission that from the point of view of the weight he would be allotted in future, it was better for a horse to win by one length than by ten. Maurice would have done better, I thought, to have chosen almost anyone else to show how to dodge the handicapper; or perhaps he did not know Corin well enough to expect him hypocritically to deny in public what he had said in private. Every jockey who had ridden the Kellar horses had learned it the hard way.

"One is always in the hands of one's jockey," Corin was saying.

"Go on," said Maurice encouragingly, leaning forward. A light somewhere in the studio lent his eyes a momentary shimmer as he moved.

Corin said, "You can slave away for weeks preparing a horse for a race and then a jockey can undo it all with one stupid mistake."

"It does the handicap good though," Maurice interrupted, laughing. The pub audience laughed too.

"Well . . ." agreed Corin, nonplused.

"If you look at it that way," Maurice continued, "there is always some compensation for a jockey's not getting the most out of a horse. Whatever the reason; trivial, like a mistake, or more serious, like a failure of resolution at a crucial point—"

"No guts, you mean?" said Corin flatly. "I'd say that that would be as obvious to a handicapper as to everyone else, and that he'd take it into account. There's a case in point now . . ." he hesitated, but Maurice did not try to stop him, so he went on more boldly, "a case now where everything a certain jockey rides goes round at the back of the field. He is afraid of falling, you see. Well, you can't tell me any handicapper thinks those particular horses are not as good as they were. Of course they are. It's just the rider who's going downhill."

I could feel the blood rush to my head and begin to pulse there. I leaned my elbows on the table and bit my knuckle. Hard.

The voices went on inexorably.

Maurice said, "What are your views on that, Mr. Jenkinson?"

And the handicapper, looking embarrassed, murmured that "Of course . . . er . . . in certain circumstances, one would er . . . overlook the occasional result."

"Occasional!" said Corin. "I wouldn't call nearly thirty races in a row occasional. Are you going to overlook them all?"

"I can't answer that," protested Jenkinson.

"What do you usually do in these cases?" Maurice asked.

"I . . . that is . . . they aren't usually as blatant as this. I may have to consult . . . er, others, before coming to a decision. But it really isn't a thing I can discuss here."

"Where better?" said Maurice persuasively. "We all know that this poor chap took a toss three weeks ago and has ridden . . . ineffectively . . . ever since. Surely you'd have to take that into account when you are handicapping those horses?"

While the camera focused on Jenkinson hesitating over his answer Corin's voice said, "I'll be interested to know what you decide. One of those horses was mine, you know. It was a shocking exhibition. Finn won't be riding for me again, or for anyone else either, I shouldn't wonder."

Jenkinson said uneasily, "I don't think we should mention names," and Maurice cut in quickly, saying, "No, no. I agree. Better not." But the damage was done.

"Well, thank you both very much for giving up your time this evening. I am sorry to say we have come nearly to the end once again . . ." He slid expertly into his minute of chitchat and his closing sentences, but I was no longer listening. Between them he and Corin had hammered in the nails on the ruins of my brief career, and watching them at it on the glaring little screen had given me a blinding headache.

I stood up stiffly as the chatter broke out again in the crowded pub and threaded my way a little unsteadily to the door. The bunch of racing enthusiasts were downing their pints and I caught a scrap of their conversation as I squeezed round them.

"Laid it on a bit thick, I thought," one of them said.

"Not thick enough," contradicted another. "I lost a quid on Finn on Tuesday. He deserves all he gets, if you ask me, the windy bastard."

I stumbled out into the street, breathing in great gulps of cold air and making a conscious effort to stand up straight. It was no use sitting down and weeping in the gutter, which would have been easy enough to do. I walked slowly back to the dark empty flat, and without switching on any lights lay down fully dressed on my bed.

The glow from the street below dimly lit the small room, the window frame throwing an angular distorted shadow on the ceiling. My head throbbed. I remembered lying there like that before, the day Grant's fist pulped my nose. I remembered pitying him, and pitying Art. It had been so easy. I groaned aloud, and the sound shocked me.

It was a long way down from my window to the street. Five stories. A long, quick way down. I thought about it.

There was a chiming clock in the flat below ours, counting away the quarter hours, and in the quiet house I could hear it clearly. It struck ten, eleven, twelve, one, two.

The window threw its shadow steadily on the ceiling. I stared up at it. Five stories down. But however bad things were I couldn't take that way, either. It wasn't for me. I shut my eyes and lay still, and finally after the long despairing hours drifted into an exhausted, uneasy, dream-filled sleep.

I woke less than two hours later, and heard the clock strike four. My headache had gone, and my mind felt as clear and sharp as the starry sky outside: washed and shining. It was like coming out of a thick fog into sunshine. Like coolness after fever. Like being reborn.

Somewhere between sleeping and waking I found I had regained myself, come back to the life-saving certainty that I was the person I thought I was, and not the cracked-up mess that everyone else believed.

And that being so, I thought in puzzlement, there must be some other explanation of my troubles. All—*all* I had to do was find it. Looking back unsympathetically on the appalling desolation in which I had so recently allowed myself to flounder, I began at last, at long last, to use my brain.

Half an hour later it was clear that my stomach was awake too, and it was so insistent to be filled that I couldn't concentrate. I got up and fetched the tins of cheese straws and marrons glacés from the kitchen, but not the snails. How hungry would one have to be, I wondered idly, to face those mollusks cold and butterless at five o'clock in the morning?

I opened the tins and lay down again, and crunched up all the cheese straws while I thought, and then I chewed half the syrupy weight-producing chestnuts. My stomach quieted, like a dragon fed its daily maiden, and outside the stars faded into the wan London dawn.

In the morning I took the advice I had given to Grant, and went to see a psychiatrist.

9

I had known the psychiatrist all my life as he was a friend of my father's and, I hoped, I knew him well enough to ring him up for help on a morning which he always reserved for golf. At eight o'clock I telephoned to his house in Wimpole Street, where he lived in a flat above his consulting rooms.

He asked after my father. He sounded in a hurry.

"Can I come and see you, sir?" I said.

"Now? No. Saturday. Golf," he said economically.

"Please . . . it won't take long."

There was a brief pause.

"Urgent?" A professional note to his question.

"Yes," I said.

"Come at once, then. I'm due at Wentworth at ten."

"I haven't shaved . . ." I said, catching sight of myself in the looking glass and realizing what a wreck I looked.

"Do you want to shave or do you want to talk?" he said, exasperated.

"Talk," I said.

"Then arrive," he said, and put down his receiver.

I took a taxi, and he opened the door to me with a corner of toast and marmalade in his hand. The eminent Mr. Claudius Mellit, whose patients usually saw him in striped trousers and black jacket, was sensibly attired for winter golf in waterproof trousers and a comfortably sloppy Norwegian sweater. He gave me a piercing preliminary glance and gestured, "Upstairs."

I followed him up. He finished his breakfast on the way. We went into his dining room, where he gave me a seat at the oval mahogany table, and some lukewarm coffee in a gold-rimmed cup.

"Now," he said, sitting down opposite me.

"Suppose . . ." I began, and stopped. It didn't seem so easy, now that I was there. What had seemed obvious and manifest at five in the morning was now tinged with doubt. The dawn hours had shown me a pattern I believed in, but in the full light of day I felt sure it was going to sound preposterous.

"Look," he said, "if you really need help, my golf can go hang. When I said on the telephone that I was in a hurry I hadn't seen the state you are in . . . and if you will excuse my saying so, your suit looks as if you had slept in it."

"Well, yes, I did," I said, surprised.

"Relax then, and tell me all." He grinned, a big bear of a man, fifty years old and formidably wise.

"I'm sorry I look so untidy and unshaved," I began.

"And sunken-eyed and hollow-cheeked," he murmured, smiling.

"But I don't feel as bad as I suppose I look. Not any more. I won't keep you away from your golf if you'll just tell me . . ."

"Yes?" He waited for me calmly.

"Suppose I had a sister," I said, "who was as good a musician as Mother and Father, and I was the only one in the entire family to lack their talent—as you know I am—and I felt they despised me for lacking it, how would you expect me to act?"

"They don't despise you," he protested.

"No . . . but if they did, would there be any way in which I could persuade them—and myself—that I had a very good excuse for not being a musician?"

"Oh, yes," he said instantly, "I'd expect you to do exactly what you have done. Find something you can do, and pursue it fanatically until in your own sphere you reach the standard of your family in theirs."

I felt as if I'd been hit in the solar plexus. So simple an explanation of my compulsion to race had never occurred to me.

"That . . . that isn't what I meant," I said helplessly. "But when I come to think of it, I see it is true." I paused. "What I really meant to ask was, could I, when I was growing up, have developed a physical infirmity to explain away my failure? Paralysis, for instance, so that I simply couldn't play a violin or a piano or any musical instrument? An apparently honorable way out?"

He looked at me for a few moments, unsmiling and intent.

"If you were a certain type of person, yes, it's possible. But not in your case. You had better stop waltzing round it and ask me your question straight out. The real question. I am very well accustomed to hypothetical questions . . . I meet them every day . . . but if you want a trustable answer you'll have to ask the real question."

"There are two," I said. I still hesitated. So very much, my whole life, depended on his answers. He waited patiently.

I said at last, "Could a boy whose family were all terrific cross-country riders develop asthma to hide the fact that he was afraid of horses?" My mouth was dry.

He didn't answer at once. He said, "What is the other question?"

"Could that boy, as a man, develop such a loathing for steeplechase jockeys that he would try to smash their careers? Even if, as you said, he had found something else which he could do extremely well?"

"I suppose this man has that sister you mentioned?"

"Yes," I said. "She is getting to be the best girl point-to-point rider for a generation."

He slouched back in his chair.

"It obviously matters so desperately to you, Robert, that I can't give you an answer without knowing more about it. I'm not giving you a couple of casual yeses, and find afterward that I've let you stir up disastrous trouble for all sorts of people. You must tell me why you ask these questions."

"But your golf," I said.

"I'll go later," he said calmly. "Talk."

So I talked. I told him what had happened to Art, and to Grant, and to Peter Cloony, and to Tick-Tock, and to myself.

I told him about Maurice Kemp-Lore. "He comes from a family who ride as soon as walk; and he's the right build for steeplechasing. But horses give him asthma, and that, everyone knows, is why he doesn't race himself. Well, it's a good reason, isn't it? Of course there are asthmatics who do ride—asthma doesn't stop people who think that racing is worth the wheezing—but no one would dream of blaming a man who didn't."

I paused, but as he made no comment, I went on: "You can't help being drawn to him. You can't imagine the spell of his personality unless you've felt it. You can see people wake up and sparkle when he speaks to them. He has the ear of everyone from the Stewards down—and I think he uses his influence to sow seeds of doubt about jockeys' characters."

"Go on," Claudius said, his face showing nothing.

"The men who seem to be especially under his spell are Corin Kellar, a trainer, and John Ballerton, a member of the ruling body. Neither of them ever has a good word to say for jockeys. I think Kemp-Lore picked them out as friends solely because they had the right sort of mean-mindedness for broadcasting every damaging opinion he insinuated into their heads. I think all the ruinous rumors start with Kemp-Lore, and that even the substance behind the rumors is mostly his work. Why isn't he content with having so much? The jockeys he is hurting like him and are pleased when he talks to them. Why does he need to destroy them?"

He said, "If this were a hypothetical case I would tell you that such a man could both hate and envy his father—and his sister—and have felt both these emotions from early childhood. But because he knows these feelings are wrong he represses them, and the aggression is unfortunately transferred onto people who show the same qualities and abilities that he hates in his father. Such individuals can be helped. They can be understood and treated, and forgiven."

"I can't forgive him," I said. "And I'm going to stop him."

He considered me. "You must make sure of your facts," he said, stroking his thumbnail down his upper lip. "At present you are just guessing. And as I've had no opportunity to talk to him, you'll get no more from me than an admission that your suspicions of Kemp-Lore may be *possibly* correct. Not even probably correct. He is a public figure of some standing. You are making a very serious accusation. You need cast-iron facts. Until you have them, there is always the chance that you have interpreted what has happened to you as malice from outside in order to explain away your own inner failure. Asthma of the mind, in fact."

"Don't psychologists ever take a simple view?" I said, sighing.

He shook his head. "Few things are simple."

"I'll get the facts, starting today," I said. I stood up. "Thank you for seeing me, and being so patient, and I'm sincerely sorry about your golf."

"I won't be very late," he assured me, ambling down the stairs and opening his front door. On the doorstep, shaking hands, he said as if making up his mind, "Be careful, Robert. Go gently. If you are right about Kemp-Lore, and it is just possible that you are, you must deal with him thoughtfully. Persuade him to ask for treatment. Don't drive him too hard. His sanity may be in your hands."

I said flatly, "I can't look at it from your point of view. I don't think of Kemp-Lore as ill, but as wicked."

"Where illness ends and crime begins . . ." He shrugged. "It has been debated for centuries, and no two people agree. But take care, take care." He turned to go in. "Remember me to your parents." He smiled and shut the door.

Round a couple of corners, first during a luxurious shave at a fresh-smelling barber's and second over a triple order of eggs and bacon in the café next door, I bent my mind to the problem of how the cast-iron facts were to be dug up. On reflection, there seemed to be precious few of them to work on, and in the digging, to start with at least, I was going to come up against the barrier of pity and contempt which my recent performances had raised. Nasty medicine, but if I wanted a cure I'd have to take it.

Using the café's telephone, I rang up Tick-Tock.

"Are you riding this afternoon?" I asked.

He said, "Do me a favor, pal. No unkind questions so early in the day. In a word—negative." A pause. "And you?" Innocently, too innocently.

"You're a bastard," I said.

"So my best friends tell me."

"I want the car," I said.

"Not if you're thinking of driving it over Beachy Head."

"I'm not," I said.

"Well, I'm relieved to hear it. But if you change your mind, let me know and I'll join you." His voice was light and mocking; the desperate truth underneath needed no stating.

"I want to call at some stables," I began.

"Whose?" he interrupted.

"Several people's . . . about six altogether, I think, apart from Axminster's. And Kellar's. I'll have to go there as well."

"You've got a nerve," said Tick-Tock.

"Thank you," I said. "You're about the only person in the country who thinks so."

"Damn it . . . I didn't mean . . ."

I grinned into the telephone. "Save it. Where's the car now?"

"Outside the window."

"I'll come down to Newbury by train and pick it up, if you'll meet me at the station," I said.

"It's no use going to any stables today," he said. "The trainers will all be at the races."

"Yes, I sincerely hope so," I agreed.

"What are you up to?" he asked suspiciously.

"Retrieving the fallen fortune of the House of Finn," I said. "I'll catch the nine-twenty. You meet it, okay?" And I put the receiver down, hearing, and ignoring, a protesting "Hey" before I cut him off.

But when I stepped off the train at Newbury he was waiting, dressed in a dandyish-waisted riding jacket of almost eighteenth-century length on top of some unbelievably narrow cavalry cord trousers. He enjoyed his moment ironically while I looked him up and down.

"Where's the cravat, the ruffles and the sword?" I asked.

He said, "You don't get the message. I'm tomorrow's man. My sword will be a do-it-yourself instant anti-radiation kit. You must fit your defense to the danger you meet." He grinned.

Young Tick-Tock, I reflected, not for the first time, took an uncompromisingly realistic view of the world.

He opened the car door and settled himself behind the wheel.

"Where to?" he said.

"You're not coming," I said.

"I certainly am. This car is half mine. Where it goes, I go." He was clearly determined. "Where to?"

"Well . . ." I got in beside him, fished out of my pocket a list I had made on the train, and showed it to him. "These are the stables I want to go to. I've tried to arrange them in order so that there isn't too much backtracking, but even so it means a lot of driving."

"Phew!" he said. "There's a lot of them. Hampshire, Sussex, Kent, Oxford, Leicester and Yorkshire. How long will you be staying in each place? We'll never cover this lot in one day. Especially as you look tired already."

I glanced at him, but he was looking down at the paper. It was true that I felt tired, but disconcerted that it should be so obvious. I had thought that the shave and breakfast and the return of self-confidence would have wiped away the ravages of the previous day and night.

"You needn't come," I began.

"We've been through all that," he interrupted. "We'll start by going to your digs and mine for overnight things, and then make for Kent. And on the way you can tell me why we're going." He calmly let in the clutch and drove off: and truth to tell I was very glad of his company.

We collected our things, and Tick-Tock pointed the Mini-Cooper's blunt nose toward the first stable on the list, Corin Kellar's, in Hampshire.

"Now," he said. "The works."

"No," I said. "I'm not going to tell you why we're going. Listen and watch, and then you tell me."

"You're a cagey blighter," he said, without arguing. He added, "I suppose you've taken into account all that about saps rushing in where angels wouldn't plonk their holy feet? I mean, to put it mildly, neither of us is in the red-carpet bracket just now. Strictly doomsville, us."

"You are so right," I said, smiling.

Tick-Tock turned his head and gave me a surprised stare.

"Keep your eyes on the road," I said mildly.

"I'll never know you," he said. "I'd have thought you'd take it very hard . . . what has happened . . . but since I picked you up at the station I've felt more cheerful than I have for weeks." His foot went down on the accelerator and he began to whistle.

We arrived at Corin's extensive, well-groomed stable while the lads were doing up the horses after the second morning exercise. Arthur, the head lad, was crossing the yard with a bucket of oats when we climbed out of the little car, and the crinkling smile with which he usually greeted me got halfway to his eyes before he remembered. I saw the embarrassment take over and the welcome fade away.

"The governor isn't here," he said awkwardly. "He's gone to the races."

"I know," I said. "Can I speak to Davey?"

Davey was the lad who looked after Shantytown.

"I suppose so," said Arthur doubtfully, "but you won't make no trouble?"

"No," I said. "No trouble. Where is he?"

"Fourth box from the end over that side," he said, pointing. Tick-Tock and I walked over, and found Davey tossing and tidying the straw bed round a big chestnut. Shantytown. We leaned over the bottom half of the door, and watched Davey's expression, too, change from warmth to disgust. He was a short, tough, sixteen-year-old boy with flaming red hair and an intolerant mouth. He turned his back on us and ran his hand down the horse's neck. Then he spat into the straw. Tick-Tock took a sharp breath and his hands clenched into fists.

I said quickly, "Davey, there's a quid for you if you feel like talking a bit."

"What about?" he said, without turning round.

"About the day I rode Shantytown at Dunstable," I said. "Three weeks ago. Do you remember?"

"I'll say I remember," he said offensively.

I ignored his tone. "Well, tell me what happened from the moment you arrived on the course until I got up on Shantytown in the parade ring."

"What the hell do you mean?" he said, wheeling round and coming over to the door. "Nothing happened. What should happen?"

I took a pound note out of my wallet and gave it to him. He looked at it for a second or two, then shrugged, and thrust it into his pocket.

"Start when you set off from here. Don't leave anything out," I said.

"Are you off your nut?" he said.

"No," I said, "and I want my quid's worth."

He shrugged again, but said, "We went in the horse box from here to Dunstable, and—"

"Did you stop on the way?" I asked.

"Yes, Joe's Caff, same as always when we go to Dunstable."

"Did you see anyone there you knew?"

"Well, Joe, and the girl who pours out the char."

"No one you wouldn't expect?" I pressed.

"No, of course not. Like I said, we got to the course and unloaded the horses, two of them, in the stables there, and went and got another cuppa and a wad in the canteen, and then I went round the bookies, like, and put ten bob on Bloggs in the first, and went up on the stands, and watched it get stuffed—sodding animal didn't try a yard—and then I went back to the stables and got Shantytown and put on his paddock clothing and led him out into the paddock . . ." His voice was bored as he recited the everyday racing routine of his job.

"Could anyone have given Shantytown anything to eat or drink in the stables, say a bucket of water just before the race?" I asked.

"Don't be so ruddy stupid. Of course not. Whoever heard of giving a horse anything to eat or drink before a race? A mouthful of water, I dare say, a couple of hours beforehand, but a bucketful . . ." The scorn in his voice suddenly changed to anger. "Here, you're not suggesting I gave him a drink, are you? Oh, no, mate, you're not putting the blame on me for the balls you made of it."

"No," I said, "no, Davey. Calm down. How tight is the security on the Dunstable stables? Would anyone but a lad or a trainer get in there?"

"No," he said, more moderately, "it's as tight as a drum. The last gateman got sacked for letting an owner in alone without a trainer, and the new man's as pernickety as they come."

"Go on, then," I said. "We've got you as far as the paddock."

"Well, I walked the horse round the assembly ring for a bit, waiting for the governor to bring the saddle up from the weighing room—" he smiled suddenly, as at some pleasant memory—"and then when he came I took Shanty into one of the saddling boxes and the governor saddled up, and then I took Shanty down into the parade ring and walked him round until they called me over and you got up on him." He stopped. "I can't see what you wanted to hear all that for."

"What happened while you were walking round the assembly ring?" I asked. "Something you enjoyed? Something you smile about when you remember it?"

He sniffed. "It's nothing you'd want to know."

I said, "The quid was for telling everything."

"Oh, very well then, but it's nothing to do with racing. It was that chap on the telly, Maurice Kemp-Lore, he came over and spoke to me and admired the horse. He said he was a friend of the owner, old man Ballerton. He patted Shanty and gave him a couple of sugar lumps, which I wasn't too keen on, mind, but you can't be narky with a chap like him, somehow, and he asked me what his chances were, and I said pretty good—more fool me—and then he went away again. That's all. I told you it wasn't anything to do with racing."

"No," I said. "Well, never mind. Thanks for trying."

I straightened up and turned away from the door, and Tick-Tock had taken a step or two toward the car when Davey said under his breath behind me, "Trying . . . you two could both do a bit more of that yourselves, if you ask me." But Tick-Tock fortunately didn't hear, and we folded ourselves back into the Mini-Cooper and drove unmourned out of the yard.

Tick-Tock exploded. "Anyone would think you'd killed your mother and robbed your grandmother, the way they look at you. Losing your nerve isn't a crime."

"Unless you can put up with a few harmless sneers you'd better get out at the next railway station," I said cheerfully, having blessedly discovered in the past half hour that they no longer hurt. "And I haven't lost my nerve. Not yet, anyway."

He opened his mouth and shut it again and flicked a glance at me, and drove another twenty miles without speaking.

We reached the next yard on my list shortly before one o'clock, and disturbed the well-to-do farmer, who trained his own horses, just as he was about to sit down to his lunch. When he opened the door to us a warm smell of stew and cabbage edged past him, and we could hear a clatter of saucepans in the kitchen. I had ridden several winners for him in the past two years before disgracing his best horse the previous week, and after he had got over the unpleasant shock of finding me on his doorstep, he asked us, in a friendly enough fashion, to go in for a drink. But I thanked him and refused, and asked where I could find the lad who looked after the horse in question. He came out to the gate with us and pointed to a house down the road.

We talked the lad out of his digs and into the car, where I gave him a pound and invited him to describe in detail what had happened on the day I had ridden his horse. He was older, less intelligent and less truculent than Davey, but not much more willing. He didn't see no sense in it, he didn't. He said so several times. Eventually I got him started, and then there was no stopping him. Detail I had asked for, and detail I got, solidly, for close on half an hour.

Sandwiched between stripping off the paddock clothing and buckling up the saddle came the news that Maurice Kemp-Lore had lounged into the saddling box, said some complimentary things to the farmer-owner about his horse, meanwhile feeding the animal some lumps of sugar, and had drifted away again leaving behind him the usual feeling of friendliness and pleasure.

"A proper corker, ain't he?" was how the lad put it.

I waited until he had reached the point when the farmer had given me a leg up onto the horse, and then stopped him and thanked him for his efforts. We left him muttering that we were welcome, but he still didn't see the point.

"How odd," said Tick-Tock pensively as we sped along the road to the next stable, eighty miles away. "How odd that Maurice Kemp-Lore . . ." He didn't finish the sentence; nor did I.

Two hours later, in Kent, we listened, for another pound, to a gaunt boy of twenty telling us what a smashing fellow that Maurice Kemp-Lore was, how interested he'd been in the horse, how kind to give him some sugar, though it wasn't really allowed in his stables, but how could you tell a man like that not to when he was being so friendly? The lad also treated us with a rather offensive superiority, but even Tick-Tock by now had become too interested to care.

"He drugged them," he said flatly, after a long silence, turning on to the Maidstone bypass. "He drugged them to make it look as if you couldn't ride them . . . to make everyone believe you'd lost your nerve."

"Yes," I agreed.

"But it's impossible," he protested vehemently. "Why on earth should he? It can't be right. It must be a coincidence that he gave sugar to three horses you rode."

"Maybe. We'll see," I said.

And we did see. We went to the stables of every horse (other than James's) that I had ridden since Shantytown, talking to every lad concerned. And in every single case we heard that Maurice Kemp-Lore had made memorable the lad's afternoon (before I had blighted it) by admiring the way the lad had looked after his horse, and by offering those tempting lumps of sugar. It took us the whole of Saturday, and all Sunday morning, and we finished the last stable on my list on the edge of the Yorkshire moors at two o'clock in the afternoon. Only because I wanted my facts to be as cast-iron as possible had we gone so far north. Tick-Tock had become convinced in Northamptonshire.

I drove us back to our respective digs in Berkshire, and the following morning, Monday, I walked up to the Axminster stables to see James.

He had just come in from supervising the morning exercise, and the cold downland air had numbed his toes and fingers.

"Come into the office," he said when he saw me waiting. His tone was neutral, but his protruding lower jaw was unrelenting. I followed him in, and he turned on an electric heater to warm his hands.

"I can't give you much to ride," he said, with his back to me. "All the owners have cried off, except one. You'd better look at this; it came this morning." He stretched out his hand, picked up a paper from his desk, and held it out to me.

I took it. It was a letter from Lord Tirrold.

Dear James,

Since our telephone conversation I have been thinking over our decision to replace Finn on Template next Saturday, and I now consider that we should reverse this and allow him to ride as originally planned. It is, I confess, at least as much for our sake as for his, since I do not want it said that I hurried to throw him out at the first possible moment, showing heartless ingratitude after his many wins on my horses. I am prepared for the disappointment of not winning the Midwinter and I apologize to you for robbing you of the chance of adding this prize to your total, but I would rather lose the race than the respect of the racing fraternity.

Yours ever,
George

I put the letter back on the desk.

"He doesn't need to worry," I said thickly. "Template will win."

"Do you mean you aren't going to ride it?" said James, turning round quickly. There was a damaging note of eagerness in his voice, and he saw that I had heard it. "I . . . I mean . . ." He tailed off.

"James," I said, sitting down unasked in one of the battered armchairs. "There are a few things I'd like you to know. First, however bad it looks, and whatever you believe, I have not lost my nerve. Second, every single horse I have ridden since that fall three weeks ago has been doped. Not enough to be very noticeable, just enough to make it run like a slug. Third, the dope has been given to all the horses by the same man. Fourth, the dope has been given to the horses on sugar lumps. I should think it was some form of sleeping draught, but I've no way of knowing for sure." I stopped abruptly.

James stood looking at me with his mouth open, the prominent lower teeth bared to the gums as his lip dropped in shocked disbelief.

I said, "Before you conclude that I am out of my mind, do me the one favor of calling in one of the lads, and listening to what he has to say."

James shut his mouth with a snap. "Which lad?"

"It doesn't really matter. Any of them whose horse I have ridden in the past three weeks."

He paused dubiously, but finally went to the door and shouted for someone to find Eddie, the lad who looked after Hugo's big chestnut. In less than a minute the boy arrived, out of breath, and with his curly fair hair sticking up in an uncombed halo.

James gave me no chance to do the questioning. He said brusquely to Eddie, "When did you last talk to Rob?"

The boy looked scared and began to stutter. "N-not since l-l-last week."

"Since last Friday?" That was the day James himself had last seen me.

"No, sir."

"Very well, then. You remember the big chestnut running badly last Wednesday week?"

"Yes, sir." Eddie treated me to a scornful glance.

"Did anyone give the chestnut a lump of sugar before the race?" There was now only interest to be heard in James's voice; the severity was masked.

"Yes, sir," said Eddie eagerly. The familiar remembering smile appeared on his grubby face, and I breathed an inward sigh of bottomless relief.

"Who was it?"

"Maurice Kemp-Lore, sir. He said how splendidly I looked after my horses, sir. He was leaning over the rails of the assembly ring and he spoke to me as I was going past. So I stopped, and he was ever so nice. He gave the chestnut some sugar, sir, but I didn't think it would matter as Mr. Hugo is always sending sugar for him anyway."

"Thank you, Eddie," said James, rather faintly. "No matter about the sugar. Run along now."

Eddie went. James looked at me blankly. The loud clock ticked.

Presently I said, "I've spent the past two days talking to the lads of all the horses I've ridden for other stables since I had that fall. Every one of them told me that Maurice Kemp-Lore gave each horse some lumps of sugar before I rode it. Ingersoll came with me. He heard them too. You've only to ask him if you can't believe it from me."

"Maurice never goes near horses at the races," James protested, "or anywhere else for that matter."

"That's precisely what helped me to understand what was happening," I said. "I talked to Kemp-Lore on the stands at Dunstable just after Shantytown and two other horses had run hopelessly for me, and he was wheezing quite audibly. He had asthma, which meant that he had recently been very close to horses. I didn't give it a thought at the time, but it means a packet to me now."

"But Maurice . . ." he repeated, unbelievingly. "It's just not possible."

"It is however possible," I said, more coldly than I had any right to, having believed it myself for twelve awful hours, "for me to fall apart from a small spot of concussion?"

"I don't know what to think," he said uncomfortably. There was a pause. There were two things I wanted James to do to help me; but in view of his ingrained disinclination to do favors for anyone, I did not think my requests would be very enthusiastically received. However, if I didn't ask I wouldn't get.

I spoke slowly, persuasively, as if the thought had just occurred to me. "Let me ride a horse for you . . . one of your own, if the owners won't have me . . . and see for yourself if Kemp-Lore tries to give it sugar. Perhaps you could stick with the horse yourself all the time? And if he comes up with his sugar lumps, maybe you could manage to knock them out of his hand before the horse eats them. Perhaps you could pick them up yourself and put them in your pocket, and give the horse some sugar lumps of your own instead? Then we would see how the horse runs."

It was too much trouble; his face showed it. He said, "That's too fantastic. I can't do things like that."

"It's simple," I said mildly; "you've only to bump his arm."

"No," he said, but not obstinately. A hopeful no, to my ears. I didn't press him, knowing from experience that he would irrevocably stick in his toes if urged too vehemently to do anything he did not want to.

I said instead, "Aren't you friendly with that man who arranges the regular dope tests at the races?" Three or four spot checks were taken at every meeting, mainly to deter trainers of doubtful reputation from pepping up or slowing down their horses with drugs. At the beginning of each afternoon the Stewards decided which horses to test—for example, the winner of the second race, the favorite in the fourth race (especially if he was beaten), and all runners in the fifth. No one, not even the Stewards, always knew in advance exactly which horses would have their saliva taken, and the value of the whole system lay in this uncertainty.

James followed my thoughts. "You mean, will I ask him if any of the horses you have ridden since your fall have been tested for dope in the normal course of events?"

"Yes," I agreed. "Could you possibly do that?"

"Yes, I'll do that," he said. "I will ring him up. But if any of them have been tested and proved negative, you do realize that it will dispose of your wild accusations absolutely?"

"I do," I agreed. "Actually, I've ridden so many beaten favorites that I can't think why such systematic doping has not already been discovered."

"You really do believe it, don't you?" said James wonderingly.

"Yes," I said, getting up and going to the door. "Yes, I believe it. And so will you, James."

But he shook his head, and I left him staring frozen-faced out the window, the incredible nature of what I had said to him still losing the battle against his own personal knowledge of Kemp-Lore. James liked the man.

10

Late that Monday evening James rang me up and told me that I could ride his own horse, Turniptop, which was due to run in the novice chase at Stratford on Avon on the following Thursday. I began to thank him, but he interrupted, "I'm doing you no favor. You know it won't win. He's never been over fences, only hurdles, and all I want is for you to give him an easy race round, getting used to the bigger obstacles. All right?"

"Yes," I said. "All right." And he rang off. There was no mention of whether he would or would not contemplate juggling with sugar lumps.

I was tired. I had spent the whole day driving to Devon and back to visit Art Mathews' beautiful widow, the ice maiden. A fruitless journey. She had been as chilly as ever. Widowhood had warmed her no more than wifehood had done. Blonde, well-bred and cold, she had answered my questions calmly and incuriously and with a complete lack of interest. Art had been dead four months. She spoke of him as though she could hardly remember what he had looked like.

No, she did not know exactly why Art had quarreled so continuously with Corin. No, she did not know why Art had thought fit to shoot himself. No, Art had not got on well with Mr. John Ballerton, but she did not know why. Yes, Art had once appeared on television on "Turf Talk." It had not been a success, she said, the shadow of an old grievance sharpening her voice. Art had been made to look a fool. Art, whose meticulous sense of honor and order had earned him only respect on the race course, had been made to look a cantankerous, mean-minded fool. No, she could not remember exactly how it had been done, but she did remember, only too well, the effect it had had on her own family and friends. They had, it appeared, loudly pitied her on her choice of husband.

But I, listening to her, inwardly pitied poor dead Art on his choice of wife.

On the following day, Tuesday, I again appropriated the Mini-Cooper, much to Tick-Tock's disgust. This time I went toward Cheltenham, and called at Peter Cloony's neat, new bungalow, turning down the narrow, winding lane from the high main road to the village in the hollow.

Peter's wife opened the door to me and asked me in with a strained smile. She no longer looked happy and rosily content. She was too thin, and her hair hung straight and wispy round her neck. It was very nearly as cold inside the house as it was outside, and she wore some tattered fur boots, thick stockings, bulky clothes, and gloves. With no lipstick and no life in her eyes, she was almost unrecognizable as the loving girl who had put me up for the night four months before.

"Come in," she said, "but I'm afraid Peter isn't here. He was given a lift to Birmingham races . . . perhaps he'll get a spare ride." She spoke without hope.

"Of course he will," I said. "He's a good jockey."

"The trainers don't seem to think so," she said despairingly. "Ever since he lost his regular job, he's barely had one ride a week. We can't live on it, how could we? If things don't change very soon, he's going to give up racing and try something else. But he only cares for horses and racing—it will break his heart if he has to leave it."

She had taken me into the sitting room. It was as bare as before. Barer. The rented television set had gone. In its place stood a baby's cot, a wickerwork basket affair on a metal stand. I went over and looked down at the tiny baby, only a small bump under the mound of blankets. He was asleep. I made admiring remarks about what I could see of him, and his mother's face momentarily livened up with pleasure.

She insisted on making us a cup of tea, and I had to wait until the questions of no milk, no sugar, no biscuits had all been settled before asking her what I really wanted to know.

I said, "That Jaguar—the one which blocked the lane and made Peter late—who did it belong to?"

"We don't know," she said. "It was very old. No one came to move it away and it stayed across the lane all that morning. In the end the police arranged for it to be towed away. I know Peter asked the police who owned it, because he wanted to tell the man just what his filthy Jaguar had cost him, but they said they hadn't yet traced him."

"You don't happen to know where the Jaguar is now?" I asked.

"I don't know if it is still there," she said, "but it used to be outside the big garage beside Timberley Station. They're the only garage round here with a breakdown truck, and they were the ones who towed it away."

I thanked her and stood up, and she came out to the car with me to say good-by. I had spent some time going through the form book, adding up the number of races Peter had ridden during the past few weeks, and I knew how little he had earned. I had brought with me a big box of groceries, butter, eggs, cheese, and so on, and a stack of tins, and also a string of plastic ducks for the baby. This collection I carried back into the bungalow and dumped on the kitchen table, ignoring her surprised protest as she followed me in.

I grinned. "They are too heavy to take back. You'll have to make the best of it."

She began to cry.

"Cheer up," I said, "things will get better soon. But, meanwhile, don't you think the bungalow is too cold for a baby? I read somewhere that some babies die every winter from breathing freezing air, even though they may be as warmly wrapped up as yours is."

She looked at me aghast, tears trickling down her cheeks.

"You ought to heat that room a little, and especially keep it warm all night, too, if he sleeps in there," I said.

"But I can't," she said jerkily, "the payments on the bungalow take nearly all we have. We can't afford a fire, except just in the evenings. Is it really true about babies dying?"

She was frightened.

"Yes, quite true," I said. I took a sealed envelope out of my pocket and gave it to her. "This is a present for the baby. Warmth. It's not a fortune, but it will pay your electricity bills for a while, and buy some coal if you want it. There's likely to be a lot of cold weather coming, so you must promise to spend most of it on keeping warm."

"I promise," she said faintly.

"Good." I smiled at her as she wiped her eyes, and then I went back to the car and drove away up the lane.

The garage at Timberley Station was a modernized affair with the front all snowy plaster and the back, when I walked round there, of badly pointed cheap brickwork. The elderly abandoned Jaguar stood there, tucked away between the burned-out remains of a Standard 8 and a pile of old tires. I went round to the front of the garage to talk to the man in charge, and I asked him if I could buy the car.

"Sorry, sir, no can do," he said breezily. He was a dapper, thirtyish man with no oil on his hands.

"Why not?" I said. "It doesn't look good for anything but the scrap heap."

"I can't sell it to you because I don't know who it belongs to," he said regretfully, "but," he brightened, "it's been here so long now that it might be mine after all . . . like unclaimed lost property. I'll ask the police."

With a bit of prompting he told me all about the Jaguar's being stuck across the lane and how his firm had fetched it.

I said, "But someone must have seen the driver after he left the car?"

"The police think he must have got a lift, and then decided the car wasn't worth coming back for. But it's in good enough order. And it wasn't hot . . . stolen, I mean."

"What's it worth?" I asked.

"To you, sir," he smiled glossily, "I'd have let it go for a hundred."

A hundred. I parted from him and strolled out onto the forecourt. Was it worth a hundred to Kemp-Lore, I wondered, to ruin Peter Cloony? Was his obsessive hatred of jockeys so fierce? But then a hundred to Kemp-Lore, I reflected, was probably a lot less than a hundred to me.

Timberley railway station (six stopping trains a day and twenty-two expresses) lay on my left. I stood and considered it. The station was nearly four miles from the top of the lane leading to Peter's village; say an hour's quick walk. Peter had found the Jaguar across the lane at eleven o'clock, and it had to have been jammed in position only seconds before he came up the hill, as his had been the first

NERVE 341

car to be obstructed. I had a vivid mental picture of Kemp-Lore parked in the gateway where the lane began to curve downward, watching Peter's house through binoculars, seeing him go out and get into his car and start on his way to the races. There wouldn't have been much time to force the Jaguar into position, lock its door, and disappear before Peter got there. Not much time; but enough.

And then? The one tremendous disadvantage Kemp-Lore had to overcome, I thought, was his own fame. His face was so well known to almost the entire British population that he could not hope to move about the country inconspicuously, and wherever he went he would be noticed and remembered. Surely, I thought, in this sparsely populated area it should be possible to find someone who had seen him.

As I was there anyway, I started with the station. Outside, I looked up the times of the stopping trains. There was, I found, a down train at 12:30, but no up train until five o'clock. The only other trains ran early in the morning and later in the evening. The booking office was shut. I found the clerk–ticket collector–porter nodding over a hot stove and a racing paper in the parcels office. A large basket of hens squawked noisily in a corner as I walked in, and he woke with a jerk and told me the next train was due in one hour and ten minutes.

I got him talking via the racing news, but there was nothing to learn. Maurice Kemp-Lore had never (more's the pity, he said) caught a train at Timberley. If it had happened when he was off duty, he'd have heard about it all right. And yes, he said, he'd been on duty the day they'd fetched the Jaguar down to the garage. Disgusting that. Shouldn't be allowed, people being rich enough to chuck their old cars in the ditch like cigarette ends.

I asked him if the station had been busy that day; if there had been a lot of passengers catching the midday train.

"A lot of passengers?" he repeated scornfully. "Never more than three or four, excepting Cheltenham race days."

"I was just wondering," I said idly, "whether the chap who left his Jaguar behind could have caught a train from here that morning."

"Not from here, he didn't," the railway man said positively. "Because, same as usual, all the people who caught the train were ladies."

"Ladies?"

"Yeh, women. Shopping in Cheltenham. We haven't had a man

catch the midday—excepting race days, of course—since young Simpkins from the garage got sent home with chickenpox last summer. Bit of a joke it is round here, see, the midday."

I gave him a hot tip for Birmingham that afternoon (which won, I was glad to see later) and left him busily putting a call through to his bookmaker on the government's telephone bill.

Timberley village pub, nearly empty, had never been stirred, they told me regretfully, by the flashing presence of Maurice Kemp-Lore.

The two transport cafés along the main road hadn't heard of any of their chaps giving him a lift.

None of the garages within ten miles had seen him, ever.

The local taxi service had never driven him. He had never caught a bus on the country route.

It wasn't hard at each place to work conversation round to Kemp-Lore, but it was never quick. By the time a friendly bus conductor had told me, over a cigarette at the Cheltenham terminus, that none of his mates had ever had such a famous man on board because they'd never have kept quiet about it (look how Bill went on for days and days when Dennis Compton took a tenpenny single), it was seven o'clock in the evening.

If I hadn't been so utterly, unreasonably sure that it was Kemp-Lore who had abandoned the Jaguar, I would have admitted that, if no one had seen him, then he hadn't been there. As it was, I was depressed by the failure of my search, but not convinced that there was nothing to search for.

The army tank carrier that had blocked Peter's and my way to Cheltenham was there accidentally: that much was clear. But Peter had got into such trouble for being late that a weapon was put straight into the hand of his enemy. He had only had to make Peter late again, and to spread his little rumors, and the deed was done. No confidence, no rides, no career for Cloony.

I found I still hoped by perseverance to dig something up, so I booked a room in a hotel in Cheltenham and spent the evening in a cinema to take my mind off food. On the telephone Tick-Tock sounded more resigned than angry to hear that he would be carless yet again. He asked how I was getting on, and when I reported no progress, he said, "If you're right about our friend, he's as sly and cunning as all get-out. You won't find his tracks too easily."

Without much hope I went down in the morning to the Cheltenham railway station and sorted out, after a little difficulty with old time sheets and the passing of a pound note, the man who had collected the tickets from the passengers on the stopping train from Timberley on the day the Jaguar was abandoned.

He was willing enough, but he too had never seen Kemp-Lore, except on television; though he hesitated while he said so.

"What is it?" I asked.

"Well, sir, I've never seen him, but I think I've seen his sister."

"What was she like?" I asked.

"Very like him, of course, sir, or I wouldn't have known who she was. And she had riding clothes on. You know—jodhpurs, I think they're called. And a scarf over her head. Pretty she looked, very pretty. I couldn't think who she was for a bit, and then it came to me, afterwards like. I didn't talk to her, see? I just took her ticket when she went through the barrier, that's all. I remember taking her ticket."

"When was it that you saw her?" I asked.

"Oh, I couldn't say. I don't rightly know when it was. Before Christmas though, sometime before Christmas, I'm certain of that."

He flipped the pound I gave him expertly into an inner pocket. "Thank you, sir, thank you indeed," he said.

I dressed and shaved with particular care on the Thursday morning as, I supposed, a sort of barrier against the reception I knew I was going to meet. It was six days since I had been racing, six days in which my shortcomings and the shreds of my riding reputation would have been brought up, pawed over and discarded. Life moved fast in the changing room; today was important, tomorrow more so; but yesterday was dead. I belonged to yesterday. I was ancient news.

Even my valet was surprised to see me, although I had written to say I was coming.

"You are riding today, then?" he said. "I was wondering if you wanted to sell your saddle; there's a boy just starting who needs one."

"I'll keep it a bit longer," I said. "I'm riding Turniptop in the fourth. Mr. Axminster's colors."

It was a strange day. As I no longer felt that I deserved the pitying glances to which I was treated, I found that they had, to a great extent, ceased to trouble me, and I even watched with fair equanimity the success of two of my ex-mounts in the first two races. The only thing I worried about was whether or not James would have both sugar lumps in his pocket and willingness in his heart.

He was so busy with his other runners that I did not exchange more than a few words with him during the first part of the afternoon, and when I went out into the parade ring to join him for Turniptop's race, he was standing alone, thoughtfully gazing into the distance.

"Maurice Kemp-Lore's here," he said abruptly.

"Yes, I know," I said. "I saw him."

"He has given sugar to several horses already."

"What?" I exclaimed.

"I have asked quite a few people . . . Maurice has been feeding sugar to any number of horses the past few weeks, not only to the ones you have ridden."

"Oh," I said weakly. Cunning as all get-out, Tick-Tock had said.

"None of the horses you rode were picked for the regulation dope test," said James, "but some of the other horses Maurice gave sugar to were tested. All negative."

"He gave doped sugar only to my mounts. The rest were camouflage," I said. It sounded improbable, but I was sure of it.

James shook his head.

"Did you . . . ?" I began without much hope. "Did he . . . Kemp-Lore . . . try to give Turniptop any sugar?"

James compressed his lips and stared into the middle distance. I positively held my breath.

"He did come into the saddling box," he said grudgingly. "He admired the horse's coat."

Turniptop ambled past glowing with good health, but before James could say any more one of the Stewards came over to talk to him, and I had no chance to find out about the sugar before it was time to mount and go out for the race.

I knew by the second fence that whether Kemp-Lore had fed him sugar or not, Turniptop was not doped. The leaden sluggishness which had afflicted my last twenty-eight mounts, and which I had been forced to believe was due to my own deficiency, had lifted like a spent thundercloud.

Turniptop leapt and sprang and surged, pulling like a train and doing his damnedest to run away with me. I could have shouted aloud with relief. He was an untidy jumper with more enthusiasm than judgment, a style which had brought him no especial grief over hurdles; but now, in his first steeplechase, he showed signs of treating fences with the same disrespect. It wouldn't really do; there's a world of difference between a single-thickness, easily knocked down hurdle and a three-foot-wide fence, solidly built of birch twigs, particularly when an open ditch lies in front of it. But Turniptop did not want to be steadied. He was eager. He was rash.

With things as they were, and with James to be convinced, I must admit that my mood matched Turniptop's exactly. We infected each other with recklessness. We took indefensible risks, and got away with them.

I kept him continually on the rails, squeezing forward into tiny openings and letting him take all the bumps that came his way. When he met a fence dead right he gained lengths over it, and when he met one wrong he scrambled through and found a foot to land on somehow. It was more like a roller-coaster ride than the sensible, well-judged race James had indicated, but it taught the tough-minded Turniptop just as much about getting himself out of trouble as going round quietly on the outside would have done.

Coming into the second to last fence, I was afraid we would win. Afraid, because I knew James wanted to sell the horse, and if he had already won a novice chase he would be less valuable than if he had not. An apparent paradox; but Turniptop, young and still green, showed great promise. Too early a win would disqualify him from entering a string of good novice chases in the following season.

It would be far, far better, I knew, to come second. To have shown what he could do but not actually to have won would have put hundreds on his value. But we had run too close a race, and at the second last the disaster of winning seemed unavoidable. There was only one other tiring horse alongside, and I could hear no others on my tail.

Turniptop rose, or rather fell, to the occasion. In spite of my urging him to put in another stride, he took off far too soon and landed with his hind feet tangled hopelessly in the birch. His forelegs buckled under the strain and he went down onto his knees, with my chin resting on his right ear and my hands touching each other round his throat. Even then his indomitable sense of balance rescued him, and he staggered back onto his feet with a terrific upthrust of his shoulders, tipping me back into the saddle, and tossing his head as if in disgust he set off again toward the winning post. The horse which had been alongside was now safely ahead, and two that had been behind me had jumped past, so that we came into the last fence in fourth position.

I had lost my irons in the debacle and couldn't get my feet into them again in time to jump, so we went over the last with them dangling and clanking in the air. I gathered him together and squeezed my legs, and Turniptop, game to the end, accelerated past two of the horses ahead and flashed into second place four strides from the post.

James waited for me to dismount in the unsaddling enclosure with a face from which all expression had studiously been wiped. Poker-faced to match, I slid from the saddle.

"Don't ever ride a race like that for me again," he said.

"No," I agreed. I undid the girth buckles and took my saddle over my arm, and at last looked into his eyes.

They gleamed, narrowed and inscrutable. He said, "You proved your point. But you could have killed my horse doing it."

I said nothing.

"And yourself," he added, implying that that was less important.

I shook my head, smiling faintly. "Not a chance," I said.

"Hm." He gave me a hard stare. "You'd better come up to the stable this evening," he said. "We can't talk about . . . what we have to talk about . . . here. There are too many people about."

As if to punctuate this remark the owner of the winner leaned over the dividing rails to admire Turniptop and I had to loop up the girths and go and weigh in, still without knowing exactly what had happened in the saddling box before the race.

Tick-Tock was standing by my peg in the changing room, one smoothly shod foot up on the bench and the Tyrolean hat pushed back on his head.

"Before you ride like that again, you might make a will leaving me your half of the car," he said. "It would solve so many legal complications."

"Oh, shut up," I said, peeling off first the crimson and white sweater, James's colors, and then the thin brown jersey underneath. I took a towel from the valet and went along to the washbasin.

"A lot of people," said Tick-Tock in a loud voice across the room, "are going to have a fine old time eating their words, and I hope it gives them indigestion." He followed me along and watched me wash, leaning languidly against the wall. "I suppose you realize that your exploits this afternoon were clearly visible to several million assorted housewives, invalids, babes in arms, and people hanging about on the pavement outside electric shops?"

"What?" I exclaimed.

"It's a fact. Didn't you really know? The last three races are filling up the spare time between 'Six for Sixth Forms' and 'Goggle with Granny.' Universal T.C. Maurice's lot. I wonder," he finished more soberly, "what he'll do when he knows you've rumbled the sugar bit?"

"He may not know," I said, toweling my chest and shoulders. "He may think it was accidental. . . . I haven't heard yet from James what happened before the race."

"Anyway," said Tick-Tock confidently, "his campaign against you is over. He won't risk going on with it after today."

I agreed with him. It just shows how little either of us understood about obsession.

James was waiting for me in the office, busy with papers at his big desk. The fire blazed hotly and the light winked on the glasses standing ready beside the whisky bottle.

He stopped writing when I came in, and got up and poured out drinks, and stood towering above me as I sat in the battered armchair by the fire. His strong heavy face looked worried.

"I apologize," he said abruptly.

"Don't," I said. "No need."

"I very nearly let Maurice give Turniptop that damned sugar," he said. "I couldn't believe him capable of a scheme as fantastic as doping every horse you ride. I mean, it's . . . it's ridiculous."

"What happened in the saddling box?" I asked.

He took a sip from his glass. "I gave Sid instructions that no one, absolutely no one, however important he was, was to give Turniptop anything to eat or drink before the race. When I reached the box with your saddle, Maurice was in the box next door and I watched him giving the horse there some sugar. Sid said no one had given Turniptop anything." He paused and drank again. "I put on your number cloth, weight pad and saddle, and began to do up with girths. Maurice came round the partition from the next box and said hello. That infectious smile of his . . . I found myself smiling back and thinking you were mad. He was wheezing a bit with asthma . . . and he put his hand in his pocket and brought out two lumps of sugar. He did it naturally, casually, and held them out to Turniptop. I had my hands full of girths and I thought you were wrong . . . but . . . I don't know . . . there was something in the way he was standing, with his arm stretched out rather stiffly and the sugar flat on the palm of his hand, that didn't look right. People who are fond of horses stroke their muzzles when they give them sugar, they don't stand as far away as possible. And if Maurice wasn't fond of horses, why was he giving them sugar? Anyway, I did decide suddenly that there would be no harm done if Turniptop didn't eat that sugar, so I dropped the girths and pretended to trip, and grabbed Maurice's arm to steady myself. The sugar fell off his hand onto the straw on the ground and I stepped on it as if by accident while I was recovering my balance."

"What did he say?" I asked, fascinated.

"Nothing," said James. "I apologized for bumping into him, but he didn't answer. Just for a second he looked absolutely furious. Then he smiled again and—" James's eyes glinted—"he said how much he admired me for giving poor Finn this one last chance."

"Dear of him," I murmured.

"I told him it wasn't exactly your last chance. I said you would be riding Template on Saturday as well. He just said, 'Oh, really?' and wished me luck and walked away."

"So the sugar was crunched up and swept out with the dirty straw," I said.

"Yes," he agreed.

"Nothing to analyze. No evidence." A nuisance.

"If I hadn't stepped on it, Maurice could have picked it up and offered it to Turniptop again. I hadn't taken any sugar with me . . . I hadn't any lumps to substitute . . . I didn't believe I would need them."

He hadn't intended to bother, I knew. But he had bothered. I would never stop feeling grateful.

We drank our whisky. James said suddenly, "Why? I don't understand why he should have gone to such lengths to discredit you. What has he got against you?"

"I am a jockey, and he is not," I said flatly. "That's all." I told him about my visit to Claudius Mellit and the answers he had given me. "It's no coincidence that you and most other trainers have had trouble finding and keeping a jockey. You've all been swayed by Kemp-Lore, either by him directly or through those two shadows of his, Ballerton and Corin Kellar, who soak up his poison like sponges and drip it out into every receptive ear. They've said it all to you. You repeated it to me yourself, not so long ago. Peter Cloony is always late, Tick-Tock doesn't try, Danny Higgs bets too heavily, Grant sold information, Finn has lost his nerve."

He stared at me, appalled.

I said, "You believed it all, James, didn't you? Even you? And so did everyone else. Why shouldn't they, with so much evident foundation for the rumors? It doesn't take much for an owner or a trainer to lose confidence in a jockey. The thought has only to be insinuated, however fleetingly, that a jockey is habitually late, or dishonest, or afraid, and very soon, very soon indeed, he is on his way out. Art. Art killed himself because Corin sacked him. Grant had a mental breakdown. Peter Cloony is so broke his wife was starving herself in a freezing-cold house. Tick-Tock makes jokes like Pagliacci."

"And you?" asked James.

"I? Well, I haven't exactly enjoyed the past three weeks."

"No," he said, as if thinking about it from my point of view for the first time. "No, I don't suppose you have."

"It's been so calculated, this destruction of jockeys," I said. "Every week in 'Turf Talk,' looking back on it, there has been some damaging reference to one jockey or another. When he had me on the program, he introduced me as an unsuccessful rider, and he meant me to stay that way. Do you remember that ghastly bit of film he showed of me? You'd never have taken me on if you'd seen that before I'd ridden for you, would you?"

He shook his head, very troubled.

I went on: "On every possible occasion—when Template won the King Chase, for instance—he has reminded everyone watching on television that I am only substituting for Pip and that I'll be out on my ear as soon as that broken leg is strong again. Fair enough, it's Pip's job and he should have it back, but that patronizing note in Kemp-Lore's voice was calculated to make everyone take it for granted that my brief spell in the limelight was thoroughly undeserved. I dare say it was, too. But I think a lot of your owners would have been readier to trust your judgment in engaging me, and less quick to chuck me overboard at the first sign of trouble, if it hadn't been for the continual deflating pinpricks Kemp-Lore had dealt out all round. And last Friday . . ." I tried, not too successfully, to keep my voice evenly conversational. "Last Friday he led Corin and that handicapper on until they said straight out that I was finished. Were you watching?"

James nodded, and poured us another drink.

"It's a matter for the National Hunt Committee," he said firmly.

"No," I said. "His father is a member of it."

James gasped sharply. "I had forgotten."

I said, "The whole Committee's a stronghold of pro-Kemp-Lore feeling. They're all sold on Maurice. Most of them wear the same old school tie." I grinned. James wore it too. "I would be very glad if you would say nothing to any of them just yet. They would take even more convincing than you did, and there aren't any facts that Kemp-Lore couldn't explain away. But I'm digging." I drank. "The day will come."

"You sound unexpectedly cheerful," he said.

"Oh, God, James." I stood up abruptly. "I wanted to kill myself last week. I'm glad I didn't. It makes me cheerful."

He looked so startled that I relaxed and laughed, and put down my glass. "Never mind," I said. "But you must understand, I don't think the National Hunt Committee meets the case at the moment. Too gentlemanly. I favor something more in the bitter-bit line for dear Maurice."

But I had as yet no useful plan, and dear Maurice still had his teeth; and they were sharp.

11

Although neither Tick-Tock nor I had any rides the next day, I pinched the car from him to go to the meeting at Ascot, and walked round the course to get the feel of the turf. There was a bitterly cold northeast wind blowing across the Heath and the ground was hard with a touch of frost in the more exposed patches. It had been a surprisingly mild winter so far, but the high clear sky spoke ominously of ice to come. One more day, that was all I asked; only one more day. But prodding the earth on the landing side of the water jump with my heel I felt it jar instead of give.

I finished the circuit, planning the race in my mind as I went. If the ground remained firm, it would be a fast-run affair, but that suited Template well, especially with top weight to carry. Lugging packets of lead around in the mud was not what his lean streamlined frame was best fitted for.

Outside the weighing room Peter Cloony stopped me. His face was white and thin and mournful, and lines were developing on his forehead.

"I'll pay you back," he said, almost belligerently. He seemed prepared to argue about it.

"All right. One day. No hurry," I said mildly.

"You shouldn't have gone behind my back and given my wife that money and the food. I wanted to send it back at once, but she wouldn't let me. We don't need charity. I don't approve of it."

"You're a fool, Peter," I said. "Your wife was right to accept what I gave her, and I'd have thought her a stubborn ass if she hadn't. And you'd better get used to the idea: a box of groceries will be delivered to your house every week until you're earning a decent screw again."

"No!" he almost shouted. "I won't have it."

"I don't see why your wife and baby should suffer because of your misplaced pride," I said. "But if it will ease your conscience, I'll tell you why I'm doing it. You'll never get much work as long as you go around with that hangdog expression. Looking weak and miserable isn't going to persuade anyone to employ you. You need to cheer up, get fit again, and prove you're worth having. Well, all I'm doing is removing one of your worries so that you can think a bit more about racing and a bit less about your cold house and empty larder. So now you can get on with it—it's all up to you. And don't ever even risk being late."

I walked off and left Peter standing with his mouth open and his eyebrows halfway to his hair.

What Kemp-Lore had pulled down I could try to rebuild, I thought. When I had arrived I had seen him in the distance, talking animatedly to one of the Stewards, who was laughing. Slim, vital, and wholesome looking, he seemed to attract the light of the day onto his fair head.

In the weighing room after the fourth race I was handed a telegram. It said: "Pick me up White Bear, Uxbridge, 6:30 p.m. Important. Ingersoll." I felt like cursing Tick-Tock soundly because Uxbridge was in the opposite direction from home. But the car was half his, after all, and I'd had more than my fair share of it during the past week.

The afternoon dragged. I hated having to watch, hated it even more after my reassuring ride on Turniptop, but I tried to take my own advice to Peter and look cheerful: and I was rewarded, as time went on, with a definite thawing of the cold shoulder. It made life much easier not finding everyone too embarrassed to speak to me; but I was also left in no doubt that most final judgments were being reserved until after Template's race. I didn't mind that. I was confident that he was the fastest chaser in training and I had James's promise that he would be guarded every second against being doped.

I dawdled after racing ended, with two hours to kill before turning up to collect Tick-Tock. I watched the men from Universal Telecast erecting their scaffolding towers, ready to televise the Midwinter the next day, and recognized the man directing them as Gordon Kildare, still in navy-blue pin-stripe suiting and still looking like a rising young executive who knew the score. He passed me with the practiced half-smile which from a man of his sort always means that he doesn't know whom he's smiling at, but smiles all the same in case he should later find out it was someone important. However, he had gone only two steps past me when he turned and came back.

"We've had you on the program," he said pleasantly. "No, don't tell me . . ." His brow furrowed; then he snapped his fingers. "Finn, that's it, Finn." But his smile at the triumph of his memory began to slip, and I knew he was also remembering what had been said about me on his program a week ago.

"Yes, Finn," I said, taking no notice. "All set for tomorrow?"

"Er, oh, yes. Busy day. Well, now, I'm sorry to have to rush off, but you know how it is—we've got the program to put out tonight and I'm due back in the studios. Maurice went ages ago."

He looked at his watch, gave me a noncommittal smile, and gracefully retreated.

I watched him drive off in the latest streamlined Ford, picturing the studio he was going to; the ranks of cameras, the dazzling lights, the plates of sandwiches; they would all be the same. And who, I wondered, was to be Kemp-Lore's victim this evening? For whom was the chopper poised, the false charm ready?

There was so little I could do against him. Pick up some of the pieces, start some counterrumors. Try to undermine his influence. All that, yes. But I didn't have his sparkle, nor his prestige, nor yet his ruthlessness. I thrust my hands into my pockets, went out to the Mini-Cooper, and drove off to fetch Tick-Tock.

Mine was only the second car in the dark park beside the White Bear. It was one of those disappointing pubs built of tidy pinkish bricks with cold lighting inside and no atmosphere. The saloon bar was empty. The public bar held only a droopy-mustached old man pursing his lips to the evening's first half-pint. I went back to the saloon bar and ordered a whisky. No Tick-Tock. I looked at my watch. Twenty to seven.

The green plastic seats round the walls were so inhospitable that I didn't wonder the pub was empty. The dark-green curtains didn't help. Nor the fluorescent strip lights on the ceiling.

I looked at my watch again.

"Are you by any chance waiting for someone, sir?" asked the characterless barman.

"Yes, I am," I said.

"You wouldn't be a Mr. Finn?"

"Yes."

"Then I've a message for you, sir. A Mr. Ingersoll telephoned just now and said he couldn't get here to meet you, sir, and he was very sorry but could you go and pick him up from the station at six-fifty-five. The station is just down the road, first turning left and straight on for half a mile."

Finishing my drink, I thanked the barman and went out to the car. I climbed into the driving seat and stretched my hand out to turn on the lights and the ignition. I stretched out my hand . . . but I didn't reach the lights.

My neck was gripped violently from behind.

There was movement then in the back of the car as the arms shifted to get a better leverage, a rustling of clothes and the scrape of a shoe across the thin carpet.

I flung up my hands and clawed but I couldn't reach the face of whoever was behind me, and my nails were useless against his gloves. Thick leather gloves. The fingers inside them were strong, and what was worse, they knew exactly where to dig in and press, each side of the neck, just above the collarbone, where the carotid arteries branched upward. Pressure on one carotid, I remembered wildly from some distant first-aid course, stops arterial bleeding from the head, but pressure on both at once blocked all blood supplies to the brain.

I hadn't a chance. My struggles were hampered by the steering wheel and gained me nothing. In the few seconds before a roaring blackness took me off, I had time for only two more thoughts. First that I should have known that Tick-Tock would never meet me in a dreary pub like that. Second, angrily, that I was dead.

I couldn't have been out very long, but it was long enough. When consciousness slowly and fuzzily returned, I found I could open neither my eyes nor my mouth. Both were covered with sticking plaster. My wrists were tied together, and my ankles, when I tried to move them, would part only a foot or two: they were hobbled together, like a gypsy pony's.

I was lying on my side, awkwardly doubled up, on the floor in the back of a car which, from the size and smell and feel, I knew to be the Mini-Cooper. It was very cold, and after a while I realized that this was because I was no longer wearing either a jacket or an overcoat. My shirt-sleeved arms were dragged forward between the the two front seats so that I couldn't reach the sticking plaster to rip it off, and I was extremely, horribly uncomfortable. I tried once as hard as I could to free my arms, lifting and jerking at the same time, but they were securely fastened, and a fist—I supposed—crashed down on them so brutally that I didn't attempt it again.

I couldn't see who was driving the car, and driving it fast, but I didn't need to. There was only one person in the world who would have set such a trap; complicated but effective, like the Jaguar in the lane. Only one person who had any reason to abduct me, however mad that reason might be. I had no illusions. Maurice Kemp-Lore did not intend that I should win the Midwinter Cup and was taking steps to prevent it.

Did he know, I wondered helplessly, that it was no accident that Turniptop had not eaten the doped sugar? Did he guess that I knew all about his anti-jockey activities? Had he heard about my trek round the stables or my inquiries about the Jaguar? If he did know these things, what was he going to do with me? To this last rather bleak question I was in no hurry to discover the answer.

When the journey had been going on for some time, the car swung suddenly to the left and bumped onto an unevenly surfaced side road, increasing my discomfort. After a while it slowed, turned again, and rolled to a stop.

Kemp-Lore got out of the car, tipped forward the driver's seat, and tugged me out after him by the wrists. I couldn't get my feet under me because of the hobble, and I fell out onto the back of my shoulders. The ground was hard and gravelly. My shirt tore, and the sharp stones scraped into my skin.

He pulled me to my feet, and I stood there swaying, blinded by the plaster on my eyes and unable to run even if I could have wrenched myself from his grasp. He had some sort of lead fixed to my tied wrists, and he began to pull me forward by it. The ground was uneven and the rope joining my ankles was very short. I kept stumbling, and twice fell down.

It was very unpleasant, falling when I couldn't see, but I managed somehow to twist before hitting the ground, landing on my shoulders instead of my face. Always he pulled my hands so far in front of me that I couldn't reach the sticking plaster: the second time I fell I made a great effort to get it off, but he wrenched my arms roughly over my head and dragged me along the ground on my back for a long way. I very painfully lost a good deal more skin.

At length he paused and let me stand up again. He still didn't speak. Not a word. And I couldn't. There was only the sound of our footsteps on the stony ground and the faint sigh of the sharp northeaster in some nearby trees. My tattered shirt was no shield against that wind, and I began to shiver.

He stopped, and there was the sound of a door being opened, and I was tugged on. This time there was a step up, as I realized a fraction too late to prevent myself falling again. I hadn't time to twist, either. I fell flat on my stomach, elbows and chest. It knocked the wind out of me and made me dizzy.

It was a wooden floor, I thought, with my cheek on it. It smelled strongly of dust, and faintly of horses. He pulled me to my feet again and I felt my wrists being hauled upward and fastened to something just above my head. When he had finished and stepped away I explored with my fingers to find out what it was; and as soon as I felt the smooth metal hooks I knew exactly the sort of place I was in.

It was a tack room. Every stable has one. It is the place where the saddles and bridles are kept, along with all the brushes and straps and bandages and rugs that horses need. From the ceiling of every tack room hangs a harness hook, a gadget something like a three-pronged anchor, which is used for hanging bridles on while they are being cleaned. There were no bridles hanging from these particular hooks. Only me. I was securely fastened at the point where they branched off their stem.

Most tack rooms are warm, heated by a stove which dries damp rugs and prevents leather getting mildewed. This tack room was very cold indeed, and in the air the ingrained smells of leather and saddle soap were overlaid by a dead sort of mustiness. It was an unused room: an empty room. The silence took on a new meaning. There were no horses moving in the boxes. It was an empty stable. I shivered from something more than cold.

I heard him step out into the gritty yard, and presently there was a familiar rattle of bolts and the clang of a stable door being opened.

After a few seconds it was shut again, and another one was opened. This again was shut, and another opened. He went on down the row, opening six doors. I thought he must be looking for something, and numbly wondered what it was, and began to hope very much that he wouldn't find it.

After the sixth stable door shut he was gone for some time, and I couldn't hear what he was doing. But the car had not been started, so I knew he must still be there. I could make no impression at all on the strands of rope twined round my wrists. They were narrow and slippery to touch, and felt like nylon, and I couldn't even find a knot, much less undo one.

Eventually he came back, and dumped down outside the door something that clattered. A bucket.

He stepped into the room and walked softly on the wooden floor. He stopped in front of me. It was very quiet everywhere. I could hear a new sound, the high faint asthmatic wheeze of the air going into his lungs. Even an empty stable, it seemed, could start him off.

Nothing happened for a while. He walked all round me, slowly, and stopped again. Walked and stopped. Making up his mind, I thought. But to do what?

He touched me once, dragging his gloved hand across my raw shoulders. I flinched, and his breath hissed sharply. He began to cough, the dry difficult asthmatic's cough. And may you choke, I thought.

He went outside, still coughing, and picked up the bucket and walked away across the yard. I heard the bucket clatter down and a tap being turned on. The water splashed into the bucket, echoing in the stillness.

Jack and Jill went up the hill, said my brain ridiculously, to fetch a pail of water. Jack fell down and broke his crown and Jill threw the water all over him.

Oh, no, I thought, oh, no, I'm so cold already.

Part of my mind said I wouldn't mind what he did to me if only he'd let me go in time to ride Template, and the rest said don't be a fool, that's the whole point, he won't let you go, and anyway if you do get away you'll be so cold and stiff after this you won't be able to ride a donkey.

He turned off the tap and came back across the yard, the water splashing as he walked. He brought the bucket with him into the tack room and stopped behind me. The handle of the bucket clanked. I ground my teeth and took a deep breath, and waited.

He threw the water. It hit me squarely between the shoulder blades and soaked me from head to foot. It was bitterly, icy cold, and it stung like murder on the skinned patches.

After a short pause he went across the yard again and refilled the bucket. I thought I was almost past caring about that. You can't be wetter than wet and you can't be colder than freezing. And my arms, with being hauled up higher than my head, were already beginning to feel heavy and to ache. I began to worry less about the immediate future and more about how long he intended to leave me where I was.

He came back with the bucket, and this time he threw the water in my face. I had been wrong about not caring. It was at least as bad as the first time, mostly because too much of it went up my nose. Couldn't he see, I thought desperately, that he was drowning me? My chest hurt. I couldn't get my breath. Surely he would pull the plaster off my mouth, surely . . . surely . . .

He didn't.

By the time a reasonable amount of air was finding its way into my heaving lungs he was across the yard again, with more water splashing into the bucket. In due course he turned the tap off, and his feet began once more to crunch methodically in my direction. Up the step and across the wooden floor. There wasn't anything I could do to stop him. My thoughts were unprintable.

He came round in front of me again. I twisted my face sideways and buried my nose against my upper arm. He poured the whole arctic bucketful over my head. After this, I thought, I am going to have more sympathy for those clowns in circuses. I hoped the poor blighters used warm water, anyway.

It seemed that he now thought I was wet enough. In any case he dumped the bucket down outside the door instead of going to fill it again, and came back and stood close beside me. His asthma was worse.

He put his hand in my hair and pulled my head back, and spoke for the first time.

He said in a low voice, with obvious satisfaction, "That should fix *you*."

He let go of my hair and went out of the room, and I heard him walk away across the yard. His footsteps faded into the distance and after a while there was the distant slam of the Mini-Cooper's door. The engine started, the car drove off, and soon I could hear it no more.

It wasn't very funny being abandoned in a trussed condition soaking wet on a cold night. I knew he wouldn't be back for hours, because it was Friday. From eight o'clock until at least 9:30 he would be occupied with his program; and I wondered in passing what effect his recent capers would have on his performance.

One thing was clear, I could not meekly stand still and wait to be released. The first necessity was obviously to get some of the sticking plaster off. I thought that as it was wet it would come away fairly easily, but it was very adhesive, and after a good deal of rubbing my mouth against my arm I only succeeded in peeling back one corner of it. It was enough to let in a precious extra trickle of air, but no good for shouting for help.

The cold was a serious problem. My wet trousers clung clammily to my legs, my shoes were full of water, and my shirt, what was left of it, was plastered against my arms and chest. Already my fingers were completely numb, and my feet were going through the stage that precedes loss of feeling. He had left the door open on purpose, I knew, and although the biting wind was not blowing straight in there were enough eddies swirling off the walls outside for me to be in a considerable draft. I shivered from head to foot.

Harness hooks. I considered their anatomy. A stem with three upward curving branches at the bottom. At the top a ring, and attached to the ring a chain. The length of the chain depended on the height of the ceiling. At the top of the chain, a staple driven into a beam. As the whole thing was solidly constructed to resist years of vigorous stablemen putting their weight on bridles while they cleaned them, it was absolutely hopeless to try to tug it straight out of the ceiling.

I had seen harness hooks which were only hitched onto their chains and would detach easily if lifted up instead of being pulled down, but after some fruitless and tiring maneuvering I knew the one I was attached to was not so obliging.

But somewhere, I thought, there must be a weak link. Literally a weak link. When they were bought, harness hooks didn't have chains on them. Chain was cut to the length needed and added when the hook was installed in the tack room. Therefore somewhere there was a join.

The bottom curve of the hooks brushed my hair, and my wrists were tied some three inches above that. It gave me very little leverage, but it was the only hope I had. I started pivoting, leaning my forearms on the hooks and twisting the chain, putting a strain on it and hearing the links rub hollowly together. In two and a half full turns, as nearly as I could judge, it locked solid. If I could turn it farther, the weak link would snap.

The theory was simple. Putting it into operation was different. For one thing, twisting the chain had shortened it, so that my arms were stretched higher above my head and gave me less leverage than ever. And for another, they had begun to ache in earnest.

I pressed round as hard as I could. Nothing happened. I unwound the chain a fraction, and forcibly jerked it tight again. The jolt ran right down my body and threw me off my feet.

I stumbled miserably upright again, and with my legs braced repeated the process. This time the jolt shook only the top part of my body. I did it again. The chain didn't break.

After that, as a respite from rattling my arms in their sockets, I got back to work on the sticking plaster and a while later dislodged the piece over my lips. It meant that at last I could open my mouth and yell.

I yelled.

No one came. My voice echoed round the tack room and sounded loud in my ears, but I feared that outside the wind would sweep it away. I shouted, on and off, for a long while. No results.

It was at this point, perhaps an hour after Kemp-Lore had gone, that I became both very frightened and very angry.

I was frightened for my hands, which I could no longer feel. I was now not only shivering but shuddering with cold, and the blood supply to my hands was having, to put it literally, an uphill job; and with the weight of my aching arms to support, the rope tying my wrists was viciously tight.

The dismal fact had to be faced that if I had to stay where I was all night my hands might be dead in the morning. My imagination trotted on unasked with scarifying pictures. Dead. Gangrenous. Amputated.

He can't have meant that, I thought suddenly. Surely he hadn't meant that all along. No one could be so savagely cruel. I remembered the satisfaction in his voice. "That will fix *you*," he had said. But I'd thought he meant for the next day only. Not for life.

Being angry gave me both strength and resolution. I would not, I absolutely would not let him get away with it. The chain had got to be broken.

I wound it up tight again and jerked. It took my breath away. I told myself not to be a baby. I loosened and jerked, loosened and jerked, pushing against the hooks, trying to twist them round with all my strength. The chain rattled, and held.

I started doing it rhythmically. Six jerks and a rest. Six jerks and a rest. On and on, six jerks and a rest, until I was sobbing.

At least, I thought, with a last flicker of humor, the exercise is making me warmer. But it was little consolation for the cracking pain in my arms and shoulders, or the red-hot pincers which seemed to have attached themselves to the back of my neck, or the bite of the rope into my wrists as the friction rubbed away the skin.

Six jerks and a rest. Six jerks and a rest. The rests got longer. Anyone who has tried crying with sticking plaster over his eyes will know that the tears run down inside the nose. When I sniffed, they came into my mouth. Salty. I got tired of the taste.

Six jerks and a rest. I wouldn't stop. I refused to stop. Six jerks. Rest. Six. Rest.

After a while I unwound the chain by turning round and round where I stood and wound it up again in the opposite direction. I thought that jolting it the other way might both snap it more quickly and be easier on my protesting muscles; but I was wrong on both counts. Eventually, I wound back again.

Time passed. Because I couldn't see I became giddy as I grew tired. I began to sway and buckle at the knees if I didn't concentrate, and neither of these things did my arms any good.

Why—jerk—wouldn't—jerk—the ruddy chain—jerk—jerk—break? I wasn't going to admit it was too much for me without struggling to the end, though the disgusting temptation gradually grew to give up the excruciating wrenching and just hang and faint away and get some peace. A temporary, deceptive, useless, dangerous peace.

I went on jerking for what seemed like hours, sometimes sobbing, sometimes cursing, sometimes maybe praying as well.

I was quite unprepared for it when it happened. One minute I was screwing up the dregs of will power for another series of jerks and the next, after a convulsive, despairing heave, I was collapsing in a tumbling heap on the floor with the harness hook clattering down on top of me, still tied to my wrists.

For a moment or two I could hardly believe it. My head was whirling, all sense of direction gone. But the floor was hard beneath my body, dusty smelling and real, damp and reassuring.

After a while, when my head cleared, I rolled into a kneeling position so that the blood was flowing down my arms at last, and put my hands between my thighs to try to warm them. They felt like lumps of frozen meat, with no sensation and no movement. The rope round my wrists didn't cut so much now that it had no weight to support, and there was room for the blood to get back into my hands, I thought, if only it would.

The unimaginable relief of having my arms down made me forget for some time how cold I was, and how wet, and how far still from getting warm and dry. I felt almost cheerful, as if I had won a major battle; and indeed, looking back on it, I know I had.

12

Kneeling very soon became uncomfortable, so I shuffled across the floor until I came to a wall, and sat with the bottom of my spine propped against it and my knees bent up.

The plaster on my eyes was still stuck tight. I tried to scrape it off by rubbing it against the rope on my wrists, but made no headway. The hooks hindered me and bumped into my face, and in the end I gave it up and concentrated again on warming my hands, alternately cradling them between my thighs and thumping them against my knees to restore the circulation.

After a time I found I could move my fingers. I still couldn't feel them at all, but movement was a tremendous step forward, and I remember smiling about it for at least ten minutes.

I put my hands up to my face and tried to scrape the plaster off with my thumbnail. My thumb slid across my cheek, checked on the edge of the plaster and, when I pushed from the elbow, bent uselessly and slithered away. I tried again. It had to be done, because until I could see where I was going I couldn't leave the tack room. It was colder outside, and my ankles were still hobbled, and wandering about blind in those conditions did not appeal to me.

I bent my head down and put my right thumb in my mouth, to warm it. Every few minutes I tested the results on the edge of the plaster and at last got to the stage where the thumb would push without bending. I needed only to prize a corner up, but even that took a long time. Eventually, however, my nail had pushed unstuck a flap big enough for me to grip between my wrists, and with several false starts and a fair selection of oaths, I managed in the end to pull the obstinate thing off.

Dazzling moonlight poured through the open door and through a window beside it. I was sitting against the end wall with the door away on my left. Above my head and all round the room there were empty wooden supports for saddles and bridles, and bare shelves and a cupboard on the wall facing me. An efficient-looking stove occupied the corner on my right, with a few dead cinders still scattered on the floor beside it.

From the center of the ceiling, pale in the moonlight, hung twenty inches of sturdy galvanized chain.

I looked down at my hands. The harness hook glinted with reflected light. No wonder it had been so difficult to break, I thought. The chain and the hook were almost new. Not the dark old rusty things I had been imagining all along. I swallowed, really shattered. It was just as well I hadn't known.

My hands themselves, including the thumb I had tried to warm, were white. Almost as white as my shirt sleeves. Almost as white as the nylon rope which wound round the hooks. Only my wrists were dark.

I stretched my feet out. More nylon rope ran from one ankle to the other; about fifteen inches of it.

My fingers wouldn't undo the knots. My pockets had been emptied; no knife, no matches. There was nothing in the tack room to cut with. I stood up stiffly, leaning against the wall, and slowly, carefully, shuffled over to the door. My foot kicked against something, and I looked down. On the edge of a patch of moonlight lay the broken link. It was a grotesquely buckled piece of silvery metal. It had given me a lot of trouble.

I went on to the door and negotiated the step. The bucket stood there, dully gray. I looked round the moonlit L-shaped yard. Four boxes stretched away to my right, and at right angles to them were two more, on the short arm of the L. Over there, too, was the tap; and beside the tap, on the ground, an object I was very glad to see. A bootscraper made of a thin metal plate bedded in concrete.

With small careful steps I made my way to it across the hard-packed gravel, the cutting wind ripping the last remnants of warmth from my body.

Leaning against the wall, and with one foot on the ground, I stretched the rope tautly over the bootscraper and began to rub it to and fro, using the other foot as a pendulum. The blade of the scraper was far from sharp and the rope was new, and it took a long time to fray it through, but it parted in the end. I knelt down and tried to do the same with the strands round my wrists, but the harness hook kept getting in the way again and I couldn't get anything like the same purchase. I stood up wearily. It looked as though I'd have to lug that tiresome piece of ironmongery around with me a while longer.

Being able to move my legs, however, gave me a marvelous sense of freedom. Stiffly, shaking with cold, I walked out of the yard and round to the house looming darkly behind it. There were no lights, and on looking closer I found the downstairs windows were all shuttered. It was as empty as the stable; an unwelcome but not unexpected discovery.

I walked a bit unsteadily past the house and down the drive. It was a long drive with no lodge at the gate, only an estate agent's board announcing that this desirable country gentleman's residence was for sale, together with some modern stabling, forty acres of arable land, and an apple orchard.

A country lane ran past the end of the drive, giving no indication as to which way lay civilization. I tried to remember from which direction the Mini-Cooper had come, but I couldn't. It seemed a very long time ago. I glanced automatically at my left wrist but there was only rope there, no watch. Since it had to be one thing or the other, I turned right. It was a deserted road with open fields on the far sides of its low hedges. No cars passed, and nowhere could I see a light. Cursing the wind and aching all over I stumbled on, hanging on to the fact that if I went far enough I was bound to come to a house in the end.

What I came to first was not a house but something much better. A telephone box. It stood alone, brightly lit inside, square and beckoning, on the corner where the lane turned into a more main road, and it solved the embarrassing problem of presenting myself at some stranger's door looking like a scarecrow and having to explain how I got into such a state.

There were a lot of people I could have called. Police, ambulance or the fire brigade, for a start; but by the time I had forced my still nearly useless hands to pull open the door far enough for me to get my foot in, I had had time to think. Once I called in authority in any form there would be unending questions to answer and statements to make, and like as not I'd end up for the night in the local cottage hospital. I hated being in hospitals.

Also, although I felt so bone-cold, it was not, I thought, actually freezing. The puddles at the side of the road had no ice on them. They would be racing at Ascot the next day. Template would turn up for the Midwinter, and James didn't know his jockey was wandering around unfit to ride.

Unfit . . . Between seeing the telephone box and clumsily picking up the receiver I came to the conclusion that the only satisfactory way to cheat Kemp-Lore of his victory was to go and ride the race, and win it if I could, and pretend that tonight's misfortunes had not happened. He had had things his own way for far too long. He was not, he was positively not, I vowed, going to get the better of me any more.

I dialed O with an effort, gave the operator my credit card number, and asked to be connected to the one person in the world who would give me the help I needed and keep quiet about it afterward, and not try to argue me out of what I intended to do.

Her voice sounded sleepy. She said, "Hello?"

"Joanna, are you busy?" I asked.

"Busy? At this hour?" she said. "Is that you, Rob?"

"Yes."

"Well, go back to bed and ring me in the morning," she said. "I was asleep. Don't you know what time it is?" I heard her yawn.

"No," I said.

"Well, it's . . . er . . . twenty to one. Good night."

"Joanna, don't go," I said urgently. "I need your help. I really do. Please don't ring off."

"What's the matter?" She yawned again.

"I . . . I . . . Joanna, come and help me. Please."

There was a little silence and she said in a more awake voice, "You've never said 'please' like that to me before. Not for anything."

"Will you come?"

"Where to?"

"I don't really know," I said despairingly. "I'm in a telephone box on a country road miles from anywhere. The telephone exchange is Hampden Row." I spelled it out for her. "I don't think it's very far from London, and somewhere on the West, probably."

NERVE 367

"You can't come back on your own?" she asked.

"No," I said. "I've no money and my clothes are wet."

"Oh." A pause. "All right, then. I'll find out where you are and come in a taxi. Anything else?"

"Bring a sweater," I said, "I'm cold. And some dry socks, if you have any. And some gloves. Don't forget the gloves. And a pair of scissors."

"Sweater, socks, gloves, scissors. Okay. You'll have to wait while I get dressed again, but I'll come as soon as I can. Stay by the telephone box."

"Yes," I said.

"I'll hurry, don't worry," she said. "Good-by."

"Good-by." I fumbled the receiver back onto its rest. However quick she was, she wouldn't arrive for an hour. Well, what was one hour more after so many? I had had no idea it was so late: the evening had certainly seemed to have been going on for an eternity, but I had lost all sense of actual time. And Kemp-Lore hadn't come back. His show had been over for hours, and he hadn't come back. The bloody, murdering bastard, I thought.

I sat down on the floor of the box and leaned gingerly against the wall beside the telephone, with my head resting on the coin box. Exercise and the bitter wind outside, inactivity and shelter inside; one looked as cold a prospect as the other. But I was too tired to walk any more if I didn't have to, so the choice was easy.

I put my hands up to my face and one by one bit my fingers. They were icy cold and yellowish white, and none of them had any feeling. They would curl and uncurl, but slowly and weakly, and that was all. I got to work on them seriously then, rubbing them up and down against my legs, bumping them on my knees, forcing them open and shut, but it seemed to make little difference. I persevered from fear that they should get worse if I didn't, and paid for it in various creaks from my sore and sorely misused shoulders.

There was a good deal to think about to take my mind off my woes. That sticking plaster, for instance. Why had he used it? The strip over my mouth, I had assumed, had been to stop me shouting for help; but when I got it off at last and shouted, there was no one to hear. No one could have heard however loud I yelled, because the stable was so far from the lane.

The strip over my eyes should have been to prevent my seeing where I was going, but why did it matter if I saw an empty yard and a deserted tack room? What would have happened differently, I wondered, if I had been able to see and talk?

To see . . . I would have seen Kemp-Lore's expression while he went about putting me out of action. I would have seen Kemp-Lore . . . that was it! It was himself he had not wanted me to see, not the place.

If that was so, it was conceivable that he had prevented me from talking simply so that he should not be trapped into answering. He had spoken only once, and that in a low, unrecognizable tone. I became convinced that he had not wanted me to hear and recognize his voice.

In that case he must have believed I did not know who had abducted me, that I didn't know who he was. He must still believe it. Which meant that he thought James had knocked Turniptop's doped sugar out of his hand by accident, that he hadn't heard about Tick-Tock and me going round all the stables, and that he didn't know I had been asking about the Jaguar. It gave me, I thought, a fractional advantage for the future. If he had left any tracks anywhere, he would not see any vital, immediate need to obliterate them. If he didn't know he was due for destruction himself, he would not be excessively on his guard.

Looking at my bloodless hands and knowing that on top of everything else I still had to face the pain of their return to life, I was aware that all the civilized brakes were off in my conscience. Helping to build up what he had broken was not enough. He himself had hammered into me the inner implacability I had lacked to avenge myself and all the others thoroughly, and do it physically and finally and without compunction.

Joanna came, in the end.

I heard a car draw up and a door slam, and her quick tread on the road. The door of the telephone box opened, letting in an icy blast, and there she was, dressed in trousers and woolly boots and a warm padded jacket, with the light falling on her dark hair and making hollows of her eyes.

I was infinitely glad to see her. I looked up at her and did my best at a big smile of welcome, but it didn't come off very well. I was shivering too much.

She knelt down and took a closer look at me. Her face went stiff with shock.

"Your hands," she said.

"Yes. Did you bring the scissors?"

Without a word she opened her handbag, took out a sensible-sized pair, and cut me free. She did it gently. She took the harness hook from between my knees and laid it on the floor, and carefully peeled from my wrists the cut pieces of rope. They were all more brown than white, stained with my blood, and where they had been there were big corrugated raw patches, dark and deep. She stared at them.

"More bits of rope down there," I said, nodding toward my feet.

She cut the pieces round my ankles, and I saw her rubbing my trouser leg between her fingers. The air had been too cold to dry them and my body had not generated enough heat, so they were still very damp.

"Been swimming?" she said flippantly. Her voice cracked.

There was a step on the road outside and a man's shape loomed up behind Joanna.

"Are you all right, miss?" he said in a reliable-sounding Cockney voice.

"Yes, thank you," she said. "Do you think you could help me get my cousin into the taxi?"

He stepped into the doorway and looked down at me, his eyes on my wrists and my hands.

"Christ!" he said.

"Very aptly put," I said.

He looked at my face. He was a big sturdy man of about fifty, weather-beaten like a sailor, with eyes that looked as if they had seen everything and found most of it disappointing.

"You've been done proper, haven't you?" he said.

"Proper," I agreed.

He smiled faintly. "Come on then. No sense in hanging about here."

I stood up clumsily and lurched against Joanna, and put my arms round her neck to save myself from falling; and as I was there it seemed a shame to miss the opportunity, so I kissed her. On the eyebrow, as it happened.

"Did you say 'cousin'?" said the taxi driver.

"Cousin," said Joanna firmly. Much too firmly.

The driver held the door open. "We'd better take him to a doctor," he said.

"No," I said. "No doctor."

Joanna said, "You need one."

"No."

"That's frostbite," said the driver, pointing to my hands.

"No," I said. "It isn't freezing. No ice on the puddles. Just cold. Not frostbite." My teeth were chattering and I could only speak in short sentences.

"What happened to your back?" asked the driver, looking at the tattered bits of shirt sticking to me.

"I . . . fell over," I said. "On some gravel."

He looked skeptical.

"It's a terrible mess, and there's a lot of dirt in it," said Joanna, peering round me and sounding worried.

"You wash it," I said. "At home."

"You need a doctor," said the driver again.

I shook my head. "I need disinfectant, aspirins and sleep."

"I hope you know what you're doing," said Joanna. "What else?"

"Sweater," I said.

"It's in the taxi," she said. "And some other clothes. You can change as we go along. The sooner you get into a hot bath the better."

"I'd be careful about that, miss," said the driver. "Don't go warming those hands up too fast or the fingers will drop off." A comforting chap. Inaccurate too, I trusted. Joanna looked more worried than ever.

We walked from the telephone box to the taxi. It was an ordinary black London taxi. I wondered what charm Joanna had used to get it so far out into the country in the middle of the night; and also, more practically, whether the meter was still ticking away. It was.

"Get in, out of the wind," she said, opening the taxi door.

I did as I was told. She had brought a suitcase, from which she now produced a thin pale-blue cardigan of her own and a padded man-sized olive-colored parka which zipped up the front. She looked at me judiciously, and out came the scissors. Some quick snips and the ruins of my shirt lay on the seat beside me. She cut two long strips off it and wound them carefully round my wrists. The taxi driver watched.

"This is a police job," he suggested.

I shook my head. "Private fight."

He held up the harness hook, which he had brought across from the telephone box.

"What sort of thing is this?" he asked.

"Throw it in the ditch," I said, averting my eyes.

"You'll be needing it for the police," he insisted.

"I told you," I said wearily, "no police."

His disillusioned face showed that he knew all about people who got themselves beaten up but wouldn't report it. He shrugged and went off into the darkness, and came back without the hook.

"It's in the ditch just behind the telephone box, if you change your mind," he said.

"Thanks," I said.

Joanna finished the bandages and helped my arms into both the garments she had brought, and fastened the fronts. The next thing the suitcase produced was a pair of fur-lined mittens which went on without too much trouble, and after that a thermos flask full of hot soup, and some cups.

I looked into Joanna's black eyes as she held the cup to my mouth. I loved her. Who wouldn't love a girl who thought of hot soup at a time like that?

The driver accepted some soup too, and stamped his feet on the ground and remarked that it was getting chilly. Joanna gave him a pained look, and I laughed.

He glanced at me appraisingly and said, "Maybe you can do without a doctor, at that." He thanked Joanna for the soup, gave her back the cup, settled himself in the driver's seat and, switching off the light inside the taxi, started to drive us back to London.

"Who did it?" said Joanna.

"Tell you later."

"All right." She didn't press. She bent down to the case and brought out some fleecy slippers, thick socks, and a pair of her own stretch pants. "Take your trousers off."

I said ironically, "I can't undo the zip."

"I forgot."

"Anyway," I said, "I'll settle for the socks; can't manage the trousers." Even I could hear the exhaustion in my voice, and Joanna without arguing got down on her knees in the swaying cab and changed my wet socks and shoes for dry ones.

"Your feet are freezing," she said.

"I can't feel them," I said. The moon shone clearly through the window and I looked at the slippers. They were too large for me; much too large for Joanna.

"Have I stepped into Brian's shoes?" I asked.

After a pause she said neutrally, "They are Brian's, yes."

"And the jacket?"

"I bought it for him for Christmas."

So that was that. It wasn't the best moment to find out.

"I didn't give it to him," she said after a moment, as if she had made up her mind about something.

"Why not?"

"It didn't seem to suit a respectable life in the outer suburbs. I gave him a gold tiepin instead."

"Very suitable," I said dryly.

"A farewell present," she said quietly.

I said sincerely, "I'm sorry." I knew it hadn't been easy for her.

She drew in a breath sharply. "Are you made of iron, Rob?"

"Iron filings," I said.

The taxi sped on.

"We had a job finding you," she said. "I'm sorry we were so long. It was such a big area, you see."

"You came, though."

"Yes."

I found sitting in the swaying taxi very uncomfortable. My arms and shoulders ached unceasingly and if I leaned back too heavily the raw bits didn't like it. After a while I gave it up, and finished the journey sitting on the floor with my head and my hands in Joanna's lap.

I was of course quite used to being knocked about. I followed, after all, an occupation in which physical damage was a fairly frequent though unimportant factor; and especially during my first season, when I was a less efficient jockey and most of the horses I rode were the worst to be had, there was rarely a time when some area of my body was not black and blue. I had broken several of the smaller bones, been kicked in tender places, and dislocated one or two joints. But none of these things had made the slightest dent on my general sense of well-being, and on my optimism that I wouldn't crash unmendably. It seemed that in common with most other jockeys I had been born with the sort of resilient constitution that could take a bang and be ready for business, if not the following day, at least a good deal quicker than the medical profession considered normal.

Practice had given me a certain routine for dealing with discomfort, which was mainly to ignore it and concentrate on something else: but this system had not operated very well that evening. It didn't work, for instance, when I sat for a while in a light armchair in Joanna's warm room with my elbows on my knees, watching my fingers gradually change color from yellowy white to smudgy charcoal, to patchy purple, and finally to red.

It began as a tingle, faint and welcome, soon after we had got back and Joanna had turned on both her powerful heaters. She had insisted at once on removing my clammy trousers and also my underpants, and on my donning her black pants, which were warm but not long enough by several inches. It was odd, in a way, letting her undress me, which she did matter-of-factly and without remark; but in another way it seemed completely natural, a throwback to our childhood, when we had been bathed together on our visits to each other's houses.

She dug out some rather powdery-looking aspirins in a bottle. There were only three of them left, which I swallowed. Then she made some black coffee and held it for me to drink. It was stiff with brandy.

"Warming," she said laconically. "Anyway, you've stopped shivering at last."

It was then that my fingers tingled, and I told her.

"Will it be bad?" she said prosaically, putting down the empty coffee mug.

"Possibly."

"You won't want me to sit and watch you, then."

I shook my head. She took the empty mug into the kitchen and was several minutes coming back with a full one for herself.

The tingle increased first to a burning sensation and then to a feeling of being squeezed in a vise, tighter and tighter, getting more and more agonizing until it felt that at any minute my fingers would disintegrate under the pressure. But there they were, harmlessly hanging in the warm air, with nothing to show for it except that they were slowly turning puce.

Joanna came back from the kitchen and wiped the sweat off my forehead.

"Are you all right?" she asked.

"Yes," I said.

She nodded, and gave me a faint edition of the smile which had had my heart doing flipflaps from boyhood, and drank her coffee.

When the pulse got going it felt as though my hands had been taken out of the vise, laid on a bench, and were being rhythmically hammered. It was terrible. And it went on too long. My head drooped.

When I looked up she was standing in front of me, watching me with an expression which I couldn't read. There were tears in her eyes.

"Is it over?" she said, blinking to disguise them.

"More or less."

We both looked at my hands, which were now a fierce red all over.

"And your feet?" she asked.

"They're fine," I said. Their awakening had been nothing.

"I'd better wash those grazes on your back," she said.

"No. In the morning."

"There's a lot of dirt in them," she protested.

"It's been there so long already that a few more hours won't hurt," I said. "I've had four anti-tetanus injections in the last two years, and there's always penicillin . . . and I'm too tired."

She didn't argue. She unzipped and helped me take off the parka, and made me get into her bed, still incongruously dressed in her black pants and blue cardigan and looking like a second-rate ballet dancer with a hangover. The sheets were rumpled from her lying in them before I had wakened her, and there was still a dent in her pillow where her head had been. I put mine there too, with an odd feeling of delight. She saw me grin, and correctly read my mind.

"It's the first time you've got into my bed," she said. "And it'll be the last."

"Have a heart, Joanna," I said.

She perched herself on the edge of the mattress and looked down at me.

"It's no good for cousins," she said.

"And if we weren't cousins?"

"I don't know . . ." She sighed. "But we are."

She bent down to kiss me good night on the forehead.

I couldn't help it; I put my arms up round her shoulders and pulled her down onto my chest and kissed her properly, mouth to mouth. It was the first time I had ever done it, and into it went all the pent-up and suppressed desire I had ever felt for her. It was too hungry, too passionate, much too desperate. I knew it, but I couldn't stop it. For a moment she seemed to relax and melt and kiss me back, but it was so brief and passing that I thought I had imagined it, and afterward her body grew rigid.

I let her go. She stood up abruptly and stared at me, her face scrubbed of any emotion. No anger, no disgust; and no love. She turned away without speaking and went across the room to the sofa, where she twisted a blanket around herself and lay down. She stretched out her hand to the table light and switched it off.

Her voice reached me across the dark room, calm, self-controlled. "Good night, Rob."

"Good night, Joanna," I said politely.

There was dead silence.

I rolled over onto my stomach and put my face in her pillow.

13

I don't know whether Joanna slept or not during the next four hours. The room was quiet. The time passed slowly.

The pulse in my hands went on throbbing violently for a while; but who cared? It was comforting, even if it hurt. I thought about all the fat red corpuscles forcing their way through the shrunken capillaries like water gushing along dry irrigation ditches after a drought. Very nice. Very life-giving. By tomorrow afternoon, I thought—correction, this afternoon—they might be fit for work. They'd got to be, that was all there was about it.

Some time after it was light I heard Joanna go into her narrow bathroom-kitchen where she brushed her teeth and made some fresh coffee. The warm roasted smell floated across to me. Saturday morning, I thought. Midwinter Cup day. I didn't leap out of bed eagerly to greet it; I turned over slowly from my stomach onto my side, shutting my eyes against the stiffness which afflicted every muscle from neck to waist, and the sharp soreness of my back and wrists. I really didn't feel very well.

She came across the room with a mug of steaming coffee and put it on the bedside table. Her face was pale and expressionless.

"Coffee," she said unnecessarily.

"Thank you."

"How do you feel?" she asked, a little too clinically.

"Alive," I said.

There was a pause.

"Oh, go on," I said. "Either slosh me one or smile . . . one or the other. But don't stand there looking tragic, as if the Albert Hall had burned down on the first night of the Proms."

"Damn it, Rob," she said, her face crinkling into a laugh.

"Truce?" I asked.

"Truce," she agreed, still smiling. She even sat down again on the edge of the bed. I shoved myself up into a sitting position, wincing somewhat from various aches, and brought a hand out from under the bedclothes to reach for the coffee.

As a hand it closely resembled a bunch of beef sausages. I produced the other one. It also was swollen. The skin on both felt very tender and they were still unnaturally red.

"Blast," I said. "What's the time?"

"About eight o'clock," she said. "Why?"

Eight o'clock. The race was at 2:30. I began counting backward. I would have to be at Ascot by at the latest 1:30, preferably earlier, and the journey down, going by taxi, would take about fifty minutes. Allow an hour for holdups. That left me precisely four and a half hours in which to get fit enough to ride, and the way I felt it was a tall order.

I began to consider ways and means. There were the Turkish baths, with heat and massage; but I had lost too much skin for that to be an attractive idea. There was a workout in a gym; a possibility, but rough. There was a canter in the Park—a good solution on any day except Saturday, when the Row would be packed with little girls on leading reins; or better still a gallop on a race horse at Epsom, but there was neither time to arrange it nor a good excuse to be found for needing it.

"What's the matter?" asked Joanna.

I told her.

"You don't mean it?" she said. "You aren't seriously thinking of racing today?"

"I seriously am."

"You're not fit to."

"That's the point. That's what we are discussing, how best to get fit."

"That isn't what I mean," she protested. "You look ill. You need a long quiet day in bed."

"I'll have it tomorrow," I said. "Today I am riding Template in the Midwinter Cup."

She began more forcefully to try to dissuade me, so I told her why I was going to ride. I told her everything, all about Kemp-Lore's anti-jockey obsession and all that had happened on the previous evening before she found me in the telephone box. It took quite a time. I didn't look at her while I told her about the tack-room episode, because for some reason it embarrassed me to describe it, even to her, and I knew then quite certainly that I was not going to repeat it to anyone else.

When I had finished she looked at me without speaking for half a minute—thirty solid seconds—and then she cleared her throat and said, "Yes, I see. We'd better get you fit, then."

I smiled at her.

"What first?" she said.

"Hot bath and breakfast," I said. "And can we have the weather forecast on?" I listened to it every morning, as a matter of routine.

She switched on the radio, which was busy with some sickening matinee music, and started tidying up the room, folding the blanket she had slept in and shaking the sofa cushions. Before she had finished the music stopped, and we heard the 8:30 news headlines, followed by the forecast.

"There was a slight frost in many parts of the country last night," said the announcer smoothly, "and more is expected tonight, especially in exposed areas. Temperatures today will reach five degrees centigrade, forty-one Fahrenheit, in most places, and the northeasterly wind will moderate slightly. It will be bright and sunny in the south. Further outlook: colder weather is expected in the next few days. And here is an announcement: The Stewards at Ascot inspected the course at eight o'clock this morning and have issued the following statement: 'Two or three degrees of frost were recorded on the race course last night, but the ground on both sides of the fences was protected by straw, and unless there is a sudden severe frost during the morning, racing is certain.'"

Joanna switched off. She said, "Are you absolutely determined to go?"

"Absolutely," I said.

"Well, I'd better tell you. I watched that program on television last night. 'Turf Talk.'"

"Did you now!" I said, surprised.

"I sometimes do, since you were on it. If I'm in. Anyway I watched last night."

"And?" I prompted.

"He," she said, neither of us needing help to know whom she meant, "talked about the Midwinter Cup nearly all the time; canned biographies of the horses and trainers, and so on. I was waiting to hear him mention you, but he didn't. He just went on and on about how superb Template is; not a word about you. But what I thought you'd like to know is that he said that as it was such an important race he personally would be commentating the finish today, and that he personally would interview the winning jockey afterward. If only you can win, he'll have to describe your doing it, which would be a bitter enough pill, and then, congratulate you publicly in full view of several million people."

I gazed at her awestruck.

"That's a great thought," I said.

"Like he interviewed you after that race on Boxing Day," she added.

"That was the race that sealed my fate with him, I imagine," I said. "And you seem to have done some fairly extensive viewing, if I may say so."

She looked taken aback. "Well, didn't I see you sitting unobtrusively at the back of a concert I gave in Birmingham one night last summer?"

"I thought those lights were supposed to dazzle you," I said.

"You'd be surprised," she said.

I pushed back the bedclothes. The black pants looked even more incongruous in the daylight.

"I'd better get going," I said. "What do you have in the way of disinfectant and bandages, and a razor?"

"Only a few bits of elastic bandage," she said apologetically, "and the razor I defuzz my legs with. There's a chemist two roads away, though, who will be open by now. I'll make a list." She wrote it on an old envelope.

"And A.P.C. tablets," I said. "They are better than just aspirins."

"Right," she said. "I won't be long."

When she had gone I got out of bed and went into the bathroom. It's easy enough to say, but it wasn't all that easy to do, since I felt as if some overzealous laundress had fed me several times through a mangle. It was exasperating, I thought bitterly, how much havoc Kemp-Lore had worked on my body by such simple means. I turned on the taps, took off the pants and socks and stepped into the bath.

The blue cardigan had stuck to my back and the shirt bandages to my wrists, so I lay down in the hot water without tugging at them and waited for them to soak off.

Gradually the heat did its customary work of unlocking the worst of the cramps, until I could rotate my shoulders and turn my head from side to side without feeling that I was tearing something adrift. Every few minutes I added more hot water, so that by the time Joanna came back I was up to my throat in it and steaming nicely, warm to the backbone and beyond.

She had dried my trousers and underpants overnight, and she pressed them for me while I eased myself out of the blue cardigan and reluctantly got out of the bath. I put on the trousers and watched her setting out her purchases on the kitchen table, a dark lock of hair falling forward into her eyes and a look of concentration firming her mouth. Quite a girl.

I sat down at the table and she bathed the abrasions with disinfectant, dried them, and covered them with large pieces of lint spread with zinc-and-castor-oil ointment which she stuck on with adhesive tape. She was neat and quick, and her touch was light.

"Most of the dirt came out in the bath luckily," she observed, busy with the scissors. "You've got quite an impressive set of muscles, haven't you? You must be strong. I didn't realize."

"At the moment I've got an impressive set of jellies." I sighed. "Very wobbly, very weak." And aching steadily, though there wasn't any point in saying so.

She went into the other room, rummaged in a drawer, and came back with another cardigan. Pale green, this time; the color suited my state of health rather well, I thought.

"I'll buy you some new ones," I said, stretching it across my chest to do up the fancy buttons.

"Don't bother," she said, "I loathe both of them."

"Thanks," I said, and she laughed.

I put the parka on again on top of the jersey and pushed the knitted cuffs up my forearms. Joanna slowly unwound the blood-stained bandages on my wrists. They still stuck a bit in spite of the soaking, and what lay underneath was a pretty disturbing sight, even to me, now that we could see it in daylight.

"I can't deal with this," she said positively. "You must go to a doctor."

"This evening," I said. "Put some more bandages on, for now."

"It's too deep," she said. "It's too easy to get it infected. You can't ride like this, Rob, really you can't."

"I can," I said. "I'll dunk them in a bowl of disinfectant for a while, and then you can wrap them up again. Nice and flat, so they won't show."

"Don't they hurt?" she said.

I didn't answer.

"Yes," she said. "Silly question." She sighed, and fetched a bowl full of warm water, pouring in solution so that it turned a milky white, and I soaked my wrists in it for ten minutes.

"That's fixed the infection," I said. "Now . . . nice and flat."

She did as I asked, fastening the ends of the bandages down with little gold safety pins. When she had finished the white cuffs looked tidy and narrow, and I knew they would be unnoticeable under racing colors.

"Perfect," I said appreciatively, pulling down the parka sleeves to cover them. "Thank you, Florence."

"And Nightingale to you, too," she said, making a face at me. "When are you going to the police?"

"I'm not. I told you," I said. "I'm not going at all. I meant what I said last night."

"But why not? Why not?" She didn't understand. "You could get him prosecuted for assault or for causing grievous bodily harm, or whatever the technical term is."

I said, "I'd rather fight my own battles. And anyway, I can't face the thought of telling the police what happened last night, or being examined by their doctors, and photographed; or standing up in court, if it came to that, and answering questions about it in public, and having the whole rotten lot printed in gory detail in the papers. I just can't face it, that's all."

"Oh," she said slowly. "I suppose it would be a bit of an ordeal, if you look at it like that. Perhaps you feel humiliated. Is that it?"

"You may be rather bruisingly right," I admitted grudgingly, thinking about it. "And I'll keep my humiliation to myself, if you don't mind."

She laughed. "You don't need to feel any," she said. "Men are funny creatures."

The pity about hot baths is that, although they loosen one up beautifully for the time being, the effect does not last; one has to consolidate the position by exercise. And exercise, my battered muscles protested, was just what they would least enjoy; all the same I did a few rather halfhearted bend-stretch arm movements while Joanna scrambled some eggs, and after we had eaten and I had shaved I went back to it with more resolution, knowing that if I didn't get onto Template's back in a reasonably supple condition he had no chance of winning. It wouldn't help anyone if I fell off at the first fence.

After an hour's work, though I couldn't screw myself up to swinging my arms round in complete circles, I did get to the stage where I could lift them above shoulder height without wanting to cry out.

Joanna washed up and tidied the flat, and soon after ten o'clock, while I was taking a breather, she said, "Are you going on with this health and beauty kick until you leave for Ascot?"

"Yes."

"Well," she said, "it's only a suggestion, but why don't we go skating instead?"

"All that ice," I said, shuddering.

She smiled. "I thought you had to remount at once, after a fall?"

I saw the point.

"Anyway," she said, "it's good, warming exercise, and far more interesting than what you've been doing."

"You're a blooming genius, my darling Joanna," I said fervently.

"Er . . . maybe," she said. "I still think you ought to be in bed."

When she was ready we went along to my family's flat where I borrowed one of my father's shirts and a tie and also his skates, which represented his only interest outside music. Then we called at the bank, since the taxi ride the night before had taken nearly all Joanna's cash, and apart from needing money myself I wanted to repay her. Lastly, we stopped at a shop to buy me a pair of brown, silk-lined leather gloves, which I put on, and finally we reached the ice rink in Queensway where we had both been members from the days when we were taken there as toddlers on afternoons too rainy for playing in the Park.

We had not skated together since we were sixteen, and it was fascinating to see how quickly we fell back into the same dancing techniques that we had practiced as children.

She was right about the exercise. After an hour of it I had loosened up from head to foot, with hardly a muscle that wasn't moving reasonably freely. She herself, sliding over the ice beside me, had color in her cheeks and a dazzling sparkle in her eyes. She looked young and vivid.

At twelve o'clock, Cinderella-like, we slid off the rink.

"All right?" she asked, smiling.

"Gorgeous," I said, admiring the clear, intelligent face turned up to mine.

She didn't know whether I meant her or the skating, which was perhaps just as well.

"I mean, how are the aches and pains?"

"Gone," I said.

"You're a liar," she said, "but at least you don't look as gray as you did."

We went to change, which for me simply meant substituting my father's shirt and tie for the pale-green cardigan, and putting back the parka on top, and the gloves. Necessary, the gloves. Although my fingers were less swollen, less red, and no longer throbbed, the skin in places was beginning to split in short thread-thin cracks.

In the foyer Joanna put the cardigan and my father's skates into her bag and zipped it up, and we went into the street. She had already told me that she would not come to Ascot with me, but would watch on television. "And mind you win," she said. "After all this."

"Can I come back to your place afterward?" I said.

"Why, yes . . . yes," she said, as if surprised that I had asked.

"Fine," I said. "Well, good-by."

"Good luck, Rob," she said seriously.

14

The third cruising taxi that I stopped just round the corner in Bayswater Road agreed to take me all the way to Ascot. During the journey, which was quick and skillfully driven, I kept the warmth and flexibility going in my arms by some minor exercises and imaginary piano playing, and if the driver saw me at it in his mirror he probably imagined I was suffering from a sad sort of St. Vitus's dance.

When I paid him at the gate, he announced that as it was his own cab he might as well stay and have a flutter on the races himself, so I arranged for him to drive me back to London at the end of the afternoon.

"Got any tips?" he said, counting my change.

"How about Template, in the big race?" I said.

"I dunno." He pursed his lips. "I dunno as I fancy that Finn. They say he's all washed."

"Don't believe all you hear," I said, smiling. "See you later."

"Right."

I went through the gate and along to the weighing room. The hands of the clock on the tower pointed to 1:05. Sid, James's head traveling lad, was standing outside the weighing-room door when I got there, and as soon as he saw me he came to meet me, and said, "You're here then."

"Yes," I said. "Why not?"

"The governor posted me here to wait for you. I had to go and tell him at once if you came. He's having lunch. There's a rumor going round that you weren't going to turn up, see?" He bustled off.

I went through the weighing room into the changing room.

"Hello," said my valet. "I thought you'd cried off."

"So you came after all," said Peter Cloony.

Tick-Tock said, "Where in hell have you been?"

"Why did everyone believe I wouldn't get here?" I asked.

"I don't know. Some rumor or other. Everyone's been saying you frightened yourself again on Thursday and you'd chucked up the idea of riding any more."

"How very interesting," I said grimly.

"Never mind that now," said Tick-Tock. "You're here, and that's that. I rang your pad this morning, but your landlady said you hadn't been back all night. I wanted to see if it was okay for me to have the car after racing today and for you to get a lift back with Mr. Axminster. I have met," he finished gaily, "a smashing girl. She's here at the races and she's coming out with me afterward."

"The car?" I said. "Oh, yes. Certainly. Meet me outside the weighing room after the last, and I'll show you where it is."

"Super," he said. "I say, are you all right?"

"Yes, of course."

"You look a bit night-afterish, to my hawk eyes," he said. "Anyway the best of luck on Template, and all that rot."

An official peered into the changing room and called me out. James was waiting in the weighing room outside.

"Where have you been?" he said.

"In London," I said. "What's this rumor about me not turning up?"

"God knows." He shrugged. "I was sure you wouldn't have stayed away without letting me know, but . . ."

"No," I said, "of course not." Not unless, I thought, I had still been hanging in a deserted tack room in the process of being crippled for life.

He dismissed the subject and began to talk about the race. "There's a touch of frost in the ground still," he said, "but that's really to our advantage." I told him I had walked round the course the day before, and knew which parts were best avoided.

"Good," he said.

I could see that for once he was excited. There was a sort of uncharacteristic shyness about his eyes, and the lower teeth gleamed in an almost perpetual half-smile. Anticipation of victory, that's what it is, I thought. And if I hadn't spent such a taxing night and morning I would have been feeling the same. As it was, I looked forward to the race without much joy, knowing from past experience that riding with injuries never made them better. Even so, I wouldn't have given up my place on Template for anything I could think of.

When I went back into the changing room to put on breeches and colors, the jockeys riding in the first race had gone out, leaving a lot of space and quiet behind them. I went along to my peg, where all my kit was out ready, and sat down for a while on the bench. My conscience ought to have been troubling me. James and Lord Tirrold had a right to expect their jockey to be in tiptop physical condition for so important a race, and, to put it mildly, he wasn't. However, I reflected wryly, looking down at my gloved hands, if we all owned up to every spot of damage we'd spend far too much time on the stands watching others win on our mounts. It wasn't the first time I had deceived an owner and trainer in this way and yet won a race, and I fervently hoped it wouldn't be the last.

I thought about the Midwinter. Much depended on how it developed, but basically I intended to start on the rails, sit tight in about fourth place all the way round, and sprint the last three furlongs. There was a new Irish mare, Emerald, that had come over with a terrific reputation and might take a lot of beating, especially as her jockey was a wily character, very clever at riding near the front and slipping the field by a hard-to-peg-back ten lengths round the last bend. If Emerald led into the last bend, I decided, Template would have to be close to her, not still waiting in fourth place. Fast though he was, it would be senseless to leave him too much to do up the straight.

It is not customary for jockeys to stay in the changing room while a race is on, and I saw the valets looking surprised that I had not gone out to watch it. I stood up, picked up the underjersey and Lord Tirrold's colors and went to change into them in the washroom. Let the valets think what they like, I thought. I wanted to change out of sight, partly because I had to do it more slowly than usual but mostly so that they shouldn't see the bandages. I pulled down the sleeves of the finely knitted green and black jersey until they hid those on my wrists.

The first race was over and the jockeys were beginning to stream into the changing room when I went back to my peg. I finished changing into breeches, nylons and boots and took my saddle and weight-cloth along to the trial scales for Mike to adjust the amount of lead needed to bring me to twelve stone.

"You've got gloves on," he pointed out.

"Yes," I said mildly, "it's a cold day. I'd better have some silk ones for riding in, though."

"Okay," he said. He produced from a hamper a bundle of whitish gloves and pulled out a pair for me.

I went along to the main scales to weigh out, and gave my saddle to Sid, who was standing there waiting for it.

He said, "The governor says I'm to saddle Template in the stable, and bring him straight down into the parade ring when it's time, and not go into the saddling boxes at all."

"Good," I said emphatically.

"We've had two private dicks and a bloody great dog patrolling the yard all night," he went on. "And another dick came with us in the horse box, and he's sitting in Template's box at this very minute. You never saw such a circus."

"How's the horse?" I asked, smiling. Evidently James was splendidly keeping his word that Template would not be doped.

"He'll eat 'em," Sid said simply. "The Irish won't know what hit them. All the lads have got their wages on him. Yeah, I know they've been a bit fed up that you were going to ride him, but I saw you turn that Turniptop inside out on Thursday and I told 'em they've nothing to worry about."

"Thanks," I said, sincerely enough: but it was just one more ounce on a load of responsibility.

The time dragged. My shoulders ached. To take my mind off that I spent time imagining the expression on Kemp-Lore's face when he saw my name up in the number frame. He would think at first it was a mistake. He would wait for it to be changed. And at any moment now, I thought maliciously, he will begin to realize that I am indeed here.

The second race was run with me still sitting in the changing room, the object of now frankly curious looks from the valets. I took the brown gloves off and put on the grayish ones. They had originally been really white, but nothing could entirely wash out a season's accumulated stains of mud and leather. I flexed my fingers. Most of the swelling had gone, and they seemed to be getting fairly strong again in spite of the cracked and tender skin.

Back came the other jockeys, talking, laughing, swearing, dealing out friendly and not so friendly abuse, yelling to the valets, dumping down their kit—the ordinary, comradely, noisy changing-room mixture—and I felt apart from it, as if I were living in a different dimension. Another slow quarter of an hour crawled by. Then an official put his head in and shouted, "Jockeys out, hurry up there, please."

I stood up, put on the parka, fastened my helmet, picked up my whip, and followed the general drift to the door. The feeling of unreality persisted.

Down in the paddock, where in June the chiffons and ribbons fluttered in the heat, stood cold little bunches of owners and trainers, most of them muffled to the eyes against the wind. It seared through the bare branches of the trees beside the parade ring, leaving a uniformity of pinched faces among the people lining the rails. The bright winter sunshine gave an illusion of warmth which blue noses and runny eyes belied. But the parka, as I had been pleased to discover, was windproof.

Lord Tirrold wore on his fine-boned face the same look of excited anticipation that I could still see on James's. They are both so sure, I thought uneasily, that Template will win. Their very confidence weakened mine.

"Well, Rob," said Lord Tirrold, shaking me too firmly by the hand, "this is it."

"Yes, sir," I agreed, "this is it."

"What do you think of Emerald?" he asked.

We watched her shamble round the parade ring with the sloppy walk and low-carried head that so often denotes a champion.

"They say she's another Kerstin," said James, referring to the best steeplechasing mare of the century.

"It's too soon to say that," said Lord Tirrold; and I wondered if the same thought sprang into his mind as into mine, that after the Midwinter it might not be too soon, after all. But he added, as if to bury the possibility, "Template will beat her."

"I think so," James agreed.

I swallowed. They were too sure. If he won, they would expect it. If he lost, they would blame me; and probably with good cause.

Template himself stalked round the parade ring in his navy-blue rug, playing up each time as he came face on to the wind, trying to turn round so that it blew on his quarters, with his lad hanging onto his leading rein like a small child on a large kite.

A bell rang, indicating that it was time for the jockeys to mount. James beckoned to the boy, who brought Template across to us and took off his rug.

"Everything all right?" James asked.

"Yes, sir."

Template's eyes were liquid clear, his ears were pricked, his muscles quivering to be off: a picture of a taut, tuned racing machine eager to get on with the job he was born for. He was not a kind horse: there was no sweetness in his makeup and he inspired admiration rather than affection; but I liked him for his fire and his aggressiveness and his unswerving will to win.

"You've admired him long enough, Rob," said James teasingly. "Get up on him."

I took off the parka and dropped it on the rug. James gave me a leg up into the saddle and I gathered the reins and put my feet into the irons.

What he read in my face I don't know, but he said suddenly, anxiously, "Is anything wrong?"

"No," I said, "everything's fine." I smiled down at him, reassuring myself as much as him.

Lord Tirrold said, "Good luck," as if he didn't think I needed it, and I touched my cap to him and turned Template away to take his place in the parade down the course.

There was a television camera on a tower not far down the course from the starting gate, and I found the thought of Kemp-Lore raging at the sight of me on his monitor set a most effective antidote to the freezing wind. We circled round for five minutes, eleven of us, while the assistant starter tightened girths and complained that anyone would think we were in perishing Siberia.

I remembered that Tick-Tock, the last time we had ridden together on the course on a cold day, had murmured, "Ascot's blasted heath. Where are the witches?" And I thought of him now, putting a brave face on his inactivity in the stands. I thought briefly of Grant, probably hating my guts while he watched the race on television, and of Peter Cloony's wife, with no set to watch on at all, and of the jockeys who had given up and gone into factories, and of Art, under the sod.

"Line up," called the starter, and we straightened into a ragged row across the course, with Template firmly on the inside, hugging the rails.

I thought of myself driven to distraction by having it drummed into me that I had lost my nerve, and I thought of myself dragged over flinty ground and tied to a piece of galvanized chain; and I didn't need any more good reasons why I had to win the Midwinter Cup.

I watched the starter's hand. He had a habit of stretching his fingers just before he pulled the lever to let the tapes up, and I had no intention of letting anyone get away before me and cut me out of the position I had acquired on the rails.

The starter stretched his fingers. I kicked Template's flanks. He was moving quite fast when we went under the rising tapes, with me lying flat along his withers to avoid being swept off like other riders who had jumped the start too effectively in the past.

The tapes whistled over my head and we were away, securely on the rails and on the inside curve for at least the next two miles.

The first three fences were the worst, as far as my comfort was concerned. By the time we had jumped the fourth—the water—I had felt the thinly healed crusts on my back tear open, had thought my arms and shoulders would split apart with the strain of controlling Template's eagerness, and had found just how much my wrists and hands had to stand from the tug of the reins.

My chief feeling, as we landed over the water, was one of relief. It was all bearable; I could contain it and ignore it, and get on with the job.

The pattern of the race was simple from my point of view, because from start to finish I saw only three other horses, Emerald and the two lightly weighted animals whom I had allowed to go on and set the pace. The jockeys of this pair, racing ahead of me nose for nose, consistently left a two-foot gap between themselves and the rails, and I reckoned that if they were still there by the time we reached the second-last fence in the straight, they would veer very slightly toward the stands, as horses usually do at Ascot, and widen the gap enough for me to get through.

My main task until then was keeping Emerald from cutting across to the rails in front of me and being able to take the opening instead of Template. I left just too little room between me and the front pair for Emerald to get in, forcing the mare to race all the way on my outside. It didn't matter that she was two or three feet in front: I could see her better there, and Template was too clever a jumper to be brought down by the half-length trick—riding into a fence half a length in front of an opponent, causing him to take off at the same moment as oneself and land on top of the fence instead of safely on the ground on the other side.

With the order unchanged we completed the whole of the first circuit and swept out to the country again. Template jumped the four fences down to Swinley Bottom so brilliantly that I kept finding myself crowding the tails of the pacemakers as we landed, and had to ease him back on the flat each time to avoid taking the lead too soon, and yet not ease him so much that Emerald could squeeze into the space between us.

From time to time I caught a glimpse of the grimness on Emerald's jockey's face. He knew perfectly well what I was doing to him, and if I hadn't beaten him to the rails and made a flying start, he would have done the same to me. Perhaps I had Kemp-Lore to thank that he hadn't even tried, I thought fleetingly; if the bonfire Kemp-Lore had made of my reputation had led the Irishman to misjudge what I would do, so much the better.

For another half mile the two horses in front kept going splendidly, but one of the jockeys picked up his whip at the third-last fence, and the other was already busy with his hands. They were dead ducks, and because of that they swung a little wide going round the last bend into the straight. The Irishman must have had his usual bend tactics too firmly fixed in his mind, for he chose that exact moment to go to the front. It was not a good occasion for that maneuver. I saw him spurt forward from beside me and accelerate, but he had to go round on the outside of the two front horses, who were themselves swinging wide, and he was wasting lengths in the process. The mare carried seven pounds less weight than Template, and on that bend she lost the advantage they should have given her.

After the bend, tackling the straight for the last time, with the second-last fence just ahead, Emerald was in the lead on the outside, then the two tiring horses, then me.

There was a three-foot gap then between the innermost pacemaker and the rails. I squeezed Template. He pricked his ears and bunched his colossal muscles and thrust himself forward into the narrow opening. He took off at the second-last fence half a length behind and landed a length in front of the tiring horse, jumping so close to him on one side and to the wings on the other that I heard the other jockey cry out in surprise as I passed.

One of Template's great advantages was his speed away from a fence. With no check in his stride he sped smoothly on, still hugging the rails, with Emerald only a length in front on our left. I urged him a fraction forward to prevent the mare from swinging over to the rails and blocking me at the last fence. She needed a two-length lead to do it safely, and I had no intention of letting her have it.

The utter joy of riding Template lay in the feeling of immense power which he generated. There was no need to make the best of things, on his back; to fiddle and scramble, and hope for others to blunder, and find nothing to spare for a finish. He had enough reserve strength for his jockey to be able to carve up the race as he wished, and there was nothing in racing, I thought, more ecstatic than that.

As we galloped toward the last fence, I knew that Template would beat Emerald if he jumped it in anything like his usual style. She was a length ahead and showing no sign of flagging, but I was still holding Template on a tight rein. Ten yards from the fence I let him go. I kicked his flanks and squeezed with the calves of my legs, and he went over the birch like an angel, smooth, surging, the nearest to flying one can get.

He gained nearly half a length on the mare, but she didn't give up easily. I sat down and rode Template for my life, and he stretched himself willingly into his flat-looking stride. He came level with Emerald halfway along the run in. She hung on grimly for a short distance, but Template would have none of it. He floated past her with an incredible increase of speed, and he won, in the end, by two clear lengths.

There are times beyond words, and that was one of them. I patted Template's sweating neck over and over. I could have kissed him. I would have given him anything. But how does one thank a horse?

How could one ever repay him, in terms he would understand, for giving one such a victory?

The two tall men were pleased all right. They stood side by side, waiting for us in the unsaddling enclosure, the same elated expression on both their faces. I smiled at them, and shook my feet out of the irons and slid onto the ground. Onto the ground: down to earth. The end of an unforgettable experience.

"Rob," said James, shaking his big head. "Rob." He slapped Template's steaming shoulder and watched me struggle to undo the girth buckles with fingers shaking from both weakness and excitement.

"I knew he'd do it," Lord Tirrold said. "What a horse! What a race!"

I had got the buckles undone at last and had pulled the saddle off over my arm when an official came over and asked Lord Tirrold not to go away, as the Cup was to be presented to him in a few minutes. To me he said, "Will you come straight out again after you have weighed in? There's a trophy for the winning jockey as well."

I nodded, and went in to sit on the scales. Now that the concentration of the race was over, I began to be aware of the extra damage it had done. Across the back of my shoulders and down my arms to the fingertips every muscle felt like lead, draggingly heavy, shot with stabbing and burning sensations. I was appallingly weak and tired, and the pain in my wrists had increased to the point where I was finding it very difficult to keep it all out of my face. A quick look revealed that the bandages were red again, and so were the cuffs of the silk gloves and parts of the fawn underjersey. But if the blood had soaked through the black jersey as well, at least it didn't show.

With a broad smile Mike took my saddle from me in the changing room and unbuckled my helmet and pulled it off my head.

"They are wanting you outside, did you know?" he said.

I nodded. He held out a comb. "Better smarten your hair a bit. You can't let the side down."

I obediently took the comb and tidied my hair, and went back outside.

The horses had been led away and in their place stood a table bearing the Midwinter Cup and other trophies, with a bunch of race-course directors and Stewards beside it.

And Maurice Kemp-Lore as well.

It was lucky I saw him before he saw me. I felt my scalp contract at the sight of him and an unexpectedly strong shock of revulsion ran right down my body. He couldn't have failed to understand it if he had seen it.

I found James at my elbow. He followed my gaze.

"Why are you looking so grim?" he said. "He didn't even try to dope Template."

"No," I agreed. "I expect he was too tied up with his television work to be sure of having time to do it."

"He has given up the whole idea," said James confidently. "He must have seen there was no chance any more of persuading anyone you had lost your nerve. Not after the way you rode on Thursday."

It was the reckless way I had ridden on Thursday that had infuriated Kemp-Lore into delivering the packet I had taken on Friday. I understood that very well.

"Have you told anyone about the sugar?" I asked James.

"No, since you asked me not to. But I think something must be done. Slander or no slander, evidence or not—"

"Will you wait," I asked, "until next Saturday? A week today? Then you can tell whomever you like."

"Very well," he said slowly. "But I still think—"

He was interrupted by the arrival at the trophy table of the day's V.I.P., a pretty Duchess, who with a few well-chosen words and a genuinely friendly smile presented the Midwinter Cup to Lord Tirrold, a silver tray to James, and a cigarette box to me. An enterprising press photographer let off a flash bulb as the three of us stood together admiring our prizes, and after that we gave them back again to the Clerk of the Course, for him to have them engraved with Template's name and our own.

I heard Kemp-Lore's voice behind me as I handed over the cigarette box, and it gave me time to arrange my face into a mildly smiling blankness before turning round. Even so, I was afraid that I wouldn't be able to look at him without showing my feelings.

I pivoted slowly on my heels and met his eyes. They were piercingly blue and very cold, and they didn't blink or alter in any way as I looked back at them. I relaxed a little, inwardly, thankful that the first difficult hurdle had been crossed. He had searched but had not read in my face that I knew it was he who had abducted me the evening before.

"Rob Finn," he said in his charming television voice, "is the jockey you just watched being carried to victory by this wonder horse, Template." He was speaking into a hand microphone from which trailed yards of black cord, and looking alternately at me and at a camera on a scaffolding tower nearby. The camera's red eye glowed. I mentally girded up my loins and prepared to forestall every disparaging opinion he might utter.

He said, "I expect you enjoyed being his passenger?"

"It was marvelous," I said emphatically, smiling a smile to outdazzle his. "It is a great thrill for any jockey to ride a horse as superb as Template. Of course," I went on amiably, before he had time to speak, "I am lucky to have had the opportunity. As you know, I have been taking Pip Pankhurst's place all these months, while his leg has been mending, and today's win should have been his. He is much better now, I'm glad to say, and we are all delighted that it won't be long before he is riding again." I spoke truthfully: whatever it meant to me in fewer rides, it would benefit the sport as a whole to have its champion back in action.

A slight chill crept into the corner of Kemp-Lore's mouth.

"You haven't been doing as well, lately—" he began.

"No," I interrupted warmly. "Aren't they extraordinary, those runs of atrocious luck in racing? Did you know that Doug Smith once rode ninety-nine losers in succession? How terrible he must have felt. It makes my twenty or so seem quite paltry."

"You weren't worried, then, by . . . er . . . by such a bad patch as you've been going through?" His smile was slipping.

"Worried?" I repeated lightheartedly. "Well, naturally I wasn't exactly delighted, but these runs of bad luck happen to everyone in racing, once in a while, and one just has to live through them until another winner comes along. Like today's," I finished with a grin at the camera.

"Most people understood it was more than bad luck," he said sharply. There was a definite crack in his jolly-chums manner, and for an instant I saw in his eyes a flash of the fury he was controlling.

It gave me great satisfaction, and because of it I smiled at him more vividly.

I said, "People will believe anything when their pockets are touched. I'm afraid a lot of people lost their money backing my mounts. It's only natural to blame the jockey—nearly everyone does when they lose."

He listened to me mending the holes he had torn in my life and he couldn't stop me without giving an impression of being a bad sport: and nothing kills the popularity of a television commentator quicker than obvious bad-sportsmanship.

He had been standing at right angles to me with his profile to the camera, but now he took a step toward me and turned so that he stood beside me on my left side. As he moved there was a fleeting set to his mouth that looked like cruelty to me, and it prepared me in some measure for what he did next.

With a large gesture which must have appeared as genuine friendship on the television screen, he dropped his right arm heavily across my shoulders, with his right thumb lying forward on my collarbone and his fingers spread out on my back.

I stood still, and turned my head slowly toward him, and smiled sweetly. Few things have ever cost me more effort.

"Tell us a bit about the race, then, Rob," he said, advancing the microphone in his left hand. "When did you begin to think you might win?"

His arm felt like a ton weight, an almost unsupportable burden on my aching muscles. I gathered my straying wits. "Oh, I thought, coming into the last fence," I said, "that Template might have the speed to beat Emerald on the flat. He can produce such a sprint at the end, you know."

"Yes, of course." He pressed his fingers more firmly into the back of my shoulder and gave what passed for a friendly shake. My head began to spin. Everything on the edge of my vision became blurred. I went on smiling, concentrating desperately on the fair, good-looking face so close to mine, and was rewarded by the expression of puzzlement and disappointment in his eyes. He knew that under his fingers, beneath two thin jerseys, were patches which must be sore if touched, but he didn't know how much or how little trouble I had had in freeing myself in the tack room. I wanted him to believe it had been none at all, that the ropes had slipped undone or the hook fallen easily out of the ceiling. I wanted to deny him even the consolation of knowing how nearly he had succeeded in preventing me from riding Template.

"And what are Template's plans for the future?" He strove to be conversational, normal. The television interview was progressing along well-trodden ways.

"There's the Gold Cup at Cheltenham," I said. I was past telling whether I sounded equally unruffled, but there was still no leap of triumph in his face, so I went on. "I expect he will run there, in three weeks' time. All being well, of course."

"And do you hope to ride him again in that?" he asked. There was an edge to his voice which stopped just short of offensiveness. He was finding it as nearly impossible to put on an appearance of affection for me as I for him.

"It depends," I said, "on whether or not Pip is fit in time . . . and on whether Lord Tirrold and Mr. Axminster want me to, if he isn't. But of course I'd like to, if I get the chance."

"You've never yet managed to ride in the Gold Cup, I believe?" He made it sound as if I had been trying unsuccessfully for years to beg a mount.

"No," I agreed. "But it has only been run twice since I came into racing, so if I get a ride in it so soon in my career I'll count myself very lucky."

His nostrils flared, and I thought in satisfaction, That got you squarely in the guts, my friend. You'd forgotten how short a time I've been a jockey.

He turned his head away from me toward the camera and I saw the rigidity in his neck and jaw and the pulse that beat visibly in his temple. I imagined he would willingly have seen me dead; yet he was enough in command of himself to realize that if he pressed my shoulder any harder I would be likely to guess it was not accidental.

Perhaps if he had been less controlled at that moment I would have been more merciful to him later. If his professionally pleasant expression had exploded into the rage he was feeling, or if he had openly dug his nails with ungovernable vindictiveness into my back, I could perhaps have believed him more mad than wicked, after all. But he knew too well where to stop; and since I could not equate madness with such self-discipline, by my standards he was sane;

sane and controlled, and therefore unlikely to destroy himself from within. I threw Claudius Mellit's plea for kid gloves finally overboard.

Kemp-Lore was speaking calmly toward the camera, finishing off his broadcast. He gave me a last, natural-looking little squeezing shake, and let his arm drop away from my shoulders. Slowly and methodically I silently repeated to myself the ten most obscene words I knew, and after that Ascot race course stopped attempting to whirl round and settled down again into bricks and mortar and grass and people, all sharp and perpendicular.

The man behind the camera on the tower held up his thumb and the red eye blinked out.

Kemp-Lore turned directly to me again and said, "Well, that's it. We're off the air now."

"Thank you, Maurice," I said, carefully constructing one last warm smile. "That was just what I needed to set me back on top of the world. A big-race win and a television interview with you to clinch it. Thank you very much." I could rub my fingers in his wounds, too.

He gave me a look in which the cultivated habit of charm struggled for supremacy over spite, and still won. Then he turned on his heel and walked away, pulling his black microphone cord along the ground after him.

It is impossible to say which of us loathed the other more.

15

I spent most of the next day in Joanna's bed. Alone, unfortunately.

She gave me a cup of coffee for breakfast, a cozy grin, and instructions to sleep. So I lazily went on snoozing in the pajamas she had bought me, dreaming about her on her own pillow, doing nothing more energetic than occasionally raising my blood pressure by thinking about Kemp-Lore.

I had arrived on her doorstep in a shaky condition the evening before, having first taken Tick-Tock and his space-age girlfriend by taxi to the boring White Bear at Uxbridge, where, as I had imagined, the Mini-Cooper stood abandoned in the car park. It had seemed to me certain that Kemp-Lore had driven to the White Bear in his own car, had used the Mini-Cooper for his excursion to the abandoned stables, and had changed back again to his own car on the return journey. His route, checked on the map, was simple: direct almost. All the same, I was relieved to find the little Mini safe and sound.

Tick-Tock's remarks about my carelessness with communal property trickled to a stop when he found my wrist watch and wallet and the other things out of my pockets on the glove shelf, and my jacket and overcoat and a length of white nylon rope on the back seat.

"Why the blazes," he said slowly, "did you leave your watch and your money and your coats here? It's a wonder they weren't pinched. And the car too."

"It's the northeast wind," I said solemnly. "Like the moon, you know. I always do mad things when there's a northeast wind."

"Northeast my aunt Fanny." He grinned, picked up the coats,

and transferred them to the waiting taxi. Then he surprisingly shoveled all my small belongings into my trousers pockets and put my watch into my gloved hand.

"You may have fooled everyone else, mate," he said lightly, "but to me you have looked like death inefficiently warmed up all day, and it's something to do with your maulers. The gloves are new . . . you don't usually wear any. What happened?"

"You work on it," I said amiably, getting back into the taxi. "If you haven't anything better to do." I glanced across at his little hepcat, and he laughed and flipped his hand, and went to help her into the Mini-Cooper.

The taxi driver, in a good mood because he had backed three winners, drove me back to Joanna's mews without a single complaint about the roundabout journey. When I paid him and added a fat tip on top he said, "Were you on a winner too, then?"

"Yes," I said. "Template."

"Funny thing that," he said. "I backed him myself, after what you said about not believing all you hear. You were quite right, weren't you? That fellow Finn's not washed up at all, not by a long chalk. He rode a hell of a race. I reckon he can carry my money again, any day." He shifted his gears gently, and drove off.

Watching his taillight bump away down the cobbled mews, I felt ridiculously happy and very much at peace. Winning the race had already been infinitely worth the cost, and the taxi driver, not knowing whom he was speaking to, had presented me with the bonus of learning that, as far as the British racing public was concerned, I was back in business.

I leaned wearily but contentedly against Joanna's doorpost, and rang her bell.

That wasn't quite the end of the most exhausting twenty-four hours of my life, however. My thoughtful cousin, anticipating correctly that I would refuse to turn out again to see a doctor, had imported one of her own. He was waiting there when I arrived, a blunt no-bedside-manner Scot with bushy eyebrows and three warts on his chin.

To my urgent protests that I was in no state to withstand his ministrations, both he and Joanna turned deaf ears. They put me into a chair, and off came my clothes again, the leather gloves and the silk racing ones I had not removed after riding, then the parka, my father's shirt and the underjersey, also not returned to Mike, then the bits of lint Joanna had stuck on in the morning, and finally the blood-soaked bandages round my wrists. Toward the end of all this rather ruthless undressing the room began spinning as Ascot had done, and I regrettably rolled off the chair onto the floor, closer to fainting than I had been the whole time.

The Scotsman picked me up and put me back on the chair and told me to pull myself together and be a man.

"You've only lost a wee bit of skin," he said sternly.

I began to laugh weakly, which didn't go down well either. He was a joyless fellow. He compressed his mouth until the warts quivered when I shook my head to his inquiries and would not tell him what had happened. But he bound me up again comfortably enough and gave me some painkilling pills which turned out to be very effective; and when he had gone I got into Joanna's bed and sank thankfully into oblivion.

Joanna worked at her painting most of the next day, and when I surfaced finally at about four o'clock in the afternoon she was singing quietly at her easel. Not the angular, spiky songs she specialized in, but a Gaelic ballad in a minor key, soft and sad. I lay and listened with my eyes shut because I knew she would stop if she found me awake. Her voice was true even at a level not much above a whisper, the result of well-exercised vocal cords and terrific breath control. A proper Finn, she is, I thought wryly. Nothing done by halves.

She came to the end of the ballad, and afterward began another. "I know where I'm going, and I know who's going with me. I know who I love, but the dear knows who I'll marry. Some say he's black, but I say he's bonny—" She stopped abruptly and said quietly but forcefully, "Damn, damn and blast." I heard her throw down her palette and brushes and go into the kitchen.

After a minute I sat up in bed and called to her.

"Yes?" she shouted, without reappearing.

"I'm starving," I said.

"Oh." She gave a laugh which ended in a choke, and called out, "All right. I'll cook."

And cook she did; fried chicken with sweet corn and pineapple and bacon. While the preliminary smells wafted tantalizingly out of the kitchen I got up and put my clothes on, and stripped her bed.

There were clean sheets in the drawer beneath, and I made it up again fresh and neat for her to get into.

She carried a tray of plates and cutlery in from the kitchen and saw the bundle of dirty sheets and the smooth bed.

"What are you doing?"

"The sofa isn't good for you," I said. "You obviously haven't slept well . . . and your eyes are red."

"That isn't . . ." she began, and thought better of it.

"It isn't lack of sleep?" I finished.

She shook her head. "Let's eat."

"Then what's the matter?" I said.

"Nothing. Nothing. Shut up and eat."

I did as I was told. I was hungry.

She watched me finish every morsel. "You're feeling better," she stated.

"Oh, yes. Much. Thanks to you."

"And you are not sleeping here tonight?"

"No."

"You can try the sofa," she said mildly. "You might as well find out what I have endured for your sake." I didn't answer at once, and she added compulsively, "I'd like you to stay, Rob. Stay."

I looked at her carefully. Was there the slightest chance, I wondered, that her gentle songs and her tears in the kitchen and now her reluctance to have me leave meant that she was at last finding the fact of our cousinship more troublesome than she was prepared for? I had always known that if she ever came to love me as I wanted and also was not able to abandon her rigid prejudice against our blood relationship it would very likely break her up. If that was what was happening to her, it was definitely not the time to walk out.

"All right," I said, smiling. "Thank you. I'll stay. On the sofa."

She became suddenly animated and talkative, and told me in great detail how the race and the interview afterward had appeared on television. Her voice was quick and light. "At the beginning of the program he said he thought your name was a mistake on the number boards, because he had heard you weren't there, and I began to worry that you had broken down on the way and hadn't got there after all. But of course you had. And afterward you looked like life-long buddies standing there with his arm round your shoulders and you smiling at him as if the sun shone out of his eyes. How did you manage it? But he was trying to needle you, wasn't he? It seemed like it to me, but then that was perhaps because I knew—" She stopped in mid-flow, and in an entirely different, sober tone of voice she said, "What are you going to do about him?"

I told her. It took some time.

She was shaken. "You can't," she said.

I smiled at her, but didn't answer.

She shivered. "He didn't know what he was up against when he picked on you."

"Will you help?" I asked. Her help was essential.

"Won't you change your mind and go to the police?" she asked seriously.

"No."

"But what you are planning . . . it's cruel."

"Yes," I agreed.

"And complicated, and a lot of work, and expensive."

"Yes. Will you make that one telephone call for me?"

She sighed and said, "You don't think you'll relent once everything has stopped hurting?"

"I'm quite certain," I said.

"I'll think about it," she said, standing up and collecting the dishes. She wouldn't let me help her wash up, so I went over to the easel to see what she had been working at all day: and I was vaguely disturbed to find it was a portrait of my mother sitting at her piano.

I was still looking at the picture when she came back.

"It's not very good, I'm afraid," she said, standing beside me. "Something seems to have gone wrong with the perspective of the piano."

"Does Mother know you are doing it?" I asked.

"Oh, no," she said.

"When did you start it?"

"Yesterday afternoon," she said.

There was a pause. Then I said, "It won't do you any good to try to convince yourself your feelings for me are maternal."

She jerked in surprise.

"I don't want mothering," I said. "I want a wife."

"I can't . . ." she said, with a tight throat.

I turned away from the picture, feeling that I had pressed her too far, too soon. Joanna abruptly picked up a turpentine-soaked rag and scrubbed at the still wet oils, wiping out all her work.

"You see too much," she said. "More than I understood myself."

I grinned at her and after a moment, with an effort, she smiled back. She wiped her fingers on the rag, and hung it on the easel.

"I'll make that telephone call," she said. "You can go ahead with . . . with what you plan to do."

On the following morning, Monday, I hired a drive-yourself car and went to see Grant Oldfield.

The hard overnight frost, which had caused the day's racing to be canceled, had covered the hedges and trees with sparkling rime, and I enjoyed the journey even though at the end of it I expected a reception as cold as the day.

I stopped outside the gate, walked up the short path through the desolate garden, and rang the bell.

It had only just struck me that the brass bell push was brightly polished when the door opened and a neat dark-haired young woman in a green wool dress looked at me inquiringly.

"I came . . ." I said. "I wanted to see . . . er . . . I wonder if you could tell me where I could find Grant Oldfield?"

"Indoors," she said. "He lives here; I'm his wife. Just a minute, and I'll get him. What name shall I say?"

"Rob Finn," I said.

"Oh," she said in surprise; and she smiled warmly. "Do come in. Grant will be so pleased to see you."

I doubted it, but I stepped into the narrow hall and she shut the door behind me. Everything was spotless and shining; it looked a different house from the one I remembered. She led the way to the kitchen and opened the door onto another area of dazzling cleanliness.

Grant was sitting at a table, reading a newspaper. He glanced up as his wife came in, and when he saw me his face too creased into a smile of surprised welcome. He stood up. He was much thinner and older looking, and shrunken in some indefinable inner way; but he was, or he was going to be soon, a whole man again.

"How are you, Grant?" I said inadequately, not understanding their friendliness.

"I'm much better, thanks," he said. "I've been home a fortnight now."

"He was in hospital," his wife explained. "They took him there the day after you brought him home. Dr. Parnell wrote to me and told me Grant was ill and couldn't help being how he was. So I came back." She smiled at Grant. "And everything's going to be all right now. Grant's got a job lined up too. He starts in two weeks, selling toys."

"Toys?" I exclaimed. Of all incongruous things, I thought.

"Yes," she said, "they thought it would be better for him to do something which had nothing to do with horses, so that he wouldn't start brooding again."

"We've a lot to thank you for, Rob," Grant said.

"Dr. Parnell told me," his wife said, seeing my surprise, "that you would have been well within your rights if you had handed him over to the police instead of bringing him here."

"I tried to kill you," Grant said in a wondering voice, as if he could no longer understand how he had felt. "I really tried to kill you, you know."

"Dr. Parnell said if you had been a different sort of person Grant could have ended up in a criminal lunatic asylum."

I said uncomfortably, "Dr. Parnell appears to have been doing too much talking altogether."

"He wanted me to understand," she said, smiling, "that you had given Grant another chance, so I ought to give him another chance too."

"Would it bother you," I said to Grant, "if I asked you a question about how you lost your job with Axminster?"

Mrs. Oldfield moved protectively to his side. "Don't bring it all back," she said anxiously, "all that resentment."

"It's all right, love," Grant said, putting his arm round her waist. "Go ahead."

"I believe you were telling the truth when you told Axminster you had not sold information to that professional punter, Lubbock," I said. "But Lubbock did get information, and did pay for it. The question is, whom was he actually handing over the money to, if he thought he was paying it to you?"

"You've got it wrong, Rob," Grant said. "I went over and over it at the time, and went to see Lubbock and got pretty angry with him."

He smiled ruefully. "And Lubbock said that until James Axminster tackled him about it he hadn't known for sure who he was buying information from. He had guessed it was me, he said. But he said I had given him the information over the telephone and he had sent the payments to me in the name of Robinson, care of a post office in London. He didn't believe I knew nothing about it, of course. He just thought I hadn't covered myself well enough and was trying to wriggle out of trouble." There was a remarkable lack of bitterness in his voice; his spell in a mental hospital, or his illness itself, seemed to have changed his personality to the roots.

"Can you give me Lubbock's address?" I asked.

"He lives in Solihull," he said slowly. "I might know the house again, but I can't remember the name of it, or the road."

"I'll find it," I said.

"Why do you want to?" he asked.

"Would it mean anything to you if I happened to prove that you were telling the truth all along?"

His face came suddenly alive from within. "I'll say it would. You can't imagine what it was like, losing that job for something I didn't do, and having no one believe me any more."

I didn't tell him that I knew exactly what it was like, only too well. I said, "I'll do my best, then."

"But you won't go back to racing?" his wife said to him anxiously. "You won't start all over again?"

"No, love. Don't worry," he said calmly. "I'm going to enjoy selling toys. You never know, we might start a toy shop of our own, next year, when I've learned the business."

I drove the thirty miles to Solihull, looked up Lubbock in the telephone directory, and rang his number. A woman answered. She told me that he was not in, but if I wanted him urgently I would probably get hold of him at the Queen's Hotel in Birmingham, as he was lunching there.

Having lost my way twice in the one-way streets I miraculously found a place to park outside the Queen's, and went in. I wrote a note on the hotel paper, asking Mr. Lubbock, whom I did not know even by sight, if he would be so very kind as to give me a few minutes of his time. Sealing the note in an envelope I asked the head porter if he would have one of the page boys find Mr. Lubbock and give it to him.

"He went into the dining room with another gentleman a few minutes ago," he said. "Here, Dickie, take this note in to Mr. Lubbock."

Dickie returned with an answer on the back of the note: Mr. Lubbock would meet me in the lounge at 2:15.

Mr. Lubbock proved to be a plumpish, middle-aged man with a gingery mustache and a thin section of lank hair brushed across a balding skull. He accepted from me a large brandy and a fat cigar with such an air of surprised irony that I was in no doubt that he was used to buying these things for jockeys, and not the other way about.

"I want to know about Grant Oldfield," I said, coming straight to the point.

"Oldfield?" he murmured, sucking flame down the cigar. "Oh, yes, I remember, Oldfield." He gave me a sharp upward glance. "You . . . er . . . you still work for the same firm, don't you? Do you want a deal, is that it? Well, I don't see why not. I'll give you the odds to a pony for every winner you put me on to. No one could say fairer than that."

"Is that what you paid Oldfield?" I said.

"Yes," he said.

"Did you give it to him personally?" I asked.

"No," he said. "But then he didn't ask me personally. He fixed it up on the telephone. He was very secretive: said his name was Robinson, and asked me to pay him in uncrossed money orders, and to send them to a post office for him to collect."

"Which one?" I asked.

He took a swig at the brandy and gave me an assessing look. "Why do you want to know?"

"It sounds a good idea," I said casually.

He shrugged. "I can't remember," he said. "Surely it's unimportant which post office it was? Somewhere in a London suburb, I know, but I can't remember where after all this time. N.E.7? N.12? Something like that."

"You wouldn't have a record of it?"

"No," he said decisively. "Why don't you ask Oldfield himself if you need to know."

I sighed. "How many times did he give you information?" I asked.

"He told me the names of about five horses altogether, I should think. Three of them won, and I sent him the money on those occasions."

"You didn't know it was Oldfield selling you tips, did you?" I said.

"It depends what you mean by 'know,'" he said. "I had a pretty good idea. Who else could it have been? But I suppose I didn't actually 'know' until Axminster said, 'I hear you have been buying information from my jockey,' and I agreed that I had."

"So you wouldn't have told anyone before that that it was Oldfield who was selling you tips?"

"Of course not."

"No one at all?" I pressed.

"No, certainly not." He gave me a hard stare. "You don't broadcast things like that, not in my business, and especially if you aren't dead sure of your facts. Just what is all this about?"

"Well . . ." I said. "I'm very sorry to have misled you, Mr. Lubbock, but I am not really in the market for information. I'm just trying to unstick a bit of the mud that was thrown at Grant Oldfield."

To my surprise he gave a fat chuckle and knocked half an inch of ash off the cigar.

"Do you know," he said, "if you'd agreed to tip me off I'd have been looking for the catch? There's some jockeys you can square, and some you can't, and in my line you get an instinct for which are which. Now you—" he jabbed the cigar in my direction—"you aren't the type."

"Thanks," I murmured.

"And more fool you," he said, nodding. "It's not illegal."

I grinned.

"Mr. Lubbock," I said, "Oldfield was not Robinson, but his career and his health were broken up because you and Mr. Axminster were led to believe that he was."

He stroked his mustache with the thumb and forefinger of his left hand, pondering.

I went on: "Oldfield has now given up all thought of riding again, but it would still mean a great deal to him to have his name cleared. Will you help to do it?"

"How?" he said.

"Would you just write a statement to the effect that you saw no evidence at any time to support your guess that in paying Robinson you were really paying Oldfield, and that at no time before James Axminster approached you did you speak of your suspicions of Robinson's identity?"

"Is that all?" he said.

"Yes."

"All right," he said. "It can't do any harm. But I think you're barking up the wrong tree. No one but a jockey would go to all that trouble to hide his identity. No one would bother if his job didn't depend on not being found out. Still, I'll write what you ask."

He unscrewed a pen, took a sheet of hotel writing paper, and in a decisive hand wrote the statement I had suggested. He signed it, and added the date and read it through.

"There you are," he said. "Though I can't see what good it will do."

I read what he had written, and folded the paper, and put it in my wallet.

"Someone told Mr. Axminster that Oldfield was selling you information," I said. "If you hadn't told anyone at all—who knew?"

"Oh." His eyes opened. "I see, yes, I see. Robinson knew. But Oldfield would never have let on . . . so Oldfield was not Robinson."

"That's about it," I agreed, standing up. "Thank you very much, Mr. Lubbock, for your help."

"Any time." He waved the diminishing cigar, smiling broadly. "See you at the races."

16

On Tuesday morning I bought a copy of the *Horse and Hound* and spent a good while telephoning to a few of the people who had advertised their hunters for sale. With three of them I made appointments to view the animal in question in two days' time.

Next I rang up one of the farmers I rode for and persuaded him to lend me his Land Rover and trailer on Thursday afternoon.

Then, having borrowed a tape measure out of Joanna's workbox —she was out at a rehearsal—I drove the hired car down to James's stables. I found him sitting in his office dealing with his paper work. The fire, newly lit in the grate, was making little headway against the raw chill in the air, and outside in the yard the lads looked frozen as they scurried about doing their horses after the second morning exercise.

"No racing again today," James remarked. "Still, we've been extraordinarily lucky this winter up to now."

He stood up and rubbed his hands, and held them out to the inadequate fire. "Some of the owners have telephoned," he said. "They're willing to have you back. I told them"—he looked at me from under his eyebrows—"that I was satisfied with your riding and that you would be on Template in the Gold Cup."

"What!" I exclaimed. "Do you mean it?"

"Yes." The glimmer deepened in his eyes.

"But . . . Pip . . ." I said.

"I've explained to Pip," he said, "that I can't take you off the horse when you've won both the King Chase and the Midwinter on him. And Pip agrees. I have arranged with him that he start again the week after Cheltenham, which will give him time to get a few races in before the Grand National. He'll be riding my runner in that—the horse he rode last year."

"It finished sixth," I said, remembering.

"Yes, that's right. Now, I've enough horses to keep both Pip and you fairly busy, and no doubt you'll get outside rides as well. It should work out all right for both of you."

"I don't know how to thank you," I said.

"Thank yourself," he said sardonically. "You earned it." He bent down and put another lump of coal on the fire.

"James," I said, "will you write something down for me?"

"Write? Oh, you'll get a contract for next season, the same as Pip."

"I didn't mean that," I said awkwardly. "It's quite different. Would you just write down that it was Maurice Kemp-Lore who told you that Oldfield was selling information about your horses, and that he said he had learned it from Lubbock?"

"Write it down?"

"Yes, please," I said.

"I don't see . . ." He gave an intent look and shrugged. "Oh, very well then." He sat down at his desk, took a sheet of paper headed with his name and address, and wrote what I asked.

"Signature and date?" he said.

"Yes, please."

He blotted the page. "What good will that do?" he said, handing it to me.

I took Mr. Lubbock's paper out of my wallet and showed it to him. He read it through three times.

"My God," he said. "It's incredible. Suppose I had checked carefully with Lubbock? What a risk Maurice took."

"It wasn't so big a risk," I said. "You wouldn't have thought of questioning what he put forward as a friendly warning. Anyway it worked. Grant got the sack."

"I'm sorry for that," James said slowly. "I wish there was something I could do about it."

"Write to Grant and explain," I suggested. "He would appreciate it more than anything in the world."

"I'll do that," he agreed, making a note.

"On Saturday morning," I said, taking back Lubbock's statement and putting it with his in my wallet, "these little documents will arrive with a plop on the Senior Steward's doormat. Of course they aren't conclusive enough to base any legal proceedings on, but they should be enough to kick friend Kemp-Lore off his pedestal."

"I should say you were right." He looked at me gravely, and then said, "Why wait until Saturday?"

"I . . . er . . . I won't be ready until then," I said evasively.

He didn't pursue it. We walked out into the yard together and looked in on some of the horses, James giving instructions, criticism and praise—in that order—to the hurrying lads. I realized how used I had grown to the efficiency and prosperity of his organization, and how much it meant to me to be a part of it.

We walked slowly along one row of boxes, and James went into the tack room at the end to talk to Sid about the cancellation of the following day's racing. Unexpectedly I stopped dead on the threshold. I didn't want to go in. I knew it was stupid, but it made no difference. Parts of me were still too sore.

The harness hook hung from the center of the ceiling, with a couple of dirty bridles swinging harmlessly on two of its curving arms. I turned my back on it and looked out across the tidy yard, and wondered if I would ever again see one without remembering.

Up in the rolling, grassy hills a mile or so away from his stable, James owned an old deserted keeper's cottage. In the past it had been the home of the man who looked after the gallops, James had told me once on a journey to the races, but as it had no electricity, no piped water and no sanitation, the new groundsman preferred, not unnaturally, to live in comfort in the village below and go up the hill to work on a motorbike.

The old cottage lay down an overgrown lane leading off a public but little-used secondary road which led nowhere except up and along the side of the hill and down again to join the main road four miles farther on. It served only two farms and one private house, and because of its quietness it was a regular route for the Axminster horses on roadwork days.

After leaving James I drove up to the cottage. I had not seen it at close quarters before, only a glimpse of its blank wall from the end of the lane as I rode by. I now found it was a four-roomed bungalow, set in a small fenced garden with a narrow path leading from the gate to the front door. There was one window to each room, two facing the front and two the back.

Getting in without a key presented no difficulty, as most of the glass in the windows was broken. I opened one and climbed in. The whole place smelled of fungus and rot, though faintly, as if the decay were only warming up for future onslaught. The walls and floor boards were still in good condition, and only one of the rooms was damp. I found that all four rooms opened onto a small central hall inside the front entrance; and as I made my tour I reflected that it could not have been more convenient if I had designed it myself.

I let myself out the front door, and walking round to the back I took out Joanna's tape and measured the window frame: three feet high, four feet wide. Then I returned to the front, counted the number of broken panes of glass, and measured one of them. That done, I returned to James and asked him to lend me the cottage for a few days to store some things for which there was no room at my digs.

"As long as you like," he agreed absently, busy with paper work.

"May I mend some of the windows, and put on a new lock, to make it more secure?" I asked.

"Help yourself," he said. "Do what you like."

I thanked him and drove into Newbury, and at a builders' merchant's waited while they made me up an order of ten panes of glass, enough putty to put them in with, several pieces of water pipe cut to a specified length, a bucket, some screws, a stout padlock, a bag of cement, a pot of green paint, a putty knife, a screw driver, a cement trowel, and a paintbrush. Loaded to the axles with that lot I returned to the cottage.

I painted the weather-beaten front door and left it open to dry, reflecting that no one could blame a keeper—or his wife for that matter—for not wanting to live in that lonely, inconvenient cul de sac.

I went into one of the back rooms and knocked out all the panes of glass which still remained in their little oblong frames. Then, outside in the garden, I mixed a good quantity of cement, using water from the rain butt, and fixed six three-foot lengths of water pipe upright in a row across the window. That done, I went round into the hall, and on the doorpost and door of the same room screwed firmly home the fittings for the padlock. On the inside of the door I unscrewed the handle and removed it.

The final job was replacing the glass in the front windows, and it took me longest to do, chipping out all the old putty and squeezing on the new; but at last it was done, and with its whole windows and fresh green door the cottage already looked more cheerful and welcoming.

I smiled to myself. I retrieved the car from where I had parked it inconspicuously behind some bushes and drove back to London.

The Scots doctor was drinking gin with Joanna when I let myself in.

"Oh, no," I said unceremoniously.

"Oh, yes, laddie," he said. "You were supposed to come and see me yesterday, remember."

"I was busy," I said.

"I'll just take a look at those wrists, if you don't mind," he said, putting down the gin and standing up purposefully.

I sighed and sat down at the table, and he unwrapped the bandages. There was blood on them again.

"I thought I told you to take it easy," he said sternly. "How do you expect them to heal? What have you been doing?"

I could have said, Screwing in screws, chipping out putty and mixing cement, but instead I rather uncooperatively muttered, "Nothing."

Irritated, he slapped on a new dressing with unnecessary force, and I winced. He snorted; but he was gentler with the second one.

"All right," he said, finishing them off. "Now, rest them a bit this time. And come and see me on Friday."

"Saturday," I said. "I won't be in London on Friday."

"Saturday morning, then. And mind you come." He picked up his glass, tossed off the gin, and said a friendly good night exclusively to Joanna.

She came back laughing from seeing him out.

"He isn't usually so unsympathetic," she said. "But I think he suspects you were engaged in some sort of sadistic disgusting orgy last week, as you wouldn't tell him how you got like that."

"And he's dead right," I said morosely. He had stirred up my wrists properly, and they hadn't been too good to start with after my labors at the cottage.

For the third night I went to bed on the sofa and lay awake in the darkness, listening to Joanna's soft sleeping breath. Every day she hesitantly asked me if I would like to stay another night in her flat, and as I had no intention of leaving while there was any chance of thawing her resistance, I accepted promptly each time, even though I was progressively finding that no bread would have been more restful. Half a loaf, in the shape of Joanna padding in and out of the bathroom in a pretty dressing gown and going to bed five yards away, was decidedly unsatisfying. But I could easily have escaped and gone to a nontantalizing sleep in my own bed in my family's flat half a mile away; if I didn't, it was my own fault, and I pointed this out to her when every morning she remorsefully apologized for being unfair.

On Wednesday morning I went to a large photographic agency and asked to see a picture of Maurice Kemp-Lore's sister Alice. I was given a bundle of photographs to choose from, varying from Alice front-view in spotted organza at a Hunt Ball to Alice back-view winning over the last fence in a point-to-point. Alice was a striking girl with dark hair, high cheekbones, small fierce eyes, and a tight aggressive mouth. A girl to avoid, as far as I was concerned. I bought a copy of a waist-length photograph which showed her watching some hunter trials, dressed in a hacking jacket and head-scarf.

On leaving the agency I went to the city offices of my parents' accountants and talked "our Mr. Stuart" in the records department into letting me use first a typewriter and then his photocopying machine.

On plain typing paper I wrote a bald account of Kemp-Lore's actions against Grant Oldfield, remarking that as a result of Axminster's relying on the apparent disinterestedness of Kemp-Lore's accusation, Oldfield had lost his job, had subsequently suffered great distress of mind, and had undergone three months' treatment in a mental hospital. I made ten copies of this statement and then on the photocopier printed ten copies each of the statements from Lubbock and James. I thanked "our Mr. Stuart" profusely and returned to Joanna's mews.

When I got back I showed Joanna the photograph of Alice Kemp-Lore, and explained who she was.

"But," said Joanna, "she isn't a bit like her brother. It can't have been her that the ticket collector saw at Cheltenham."

"No," I said. "It was Kemp-Lore himself. Could you draw me a picture of him wearing a headscarf?"

She found a piece of cartridge paper and with concentration made a reasonable likeness in charcoal of the face I now unwillingly saw in dreams.

"I've only seen him on television," she said. "It isn't very good."

She began to sketch in a headscarf, adding with a few strokes an impression of a curl over the forehead. Then, putting her head on one side and considering her work, she emphasized the lips so that they looked dark and full.

"Lipstick," she murmured, explaining. "How about clothes?" Her charcoal hovered over the neck.

"Jodhpurs and hacking jacket," I said. "The only clothes which look equally right on men and women."

"Crumbs," she said, staring at me. "It was easy, wasn't it? On with the headscarf and lipstick and exit the immediately recognizable Kemp-Lore."

I nodded. "Except that he still reminded people of himself."

She drew a collar and tie and the shoulders of a jacket with revers. The portrait grew into a likeness of a pretty young woman dressed for riding. It made my skin crawl.

I found Joanna regarding me with sympathetic eyes.

"You can hardly bear to look at him, can you?" she said. "And you talk in your sleep."

I rolled up the picture, bounced it on the top of her head, and said lightly, "Then I'll buy you some earplugs."

"He was taking a big risk, all the same, pretending to be a girl," she said, smiling.

"I don't suppose he did it a minute longer than he had to," I agreed. "Just long enough to get from Timberley to Cheltenham."

I filled ten long envelopes with the various statements, and sealed them. I addressed one to the Senior Steward and four others to influential people on the National Hunt Committee. One to the Chairman of Universal Telecast, one to John Ballerton, and one to Corin Kellar, to show them their idol's clay feet. One to James. And one to Maurice Kemp-Lore.

"Can't he get you for libel?" asked Joanna, looking over my shoulder.

"Not a chance," I said. "There's a defense in libel actions called justification, which roughly means that if a man has done something dishonest you are justified in disclosing it. You have to prove that it is true, that's all."

"I hope you are right," she said dubiously, sticking on some stamps.

"Don't worry. He won't sue me," I said positively.

I stacked nine of the envelopes into a neat pile on the bookshelf and propped the tenth, the unstamped one for Kemp-Lore, up on end behind them.

"We'll post that lot on Friday," I said. "And I'll deliver the other one myself."

At 8:30 on Thursday morning Joanna made the telephone call upon which so much depended.

I dialed the number of Kemp-Lore's London flat. There was a click as soon as the bell started ringing, and an automatic answering device invited us to leave a recorded message. Joanna raised her eyebrows: I shook my head, and she put down the receiver without saying anything.

"Out," I said unnecessarily. "Damn."

I gave her the number of Kemp-Lore's father's house in Essex and she was soon connected and talking to someone there. She nodded to me and put her hand over the mouthpiece, and said, "He's there. They've gone to fetch him. I . . . I hope I don't mess it up."

I shook my head encouragingly. We had rehearsed pretty thoroughly what she was going to say. She licked her lips and looked at me with anxious eyes.

"Oh? Mr. Kemp-Lore?" She could do a beautiful Cockney-suburban accent, not exaggerated and very convincing. "You don't know me, but I wondered if I could tell you something that you could use on your program in the newsy bits at the end? I do admire your program, I do really. It's ever so good, I always think—"

His voice clacked, interrupting the flow.

"What information?" repeated Joanna. "Oh, well, you know all the talk there's been about athletes using them pep pills and injections and things, well, I wondered if you wanted to know about jockeys doing it too. . . . One jockey, actually that I know of, but I expect they all do it if the truth were known. . . . Which jockey? . . . Oh . . . er, Robbie Finn, you know, the one you talked to on the telly on Saturday after he won that race. Pepped to the eyebrows as usual he was, didn't you guess? You was that close to him I thought you must have. . . . How do I know? Well, I do know. . . . You want to know how I know. . . . Well, it's a bit dodgy, like, but it was me got some stuff for him once. I work in a doctor's dispensary—cleaning, you see—and he told me what to take and I got it for him. But now look here, I don't want to get into trouble, I didn't mean to let on about that. . . . I think I'd better ring off. . . . Don't ring off? You won't say nothing about it then, you know, me pinching the stuff?

"Why am I telling you? . . . Well, he don't come to see me no more, that's why." Her voice was superbly loaded with jealous spite. "After all I've done for him. I did think of telling one of the newspapers, but I thought I'd see if you was interested first. I can tell them if you'd rather. . . . Check, what do you mean check? . . . You can't take my word for it on the telephone? Well, yes, you can come and see me if you want to. . . . No, not today, I'm at work all day. Yes, all right, tomorrow morning then.

"How do you get there? . . . Well, you go to Newbury and then out toward Hungerford . . ." She went on with the directions slowly while he wrote them down. "And it's the only cottage along there, you can't miss it. Yes, I'll wait in for you, about eleven o'clock, all right then. What's my name? . . . Doris Jones. Yes, that's right. Mrs. Doris Jones. Well, ta-ta then." The telephone clicked and buzzed as he disconnected.

She put the receiver down slowly, looking at me with a serious face.

"Hook, line and sinker," she said.

When the banks opened I went along and drew out one hundred and fifty pounds. As Joanna had said, what I was doing was complicated and expensive; but complications and expense had achieved top-grade results for Kemp-Lore, and at least I was paying him the compliment of copying his methods. I grudged the money not at all: what is money for, if not to get what you want? What I wanted, admirable or not, was to pay him in his own coin.

I drove off to the Bedfordshire farmer who promised to lend me his Land Rover and trailer. It was standing ready in the yard when I arrived at noon, and before I left I bought from the farmer two bales of straw and one of hay, which we stowed in the back of the Land Rover. Then, promising to return that evening, I started away to the first of my appointments with the *Horse and Hound* advertisers.

The first hunter, an old gray gelding in Northamptonshire, was so lame that he could hardly walk out of his box and he was no bargain even at the fifty pounds they were asking for him. I shook my head, and pressed on into Leicestershire.

The second appointment proved to be with a brown mare, sound in limb but noisy in wind, as I discovered when I cantered her across a field. She was big, about twelve years old and gawky, but quiet to handle and not too bad to look at, and she was for sale only because she could not go as fast as her ambitious owner liked. I haggled him from the hundred he had advertised her for down to eighty-five pounds, and clinched the deal. Then I loaded the mare, whose name, her ex-owner said, was Buttonhook, into the trailer and turned my face south again to Berkshire.

Three hours later, at half past five in the afternoon, I turned the Land Rover into the lane to the cottage, and bumped Buttonhook to a standstill on the rough ground behind the bushes beyond the building. She had to wait in the trailer while I got the straw and spread it thickly over the floor boards in the room with the water pipes cemented over the window, and again while I filled her a bucket of water out of the rain butt and carried an armful of hay into the room and put it in the corner behind the door.

She was an affectionate old thing, I found. She came docilely out of the trailer and made no fuss when I led her up the little garden path and in through the front door of the cottage and across the little hall into the room prepared for her. I gave her some sugar and rubbed her ears, and she butted her head playfully against my chest. After a while, as she seemed quite content in her unusual and not very spacious box, I went out into the hall, shut the door, and padlocked her in. Then I walked round the outside of the cottage and shook the water pipe bars to see if they were secure, as the frosty air might have prevented the cement from setting properly. But they were immovably fixed.

The mare came to the window and tried to poke her muzzle through the glassless squares of the window frame and through the bars outside them, but the maze defeated her. I put my hand through and fondled her muzzle, and she blew contentedly down her nostrils. Then she turned and went over to the corner where her hay was, and quietly and trustfully put her head down to eat.

I dumped the rest of the straw and hay in one of the front rooms of the cottage, shut the front door, maneuvered the trailer round with some difficulty into the lane again, and set off back to Bedfordshire. In due course I delivered the Land Rover and trailer to their owner, thanked him, and drove the hired car back to Joanna's mews.

When I went in, she kissed me. She sprang up from the sofa where she had been sitting reading, and kissed me lightly on the mouth. It was utterly spontaneous; without thought: and it was a great surprise to both of us. I put my hands on her arms and smiled incredulously down into her black eyes, and watched the surprise there turn to confusion and the confusion to panic. I took my hands away and turned my back on her to give her time, taking off the parka and saying casually over my shoulder, "The lodger is installed in the cottage. A big brown mare with a nice nature."

I hung up the parka in the closet.

"I was just . . . glad to see you back," she said in a high voice.

"That's fine," I said lightly. "Can I rustle up an egg, do you think?"

"There are some mushrooms for an omelette," she said, more normally.

"Terrific," I said, going into the kitchen. "Not peeled, by any chance?"

"Damn it, no," she said, following me and beginning to smile. She made the omelette for me and I told her about Buttonhook, and the difficult moment passed.

Later she announced that she was coming down to the cottage with me when I went in the morning.

"No," I said.

"Yes." She nodded. "He is expecting Mrs. Doris Jones to open the door to him. It will be much better if she does."

I couldn't budge her.

"And," she said, "I don't suppose you've thought of putting curtains in the windows? If you want him to walk into your parlor you'll have to make it look normal. He probably has a keen nose for rats." She fished some printed cotton material out of a drawer and held it up. "I've never used this. We can pin it up to look like curtains."

She busily collected some drawing pins and scissors, and then rolled up the big rag rug which the easel stood on and took a flower picture off the wall.

"What are those for?" I said.

"To furnish the hall, of course. It's got to look right."

"Okay, genius," I said, giving in. "You can come."

We put all the things she had gathered into a tidy pile by the door, and I added two boxes of cubed sugar from her cupboard, the big electric torch she kept in case of power cuts, and a broom.

After that springing kiss, the sofa was more of a wasteland than ever.

17

We set off early and got down to the cottage before nine, because there was a good deal to be done before Kemp-Lore arrived.

I hid the car behind the bushes again, and we carried the rug and the other things indoors. Buttonhook was safe and sound in her room, and was delighted to see us, neighing purringly in her throat when we opened the door. While I tossed her straw and fetched her some more hay and water, Joanna said she would clean the windows at the front of the cottage, and presently I heard her humming softly as she wiped away the grime of years.

The putty round the new panes had hardened well, and after I had finished Buttonhook, and Joanna was stepping back admiring the sparkle of the glass, I fetched the paint and began the tedious job of covering the patchwork of old decayed black paint and pale new putty with a bright green skin. Joanna watched me for a while and then went indoors. She put down the rug in the little hall, and I heard her banging a nail into the wall to hang up the picture just inside the front door where no visitor could fail to see it. After that she worked on the inside of the windows while I painted their outsides. She cut the flowery material into lengths and pinned it so that it hung like curtains at the sides.

When we had both finished we stood at the gate in front of the cottage admiring our handiwork. With its fresh paint, pretty curtains, and the rug and picture showing through the half-open door, it looked well cared for and homely.

"Has it got a name?" Joanna asked.

"I don't think so. It's always called the keeper's cottage, as far as I know," I said.

"We should name it Sundew," she said.

"After the Grand National winner?" I said, puzzled.

"No," she said soberly, "the carnivorous plant."

I put my arm round her waist. She didn't stir.

"You will be careful, won't you?" she said.

"Yes, I will," I assured her. I looked at my watch. It was twenty minutes to eleven. "We'd better go indoors in case he comes early."

We went in and shut the front door and sat on the remains of the hay bale in the front room, giving ourselves a clear view of the front gate.

A minute or two ticked by in silence. Joanna shivered.

"Are you too cold?" I said with concern. There had been another frost during the night and there was of course no heating in the cottage. "We should have brought a stove."

"It's nerves as much as cold," she said, shivering again.

I put my arm round her shoulders. She leaned comfortably against me, and I kissed her cheek. Her black eyes looked gravely, warily into mine.

"It isn't incest," I said.

Her eyelids flickered in shock, but she didn't move.

"Our fathers may be brothers," I said, "but our mothers are not related to them or to each other."

She said nothing. I had a sudden feeling that if I lost this time I had lost forever, and a leaden chill of despair settled in my stomach.

"No one forbids marriage between cousins," I said slowly. "The law allows it and the Church allows it, and you can be sure they wouldn't if there were anything immoral in it. And in a case like ours, the medical profession raises no objection either. If there were a good genetic reason why we shouldn't marry, it would be different. But you know there isn't." I paused, but she still looked at me gravely and said nothing. Without much hope I said, "I don't really understand why you feel the way you do."

"It's instinct," she said. "I don't understand it myself. It's just that I have always thought of it as wrong—and impossible."

There was a little silence.

I said, "I think I'll sleep in my digs down here in the village tonight, and ride out at exercise with the horses tomorrow morning. I've been neglecting my job this week."

She sat up straight, pulling free of my arm.

"No," she said abruptly. "Come back to the flat."

"I can't. I can't any more," I said.

She stood up and went over to the window and looked out. Minutes passed. Then she turned round and perched on the window sill with her back to the light, and I couldn't see her expression.

"It's an ultimatum, isn't it?" she said shakily. "Either I marry you or you clear out altogether? No more having it both ways, like you've given me this past week."

"It isn't a deliberate ultimatum," I protested. "But we can't go on like this forever. At least, I can't. Not if you know beyond any doubt that you'll never change your mind."

"Before last weekend there wasn't any problem as far as I was concerned," she said. "You were just something I couldn't have—like oysters, which give me indigestion—something nice, but out of bounds. And now—" she tried to laugh—"now it's as if I've developed a craving for oysters. And I'm in a thorough muddle."

"Come here," I said persuasively. She walked across and sat down again beside me on the hay bale. I took her hand.

"If we weren't cousins, would you marry me?" I held my breath.

"Yes," she said simply. No reservations, no hesitation any more.

I turned toward her and put my hands on the sides of her head and tilted her face up. There wasn't any panic this time. I kissed her; gently, and with love.

Her lips trembled, but there was no rigidity in her body, no blind instinctive retreat as there had been a week ago. I thought, If seven days can work such a change, what could happen in seven weeks?

I hadn't lost after all. The chill in my stomach melted away. I sat back on the bale, holding Joanna's hand again and smiling at her.

"It will be all right," I said. "Our being cousins won't worry you in a little while."

She looked at me wonderingly for a moment and then unexpectedly her lips twitched at the corners.

"I believe you," she said, "because I've never known anyone more determined in all my life. You've always been like that. You don't care what trouble you put yourself to to get what you want—like riding in that race last Saturday, and fixing up this fly trap of a cottage, and living with me how you have this week—so my instinct against blood relatives marrying, wherever it is seated, will have to start getting used to the idea that it is wrong, I suppose, otherwise I'll find myself being dragged by you along to Claudius Mellit to be psychoanalyzed or brainwashed, or something. I will try," she finished, sighing, "not to keep you waiting very long."

"In that case," I said, matching her lightheartedness, "I'll go on sleeping on your sofa as often as possible, so as to be handy when the breakthrough occurs."

She laughed without strain. "Starting tonight?" she asked.

"I guess so," I said, smiling. "I never did like my digs much."

"Ouch," she said.

"But I'll have to come back here on Sunday evening in any case. As James has given me my job back, the least I can do is show some interest in his horses."

We went on sitting on the hay bale, talking calmly as if nothing had happened; and nothing had, I thought, except a miracle that one could reliably build a future on, the miracle that Joanna's hand now lay intimately curled in mine without her wanting to remove it.

The minutes ticked away toward eleven o'clock.

"Suppose he doesn't come?" she said.

"He will."

"I almost hope he doesn't," she said. "Those letters would be enough by themselves."

"You won't forget to post them when you get back, will you?" I said.

"Of course not," she said. "But I wish you'd let me stay."

I shook my head. We sat on, watching the gate. The minute hand crept round to twelve on my watch, and passed it.

"He's late," she said.

Five past eleven. Ten past eleven.

"He isn't coming," Joanna murmured.

"He'll come," I said.

"Perhaps he got suspicious and checked up and found there wasn't any Mrs. Doris Jones living in the keeper's cottage," she said.

"There shouldn't be any reason for him to be suspicious," I pointed out. "He clearly didn't know at the end of that television interview with me last Saturday that I was on to him, and nothing I've done since should have got back to him, and James and Tick-Tock promised to say nothing to anyone about the doped sugar. As far as Kemp-Lore should know, he is unsuspected and undiscovered. If he feels as secure as I am sure he does, he'll never pass up an opportunity to learn about something as damaging as pep pills. So he'll come."

A quarter past eleven.

He had to come. I found that all my muscles were tense as if I were listening for him with my whole body, not only my ears. I flexed my toes inside my shoes and tried to relax. There were traffic jams, breakdowns, detours, any number of things to delay him. It was a long way, and he could easily have misjudged the time it would take.

Twenty past eleven.

Joanna sighed and stirred. Neither of us spoke for ten minutes. At 11:30 she said again, "He isn't coming."

I didn't answer.

At 11:33 the sleek cream nose of an Aston Martin slid to a stop at the gate and Maurice Kemp-Lore stepped out. He stretched himself, stiff from driving, and glanced over the front of the cottage. He wore a beautifully cut hacking jacket and cavalry twill trousers, and there were poise and grace in his every movement.

"Glory, he's handsome," breathed Joanna in my ear. "What features! What coloring! Television doesn't do him justice. It's difficult to think of anyone who looks so young and noble doing any harm."

"He's thirty-three," I said, "and Nero died at twenty-nine."

"You know the oddest things," she murmured.

Kemp-Lore unlatched the garden gate, walked up the short path, and banged the knocker on the front door.

We stood up. Joanna picked a piece of hay off her skirt, swallowed, gave me a half-smile, and walked unhurriedly into the hall. I followed her and stood against the wall where I would be hidden when the front door opened.

Joanna licked her lips.

"Go on," I whispered.

She put her hand on the latch, and opened the door.

"Mrs. Jones?" the honey voice said. "I'm so sorry I'm a little late."

"Won't you come in, Mr. Kemp-Lore," said Joanna in her Cockney-suburban accent. "It's ever so nice to see you."

"Thank you," he said, stepping over the threshold. Joanna took two paces backward and Kemp-Lore followed her into the hall.

Slamming the front door with my foot, I seized Kemp-Lore from behind by both elbows, pulling them backward and forcing him forward at the same time. Joanna opened the door of Buttonhook's room and I brought my foot into the small of Kemp-Lore's back and gave him an almighty push. He staggered forward through the door and I had a glimpse of him falling face downward in the straw before I had the door shut again and the padlock firmly clicking into place.

"That was easy enough," I said with satisfaction. "Thanks to your help."

Kemp-Lore began kicking the door.

"Let me out!" he shouted. "What do you think you're doing?"

"He didn't see you," said Joanna softly.

"No," I agreed. "I think we'll leave him in ignorance while I take you into Newbury to catch the train."

"Is it safe?" she said, looking worried.

"I won't be away long," I promised. "Come on."

Before driving her down to Newbury I moved Kemp-Lore's car along and off the lane until it was hidden in the bushes. The last thing I wanted was some stray inquisitive local inhabitant going along to the cottage to investigate. Then I took Joanna to the station and drove straight back again, a matter of twenty minutes each way, and parked in the bushes as usual.

Walking quietly I went along the side of the cottage and round to the back.

Kemp-Lore's hands stuck out through the glassless window frames, gripping the water pipe bars and shaking them vigorously. They had not budged in their cement.

He stopped abruptly when he saw me and I watched the anger in his face change to blank surprise.

"Who did you expect?" I said.

"I don't know what's going on," he said. "Some damn fool of a woman locked me in here nearly an hour ago and went away and left me. You can let me out. Quickly." His breath wheezed sharply in his throat. "There's a horse in here," he said, looking over his shoulder, "and they give me asthma."

"Yes," I said steadily, without moving. "Yes, I know."

It hit him then. His eyes widened.

"It was you . . . who pushed me . . ."

"Yes," I said.

He stood staring at me through the crisscross of window frames and bars.

"You did it on purpose? You put me in here with a horse on purpose?" His voice rose.

"Yes," I agreed.

"Why?" he cried. He must have known the answer already, but when I didn't reply he said again, almost in a whisper, "Why?"

"I'll give you half an hour to think about it," I said, turning to walk away.

"No!" he exclaimed. "My asthma's bad. Let me out at once." I turned back and stood close to the window. His breath whistled fiercely, but he had not even loosened his collar and tie. He was in no danger.

"Don't you have some pills?" I said.

"Of course. I've taken them. But they won't work with a horse so close. Let me out."

"Stand by the window," I said, "and breathe the fresh air."

"It's cold," he objected. "This place is like an icehouse."

I smiled. "Maybe it is," I said. "But then you are fortunate. You can move about to keep warm, and you have your jacket on—and I have not poured three bucketfuls of cold water over your head."

He gasped sharply, and it was then, I think, that he began to realize that he was not going to escape lightly or easily from his prison.

Certainly, when I returned to him after sitting on the hay bale for half an hour listening to him alternately kicking the door and yelling for help out the window, he was no longer assuming that I had lured him all the way from London and gone to the trouble of converting a cottage room into a loose box merely to set him free again at his first squawk.

When I walked round to the window I found him fending off Buttonhook, who was putting her muzzle affectionately over his shoulder. I laughed callously, and he nearly choked with rage.

"Get her away from me!" he screamed. "She won't leave me alone. I can't breathe."

He clung onto a bar with one hand, and chopped at Buttonhook with the other.

"If you don't make so much noise she'll go back to her hay," I observed.

He glared at me through the bars, his face distorted with rage and hate and fright. His asthma was much worse. He had unbuttoned his shirt collar and pulled down his tie, and I could see his throat heaving.

I put the box of sugar cubes I was carrying on the inner window sill, withdrawing my hand quickly as he made a grab at it.

"Put some sugar on her hay," I said. "Go on," I added, as he hesitated. "This lot isn't doped."

His head jerked up. I looked bitterly into his staring eyes.

"Twenty-eight horses," I said, "starting with Shantytown. Twenty-eight sleepy horses who all ate some sugar from your hand before they raced."

Savagely he picked up the box of sugar, tore it open, and sprinkled the cubes on the pile of hay at the other end of the room. Buttonhook, following him, put her head down and began to crunch. He came back to the window, wheezing laboriously.

"You won't get away with this," he said. "You'll go to jail for this. I'll see you pilloried for this."

"Save your breath," I said brusquely. "I've a good deal to say to you. After that, if you want to complain to the police about the way I've treated you, you're welcome."

"You'll be in jail so fast you won't know what hit you," he said, the breath hissing through his teeth. "Now, hurry up and say whatever it is you want to say."

"Hurry?" I said slowly. "Well, now, it's going to take some time."

"You'll have to let me out by two-thirty at the latest," he said unguardedly. "I've got rehearsals at five today."

I smiled at him. I could feel it wasn't a pleasant smile.

I said, "It isn't an accident that you are here on a Friday."

His jaw literally dropped. "The program . . ." he said.

"Will have to go on without you," I agreed.

"But you can't," he shouted, gasping for enough breath, "you can't do that!"

"Why not?" I said mildly.

"It's . . . it's television!" he shouted, as if I didn't know. "Millions of people are expecting to see the program."

"Then millions of people are going to be disappointed," I said.

He stopped shouting and took three gulping, wheezing breaths.

"I know," he said, with a visible effort at moderation and at getting back to normal, "that you don't really mean to keep me here so long that I can't get to the studio in time for the program. All right, then." He paused for a couple of wheezes. "If you let me go in good time for the rehearsals, I won't report you to the police as I threatened. I'll overlook all this."

"I think you had better keep quiet and listen," I said. "I suppose you'll find it hard to realize, but I don't give a damn for your influence, or for the pinnacle the British public have seen fit to put you on, or for your dazzling synthetic personality. They are a fraud. Underneath there is only a sick mess of envy and frustration and spite. But I wouldn't have found you out if you hadn't doped twenty-eight horses I rode and told everyone I had lost my nerve. And you can spend this afternoon reflecting that you wouldn't be missing your program tonight if you hadn't tried to stop me riding Template."

He stood stock-still, his face pallid and suddenly sweating.

"You mean it," he whispered.

"Indeed I do," I said.

"No," he said. A muscle in his cheek started twitching. "No. You can't. You did ride Template. You must let me do the program."

"You won't be doing any more programs," I said. "Not tonight or any night. I didn't bring you here just for a personal revenge, though I don't deny I felt like killing you last Friday night. I brought you here on behalf of Art Mathews and Peter Cloony and Grant Oldfield. I brought you because of Danny Higgs and Ingersoll, and every other jockey you have hit where it hurts. In various ways you saw to it that they lost their jobs; so now you are going to lose yours."

For the first time he was speechless. His lips moved but no sound came out except the high asthmatic whine of his breathing. His eyes seemed to fall back in their sockets and his lower jaw hung slack, making hollows of his cheeks. He looked like a death's-head caricature of the handsome charmer he had been.

I took out of my pocket the long envelope addressed to him and held it to him through the bars. He took it mechanically, with slack fingers.

"Open it," I said.

He pulled out the sheets of paper and read them. He read them through twice, though his face showed from the first that he understood the extent of the disaster. The haggard hollows deepened.

"As you will see," I said, "those are photostat copies. More like them are in the post to the Senior Steward and to your boss at Universal Telecast, and to several other people as well. They will get them tomorrow morning. And they will no longer wonder why you failed to turn up for your program tonight."

He still seemed unable to speak, and his hands shook convulsively. I passed to him through the bars the rolled-up portrait Joanna had drawn of him. He opened it, and it was clearly another blow.

"I brought it to show you," I said, "so that you would realize beyond any doubt that I know exactly what you have been doing. All along you have found that having an instantly recognizable face was a big handicap when it came to doing things you couldn't explain away, like ramming an old Jaguar across Peter Cloony's lane."

His head jerked back, as if it still surprised him that I knew so much.

I said calmly, "A ticket collector at Cheltenham said you were pretty."

I smiled faintly. He looked very far from pretty at that moment.

"As for that Jaguar," I said, "I haven't had time yet to find out where it came from, but it can be done. It's only a question of asking. Advertising its number in the trade papers, tracing its former owner —that sort of thing. Tedious, I dare say, but definitely possible, and if necessary I will do it. No one would forget having you for a customer.

"You must have bought it in the week after the tank carrier blocked Cloony's lane, because that is what gave you the idea. Do you think you can explain away the time sequence of acquiring the Jaguar and abandoning it exactly where and when and how you did? And disappearing from the scene immediately afterward?"

His mouth hung open and the muscle twitched in his cheek.

"Most of your vicious rumors," I said, changing tack, "were spread for you by Corin Kellar and John Ballerton, who you found would foolishly repeat every thought that you put into their heads. I hope you know Corin well enough to realize that he never stands by his friends. When the contents of the letter he will receive in the morning sink into that rat brain of his, and he finds that other people have had letters like it, there won't be anyone spewing out more damaging truth about you than him. He will start telling everyone, for instance, that it was you who set him at loggerheads with Art Mathews. There won't be any stopping him.

"You see," I finished after a pause, "I think it is only justice that as far as possible you should suffer exactly what you inflicted on other people."

He spoke at last. The words came out in a wheezing croak, and he was past caring what admissions he made. "How did you find it out?" he said disbelievingly. "You didn't know last Friday, you couldn't see . . ."

"I did know last Friday," I said, "I knew just how far you had gone to smash Peter Cloony, and I knew you hated me enough to give yourself asthma doping my mounts. I knew the dope business had gone sour on you when it came to Turniptop at Stratford. And you may care to learn that it was no accident that James Axminster jogged your arm and stepped on the sugar lumps; I asked him to, and told him what you were doing. I knew all about your curdled, obsessive jealousy of jockeys. I didn't need to see you last Friday to know you. There wasn't anyone else with any reason to want me out of action."

"You can't have known all that," he said obstinately, clinging to it as if it mattered. "You didn't know the next day when I interviewed you after the race . . ." His voice trailed off into a wheeze and he stared at me hopelessly through the bars.

"You aren't the only one who can smile and hate at the same time," I said neutrally. "I learned it from you."

He made a sound like a high-pitched moan, and turned his back toward me with his arms bent upward and folded over his head in an attitude of utmost misery and despair. It may be regrettable, but I felt no pity for him at all.

I walked away from his window, round the cottage and in at the front door, and sat down again on the hay in the front room. I looked at my watch. It was a quarter to two. The afternoon stretched lengthily ahead.

Kemp-Lore had another spell of screaming for help through the window, but no one came; then he tried the door again, but there was no handle on his side of it for him to pull, and it was too solidly constructed for him to kick his way through. Buttonhook grew restive again from the noise and started pawing the ground, and Kemp-Lore shouted to me furiously to let him out, let him out, let him out.

NERVE

Joanna's great fear had been that his asthma would make him seriously ill, and she had repeatedly warned me to be careful; but I judged that while he had enough breath for so much yelling he was in no real danger, and I sat and listened to him without relenting. The slow hours passed, punctuated only by the bursts of fury from the back room, while I stretched myself comfortably across the hay and daydreamed about marriage to my cousin.

At about five o'clock he was quiet for a long time. I got up and walked round the outside of the cottage and looked in through the window. He was lying face down in the straw near the door, not moving at all.

I watched him for a few minutes and called his name, but as he still did not stir I began to be alarmed, and decided I would have to make sure he was all right. I returned to the hall, and having shut the front door firmly behind me, I unlocked the padlock on the back room. The door swung inward, and Buttonhook, lifting her head, greeted me with a soft whinny.

Kemp-Lore was alive, that at least was plain. The sound of his high, squeezed breath rose unmistakably from his still form. I bent down beside him to see into just how bad a spasm he had been driven, but I never did get around to turning him over or feeling his pulse. As soon as I was down on one knee beside him he heaved himself up and into me, knocking me sprawling off balance, and sprang like lightning for the door.

I caught his shoe as it zipped across three inches from my face and yanked him back. He fell heavily on top of me and we rolled toward Buttonhook, with me trying to pin him down on the floor and he fighting like a tiger to get free. The mare was frightened. She cowered back against the wall to get out of our way, but it was a small room and our struggling took us among Buttonhook's feet and under her belly. She stepped gingerly over us and made cautiously for the open door.

Kemp-Lore's left hand was clamped round my right wrist, a circumstance which hindered me considerably. If he'd been clairvoyant he couldn't have struck on anything better calculated to cause me inconvenience. I hit him in the face and neck with my left hand, but I was too close to get any weight behind it and was also fairly occupied dodging the blows he aimed at me in return.

After he had lost the advantage of surprise, he seemed to decide he could only get free of me by lacing his fingers in my hair and banging my head against the wall, and this he tried repeatedly to do. He was staggeringly strong, more than I would have believed possible in view of his asthma, and the fury and desperation which fired him blazed in his blue eyes like a furnace.

If my hair hadn't been so short he would probably have succeeded in knocking me out, but his fingers kept slipping when I twisted my head violently in his grasp, and the third time my ear grazed the plaster I managed at last to wrench my right hand free as well.

After that, hauling off a fraction, I landed a socking right jab in his short ribs, and the air whistled out of his lungs screeching like an express train. He went a sick gray-green color and fell slackly off me, gasping and retching and clawing his throat for air.

I got to my feet and hauled him up, and staggered with him over to the window, holding him where the fresh cold air blew into his face. After three or four minutes his color improved and the terrifying heaving lessened, and some strength flowed back into his sagging legs.

I clamped his fingers round the window frames and let go of him. He swayed a bit, but his hands held, and after a moment I walked dizzily out of the room and padlocked the door behind me.

Buttonhook had found her way into the front room and was placidly eating the hay. I leaned weakly against the wall and watched her for a while, cursing myself for the foolish way I had nearly got myself locked into my own prison. I was badly shaken, not only by the fight itself but by the strength with which Kemp-Lore had fought and by the shocking effect my last blow had had on him. I ought to have had more sense, I knew, than to hit an asthmatic with that particular punch.

There was no sound from the back room. I straightened up and walked round to the window. He was standing there, holding onto the frames where I had put him, and there were tears running down his cheeks.

He was breathing safely enough, the asthma reduced to a more manageable wheeze, and I imagined it would not get any worse from then on, as Buttonhook was no longer in the room with him.

"Damn you," he said. Another tear spilled over. "Damn you. Damn you."

There wasn't anything to say.

I went back to Buttonhook, and put on her halter. I had meant to deal with her later, after I had let Kemp-Lore go, but in the changed circumstances I decided to do it straightaway, while it was still light. Leading her out the front door and through the gate, I jumped on to her back and rode her away up past the two cars hidden in the bushes and along the ridge of the hill.

A mile farther on I struck the lane which led up to the Downs, and turning down that came soon to a gate into a field owned by a farmer I had often ridden for. Slipping off Buttonhook I opened the gate, led her through, and turned her loose.

She was so amiable that I was sorry to part with her, but I couldn't keep her in the cottage, I couldn't stable an elderly hunter in James's yard and expect his lads to look after her, I couldn't find a snap buyer for her at six o'clock in the evening; and I frankly didn't know what else to do with her. I fondled her muzzle and patted her neck and fed her a handful of sugar. Then I slapped her on the rump and watched my eighty-five quid kick up her heels and canter down the field like a two-year-old. The farmer would no doubt be surprised to find an unclaimed brown mare on his land, but it would not be the first time a horse had been abandoned in that way, and I hadn't any doubt that he would give her a good home.

I turned away and walked back along the hill to the cottage. It was beginning to get dark, and the little building lay like a shadow in the hollow as I went down to it through the trees and bushes. All was very quiet, and I walked softly through the garden to the back window.

He was still standing there. When he saw me he said quite quietly, "Let me out."

I shook my head.

"Well, at least go and telephone the company, and tell them I'm ill. You can't let them all wait and wait for me to come, right up to the last minute."

I didn't answer.

"Go and telephone," he said again.

I shook my head.

He seemed to crumple inside. He stretched his hands through the bars and rested his head against the window frames.

"Let me out."

I said nothing.

"For pity's sake," he said, "let me out."

For pity's sake.

I said, "How long did you intend to leave me in that tack room?"

His head snapped up as if I'd hit him. He drew his hands back and gripped the bars.

"I went back to untie you," he said, speaking quickly, wanting to convince me. "I went back straight after the program was over, but you'd gone. Someone found you and set you free pretty soon, I suppose, since you were able to ride the next day."

"And you went back to find the tack room empty?" I said. "So you knew I had come to no harm?"

"Yes," he said eagerly. "Yes, that's what happened. I wouldn't have left you there very long, because of the rope stopping your circulation."

"You did think there was some danger of that, then?" I said innocently.

"Yes, of course there was, and that's why I wouldn't have left you there too long. If someone hadn't freed you first, I'd have let you go in good time. I only wanted to hurt you enough to stop you riding." His voice was disgustingly persuasive, as if what he was saying were not abnormal.

"You're a liar," I said calmly. "You didn't go back to untie me after the show. You would have found me still there if you had. In fact it took me until midnight to get free, because no one came. Then I found a telephone and rang up for a car to fetch me, but by the time it reached me, which was roughly two o'clock, you had still not returned. When I got to Ascot the following day everyone was surprised to see me. There was a rumor, they said, that I wouldn't turn up. You even mentioned on television that my name in the number frames was a mistake. Well, no one but you had any reason to believe that I wouldn't arrive at the races: so when I heard that rumor I knew that you had not gone back to untie me, not even in the morning. You thought I was still swinging from that hook, in God knows what state. And, as I understand it, you intended to leave me there indefinitely, until someone found me by accident . . . or until I was dead."

"No," he said faintly.

I looked at him without speaking for a moment, and then turned to walk away.

"All right!" he screamed suddenly, banging on the bars with his fists. "All right! I didn't care whether you lived or died. Do you like that? Is that what you want to hear? I didn't care if you died. I thought of you hanging there with your arms going black . . . with the agony going on and on . . . and I didn't care. I didn't care enough to stay awake. I went to bed. I went to sleep. I didn't care. I didn't care. And I hope you like it."

His voice cracked, and he sank down inside the room so that all I could see in the gathering dusk was the top of his fair head and the hands gripping the bars with the knuckles showing white through the skin.

"I hope you like it," he said brokenly.

I didn't like it. Not one little bit. It made me feel distinctly sick.

I went slowly round into the front room and sat down again on the hay. I looked at my watch. It was a quarter past six. Still three hours to wait: three hours in which the awful truth would dawn on Kemp-Lore's colleagues in the television studio, three hours of anxious speculation and stopgap planning, culminating in the digging out of a bit of old film to fill in the empty fifteen minutes and the smooth announcement: "We regret that owing to the—er—illness of Maurice Kemp-Lore there will be no 'Turf Talk' tonight."

Or ever again, mates, I thought, if you did but know it.

As it grew dark, the air got colder. It had been frosty all day, but with the disappearance of the sun the evening developed a subzero bite, and the walls of the unlived-in cottage seemed to soak it up. Kemp-Lore began kicking the door again.

"I'm cold," he shouted. "It's too cold."

"Too bad," I said under my breath.

"Let me out!" he yelled.

I lay on the hay without moving. The wrist which he had latched onto while we fought was uncomfortably sore, and blood seeped through the bandage again. What the Scots doctor would have to say when he saw it I hated to think. The three warts would no doubt quiver with disapproval. I smiled at the picture.

Kemp-Lore kicked the door for a long time, trying to break through it, but he didn't succeed. At the same time he wasted a good deal of breath yelling that he was cold and hungry and that I was to let him out. I made no reply to him at all, and after about an hour of it the kicking and shouting stopped, and I heard him slither down the door as if exhausted and begin sobbing with frustration.

I stayed where I was and listened while he went on and on moaning and weeping in desolation. I listened to him without emotion; for I had cried too, in the tack room.

The hands crawled round the face of my watch.

At a quarter to nine, when nothing could any longer save his program and even a message explaining his absence could scarcely be telephoned through in time, Kemp-Lore's decreasing sobs faded away altogether, and the cottage was quiet.

I got stiffly to my feet and went out into the front garden, breathing deeply in the clear air with an easing sense of release. The difficult day was over, and the stars were bright in the frosty sky. It was a lovely night.

I walked along to the bushes and started Kemp-Lore's car, turning it and driving it back to the gate. Then for the last time I walked round the cottage to talk to him through the window, and he was standing there already, his face a pale blur behind the window frames.

"My car," he said hysterically. "I heard the engine. You're going to drive away in my car and leave me."

I laughed. "No. You are going to drive it away yourself. As fast and as far as you like. If I were you, I'd drive to the nearest airport and fly off. No one is going to like you very much when they've read those letters in the morning, and it will be only a day or two before the newspapers get on to it. As far as racing goes, you will certainly be warned off. Your face is too well known in Britain for you to hide or change your name or get another job. And as you've got all night and probably most of tomorrow before the storm breaks and people start eying you with sneers and contempt, you can pack up and skip the country quite easily, without any fuss."

"You mean . . . I can go? Just go?" He sounded astounded.

"Just go," I said, nodding. "If you go quickly enough, you'll avoid the inquiry the Stewards are bound to hold and you'll avoid any charge they might think of slapping on you. You can get away to some helpful distant country where they don't know you, and you can start again from scratch."

"I suppose I haven't much choice," he muttered. His asthma was almost unnoticeable.

"And find a country where they don't have steeplechasing," I finished.

He moaned sharply, and crashed his fists down on the window frame.

I went round into the cottage and in the light of Joanna's big torch unlocked the padlock and pushed open the door. He turned from the window and walked unsteadily toward me across the straw, shielding his ravaged face from the light. He went through the door, passed me without a glance, and stumbled down the path to his car; and I walked down the path behind him, shining the torch ahead. I propped the torch on top of the gatepost so as to leave my hands free in case I needed to use them, but there didn't seem to be much fight left in him.

He paused when he was sitting in his car, and with the door still wide open looked out at me.

"You don't understand," he said, his voice shaking. "When I was a boy I wanted to be a jockey. I wanted to ride in the Grand National, like my father. And then there was this thing about falling off: I'd see the ground rushing past under my horse and there would be this terrible sort of pain in my guts, and I sweated until I could pull up and get off. And then I'd be sick."

He made a moaning noise and clutched his stomach at the memory. His face twisted. Then he said suddenly, fiercely, "It made me feel good to see jockeys looking worried. I broke them up, all right. It made me feel warm inside. Big."

He looked up at me with renewed rage, and his voice thickened venomously.

"I hated you more than all the others. You rode too well for a new jockey and you were getting on too quickly. Everyone was saying, 'Give Finn the bad horses to ride, he doesn't know what fear is.' It made me furious when I heard that. So I had you on my program, remember? I meant to make you look a fool. It worked with Mathews, why not with you? But Axminster took you up and then Pankhurst broke his leg. . . . I wanted to smash you so much that it gave me headaches. You walked about with that easy confidence of yours as if you took your strength for granted, and too many people were getting to say you'd be champion one day. . . .

"I waited for you to have a fall that looked fairly bad, and then I used the sugar. It worked. You know it worked. I felt ten feet tall, looking at your white face and listening to everyone sniggering about you. I watched you find out how it felt. I wanted to see you writhe when everyone you cared for said—as my father said to all his friends —that it was a pity about you . . . a pity you were a sniveling little coward, a pity you had no nerve . . . no nerve . . ."

His voice died away, and his hollowed eyes were wide, unfocused, as if he were staring back into an unbearable past.

I stood looking down at the wreck of what could have been a great man. All that vitality, I thought; all that splendid talent wasted for the sake of hurting people who had not hurt him.

Such individuals could be understood, Claudius Mellit had said. Understood, and treated, and forgiven.

I could understand him in a way, I supposed, because I was myself the changeling in a family. But my father had rejected me kindly, and I felt no need to watch musicians suffer.

Treated . . . The treatment I had given him that day might not have cured the patient, but he would no longer spread his disease, and that was all I cared about.

Without another word I shut the car door on him and gestured to him to drive away. He gave me one more incredulous glance as if he still found it impossible that I should let him go, and began to fumble with the light switches, the ignition, and the gears.

I hoped he was going to drive carefully. I wanted him to live. I wanted him to live for years, thinking about what he had thrown away. Anything else would be too easy, I thought.

The car began to roll, and I caught a last glimpse of the famous profile, the eclipsed, exiled profile, as he slid away into the dark. The brake lights flashed red as he paused at the end of the lane, then he turned out into the road and was gone. The sound of his engine died away.

I took the torch from the gatepost and walked up the path to the quiet cottage, to sweep it clean.

Forgiveness, I thought. That was something else again.

It would take a long time to forgive.

THREE

ODDS AGAINST

1

I was never particularly keen on my job before the day I got shot and nearly lost it, along with my life. But the .38 slug of lead which made a pepper shaker out of my intestines left me with fire in my belly in more ways than one. Otherwise I should never have met Zanna Martin, and would still be held fast in the spider threads of departed joys, of no use to anyone, least of all myself.

It was the first step to liberation, that bullet, though I wouldn't have said so at the time. I stopped it because I was careless. Careless because bored.

I woke up gradually in the hospital, in a private room for which I got a whacking great bill a few days later. Even before I opened my eyes I began to regret I had not left the world completely. Someone had lit a bonfire under my navel.

A fierce conversation was being conducted in unhushed voices over my head. With woolly wits, the anesthetic still drifting inside my skull like puffball clouds in a summer sky, I tried unenthusiastically to make sense of what was being said.

"Can't you give him something to wake him more quickly?"

"No."

"We can't do much until we have his story, you must see that. It's nearly seven hours since you finished operating. Surely—"

"And he was all of four hours on the table before that. Do you want to finish off what the shooting started?"

"Doctor—"

"I am sorry, but you'll have to wait."

There's my pal, I thought. They'll have to wait. Who wants to hurry back into the dreary world? Why not go to sleep for a month and take things up again after they've put the bonfire out? I opened my eyes reluctantly.

It was night. A globe of electric light shone in the center of the ceiling. That figured. It had been morning when Jones-boy found me still seeping gently onto the office linoleum and went to telephone, and it appeared that about twelve hours had passed since they stuck the first blessed needle into my arm. Would a twenty-four-hour start, I wondered, be enough for a panic-stricken ineffectual little crook to get himself undetectably out of the country?

There were two policemen on my left, one in uniform, one not. They were both sweating, because the room was hot. The doctor stood on the right, fiddling with a tube which ran from a bottle into my elbow. Various other tubes sprouted disgustingly from my abdomen, partly covered by a light sheet. Drip and drainage, I thought sardonically. How absolutely charming.

Radnor was watching me from the foot of the bed, taking no part in the argument still in progress between medicine and the law. I wouldn't have thought I rated the boss himself attendant at the bedside, but then I suppose it wasn't every day that one of his employees got himself into such a spectacular mess.

He said, "He's conscious again, and his eyes aren't so hazy. We might get some sense out of him this time." He looked at his watch.

The doctor bent over me, felt my pulse, and nodded. "Five minutes, then. Not a second more."

The plainclothes policeman beat Radnor to it by a fraction of a second. "Can you tell us who shot you?"

I still found it surprisingly difficult to speak, but not as impossible as it had been when they asked me the same question that morning. Then, I had been too far gone. Now, I was apparently on the way back. Even so, the policeman had plenty of time to repeat his question, and to wait some more, before I managed to answer.

"Andrews."

It meant nothing to the policeman, but Radnor looked astonished and also disappointed.

"Thomas Andrews?" he asked.

"Yes."

Radnor explained to the police. "I told you that Halley here and another of my operatives set some sort of a trap intending to clear up an intimidation case we are investigating. I understand they were hoping for a big fish, but it seems now they caught a tiddler. Andrews is small stuff, a weak sort of youth used for running errands. I would never have thought he would carry a gun, much less that he would use it."

Me neither. He had dragged the revolver clumsily out of his jacket pocket, pointed it shakily in my direction, and used both hands to pull the trigger. If I hadn't seen that it was only Andrews who had come to nibble at the bait I wouldn't have ambled unwarily out of the darkness of the washroom to tax him with breaking into the Cromwell Road premises of Hunt Radnor Associates at one o'clock in the morning. It simply hadn't occurred to me that he would attack me in any way.

By the time I realized that he really meant to use the gun and was not waving it about for effect, it was far too late. I had barely begun to turn to flip off the light switch when the bullet hit, in and out diagonally through my body. The force of it spun me onto my knees and then forward onto the floor.

As I went down he ran for the door, stiff-legged, crying out, with circles of white showing wild round his eyes. He was almost as horrified as I was at what he had done.

"At what time did the shooting take place?" asked the policeman formally.

After another pause I said, "One o'clock, about."

The doctor drew in a breath. He didn't need to say it; I knew I was lucky to be alive. In a progressively feeble state I'd lain on the floor through a chilly September night looking disgustedly at a telephone on which I couldn't summon help. The office telephones all worked through a switchboard. This might have been on the moon as far as I was concerned, instead of along the passage, down the curving stairs and through the door to the reception desk, with the girl who worked the switches fast asleep in bed.

The policeman wrote in his notebook. "Now sir, I can get a description of Thomas Andrews from someone else so as not to trouble you too much now, but I'd be glad if you can tell me what he was wearing."

"Black jeans, very tight. Olive-green jersey. Loose black jacket." I paused. "Black fur collar, black and white checked lining. All shabby . . . dirty." I tried again. "He had gun in jacket pocket right side . . . took it with him . . . no gloves . . . can't have a record."

"Shoes?"

"Didn't see. Silent, though."

"Anything else?"

I thought. "He had some badges . . . place names, skull and crossbones, things like that . . . sewn on his jacket, left sleeve."

"I see. Right. We'll get on with it then." He snapped shut his notebook, smiled briefly, turned, and walked to the door, followed by his uniformed ally, and by Radnor, presumably for Andrews' description.

The doctor took my pulse again, and slowly checked all the tubes. His face showed satisfaction.

He said cheerfully, "You must have the constitution of a horse."

"No," said Radnor, coming in again and hearing him. "Horses are really quite delicate creatures. Halley has the constitution of a jockey. A steeplechase jockey. He used to be one. He's got a body like a shock absorber . . . had to have to deal with all the fractures and injuries he got racing."

"Is that what happened to his hand? A fall in a steeplechase?"

Radnor's glance flicked to my face and away again, uncomfortably. They never mentioned my hand to me in the office if they could help it. None of them, that is, except my fellow trap-setter Chico Barnes, who didn't care what he said to anyone.

"Yes," Radnor said tersely. "That's right." He changed the subject. "Well, Sid, come and see me when you are better. Take your time." He nodded uncertainly to me, and he and the doctor, with a joint backward glance, ushered each other out of the door.

So Radnor was in no hurry to have me back. I would have smiled if I'd had the energy. When he first offered me the job I guessed that somewhere in the background my father-in-law was pulling strings; but I had been in a why-not mood at the time. Nothing mattered very much.

"Why not?" I said to Radnor, and he put me on his payroll as an investigator, racing section, ignoring my complete lack of experience, and explained to the rest of the staff that I was there in an advisory capacity, owing to my intimate knowledge of the game. They had taken it very well, on the whole. Perhaps they realized, as I did, that my employment was an act of pity. Perhaps they thought I should be too proud to accept that sort of pity. I wasn't, I didn't care one way or the other.

Radnor's agency ran Missing Persons, Guard, and Divorce departments, and also a section called Bona Fides, which was nearly as big as the others put together. Most of the work was routine painstaking inquiry stuff, sometimes leading to civil or divorce action, but oftener merely to a discreet report sent to the client. Criminal cases, though accepted, were rare. The Andrews business was the first for three months.

The Racing section was Radnor's special baby. It hadn't existed, I'd been told, when he bought the agency with an army gratuity after the war and developed it from a dingy three-roomed affair into something like a national institution. Radnor printed "Speed, Results, and Secrecy" across the top of his stationery; promised them, and delivered them. A lifelong addiction to racing, allied to six youthful rides in point-to-points, had led him not so much to ply for hire from the Jockey Club and the National Hunt Committee as to indicate that his agency was at their disposal. The Jockey Club and the National Hunt Committee tentatively wet their feet, found the water beneficial, and plunged right in. The Racing section blossomed. Eventually private business outstripped the official, especially when Radnor began supplying pre-race guards for fancied horses.

By the time I joined the firm, "Bona Fides: Racing" had proved so successful that it had spread from its own big office into the room next door. For a reasonable fee a trainer could check on the character and background of a prospective owner, a bookmaker on a client, a client on a bookmaker, anybody on anybody. The phrase "O.K.'d by Radnor" had passed into racing slang. Genuine, it meant. Trustworthy. I had even heard it applied to a horse.

They had never given me a Bona Fides assignment. This work was done by a bunch of inconspicuous middle-aged retired policemen who took minimum time to get results. I'd never been sent to sit all night outside the box of a hot favorite, though I would have done it willingly. I had never been put on a racecourse security patrol. If the stewards asked for operators to keep tabs on undesirables at race meetings, I didn't go. If anyone had to watch for pickpockets in Tattersalls, it wasn't me. Radnor's two unvarying excuses for giving me nothing to do were first that I was too well known to the whole racing world to be inconspicuous, and second, that even if I didn't seem to care, he was not going to be the one to give an ex-champion jockey tasks which meant a great loss of face.

As a result I spent most of my time kicking around the office reading other people's reports. When anyone asked me for the informed advice I was supposedly there to give, I gave it; if anyone asked what I would do in a certain set of circumstances, I told them. I got to know all the operators and gossiped with them when they came into the office. I always had the time. If I took a day off and went to the races nobody complained. I sometimes wondered whether they even noticed.

At intervals I remarked to Radnor that he didn't have to keep me, as I so obviously did nothing to earn my salary. He replied each time that he was satisfied with the arrangement, if I was. I had the impression that he was waiting for something, but if it wasn't for me to leave, I didn't know what. On the day I walked into Andrews' bullet I had been with the agency in this fashion for exactly two years.

A nurse came in to check the tubes and take my blood pressure. She was starched and efficient. She smiled, but didn't speak. I waited for her to say that my wife was outside asking about me anxiously. She didn't say it. My wife hadn't come. Wouldn't come. If I couldn't hold her when I was properly alive, why should my near-death bring her running? Jenny. My wife. Still my wife in spite of three years' separation. Regret, I think, held both of us back from the final step of divorce: we had been through passion, delight, dissension, anger and explosion. Only regret was left, and it wouldn't be strong enough to bring her to the hospital. She'd seen me in too many hospitals before. There was no more drama, no more impact, in my form recumbent, even with tubes. She wouldn't come. Wouldn't telephone. Wouldn't write. It was stupid of me to want her to.

Time passed slowly and I didn't enjoy it, but eventually all the tubes except the one in my arm were removed and I began to heal. The police didn't find Andrews, Jenny didn't come, Radnor's typists sent me a get-well card, and the hospital sent the bill.

Chico slouched in one evening, his hands in his pockets and the usual derisive grin on his face. He looked me over without haste and the grin, if anything, widened.

"Rather you than me, mate," he said.

"Go to bloody hell."

He laughed. And well he might. I had been doing his job for him because he had a date with a girl, and Andrews' bullet should have been his bellyache, not mine.

"Andrews," he said musingly. "Who'd have thought it? Sodding little weasel. All the same, if you'd done what I said and stayed in the washroom, and taken his photo quiet-like on the old infrared, we'd have picked him up later nice and easy and you'd have been lolling on your arse around the office as usual instead of sweating away in here."

"You needn't rub it in," I said. "What would you have done?"

He grinned. "The same as you, I expect. I'd have reckoned it would only take the old one-two for that little worm to come across with who sent him."

"And now we don't know."

"No." He sighed. "And the old man ain't too sweet about the whole thing. He did know I was using the office as a trap, but he didn't think it would work, and now this has happened he doesn't like it. He's leaning over backwards, hushing the whole thing up. They might have sent a bomb, not a sneak thief, he said. And of course Andrews bust a window getting in, which I've probably got to pay for. Trust the little sod not to know how to pick a lock."

"I'll pay for the window," I said.

"Yeah," he grinned. "I reckoned you would if I told you."

He wandered round the room, looking at things. There wasn't much to see.

"What's in that bottle dripping into your arm?"

"Food of some sort, as far as I can gather. They never give me anything to eat."

"Afraid you might bust out again, I expect."

"I guess so," I agreed.

He wandered on. "Haven't you got a telly then? Cheer you up a bit, wouldn't it, to see some other silly buggers getting shot?" He looked at the chart on the bottom of the bed. "Your temperature was one hundred and two this morning, did they tell you? Do you reckon you're going to kick it?"

"No."

"Near thing, from what I've heard. Jones-boy said there was enough of your life's blood dirtying up the office floor to make a tidy few black puddings."

I didn't appreciate Jones-boy's sense of humor.

Chico said, "Are you coming back?"

"Perhaps."

He began tying knots in the cord of the window blind. I watched him, a thin figure imbued with so much energy that it was difficult for him to keep still. He had spent two fruitless nights watching in the washroom before I took his place, and I knew that if he hadn't been dedicated to his job he couldn't have borne such inactivity. He was the youngest of Radnor's team. About twenty-four, he believed, though as he had been abandoned as a child on the steps of a police station in a push-chair, no one knew for certain.

If the police hadn't been so kind to him, Chico sometimes said, he would have taken advantage of his later opportunities and turned delinquent. He never grew tall enough to be a copper. Radnor's was the best he could do. And he did very well by Radnor. He put two and two together quickly and no one on the staff had faster physical reactions. Judo and wrestling were his hobbies, and along with the regular throws and holds he had been taught some strikingly dirty tricks. His smallness bore no relation whatever to his effectiveness in his job.

"How are you getting on with the case?" I asked.

"What case? Oh . . . that. Well, since you got shot the heat's off, it seems. Brinton's had no threatening calls or letters since the other night. Whoever was leaning on him must have got the wind up. Anyway, he's feeling a bit safer all of a sudden and he's carping a lot to the old man about fees. Another day or two, I give it, and there won't be no one holding his hand at night. Anyway, I've been pulled off it. I'm flying from Newmarket to Ireland tomorrow, sharing a stall with a hundred thousand pounds' worth of stallion."

Escort duty was another little job I never did. Chico liked it, and went often. As he had once thrown a fifteen-stone would-be nobbler over a seven-foot wall, he was always much in demand.

"You ought to come back," he said suddenly.

"Why?" I was surprised.

"I don't know. . . ." He grinned. "Silly, really, when you do sweet off all, but everybody seems to have got used to you being around. You're missed, kiddo, you'd be surprised."

"You're joking, of course."

"Yeah. . . ." He undid the knots in the window cord, shrugged, and thrust his hands into his trouser pockets. "God, this place gives you the willies. It reeks of warm disinfectant. Creepy. How much longer are you going to lie here rotting?"

"Days," I said mildly. "Have a good trip."

"See you." He nodded, drifting in relief to the door. "Do you want anything? I mean books or anything?"

"Nothing, thanks."

"Nothing . . . that's just your form, Sid, mate. You don't want nothing." He grinned and went.

I wanted nothing. My form. My trouble. I'd had what I wanted most in the world and lost it irrevocably. I'd found nothing else to want. I stared at the ceiling, waiting for time to pass. All I wanted was to get back onto my feet and stop feeling as though I had eaten a hundredweight of green apples.

Three weeks after the shooting I had a visit from my father-in-law. He came in the late afternoon, bringing with him a small parcel which he put without comment on the table beside the bed.

"Well, Sid, how are you?" He settled himself into an easy chair, crossed his legs and lit a cigar.

"Cured, more or less. I'll be out of here soon."

"Good. Good. And your plans are . . . ?"

"I haven't any."

"You can't go back to the agency without some . . . er, convalescence," he remarked.

"I suppose not."

"You might prefer somewhere in the sun," he said, studying the cigar. "But I would like it if you could spend some time with me at Aynsford."

I didn't answer immediately.

"Will . . . ?" I began and stopped, wavering.

"No," he said. "She won't be there. She's gone out to Athens to stay with Jill and Tony. I saw her off yesterday. She sent you her regards."

"Thanks," I said dryly. As usual I did not know whether to be glad or sorry that I was not going to meet my wife. Nor was I sure that this trip to see her sister Jill was not as diplomatic as Tony's job in the Corps.

"You'll come, then? Mrs. Cross will look after you splendidly."

"Yes, Charles, thank you. I'd like to come for a little while."

He gripped the cigar in his teeth, squinted through the smoke, and took out his diary.

"Let's see, suppose you leave here in, say, another week. . . . No point in hurrying out before you're fit to go. That brings us to the twenty-sixth . . . hm . . . now, suppose you come down a week on Sunday, I'll be at home all that day. Will that suit you?"

"Yes, fine, if the doctors agree."

"Right, then." He wrote in the diary, put it away and took the cigar carefully out of his mouth, smiling at me with the usual inscrutable blankness in his eyes. He sat easily in his dark city suit, Rear Admiral Charles Roland, R.N., retired, a man carrying his sixty-six years lightly. War photographs showed him tall, straight, bony almost, with a high forehead and thick dark hair. Time had grayed the hair, which in receding left his forehead higher than ever, and had added weight where it did no harm. His manner was ordinarily extremely charming and occasionally patronizingly offensive. I had been on the receiving end of both.

He relaxed in the armchair, talking unhurriedly about steeplechasing.

"What do you think of that new race at Sandown? I don't know about you, but I think it's framed rather awkwardly. They're bound to get a tiny field with those conditions, and if Devil's Dyke doesn't run after all the whole thing will be a non-crowd puller par excellence."

His interest in this game only dated back a few years, but recently to his pleasure he had been invited by one or two courses to act as a Steward. Listening to his easy familiarity with racing problems and racing jargon, I was in a quiet inward way amused. It was impossible to forget his reaction long ago to Jenny's engagement to a jockey, his unfriendly rejection of me as a future son-in-law, his absence from our wedding, the months afterward of frigid disapproval, the way he had seldom spoken to or even looked at me.

I believed at the time that it was sheer snobbery, but it wasn't as simple as that. Certainly he didn't think me good enough, but not only, or even mainly, on a class distinction level; and probably we would never have understood each other, or come eventually to like each other, had it not been for a wet afternoon and a game of chess.

Jenny and I went to Aynsford for one of our rare, painful Sunday visits. We ate our roast beef in near silence, Jenny's father staring rudely out of the window and drumming his fingers on the table. I made up my mind that we wouldn't go again. I'd had enough. Jenny could visit him alone.

After lunch she said she wanted to sort out some of her books now that we had a new bookcase, and disappeared upstairs. Charles Roland and I looked at each other in dislike, the afternoon stretching drearily ahead and the downpour outside barring retreat into the garden and park beyond.

"Do you play chess?" he asked in a bored, expecting-the-answer-no voice.

"I know the moves," I said.

He shrugged (it was more like a squirm), but clearly thinking that it would be less trouble than making conversation, he brought a chess set out and gestured to me to sit opposite him. He was normally a good player, but that afternoon he was bored and irritated and inattentive, and I beat him quite early in the game. He couldn't believe it. He sat staring at the board, fingering the bishop with which I'd got him in a classic discovered check.

"Where did you learn?" he said eventually, still looking down.

"Out of a book."

"Have you played a great deal?"

"No, not much. Here and there." But I'd played with some good players.

"Hm." He paused. "Will you play again?"

"Yes, if you like."

We played. It was a long game and ended in a draw, with practically every piece off the board. A fortnight later he rang up and asked us, next time we came, to stay overnight. It was the first twig of the olive branch. We went more often and more willingly to Aynsford after that. Charles and I played chess occasionally and won a roughly equal number of games, and he began rather tentatively to go to the races. Ironically from then on our mutual respect grew strong enough to survive even the crash of Jenny's and my marriage, and Charles's interest in racing expanded and deepened with every passing year.

"I went to Ascot yesterday," he was saying, tapping off his cigar. "It wasn't a bad crowd, considering the weather. I had a drink with that handicap fellow, John Pagan. Nice chap. He was very pleased with himself because he got six abreast over the last in the handicap hurdle. There was an objection after the three-mile chase—flagrant bit of crossing on the run-in. Carter swore blind he was leaning and couldn't help it, but you can never believe a word he says. Anyway, the Stewards took it away from him. The only thing they could do. Wally Gibbons rode a brilliant finish in the handicap hurdle and then made an almighty hash of the novice chase."

"He's heavy-handed with novices," I agreed.

"Wonderful course, that."

"The tops." A wave of weakness flowed outward from my stomach. My legs trembled under the bedclothes. It was always happening. Infuriating.

"Good job it belongs to the Queen and is safe from the land-grabbers." He smiled.

"Yes, I suppose so. . . ."

"You're tired," he said abruptly. "I've stayed too long."

"No," I protested. "Really, I'm fine."

He put out the cigar, however, and stood up. "I know you too well, Sid. Your idea of fine is not the same as anyone else's. If you're not well enough to come to Aynsford a week on Sunday you'll let me know. Otherwise I'll see you then."

"Yes, O.K."

He went away, leaving me to reflect that I did still tire infernally easily. Must be old age, I grinned to myself, old age at thirty-one. Old tired battered Sid Halley, poor old chap. I grimaced at the ceiling.

A nurse came in for the evening jobs.

"You've got a parcel," she said brightly, as if speaking to a retarded child. "Aren't you going to open it?"

I had forgotten about Charles's parcel.

"Would you like me to open it for you? I mean, you can't find things like opening parcels very easy with a hand like yours."

She was only being kind. "Yes," I said. "Thank you."

She snipped through the wrappings with scissors from her pocket and looked dubiously at the slim dark book she found inside.

"I suppose it is meant for you? I mean somehow it doesn't seem like things people usually give patients."

She put the book into my right hand and I read the title embossed in gold on the cover. *Outline of Company Law.*

"My father-in-law left it on purpose. He meant it for me."

"Oh well, I suppose it's difficult to think of things for people who can't eat grapes and such." She bustled around, efficient and slightly bullying, and finally left me alone again.

Outline of Company Law. I riffled through the pages. It was certainly a book about company law. Solidly legal. Not light entertainment for an invalid. I put the book on the table.

Charles Roland was a man of subtle mind, and subtlety gave him pleasure. It hadn't been my parentage that he had objected to so much as what he took to be Jenny's rejection of his mental standards in choosing a jockey for a husband. He'd never met a jockey before, disliked the idea of racing, and took it for granted that everyone engaged in it was either a rogue or a moron. He'd wanted both his daughters to marry clever men, clever more than handsome or well-born or rich, so that he could enjoy their company. Jill had obliged him with Tony, Jenny disappointed him with me: that was how he saw it, until he found that at least I could play chess with him now and then.

Knowing his subtle habits, I took it for granted that he had not idly brought such a book and hadn't chosen it or left it by mistake. He meant me to read it for a purpose. Intended it to be useful to me —or to him—later on. Did he think he could maneuver me into business, now that I hadn't distinguished myself at the agency? A nudge, that book was. A nudge in some specific direction.

I thought back over what he had said, looking for a clue. He'd been insistent that I should go to Aynsford. He'd sent Jenny to Athens. He'd talked about racing, about the new race at Sandown, about Ascot, John Pagan, Carter, Wally Gibbons . . . nothing there that I could see had the remotest connection with company law.

I sighed, shutting my eyes. I didn't feel too well. I didn't have to read the book, or go wherever Charles pointed. And yet . . . why not? There was nothing I urgently wanted to do instead. I decided to do my stodgy homework. Tomorrow.

Perhaps.

2

Four days after my arrival at Aynsford I came downstairs from an afternoon's rest to find Charles delving into a large packing case in the center of the hall. Strewn round on the half-acre of parquet was a vast amount of wood shavings, white and curly, and arranged carefully on a low table beside him were the first trophies out of the lucky dip, appearing to me to be dull chunks of rock.

I picked one of them up. One side had been ground into a smooth face and across the bottom of this was stuck a neat label. "Porphyry" it said, and beneath, "Carver Mineralogy Foundation."

"I didn't know you had an obsessive interest in quartz."

He gave me one of his blank stares which I knew didn't mean that he hadn't heard or understood what I'd said, but that he didn't intend to explain.

"I'm going fishing," he said, plunging his arms back into the box.

So the quartz was bait. I put down the porphyry and picked up another piece. It was small, the size of a squared-off egg, and beautiful, as clear and translucent as glass. The label said simply "Rock Crystal."

"If you want something useful to do," said Charles, "you can write out what sort they all are on the plain labels you will find on my desk, and then soak the Foundation's labels off and put the new ones on. Keep the old ones, though. We'll have to replace them when all this stuff goes back."

"All right," I agreed.

The next chunk I picked up was heavy with gold. "Are these valuable?" I asked.

"Some are. There's a booklet somewhere. But I told the Foundation they'd be safe enough. I said I'd have a private detective in the house all the time guarding them."

I laughed and began writing the new labels, working from the inventory. The lumps of quartz overflowed from the table onto the floor before the box was empty.

"There's another box outside," Charles observed.

"Oh no!"

"I collect quartz," said Charles with dignity, "and don't you forget it. I've collected it for years. Years. Haven't I?"

"Years," I agreed. "You're an authority. Who wouldn't be an authority on rocks, after a life at sea?"

"I've got exactly one day to learn them in," said Charles, smiling. "They've come later than I asked. I'll have to be word-perfect by tomorrow night."

He fetched the second lot, which was much smaller and was fastened with important-looking seals. Inside were uncut gem quartz crystals, mounted on small individual black plinths. Their collective value was staggering. The Carver Foundation must have taken the private detective bit seriously. They'd have held tight to their rocks if they'd seen my state of health.

We worked for some time changing the labels while Charles muttered their names like incantations under his breath. "Chrysoprase, aventurine, agate, onyx, chalcedony, tiger's-eye, carnelian, citrine, rose, plasma, basanite, bloodstone, chert. Why the hell did I start this?"

"Well, why?"

I got the blank stare again. He wasn't telling. "You can test me on them," he said.

We carried them piece by piece into the dining room, where I found the glass-doored bookshelves on each side of the fire had been cleared of their yards of leather-bound classics.

"They can go up there later," said Charles, covering the huge dining-room table with a thick felt. "Put them on the table for now."

When they were all arranged he walked slowly round learning them. There were about fifty altogether. I tested him after a while, at his request, and he muddled up and forgot about half of them. They were difficult, because so many looked alike.

He sighed. "It's time we had a noggin and you went back to bed." He led the way into the little sitting room he occasionally referred to as the wardroom, and poured a couple of stiffish brandies. He raised his glass to me and appreciatively took a mouthful. There was a suppressed excitement in his expression, a glint in the unfathomable eyes. I sipped the brandy, wondering with more interest what he was up to.

"I have a few people coming for the weekend," he said casually, squinting at his glass. "A Mr. and Mrs. Rex van Dysart, a Mr. and Mrs. Howard Kraye, and my cousin Viola, who will act as hostess."

"Old friends?" I murmured, having ever heard only of Viola.

"Not very," he said smoothly. "They'll be here in time for dinner tomorrow night. You'll meet them then."

"But I'll make it an odd number. . . . I'll go up before they come and stay out of your way for most of the weekend."

"No," he said sharply. Much too vehemently. I was surprised. Then it came to me suddenly that all he had been doing with his rocks and his offer of a place for my convalescence was to engineer a meeting between me and the weekend guests. He offered me rest. He offered Mr. van Dysart, or perhaps Mr. Kraye, rocks. Both of us had swallowed the hook. I decided to give the line a tug, to see just how determined was the fisherman.

"I'd be better upstairs. You know I can't eat normal meals." My diet at that time consisted of brandy, beef juice, and some vacuum-packed pots of stuff which had been developed for feeding astronauts. Apparently none of these things affected the worst-shot-up bits of my digestive tract.

"People loosen up over the dinner table . . . they talk more, and you get to know them better." He was carefully unpersuasive.

"They'll talk to you just as well if I'm not there—better in fact. And I couldn't stand watching you all tuck into steaks."

He said musingly, "You can stand anything, Sid. But I think you'd be interested. Not bored, I promise you. More brandy?"

I shook my head, and relented. "All right, I'll be there at dinner, if you want it."

He relaxed only a fraction. A controlled and subtle man. I smiled at him, and he guessed that I'd been playing him along.

"You're a bastard," he said.

From him, it was a compliment.

The transistor beside my bed was busy with the morning news as I slowly ate my breakfast pot of astronaut paste.

"The race meeting scheduled for today and tomorrow at Seabury," the announcer said, "has had to be abandoned. A tanker carrying liquid chemical crashed and overturned at dusk yesterday afternoon on a road crossing the racecourse. There was considerable damage to the turf, and after an examination this morning, the Stewards regretfully decided that it was not fit to be raced on. It is hoped to replace the affected turf in time for the next meeting in a fortnight's time, but an announcement will be made about this at a later date. And here is the weather forecast. . . ."

Poor Seabury, I thought, always in the wars. It was only a year since their stable block had been burned down on the eve of a meeting. They had had to cancel then too, because temporary stables could not be erected overnight and the National Hunt Committee in consultation with Radnor had decided that indiscriminate stabling in the surrounding district was too much of a security risk.

It was a nice track to ride on, a long circuit with no sharp bends, but there had been trouble with the surface in the spring, a drain of some sort had collapsed during a hurdle race: the forefeet of one unfortunate horse had gone right through into it to a depth of about eighteen inches and he had broken a leg. In the resulting pile-up two more horses had been injured and one jockey badly concussed. Maps of the course didn't even warn that the drain existed, and I'd heard trainers wondering whether there were any more antique waterways ready to collapse with as little notice. The executive, on their side, naturally swore there weren't.

For some time I lay daydreaming, racing round Seabury again in my mind, and wishing uselessly, hopelessly, achingly, that I could do it again in fact.

Mrs. Cross tapped on the door and came in. She was a quiet, unobtrusive mouse of a woman with soft brown hair and a slight outward cast in her gray-green eyes. Although she seemed to have no spirit whatever and seldom spoke, she ran the place like oiled machinery, helped by a largely invisible squad of "dailies." She had the great virtue to me of being fairly new in the job and impartial on the subject of Jenny and me. I wouldn't have trusted her predecessor, who had been fanatically fond of Jenny, not to have added cascara to my beef juice.

"The Admiral would like to know if you are feeling well today, Mr. Halley," said Mrs. Cross primly, picking up my breakfast tray.

"Yes, I am, thank you." More or less.

"He said, then, when you're ready would you join him in the dining room?"

"The rocks?"

She gave me a small smile. "He was up before me this morning, and had his breakfast on a tray in there. Shall I tell him you'll come down?"

"Please."

When she had gone, and while I was slowly dressing, the telephone bell rang. Not long afterward, Charles himself came upstairs.

"That was the police," he said abruptly with a frown. "Apparently they've found a body and they want you to go and identify it."

"Whose body, for heaven's sake?"

"They didn't say. They said they would send a car for you immediately though. I gathered they really rang here to locate you."

"I haven't any relatives. It must be a mistake."

He shrugged. "We'll know soon, anyway. Come down now and test me on the quartz. I think I've got it taped at last."

We went down to the dining room, where I found he was right. He went round the whole lot without a mistake. I changed the order in which they stood, but it didn't throw him. He smiled, very pleased with himself.

"Word-perfect," he said. "Let's put them up on the shelves now. At least, we'll put all the least valuable ones up there, and the gem stones in the bookcase in the drawing room—that one with the curtains inside the glass doors."

"They ought to be in a safe." I had said it yesterday evening as well.

"They were quite all right on the dining-room table last night, in spite of your fears."

"As the consultant private detective in the case I still advise a safe."

He laughed. "You know bloody well I haven't got a safe. But as consultant private detective you can guard the things properly tonight. You can put them under your pillow. How's that?"

"O.K." I nodded.

"You're not serious?"

"Well, no . . . they'd be too hard under the pillow."

"Damn it. . . ."

"But upstairs, either with you or me, yes. Some of those stones really are valuable. You must have had to pay a big insurance premium on them."

"Er . . . no," admitted Charles. "I guaranteed to replace anything which was damaged or lost."

I goggled. "I know you're rich, but . . . you're an absolute nut. Get them insured at once. Have you any idea what each specimen is worth?"

"No, as a matter of fact . . . no. I didn't ask."

"Well, if you've got a collector coming to stay, he'll expect you to remember how much you paid for each."

"I thought of that," he interrupted. "I inherited them all from a distant cousin. That covers a lot of ignorance, not only costs and values but about crystallography and distribution and rarity, and everything specialized. I found I couldn't possibly learn enough in one day. Just to be able to show some familiarity with the collection should be enough."

"That's fair enough. But you ring the Carver Foundation at once and find out what the stones are worth just the same, and then get straight onto your broker. The trouble with you, Charles, is that you are too honest. Other people aren't. This is the bad, rough world you're in now, not the navy."

"Very well," he said amicably. "I'll do as you say. Hand me that inventory."

He went to telephone and I began putting the chunks of quartz on the empty bookshelves, but before I had done much the front doorbell rang. Mrs. Cross went to answer it and presently came to tell me that a policeman was asking for me.

I put my useless, deformed left hand into my pocket, as I always did with strangers, and went into the hall. A tall, heavy young man in uniform stood there, giving the impression of trying not to be overawed by his rather grand surroundings. I remembered how it felt.

"Is it about this body?" I asked.

"Yes, sir, I believe you are expecting us."

"Whose body is it?"

"I don't know, sir. I was just asked to take you."

"Well . . . where to?"

"Epping Forest, sir."

"But that's miles away," I protested.

"Yes, sir," he agreed, with a touch of gloom.

"Are you sure it's me that's wanted?"

"Oh, positive, sir."

"Well, all right. Sit down a minute while I get my coat and say where I am going."

The policeman drove on his gears, which I found tiring. It took two hours to go from Aynsford, west of Oxford, to Epping Forest, and it was much too long. Finally, however, we were met at a crossroads by another policeman on a motorcycle, and followed him down a twisting secondary road. The forest stretched away all round, bare-branched and mournful in the gray, damp day.

Round the bend we came on a row of two cars and a van, parked. The motorcyclist stopped and dismounted, and the policeman and I got out.

"ETA 12.15," said the motorcyclist, looking at his watch. "You're late. The brass has been waiting here twenty minutes."

"Traffic like caterpillars on the A.40," said my driver defensively.

"You should have used your bell," the motorcyclist grinned. "Come on. It's over this way."

He led us down a barely perceptible track into the wood. We walked on dead brown leaves, rustling. After about half a mile we came to a group of men standing round a screen made of hessian. They were stamping their feet to keep warm and talking in quiet voices.

"Mr. Halley?" One of them shook hands, a pleasant, capable-looking man in middle age who introduced himself as Chief Inspector Cornish. "We're sorry to bring you here all this way, but we want you to see the er . . . remains . . . before we move them. I'd better warn you, it's a perfectly horrible sight." He gave a very human shudder.

"Who is it?" I asked.

"We're hoping you can tell us that, for sure. We think . . . but we'd like you to tell us without us putting it into your head. All right? Now?"

I nodded. He showed me round the screen.

It was Andrews. What was left of him. He had been dead a long time, and the Epping Forest scavengers seemed to have found him tasty. I could see why the police had wanted me to see him *in situ*. He was going to fall to pieces as soon as they moved him.

"Well?"

"Thomas Andrews," I said.

They relaxed. "Are you sure? Positive?"

"Yes."

"It's not just the clothes?"

"No. The shape of the hairline. Protruding ears. Exceptionally rounded helix, vestigial lobes. Very short eyebrows, thick near the nose. Spatulate thumbs, white marks across nails. Hair growing on backs of phalanges."

"Good," said Cornish. "That's conclusive, I'd say. We made a preliminary identification fairly early because of the clothes—they were detailed on the wanted-for-questioning list, of course. But our first inquiries were negative. He seems to have no family, and no one could remember that he had any distinguishing marks—no tattoos, no scars, no operations, and as far as we could find out he hadn't been to a dentist all his life."

"It was intelligent of you to check all that before you gave him to the pathologist," I remarked.

"It was the pathologist's idea, actually." He smiled.

"Who found him?" I asked.

"Some boys. It's usually boys who find bodies."

"When?"

"Three days ago. But obviously he's been here weeks, probably from very soon after he took a pot at you."

"Yes. Is the gun still in his pocket?"

Cornish shook his head. "No sign of it."

"You don't know yet how he died?" I asked.

"No, not yet. But now you've identified him we can get on with it."

We went out from behind the screen and some of the other men went in with a stretcher. I didn't envy them.

Cornish turned to walk back to the road with me, the driver following at a short distance. We went fairly slowly, talking about Andrews, but it seemed more like eight miles than eight hundred yards. I wasn't quite ready for jolly country rambles.

As we reached the cars he asked me to lunch with him. I shook my head, explained about the diet, and suggested a drink instead.

"Fine," he said. "We could both do with one after that." He jerked his head in the direction of Andrews. "There's a good pub down the road this way. Your driver can follow us."

He climbed into his car and we drove after him.

In the bar, equipped with a large brandy and water for me and a whisky and sandwiches for him, we sat at a black oak table, on chintzy chairs, surrounded by horse brasses, hunting horns, warming pans and pewter pots.

"It's funny, meeting you like this," said Cornish, in between bites. "I've watched you so often racing. You've won a tidy bit for me in your time. I hardly missed a meeting on the old Dunstable course, before they sold it for building. I don't get so much racing now, it's so far to a course. Nowhere now to slip along to for a couple of hours in an afternoon." He grinned cheerfully and went on, "You gave us some rare treats at Dunstable. Remember the day you rode that dingdong finish on Brushwood?"

"I remember," I said.

"You literally picked that horse up and carried him home." He took another bite. "I never heard such cheering. There's no mistake about it, you were something special. Pity you had to give it up."

"Yes. . . ."

"Still, I suppose that's a risk you run steeplechasing. There is always one crash too many."

"That's right."

"Where was it you finally bought it?"

"At Stratford-on-Avon, two years ago last May."

He shook his head sympathetically. "Rotten bad luck."

I smiled. "I'd had a pretty good run, though, before that."

"I'll say you did." He smacked his palm on the table. "I took the Missus down to Kempton on Boxing Day, three or four years ago. . . ." He went on talking with enjoyment about races he had watched, revealing himself as a true enthusiast, one of the people without whose interest all racing would collapse. Finally, regretfully, he finished his whisky and looked at his watch. "I'll have to get back. I've enjoyed meeting you. It's odd how things turn out, isn't it? I don't suppose you ever thought when you were riding that you would be good at this sort of work."

"What do you mean, good?" I asked, surprised.

"Hm? Oh, Andrews of course. That description of his clothes you gave after he had shot you. And identifying him today. Most professional. Very efficient." He grinned.

"Getting shot wasn't very efficient," I pointed out.

He shrugged. "That could happen to anyone, believe me. I shouldn't worry about that."

I smiled, as the driver drove me back to Aynsford, at the thought that anyone could believe me good at detective work. There was a simple explanation of my being able to describe and identify—I had read so many of the Missing Persons and Divorce files. The band of ex-policemen who compiled them knew what to base identification on, the unchanging things like ears and hands, not hair color or the wearing of spectacles or a mustache. One of them had told me without pride that wigs, beards, face-padding, and the wearing of or omission of cosmetics made no impression on him, because they were not what he looked at. "Ears and fingers," he said, "they can't disguise those. They never think of trying. Stick to ears and fingers, and you don't go far wrong."

Ears and fingers were just about all there was left of Andrews to identify. The unappetizing gristly bits.

The driver decanted me at Charles's back door and I walked along the passage to the hall. When I had one foot on the bottom tread of the staircase Charles himself appeared at the drawing-room door.

"Oh, hullo, I thought it might be you. Come in here and look at these."

Reluctantly leaving the support of the bannisters I followed him into the drawing room.

"There," he said, pointing. He had fixed up a strip of light inside his bookcase and it shone down onto the quartz gems, bringing them to sparkling life. The open doors with their red silk curtains made a softly glowing frame. It was an eye-catching and effective arrangement, and I told him so.

"Good. The light goes on automatically when the doors are open. Nifty, don't you think?" He laughed. "And you can set your mind at rest. They are now insured."

"That's good."

He shut the doors of the bookcase and the light inside went out.

The red curtains discreetly hid their treasure. Turning to me, more seriously he said, "Whose body?"

"Andrews'."

"The man who shot you? How extraordinary. Suicide?"

"No, I don't think so. The gun wasn't there, anyway."

He made a quick gesture toward the chair. "My dear Sid, sit down, sit down. You look like d . . . er . . . a bit worn out. You shouldn't have gone all that way. Put your feet up, I'll get you a drink." He fussed over me like a mother hen, fetching me first water, then brandy, and finally a cup of warm beef juice from Mrs. Cross, and sat opposite me watching while I dispatched it.

"Do you like that stuff?" he asked.

"Yes, luckily." I grinned.

"We used to have it when we were children. A ritual once a week. My father used to drain it out of the Sunday joint, propping the dish on the carving fork. We all loved it, but I haven't had any for years."

"Try some?" I offered him the cup.

He took it and tasted it. "Yes, it's good. Takes me back sixty years. . . ." He smiled companionably, relaxing in his chair, and I told him about Andrews and the long-dead state he was in.

"It sounds," he said slowly, "as if he might have been murdered."

"I wouldn't be surprised. He was young and healthy. He wouldn't just lie down and die of exposure in Hertfordshire."

Charles laughed.

"What time are your guests expected?" I asked, glancing at the clock. It was just after five.

"About six."

"I think I'll go up and lie on my bed for a while, then."

"You are all right, Sid, aren't you? I mean, really all right?"

"Oh yes. Just tired."

"Will you come down to dinner?" There was the faintest undercurrent of disappointment in his casual voice. I thought of all his hard work with the rocks and the amount of maneuvering he had done. Besides, I was getting definitely curious myself about his intentions.

"Yes," I nodded, getting up. "Lay me a teaspoon."

I made it upstairs and lay on my bed, sweating. And cursing. Although the bullet had missed everything vital in tearing holes through my gut, it had singed and upset a couple of nerves. They had warned me in the hospital that it would be some time before I felt well. It didn't please me that so far they were right.

I heard the visitors arrive, heard their loud cheerful voices as they were shown up to their rooms, the doors shutting, the bath waters running, the various bumps and murmurs from the adjoining rooms; and eventually the diminishing chatter as they finished changing and went downstairs past my door. I heaved myself off the bed, took off the loose-waisted slacks and jersey shirt I felt most comfortable in, and put on a white cotton shirt and dark gray suit.

My face looked back at me, pale, gaunt and dark-eyed, as I brushed my hair. A bit of a death's-head at the feast. I grinned nastily at my reflection. It was only a slight improvement.

3

By the time I got to the foot of the stairs, Charles and his guests were coming across the hall from the drawing room to the dining room. The men all wore dinner jackets and the women, long dresses. Charles deliberately hadn't warned me, I reflected. He knew my convalescent kit didn't include a black tie.

He didn't stop and introduce me to his guests, but nodded slightly and went straight on into the dining room, talking with charm to the rounded, fluffy little woman who walked beside him. Behind came Viola and a tall dark girl of striking good looks. Viola, Charles's elderly widowed cousin, gave me a passing half-smile, embarrassed and worried. I wondered what was the matter: normally she greeted me with affection, and it was only a short time since she had written warm wishes for my recovery. The girl beside her barely glanced in my direction, and the two men bringing up the rear didn't look at me at all.

Shrugging, I followed them into the dining room. There was no mistaking the place laid for me: it consisted, in actual fact, of a spoon, a mat, a glass, and a fork, and it was situated in the center of one of the sides. Opposite me was an empty gap. Charles seated his guests, himself in his usual place at the end of the table with fluffy Mrs. van Dysart on his right, and the striking Mrs. Kraye on his left. I sat between Mrs. Kraye and Rex van Dysart. It was only gradually that I sorted everyone out. Charles made no introductions whatever.

The groups at each end of the table fell into animated chat and paid me as much attention as a speed limit. I began to think I would go back to bed.

The manservant whom Charles engaged on these occasions served small individual tureens of turtle soup. My tureen, I found, contained more beef juice. Bread was passed, spoons clinked, salt and pepper were shaken and the meal began. Still no one spoke to me, though the visitors were growing slightly curious. Mrs. van Dysart flicked her sharp china-blue eyes from Charles to me and back again, inviting an introduction. None came. He went on talking to the two women with almost overpowering charm, apparently oblivious.

Rex van Dysart on my left offered me bread, with lifted eyebrows and a faint noncommittal smile. He was a large man with a flat white face, heavy black rimmed spectacles and a domineering manner. When I refused the bread he put the basket down on the table, gave me the briefest of nods, and turned back to Viola.

Even before he brought quartz into his conversation I guessed it was for Howard Kraye that the show was being put on; and I disliked him on sight with a hackle-raising antipathy that disconcerted me. If Charles was planning that I should ever work for, or with, or near Mr. Kraye, I thought, he could think again.

He was a substantial man of about forty-eight to fifty, with shoulders, waist and hips all knocking forty-four. The dinner jacket sat on him with the ease of a second skin, and when he shot his cuffs occasionally he did so without affectation, showing off noticeably well-manicured hands.

He had tidy gray-brown hair, straight eyebrows, narrow nose, small firm mouth, rounded freshly shaven chin, and very high unwrinkled lower eyelids, which gave him a secret, shuttered look.

A neat enclosed face like a mask, with perhaps something rotten underneath. You could almost smell it across the dinner table. I guessed, rather fancifully, that he knew too much about too many vices. But on top he was smooth. Much too smooth. In my book, a nasty type of phony. I listened to him talking to Viola.

". . . So when Doria and I got to New York I looked up those fellows in that fancy crystal palace on First Avenue and got them moving. You have to give the clotheshorse diplomats a lead, you know, they've absolutely no initiative of their own. Look, I told them, unilateral action is not only inadvisable, it's impracticable. But they are so steeped in their own brand of pragmatism that informed opinion has as much chance of osmosing as mercury through rhyolite. . . ."

Viola was nodding wisely while not understanding a word. The pretentious rigmarole floated comfortably over her sensible head and left her unmoved. But its flashiness seemed to me to be part of a gigantic confidence trick: one was meant to be enormously impressed. I couldn't believe that Charles had fallen under his spell; it was impossible. Not my subtle, clever, coolheaded father-in-law. Mr. van Dysart, however, hung on every word.

By the end of the soup his wife at the other end of the table could contain her curiosity no longer. She put down her spoon and with her eyes on me, said to Charles in a low but clearly audible voice, "Who is that?"

All the heads turned toward him, as if they had been waiting for the question. Charles lifted his chin and spoke distinctly, so that they should all hear the answer.

"That," he said, "is my son-in-law." His tone was light, amused, and infinitely contemptuous; and it jabbed raw on a nerve I had thought long-dead. I looked at him sharply, and his eyes met mine, blank and expressionless.

My gaze slid up over and past his head to the wall behind him. There, for some years, and certainly that morning, had hung an oil painting of me on a horse going over a fence at Cheltenham. In its place there was now an old-fashioned seascape, brown with Victorian varnish.

Charles was watching me. I looked back at him briefly and said nothing. I suppose he knew I wouldn't. My only defense against his insults long ago had been silence, and he was counting on my instant reaction being the same again.

Mrs. van Dysart leaned forward a little, and with waking malice murmured, "Do go on, Admiral."

Without hesitation Charles obeyed her, in the same flaying voice. "He was fathered, as far as he knows, by a window cleaner on a nineteen-year-old unmarried girl from the Liverpool slums. She later worked, I believe, as a packer in a biscuit factory."

"Admiral, no!" exclaimed Mrs. van Dysart breathlessly.

"Indeed yes," nodded Charles. "As you might guess, I did my best to stop my daughter making such an unsuitable match. He is small, as you see, and he has a crippled hand. Working class and undersized . . . but my daughter was determined. You know what girls are." He sighed.

"Perhaps she was sorry for him," suggested Mrs. van Dysart.

"Maybe," said Charles. He hadn't finished, and wasn't to be deflected. "If she had met him as a student of some sort, one might have understood it . . . but he isn't even educated. He finished school at fifteen to be apprenticed to a trade. He has been unemployed now for some time. My daughter, I may say, has left him."

I sat like stone, looking down at the congealed puddle at the bottom of my soup dish, trying to loosen the clamped muscles in my jaw, and to think straight. Not four hours ago he'd shown concern for me and had drunk from my cup. As far as I could ever be certain of anything, his affection for me was genuine and unchanged. So he must have a good reason for what he was doing to me now. At least I hoped so.

I glanced at Viola. She hadn't protested. She was looking unhappily down at her place. I remembered her embarrassment out in the hall, and I guessed that Charles had warned her what to expect. He might have warned me too, I thought grimly.

Not unexpectedly, they were all looking at me. The dark and beautiful Doria Kraye raised her lovely eyebrows and in a flat, slightly nasal voice, remarked, "You don't take offense, then." It was halfway to a sneer. Clearly she thought I ought to take offense, if I had any guts.

"He is not offended," said Charles easily. "Why should the truth offend?"

"Is it true then," asked Doria down her flawless nose, "that you are illegitimate, and all the rest?"

I took a deep breath and eased my muscles.

"Yes."

There was an uncomfortable short silence. Doria said, "Oh," blankly, and began to crumble her bread.

On cue, and no doubt summoned by Charles's foot on the bell, the manservant came in to remove the plates, and conversation trickled back to the party like cigarette smoke after a cancer scare.

I sat thinking of the details Charles had left out: the fact that my twenty-year-old father, working overtime for extra cash, had fallen from a high ladder and been killed three days before his wedding day, and that I had been born eight months later. The fact that my young mother, finding that she was dying from some obscure kidney ailment, had taken me from grammar school at fifteen, and because I was small for my age had apprenticed me to a racehorse trainer in Newmarket, so that I should have a home and someone to turn to when she had gone. They had been good enough people, both of them, and Charles knew that I thought so.

The next course was some sort of fish smothered in mushroom-colored sauce. My astronauts' delight, coming at the same time, didn't look noticeably different, as it was not in its pot, but out on a plate. Dear Mrs. Cross, I thought fervently, I could kiss you. I could eat it this way with a fork, singlehanded. The pots needed to be held —in my case inelegantly hugged between forearm and chest—and at that moment I would have starved rather than taken my left hand out of my pocket.

Fluffy Mrs. van Dysart was having a ball. Clearly she relished the idea of me sitting there practically isolated, dressed in the wrong clothes, and an object of open derision to her host. With her fair frizzy hair, her baby-blue eyes and her rose-pink silk dress embroidered with silver, she looked as sweet as sugar icing. What she said showed that she thoroughly understood the pleasures of keeping a whipping boy.

"Poor relations are such a problem, aren't they?" she said to Charles sympathetically, and intentionally loud enough for me to hear. "You can't neglect them in our position, in case the Sunday papers get hold of them and pay them to make a smear. And it's especially difficult if one has to keep them in one's own house. One can't, I suppose, put them to eat in the kitchen, but there are so many occasions when one could do without them. Perhaps a tray upstairs is the best thing."

"Ah, yes," nodded Charles smoothly, "but they won't always agree to that."

I half choked on a mouthful, remembering the pressure he had exerted to get me downstairs. And immediately I felt not only reassured but deeply interested. This, then, was what he had been so industriously planning, the destruction of me as a man in the eyes of his guests. He would no doubt explain why in his own good time. Meanwhile I felt slightly less inclined to go back to bed.

I glanced at Kraye, and found his greenish-amber eyes steady on my face. It wasn't as overt as in Mrs. van Dysart's case, but it was there: pleasure. My toes curled inside my shoes. Interested or not, it went hard to sit tight before that loathsome, taunting half-smile. I looked down, away, blotting him out.

He gave a sound halfway between a cough and a laugh, turned his head, and began talking down the table to Charles about the collection of quartz.

"So sensible of you, my dear chap, to keep them all behind glass, though most tantalizing to me from here. Is that a geode, on the middle shelf? The reflection, you know . . . I can't quite see."

"Er . . ." said Charles, not knowing any more than I did what a geode was. "I'm looking forward to showing them to you. After dinner, perhaps? Or tomorrow?"

"Oh, tonight, I'd hate to postpone such a treat. Did you say that you had any felspar in your collection?"

"No," said Charles uncertainly.

"No, well, I can see it is a small specialized collection. Perhaps you are wise in sticking to silicon dioxide."

Charles glibly launched into the cousinly-bequest alibi for ignorance, which Kraye accepted with courtesy and disappointment.

"A fascinating subject, though, my dear Roland. It repays study. The earth beneath our feet, the fundamental sediment from the Triassic and Jurassic epochs, is our priceless inheritance, the source of all our life and power. . . . There is nothing which interests me so much as land."

Doria on my right gave the tiniest of snorts, which her husband didn't hear. He was busy constructing another long, polysyllabic and largely unintelligible chat on the nature of the universe.

I sat unoccupied through the steaks, the meringue pudding, the cheese and the fruit. Conversations went on on either side of me and occasionally past me, but a deaf-mute could have taken as much part as I did. Mrs. van Dysart commented on the difficulties of feeding poor relations with delicate stomachs and choosy appetites. Charles neglected to tell her that I had been shot and wasn't poor, but agreed that a weak digestion in dependents was a moral fault. Mrs. van Dysart loved it. Doria occasionally looked at me as if I were an interesting specimen of low life. Rex van Dysart again offered me the bread; and that was that. Finally Viola shepherded Doria and Mrs. van Dysart out to have coffee in the drawing room and Charles offered his guests port and brandy. He passed me the brandy bottle with an air of irritation and compressed his lips in disapproval when I took some. It wasn't lost on his guests.

After a while he rose, opened the glass bookcase doors, and showed the quartzes to Kraye. Piece by piece the two discussed their way along the rows, with van Dysart standing beside them exhibiting polite interest and hiding his yawns of boredom. I stayed sitting down. I also helped myself to some more brandy.

Charles kept his end up very well and went through the whole lot without a mistake. He then transferred to the drawing room, where his gem cabinet proved a great success. I tagged along, sat in an unobtrusive chair and listened to them all talking, but I came to no conclusions except that if I didn't soon go upstairs I wouldn't get there under my own steam. It was eleven o'clock and I had had a long day. Charles didn't look round when I left the room.

Half an hour later, when his guests had come murmuring up to their rooms, he came quietly through my door and over to the bed. I was still lying on top of it in my shirt and trousers, trying to summon some energy to finish undressing.

He stood looking down at me, smiling.

"Well?" he said.

"It is you," I said, "who is the dyed-in-the-wool, twenty-four-carat, unmitigated bastard."

He laughed. "I thought you were going to spoil the whole thing when you saw your picture had gone." He began taking off my shoes and socks. "You looked as bleak as the Bering Strait in December. Pajamas?"

"Under the pillow."

He helped me undress in his quick neat naval fashion.

"Why did you do it?" I said.

He waited until I was lying between the sheets, then he perched on the edge of the bed.

"Did you mind?"

"Hell, Charles . . . of course. At first anyway."

"I'm afraid it came out beastlier than I expected, but I'll tell you why I did it. Do you remember that first game of chess we had? When you beat me out of sight? You know why you won so easily?"

"You weren't paying enough attention."

"Exactly. I wasn't paying enough attention, because I didn't think you were an opponent worth bothering about. A bad tactical error." He grinned. "An admiral should know better. If you underrate a strong opponent you are at a disadvantage. If you grossly underrate him, if you are convinced he is of absolutely no account, you prepare no defense and are certain to be defeated." He paused for a moment, and went on. "It is therefore good strategy to delude the enemy into believing you are too weak to be considered. And that is what I was doing tonight on your behalf."

He looked at me gravely. After some seconds I said, "At what game, exactly, do you expect me to play Howard Kraye?"

He sighed contentedly, and smiled. "Do you remember what he said interested him most?"

I thought back. "Land."

Charles nodded. "Land. That's right. He collects it. Chunks of it, yards of it, acres of it. . . ." He hesitated.

"Well?"

"You can play him," he said slowly, "for Seabury Racecourse."

The enormity of it took my breath away.

"What?" I said incredulously. "Don't be silly. I'm only—"

"Shut up," he interrupted. "I don't want to hear what you think you are only. You're intelligent, aren't you? You work for a detective agency? You wouldn't want Seabury to close down? Why shouldn't you do something about it?"

"But I imagine he's after some sort of take-over bid, from what you say. You want some powerful city chap or other to oppose him, not . . . me."

"He is very much on his guard against powerful chaps in the city, but wide open to you."

I stopped arguing because the implications were pushing into the background my inadequacy for such a task.

"Are you sure he is after Seabury?" I asked.

"Someone is," said Charles. "There has been a lot of buying and selling of the shares lately, and the price per share is up although they haven't paid a dividend this year. The clerk of the course told me about it. He said that the directors are very worried. On paper, there is no great concentration of shares in any one name, but there wasn't at Dunstable either. There, when it came to a vote on selling out to a land developer, they found that about twenty various nominees were in fact all agents for Kraye. He carried enough of the other shareholders with him, and the racecourse was lost to housing."

"It was all legal, though?"

"A wangle; but legal, yes. And it looks like it's happening again."

"But what's to stop him, if it's legal?"

"You might try."

I stared at him in silence. He stood up and straightened the bedcover neatly. "It would be a pity if Seabury went the way of Dunstable." He went toward the door.

"Where does van Dysart fit in?" I asked.

"Oh," he said, turning, "nowhere. It was Mrs. van Dysart I wanted. She has a tongue like a rattlesnake. I knew she would help me tear you to pieces." He grinned. "She'll give you a terrible weekend, I'm glad to say."

"Thanks very much," I said sarcastically. "Why didn't you tell me all this before? When you so carefully left me that book on company law for instance? Or at least this evening when I came back from seeing Andrews, so that I could have been prepared, at dinner?"

He opened the door and smiled across the room, his eyes blank again.

"Sleep well," he said. "Good night, Sid."

Charles took the two men out shooting the following morning and Viola drove their wives into Oxford to do some shopping and visit an exhibition of Venetian glass. I took the opportunity of having a good look round the Krayes' bedroom.

It wasn't until I'd been there for more than ten minutes that it struck me that two years earlier I wouldn't have dreamed of doing such a thing. Now I had done it as a matter of course, without thinking twice. I grinned sardonically. Evidently even in just sitting around in a detective agency one caught an attitude of mind. I realized, moreover, that I had instinctively gone about my search methodically and with a careful touch. In an odd way it was extremely disconcerting.

I wasn't of course looking for anything special: just digging a little into the Krayes' characters. I wouldn't even concede in my own mind that I was interested in the challenge Charles had so elaborately thrown down. But all the same I searched, and thoroughly.

Howard Kraye slept in crimson pajamas with his initials embroidered in white on the pocket. His dressing gown was of crimson brocade with a black quilted collar and black tassels on the belt. His washing things, neatly arranged in a large fitted toilet case in the adjoining bathroom, were numerous and ornate. He used pine-scented after-shave lotion, cologne friction rub, lemon hand cream, and an oily hair dressing, all from gold-topped cut-glass bottles. There were also medicated soap tablets, special formula toothpaste, talcum powder in a gilt container, deodorant, and a supersonic-looking electric razor. He wore false teeth and had a spare set. He had brought a half-full tin of laxatives, some fruit salts, a bottle of mouthwash, some antiseptic foot powder, penicillin throat lozenges, a spot-sealing stick, digestive tablets and an eye bath. The body beautiful, in and out.

All his clothes, down to his vests and pants, had been made to measure, and he had brought enough to cover every possibility of a country weekend. I went through the pockets of his dinner jacket and the three suits hanging beside it, but he was a tidy man and they were all empty, except for a nail file in each breast pocket. His six various pairs of shoes were handmade and nearly new. I looked into each shoe separately, but except for trees they were all empty.

In a drawer I found neatly arranged his stock of ties, handkerchiefs, and socks: all expensive. A heavy chased silver box contained cuff links, studs, and tiepins; mostly of gold. He had avoided jewels, but one attractive pair of cuff links was made from pieces of what I now knew enough to identify as tiger's-eye. The backs of his hairbrushes were beautiful slabs of the gem stone, smoky quartz. A few brown and gray hairs were lodged in between the bristles.

There remained only his luggage, four lavish suitcases standing in a neat row beside the wardrobe. I opened each one. They were all empty except for the smallest, which contained a brown calf attaché case. I looked at it carefully before I touched it, but as Kraye didn't seem to have left any telltales like hairs or pieces of cotton attached, I lifted it out and put it on one of the beds. It was locked, but I had learned how to deal with such drawbacks. A lugubrious ex-police sergeant on Radnor's payroll gave me progressively harder lessons in lock-picking every time he came into the office between jobs, moaning all the while about the damage London soot did to his chrysanthemums. My one-handedness he had seen only as a challenge, and had invented a couple of new techniques and instruments entirely for my benefit. Recently he had presented me with a collection of fine delicate keys which he had once removed from a burglar, and had bullied me until I carried them with me everywhere. They were in my room. I went and fetched them and without much trouble opened the case.

It was as meticulously tidy as everything else, and I was particularly careful not to alter the position or order of any of the papers. There were several letters from a stockbroker, a bunch of share transfer certificates, various oddments, and a series of typed sheets, headed with the previous day's date, which were apparently an up-to-the-minute analysis of his investments. He seemed to be a rich man and to do a good deal of buying and selling. He had money in oils, mines, property and industrial stocks. There was also a sheet headed simply S.R., on which every transaction was a purchase. Against each entry was a name and the address of a bank. Some names occurred three or four times, some only once.

Underneath the papers lay a large thick brown envelope inside which were two packets of new ten-pound notes. I didn't count, but there couldn't have been fewer than a hundred of them. The envelope was at the bottom of the case except for a writing board with slightly used white blotting paper held by crocodile and gold corners. I pulled up the board and found underneath it two more sheets of paper, both covered with dates, initials, and sums of money.

I let the whole lot fall back into place, made sure that everything looked exactly as I had found it, relocked the case, and put it back into its covering suitcase.

The divine Doria, I found, was far from being as tidy as her husband. All her things were in a glorious jumble, which made leaving them undisturbed a difficult job, but also meant that she would be less likely than her husband to notice if anything were slightly out of place.

Her clothes, though they looked and felt expensive, were bought ready-made and casually treated. Her washing things consisted of a plastic zipped case, a flannel, a toothbrush, bath essence, and a puffing bottle of talc. Almost stark beside Howard's collection. No medicine. She appeared to wear nothing in bed, but a pretty white quilted dressing gown hung half off a hanger behind the bathroom door.

She had not completely unpacked. Suitcases propped on chairs and stools still held stirred-up underclothes and various ultra-feminine equipment which I hadn't seen since Jenny left.

The top of the dressing table, though the daily seemed to have done her best to dust it, was an expensive chaos. Pots of cosmetics, bottles of scent and hair spray stood on one side, a box of tissues, a scarf, and the cluttered tray out of the top of a dressing case filled the other. The dressing case itself, of crocodile with gold clips, stood on the floor. I picked it up and put it on the bed. It was locked. I unlocked it, and looked inside.

Doria was quite a girl. She possessed two sets of false eyelashes, spare fingernails, and a hairpiece on a tortoise-shell headband. Her big jewel case, the one tidy thing in her whole luggage, contained on the top layer the sapphire and diamond earrings she had worn the previous evening, along with a diamond sunburst brooch and a sapphire ring; and on the lower layer a second necklace, bracelet, earrings, brooch and ring all of gold, platinum and citrine. The yellow jewels were uncommon, barbaric in design, and had no doubt been made especially for her.

Under the jewel case were four paperback novels so pornographic in content as to raise doubts about Kraye's ability as a lover. Jenny had held that a truly satisfied woman didn't need to read dirty sex. Doria clearly did.

Alongside the books was a thick leather-covered diary to which the beautiful Mrs. Kraye had confided the oddest thoughts. Her life seemed to be as untidy as her clothes, a mixture of ordinary social behavior, dream fantasy and a perverted marriage relationship. If the diary were to be believed, she and Howard obtained deeper pleasure, both of them, from his beating her than from the normal act of love. Well, I reflected, at least they were well matched. Some of the divorces which Hunt Radnor Associates dealt with arose because one partner alone was pain-fixated, the other being revolted.

At the bottom of the case were two other objects of interest. First, coiled in a brown velvet bag, the sort of leather strap used by schoolmasters, at whose purpose, in view of the diary, it was easy to guess; and second, in a chocolate box, a gun.

4

Telephoning for the local taxi to come and fetch me, I went to Oxford and bought a camera. Although the shop was starting a busy Saturday afternoon, the boy who served me tackled the problem of a one-handed photographer with enthusiasm and as if he had all the time in the world. Between us we sorted out a minature German 16 mm. camera, three inches long by one and a half wide, which I could hold, set, snap and wind with one hand with the greatest ease.

He gave me a thorough lesson in how to work it, added an inch to its length in the shape of a screwed-on photoelectric light meter, loaded it with film, and slid it into a black case so small that it made no bulge in my trouser pocket. He also offered to change the film later if I couldn't manage it. We parted on the best of terms.

When I got back everyone was sitting round a cozy fire in the sitting room, eating crumpets. Very tantalizing. I loved crumpets.

No one took much notice when I went in and sat down on the fringe of the circle except Mrs. van Dysart, who began sharpening her claws. She got in a couple of quick digs about spongers marrying girls for their money, and Charles didn't say that I hadn't. Viola looked at me searchingly, worry opening her mouth. I winked, and she shut it again in relief.

I gathered that the morning's bag had been the usual mixture (two brace of pheasant, five wild duck and a hare), because Charles preferred a rough shoot over his own land to organized affairs with beaters. The women had collected a poor opinion of Oxford shop assistants and a booklet on the manufacture of fifteenth-century Italian glass. All very normal for a country weekend. It was my snooping that seemed unreal. That, and the false position Charles had steered me into.

Kraye's gaze, and finally his hands, strayed back to the gem bookshelves. Again the door was opened, Charles's trick lighting working effectively, and one by one the gems were brought out, passed round and closely admired. Mrs. van Dysart seemed much attached to a spectacular piece of rose quartz, playing with it to make light strike sparks from it, and smoothing her fingers over the glossy surface.

"Rex, you must collect some of this for me!" she ordered, her will showing like iron inside the fluff; and masterful-looking Rex nodded his meek agreement.

Kraye was saying, "You know, Roland, these are really remarkably fine specimens. Among the best I've ever seen. Your cousin must have been extremely fortunate and influential to acquire so many fine crystals."

"Oh, indeed he was," agreed Charles equably.

"I should be interested if you ever think of realizing on them . . . a first option, perhaps?"

"You can have a first option by all means," smiled Charles. "But I shan't be selling them, I assure you."

"Ah well, so you say now. But I don't give up easily. . . . I shall try you later. But don't forget, my first option?"

"Certainly," said Charles. "My word on it."

Kraye smiled at the stone he held in his hands, a magnificent raw amethyst like a cluster of petrified violets.

"Don't let this fall into the fire," he said. "It would turn yellow." He then treated everyone to a lecture on amethysts which would have been interesting had he made any attempt at simplicity: but blinding by words was with him either a habit or a policy. I wasn't certain which.

". . . Manganese, of course occurring in geodes or agate nodules in South America or Russia, but with such a world-wide distribution it was only to be expected that elementary societies should ascribe to it supra rational inherencies and attributes. . . ."

I suddenly found him looking straight at me, and I knew my expression had not been one of impressed admiration. More like quizzical sarcasm. He didn't like it. There was a quick flash in his eyes.

"It is symptomatic of the slum mentality," he remarked, "to scoff at what it can't comprehend."

"Sid," said Charles sharply. "I'm sure you must have something else to do. We can let you go until dinner."

I stood up. The natural anger rose quickly, but only as far as my teeth. I swallowed. "Very well," I muttered.

"Before you go, Sid," said Mrs. van Dysart from the depths of a sofa, ". . . Sid, what a deliciously plebeian name, so suitable. . . . Put these down on the table for me."

She held out both hands, one stone in each and another balanced between them. I couldn't manage them all, and dropped them.

"Oh dear," said Mrs. van Dysart, acidly sweet, as I knelt and picked them up, putting them one by one on the table, "I forgot you were disabled, so silly of me." She hadn't forgotten. "Are you sure you can't get treatment for whatever is wrong with you? You ought to try some exercises, they'd do you the world of good. All you need is a little perseverance. You owe it to the Admiral, don't you think, to *try?*"

I didn't answer, and Charles at least had the grace to keep quiet.

"I know a very good man," went on Mrs. van Dysart. "He used to work for the army . . . excellent at getting malingerers back into service. Now he's the sort of man who'd do you good. What do you think, Admiral, shall I fix it up for your son-in-law to see him?"

"Er . . . ," said Charles, "I don't think it would work."

"Nonsense." She was brisk and full of smiles. "You can't let him lounge about doing nothing for the rest of his life. A good bracing course of treatment, that's what he needs. Now," she said turning to me, "so that I know exactly what I'm talking about when I make an appointment, let's see this precious crippled hand of yours."

There was a tiny pause. I could feel their probing eyes, their unfriendly curiosity.

"No," I said calmly. "Excuse me, but no."

As I walked across the room and out of the door her voice floated after me. "There you are, Admiral, he doesn't *want* to get better. They're all the same. . . ."

I lay on my bed for a couple of hours rereading the book on company law, especially, now, the section on take-overs. It was no easier going than it had been in the hospital, and now that I knew why I was reading it, it seemed more involved, not less. If the directors of Seabury were worried, they would surely have called in their own investigator. Someone who knew his way round the stock markets like I knew my way round the track. An expert. I wasn't at all the right sort of person to stop Kraye, even if indeed anyone could stop him. And yet . . . I stared at the ceiling, taking my lower lip between my teeth. And yet . . . I did have a wild idea. . . .

Viola came in, knocking as she opened the door.

"Sid, dear, are you all right? Can I do anything for you?" She shut the door, gentle, generous, and worried.

I sat up and swung my legs over the side of the bed. "No, thanks, I'm fine."

She perched on the arm of an easy chair, looked at me with her kind, slightly mournful brown eyes, and said a little breathlessly, "Sid, why are you letting Charles say such terrible things about you? It isn't only when you are there in the room; they've been, oh, almost sniggering about you behind your back. Charles and that frightful Mrs. van Dysart. . . . What has happened between you and him? When you nearly died he couldn't have been more worried if you'd been his own son . . . but now he is so cruel, and terribly unfair."

"Dear Viola, don't worry. It's only some game that Charles is playing, and I go along with him."

"Yes," she said, nodding. "He warned me. He said that you were both going to lay a smoke screen and that I was on no account to say a single word in your defense the whole weekend. But it wasn't true, was it? When I saw your face, when Charles said that about your poor mother, I knew you didn't know what he was going to do."

"Was it so obvious?" I said ruefully. "Well, I promise you I haven't quarreled with him. Will you just be a dear and do exactly as he asked? Don't say a single word to any of them about . . . um . . . the more successful bits of my life history, or about my job at the agency, or about the shooting. You didn't today, did you, on the trip to Oxford?" I finished with some anxiety.

She shook her head. "I thought I'd talk to you first."

"Good." I grinned.

"Oh dear," she cried, partly in relief, partly in puzzlement. "Well, in that case, Charles asked me to pop in and make sure you would come down to dinner."

"Oh he did, did he? Afraid I'll throw a boot at him, I should think, after sending me out of the room like that. Well, you just pop back to Charles and say that I'll come down to dinner on condition that he organizes some chemmy afterwards, and includes me out."

Dinner was a bit of a trial: with their smoked salmon and pheasant the guests enjoyed another round of Sid-baiting. Both the Krayes, egged on by Charles and the fluffy harpy beside him, had developed a pricking skill for this novel weekend parlor game, and I heartily wished Charles had never thought of it. However, he kept his side of the bargain by digging out the chemin-de-fer shoe, and after the coffee, the brandy, and another inspection of the dining-room quartzes, he settled his guests firmly round the table in the drawing room.

Upstairs, once the shoe was clicking regularly and the players were well involved, I went and collected Kraye's attaché case and took it along to my room.

Because I was never going to get another chance and did not want to miss something I might regret later, I photographed every single paper in the case. All the stockbroker's letters and all the investment reports. All the share certificates, and also the two separate sheets under the writing board.

Although I had an ultra-bright light bulb and the exposure meter to help me get the right setting, I took several pictures at different light values of the papers I considered the most important in order to be sure of getting the sharpest possible result. The little camera handled beautifully, and I found I could change the films in their tiny casettes without much difficulty. By the time I had finished I had used three whole films of twenty exposures on each. It took me a long time, as I had to put the camera down between each shot to move the next paper into my pool of light, and also had to be very careful not to alter the order in which the papers had lain in the case.

The envelope of ten-pound notes kept me hoping like crazy that Howard Kraye would not lose heavily and come upstairs for replacements. It seemed to me at the time a ridiculous thing to do, but I took the two flat blocks of tenners out of the envelope, and photographed them as well. Putting them back I flipped through them: the notes were new, consecutive, fifty to a packet. One thousand pounds to a penny.

When everything was back in the case I sat looking at the contents for a minute, checking their position against my visual memory of how they looked when I first saw them. At last satisfied, I shut the case, locked it, rubbed it over to remove any finger marks I might have left, and put it back where I had found it.

After that I went downstairs to the dining room for the brandy I had refused at dinner. I needed it. Carrying the glass, I listened briefly outside the drawing-room door to the murmurs and clicks from within and went upstairs again, to bed.

Lying in the dark I reviewed the situation. Howard Kraye, drawn by the bait of a quartz collection, had accepted an invitation to a quiet weekend in the country with a retired admiral. With him he had brought a selection of private papers. As he had no possible reason to imagine that anyone in such innocent surroundings would spy on him, the papers might be very private indeed. So private that he felt safest when they were with him? Too private to leave at home? It would be nice to think so.

At that point, imperceptibly, I fell asleep.

The nerves in my abdomen wouldn't give up. After about five hours of fighting them unsuccessfully I decided that staying in bed all morning thinking about it was doing no good, and got up and dressed.

Drawn partly against my will, I walked along the passage to Jenny's room, and went in. It was the small sunny room she had had as a child. She had gone back to it when she left me and it was all hers alone. I had never slept there. The single bed, the relics of childhood, girlish muslin frills on curtains and dressing table, everything shut me out. The photographs round the room were of her father, her dead mother, her sister, brother-in-law, dogs and horses, but not of me. As far as she could, she had blotted out her marriage.

I walked slowly round touching her things, remembering how much I had loved her. Knowing, too, that there was no going back, and that if she walked through the door at that instant we would not fall into each other's arms in tearful reconciliation.

Removing a one-eyed teddy bear I sat down for a while on her pink armchair. It's difficult to say just where a marriage goes wrong, because the accepted reason often isn't the real one. The rows Jenny and I had had were all ostensibly caused by the same thing: my ambition. Grown finally too heavy for flat racing, I had switched entirely to steeplechasing the season before we married, and I wanted to be champion jumping jockey. To this end I was prepared to eat little, drink less, go to bed early, and not make love if I were racing the next day. It was unfortunate that she liked late-night parties and dancing more than anything else. At first she gave them up willingly, then less willingly, and finally in fury. After that, she started going on her own.

In the end she told me to choose between her and racing. But by then I was indeed champion jockey, and had been for some time, and I couldn't give it up. So Jenny left. It was just life's little irony that six months later I lost the racing as well. Gradually since then I had come to realize that a marriage didn't break up just because one half liked parties and the other didn't. I thought now that Jenny's insistence on a gay time was the result of my having failed her in some basic, deeply necessary way. Which did nothing whatsoever for my self-respect or my self-confidence.

I sighed, stood up, replaced the teddy bear, and went downstairs to the drawing room. Eleven o'clock on a windy autumn morning.

Doria was alone in the big comfortable room, sitting on the window seat and reading the Sunday papers, which lay around her on the floor in a haphazard mess.

"Hello," she said, looking up. "What hole did you crawl out of?"

I walked over to the fire and didn't answer.

"Poor little man, are his feelings hurt then?"

"I do have feelings, the same as anyone else."

"So you actually can talk?" she said mockingly. "I'd begun to wonder."

"Yes, I can talk."

"Well, now, tell me all your troubles, little man."

"Life is just a bowl of cherries."

She uncurled herself from the window seat and came across to the fire, looking remarkably out of place in skin-tight leopard-printed pants and a black silk shirt.

She was the same height as Jenny, the same height as me, just touching five foot six. As my smallness had always been an asset for racing, I never looked on it as a handicap for life in general, either physical or social. Neither had I ever really understood why so many people thought that height for its own sake was important. But it would have been naïve not to take note of the widespread extraordinary assumption that the mind and heart could be measured by tallness. The little man with the big emotion was a stock comic figure.

It was utterly irrational. What difference did three or four inches of leg bone make to a man's essential nature? Perhaps I had been fortunate in coming to terms early with the effect of poor nutrition in a difficult childhood; but it did not stop me understanding why other short men struck back in defensive aggression. There were the pinpricks, for instance, of girls like Doria calling one "little" and intending it as an insult.

"You've dug yourself into a cushy berth here, haven't you?" she said, taking a cigarette from the silver box on the mantelpiece.

"I suppose so."

"If I were the Admiral I'd kick you out."

"Thank you," I said, neglecting to offer her a light. With a mean look she found a box of matches and struck one for herself.

"Are you ill, or something?"

"No. Why?"

"You eat those faddy health foods, and you look such a sickly little creature. . . . I just wondered." She blew the smoke down her nose. "The Admiral's daughter must have been pretty desperate for a wedding ring."

"Give her her due," I said mildly. "At least she didn't pick a rich father figure twice her age."

I thought for a moment she meant to go into the corny routine of smacking my face, but as it happened she was holding the cigarette in the hand she needed.

"You little shit," she said instead. A charming girl, altogether.

"I get along."

"Not with me, you don't." Her face was tight. I had struck very deep, it seemed.

"Where is everyone else?" I asked, gesturing around the empty room.

"Out with the Admiral somewhere. And you can take yourself off again too. You're not wanted in here."

"I'm not going. I live here, remember?"

"You went quick enough last night," she sneered. "When the Admiral says jump, you jump. But fast, little man. And that I like to see."

"The Admiral," I pointed out, "is the hand that feeds. I don't bite it."

"Bootlicking little creep."

I grinned at her nastily and sat down in an armchair. I still didn't feel too good. Pea green and clammy, to be exact. Nothing to be done though, but wait for it to clear off.

Doria tapped ash off her cigarette and looked at me down her nose, thinking up her next attack. Before she could launch it, however, the door opened and her husband came in.

"Doria," he said happily, not immediately seeing me in the armchair, "where have you hidden my cigarette case? I shall punish you for it."

She made a quick movement toward me with her hand and Howard saw me and stopped dead.

"What are you doing here?" he said brusquely, the fun-and-games dying abruptly out of his face and voice.

"Passing the time."

"Clear out, then. I want to talk to my wife."

I shook my head and stayed put.

"Short of picking him up and throwing him out bodily," said Doria, "you won't get rid of him. I've tried."

Kraye shrugged. "Roland puts up with him. I suppose we can too." He picked up one of the newspapers and sat down in an armchair facing me. Doria wandered back to the window seat, pouting. Kraye straightened up the paper and began to read the front page. Across the back page, the racing page, facing me across the fireplace, the black, bold headlines jumped out.

"ANOTHER HALLEY?"

Underneath, side by side, were two photographs: one of me, and the other of a boy who had won a big race the day before.

It was by then essential that Kraye should not discover how Charles had misrepresented me; it had gone much too far to be explained away as a joke. The photograph was clearly printed for once. I knew it well. It was an old one which the papers had used several times before, chiefly because it was a good likeness. Even if none of the guests read the racing column, as Doria obviously hadn't, it might catch their eye in passing, through being in such a conspicuous place.

Kraye finished reading the front page and began to turn the paper over.

"Mr. Kraye," I said. "Do you have a very big quartz collection yourself?"

He lowered the paper a little and gave me an unenthusiastic glance.

"Yes, I have," he said briefly.

"Then could you please tell me what would be a good thing to give the Admiral to add to his collection? And where would I get it, and how much would it cost?"

The paper folded over, hiding my picture. He cleared his throat and with strained politeness started to tell me about some obscure form of crystal which the Admiral didn't have. Press the right button, I thought . . . Doria spoiled it. She walked jerkily over to Kraye and said crossly, "Howard, for God's sake. The little creep is buttering you up. I bet he wants something. You're a sucker for anyone who will talk about rocks."

"People don't make a fool of me," said Kraye flatly, his eyes narrowing in irritation.

"No. I only want to please the Admiral," I explained.

"He's a sly little beast," said Doria. "I don't like him."

Kraye shrugged, looked down at the newspaper and began to unfold it again.

"It's mutual," I said casually. "You daddy's doll."

Kraye stood up slowly and the paper slid to the floor, front page up.

"What did you say?"

"I said I didn't think much of your wife."

He was outraged, as well he might be. He took a single step across the rug, and there was suddenly something more in the room than three guests sparring round a Sunday-morning fire.

Even though I was as far as he knew an insignificant fly to swat, a clear quality of menace flowed out of him like a radio signal. The calm social mask had disappeared along with the wordy, phony, surface personality. The vague suspicion I had gained from reading his papers, together with the antipathy I had felt for him all along, clarified into belated recognition: this was not just a smooth speculator operating near the legal border line, but a full-blown, powerful, dangerous big-time crook.

Trust me, I thought, to prod an anthill and find a hornets' nest. Twist the tail of a grass snake and find a boa constrictor. What on earth would he be like, I wondered, if one did more to cross him than disparage his choice of wife?

"He's sweating," said Doria, pleased. "He's afraid of you."

"Get up," he said.

As I was sure that if I stood up he would simply knock me down again, I stayed where I was.

"I'll apologize," I said.

"Oh, no," said Doria, "that's much too easy."

"Something subtle," suggested Kraye, staring down.

"I know!" Doria was delighted with her idea. "Let's get that hand out of his pocket."

They both saw from my face that I would hate that more than anything. They both smiled. I thought of bolting, but it meant leaving the paper behind.

"That will do very nicely," said Kraye. He leaned down, twined one hand into the front of my jersey shirt and the other into my hair, and pulled me to my feet. The top of my head reached about to his chin. I wasn't in much physical shape for resisting, but I took a half-hearted swipe at him as I came up. Doria caught my swinging arm and twisted it up behind my back, using both of hers and an uncomfortable amount of pressure. She was a strong, healthy girl with no inhibitions about hurting people.

"That'll teach you to be rude to me," she said with satisfaction.

I thought of kicking her shins, but it would only have brought more retaliation. I also wished Charles would come back at once from wherever he was.

He didn't.

Kraye transferred his grip from my hair to my left forearm and began to pull. That arm was no longer much good, but I did my best. I tucked my elbow tight against my side, and my hand stayed in my pocket.

"Hold him harder," he said to Doria. "He's stronger than he looks." She levered my arm up another inch and I started to roll round to get out of it. But Kraye still had his grasp on the front of my jersey, with his forearm leaning across under my throat, and between the two of them I was properly stuck. All the same, I found I couldn't just stand still and let them do what I so much didn't want them to.

"He squirms, doesn't he?" said Doria cheerfully.

I squirmed and struggled a good deal more—until they began getting savage with frustration, and I was panting. It was my wretched stomach which finished it. I began to feel too ill to go on. With a terrific jerk Kraye dragged my hand out.

"Now," he said triumphantly.

He gripped my elbow fiercely and pulled the jersey sleeve up from my wrist. Doria let go of my right arm and came to look at their prize. I was shaking with rage, pain, humiliation . . . heaven knows what.

"Oh," said Doria blankly. "Oh."

She was no longer smiling, nor was her husband. They looked steadily at the wasted, flabby, twisted hand, and at the scars on my forearm, wrist and palm, not only the terrible jagged marks of the original injury but the several tidier ones of the operations I had had since. It was a mess, a right and proper mess.

"So that's why the Admiral lets him stay, the nasty little beast," said Doria, screwing up her face in distaste.

"It doesn't excuse his behavior," said Kraye. "I'll make sure he keeps that tongue of his still, in future."

He stiffened his free hand and chopped the edge of it down across the worst part, the inside of my wrist. I jerked in his grasp.

"Ah . . . ," I said. "Don't."

"He'll tell tales to the Admiral," said Doria warningly, "if you hurt him too much. It's a pity, but I should think that's about enough."

"I don't agree, but—"

There was a scrunch on the gravel outside, and Charles's car swept past the window, coming back.

Kraye let go of my elbow with a shake. I went weakly down on my knees on the rug, and it wasn't all pretense.

"If you tell the Admiral about this, I'll deny it," said Kraye, "and we know who he'll believe."

I did know who he'd believe, but I didn't say so. The newspaper which had caused the whole rumpus lay close beside me on the rug. The car doors slammed distantly. The Krayes turned away from me toward the window, listening. I picked up the paper, got to my feet, and set off for the door. They didn't try to stop me in any way. They didn't mention the newspaper either. I opened the door, went through, shut it, and steered a slightly crooked course across the hall to the wardroom. Upstairs was too far. I shut the wardroom door behind me, hid the newspaper, slid into Charles's favorite armchair, and waited for my various miseries, mental and physical, to subside.

Some time later Charles came in to fetch some fresh packages of cigarettes.

"Hullo," he said over his shoulder, opening the cupboard. "I thought you were still in bed. Mrs. Cross said you weren't very well this morning. It isn't at all warm in here. Why don't you come into the drawing room?"

"The Krayes . . ." I stopped.

"They won't bite you." He turned round, cigarette in hand. He looked at my face. "What's so funny?" and then more sharply, looking closer. "What's the matter?"

"Oh, nothing. Have you seen today's Sunday *Hemisphere?*"

"No, not yet. Do you want it? I thought it was in the drawing room with the other papers."

"No, it's in the top drawer of your desk. Take a look."

Puzzled, he opened the drawer, took out the paper, and unfolded it. He went to the racing section unerringly.

"My God!" he said, aghast. "Today of all days." His eyes skimmed down the page and he smiled. "You've read this, of course?"

I shook my head. "I just took it to hide it."

He handed me the paper. "Read it then. It'll be good for your ego. They won't let you die! 'Young Finch,'" he quoted, "'showed much of the judgment and miraculous precision of the great Sid.' How about that? And that's just the start."

"Yeah, how about it?" I grinned. "Count me out for lunch, if you don't mind, Charles. You don't need me there any more."

"All right, if you don't feel like it. They'll be gone by six at the latest, you'll be glad to hear." He smiled and went back to his guests.

I read the newspaper before putting it away again. As Charles had said, it was good for the ego. I thought the columnist, whom I'd known for years, had somewhat exaggerated my erstwhile powers. A case of the myth growing bigger than the reality. But still, it was nice. Particularly in view of the galling, ignominious end to the roughhouse in which the great Sid had so recently landed himself.

On the following morning Charles and I changed back the labels on the chunks of quartz and packed them up ready to return to the Carver Foundation. When we had finished we had one label left over.

"Are you sure we haven't put one stone in the box without changing the label?" said Charles.

"Positive."

"I suppose we'd better check. I'm afraid that's what we've done."

We took all the chunks out of the big box again. The gem collection, which Charles under protest had taken to bed with him each night, was complete; but we looked through them again too to make sure the missing rock had not got among them by mistake. It was nowhere to be found.

"St. Luke's stone," I read from the label. "I remember where that was, up on the top shelf on the right-hand side."

"Yes," agreed Charles, "a dull-looking lump about the size of a fist. I do hope we haven't lost it."

"We have lost it," I remarked. "Kraye's pinched it."

"Oh no," Charles exclaimed. "You can't be right."

"Go and ring up the Foundation, and ask them what the stone is worth."

He shook his head doubtfully, but went to the telephone and came back frowning.

"They say it hasn't any intrinsic value, but it's an extremely rare form of meteorite. It never turns up in mines or quarrying of course. You have to wait for it to fall from the heavens, and then find it. Very tricky."

"A quartz which friend Kraye didn't have."

"But he surely must know I'd suspect him?" Charles protested.

"You'd never have missed it, if it had really been part of your cousin's passed-on collection. There wasn't any gap on the shelf just now. He'd moved the others along. He couldn't know you would check carefully almost as soon as he had gone."

Charles sighed. "There isn't a chance of getting it back."

"No," I agreed.

"Well, it's a good thing you insisted on the insurance," he said. "Carver's valued that boring-looking lump more than all the rest put together. Only one other meteorite like it has ever been found: the St. Mark's stone." He smiled suddenly. "We seem to have mislaid the equivalent of the penny black."

5

Two days later I went back through the porticoed, columned doorway of Hunt Radnor Associates a lot more alive than when I last came out.

I got a big hullo from the girl on the switchboard, went up the curving staircase very nearly whistling, and was greeted by a barrage of ribald remarks from the Racing Section. What most surprised me was the feeling I had of coming home: I had never thought of myself as really belonging to the agency before, even though down at Aynsford I had realized that I very much didn't want to leave it. A bit late, that discovery. The skids were probably under me already.

Chico grinned widely. "So you made it."

"Well . . . yes."

"I mean, back here to the grindstone."

"Yeah."

"But," he cast a rolling eye at the clock, "late as usual."

"Go stuff yourself," I said.

Chico threw out an arm to the smiling department. "Our Sid is back, his normal charming bloody self. Work in the agency can now begin."

"I see I still haven't got a desk," I observed, looking round. No desk. No roots. No real job. As ever.

"Sit on Dolly's, she's kept it dusted for you."

Dolly looked at Chico, smiling, the mother-hunger showing too vividly in her great blue eyes. She might be the second-best head of department the agency possessed, with a cross-referencing filing-index mind like a computer, she might be a powerful, large, self-assured woman of forty-odd with a couple of marriages behind her and an ever hopeful old bachelor at her heels, but she still counted her life a wasteland because her body couldn't produce children. Dolly was a terrific worker, overflowing with intensely female vitality, excellent drinking company, and very, very sad.

Chico didn't want to be mothered. He was prickly about mothers. All of them in general, not just those who abandoned their tots in push-chairs at police stations near Barnes Bridge. He jollied Dolly along and deftly avoided her tentative maternal invitations.

I hitched a hip onto a long-accustomed spot on the edge of Dolly's desk, and swung my leg.

"Well, Dolly, my love, how's the sleuthing trade?" I said.

"What we need," she said with mock tartness, "is a bit more work from you and a lot less lip."

"Give me a job, then."

"Ah, now." She pondered. "You could . . . ," she began, then stopped. "Well, no . . . perhaps not. And it had better be Chico who goes to Lambourn; some trainer there wants a doubtful lad checked on. . . ."

"So there's nothing for me?"

"Er . . . well . . . ," said Dolly. "No." She had said no a hundred times before. She had never once said yes.

I made a face at her, picked up her telephone, pressed the right button, and got through to Radnor's secretary.

"Joanie? This is Sid Halley. Yes . . . back from Beyond, that's right. Is the old man busy? I'd like a word with him."

"Big deal," said Chico.

Joanie's prim voice said, "He's got a client with him just now. When she's gone I'll ask him, and ring you back."

"O.K." I put down the receiver.

Dolly raised her eyebrows. As head of the department she was my immediate boss, and in asking direct for a session with Radnor I was blowing agency protocol a raspberry. But I was certain that her constant refusal to give me anything useful to do was a direct order from Radnor. If I wanted the drain unblocked I would have to go and pull out the plug. Or go on my knees to stay at all.

"Dolly, love, I'm tired of kicking my heels. Even against your well-worn desk, though the view from here is ravishing." She was wearing, as she often did, a crossover cream silk shirt: it crossed over at a point which on a young girl would have caused a riot. On

Dolly it still looked pretty potent, owing to the generosity of nature and the disposal of her arrangements.

"Are you chucking it in?" said Chico, coming to the point.

"It depends on the old man," I said. "He may be chucking me out."

There was a brief, thoughtful silence in the department. They all knew very well how little I did. How little I had been content to do. Dolly looked blank, which wasn't helpful.

Jones-boy clattered in with a tray of impeccable unchipped tea mugs. He was sixteen; noisy, rude, anarchistic, callous, and probably the most efficient office boy in London. His hair grew robustly heavy down to his shoulders, wavy and fanatically clean, dipping slightly in an expensive styling at the back. From behind he looked like a girl, which never disconcerted him. From in front his bony, acned face proclaimed him unprepossessing male. He spent half his pay packet and his Sundays in Carnaby Street and the other half on week nights chasing girls. According to him, he caught them. No girls had so far appeared in the office to corroborate his story.

Under the pink shirt beat a stony heart; inside the sprouting head hung a big "So what?" Yet it was because this amusing, ambitious, unsocial creature invariably arrived well before his due hour to get his office arrangements ready for the day that he had found me before I died. There was a moral there, somewhere.

He gave me a look. "The corpse has returned, I see."

"Thanks to you," I said idly, but he knew I meant it. He didn't care, though.

He said, "Your blood and stuff ran through a crack in the linoleum and soaked the wood underneath. The old man was wondering if it would start dry rot or something."

"Jones-boy," protested Dolly, looking sick. "Get the hell out of here, and shut up."

The telephone rang on her desk. She picked it up and listened, said, "All right," and disconnected.

"The old man wants to see you. Right away."

"Thanks." I stood up.

"The flipping boot?" asked Jones-boy interestedly.

"Keep your snotty nose out," said Chico.

"And balls to you. . . ."

I went out smiling, hearing Dolly start to deal once again with the running dogfight Chico and Jones-boy never tired of. Downstairs, across the hall, into Joanie's little office and through into Radnor's.

He was standing by the window, watching the traffic doing its nut in Cromwell Road. This room, where the clients poured out their troubles, was restfully painted a quiet gray, carpeted and curtained in crimson and furnished with comfortable armchairs, handy little tables with ash trays, pictures on the walls, ornaments, and vases of flowers. Apart from Radnor's small desk in the corner, it looked like an ordinary sitting room, and indeed everyone believed that he had bought the room intact with the lease, so much was it what one would expect to find in a graceful, six-storied, late Victorian town house. Radnor had a theory that people exaggerated and distorted facts less in such peaceful surroundings than in the formality of a more orthodox office.

"Come in, Sid," he said. He didn't move from the window, so I joined him there. He shook hands.

"Are you sure you're fit enough to be here? You haven't been as long as I expected. Even knowing you . . ." He smiled slightly, with watching eyes.

I said I was all right. He remarked on the weather, the rush hour and the political situation, and finally worked round to the point we both knew was at issue.

"So, Sid, I suppose you'll be looking around a bit now?"

Laid on the line, I thought.

"If I wanted to stay here . . ."

"If? Hm, I don't know." He shook his head very slightly.

"Not on the same terms, I agree."

"I'm sorry it hasn't worked out." He sounded genuinely regretful, but he wasn't making it easy.

I said with careful calm, "You've paid me for nothing for two years. Well, give me a chance now to earn what I've had. I don't really want to leave."

He lifted his head slightly like a pointer to a scent, but he said nothing. I ploughed on.

"I'll work for you for nothing, to make up for it. But only if it's real, decent work. No more sitting around. It would drive me mad."

He gave me a hard stare and let out a long breath like a sigh.

"Good God. At last," he said. "And it took a bullet to do it."

"What do you mean?"

"Sid, have you ever seen a zombie wake up?"

"No," I said ruefully, understanding him. "It hasn't been as bad as that?"

He shrugged one shoulder. "I saw you racing, don't forget. You notice when a fire goes out. We've had the pleasant, flippant ashes drifting round this office, that's all." He smiled deprecatingly at his flight of fancy: he enjoyed making pictures of words. It wasted a lot of office time, on the whole.

"Consider me alight again, then." I grinned. "And I've brought a puzzle back with me. I want very much to sort it out."

"A long story?"

"Fairly, yes."

"We'd better sit down, then."

He waved me to an armchair, sank into one himself, and prepared to listen with the stillness and concentration which sent him time and time again to the core of a problem.

I told him about Kraye's dealing in racecourses. Both what I knew and what I guessed. When at length I finished he said calmly, "Where did you get hold of this?"

"My father-in-law, Charles Roland, tossed it at me while I was staying with him last weekend. He had Kraye as a house guest." The subtle old fox, I thought, throwing me in at the deep end: making me wake up and swim.

"And Roland got it from where?"

"The clerk of the course at Seabury told him that the directors were worried about too much share movement, that it was Kraye who got control of Dunstable, and they were afraid he was at it again."

"But the rest, what you've just told me, is your own supposition?"

"Yes."

"Based on your appraisal of Kraye over one weekend?"

"Partly on what he showed me of his character, yes. Partly on what I read of his papers. . . ." With some hesitation I told him about my snooping and the photography. ". . . The rest, I suppose, a hunch."

"Hmm. It needs checking. . . . Have you brought the films with you?"

I nodded, took them out of my pocket, and put them on the little table beside me.

"I'll get them developed." He drummed his fingers lightly on the arm of the chair, thinking. Then, as if having made a decision, said more briskly, "Well, the first thing we need is a client."

"A client?" I echoed absent-mindedly.

"Of course. What else? We are not the police. We work strictly for profit. Ratepayers don't pay the overheads and salaries in this agency. The clients do."

"Oh . . . , yes, of course."

"The most likely client in this case is either Seabury Racecourse executive, or perhaps the National Hunt Committee. I think I should sound out the Senior Steward first, in either case. No harm in starting at the top."

"He might prefer to try the police," I said, "free."

"My dear Sid, one thing people want when they employ private investigators is privacy. They pay for privacy. When the police investigate something, everyone knows about it. When we do, they don't. That's why we sometimes get criminal cases when it would undoubtedly be cheaper to go to the police."

"I see. So you'll try the Senior Steward—"

"No," he interrupted. "You will."

"I?"

"Naturally. It's your case."

"But it's your agency—he is used to negotiating with you."

"You know him too," he pointed out.

"I used to ride for him, and that puts me on a bad footing for this sort of thing. I'm a jockey to him, an ex-jockey. He won't take me seriously."

Radnor shrugged a shoulder. "If you want to take on Kraye, you need a client. Go and get one."

I knew very well that he never sent even senior operatives, let alone inexperienced ones, to arrange or angle for an assignment, so that for several moments I couldn't really believe that he intended me to go. But he said nothing else, and eventually I stood up and went toward the door.

"Sandown races are on today," I said tentatively. "He's sure to be there."

"A good opportunity." He looked straight ahead, not at me.

"I'll try it, then."

"Right."

He wasn't letting me off. But then he hadn't kicked me out either. I went through the door and shut it behind me, and while I was still hesitating in disbelief I heard him inside the room give a sudden guffaw, a short, sharp, loud, triumphant snort of laughter.

I walked back to my flat, collected the car, and drove down to Sandown. It was a pleasant day, dry, sunny, and warm for November, just right for drawing a good crowd for steeplechasing.

I turned in through the racecourse gates, spirits lifting, parked the car (a Mercedes 230 SL with automatic gears, power-assisted steering, and a strip on the back saying NO HAND SIGNALS), and walked round to join the crowd outside the weighing-room door. I could no longer go through it. It had been one of the hardest things to get used to, the fact that all the changing rooms and weighing rooms which had been my second homes for fourteen years were completely barred to me from the day I rode my last race. You didn't lose just a job when you handed in your jockey's license, you lost a way of life.

There were a lot of people to talk to at Sandown, and as I hadn't been racing for six weeks I had a good deal of gossip to catch up on. No one seemed to know about the shooting, which was fine by me, and I didn't tell them. I immersed myself very happily in the racecourse atmosphere and for an hour Kraye retreated slightly into the background.

Not that I didn't keep an eye on my purpose, but until the third race the Senior Steward, Viscount Hagbourne, was never out of a conversation long enough for me to catch him.

Although I had ridden for him for years and had found him undemanding and fair, he was in most respects still a stranger. An aloof, distant man, he seemed to find it difficult to make ordinary human contacts, and unfortunately he had not proved a great success as Senior Steward. He gave the impression, not of power in himself, but of looking over his shoulder at power behind: I'd have said he was afraid of incurring the disapproval of the little knot of rigidly determined men who in fact ruled racing themselves, regardless of who might be in office at the time. Lord Hagbourne postponed making decisions until it was almost too late to make them, and there was still a danger after that that he would change his mind. But all the same he was the front man until his year of office ended, and with him I had to deal.

At length I fielded him neatly as he turned away from the clerk of the course and forestalled a trainer who was advancing upon him with a grievance. Lord Hagbourne, with one of his rare moments of humor, deliberately turned his back on the grievance and consequently greeted me with more warmth than usual.

"Sid, nice to see you. Where have you been lately?"

"Holidays," I explained succinctly. "Look, sir, can I have a talk with you after the races? There's something I want to discuss urgently."

"No time like the present," he said, one eye on the grievance. "Fire away."

"No, sir. It needs time and all your attention."

"Hm?"

The grievance was turning away. "Not today, Sid, I have to get home. What is it? Tell me now."

"I want to talk to you about the take-over bid for Seabury racecourse."

He looked at me, startled. "You want . . . ?"

"That's right. It can't be said out here where you will be needed at any moment by someone else. If you could just manage twenty minutes at the end of the afternoon . . . ?"

"Er . . . what is your connection with Seabury?"

"None in particular, sir. I don't know if you remember, but I've been connected" (a precise way of putting it) "with Hunt Radnor Associates for the last two years. Various . . . er . . . facts about Seabury have come our way and Mr. Radnor thought you might be interested. I am here as his representative."

"Oh, I see. Very well, Sid, come up to the Stewards' tearoom after the last. If I'm not there, wait for me. Right?"

"Yes. Thank you."

I walked down the slope and then up the iron staircase to the jockeys' box in the stand, smiling at myself. Representative. A nice big important word. It covered anything from an ambassador down. Commercial travelers had rechristened themselves with its rolling syllables years ago; they had done it because of the jokes, of course. It didn't sound the same, somehow, starting off with "Did you hear the one about the representative who stopped at a lonely farmhouse? . . ." Rodent officers, garbage disposal and sanitary staff: pretty new names for rat catchers, dustmen and road sweepers. So why not for me?

"Only idiots laugh at nothing," said a voice in my ear. "What the hell are you looking so pleased about all of a sudden? And where the blazes have you been this last month?"

"Don't tell me you've missed me?" I grinned, not needing to look round. We went together through the door of the high-up jockeys' box, two of a kind, and stood looking out over the splendid racecourse.

"Best view in Europe." He sighed. Mark Witney, thirty-eight years old, racehorse trainer. He had a face battered like a boxer's from too many racing falls, and in the two years since he hung up his boots and stopped wasting he had put on all of forty pounds. A fat, ugly man. We had a host of memories in common, a host of hard-ridden races. I liked him a lot.

"How's things?" I said.

"Oh, fair, fair. They'll be a damn sight better if that animal of mine wins the fifth."

"He must have a good chance."

"He's a damn certainty, boy. A certainty. If he doesn't fall over his goddamned legs. Clumsiest sod this side of Hades." He lifted his race glasses and looked at the number board. "I see poor old Charlie can't do the weight again on that thing of Bob's. . . . That boy of Plumtree's is getting a lot of riding just now. What do you think of him?"

"He takes too many risks," I said. "He'll break his neck."

"Look who's talking. No, seriously, I'm considering taking him on. What do you think?" He lowered his glasses. "I need someone available regularly from now on and all the ones I'd choose are already tied up."

"Well, you could do better, you could do worse, I suppose. He's a bit flashy for me, but he can ride, obviously. Will he do as he's told?"

He made a face. "You've hit the bull's-eye. That's the snag. He always knows best."

"Pity."

"Can you think of anyone else?"

"Um . . . what about that boy Cotton? He's too young really.

But he's got the makings. . . ." We drifted out in amiable chat, discussing his problem, while the box filled up around us and the horses went down to the start.

It was a three-mile chase, and one of my ex-mounts was favorite. I watched the man who had my old job ride a very pretty race, and with half my mind thought about housing estates. Sandown itself had survived, some years ago, a bid to cover its green tempting acres with little boxes. Sandown had powerful friends. But Hurst Park, Manchester and Birmingham racecourses had all gone under the rolling tide of bricks and mortar, lost to the double-barreled persuasive arguments that shareholders liked capital gains and people needed houses. To defend itself from such a fate Cheltenham Racecourse had transformed itself from a private, dividend-paying company into a non-profit-making holdings trust, and other racecourses had followed their lead.

But not Seabury. And Seabury was deep in a nasty situation. Not Dunstable, and Dunstable Racecourse was now a tidy dormitory for the Vauxhall workers of Luton.

Most British racecourses were, or had been, private companies, in which it was virtually impossible for an outsider to acquire shares against the will of the members. But four—Dunstable, Seabury, Sandown and Chepstow—were public companies, and their shares could be bought in open market, through the stock exchange.

Sandown had been played for in a straightforward and perfectly honorable way, and plans to turn it into suburban housing had been turned down by the local and county councils. Sandown flourished, made a good profit, paid a 10 per cent dividend, and was probably now impregnable. Chepstow was surrounded by so much other open land that it was in little danger from developers. But little Dunstable had been an oasis inside a growing industrial area.

Seabury was on the flat part of the south coast, flanked on every side by miles of warm little bungalows representing the dreams and savings of people in retirement. At twelve bungalows to the acre —elderly people liked tiny gardens—there must be room on the spacious racecourse for over three thousand more. Add six or seven hundred pounds to the building price of each bungalow for the plot it stood on, and you scooped something in the region of two million.

The favorite won and was duly cheered, I clattered down the iron staircase with Mark, and we went and had a drink together.

"Are you sending anything to Seabury next week?" I asked. Seabury was one of his nearest meetings.

"Perhaps. I don't know. It depends if they hold it at all, of course. But I've got mine entered at Lingfield as well, and I think I'll send them there instead. It's a much more prosperous-looking place, and the owners like it better. Good lunch and all that. Seabury's so dingy these days. I had a hard job getting old Carmichael to agree to me running his horse there at the last meeting—and look what happened. The meeting was off and we'd missed the other engagement at Worcester too. It wasn't my fault, but I'd persuaded him that he stood more chance at Seabury, and he blamed me because in the end the horse stayed at home eating his head off for nothing. He says there's a jinx on Seabury, and I've a couple more owners who don't like me entering their horses there. I've told them that it's a super track from the horses' point of view, but it doesn't make much difference, they don't know it like we do."

We finished our drinks and walked back toward the weighing room. His horse scrambled home in the fifth by a whisker and I saw him afterward in the unsaddling enclosure beaming like a Halloween pumpkin.

After the last race I went to the Stewards' tearoom. There were several Stewards with their wives and friends having tea, but no Lord Hagbourne. The Stewards pulled out a chair, gave me a welcome, and talked, as ever, about the racing. Most of them had ridden as amateurs in their day, one against me in the not too distant past, and I knew them all well.

"Sid, what do you think of the new-type hurdles?"

"Oh, much better. Far easier for a young horse to see."

"Do you know of a good young chaser I could buy?"

"Didn't you think Hayward rode a splendid race?"

"I watched the third down at the Pond, and believe me that chestnut took off outside the wings. . . ."

". . . do you think we ought to have had him in, George?"

". . . heard that Green bust his ribs again yesterday . . ."

"Don't like that breed, never did, not genuine. . . ."

"Miffy can't seem to go wrong, he'd win with a cart horse. . . ."

"Can you come and give a talk to our local pony club, Sid? I'll write you the details. What date would suit you?"

Gradually they finished their tea, said good-bye, and left for home. I waited. Eventually he came, hurrying, apologizing, explaining what had kept him.

"Now," he said, biting into a sandwich. "What's it all about, eh?"

"Seabury."

"Ah yes, Seabury. Very worrying. Very worrying indeed."

"A Mr. Howard Kraye has acquired a large number of shares—"

"Now hold on a minute, Sid. That's only a guess, because of Dunstable. We've been trying to trace the buyer of Seabury shares through the stock exchange, and we can find no definite lead to Kraye."

"Hunt Radnor Associates do have that lead."

He stared. "Proof?"

"Yes."

"What sort?"

"Photographs of share transfer certificates." And heaven help me, I thought, if I've messed them up.

"Oh," he said somberly. "While we weren't sure, there was some hope we were wrong. Where did you get these photographs?"

"I'm not at liberty to say, sir. But Hunt Radnor Associates would be prepared to make an attempt to forestall the takeover of Seabury."

"For a fat fee, I suppose," he said dubiously.

"I'm afraid so, sir, yes."

"I don't connect you with this sort of thing, Sid." He moved restlessly and looked at his watch.

"If you would forget about me being a jockey, and think of me as having come from Mr. Radnor, it would make things a lot easier. How much is Seabury worth to National Hunt racing?"

He looked at me in surprise, but he answered the question, though not in the way I meant.

"Er . . . well, you know it's an excellent course, good for horses and so on."

"It didn't show a profit this year, though."

"There was a great deal of bad luck."

"Yes. Too much to be true, don't you think?"

"What do you mean?"

"Has it ever occurred to the National Hunt Committee that bad luck can be . . . well, arranged?"

"You aren't seriously suggesting that Kraye . . . I mean that anyone would damage Seabury on purpose? In order to make it show a loss?"

"I am suggesting that it is a possibility. Yes."

"Good God." He sat down rather abruptly.

"Malicious damage," I said. "Sabotage, if you like. There's a great deal of industrial precedent. Hunt Radnor Associates investigated a case of it only last year in a small provincial brewery where the fermentation process kept going wrong. A prosecution resulted, and the brewery was able to remain in business."

He shook his head. "It is quite ridiculous to think that Kraye would be implicated in anything like that. He belongs to one of my clubs. He's a wealthy, respected man."

"I know, I've met him," I said.

"Well then, you must be aware of what sort of person he is."

"Yes." Only too well.

"You can't seriously suggest—" he began.

"There would be no harm in finding out," I interrupted. "You'll have studied the figures. Seabury's quite a prize."

"How do you see the figures, then?" It seemed he genuinely wanted to know, so I told him.

"Seabury Racecourse has an issued share capital of eighty thousand pounds in fully paid-up one-pound shares. The land was bought when that part of the coast was more or less uninhabited, so that this sum bears absolutely no relation to the present value of the place. Any company in that position is just asking for a take-over.

"A buyer would in theory need fifty-one per cent of the shares to be certain of gaining control, but in practice, as was found at Dunstable, forty would be plenty. It could probably be swung on a good deal less, but from the point of view of the buyer, the more he got his hands on before declaring his intentions, the bigger would be his profit.

"The main difficulty in taking over a racecourse company—its only natural safeguard, in fact—is that the shares seldom come on the market. I understand that it isn't always by any means possible to buy even a few on the stock exchange, as people who own them tend to be fond of them, and as long as the shares pay any dividend, however small, they won't sell. But it's obvious that not everyone can afford to have bits of capital lying around unproductively, and once the racecourse starts showing a loss, the temptation grows to transfer to something else.

"Today's price of Seabury shares is thirty shillings, which is about four shillings higher than it was two years ago. If Kraye can manage to get hold of a forty per cent holding at an average price of thirty shillings, it will cost him only about forty-eight thousand pounds.

"With a holding that size, aided by other shareholders tempted by a very large capital gain, he can outvote any opposition, and sell the whole company to a land developer. Planning permission would almost certainly be granted, as the land is not beautiful, and is surrounded already by houses. I estimate that a developer would pay roughly a million for it, as he could double that by selling off all those acres in tiny plots. There's the capital gains tax, of course, but Seabury shareholders stand to make eight hundred per cent on their original investment, if the scheme goes through. Four hundred thousand gross for Mr. Kraye, perhaps. Did you ever find out how much he cleared at Dunstable?"

He didn't answer.

I went on, "Seabury used to be a busy, lively, successful place, and now it isn't. It's a suspicious coincidence that as soon as a big buyer comes along the place goes downhill fast. They paid a dividend of only sixpence per share last year, a gross yield of under one and three-quarters per cent at today's price, and this year they showed a loss of three thousand, seven hundred and fourteen pounds. Unless something is done soon, there won't be a next year."

He didn't reply at once. He stared at the floor for a long time with the half-eaten sandwich immobile in his hand.

Finally he said, "Who did the arithmetic? Radnor?"

"No . . . I did. It's very simple. I went to Company House in the city yesterday and looked up the Seabury balance sheets for the last few years, and I rang for a quotation of today's share price from a stockbroker this morning. You can easily check it."

"Oh, I don't doubt you. I remember now, there was a rumor that you made a fortune on the stock exchange by the time you were twenty."

"People exaggerate so." I smiled. "My old governor, where I was apprenticed, started me off investing, and I was a bit lucky."

"Hm."

There was another pause while he hesitated over his decision. I didn't interrupt him, but I was much relieved when finally he said, "You have Radnor's authority for seeing me, and he knows what you have told me?"

"Yes."

"Very well." He got up stiffly and put down the unfinished sandwich. "You can tell Radnor that I agree to an investigation being made, and I think I can vouch for my colleagues agreeing. You'll want to start at once, I suppose."

I nodded.

"The usual terms?"

"I don't know," I said. "Perhaps you would get onto Mr. Radnor about that."

As I didn't know what the usual terms were, I didn't want to discuss them.

"Yes, all right. And Sid . . . it's understood that there is to be no leak about this? We can't afford to have Kraye slapping a libel or slander action on us."

"The agency is always discreet," I said, with an outward and an inward smile. Radnor was right. People paid for privacy. And why not?

6

The racing section was quiet when I went in next morning, mostly because Chico was out on an escort job. All the other heads, including Dolly's, were bent studiously over their desks.

She looked up and said with a sigh, "You're late again." It was ten to ten. "The old man wants to see you."

I made a face at her and retraced my way down the staircase. Joanie looked pointedly at her watch.

"He's been asking for you for half an hour."

I knocked and went in. Radnor was sitting behind his desk, reading some papers, pencil in hand. He looked at me and frowned.

"Why are you so late?"

"I had a pain in me tum," I said flippantly.

"Don't be funny," he said sharply, and then, more reasonably, "Oh . . . I suppose you're not being funny."

"No. But I'm sorry about being late." I wasn't a bit sorry, however, that it had been noticed; before, no one would have said a thing if I hadn't turned up all day.

"How did you get on with Lord Hagbourne?" Radnor asked. "Was he interested?"

"Yes. He agreed to an investigation. I said he should discuss terms with you."

"I see." He flicked a switch on the small box on his desk. "Joanie, see if you can get hold of Lord Hagbourne. Try the London flat number first."

"Yes, sir," her voice came tinnily out of the speaker.

"Here," said Radnor, picking up a shallow brown cardboard box. "Look at these."

The box contained a thick wad of large glossy photographs. I looked at them one by one and heaved a sigh of relief. They had all come out sharp and clear, except some of the ones I had duplicated at varying exposures.

The telephone on Radnor's desk rang once, quietly. He lifted the receiver.

"Oh, good morning, Lord Hagbourne. Radnor here. Yes, that's right. . . ." He gestured to me to sit down, and I stayed there listening while he negotiated terms in a smooth, civilized, deceptively casual voice.

"And of course in a case like this, Lord Hagbourne, there's one other thing: we make a small surcharge if our operatives have to take out-of-the-ordinary risks. . . . Yes, as in the Canlas case, exactly. Right then, you shall have a preliminary report from us in a few days. Yes . . . good-bye."

He put down the receiver, bit his thumbnail thoughtfully for a few seconds, and said finally, "Right, then, Sid. Get on with it."

"But—" I began.

"But nothing," he said. "It's your case. Get on with it."

I stood up, holding the packet of photographs. "Can I . . . can I use Bona Fides and so on?"

He waved his hand permissively. "Sid, use every resource in the agency you need. Keep an eye on expenses though, we don't want to price ourselves out of business. And if you want legwork done, arrange it through Dolly or the other department heads. Right?"

"Won't they think it odd? I mean . . . I don't amount to much round here."

"And whose fault is that? If they won't do what you ask, refer them to me." He looked at me expressionlessly.

"All right." I walked to the door. "Er . . . who . . . ," I said, turning the knob, "gets the danger money? The operative or the agency?"

"You said you would work for nothing," he observed dryly.

I laughed. "Just so. Do I get expenses?"

"That car of yours drinks petrol."

"It does twenty," I protested.

"The agency rate is based on thirty. You can have that. And other expenses, yes. Put in a chit to accounts."

"Thanks."

He smiled suddenly, the rare sweet smile so incongruous to his military bearing, and launched into another elaborate metaphor.

"The tapes are up," he said. "What you do with the race depends on your skill and timing, just as it always used to. I've backed you with the agency's reputation for getting results, and I can't afford to lose my stake. Remember that."

"Yes," I said soberly. "I will."

I thought, as I took my stupidly aching stomach up two stories to Bona Fides, that it was time Radnor had a lift installed; and was glad I wasn't bound for Missing Persons away in the rarefied air of the fifth floor. There was a lot more character, I supposed, in the splendidly proportioned, solidly built town house that Radnor had chosen on a corner site on Cromwell Road, but a flat half acre of modern office block would have been easier on his staff. And about ten times as expensive, no doubt.

The basement, to start at the bottom, was—except for the kitchen—given over entirely to files and records. On the ground floor, besides Radnor himself and Joanie, there were two interview-cum-waiting rooms, and also the Divorce Section. On the first floor, the Racing Section, Accounts, another interview room and the general secretarial department. Up one was Bona Fides, and above that, on the two smaller top floors, Guard and Missing Persons. Missing Persons alone had room to spare. Bona Fides, splitting at the seams, was encroaching on Guard. Guard was sticking in its toes.

Jones-boy, who acted as general messenger, must have had legs like iron from pounding up and down the stairs, though thanks to a tiny service lift used long ago to take nursery food to top-floor children, he could haul his ten trays up from landing to landing instead of carrying them.

In Bona Fides there was the usual chatter of six people talking on the telephone all at once. The department head, receiver glued to one ear and finger stuck in the other, was a large bald-headed man with half-moon spectacles sitting halfway down a prominent nose. As always, he was in his shirt sleeves, teamed with a frayed pullover and baggy gray flannels. No tie. He seemed to have an inexhaustible supply of old clothes but never any new ones, and Jones-boy had a theory that his wife dressed him from jumble sales.

I waited until he had finished a long conversation with a managing director about the character of the proposed production manager of a glass factory. The invaluable thing about Jack Copeland was his quick and comprehensive grasp of what dozens of jobs entailed. He was speaking to the glass manufacturer as if he had grown up in the industry; and in five minutes, I knew, he might be advising just as knowledgeably on the suitability of a town clerk. His summing up of a man went far beyond the basic list of honesty, conscientiousness, normality and prudence, which was all that many employers wanted. He liked to discover his subject's reaction under stress, to find out what he disliked doing, and what he often forgot. The resulting footnotes to his reports were usually the most valuable part of them, and the faith large numbers of industrial firms had in him bore witness to his accuracy.

He wielded enormous power but did not seem conscious of it, which made him much liked. After Radnor, he was the most important person in the agency.

"Jack," I said, as he put down the receiver. "Can you check a man for me, please?"

"What's wrong with the Racing Section, pal?" he said, jerking his thumb toward the floor.

"He isn't a racing person."

"Oh? Who is it?"

"A Howard Kraye. I don't know if he has a profession. He speculates on the stock market. He is a rabid collector of quartz." I added Kraye's London address.

He scribbled it all down fast.

"O.K., Sid. I'll put one of the boys on to it and let you have a prelim. Is it urgent?"

"Fairly."

"Right." He tore the sheet off the pad. "George? You still doing that knitting-wool client's report? When you've finished, here's your next one."

"George," I said. "Be careful."

They both looked at me, suddenly still.

"An unexploded bomb," I observed. "Don't set him off."

George said cheerfully, "Makes a nice change from knitting wool. Don't worry, Sid. I'll walk on eggs."

Jack Copeland peered at me closely through the half specs.

"You've cleared it with the old man, I suppose?"

"Yes." I nodded. "It's a query fraud. He said to check with him if you wanted to."

He smiled briefly. "No need, I guess. Is that all then?"

"For the moment, yes, thanks."

"Just for the record, is this your own show, or Dolly's, or whose?"

"I suppose . . . mine."

"Uh-huh," he said accenting the second syllable. "The winds of change, if I read it right?"

I laughed. "You never know."

Down in the Racing Section I found Dolly supervising the reshuffling of the furniture. I asked what was going on, and she gave me a flashing smile.

"It seems you're in, not out. The old man just rang to say you needed somewhere to work, and I've sent Jones-boy upstairs to pinch a table from Missing Persons. That'll do for now, won't it? There isn't a spare desk in the place."

A series of bangs from outside heralded the return of Jones-boy, complete with a spindly plywood affair in a sickly lemon color. "How that lot ever find a missing person I'll never know. I bet they don't even find their missing junk."

He disappeared and came back shortly with a chair.

"The things I do for you!" he said, setting it down in front of me. "A dim little bird in the typing pool is now squatting on a stool. I chatted her up a bit."

"What this place needs is some more equipment," I murmured.

"Don't be funny," said Dolly. "Every time the old man buys one desk he takes on two assistants. When I first came here fifteen years ago we had a whole room each, believe it or not."

The rearranged office settled down again, with my table wedged into a corner next to Dolly's desk. I sat behind it and spread out the photographs to sort them. The people who developed and printed all the agency's work had come up with their usual excellent job, and it amazed me that they had been able to enlarge the tiny negatives up to nine-by-seven-inch prints and get a clearly readable result.

I picked out all the fuzzy ones, the duplicates at the wrong exposures, tore them up, and put the pieces in Dolly's wastepaper basket. That left me with fifty-one pictures of the contents of Kraye's attaché case. Innocent enough to the casual eye, but they turned out to be dynamite.

The two largest piles, when I had sorted them out, were Seabury share transfer certificates, and letters from Kraye's stockbroker. The paper headed S.R. revealed itself to be a summary in simple form of the share certificates, so I added it to that pile. I was left with the photographs of the bank notes, of share dealings which had nothing to do with Seabury, and the two sheets of figures I had found under the writing board at the bottom of the case.

I read through all the letters from the stockbroker, a man called Ellis Bolt, who belonged to a firm known as Charing, Street and King. Bolt and Kraye were on friendly terms; the letters referred sometimes to social occasions on which they had met; but for the most part the typewritten sheets dealt with the availability and prospects of various shares (including Seabury), purchases made or proposed, and references to tax, stamp duty, and commission.

Two letters had been written in Bolt's own hand. The first, dated ten days ago, said briefly:

Dear H.
Shall wait with interest for the news on Friday.

E.

The second, which Kraye must have received on the morning he went to Aynsford, read:

Dear H.
I have put the final draft in the hands of the printers, and the leaflets should be out by the end of next week, or the Tuesday following at the latest. Two or three days before the next meeting, anyway. That should do it, I think. There would be a lot of unrest should there be another hitch, but surely you will see to that.

E.

"Dolly," I said. "May I borrow your phone?"
"Help yourself."

I rang upstairs to Bona Fides. "Jack? Can I have a rundown on another man as well? Ellis Bolt, stockbroker, works for a firm called Charing, Street and King." I gave him the address. "He's a friend of Kraye's. Same care needed, I'm afraid."

"Right. I'll let you know."

I sat staring down at the two harmless-looking letters.

"Shall wait with interest for the news on Friday." It could mean any news, anything at all. It also could mean the News; and on the radio on Friday I had heard that Seabury Races were off because a lorry carrying chemicals had overturned and burned the turf.

The second letter was just as tricky. It could easily refer to a shareholder's meeting at which a hitch should be avoided at all costs. Or it could refer to a race meeting—at Seabury—where another hitch could affect the sale of shares yet again.

It was like looking at a conjuring trick: from one side you saw a normal object, but from the other, a sham.

If it were a sham, Mr. Ellis Bolt was in a criminal career up to his eyebrows. If it was just my suspicious mind jumping to hasty conclusions I was doing an old-established respectable stockbroker a shocking injustice.

I picked up Dolly's telephone again and got an outside line.

"Charing, Street and King, good morning," said a quiet female voice.

"Oh, good morning. I would like to make an appointment to see Mr. Bolt and discuss some investments. Would that be possible?"

"Certainly, yes. This is Mr. Bolt's secretary speaking. Could I have your name?"

"Halley. John Halley."

"You would be a new client, Mr. Halley?"

"That's right."

"I see. Well, now, Mr. Bolt will be in the office tomorrow afternoon, and I could fit you in at three thirty. Would that suit you?"

"Thank you. That's fine. I'll be there."

I put down the receiver and looked tentatively at Dolly.

"Would it be all right with you if I go out for the rest of the day?"

She smiled. "Sid, dear, you're very sweet, but you don't have to ask my permission. The old man made it very clear that you're on your own now. You're not accountable to me or anyone else in the agency, except the old man himself. I'll grant you I've never known him give anyone quite such a free hand before, but there you are, my love, you can do what you like. I'm your boss no longer."

"You don't mind?" I asked.

"No," she said thoughtfully. "Come to think of it, I don't. I've a notion that what the old man has always wanted of you in this agency is a partner."

"Dolly!" I was astounded. "Don't be ridiculous."

"He's not getting any younger," she pointed out.

I laughed. "So he picked on a broken-down jockey to help him out."

"He picks on someone with enough capital to buy a partnership, someone who's been to the top of one profession and has the time in years to get to the top of another."

"You're raving, Dolly, dear. He nearly chucked me out yesterday morning."

"But you're still here, aren't you? More here than ever before. And Joanie said he was in a fantastically good mood all day yesterday, after you'd been in to see him."

I shook my head, laughing. "You're too romantic. Jockeys don't turn into investigators any more than they turn into . . ."

"Well, what?" she prompted.

"Into auctioneers, then . . . or accountants."

She shook her head. "You've already turned into an investigator, whether you know it or not. I've been watching you these two years, remember? You look as if you're doing nothing, but you've soaked up everything the bloodhounds have taught you like a hungry sponge. I'd say, Sid love, if you don't watch out, you'll be part of the fixtures and fittings for the rest of your life."

But I didn't believe her, and I paid no attention to what she had said.

I grinned. "I'm going down to take a look at Seabury Racecourse this afternoon. Like to come?"

"Are you kidding?" she sighed. Her in-tray was six inches deep. "I could have just done with a ride in that rocket car of yours, and a breath of sea air."

I stacked the photographs together and returned them to the box, along with the negatives. There was a drawer in the table, and I pulled it open to put the photographs away. It wasn't empty. Inside lay a packet of sandwiches, some cigarettes, and a flat half bottle of whisky.

I began to laugh. "Someone," I said, "will shortly come rampaging down from Missing Persons looking for his missing lunch."

Seabury Racecourse lay about half a mile inland, just off a trunk road to the sea. Looking backward from the top of the stands one could see the wide silver sweep of the English Channel. Between and on both sides the crowded rows of little houses seemed to be rushing toward the coast like Gadarene swine. In each little unit a retired schoolmaster or civil servant or clergyman—or their widows —thought about the roots they had pulled up from wherever it had been too cold or too dingy for their old age, and sniffed the warm south salt-laden air.

They had made it. Done what they'd always wanted. Retired to a bungalow by the sea.

I drove straight in through the open racecourse gate and stopped outside the weighing room. Climbing out, I stretched, and walked over to knock on the door of the racecourse manager's office.

There was no reply. I tried the handle. It was locked. So was the weighing-room door, and everything else.

Hands in pockets, I strolled round the end of the stands to look at the course. Seabury was officially classified in Group Three: that is to say, lower than Doncaster and higher than Windsor when it came to receiving aid from the Betting Levy Board.

It had less than Grade Three stands: wooden steps with corrugated tin roofs for the most part, and drafts from all parts of the compass. But the track itself was a joy to ride on, and it had always seemed a pity to me that the rest of the amenities didn't match it.

There was no one about near the stands. Down at one end of the course, however, I could see some men and a tractor, and I set off toward them, walking down inside the rails, on the grass. The going was just about perfect for November racing, soft but springy underfoot, exactly right for tempting trainers to send their horses to the course in droves. In ordinary circumstances, that was. But as things stood at present, more trainers than Mark Witney were sending their horses elsewhere. A course which didn't attract runners didn't attract crowds to watch them. Seabury's gate receipts had been falling off for some time, but its expenses had risen; and therein lay its loss.

Thinking about the sad tale I had read in the balance sheets, I reached the men working on the course. They were digging up a great section of it and loading it onto a trailer behind the tractor. There was a pervasive unpleasant smell in the air.

An irregular patch about thirty yards deep, stretching nearly the whole width of the course, had been burned brown and killed. Less than half of the affected turf had already been removed, showing the grayish chalky mud underneath, and there was still an enormous amount to be shifted. I didn't think there were enough men working on it for there to be a hope of its being returfed and ready to race on in only eight days' time.

"Good afternoon," I said to the men in general. "What a horrible mess."

One of them thrust his spade into the earth and came over, rubbing his hands on the sides of his trousers.

"Anything you want?" he said, with fair politeness.

"The racecourse manager. Captain Oxon."

His manner shifted perceptibly toward the civil. "He's not here today, sir. Hey! Aren't you Sid Halley?"

"That's right."

He grinned, doing another quick change, this time toward brotherhood. "I'm the foreman. Ted Wilkins." I shook his outstretched hand. "Captain Oxon's gone up to London. He said he wouldn't be back until tomorrow."

"Never mind," I said. "I was just down in this part of the world and I thought I'd drop in and have a look at the poor old course."

He turned with me to look at the devastation. "Shame, isn't it?"

"What happened, exactly?"

"The tanker overturned on the road over there." He pointed, and we began to walk toward the spot, edging round the dug-up area. The road, a narrow secondary one, ran across near the end of the racecourse, with a side semicircle of track on the far side of it. During the races the hard road surface was covered thickly with tan or peat, or with thick green matting, which the horses galloped over without any trouble. Although not ideal, it was an arrangement to be found on many courses throughout the country, most famously with the Melling Road at Aintree, and reaching a maximum with five road crossings at Ludlow.

"Just here," said Ted Wilkins, pointing. "Worst place it could possibly have happened, right in the middle of the track. The stuff just poured out of the tanker. It turned right over, see, and the hatch thing was torn open in the crash."

"How did it happen?" I asked. "The crash, I mean?"

"No one knows, really."

"But the driver? He wasn't killed, was he?"

"No, he wasn't even hurt much. Just shook up a bit. But he

couldn't remember what happened. Some people in a car came driving along after dark and nearly ran into the tanker. They found the driver sitting at the side of the road, holding his head and moaning. Concussion, it was, they say. They reckon he hit his head somehow when his lorry went over. Staggers me how he got out of it so lightly, the cab was fair crushed, and there was glass everywhere."

"Do tankers often drive across here? Lucky it's never happened before, if they do."

"They used not to," he said, scratching his head. "But they've been over here quite regularly now for a year or two. The traffic on the London road's getting chronic, see?"

"Oh . . . did it come from a local firm, then?"

"Down the coast a bit. Intersouth Chemicals, that's the firm it belonged to."

"How soon do you think we'll be racing here again?" I asked, turning back to look at the track. "Will you make it by next week?"

He frowned. "Strictly between you and me, I don't think there's a bleeding hope. What we needed, as I said to the Captain, was a couple of bulldozers, not six men with spades."

"I would have thought so too."

He sighed. "He just told me we couldn't afford them and to shut up and get on with it. And that's what we've done. We'll just about have cut out all the dead turf by next Wednesday, at this rate of going on."

"That doesn't leave any time for new turf to settle," I remarked.

"It'll be a miracle if it's laid, let alone settled," he agreed gloomily.

I bent down and ran my hand over a patch of brown grass. It was decomposing and felt slimy. I made a face, and the foreman laughed.

"Horrible, isn't it? It stinks, too."

I put my fingers to my nose and wished I hadn't. "Was it slippery like this right from the beginning?"

"Yes, that's right. Hopeless."

"Well, I won't take up any more of your time," I said, smiling. "I'll tell Captain Oxon you came. Pity you missed him."

"Don't bother him. He must have a lot to worry about just now."

"One bloody crisis after another." He nodded. "So long, then." He went back to his spade and his heartbreaking task, and I retraced the quarter mile up the straight to the deserted stands.

I hesitated for a while outside the weighing room, wondering whether to pick the lock and go in, and knowing it was mainly nostalgia that urged me to do it, not any conviction that it would be a useful piece of investigation. There would always be the temptation, I supposed, to use dubious professional skills for one's own pleasure. Like doctors sniffing ether. I contented myself with looking through the windows.

The deserted weighing room looked the same as ever: a large bare expanse of wooden board floor, with a table and some upright chairs in one corner, and the weighing machine itself on the left. Racecourse weighing machines were not all of one universal design. There weren't any left of the old type where the jockeys stood on a platform while weights were added to the balancing arm. That whole process was much too slow. Now there were either seats slung from above, in which one felt much like a bag of sugar, or chairs bolted to a base plate on springs: in both these cases the weight was quickly indicated by a pointer which swung round a gigantic clock face. In essence, modern kitchen scales vastly magnified.

The scales at Seabury were the chair-on-base-plate type, which I'd always found simplest to use. I recalled a few of the before-and-after occasions when I had sat on that particular spot. Some good, some bad, as always with racing.

Shrugging, I turned away. I wouldn't, I thought, ever be sitting there again. And no one walked over my grave.

Climbing into the car, I drove to the nearest town, looked up the whereabouts of Intersouth Chemicals, and an hour later was speaking to the personnel manager. I explained that on behalf of the National Hunt Committee I had just called in passing to find out if the driver of the tanker had fully recovered, or had remembered anything else about the accident.

The manager, fat and fiftyish, was affable but unhelpful. "Smith's left," he said briefly. "We gave him a few days off to get over the accident, and then he came back yesterday and said his wife didn't fancy him driving chemicals any more, and he was packing it in." His voice held a grievance.

"Had he been with you long?" I asked sympathetically.

"About a year."

"A good driver, I suppose?"

"Yes, about average for the job. They have to be good drivers, or we don't use them, you see. Smith was all right, but nothing special."

"And you still don't really know what happened?"

"No," he sighed. "It takes a lot to tip one of our tankers over. There was nothing to learn from the road. It was covered with oil and petrol and chemical. If there had ever been any marks, skid marks I mean, they weren't there after the breakdown cranes had lifted the tanker up again, and the road was cleared."

"Do your tankers use that road often?"

"They have done recently, but not any more after this. As a matter of fact, I seem to remember it was Smith himself who found that way round. Going over the racecourse missed out some bottleneck at a junction, I believe. I know some of the drivers thought it a good idea."

"They go through Seabury regularly, then?"

"Sure, often. Straight line to Southampton and round to the oil refinery at Fawley."

"Oh? What exactly was Smith's tanker carrying?"

"Sulfuric acid. It's used in refining petrol, among other things."

Sulfuric acid. Dense, oily, corrosive to the point of charring. Nothing more instantly lethal could have poured out over Seabury's turf. They could have raced had it been a milder chemical, put sand or tan on the dying grass and raced over the top. But no one would risk a horse on ground soaked with sulfuric acid.

I said, "Could you give me Smith's address? I'll call round and see if his memory has come back."

"Sure." He searched in a file and found it for me. "Tell him he can have his job back if he's interested. Another of the men gave notice this morning."

I said I would, thanked him, and went to Smith's address, which proved to be two rooms upstairs in a suburban house. But Smith and his wife no longer lived there. Packed up and gone yesterday, I was told by a young woman in curlers. No, she didn't know where they went. No, they didn't leave a forwarding address, and if I was her I wouldn't worry about his health as he'd been laughing and drinking and playing records till all hours the day after the crash, his concussion having cured itself pretty quick. Reaction, he'd said when she complained of the noise, against not being killed.

It was dark by then, and I drove slowly back into London against the stream of headlights pouring out. Back to my flat in a modern block, a short walk from the office, down the ramp into the basement garage, and up in the lift to the fifth floor, home.

There were two rooms facing south, bedroom and sitting room, and two behind them, bathroom and kitchen, with windows into an inner well. A pleasant sunny place, furnished in blond wood and cool colors, centrally heated, cleaning included in the rent. A regular order of groceries arrived week by week directly into the kitchen through a hatch, and rubbish disappeared down a chute. Instant living. No fuss, no mess, no strings. And damnably lonely, after Jenny.

Not that she had ever been in the place; she hadn't. The house in the Berkshire village where we had mostly lived had been too much of a battleground, and when she walked out I sold it, with relief. I'd moved into the new flat shortly after going to the agency, because it was close. It was also expensive, but I had no fares to pay.

I mixed myself a brandy with ice and water, sat down in an armchair, put my feet up, and thought about Seabury. Seabury, Captain Oxon, Ted Wilkins, Intersouth Chemicals, and a driver called Smith.

After that I thought about Kraye. Nothing pleasant about him, nothing at all. A smooth, phony crust of sophistication hiding ruthless greed; a seething passion for crystals, ditto for land; an obsession with the cleanliness of his body to compensate for the murk in his mind; unconventional sexual pleasures; and the abnormal quality of being able to look carefully at a crippled hand and *then hit it*.

No, I didn't care for Howard Kraye one little bit.

7

"Chico," I said. "How would you overturn a lorry on a predetermined spot?"

"Huh? That's easy. All you'd need would be some heavy lifting gear. A big hydraulic jack. A crane. Anything like that."

"How long would it take?"

"You mean, supposing the lorry and the crane were both in position?"

"Yes."

"Only a minute or two. What sort of lorry?"

"A tanker."

"A petrol job?"

"A bit smaller than the petrol tankers. More the size of milk ones."

"Easy as kiss your hand. They've got a low center of gravity, mind. It'd need a good strong lift. But dead easy, all the same."

I turned to Dolly. "Is Chico busy today, or could you spare him?"

Dolly leaned forward, chewing the end of a pencil and looking at her day's chart. The crossover blouse did its stuff.

"I could send someone else to Kempton. . . ." She caught the direction of my eyes and laughed, and retreated a whole half inch. "Yes, you can have him." She gave him a fond glance.

"Chico," I said. "Go down to Seabury and see if you can find any trace of heavy lifting gear having been seen near the racecourse last Friday . . . those little bungalows are full of people with nothing to do but watch the world go by. You might check whether anything was hired locally, but I suppose that's a bit much to hope for. The road would have to have been closed for a few minutes before the tanker went over, I should think. See if you can find anyone who noticed anything like that . . . detour signs, for instance. And after that, go to the council offices and see what you can dig up among their old maps on the matter of drains." I told him the rough position of the subsiding trench which had made a slaughterhouse of the hurdle race, so that he should know what to look for on the maps. "And be discreet."

"Teach your grandmother to suck eggs." He grinned.

"Our quarry is rough."

"And you don't want him to hear us creep up behind him?"

"Quite right."

"Little Chico," he said truthfully, "can take care of himself."

After he had gone I telephoned Lord Hagbourne and described to him in no uncertain terms the state of Seabury's turf.

What they need is some proper earth-moving equipment, fast, and apparently there's nothing in the kitty to pay for it. Couldn't the Levy Board . . . ?"

"The Levy Board is no fairy godmother," he interrupted. "But I'll see what can be done. Less than half cleared, you say? Hmm. However, I understand that Captain Oxon assured Weatherbys that the course would be ready for the next meeting. Has he changed his mind?"

"I didn't see him, sir. He was away for the day."

"Oh." Lord Hagbourne's voice grew a shade cooler. "Then he didn't ask you to enlist my help?"

"No."

"I don't see that I can interfere then. As racecourse manager it is his responsibility to decide what can be done and what can't, and I think it must be left like that. Mm, yes. And of course he will consult the clerk of the course if he needs advice."

"The clerk of the course is Mr. Fotherton, who lives in Bristol. He is clerk of the course there, too, and he's busy with the meetings there tomorrow and Monday."

"Er, yes, so he is."

"You could ring Captain Oxon up in an informal way and just ask how the work is getting on," I suggested.

"I don't know—"

"Well, sir, you can take my word for it that if things dawdle on at the same rate down there, there won't be any racing at Seabury next weekend. I don't think Captain Oxon can realize just how slowly those men are digging."

"He must," he protested. "He assured Weatherbys—"

"Another last-minute cancellation will kill Seabury off," I said with some force.

There was a moment's pause. Then he said reluctantly, "Yes, I suppose it might. All right then. I'll ask Captain Oxon and Mr. Fotherton if they are both satisfied with the way things are going."

And I couldn't pin him down to any more direct action than that, which was certainly not going to be enough. Protocol would be the death of Seabury, I thought.

Monopolizing Dolly's telephone, I next rang up the Epping police and spoke to Chief Inspector Cornish.

"Any more news about Andrews?" I asked.

"I suppose you have a reasonable personal interest." His chuckle came down the wire. "We found he did have a sister after all. We called her at the inquest yesterday for identification purposes as she is a relative, but if you ask me she didn't really know. She took one look at the bits in the mortuary and was sick on the floor."

"Poor girl, you couldn't blame her."

"No. She didn't look long enough though to identify anyone. But we had your identification for sure, so we hadn't the heart to make her go in again."

"How did he die? Did you find out?"

"Indeed we did. He was shot in the back. The bullet ricocheted off a rib and lodged in the sternum. We got the experts to compare it with the one they dug out of the wall of your office. Your bullet was a bit squashed by the hard plaster, but there's no doubt that they are the same. He was killed with the gun he used on you."

"And was it there, underneath him?"

"Not a sign of it. They brought in 'murder by persons unknown.' And between you and me, that's how it's likely to stay. We haven't a lead to speak of."

"What lead do you have?" I asked.

His voice had a smile in it. "Only something his sister told us. She has a bed-sitter in Islington, and he spent the evening there before breaking into your place. He showed her the gun. She says he was proud of having it; apparently he was a bit simple. All he told her was that a big chap had lent it to him to go out and fetch something, and he was to shoot anyone who got in his way. She didn't believe him. She said he was always making things up, always had, all his life. So she didn't ask him anything about the big chap, or about where he was going, or anything at all."

"A bit casual," I said. "With a loaded gun under her nose."

"According to the neighbors she was more interested in a stream of men friends than in anything her brother did."

"Sweet people, neighbors."

"You bet. Anyway we checked with anyone we could find who had seen Andrews the week he shot you, and he hadn't said a word to any of them about a gun or a 'big chap,' or an errand in Cromwell Road."

"He didn't go back to his sister afterwards?"

"No, she'd told him she had a guest coming."

"At one in the morning? The neighbors must be right. You tried racecourses, of course? Andrews is quite well known there, as a sort of spivvy odd-job messenger boy."

"Yes, we mainly tried the racecourses. No results. Everyone seemed surprised that such a harmless person should have been murdered."

"Harmless!"

He laughed. "If you hadn't thought him harmless, you'd have kept out of his way."

"You're so right," I said with feeling. "But now I see a villain in every respectable citizen. It's very disturbing."

"Most of them are villains, in one way or another," he said cheerfully. "Keeps us busy. By the way, what do you think of Sparkle's chances this year in the Henessy? . . ."

When eventually I put the telephone down Dolly grabbed it with a sarcastic "Do you mind?" and asked the switchboard girl to get her three numbers in a row, "without interruptions from Halley." I grinned, got the packet of photographs out of the plywood table drawer, and looked through them again. They didn't tell me any more than before. Ellis Bolt's letters to Kraye. Now you see it, now you don't. A villain in every respectable citizen. Play it secretly, I thought, close to the chest, in case the eyes looking over your shoulder give you away. I wondered why I was so oppressed by a vague feeling of apprehension, and decided in irritation that a bullet in the stomach had made me nervous.

When Dolly finished her calls I took the receiver out of her hand and got through to my bank manager.

"Mr. Harper? This is Sid Halley . . . yes, fine thanks, and you? Good. Now, would you tell me just how much I have in both my accounts, deposit and current?"

"They're quite healthy, actually," he said in his gravelly bass voice. "You've had several dividends in lately. Hang on a minute, and I'll send for the exact figures." He spoke to someone in the background and then came back. "It's time you reinvested some of it."

"I do have some investments in mind," I agreed. "That's what I want to discuss with you. I'm planning to buy some shares this time from another stockbroker, not through the bank. Er . . . please don't think that I'm dissatisfied; how could I be, when you've done so well for me. It's something to do with my work at the agency."

"Say no more. What exactly do you want?"

"Well, to give you as a reference," I said. "He's sure to want one, but I would be very grateful if you would make it as impersonal and as strictly financial as possible. Don't mention either my past occupation or my present one. That's very important."

"I won't, then. Anything else?"

"Nothing . . . oh, yes. I've introduced myself to him as John Halley. Would you refer to me like that if he gets in touch with you?"

"Right. I'll look forward to hearing from you one day what it's all about. Why don't you come in and see me? I've some very good cigars." The deep voice was amused. "Ah, here are the figures. . . ." He told me the total, which for once was bigger than I expected. That happy state of affairs wouldn't last very long, I reflected, if I had to live for two years without any salary from Radnor. And no one's fault but my own.

Giving Dolly back her telephone with an ironic bow, I went upstairs to Bona Fides. Jack Copeland's mud-colored jersey had a dark blue darn on the chest and a fraying stretch of ribbing on the hip. He was picking at a loose thread and making it worse.

"Anything on Kraye yet?" I asked. "Or is it too early?"

"George has got something on the prelim, I think," he answered. "Anybody got any scissors?" A large area of jersey disintegrated into ladders. "Blast."

Laughing, I went over to George's desk. The prelim was a sheet of handwritten notes in George's concertinaed style. "Leg mat, 2 yrs. 2 prev, 1 div, 1 sui dec.," it began, followed by a list of names and dates.

"Oh, yeah?" I said.

"Yeah." He grinned. Kraye was legally married to Doria Dawn, nee Easterman, two years ago. Before that he had two other wives. One killed herself; the other divorced him for cruelty." He pointed to the names and dates.

"So clear," I agreed. "When you know how."

"If you weren't so impatient you'd have had a legible typed report. But as you're here . . ." He went on down the page pointing. "Geologists think him a bit eccentric . . . quartz has no intrinsic value, most of it's much too common, except for the gem stones, but Kraye goes round trying to buy chunks of it if they take his fancy. They know him quite well along the road at the Geology Museum. But not a breath of any dirty work. Clubs: he belongs to these three, not overliked, but most members think he's a brilliant fellow, talks very well. He gambles at Crockfords, ends up about all square over the months. He travels, always first class, usually by boat, not air. No job or profession, can't trace him on any professional or university lists. Thought to live on investments, playing the stock market, etc. Not much liked, but considered by most a clever, cultured man, by one or two a hypocritical gasbag."

"No talk of him being crooked in any way?"

"Not a word. You want him dug deeper?"

"If you can do it without him finding out."

George nodded. "Do you want him tailed?"

"No, I don't think so. Not at present." A twenty-four-hour tail was heavy on man-power, and expensive to the client, quite apart from the risk of the quarry noticing and being warned of the hunt. "Anything on his daily life?" I asked.

George shook his head. "Nothing. Nobody who knows him now has known him longer than about ten years. He either wasn't born in Britain, or his name at birth wasn't Kraye. No known relatives."

"You've done marvels, George. All this in one day."

"Contacts, chum, contacts. A lot of phoning, a bit of pubbing, a touch of gossip with the local tradesmen—nothing to it."

Jack, moodily poking his fingers through the cobweb remains of his jersey, looked at me over the half-moon specs and said that there wasn't a prelim on Bolt yet because ex-sergeant Lamar, who was working on it, hadn't phoned in.

"If he does," I said, "let me know? I've an appointment with Bolt at three thirty. It would be handy to know the setup before I go."

"O.K."

After that I went down and looked out of the windows of the Racing Section for half an hour, idly watching life go by in Cromwell Road and wondering just what sort of mess I was making of the Kraye investigation. A novice chaser in the Grand National, I thought wryly; that was me. Though, come to think of it, I had once ridden a novice in the National, and got round, too. Slightly cheered, I took Dolly out to a drink and a sandwich in the snack bar at the Air Terminal, where we sat and envied the people starting off on their travels. So much expectation in the faces, as if they could fly away and leave their troubles on the ground. An illusion, I thought sourly. Your troubles flew with you; a drag in the mind . . . a deformity in the pocket.

I laughed and joked with Dolly, as usual. What else can you do?

The firm of Charing, Street and King occupied two rooms in a large block of offices belonging to a bigger firm, and consisted entirely of Bolt, his clerk and a secretary.

I was shown the door of the secretary's office, and went into a dull, tidy, fog-colored box of a room with cold fluorescent lighting and a close-up view of the fire escape through the grimy window. A woman sat at a desk by the right-hand wall, facing the window, with her back toward me. A yard behind her chair was a door with ELLIS BOLT painted on a frosted glass panel. It occurred to me that she was most awkwardly placed in the room, but that perhaps she liked sitting in a potential draft and having to turn around every time someone came in.

She didn't turn round, however. She merely moved her head round a fraction toward me and said, "Yes?"

"I have an appointment with Mr. Bolt," I said. "At three thirty."

"Oh, yes, you must be Mr. Halley. Do sit down. I'll see if Mr. Bolt is free now."

She pointed to an easy chair a step ahead of me, and flipped a switch on her desk. While I listened to her telling Mr. Bolt I was there, in the quiet voice I had heard on the telephone, I had time to see she was in her late thirties, slender, upright in her chair, with a smooth wing of straight, dark hair falling down beside her cheek. If anything, it was too young a hair style for her. There were no rings on her fingers, and no nail varnish either. Her clothes were dark and uninteresting. It seemed as though she were making a deliberate attempt to be unattractive, yet her profile, when she half turned and told me Mr. Bolt would see me, was pleasant enough. I had a glimpse of one brown eye quickly cast down, the beginning of a smile on pale lips, and she presented me again squarely with the back of her head.

Puzzled, I opened Ellis Bolt's door and walked in. The inner office wasn't much more inspiring than the outer; it was larger and there was a new green square of carpet on the linoleum, but the grayish walls prevailed, along with the tidy dullness. Through the two windows was a more distant view of the fire escape of the building across the alley. If a drab conventional setting equaled respectability, Bolt was an honest stockbroker; and Lamar, who had phoned in just before I left, had found nothing to suggest otherwise.

Bolt was on his feet behind his desk, hand outstretched. I shook it, he gestured me to a chair with arms, and offered me a cigarette.

"No, thank you, I don't smoke."

"Lucky man," he said benignly, tapping ash off one he was half through and settling his pin-striped bulk back into his chair.

His face was rounded at every point, large round nose, round cheeks, round heavy chin; no planes, no impression of bone structure underneath. He had exceptionally heavy eyebrows, a full, mobile mouth, and a smug, self-satisfied expression.

"Now, Mr. Halley, I believe in coming straight to the point. What can I do for you?"

He had a mellifluous voice, and he spoke as if he enjoyed the sound of it.

I said, "An aunt has given me some money now rather than leave it to me in her will, and I want to invest it."

"I see. And what made you come to me? Did someone recommend . . . ?" He tailed off, watching me with eyes that told me he was no fool.

"I'm afraid . . ." I hesitated, smiling apologetically to take the offense out of the words, "that I literally picked you with a pin. I don't know any stockbrokers. I didn't know how to get to know one, so I picked up a classified directory and stuck a pin into the list of names, and it was yours."

"Ah," he said paternally, observing the bad fit of Chico's second-best suit, which I had borrowed for the occasion, and listening to me reverting to the accent of my childhood.

"Can you help me?" I asked.

"I expect so, I expect so. How much is this, er, gift?" His voice was minutely patronizing, his manner infinitesimally bored. His time, he suspected, was being wasted.

"Fifteen hundred pounds."

He brightened a very little. "Oh, yes, definitely, we can do something with that. Now, do you want growth stock or a high rate of yield?"

I looked vague. He told me quite fairly the difference between the two and offered no advice.

"Growth, then," I said, tentatively. "Turn it into a fortune in time for my old age."

He smiled without much mirth, and drew a sheet of paper toward him.

"Could I have your full name?"

"John Halley . . . John Sidney Halley," I said truthfully. He wrote it down.

"Address?" I gave it.

"And your bank?" I told him that too.

"And I'll need a reference, I'm afraid."

"Would the bank manager do?" I asked. "I've had an account there for two years. He knows me quite well."

"Excellent." He screwed up his pen. "Now, do you have any idea what companies you'd like shares in, or will you leave it to me?"

"Oh, I'll leave it to you. If you don't mind, that is. I don't know anything about it, you see, not really. Only it seems silly to leave all that money around doing nothing."

"Quite, quite." He was bored with me. I thought with amusement that Charles would appreciate my continuing his strategy of the weak front. "Tell me, Mr. Halley, what do you do for a living?"

"Oh . . . um . . . I work in a shop," I said. "In the men's wear. Very interesting, it is."

"I'm sure it is." There was a yawn stuck in his throat.

"I'm hoping to be made an assistant buyer next year," I said eagerly.

"Splendid. Well done." He'd had enough. He got cumbrously to his feet and ushered me to the door. "All right, Mr. Halley, I'll invest your money safely for you in good long-term growth stock, and send you the papers to sign in due course. You'll hear from me in a week or ten days. All right?"

"Yes, Mr. Bolt, thank you very much indeed," I said. He shut the door gently behind me.

There were now two people in the outer office. The woman with her back still turned, and a spare, middle-aged man with a primly folded mouth, and tough stringy tendons pushing his collar away from his neck. He was quite at home, and with an incurious, unhurried glance at me he went past into Bolt's office. The clerk, I presumed.

The woman was typing addresses on envelopes. The twenty or so that she had done lay in a slithery stack on her left; on her right an open file provided a list of names. I looked over her shoulder casually, and then with quickened interest. She was working down the first page of a list of Seabury shareholders.

"Do you want something, Mr. Halley?" she asked politely, pulling one envelope from the typewriter and inserting another with a minimum of flourish.

"Well, er, yes," I said diffidently. I walked round to the side of her desk and found that one couldn't go on round to the front of it: a large old-fashioned table with bulbous legs filled all the space between the desk and the end of the room. I looked at this arrangement with some sort of understanding and with compassion.

"I wondered," I said, "if you could be very kind and tell me something about investing money, and so on. I didn't like to ask Mr. Bolt too much, he's a busy man. And I'd like to know a bit about it."

"I'm sorry, Mr. Halley." Her head was turned away from me, bent over the Seabury investors. "I've a job to do, as you see. Why don't you read the financial columns in the papers, or get a book on the subject?"

I had a book all right. *Outline of Company Law*. One thing I had learned from it was that only stockbrokers—apart from the company involved—could send circulars to shareholders. It was illegal if private citizens did it. Illegal for Kraye to send letters to Seabury shareholders offering to buy them out: legal for Bolt.

"Books aren't as good as people at explaining things," I said. "If you are busy now, could I come back when you've finished work and take you out for a meal? I'd be so grateful if you would, if you possibly could."

A sort of shudder shook her. "I'm sorry, Mr. Halley, but I'm afraid I can't."

"If you will look at me, so that I can see all of your face," I said, "I will ask you again."

Her head went up with a jerk at that, but finally she turned round and looked at me.

I smiled. "That's better. Now, how about coming out with me this evening?"

"You guessed?"

I nodded. "The way you've got your furniture organized. Will you come?"

"You still want to?"

"Well, of course. What time do you finish?"

"About six, tonight."

"I'll come back. I'll meet you at the door, down in the street."

"All right," she said. "If you really mean it, thank you. I'm not doing anything else tonight. . . ."

Years of hopeless loneliness showed raw in the simple words. Not doing anything else, tonight or most nights. Yet her face wasn't horrific; not anything as bad as I had been prepared for. She had lost an eye, and wore a false one. There had been some extensive burns and undoubtedly some severe fracture of the facial bones, but plastic surgery had repaired the damage to a great extent, and it had all been a long time ago. The scars were old. It was the inner wound which hadn't healed. Well . . . I knew a bit about that myself, on a smaller scale.

8

She came out of the door at ten past six wearing a neat well-cut dark overcoat and with a plain silk scarf covering her hair, tied under her chin. It hid only a small part of the disaster to her face, and seeing her like that, defenseless, away from the shelter she had made in her office, I had an uncomfortably vivid vision of the purgatory she suffered day in and day out on the journeys to work.

She hadn't expected me to be there. She didn't look round for me when she came out, but turned directly up the road toward the tube station. I walked after her and touched her arm. Even in low heels she was taller than I.

"Mr. Halley!" she said. "I didn't think—"

"How about a drink first?" I said. "The pubs are open."

"Oh no—"

"Oh yes. Why not?" I took her arm and steered her firmly across the road into the nearest bar. Dark oak, gentle lighting, brass pump handles, and the lingering smell of lunchtime cigars: a warm beckoning stop for city gents on their way home. There were already half a dozen of them, prosperous and dark-suited, adding fizz to their spirits.

"Not here," she protested.

"Here." I held a chair for her to sit on at a small table in a corner, and asked her what she would like to drink.

"Sherry, then . . . dry."

I took the two glasses over one at a time, sherry for her, brandy for me. She was sitting on the edge of the chair, uncomfortably, and it was not the one I had put her in. She had moved round so that she had her back to everyone except me.

"Good luck, Miss . . . ?" I said, lifting my glass.

"Martin. Zanna Martin."

"Good luck, Miss Martin." I smiled.

Tentatively she smiled back. It made her face much worse: half the muscles on the disfigured right side didn't work and could do nothing about lifting the corner of her mouth or crinkling the skin round the socket of her eye. Had life been even ordinarily kind she would have been a pleasant-looking, assured woman in her late thirties with a loving husband and a growing family: years of heartbreak had left her a shy, lonely spinster who dressed and moved as though she would like to be invisible. Yet, looking at the sad travesty of her face, one could neither blame the young men who hadn't married her nor condemn her own efforts at effacement.

"Have you worked for Mr. Bolt long?" I asked peaceably, settling back lazily into my chair and watching her gradually relax into her own.

"Only a few months. . . ." She talked for some time about her job in answer to my interested questions, but unless she was supremely artful, she was not aware of anything shady going on in Charing, Street and King. I mentioned the envelopes she had been addressing, and asked what was going into them.

"I don't know yet," she said. "The leaflets haven't come from the printers."

"But I expect you typed the leaflet anyway," I said idly.

"No, actually I think Mr. Bolt did that one himself. He's quite helpful in that way, you know. If I'm busy he'll often do letters himself."

Will he, I thought. Will he, indeed. Miss Martin, as far as I was concerned, was in the clear. I bought her another drink and extracted her opinion about Bolt as a stockbroker. Sound, she said, but not busy. She had worked for other stockbrokers, it appeared, and knew enough to judge.

"There aren't many stockbrokers working on their own any more," she explained, "and . . . well, I don't like working in a big office, you see . . . and it's getting more difficult to find a job which suits me. So many stockbrokers have joined up into partnerships of three or more; it reduces overheads terrifically, of course, and it means that they can spend more time in the House. . . ."

"Where are Mr. Charing, Mr. Street, and Mr. King?" I asked.

Charing and Street were dead, she understood, and King had retired some years ago. The firm now consisted simply and solely of Ellis Bolt. She didn't really like Mr. Bolt's offices being contained inside of those of another firm. It wasn't private enough, but it was the usual arrangement nowadays. It reduced overhead so much. . . .

When the city gents had mostly departed to the bosoms of their families, Miss Martin and I left the pub and walked through the empty city streets toward the Tower. We found a quiet little restaurant where she agreed to have dinner. As before, she made a straight line for a corner table and sat with her back to the room.

"I'm paying my share," she announced firmly when she had seen the prices on the menu. "I had no idea this place was so expensive or I wouldn't have let you choose it. Mr. Bolt mentioned that you worked in a shop."

"There's Aunty's legacy," I pointed out. "The dinner's on Aunty."

She laughed. It was a happy sound if you didn't look at her, but I found I was already able to talk to her without continually, consciously thinking about her face. One got used to it after a very short while. Sometime, I thought, I would tell her so.

I was still on a restricted diet, which made social eating difficult enough without one-handedness thrown in, but did very well on clear soup and Dover sole, expertly removed from the bone by a waiter. Miss Martin, shedding inhibitions visibly, ordered lobster cocktail, fillet steak, and peaches in kirsch. We drank wine, coffee and brandy, and took our time.

"Oh!" she said ecstatically at one point. "It is so long since I had anything like this. My father used to take me out now and then, but since he died . . . well, I can't go to places like this by myself. I sometimes eat in a café round the corner from my rooms, they know me there . . . it's very good food really, chops, eggs and chips . . . you know . . . things like that." I could picture her there, sitting alone with her ravaged head turned to the wall. Lonely unhappy Miss Martin. I wished I could do something—anything—to help her.

Eventually, when she was stirring her coffee, she said simply, "It was a rocket, this." She touched her face. "A firework. The bottle it was standing in tipped over just as it went off, and it came straight at me. It hit me on the cheek bone and exploded. It wasn't anybody's fault. I was sixteen."

"They made a good job of it," I said.

She shook her head, smiling the crooked tragic smile. "A good job from what it was, I suppose, but . . . they said if the rocket had struck an inch higher it would have gone through my eye into my brain and killed me. I often wish it had."

She meant it. Her voice was calm. She was stating a fact.

"Yes," I said.

"It's strange, but I've almost forgotten about it this evening, and that doesn't often happen when I'm with anyone."

"I'm honored."

She drank her coffee, put down her cup, and looked at me thoughtfully.

She said, "Why do you keep your hand in your pocket all the time?"

I owed it to her, after all. I put my hand palm upward on the table, wishing I didn't have to.

She said "Oh!" in surprise, and then, looking back at my face, "So you do know. That's why I feel so . . . so easy with you. You do understand."

I shook my head. "Only a little. I have a pocket; you haven't. I can hide." I rolled my hand over (the back of it was less off-putting) and finally retreated it onto my lap.

"But you can't do the simplest things," she exclaimed. Her voice was full of pity. "You can't tie your shoelaces, for instance. You can't even eat steak in a restaurant without asking someone else to cut it up for you—"

"Shut up," I said abruptly. "Shut up, Miss Martin. Don't you dare to do to me what you can't bear yourself."

"Pity . . . ," she said, biting her lip and staring at me unhappily. "Yes, it's so easy to give—"

"And embarrassing to receive." I grinned at her. "And my shoes don't have shoelaces. They're out of date, for a start."

"You can know as well as I do what it feels like, and yet do it to someone else . . ." She was very upset.

"Stop being miserable. It was kindness. Sympathy."

"Do you think," she said hesitantly, "that pity and sympathy are the same thing?"

"Very often, yes. But sympathy is discreet and pity is tactless. Oh . . . I'm so sorry." I laughed. "Well, it was sympathetic of you to feel sorry I can't cut up my own food, and tactless to say so. The perfect example."

"It wouldn't be so hard to forgive people for just being tactless," she said thoughtfully.

"No," I agreed, surprised. "I suppose it wouldn't."

"It might not hurt so much . . . just tactlessness?"

"It mightn't."

"And curiosity—that might be easier, too, if I just thought of it as bad manners, don't you think? I mean tactlessness and bad manners wouldn't be so hard to stand. In fact *I* could be sorry for *them,* for not knowing better how to behave. Oh why, why didn't I think of that years ago, when it seems so simple now. So sensible."

"Miss Martin," I said with gratitude. "Have some more brandy. You're a liberator."

"How do you mean?"

"Pity is bad manners and can be taken in one's stride, as you said."

"You said it," she protested.

"Indeed I didn't, not like that."

"All right," she said with gaiety, "we'll drink to a new era. A bold front to the world. I will put my desk back to where it was before I joined the office, facing the door. I'll let every caller see me. I'll—" Her brave voice nearly cracked. "I'll just think poorly of their manners if they pity me too openly. That's settled."

We had some more brandy. I wondered inwardly whether she would have the same resolve in the morning, and doubted it. There had been so many years of hiding. She too, it seemed, was thinking along the same lines.

"I don't know that I can do it alone. But if you will promise me something, then I can."

"Very well," I said incautiously. "What?"

"Don't put your hand in your pocket tomorrow. Let everyone see it."

I couldn't. Tomorrow I would be going to the races. I looked at her, appalled, and really understood only then what she had to bear, and what it would cost her to move her desk. She saw the refusal in my face, and some sort of light died in her own. The gaiety collapsed, the defeated, defenseless look came back, the liberation was over.

"Miss Martin . . ." I swallowed.

"It doesn't matter," she said tiredly. "It doesn't matter. And anyway, it's Saturday tomorrow. I only go in for a short while to see to the mail and anything urgent from today's transactions. There wouldn't be any point in changing the desk."

"And on Monday?"

"Perhaps." It meant no.

"If you'll change it tomorrow and do it all next week, I'll do what you ask," I said, quaking at the thought of it.

"You can't," she said sadly. "I can see that you can't."

"If you can, I must."

"But I shouldn't have asked you . . . you work in a shop."

"Oh." That I had forgotten. "It won't matter."

An echo of her former excitement crept back.

"Do you really mean it?"

I nodded. I had wanted to do something—anything—to help her. Anything. My God.

"Promise?" she said doubtfully.

"Yes. And you?"

"All right," she said, with returning resolution. "But I can only do it if I know you are in the same boat. I couldn't let you down then, you see."

I paid the bill, and although she said there was no need, I took her home. We went on the underground to Finchley. She made straight for the least conspicuous seat and sat presenting the good side of her face to the carriage. Then, laughing at herself, she apologized for doing it.

"Never mind," I said, "the new era doesn't start until tomorrow," and hid my hand like a proper coward.

Her room was close to the station (a deliberately short walk, I guessed) in a large, prosperous-looking suburban house. At the gate she stopped.

"Will . . . er . . . I mean, would you like to come in? It's not very late . . . but perhaps you are tired."

She wasn't eager, but when I accepted she seemed pleased.

"This way, then."

We went through a bare tidy garden to a black-painted front door adorned with horrible stained-glass panels. Miss Martin fumbled endlessly in her bag for her key and I reflected idly that I could have picked that particular lock as quickly as she opened it legally. Inside there was a warm hall smelling healthily of air freshener, and at the end of a passage off it, a door with a card saying "Martin."

Miss Martin's room was a surprise. Comfortable, large, close carpeted, newly decorated, and alive with color. She switched on a standard lamp and a rosy table lamp, and drew burnt orange curtains over the black expanse of French windows. With satisfaction she showed me the recently built tiny bathroom leading out of her room, and the suitcase-sized kitchen beside it, both of which additions she had paid for herself. The people who owned the house were very understanding, she said. Very kind. She had lived there for eleven years. It was home.

Miss Martin had no mirrors in her home. Not one.

She bustled in her little kitchen, making more coffee: for something to do, I thought. I sat relaxed on her long comfortable modern sofa and watched how, from long habit, she leaned forward most of the time so that the heavy shoulder-length dark hair swung down to hide her face. She brought the tray and set it down, and sat on the sofa carefully on my right. One couldn't blame her.

"Do you ever cry?" she said suddenly.

"No."

"Not . . . from frustration?"

"No." I smiled. "Swear."

She sighed. "I used to cry often. I don't any more, though. Getting older, of course. I'm nearly forty. I've got resigned now to not getting married. I knew I was resigned to it when I had the bathroom and kitchen built. Up to then, you see, I'd always pretended to myself that one day . . . one day, perhaps . . . but I don't expect it any more, not any more."

"Men are fools," I said inadequately.

"I hope you don't mind me talking like this? It's so seldom that I have anyone in here, and practically never anyone I can really talk to. . . ."

I stayed for an hour, listening to her memories, her experiences, her whole shadowed life. What, I chided myself, had ever happened to me that was one tenth as bad? I had had far more ups than downs.

At length she said, "How did it happen with you? Your hand. . . ."

"Oh, an accident. A sharp bit of metal." A razor-sharp racing horseshoe attached to the foot of a horse galloping at thirty miles an hour, to be exact. A hard kicking slash as I rolled on the ground from an easy fall. One of those things.

Horses race in thin light shoes called plates, not the heavy ones they normally wear; blacksmiths change them before and after, every time a horse runs. Some trainers save a few shillings by using the same racing plates over and over again, so that the leading edge gradually wears down to the thickness of a knife. But jagged knives, not smooth. They can cut you open like a hatchet.

I'd really known at once when I saw my stripped wrist, with the blood spurting out in a jet and the broken bones showing white, that I was finished as a jockey. But I wouldn't give up hope, and insisted on the surgeons' sewing it all up, even though they wanted to take my hand off there and then. It would never be any good, they said; and they were right. Too many of the tendons and nerves were severed. I persuaded them to try twice later on to rejoin and graft some of them and both times it had been a useless agony. They had refused to consider it again.

Miss Martin hesitated on the brink of asking for details, and fortunately didn't. Instead she said, "Are you married? Do you know, I've talked so much about myself that I don't know a thing about you."

"My wife's in Athens, visiting her sister."

"How lovely," Miss Martin sighed. "I wish . . ."

"You'll go one day," I said firmly. "Save up, and go in a year or two. On a bus tour or something. With people anyway. Not alone."

I looked at my watch, and stood up. "I've enjoyed this evening a great deal. Thank you so much for coming out with me."

She stood and formally shook hands, not suggesting another meeting. So much humility, I thought, so little expectation. Poor, poor Miss Martin.

"Tomorrow morning . . ." she said tentatively, at the door.

"Tomorrow," I nodded. "Move that desk. And I . . . I promise I won't forget."

I went home cursing that fate had sent me someone like Miss Martin. I had expected Charing, Street and King's secretary to be young, perhaps pretty, a girl I could take to a café and the pictures and flirt with, with no great involvement on either side. Instead it looked as if I should have to pay more than I'd meant to for my inside information on Ellis Bolt.

9

"Now look," said Lord Hagbourne, amid the bustle of Kempton races, "I've had a word with Captain Oxon and he's satisfied with the way things are going. I really can't interfere any more. Surely you understand that?"

"No, sir, I don't. I don't think Captain Oxon's feelings are more important than Seabury Racecourse. The course should be put right quickly, even if it means overruling him."

"Captain Oxon," he said with a touch of sarcasm, "knows more about his job than you do. I give more weight to his assurance than to your quick look at the track."

"Then couldn't you go and see for yourself? While there is still time."

He didn't like being pushed. His expression said so, plainly. There was no more I could say, either, without risking his ringing up Radnor to cancel the whole investigation.

"I may . . . er . . . I may find time on Monday," he said at last, grudgingly. "I'll see. Have you found anything concrete to support your idea that Seabury's troubles were caused maliciously?"

"Not yet, sir."

"A bit farfetched, if you ask me," he said crossly. "I said so to begin with, as you remember. If you don't turn something up pretty soon . . . it's all expense, you know."

He was intercepted by a passing Steward who took him off to another problem, leaving me grimly to reflect that so far there was a horrid lack of evidence of any sort. What there was was negative.

George had still found no chink in Kraye's respectability, ex-sergeant Lamar had given Bolt clearance, and Chico had come back from Seabury with no results all along the line.

We'd met in the office that morning before I went to Kempton.

"Nothing," said Chico. "I wagged my tongue off, knocking at every front door along that road. Not a soggy flicker. The bit that crosses the racecourse wasn't closed by diversion notices, that's for sure. There isn't much traffic along there, of course. I counted it. Only forty to the hour, average. Still, that's too much for at least some of the neighbors not to notice if there'd been anything out of the ordinary."

"Did anyone see the tanker before it overturned?"

"They're always seeing tankers nowadays. Several complaints about it, I got. No one noticed that one, especially."

"It can't be coincidence. Just at that spot at that time where it would do most harm. And the driver packing up and moving a day or two afterwards, with no forwarding address."

"Well . . ." Chico scratched his ear reflectively. "I got no dice with the hiring of lifting gear either. There isn't much to be had, and what there was was accounted for. None of the little bungalows saw anything in that line, except the breakdown cranes coming to lift the tanker up again."

"How about the drains?"

"No drains," he said. "A blank back to doomsday."

"Good."

"Come again?"

"If you'd found them on a map the hurdle race accident would have been a genuine accident. This way, they reek of tiger traps."

"A spot of spadework after dark? Dodgy stuff."

I frowned. "Yes. And it had to be done long enough before the race meeting for the ground to settle, so that the line of the trench didn't show."

"And strong enough for a tractor to roll over it."

"Tractor?"

"There was one on the course yesterday, pulling a trailer of dug-up turf."

"Oh yes, of course. Yes, strong enough to hold a tractor . . . but wheels wouldn't pierce the ground like a horse's legs. The weight is more spread."

"True enough."

"How fast was the turf-digging going?" I asked.

"Fast? You're joking."

It was depressing. So was Lord Hagbourne's shilly-shallying. So, acutely, was the whole day, because I kept my promise to Miss Martin. Pity, curiosity, surprise, embarrassment and revulsion, I encountered the lot. I tried hard to look on some of the things that were said as tactlessness or bad manners, but it didn't really work. Telling myself it was idiotic to be so sensitive didn't help either. If Miss Martin hadn't kept her side of the bargain, I thought miserably, I would throttle her.

Halfway through the afternoon I had a drink in the big upstairs bar with Mark Witney.

"So that's what you've been hiding all this time in pockets and gloves," he said.

"Yes."

"Bit of a mess," he commented.

"I'm afraid so."

"Does it hurt still?"

"No, only if I knock it. And it aches sometimes."

"Mm," he said sympathetically. "My ankle still aches too. Joints are always like that; they mend, but they never forgive you." He grinned. "The other half? There's time; I haven't a runner until the fifth."

We had another drink, talking about horses, and I reflected that it would be easy if they were all like him.

"Mark," I said as we walked back to the weighing room, "do you remember whether Dunstable ran into any sort of trouble before it packed up?"

"That's going back a bit." He pondered. "Well, it certainly wasn't doing so well during the last year or two, was it? The attendances had fallen off, and they weren't spending any money on paint."

"But no specific disasters?"

"The clerk of the course took an overdose, if you call that a disaster. Yes, I remember now, the collapse of the place's prosperity was put down to the clerk's mental illness. Brinton, I think his name was. He'd been quietly going loco and making hopeless decisions all over the place."

"I'd forgotten," I said glumly. Mark went into the weighing room and I leaned against the rails outside. A suicidal clerk of the course could hardly have been the work of Kraye, I thought. It might have given him the idea of accelerating the demise of Seabury, though. He'd had plenty of time over Dunstable, but owing to a recent political threat of nationalization of building land, he might well be in a hurry to clinch Seabury. I sighed, disregarded as best I could a stare of fascinated horror from the teen-age daughter of a man I used to ride for, and drifted over to look at the horses in the parade ring.

At the end of the too-long afternoon I drove back to my flat, mixed a bigger drink than usual, and spent the evening thinking, without any world-shattering results. Late the next morning, when I was similarly engaged, the doorbell rang, and I found Charles outside.

"Come in," I said with surprise: he rarely visited the flat, and was seldom in London at weekends. "Like some lunch? The restaurant downstairs is quite good."

"Perhaps. In a minute." He took off his overcoat and gloves and accepted some whisky. There was something unsettled in his manner, a ruffling of the smooth, urbane exterior, a suggestion of a troubled frown on the high domed forehead.

"O.K.," I said. "What's the matter?"

"Er . . . I've just driven up from Aynsford. No traffic at all, for once. Such a lovely morning, I thought the drive would be . . . oh damn it," he finished explosively, putting down his glass with a bang. "To get it over quickly, Jenny telephoned from Athens last night. She's met some man there. She asked me to tell you she wants a divorce."

"Oh," I said. How like her, I thought, to get Charles to wield the ax. Practical Jenny, eager for a new fire, hacking away the deadwood. And if some of the wood was still alive, too bad.

"I must say," said Charles, relaxing, "you make a thorough job of it."

"Of what?"

"Of not caring what happens to you."

"I do care."

"No one would suspect it," he sighed. "When I tell you your wife wants to divorce you, you just say, 'Oh.' When that happened"—he nodded to my arm—"the first thing you said to me afterwards when I arrived full of sorrow and sympathy was, if I remember correctly, and I do, 'Cheer up, Charles. I had a good run for my money.'"

"Well, so I did." Always, from my earliest childhood, I had instinctively shied away from too much sympathy. I didn't want it. I distrusted it. It made you soft inside, and an illegitimate child couldn't afford to be soft. One might weep at school, and one's spirit would never recover from so dire a disgrace. So the poverty and the snickers, and later the lost wife and the smashed career, had to be passed off with a shrug, and what one really felt about it had to be locked up tightly inside, out of view. Silly, really, but there it was.

We lunched companionably together downstairs, discussing in civilized tones the mechanics of divorce. Jenny, it appeared, did not want me to use the justified grounds of desertion. I, she said, should "arrange things" instead. I must know how to do it, working for the agency. Charles was apologetic: Jenny's prospective husband was in the diplomatic service like Tony, and would prefer her not to be the guilty party.

Had I, Charles inquired delicately, already been . . . er . . . unfaithful to Jenny? No, I replied, watching him light his cigar, I was afraid I hadn't. For much of the time, owing to one thing and another, I hadn't felt well enough. That, he agreed with amusement, was a reasonable excuse.

I indicated that I would fix things as Jenny wanted, because it didn't affect my future as it did hers. She would be grateful, Charles said. I thought, knowing her, she would very likely take it for granted.

When there was little else to say on that subject, we switched to Kraye. I asked Charles if he had seen him again during the week.

"Yes, I was going to tell you. I had lunch with him in the Club on Thursday. Quite accidentally. We both just happened to be there alone."

"That's where you met him first, in your club?"

"That's right. Of course he thanked me for the weekend and so on. Talked about the quartz. Very interesting collection, he said. But not a murmur about the St. Luke's stone. I would have liked to have asked him straight out, just to see his reaction." He tapped off the ash, smiling. "I did mention you, though, in passing, and he switched on all the charm and said you had been extremely insulting to him and his wife, but that of course you hadn't spoiled his enjoyment. Very nasty, I thought it. He was causing bad trouble for you. Or at least, he intended to."

"Yes," I said cheerfully. "But I did insult him, and I also spied on him. Anything he says of me is fully merited." I told Charles how I had taken the photographs, and all that I had discovered or guessed during the past week. His cigar went out. He looked stunned.

"Well, you wanted me to, didn't you?" I said. "You started it. What did you expect?"

"It's only that I had almost forgotten . . . this is what you used to be like, always. Determined. Ruthless, even." He smiled. "My game for convalescence has turned out better than I expected."

"God help your other patients," I said, "if Kraye is standard medicine."

We walked along the road toward where Charles had left his car. He was going straight home again.

I said, "I hope that in spite of the divorce I shall see something of you? I should be sorry not to. As your ex-son-in-law, I can hardly come to Aynsford any more."

He looked startled. "I'll be annoyed if you don't, Sid. Jenny will be living all round the world, like Jill. Come to Aynsford whenever you want."

"Thank you," I said. I meant it, and it sounded like it.

He stood beside his car, looking down at me from his straight six feet.

"Jenny," he said casually, "is a fool."

I shook my head. Jenny was no fool. Jenny knew what she wanted, and it wasn't me.

When I went into the office (on time) the following morning, the girl on the switchboard caught me and said Radnor wanted me straight away.

"Good morning," he said. "I've just had Lord Hagbourne on the telephone telling me it's time we got results and that he can't go to Seabury today because his car is being serviced. Before you explode, Sid . . . I told him that you would take him down there now, at once, in your own car. So get a move on."

I grinned. "I bet he didn't like that."

"He couldn't think of an excuse fast enough. Get round and collect him before he comes up with one."

"Right."

I made a quick detour up to the Racing Section where Dolly was adjusting her lipstick. No crossover blouse today. A disappointment.

I told her where I was going and asked if I could use Chico.

"Help yourself," she said resignedly. "If you can get a word in edgeways. He's along in Accounts arguing with Jones-boy."

Chico, however, listened attentively and repeated what I had asked him. "I'm to find out exactly what mistakes the clerk of the course at Dunstable made, and make sure that they and nothing else were the cause of the course losing money."

"That's right. And dig out the file on Andrews and the case you were working on when I got shot."

"But that's all dead," he protested, "the file's down in records in the basement."

"Send Jones-boy down for it," I suggested, grinning. "It's probably only a coincidence, but there is something I want to check. I'll do it tomorrow morning. O.K.?"

"If you say so, chum."

Back at my flat, I filled up with Extra and made all speed round to Beauchamp Place. Lord Hagbourne, with a civil but cool good morning, lowered himself into the passenger seat, and we set off for Seabury. It took him about a quarter of an hour to get over having been maneuvered into something he didn't want to do, but at the end of that time he sighed and moved in his seat and offered me a cigarette.

"No, thank you, sir. I don't smoke."

"You don't mind if I do?" He took one out.

"Of course not."

"This is a nice car," he remarked, looking round.

"It's nearly three years old now. I bought it the last season I was riding. It's the best I've ever had, I think."

"I must say," he said inoffensively, "that you manage extremely well. I wouldn't have thought that you could drive a car like this with only one effective hand."

"Its power makes it easier, actually. I took it across Europe last spring . . . good roads, there."

We talked on about cars and holidays, then about theaters and books, and he seemed for once quite human. The subject of Seabury we carefully bypassed. I wanted to get him down there in a good mood—the arguments, if any, could take place on the way back—and it seemed as if he was of the same mind.

The state of Seabury's track reduced him to silent gloom. We walked down to the burnt piece with Captain Oxon, who was bearing himself stiffly and being pointedly polite. I thought he was a fool: he should have fallen on the Senior Steward and begged for instant help.

Captain Oxon, whom I had not met before, though he said he knew me by sight, was a slender, pleasant-looking man of about fifty, with a long pointed chin and a slight tendency to watery eyes. The present offended obstinacy of his expression looked more like childishness than real strength. A colonel *manqué*, I thought uncharitably, and no wonder.

"I know it's not really my business," I said, "but surely a bulldozer would shift what's left of the burnt bit in a couple of hours? There isn't time to settle new turf, but you could cover the whole area with some tons of tan and race over it quite easily, like that. You must be getting tan anyway, to cover the road surface. Surely you could just increase the order?"

Oxon looked at me with irritation. "We can't afford it."

"You can't afford another cancellation at the last minute," I corrected.

"We are insured against cancellations."

"I doubt whether an insurance company would stand this one," I said. "They'd say you could have raced if you'd tried hard enough."

"It's Monday now," remarked Lord Hagbourne thoughtfully. "Racing's due on Friday. Suppose we call in a bulldozer tomorrow; the tan can be unloaded and spread on Wednesday and Thursday. Yes, that seems sound enough."

"But the cost—" began Oxon.

"I think the money must be found," said Lord Hagbourne. "Tell Mr. Fotherton when he comes over that I have authorized the expenditure. The bills will be met, in one way or another. But I do think there is no case for not making an effort."

It was on the tip of my tongue to point out that if Oxon had arranged for the bulldozer on the first day he could have saved the price of casual labor from six hand-diggers for a week, but as the battle was already won, I nobly refrained. I continued to think, however, that Oxon was a fool. Usually the odd custom of giving the managerships of racecourses to ex-army officers worked out well, but conspicuously not in this case.

The three of us walked back up to the stands, Lord Hagbourne pausing and pursing his lips at their dingy appearance. I reflected that it was a pity Seabury had a clerk of the course whose heart and home were far away on the thriving course at Bristol. If I'd been arranging things, I'd have seen to it a year ago, when the profits turned to loss, that Seabury had a new clerk entirely devoted to its own interests, someone moreover whose livelihood depended on its staying open. The bungle, delay, muddle, too much politeness and failure to take action showed by the Seabury executive had been of inestimable value to the quietly burrowing Kraye.

Mr. Fotherton might have been worried, as he said, but he had done little except mention it in passing to Charles in his capacity as Steward at some other meeting. Charles, looking for something to divert my mind from my stomach, and perhaps genuinely anxious about Seabury, had tossed the facts to me. In his own peculiar way, naturally.

The casualness of the whole situation was horrifying. I basely wondered whether Fotherton himself had a large holding in Seabury shares and therefore a vested interest in its demise. Planning a much closer scrutiny of the list of shareholders, I followed Lord Hagbourne and Captain Oxon round the end of the stands, and we walked the three hundred yards or so through the racecourse gates and down the road to where Captain Oxon's flat was situated above the canteen in the stable block.

On Lord Hagbourne's suggestion he rang up a firm of local contractors while we were still there, and arranged for the urgent earth-moving to be done the following morning. His manner was still ruffled, and it didn't improve things when I declined the well-filled ham and chutney sandwiches he offered, though I would have adored to have eaten them, had he but known. I had been out of hospital for a fortnight, but I had another fortnight to go before things like new bread, ham, mustard and chutney were due back on the agenda. Very boring.

After the sandwiches Lord Hagbourne decided on a tour of inspection, so we all three went first round the stable block, into the lads' hostel, through the canteen to the kitchen, and into all the stable administrative offices. Everywhere the story was the same. Except for the rows of wooden boxes which had been thrown up cheaply after the old ones burned down, there was no recent maintenance and no new paint.

Then we retraced our steps up the road, through the main gate, and across to the long line of stands with the weighing room, dining rooms, bars and cloakrooms built into the back. At one end were the secretary's office, the press room and the Stewards' room; at the other, the first-aid room and a store. A wide tunnel like a passage ran centrally through the whole length of the building, giving secondary access on one side to many of the rooms, and on the other to the steps of the stands themselves. We painstakingly covered the lot, even down to the boiler room and the oil bunkers, so I had my nostalgic look inside the weighing room and changing room after all.

The whole huge block was dankly cold, very drafty, and smelled of dust. Nothing looked new, not even the dirt. For inducing depression it was hard to beat, but the dreary buildings along in the cheaper rings did a good job of trying.

Captain Oxon said the general dilapidation was mostly due to the sea air, the racecourse being barely half a mile from the shore, and no doubt in essence he was right. The sea air had had a free hand for far too long.

Eventually we returned to where my car was parked inside the gate, and looked back to the row of stands: forlorn, deserted, decaying on a chilly early November afternoon, with a salt-laden drizzle just beginning to blur the outlines.

"What's to be done?" said Lord Hagbourne glumly, as we drove through the rows of bungalows on our way home.

"I don't know." I shook my head.

"The place is dead."

I couldn't argue. Seabury had suddenly seemed to me to be past saving. The Friday and Saturday fixtures could be held now, but as things stood the gate money would hardly cover expenses. No company could go on taking a loss indefinitely. Seabury could plug the gap at present by drawing on their reserve funds, but as I'd seen from their balance sheets at Company House, the reserves only amounted to a few thousands. Matters were bound to get worse. Insolvency waited round a close corner. It might be more realistic to admit that Seabury had no future and to sell the land at the highest price offered as soon as possible. People were, after all, crying out for flat land at the seaside. And there was no real reason why the shareholders shouldn't be rewarded for their long loyalty and recent poor dividends and receive eight pounds for each one they had invested. Many would gain if Seabury came under the hammer, and no one would lose. Seabury was past saving: best to think only of the people who would benefit.

My thoughts stopped with a jerk. This, I realized, must be the attitude of the clerk, Mr. Fotherton, and of the manager, Oxon, and of all the executives. This explained why they had made surprisingly little attempt to save the place. They had accepted defeat easily and seen it to be not only harmless but, to many, usefully profitable. As it had been with other courses, big courses like Hurst Park and Birmingham, so it should be with Seabury.

What did it matter that yet another joined the century's ghost ranks of Cardiff, Derby, Bournemouth, Newport? What did it matter if busy people like Inspector Cornish of Dunstable couldn't go racing much because their local course had vanished? What did it matter if Seabury's holidaymakers went to the bingo halls instead?

Chasing owners, I thought, should rise up in a body and demand that Seabury should be preserved, because no racecourse was better for their horses. But of course they wouldn't. You could tell owners how good it was, but unless they were horsemen themselves, it didn't register. They only saw the rotten amenities of the stands, not the splendidly sited well-built fences that positively invited their horses to jump. They didn't know how their horses relished the short springy turf underfoot, or found the arc and cambers of the bends perfect for maintaining an even speed. Corners at many other racecourses threw horses wide and broke up their stride, but not those at Seabury. The original course builder had been brilliant, and regular visits from the inspector of courses had kept his work fairly intact. Fast, true-run, unhazardous racing, that's what Seabury gave.

Or had given, before Kraye.

Kraye and the executive's inertia between them. . . . I stamped on the accelerator in a surge of anger and the car swooped up the side of the South Downs like a bird. I didn't often drive fast any more: I did still miss having two hands on the wheel. At the top, out of consideration for my passenger's nerves, I let the speedometer ribbon slide back to fifty.

He said, "I feel like that about it too."

I glanced at him in surprise.

"The whole situation is infuriating," he said. "Such a good course basically, and nothing to be done."

"It could be saved," I said.

"How?"

"A new attitude of mind. . . ." I trailed off.

"Go on," he said. But I couldn't find the words to tell him politely that he ought to chuck out all the people in power at Seabury; too many of them were probably his ex-school chums or personal friends.

"Suppose," he said after a few minutes, "that you had a free hand, what would you do?"

"One would never get a free hand. That's half the trouble. Someone makes a good suggestion, and someone else squashes it. They end up, often as not, by doing nothing."

"No, Sid, I mean you personally. What would you do?"

"I?" I grinned. "What I'd do would have the National Hunt Committee swooning like Victorian maidens."

"I'd like to know."

"Seriously?"

He nodded. As if he could ever be anything else but serious.

I sighed. "Very well, then. I'd pinch every good crowd-pulling idea that any other course has thought of and put them all into operation on the same day."

"What, for instance?"

"I'd take the whole of the reserve fund and offer it as a prize for a big race. I'd make sure the race was framed to attract the really top chasers. Then I'd go round to their trainers personally and explain the situation, and beg for their support. I'd go to some of the people who sponsor Gold Cup races and cajole them into giving five-hundred-pound prizes for all the other races on that day. I'd make the whole thing into a campaign. I'd get Save Seabury discussed on television, and in the sports columns of newspapers. I'd get people interested and involved. I'd make helping Seabury the smart thing to do. I'd get someone like the Beatles to come and present the trophies. I'd advertise free car-parking and free race cards, and on the day I'd have the whole place bright with flags and bunting and tubs of flowers to hide the lack of paint. I'd make sure everyone on the staff understood that a friendly welcome must be given to the customers. And I'd insist that the catering firm use its imagination. I'd fix the meeting for the beginning of April, and pray for a sunny spring day. That," I said, running down, "would do for a start."

"And afterwards?" He was noncommittal.

"A loan, I suppose. Either from a bank or from private individuals. But the executive would have to show first that Seabury could be a success again, like it used to be. No one falls over himself to lend to a dying business. The revival has to come before the money, if you see what I mean."

"I do see," he agreed slowly, "but . . ."

"Yes. But. It always comes to 'but.' But no one at Seabury is going to bother."

We were silent for a long way.

Finally I said, "This meeting on Friday and Saturday—it would be a pity to risk another last-minute disaster. Hunt Radnor Associates could arrange for some sort of guard on the course. Security patrols, that kind of thing."

"Too expensive," he said promptly. "And you've not yet proved that it is really needed. Seabury's troubles still look like plain bad luck to me."

"Well, a security patrol might prevent any more of it."

"I don't know. I'll have to see." He changed the subject then, and talked firmly about other races on other courses all the way back to London.

10

Dolly lent me her telephone with resignation on Tuesday morning, and I buzzed the switchboard for an internal call to Missing Persons.

"Sammy?" I said. "Sid Halley, down in Racing. Are you busy?"

"The last teen-ager has just been retrieved from Gretna. Fire away. Who's lost?"

"A man called Smith."

Some mild blasphemy sped three stories down the wire.

I laughed. "I think his name really is Smith. He's a driver by trade. He's been driving a tanker for Intersouth Chemicals for the last year. He left his job and his digs last Wednesday; no forwarding address." I told him about the crash, the suspected concussion and the revelry by night.

"You don't think he was planted on purpose on the job a year ago? His name likely wouldn't be Smith in that case . . . make it harder."

"I don't know. But I think it's more likely he was a bona fide Intersouth driver who was offered a cash payment for exceptional services rendered."

"O.K., I'll try that first. He might give Intersouth as a reference, in which case they'll know if he applies for another job somewhere, or I might trace him through his union. The wife might have worked, too. I'll let you know."

"Thanks."

"Don't forget, when the old man buys you a gold-plated executive desk I want my table back."

"You'll want forever," I said, smiling. It had been Sammy's lunch.

On the table in question lay the slim file on the Andrews case that Jones-boy had unearthed from the basement. I looked round the room.

"Where's Chico?" I asked.

Dolly answered. "Helping a bookmaker to move house."

"He's doing *what?*" I goggled.

"That's right. Long-standing date. The bookmaker is taking his safe with him and wants Chico to sit on it in the furniture van. It had to be Chico, he said. No one else would do. The paying customer is always right, so Chico's gone."

"Damn."

She reached into a drawer. "He left you a tape," she said.

"Undamn, then."

She grinned and handed it to me, and I took it over to the recorder, fed it through onto the spare reel, and listened to it in the routine office way, through the earphones.

"After wearing my plates down to the ankles," said Chico's cheerful voice, "I found out that the worst things your clerk of the course did at Dunstable were to frame a lot of races that did the opposite of attract any decent runners, and be stinking rude to all and sundry. He was quite well liked up to the year before he killed himself. Then everyone says he gradually got more and more crazy. He was so rude to people who worked at the course that half of them wouldn't put up with it and left. And the local tradesmen practically spat when I mentioned his name. I'll fill you in when I see you, but there wasn't anything like Seabury—no accidents or damage or anything like that."

Sighing, I wiped the tape clean and gave it back to Dolly. Then I opened the file on my table and studied its contents.

A Mr. Mervyn Brinton of Reading, Berkshire, had applied to the agency for personal protection, having had reason to believe that he was in danger of being attacked. He had been unwilling to say why he might be attacked, and refused to have the agency make inquiries. All he wanted was a bodyguard. There was a strong possibility, said the report, that Brinton had tried a little amateurish blackmail, which had backfired. He had at length revealed that he possessed a certain letter, and was afraid of being attacked and having it stolen. After much persuasion by Chico Barnes, who pointed out that Brinton could hardly be guarded for the rest of his life, Brinton had agreed to inform a certain party that the letter in question was lodged in a particular desk drawer in the Racing Section of Hunt Radnor Associates. In fact it was not; and had not at any time been seen by anyone working for the agency. However, Thomas Andrews came, or was sent, to remove the letter, was interrupted by J. S. Halley (whom he wounded by shooting), and subsequently made his escape. Two days later Brinton telephoned to say he no longer required a bodyguard, and as far as the agency was concerned the case was then closed.

The foregoing information had been made available to the police in their investigation into the shooting of Halley.

I shut the file. A drab little story, I thought, of a pathetic little man playing out of his league.

Brinton.

The clerk of the course at Dunstable had also been called Brinton.

I sat gazing at the short file. Brinton wasn't an uncommon name. There was probably no connection at all. Brinton of Dunstable had died a good two years before Brinton of Reading had asked for protection. The only visible connection was that at different ends of the scale both the Dunstable Brinton and Thomas Andrews had earned their living on the racecourse. It wasn't much. Probably nothing. But it nagged.

I went home, collected the car, and drove to Reading.

A nervous, gray-haired elderly man opened the front door on a safety chain, and peered through the gap.

"Yes?"

"Mr. Brinton?"

"What is it?"

"I'm from Hunt Radnor Associates. I'd be most grateful for a word with you."

He hesitated, chewing an upper lip adorned with an untidy pepper-and-salt mustache. Anxious brown eyes looked me up and down and went past me to the white car parked by the curb.

"I sent a check," he said finally.

"It was quite in order," I assured him.

"I don't want any trouble . . . it wasn't my fault that that man was shot." He didn't sound convinced.

"Oh, no one blames you for that," I said. "He's perfectly all right now. Back at work, in fact."

His relief showed, even through the crack. "Very well," he said, and pushed the door shut to take off the chain.

I followed him into the front room of his tall terrace house. The air smelled stale and felt still, as if it had been hanging in the same spot for days. The furniture was of the hard-stuffed and brown shellacked substantial type that in my plywood childhood I had thought the peak of living, unobtainable; and there were cases of tropical butterflies on the walls, and carved ornaments from somewhere like Java or Borneo on several small tables. A life abroad, retirement at home, I thought. From color and heat to suburban respectability in Reading.

"My wife has gone out shopping," he said, still nervously. "She'll be back soon." He looked hopefully out of the lace-curtained window, but Mrs. Brinton didn't oblige him by coming to his support.

I said, "I just wanted to ask you, Mr. Brinton, if you were by any chance related to a Mr. William Brinton, one-time clerk of Dunstable racecourse."

He gave me a long agonized stare, and to my consternation sat down on his sofa and began to cry, his shaking hands covering his eyes and the tears splashing down onto his tweed-clad knees.

"Please . . . Mr. Brinton . . . I'm so sorry," I said awkwardly.

He snuffled and coughed, and dragged a handkerchief out to wipe his eyes. Gradually the paroxysm passed, and he said indistinctly, "How did you find out? I told you I didn't want anyone asking questions."

"It was quite accidental. Nobody asked any questions, I promise you. Would you like to tell me about it? Then I don't think any questions will need to be asked at all, from anyone else."

"The police . . . ," he said doubtfully, on a sob. "They came before. I refused to say anything, and they went away."

"Whatever you tell me will be in confidence."

"I've been such a fool. I'd like to tell someone, really."

I pictured the strung-up, guilt-ridden weeks he'd endured, and the crying fit became not only understandable but inevitable.

"It was the letter, you see," he said, sniffling softly. "The letter William began to write to me, though he never sent it. I found it in a whole trunk of stuff that was left when he . . . killed himself. I was in Sarawak then, you know, and they sent me a cable. It was a shock . . . one's only brother doing such a . . . a terrible thing. He was younger than me. Seven years. We weren't very close, except when we were children. I wish . . . but it's too late now. Anyway, when I came home I fetched all his stuff round from where it had been stored and put it up in the attic here, all his racing books and things. I didn't know what to do with them, you see. I wasn't interested in them, but it seemed . . . I don't know . . . I couldn't just burn them. It was months before I bothered to sort them out, and then I found the letter. . . ." His voice faltered and he looked at me appealingly, wanting to be forgiven.

"Kitty and I had found my pension didn't go anywhere near as far as we'd expected. Everything is so terribly expensive. The rates . . . we decided we'd have to sell the house again though we'd only just bought it, and Kitty's family are all close. And then . . . I thought . . . perhaps I could sell the letter instead."

"And you got threats instead of money," I said.

"Yes. It was the letter itself which gave me the idea." He chewed his mustache.

"And now you no longer have it," I said matter-of-factly, as if I knew for certain and wasn't guessing. "When you were first threatened you thought you could still sell the letter if Hunt Radnor kept you safe, and then you got more frightened and gave up the letter, and then canceled the protection because the threats had stopped."

He nodded unhappily. "I gave them the letter because that man was shot. . . . I didn't realize anything like that would happen. I was horrified. It was terrible. I hadn't thought it could be so dangerous, just selling a letter. . . . I wish I'd never found it. I wish William had never written it."

So did I, as it happened.

"What did the letter say?" I asked.

He hesitated, his fear showing. "It might cause more trouble. They might come back."

"They won't know you've told me," I pointed out. "How could they?"

"I suppose not." He looked at me, making up his mind. There's one thing about being small: no one is ever afraid of you. If I'd been big and commanding I don't think he'd have risked it. As it was, his face softened and relaxed and he threw off the last threads of reticence.

"I know it by heart," he said. "I'll write it down for you, if you like. It's easier than saying it."

I sat and waited while he fetched a ball-point pen and a pad of large writing paper and got on with his task. The sight of the letter materializing again in front of his eyes affected him visibly, but whether to fear or remorse or sorrow, I couldn't tell. He covered one side of the page, then tore it off the pad and shakily handed it over.

I read what he had written. I read it twice. Because of these short desperate sentences, I reflected unemotionally, I had come within spitting distance of St. Peter.

"That's fine," I said. "Thank you very much."

"I wish I'd never found it," he said again. "Poor William."

"Did you go to see this man?" I asked, indicating the letter as I put it away in my wallet.

"No, I wrote to him . . . he wasn't hard to find."

"And how much did you ask for?"

Shamefaced, he muttered, "Five thousand pounds."

Five thousand pounds had been wrong, I thought. If he'd asked fifty thousand, he might have had a chance. But five thousand didn't put him among the big-power boys, it just revealed his mediocrity. No wonder he had been stamped on, fast.

"What happened next?" I asked.

"A big man came for the letter, about four o'clock one afternoon. It was awful. I asked him for the money and he just laughed in my face and pushed me into a chair. No money, he said, but if I didn't hand over the letter at once he'd . . . he'd teach me a thing or two. That's what he said, teach me a thing or two. I explained that I had put the letter in my box at the bank and that the bank was closed and that I couldn't get it until the next morning. He said that he would come to the bank with me the next day, and then he went away."

"And you rang up the agency almost at once? Yes. What made you choose Hunt Radnor?"

He looked surprised. "It was the only one I knew about. Are there any others? I mean, most people have heard of Hunt Radnor, I should think."

"I see. So Hunt Radnor sent you a bodyguard, but the big man wouldn't give up."

"He kept telephoning . . . then your man suggested setting a trap in his office, and in the end I agreed. Oh, I shouldn't have let him, I was such a fool. I knew all the time, you see, who was threatening me, but I couldn't tell your agency because I would have had to admit I'd tried to get money . . . illegally."

"Yes. Well, there's only one more thing. What was he like, the man who came and threatened you?"

Brinton didn't like even the memory of him. "He was very strong. Hard. When he pushed me it was like a wall. I'm not . . . I mean, I've never been good with my fists, or anything like that. If he'd started hitting me I couldn't have stopped him."

"I'm not blaming you for not standing up to him," I pointed out. "I just want to know what he looked like."

"Very big," he said vaguely. "Huge."

"I know it's several weeks ago now, but can't you possibly remember more than that? How about his hair? Anything odd about his face? How old? What class?"

He smiled for the first time, the sad wrinkles folding for a moment into some semblance of faded charm. If he'd never taken his first useless step into crime, I thought, he might still have been a nice gentle innocuous man, fading without rancor toward old age, troubled only by how to make a little pension go a long way. No tearing, destructive guilt.

"It's certainly easier when you ask questions like that. He was beginning to go bald, I remember now. And he had big blotchy freckles on the backs of his hands. It's difficult to know about his age. Not a youth, though; more than thirty, I think. What else did you ask? Oh yes, class. Working class, then."

"English?"

"Oh yes, not foreign. Sort of cockney, I suppose."

I stood up, thanked him, and began to take my leave. He said, begging me still for reassurance, "There won't be any more trouble?"

"Not from me or the agency."

"And the man who was shot?"

"Not from him either."

"I tried to tell myself it wasn't my fault . . . but I haven't been able to sleep. How could I have been such a fool? I shouldn't have let that young man set any trap. . . . I shouldn't have called in your agency . . . and it cost another chunk of our savings. . . . I ought never to have tried to get money for that letter."

"That's true, Mr. Brinton, you shouldn't. But what's done is done, and I don't suppose you'll start anything like that again."

"No, no," he said with pain. "I wouldn't. Ever. These last few weeks have been . . ." His voice died. Then he said more strongly, "We'll have to sell the house now. Kitty likes it here, of course. But what I've always wanted myself is a little bungalow by the sea."

When I reached the office I took out the disastrous letter and read it again, before adding it to the file. Being neither the original nor a photocopy, but only a reproduction from memory, it wasn't of the slightest use as evidence. In the elder Brinton's small tidy script, a weird contrast to the heartbroken contents, it ran:

Dear Mervy, dear big brother,

I wish you could help me, as you did when I was little. I have spent fifteen years building up Dunstable Racecourse, and a man called Howard Kraye is making me destroy it. I have to frame races which nobody likes. Very few horses come now, and the gate receipts are falling fast. This week I must see that the racecard goes to the printers too late, and the press-room telephones will all be out of order. There will be a terrible muddle. People must think I am mad. I can't escape him. He is paying me as well, but I must do as he says. I can't help my nature, you know that. He has found out about a boy I was living with, and I could be prosecuted. He wants the racecourse to sell for housing. Nothing can stop him getting it. My racecourse, I love it.

I know I shan't send this letter. Mervy, I wish you were here. I haven't anyone else. Oh dear God, I can't go on much longer, I really can't.

At five to six that afternoon I opened the door of Zanna Martin's office. Her desk was facing me and so was she. She raised her head, recognized me, and looked back at me in a mixture of pride and embarrassment.

"I did it," she said. "If you didn't, I'll kill you."

She had combed her hair even further forward, so that it hung close round her face, but all the same one could see the disfigurement at first glance. I had forgotten, in the days since Friday, just how bad it was.

"I felt the same about you," I said, grinning.

"You really did keep your promise?"

"Yes, I did. All day Saturday and Sunday, most of yesterday and most of today, and very nasty it is, too."

She sighed with relief. "I'm glad you've come. I nearly gave it up this morning. I thought you wouldn't do it, and you'd never come back to see if I had, and that I was being a proper idiot."

"Well, I'm here," I said. "Is Mr. Bolt in?"

She shook her head. "He's gone home. I'm just packing up."

"Finished the envelopes?" I said.

"Envelopes? Oh, those I was doing when you were here before? Yes, they're all done."

"And filled and sent?"

"No, the leaflets haven't come back from the printers yet, much to Mr. Bolt's disgust. I expect I'll be doing them tomorrow."

She stood up, tall and thin, put on her coat and tied the scarf over her hair.

"Are you going anywhere this evening?" I asked.

"Home," she said decisively.

"Come out to dinner," I suggested.

"Aunty's legacy won't last long, the way you spend. I think Mr. Bolt has already invested your money. You'd better save every penny until after settlement day."

"Coffee, then, and the flicks?"

"Look," she said hesitantly, "I sometimes buy a hot chicken on my way home. There's a fish-and-chips shop next to the station that sells them. Would you . . . would you like to come and help me eat it? In return, I mean, for Friday night."

"I'd enjoy that," I said, and was rewarded by a pleased, half-incredulous laugh.

"Really?"

"Really."

As before, we went to Finchley by underground, but this time Miss Martin sat boldly where her whole face showed. To try to match her fortitude, I rested my elbow on the seat arm between us. She looked at my hand and then at my face, gratefully, almost as if we were sharing an adventure.

As we emerged from the tube station she said, "You know, it makes a great deal of difference if one is accompanied by a man, even—" she stopped abruptly.

"Even," I finished, smiling, "if he is smaller than you and also damaged."

"Oh dear . . . and much younger, as well." Her real eye looked at me with rueful amusement. The glass one stared stonily ahead. I was getting used to it again.

"Let me buy the chicken," I said, as we stopped outside the shop. The smell of hot chips mingled with diesel fumes from a passing lorry. Civilization, I thought. Delightful.

"Certainly not." Miss Martin was firm and bought the chicken herself. She came out with it wrapped in newspaper. "I got a few chips and a packet of peas," she said.

"And I," I said firmly, as we came to an off-license, "am getting some brandy." What chips and peas would do to my digestion I dared not think.

We walked round to the house with the parcels and went through into her room. She moved with a light step.

"In that cupboard over there," she said, pointing, as she peeled off her coat and scarf, "there are some glasses and a bottle of sherry. Will you pour me some? I expect you prefer brandy, but have some sherry if you'd like. I'll just take these things into the kitchen and put them to keep hot."

While I unscrewed the bottles and poured the drinks I heard her lighting her gas stove and unwrapping the parcels. There was dead quiet as I walked across the room with her sherry, and when I reached the door I saw why. She held the chicken in its piece of greaseproof paper absently in one hand; the bag of chips lay open on the table with the box of peas beside it; and she was reading the newspaper they had all been wrapped in.

She looked up at me in bewilderment.

"You," she said. "It's you. This is you."

I looked down where her finger pointed. The fish-and-chips shop had wrapped up her chicken in the Sunday *Hemisphere*.

"Here's your sherry," I said, holding it out to her.

She put down the chicken and took the glass without appearing to notice it.

"Another Halley," she said. "It caught my eye. Of course I read it. And it's your picture, and it even refers to your hand. You are Sid Halley."

"That's right." There was no chance of denying it.

"Good heavens. I've known about you for years. Read about you. I saw you on television, often. My father loved watching the racing, we always had it on when he was alive—" She broke off and then said with increased puzzlement, "Why on earth did you say your name was John and that you worked in a shop? Why did you come to see Mr. Bolt? I don't understand."

"Drink your sherry, put your chicken in the oven before it freezes and I'll tell you." There was nothing else to do: I didn't want to risk her brightly passing on the interesting tidbit of news to her employer.

Without demur she put the dinner to heat, came to sit on the sofa, opposite to where I apprehensively waited in an armchair, and raised her eyebrows in expectation.

"I don't work in a shop," I admitted. "I am employed by a firm called Hunt Radnor Associates."

Like Brinton, she had heard of the agency. She stiffened her whole body and began to frown. As casually as I could, I told her about Kraye and the Seabury shares; but she was no fool and she went straight to the heart of things.

"You suspect Mr. Bolt too. That's why you went to see him."

"Yes, I'm afraid so."

"And me? You took me out simply and solely to find out about him?" Her voice was bitter.

I didn't answer at once. She waited, and somehow her calmness was more piercing than tears or temper could have been. She asked so little of life.

At last I said, "I went to Bolt's office as much to take out his secretary as to see Bolt himself, yes."

The peas boiled over, hissing loudly. She stood up slowly. "At least that's honest."

She went into the tiny kitchen and turned out the gas under the saucepan.

I said, "I came to your office this afternoon because I wanted to look at those leaflets Bolt is sending to Seabury shareholders. You told me at once that they hadn't come from the printers. I didn't need to accept your invitation to supper after that. But I'm here."

She stood in the kitchen doorway, holding herself straight with an all too apparent effort.

"I suppose you lied about that too," she said in a quiet rigidly controlled voice, pointing to my arm. "Why? Why did you play such a cruel game with me? Surely you could have got your information without that. Why did you make me change my desk round?

I suppose you were laughing yourself sick all day Saturday thinking about it."

I stood up. Her hurt was dreadful.

I said, "I went to Kempton races on Saturday."

She didn't move.

"I kept my promise."

She made a slight gesture of disbelief.

"I'm sorry," I said helplessly.

"Yes. Good night, Mr. Halley. Good night."

I went.

11

Radnor held a Seabury conference the next morning, Wednesday, consisting of himself, Dolly, Chico and me; the result, chiefly, of my having the previous afternoon finally wrung grudging permission from Lord Hagbourne to arrange a twenty-four-hour guard at Seabury for the coming Thursday, Friday and Saturday.

The bulldozing had been accomplished without trouble, and a call to the course that morning had established that the tan was arriving in regular lorry loads and was being spread. Racing, bar any last-minute accidents, was now certain. Even the weather was cooperating. The glass was rising; the forecast was dry, cold and sunny.

Dolly proposed a straight patrol system, and Radnor was inclined to agree. Chico and I had other ideas.

"If anyone intended to sabotage the track," Dolly pointed out, "they would be frightened off by a patrol. Same thing if they were planning something in the stands themselves."

Radnor nodded. "Safest way of making sure racing takes place. I suppose we'll need at least four men to do it properly."

I said, "I agree that we need a patrol tonight, tomorrow night and Friday night, just to play safe. But tomorrow, when the course will be more or less deserted . . . what we need is to pinch them at it, not frighten them off. There's no evidence yet that could be used in a court of law. If we could catch them in mid-sabotage, so to speak, we'd be much better off."

"That's right," said Chico. "Hide and pounce. Much better than scaring them away."

"I seem to remember," said Dolly with a grin, "that the last time you two set a trap the mouse shot the cheese."

"Oh God, Dolly, you slay me," said Chico, laughing warmly and for once accepting her affection.

Even Radnor laughed. "Seriously, though," he said, "I don't see how you can. A racecourse is too big. If you are hiding you can only see a small part of it. And surely if you show yourself your presence would act like any other patrol to stop anything plainly suspicious being done? I don't think it's possible."

"Um," I said. "But there's one thing I can still do better than anyone else in this agency."

"And what's that?" said Chico, ready to argue.

"Ride a horse."

"Oh," said Chico. "I'll give you that, chum."

"A horse," said Radnor thoughtfully. "Well, that's certainly an idea. Nobody's going to look suspiciously at a horse on a racecourse, I suppose. Mobile, too. Where would you get one?"

"From Mark Witney. I could borrow his hack. Seabury's his local course. His stables aren't many miles away."

"But can you still—?" began Dolly, and broke off. "Well, don't glare at me like that, all of you. I can't ride with two hands, let alone one."

"A man called Gregory Philips had his arm amputated very high up," I said, "and went on racing in point-to-points for years."

"Enough said," said Dolly. "How about Chico?"

"He can wear a pair of my jodhpurs. Protective coloring. And lean nonchalantly on the rails."

"Stick insects," said Chico cheerfully.

"That's what you want, Sid?" said Radnor.

I nodded. "Look at it from the worst angle: we haven't anything on Kraye that will stand up. We might not find Smith, the tanker driver, and even if we do, he has everything to lose by talking and nothing to gain. When the racecourse stables burned down a year ago, we couldn't prove it wasn't an accident; an illicit cigarette end. Stable lads do smoke, regardless of bans.

"The so-called drain which collapsed—we don't know if it was dug a day, a week, or six weeks before it did its work. That letter William Brinton of Dunstable wrote to his brother, it's only a copy from memory that we've got, no good at all for evidence. All it proves, to our own satisfaction, is that Kraye is capable of anything. We can't show it to Lord Hagbourne, because I obtained it in confidence, and he still isn't a hundred per cent convinced that Kraye has done more than buy shares. As I see it, we've just got to give the enemy a chance to get on with their campaign."

"You think they will, then?"

"It's awfully likely, isn't it? This year there isn't another Seabury meeting until February. A three months' gap. And if I read it right, Kraye is in a hurry now because of the political situation. He won't want to spend fifty thousand buying Seabury and then find building land has been nationalized overnight. If I were him, I'd want to clinch the deal and sell to a developer as quickly as possible. According to the photographs of the share transfers, he already holds twenty-three per cent of the shares. This is almost certainly enough to swing the sale of the company if it comes to a vote. But he's greedy. He'll want more. But he'll only want more if he can get it soon. Waiting for February is too risky. So yes, I do think if we give him a chance that he will organize some more damage this week."

"It's a risk," said Dolly. "Suppose something dreadful happens and we neither prevent it nor catch anyone doing it?"

They kicked it round among the three of them for several more minutes, the pros and cons of the straight patrols versus cat and mouse. Finally Radnor turned back to me and said, "Sid?"

"It's your agency," I said seriously. "It's your risk."

"But it's your case. It's still your case. You must decide."

I couldn't understand him. It was all very well for him to have given me a free hand so far, but this wasn't the sort of decision I would have ever expected him to pass on.

Still . . . "Chico and I, then," I said. "We'll go alone tonight and stay all day tomorrow. I don't think we'll let even Captain Oxon know we're there. Certainly not the foreman, Ted Wilkins, or any of the other men. We'll come in from the other side from the stands, and I'll borrow the horse for mobility. Dolly can arrange official patrol guards with Oxon for tomorrow night—suggest he gives them a warm room, Dolly. He ought to have the central heating on by then."

"Friday and Saturday?" asked Radnor, noncommittally.

"Full guards, I guess. As many as Lord Hagbourne will sub for. The race-going crowds make cat-and-mouse impossible."

"Right," said Radnor, decisively. "That's it, then."

When Dolly, Chico and I had got as far as the door he said, "Sid, you wouldn't mind if I had another look at those photographs? Send Jones-boy down with them if you're not needing them."

"Sure," I agreed. "I've pored over them till I know them by heart. I bet you'll spot something at once that I've missed."

"It often works that way," he said, nodding.

The three of us went back to the Racing Section, and via the switchboard I traced Jones-boy, who happened to be in Missing Persons. While he was on his way down I flipped through the packet of photographs yet again. The share transfers, the summary with the list of bank accounts, the letters from Bolt, the ten-pound notes, and the two sheets of dates, initials and figures from the very bottom of the attaché case. It had been clear all along that these last were lists either of receipts or expenditures, but by now I was certain they were the latter. A certain W.L.B. had received regular sums of fifty pounds a month for twelve months, and the last date for W.L.B. was four days before William Leslie Brinton, clerk of Dunstable Racecourse, had taken the quickest way out. Six hundred pounds and a threat; the price of a man's soul.

Most of the other initials meant nothing to me, except the last one, J.R.S., which looked as if they could be the tanker driver's. The first entry for J.R.S., for one hundred pounds, was dated the day before the tanker overturned at Seabury, the day before Kraye went to Aynsford for the weekend.

In the next line, the last of the whole list, a further sum of one hundred and fifty pounds was entered against J.R.S. The date of this was that of the following Tuesday, three days after I had taken the photographs. Smith had packed up and vanished from his job and his digs on that Tuesday.

Constantly recurring among the other varying initials were two Christian names, Leo and Fred. Each of these was on the regular payroll, it seemed. Either Leo or Fred, I guessed, had been the big man who had visited and frightened Mervyn Brinton. Either Leo or Fred was the "big chap" who had sent Andrews with a gun to Cromwell Road.

I had a score to settle with either Leo or Fred.

Jones-boy came in for the photographs. I tapped them together back into their box and gave them to him.

"Where, you snotty-nosed little coot, is our coffee?" said Chico rudely. We had been downstairs when Jones-boy did his rounds.

"Coots are bald," observed Dolly coyly, eyeing Jones-boy's luxuriant locks.

Jones-boy unprintably told Chico where he could find his coffee.

Chico advanced a step, saying, "You remind me of the people sitting on the walls of Jerusalem." He had been raised in a church orphanage, after all.

Jones-boy also knew the more basic bits of Isaiah. He said callously, "You did it on the doorstep of Barnes cop shop, I believe."

Chico furiously lashed out a fist to Jones-boy's head. Jones-boy jumped back, laughed insultingly, and the box he was holding flew high out of his hand, opening as it went.

"Stop it you two, damn you," shouted Dolly, as the big photographs floated down onto her desk and onto the floor.

"Babes in the wood," remarked Jones-boy, in great good humor from having got the best of the slinging match. He helped Dolly and me pick up the photographs, shuffled them back into the box in no sort of order, and departed grinning.

"Chico," said Dolly severely, "you ought to know better."

"The bossy-mother routine bores me sick," said Chico violently.

Dolly bit her lip and looked away. Chico stared at me defiantly, knowing very well he had started the row and was in the wrong.

"As one bastard to another," I said mildly, "pipe down."

Not being able to think of a sufficiently withering reply fast enough Chico merely scowled and walked out of the room. The show was over. The office returned to normal. Typewriters clattered, someone used the tape recorder, someone else the telephone. Dolly sighed and began to draw up her list for Seabury. I sat and thought about Leo. Or Fred. Unproductively.

After a while I ambled upstairs to Bona Fides, where the usual amount of telephone shouting filled the air. George, deep in a mysterious conversation about moth balls, saw me and shook his head. Jack Copeland, freshly attired in a patchily faded green sleeveless pull-over, took time out between calls to say that they were sorry, but they'd made no progress with Kraye. He had, Jack said, very craftily covered his tracks about ten years back. They would keep digging, if I liked. I liked.

Up in Missing Persons Sammy said it was too soon for results on Smith.

When I judged that Mark Witney would be back in his house after exercising his second lot of horses, I rang him up and asked him to lend me his hack, a pensioned-off old steeplechaser of the first water.

"Sure," he said. "What for?"

I explained what for.

"You'd better have my horse box as well," he commented. "Suppose it pours with rain all night? Give you somewhere to keep dry, if you have the box."

"But won't you be needing it? The forecast says clear and dry anyway."

"I won't need it until Friday morning. I haven't any runners until Seabury. And only one there, I may say, in spite of it being so close. The owners just won't have it. I have to go all the way to Banbury on Saturday. Damn silly with another much better course on my doorstep."

"What are you running at Seabury?"

He told me, at great and uncomplimentary length, about a half-blind, utterly stupid, one-paced habitual non-jumper with which he proposed to win the novice chase. Knowing him, I guessed he would. We agreed that Chico and I should arrive at his place at about eight that evening, and I rang off.

After that I left the office, went across London by underground to Company House in the city, and asked for the files of Seabury Racecourse. In a numbered chair at a long table, surrounded by earnest men and women clerks poring over similar files and making copious notes, I studied the latest list of investors. Apart from Kraye and his various aliases, which I now recognized on sight from long familiarity with the share-transfer photographs, there were no large blocks in single ownership. No one else held more than 3 per cent of the total: and as 3 per cent meant that roughly £2500 was lying idle and not bringing in a penny in dividends, it was easy to see why no one wanted a larger holding.

Fotherton's name was not on the list. Although this was not conclusive, because a nominee name like "Mayday Investments" could be anyone at all, I was more or less satisfied that Seabury's clerk was not gambling on Seabury's death. All the big share movements during the past year had been to Kraye, and no one else.

A few of the small investors, holding two hundred or so shares each, were people I knew personally. I wrote down their names and addresses, intending to ask them to let me see Bolt's circular letter when it arrived. Slower than via Zanna Martin, but surer.

My mind shied away from Miss Martin. I'd had a bad night thinking about her. Her and Jenny, both.

Back in the office I found it was the tail end of the lunch hour, with nearly all the desks still empty. Chico alone was sitting behind his, biting his nails.

"If we're going to be up all night," I suggested, "we'd better take the afternoon off for sleep."

"No need."

"Every need. I'm not as young as you."

"Poor old grandpa." He grinned suddenly, apologizing for the morning. "I can't help it. That Jones-boy gets on my wick."

"Jones-boy can look after himself. It's Dolly—"

"It's not my bloody fault she can't have kids."

"She wants kids like you want a mother."

"But I don't—" he began indignantly.

"Your own," I said flatly. "Like you want your own mother to have kept you and loved you. Like mine did."

"You had every advantage, of course."

"That's right."

He laughed. "Funny thing is I like old Dolly, really. Except for the hen bit."

"Who wouldn't?" I said amicably. "You can sleep on my sofa."

He sighed. "You're going to be less easy than Dolly to work for, I can see that."

"Eh?"

"Don't kid yourself, mate. Sir, I mean." He was lightly ironic.

The other inmates of the office drifted back, including Dolly, with whom I fixed for Chico to have the afternoon free. She was cool to him and unforgiving, which I privately thought would do them both good.

She said, "The first official patrol will start on the racecourse tomorrow at six P.M. Shall I tell them to find you and report?"

"No," I said defiantly. "I don't know where I'll be."

"It had better be the usual then," she said. "They can report to the old man at his home number when they start the job, and again at six A.M. when they go off and the next lot take over."

"And they'll ring him in between if anything happens?" I said.

"Yes. As usual."

"It's as bad as being a doctor," I said smiling.

Dolly nodded, and half to herself she murmured, "You'll find out."

Chico and I walked round to my flat, pulled the curtains, and did our best to sleep. I didn't find it easy at two-thirty in the afternoon: it was the time for racing, not rest. It seemed to me that I had barely drifted off when the telephone rang. I looked at my watch on my way to answer it in the sitting room and found it was only ten to five. I had asked for a call at six.

It was not the telephone exchange, however, but Dolly.

"A message has come for you by hand, marked 'very urgent.' I thought you might want it before you go to Seabury."

"Who brought it?"

"A taxi driver."

"Shunt him round here, then."

"He's gone, I'm afraid."

"Who's the message from?"

"I've no idea. It's a plain brown envelope, the size we use for interim reports."

"Oh. All right, I'll come back."

Chico had drowsily propped himself up on one elbow on the sofa.

"Go to sleep again," I said. "I've got to go and see something in the office. Won't be long."

When I reached the Racing Section again I found that whatever had come for me, something else had gone. The shaky lemon-colored table. I was deskless again.

"Sammy said he was sorry," explained Dolly, "but he has a new assistant and nowhere to park him."

"I had things in the drawer," I complained. Shades of Sammy's lunch, I thought.

"They're here," Dolly said, pointing to a corner of her desk. "There was only the Brinton file, a half bottle of brandy, and some pills. Also I found this on the floor." She held out a flat, crackly cellophane packet.

"The negatives of those photographs are in here," I said, taking it from her. "They were in the box, though."

"Until Jones-boy dropped it."

"Oh yes." I put the packet of negatives inside the Brinton file and pinched a large rubber band from Dolly to snap round the outside.

"How about that mysterious very urgent message?" I asked.

Dolly silently and considerately slit open the envelope in question, drew out the single sheet of paper it contained and handed it to me. I unfolded it and stared at it in disbelief.

It was a circular, headed Charing, Street and King, Stockbrokers, dated with the following day's date, and it ran:

Dear Sir or Madam,

We have various clients wishing to purchase small parcels of shares in the following lists of minor companies. If you are considering selling your interests in any of these, we would be grateful if you would get in touch with us. We would assure you of a good fair price, based on today's quotation.

There followed a list of about thirty companies, of which I had heard of only one. Tucked in about three-quarters of the way down was Seabury Racecourse.

I turned the page over. Zanna Martin had written on the back in a hurried hand.

This is only going to Seabury shareholders. Not to anyone owning shares in the other companies. The leaflets came from the printers this morning, and are to be posted tomorrow. I hope it is what you want. I'm sorry about last night.

Z.M.

"What is it?" asked Dolly.

"A free pardon," I said lightheartedly, slipping the circular inside the Brinton file along with the negatives. "Also confirmation that Ellis Bolt is not on the side of the angels."

"You're a nut," she said. "And take these things off my desk. I haven't room for them."

I put the pills and brandy in my pocket and picked up the Brinton file.

"Is that better?"

"Thank you, yes."

"So long, then, my love. See you on Friday."

On the walk back to the flat I decided suddenly to go and see Miss Martin. I went straight down to the garage for my car without going up and waking Chico again, and made my way eastward to the city for the second time that day. The rush-hour traffic was so bad that I was afraid I would miss her, but in fact she was ten minutes late leaving the office and I caught her up just before she reached the underground station.

"Miss Martin," I called. "Would you like a lift home?"

She turned round in surprise.

"Mr. Halley!"

"Hop in."

She hopped. That is to say, she opened the door, picked up the Brinton file which was lying on the passenger seat, sat down, tidily folded her coat over her knees, and pulled the door shut again. The bad side of her face was toward me, and she was very conscious of it. The scarf and the hair were gently pulled forward.

I took a pound and a ten-shilling note out of my pocket and gave them to her. She took them smiling.

"The taxi man told our switchboard girl you gave him that for bringing the leaflet. Thank you very much." I swung out through the traffic and headed for Finchley.

She answered obliquely. "That wretched chicken is still in the oven, stone cold. I just turned the gas out yesterday, after you'd gone."

"I wish I could stay this evening instead," I said, "but I've got a job on for the agency."

"Another time," she said tranquilly. "Another time, perhaps. I understand that you couldn't tell me at first who you worked for, because you didn't know whether I was an . . . er, an accomplice of Mr. Bolt's, and afterwards you didn't tell me for fear of what actually happened, that I would be upset. So that's that."

"You are generous."

"Realistic, even if a bit late."

We went a little way in silence. Then I asked, "What would happen to the shares Kraye owns if it were proved he was sabotaging the company? If he were convicted, I mean. Would his shares be confiscated, or would he still own them when he came out of jail?"

"I've never heard of anyone's shares being confiscated," she said, sounding interested. "But surely that's a long way in the future?"

"I wish I knew. It makes a good deal of difference to what I should do now."

"How do you mean?"

"Well . . . an easy way to stop Kraye buying too many more shares would be to tell the racing press and the financial press that a take-over is being attempted. The price would rocket. But Kraye already holds twenty-three per cent, and if the law couldn't take it away from him, he would either stick to that and vote for a sell-out, or if he got cold feet he could unload his shares at the higher price and still make a fat profit. Either way, he'd be sitting pretty financially, in jail or out. And either way Seabury would be built on."

"I suppose this sort of thing's happened before?"

"Take-overs, yes, several. But only one other case of sabotage. At Dunstable. Kraye again."

"Haven't any courses survived a take-over bid?"

"Only Sandown, publicly. I don't know of any others, but they may have managed it in secrecy."

"How did Sandown do it?"

"The local council did it for them. Stated loudly that planning permission would not be given for building. Of course the bid collapsed then."

"It looks as though the only hope for Seabury, in that case, is that the council there will act in this same way. I'd try a strong lobby, if I were you."

"You're quite a girl, Miss Martin," I said, smiling. "That's a very good idea. I'll go and dip a toe into the climate of opinion at the Town Hall."

She nodded approvingly. "No good lobbying against the grain. Much better to find out which way people are likely to move before you start pushing!"

Finchley came into sight. I said, "You do realize, Miss Martin, that if I am successful at my job, you will lose yours?"

She laughed. "Poor Mr. Bolt. He's not at all bad to work for. But don't worry about my job. It's easy for an experienced stockbroker's secretary to get a good one, I assure you."

I stopped at her gate, looking at my watch. "I'm afraid I can't come in. I'm already going to be a bit late."

She opened the door without ado and climbed out. "Thank you

for coming at all." She smiled, shut the door crisply, and waved me away.

I drove back to my flat as fast as I could, fuming slightly at the traffic. It wasn't until I switched off the engine down in the garage and leaned over to pick it up that I discovered the Brinton file wasn't there. And then remembered Miss Martin holding it on her lap during the journey, and me hustling her out of the car. Miss Martin still had Brinton's file. I hadn't time to go back for it, and I couldn't ring her up because I didn't know the name of the owner of the house she lived in. But surely, I reassured myself, surely the file would be safe enough where it was until Friday.

12

Chico and I sat huddled together for warmth in some gorse bushes and watched the sun rise over Seabury Racecourse. It had been a cold clear night with a tingle of naught degrees centigrade about it, and we were both shivering.

Behind us, among the bushes and out of sight, Revelation, onetime winner of the Cheltenham Gold Cup, was breakfasting on meager patches of grass. We could hear the scrunch when he bit down close to the roots, and the faint chink of the bridle as he ate. For some time Chico and I had been resisting the temptation to relieve him of his nice warm rug.

"They might try something now," said Chico hopefully. "First light, before anyone's up."

Nothing had moved in the night, we were certain of that. Every hour I had ridden Revelation at a careful walk round the whole of the track itself, and Chico had made a plimsoll-shod inspection of the stands at one with the shadows. There had been no one about. Not a sound but the stirring breeze, not a glimmer of light but from the stars and a waning moon.

Our present spot, chosen as the sky lightened and some concealment became necessary, lay at the furthest spot from the stands, at the bottom of the semicircle of track cut off by the road which ran across the course. Scattered bushes and scrub filled the space between the track and boundary fence, enough to shield us from all but closely prying eyes. Behind the boundary fence were the little back gardens of the first row of bungalows. The sun rose bright and yellow away to our left and the birds sang around us. It was half past seven.

"It's going to be a lovely day," said Chico.

At ten past nine there was some activity up by the stands and the tractor rolled onto the course pulling a trailer. I unshipped my race glasses, balanced them on my bent-up knees, and took a look. The trailer was loaded with what I guessed were hurdles, and was accompanied by three men on foot.

I handed the glasses to Chico without comment, and yawned.

"Lawful occasions," he remarked, bored.

We watched the tractor and trailer lumber slowly round the far end of the course, pause to unload, and return for a refill. On its second trip it came close enough for us to confirm that it was in fact the spare hurdles that were being dumped in position, four or five at each flight, ready to be used if any were splintered in the races. We watched for a while in silence. Then I said slowly, "Chico, I've been blind."

"Huh?"

"The tractor," I said. "The tractor. Under our noses all the time."

"So?"

"So the sulfuric acid tanker was pulled over by a tractor. No complicated lifting gear necessary. Just a couple of ropes or chains slung over the top of the tanker and fastened round the axles. Then you unscrew the hatches and stand well clear. Someone drives the tractor at full power up the course, over goes the tanker and out pours the juice. And Bob's your uncle!"

"Every racecourse has a tractor," said Chico thoughtfully.

"That's right."

"So no one would look twice at a tractor on a racecourse. Quite. No one would remark on any tracks it left. No one would mention seeing one on the road. So if you're right, and I'd say you certainly are, it wouldn't necessarily have been that tractor, the racecourse tractor, which was used."

"I'll bet it was, though." I told Chico about the photographed initials and payments. "Tomorrow I'll check the initials of all the workmen here from Ted Wilkins downwards against that list. Any one of them might have been paid just to leave the tractor on the course, lying handy. The tanker went over on the evening before the meeting, like today. The tractor would have been in use then too. Warm and full of fuel. Nothing easier. And afterwards, straight on up the racecourse, and out of sight."

"It was dusk," agreed Chico. "As long as no one came along the road in the minutes it took to unhitch the ropes or chains afterwards, they were clear. No traffic diversions, no detours, nothing."

We sat watching the tractor lumbering about, gloomily realizing we couldn't prove a word of it.

"We'll have to move," I said presently. "There's a hurdle just along there, about fifty yards away, where those wings are. They'll be down here over the road soon."

We adjourned with Revelation back to the horse box half a mile away down the road to the west and took the opportunity to eat our own breakfast. When we had finished Chico went back first, strolling along confidently in my jodhpurs, boots and polo-necked jersey, the complete horseman from head to foot. He had never actually sat on a horse in his life.

After a while I followed on Revelation. The men had brought the hurdles down into the semicircular piece of track and had laid them in place. They were now moving further away up the course, unloading the next lot. Unremarked, I rode back to the bushes and dismounted. Of Chico there was no sign for another half hour, and then he came whistling across from the road with his hands in his pockets.

When he reached me he said, "I had another look round the stands. Rotten security, here. No one asked me what I was doing. There are some women cleaning here and there, and some are working in the stable block, getting the lads' hostel ready, things like that. I said good morning to them, and they said good morning back." He was disgusted.

"Not much scope for saboteurs," I said morosely. "Cleaners in the stands and workmen on the course."

"Dusk tonight," nodded Chico. "That's the most likely time now."

The morning ticked slowly away. The sun rose to its low November zenith and shone straight into our eyes. I passed the time by taking a photograph of Revelation and another of Chico. He was fascinated by the tiny camera and said he couldn't wait to get one like it. Eventually I put it back into my breeches pocket, and shading my eyes against the sun took my hundredth look up the course.

Nothing. No men, no tractor. I looked at my watch. One o'clock. Lunch hour. More time passed.

Chico picked up the race glasses and swept the course.

"Be careful," I said idly. "Don't look at the sun with those. You'll hurt your eyes."

"Do me a favor."

I yawned, feeling the sleepless night catch up.

"There's a man on the course," he said. "One. Just walking."

He handed me the glasses and I took a look. He was right. One man was walking alone across the racecourse; not round the track but straight across the rough grass in the middle. He was too far away for his features to be distinguishable and in any case he was wearing a fawn duffel coat with the hood up. I shrugged and lowered the glasses. He looked harmless enough.

With nothing better to do we watched him reach the far side, duck under the rails, and move along until he was standing behind one of the fences with only his head and shoulders in our sight.

Chico remarked that he should have attended to nature in the gents' before he left the stands. I yawned again, smiling at the same time. The man went on standing behind the fence.

"What on earth is he doing?" said Chico, after about five minutes.

"He isn't doing anything," I said, watching through the glasses. "He's just standing there looking this way."

"Do you think he's spotted us?"

"No, he couldn't. He hasn't any binocs, and we are in the bushes."

Another five minutes passed in inactivity.

"He must be doing *something*," said Chico, exasperated.

"Well, he isn't," I said.

Chico took a turn with the glasses. "You can't see a damn thing against the sun," he complained. "We should have camped up the other end."

"In the car park?" I suggested mildly. "The road to the stables and the main gates runs along the other end. There isn't a scrap of cover."

"He's got a flag," said Chico suddenly. "Two flags. One in each hand. White on the left, orange on the right. He seems to be waving them alternately. He's just some silly nit of a racecourse attendant practicing calling up the ambulance and the vet." He was disappointed.

I watched the flags waving, first white, then orange, then white, then orange, with a gap of a second or two between each wave. It certainly wasn't any form of recognizable signaling: nothing like semaphore. They were, as Chico had said, quite simply the flags used after a fall in a race: white to summon the ambulance for the jockey, orange to get attention for a horse. He didn't keep it up very long. After about eight waves altogether he stopped, and in a moment or two began to walk back across the course to the stands.

"Now what," said Chico, "do you think all that was in aid of?"

He swept the glasses all round the whole racecourse yet again. "There isn't a soul about except him and us."

"He's probably been standing by a fence for months waiting for a chance to wave his flags, and no one has been injured anywhere near him. In the end, the temptation proved too much."

I stood up and stretched, went through the bushes to Revelation, undid the halter with which he was tethered to the bushes, unbuckled the surcingle and pulled off his rug.

"What are you doing?" said Chico.

"The same as the man with the flags. Succumbing to an intolerable temptation. Give me a leg up." He did what I asked, but hung on to the reins.

"You're mad. You said in the night that they might let you do it after this meeting, but they'd never agree to it before. Suppose you smash the fences?"

"Then I'll be in almighty trouble," I agreed. "But here I am on a super jumper looking at a heavenly course on a perfect day, with everyone away at lunch." I grinned. "Leave go."

Chico took his hand away. "It's not like you," he said doubtfully.

"Don't take it to heart," I said flippantly, and touched Revelation into a walk.

At this innocuous pace the horse and I went out onto the track and proceeded in the direction of the stands. Counterclockwise, the way the races were run. Still at a walk we reached the road and went across its uncovered Tarmac surface. On the far side of the road lay the enormous dark brown patch of tan, spread thick and firm where the burnt turf had been bulldozed away. Horses would have no difficulty in racing over it.

Once on the other side, on the turf again, Revelation broke into a trot. He knew where he was. Even with no crowds and no noise the fact of being on a familiar racecourse was exciting him. His ears were pricked, his step springy. At fourteen he had been already a year in retirement, but he moved beneath me like a four-year-old. He too, I guessed fancifully, was feeling the satanic tug of pleasure about to be illicitly snatched.

Chico was right, of course. I had no business at all to be riding on the course so soon before a meeting. It was indefensible. I ought to know better. I did know better. I eased Revelation gently into a canter.

There were three flights of hurdles and three fences more or less side-by-side up the straight, and the water jump beyond that. As I wasn't sure that Revelation would jump the fences in cold blood on his own (many horses won't), I set him at the hurdles.

Once he had seen these and guessed my intention I doubt if I could have stopped him, even if I'd wanted to. He fairly ate up the first flight and stretched out eagerly for the second. After that I gave him a choice, and of the two obstacles lying ahead, he opted for the fence. It didn't seem to bother him that he was on his own. They were excellent fences and he was a Gold Cup winner, born and bred for the job and being given an unexpected, much-missed treat. He flew the fence with all his former dash and skill.

As for me, my feelings were indescribable. I'd sat on a horse a few times since I'd given up racing, but never found an opportunity of doing more than riding out quietly at morning exercise with Mark's string. And here I was, back in my old place, doing again what I'd ached for in the two and a half years. I grinned with irrepressible joy and got Revelation to lengthen his stride for the water jump.

He took it with feet to spare. Perfect. There were no irate shouts from the stands on my right, and we swept away on round the top bend of the course, fast and free. Another fence at the end of the bend—Revelation floated it—and five more stretching away down the far side. It was at the third of these, the open ditch, that the man had been standing and waving the flags.

It's an undoubted fact that emotions pass from rider to horse, and Revelation was behaving with the same reckless exhilaration which gripped me, so after two spectacular leaps over the next two fences we both sped onward with arms open to fate. There ahead was the guard rail, the four-foot-wide open ditch and the four-foot-six fence rising on the far side of it. Revelation, knowing all about it, automatically put himself right to jump.

It came, the blinding flash in the eyes, as we soared into the air. White, dazzling, brain-shattering light, splintering the day into a million fragments and blotting out the world in a blaze as searing as the sun.

I felt Revelation falling beneath me and rolled instinctively, my eyes open and quite unable to see. Then there was the rough crash on the turf and the return of vision from light to blackness and up through gray to normal sight.

I was on my feet before Revelation, and I still had hold of the reins. He struggled up, bewildered and staggering, but apparently unhurt. I pulled him forward into an unwilling trot to make sure of his legs, and was relieved to find them whole and sound. It only remained to remount as quickly as possible, and this was infuriatingly difficult. With two hands I could have jumped up easily; as it was I scrambled untidily back into the saddle at the third attempt, having lost the reins altogether and bashed my stomach on the pommel of the saddle into the bargain. Revelation behaved very well, all things considered. He trotted only fifty yards or so in the wrong direction before I collected myself and the reins into a working position and turned him round. This time we by-passed the fence and all subsequent ones: I cantered him first down the side of the track, slowed to a trot to cross the road, and steered then not on round the bottom semicircle but off to the right, heading for where the boundary fence met the main London road.

Out of the corner of my eye I saw Chico running in my direction across the rough grass. I waved him toward me with a sweep of the arm and reined in and waited for him where our paths converged.

"I thought you said you could bloody well ride," he said, scarcely out of breath from the run.

"Yeah," I said. "I thought so once."

He looked at me sharply. "You fell off. I was watching. You fell off like a baby."

"If you were watching . . . the horse fell, if you don't mind. There's a distinction. Very important to jockeys."

"Nuts," he said. "You fell off."

"Come on," I said, walking Revelation toward the boundary fence. "There's something to find." I told Chico what. "In one of those bungalows, I should think. At a window or on the roof, or in a garden."

"Sods," said Chico forcefully. "The dirty sods."

I agreed with him.

It wasn't very difficult, because it had to be within a stretch of only a hundred yards or so. We went methodically along the boundary fence toward the London road, stopping to look carefully into every separate little garden, and at every separate little house. A fair number of inquisitive faces looked back.

Chico saw it first, propped into a high leafless branch of a tree growing well back in the second-to-last garden. Traffic whizzed along the London road only ten yards ahead, and Revelation showed signs of wanting to retreat.

"Look," said Chico, pointing upward.

I looked, fighting a mild battle against the horse. It was five feet high, three feet wide, and polished to a spotless brilliance. A mirror.

"Sods," said Chico again.

I nodded, dismounted, led Revelation back to where the traffic no longer fretted him, and tied the reins to the fence. Then Chico and I walked along to the London road and round into the road of bungalows. Napoleon Close, it said. Napoleon wasn't *that* close, I reflected, amused.

We rang the door of the second bungalow. A man and a woman both came to the door to open it, elderly, gentle, inoffensive and inquiring.

I came straight to the point, courteously. "Do you know you have a mirror in your tree?"

"Don't be silly," said the woman, smiling as at an idiot. She had flat wavy gray hair and was wearing a sloppy black cardigan over a brown wool dress. No color sense, I thought.

"You'd better take a look," I suggested.

"It's not a mirror, you know," said the husband, puzzled. "It's a placard. One of those advertisement things."

"That's right," said his wife contrapuntally. "A placard."

"We agreed to lend our tree—"

"For a small sum, really . . . only our pension—"

"A man put up the framework—"

"He said he would be back soon with the poster—"

"A religious one, I believe. A good cause—"

"We wouldn't have done it otherwise—"

Chico interrupted. "I wouldn't have thought it was a good place for a poster. Your tree stands further back than the others. It isn't conspicuous."

"I did think—" began the man doubtfully, shuffling in his checked, woolly bedroom slippers.

"But if he was willing to pay rent for your particular tree, you didn't want to put him off," I finished. "An extra quid or two isn't something you want to pass on next door."

They wouldn't have put it so bluntly, but they didn't demur.

"Come and look," I said.

They followed me round along the narrow path beside their bungalow wall and into their own back garden. The tree stood halfway to the racecourse boundary fence, the sun slanting down through the leafless branches. We could see the wooden back of the mirror, and the ropes which fastened it to the tree trunk. The man and his wife walked round to the front, and their puzzlement increased.

"He said it was for a poster," repeated the man.

"Well," I said as matter-of-factly as I could, "I expect it is for a poster, as he said. But at the moment, you see, it is a mirror. And it's pointing straight out over the racecourse; and you know how mirrors reflect the sunlight? We just thought it might not be too safe, you know, if anyone got dazzled, so we wondered if you would mind us moving it?"

"Why, goodness," agreed the woman, looking with more awareness at our riding clothes, "no one could see the racing with light shining in their eyes."

"Quite. So would you mind if we turned the mirror round a bit?"

"I can't see that it would hurt, Dad," she said doubtfully.

He made a nondescript assenting movement with his hand, and Chico asked how the mirror had been put up in the tree in the first place. The man had brought a ladder with him, they said, and no, they hadn't one themselves. Chico shrugged, placed me beside the tree, put one foot on my thigh, one on my shoulder, and was up in the bare branches like a squirrel. The elderly couple's mouths sagged open.

"How long ago?" I asked. "When did the man put up the mirror?"

"This morning," said the woman, getting over the shock. "He came back just now, too, with another rope or something. That's when he said he'd be back with the poster."

So the mirror had been hauled up into the tree while Chico and I had been obliviously sitting in the bushes, and adjusted later when the sun was at the right angle in the sky. At two o'clock. The time, the next day, of the third race, the handicap steeplechase. Some handicap, I thought, a smash of light in the eyes.

White flag: a little bit to the left. Orange flag: a little bit to the right. No flag: dead on target.

Come back tomorrow afternoon and clap a religious poster over the glass as soon as the damage was done, so that even the most thorough search wouldn't reveal a mirror. Just another jinx on Seabury Racecourse. Dead horses, crushed and trampled jockeys. A jinx. Send my horses somewhere else, Mr. Witney, something always goes wrong at Seabury.

I was way out in one respect. The religious poster was not due to be put in place the following day.

13

"I think," I said gently to the elderly couple, "that it might be better if you went indoors. We will explain to the man who is coming what we are doing to his mirror."

Dad glanced up the path toward the road, put his arm protectively round his wife's woolly shoulders, and said gratefully, "Er . . . yes . . . yes."

They shuffled rapidly through the back door into the bungalow just as a large man carrying an aluminum folding ladder and a large rolled-up paper came barging through their front gate. There had been the squeak of his large, plain, dark blue van stopping, the hollow crunch of the handbrake being forcibly applied, the slam of the door and the scrape of the ladder being unloaded. Chico in the tree crouched quite still, watching.

I was standing with my back to the sun, but it fell full on the big man's face when he came into the garden. It wasn't the sort of face one would naturally associate with religious posters. He was a cross between a heavyweight wrestler and Mount Vesuvius. Craggy, brutally strong and not far off erupting.

He came straight toward me across the grass, dropped the ladder beside him, and said inquiringly, "What goes on?"

"The mirror," I said, "comes down."

His eyes narrowed in sudden awareness and his body stiffened. "There's a poster going over it," he began quite reasonably, lifting the paper roll. Then with a rush the lava burst out, the paper flew wide, and the muscles bunched into action.

It wasn't much of a fight. He started out to hit my face, changed his mind, and ploughed both fists in below the belt. It was quite a long way down for him. Doubling over in pain onto the lawn, I picked up the ladder, and gave him a swinging swipe behind the knees.

The ground shook with the impact. He fell on his side, his coat swinging open. I lunged forward, snatching at the pistol showing in the holster beside his ribs. It came loose, but he brushed me aside with an arm like a telegraph pole. I fell, sprawling. He rolled over into a crouch, picked up the gun from the grass and sneered down into my face. Then he stood up like a released spring and on the way with force and deliberation booted his toecap into my navel. He also clicked back the catch on his gun.

Up in the tree Chico yelled. The big man turned and took three steps toward him, seeing him for the first time. With a choice of targets, he favored the one still in a state to resist. The hand with the pistol pointed at Chico.

"Leo," I shouted. Nothing happened. I tried again.

"Fred!"

The big man turned his head a fraction back to me and Chico jumped down onto him from ten feet up.

The gun went off with a double crash and again the day flew apart in shining splintering fragments. I sat on the ground with my knees bent up, groaning quietly, cursing fluently, and getting on with my business.

Drawn by the noise, the inhabitants of the bungalows down the line came out into their back gardens and looked in astonishment over the fences. The elderly couple stood palely at their window, their mouths again open. The big man had too big an audience now for murder.

Chico was overmatched for size and nearly equaled in skill. He and the big man threw each other round a bit while I crept doubled up along the path into the front garden as far as the gate, but the battle was a foregone conclusion, bar the retreat.

He came alone, crashing up the path, saw me hanging on to the gate and half raised the gun. But there were people in the road now, and more people peering out of opposite windows. In scorching fury he whipped at my head with the barrel, and I avoided it by letting go of the gate and collapsing on the ground again. Behind the gate, with the bars nice and comfortingly between me and his boot.

He crunched across the pavement, slammed into the van, cut his cogs to ribbons and disappeared out onto the London road in a cloud of dust.

Chico came down the garden path staggering, with blood sloshing out of a cut eyebrow. He looked anxious and shaken.

"I thought you said you could bloody well fight," I mocked him.

He came to a halt beside me on his knees. "Blast you." He put his fingers to his forehead and winced at the result.

I grinned at him.

"You were running away," he said.

"Naturally."

"What have you got here?" He took the little camera out of my hand. "Don't tell me," he said, his face splitting into an unholy smile. "Don't tell me."

"It's what we came for, after all."

"How many?"

"Four of him. Two of the van."

"Sid, you slay me, you really do."

"Well," I said, "I feel sick." I rolled over and retched what was left of my breakfast onto the roots of the privet hedge. There wasn't any blood. I felt a lot better.

"I'll go and get the horse box," said Chico, "and pick you up."

"You'll do nothing of the sort," I said, wiping my mouth on a handkerchief. "We're going back into the garden. I want that bullet."

"It's halfway to Seabury," he protested, borrowing my handkerchief to mop the blood off his eyebrow.

"What will you bet?" I said. I used the gate again to get up, and after a moment or two was fairly straight. We presented a couple of reassuring grins to the audience, and retraced our way down the path into the back garden.

The mirror lay in sparkling pointed fragments all over the lawn.

"Pop up the tree and see if the bullet is there, in the wood. It smashed the mirror. It might be stuck up there. If not, we'll have to comb the grass."

Chico went up the aluminum ladder that time.

"Of all the luck," he called. "It's here." I watched him take a penknife out of his pocket and carefully cut away at a section just off-center of the backboard of the ex-mirror. He came down and held the little misshapen lump out to me on the palm of his hand. I put it carefully away in the small waist pocket of my breeches.

The elderly couple had emerged like tortoises from their bungalow. They were scared and puzzled, understandably. Chico offered to cut down the remains of the mirror, and did, but we left them to clear up the resulting firewood.

As an afterthought, however, Chico went across the garden and retrieved the poster from a soggy winter rosebed. He unrolled it and showed it to us, laughing.

BLESSED ARE THE MEEK, FOR THEY SHALL INHERIT THE EARTH.

"One of them," said Chico, "has a sense of humor."

Much against his wishes, we returned to our observation post in the scrubby gorse.

"Haven't you had enough?" he said crossly.

"The patrols don't get here till six," I reminded him. "And you yourself said that dusk would be the likely time for them to try something."

"But they've already done it."

"There's nothing to stop them from rigging up more than one booby trap," I pointed out. "Especially as that mirror thing wouldn't have been one hundred per cent reliable, even if we hadn't spotted it. It depended on the sun. Good weather forecast, I know, but weather forecasts are as reliable as a perished hot-water bottle. A passing cloud would have wrecked it. I would think they have something else in mind."

"Cheerful," he said resignedly. He led Revelation away along the road to stow him in the horse box, and was gone a long time.

When he came back he sat down beside me and said, "I went all round the stables. No one stopped me or asked what I was doing. Don't they have *any* security here? The cleaners have all gone home, but there's a woman cooking in the canteen. She said I was too early, to come back at half past six. There wasn't anyone about in the stands block except an old geezer with snuffles mucking about with the boiler."

The sun was lower in the sky and the November afternoon grew colder. We shivered a little and huddled inside our jerseys.

Chico said, "You guessed about the mirror before you set off round the course."

"It was a possibility, that's all."

"You could have ridden along the boundary fence, looking into the gardens like we did afterwards, instead of haring off over all those jumps."

I grinned faintly. "Yes. As I told you, I was giving in to temptation."

"Screwy. You must have known you'd fall."

"Of course I didn't. The mirror mightn't have worked very effectively. Anyway, it's better to test a theory in a practical way. And I just wanted to ride round there. I had a good excuse if I were hauled up for it. So I went. And it was grand. So shut up."

He laughed. "All right." Restlessly he stood up again and said he would make another tour. While he was gone I watched the racecourse with and without the binoculars, but not a thing moved on it.

He came back quietly and dropped down beside me.

"As before," he said.

"Nothing here, either."

He looked at me sideways. "Do you feel as bad as you look?"

"I shouldn't be surprised," I said. "Do you?"

He tenderly touched the area round his cut eyebrow. "Worse. Much worse. Soggy bad luck, him slugging away at your belly like that."

"He did it on purpose," I said idly, "and it was very informative."

"Huh?"

"It showed he knew who I was. He wouldn't have needed to have attacked us like that if we'd just been people come over from the racecourse to see if we could shift the mirror. But when he spoke to me he recognized me, and he knew I wouldn't be put off by any poster eyewash. And his sort don't mildly back down and retreat without paying you off for getting in their way. He just hit where he knew it would have most effect. I actually saw him think it."

"But how did he know?"

"It was he who sent Andrews to the office," I said. "He was the man Mervyn Brinton described: big, going a bit bald, freckles on the back of his hands, cockney accent. He was strong-arming Brinton, and he sent Andrews to get the letter that was supposed to be in the office. Well, Andrews knew me, and I knew him. He must have gone back and told our big friend Fred that he had shot me in the stomach. My death wasn't reported in the papers, so Fred knew I was still alive and would put the finger on Andrews at once. Andrews wasn't exactly a good risk to Fred, just a silly spiv with no sense, so Fred, I guess, marched him straight off to Epping Forest and left him for the birds. Who did a fair job, I'll give them that."

"Do you think," said Chico slowly, "that the gun Fred had today . . . is that why you wanted the bullet?"

I nodded. "That's right. I tried for the gun too, but no dice. If I'm going on with this sort of work, pal, you'll have to teach me a spot of judo."

He looked down doubtfully. "With that hand?"

"Invent a new sport," I said. "One-armed combat."

"I'll take you to the club," he said, smiling. "There's an old Jap there who'll find a way if anyone can."

"Good."

Up at the far end of the racecourse a horse box turned in off the main road and trundled along toward the stables. The first of the next day's runners had apparently arrived.

Chico went to have a look.

I sat on in fading daylight, watching nothing happen, hugging myself against the cold and the reawakened grinding ache in my gut, and thinking evil thoughts about Fred. Not Leo. Fred.

There were four of them, I thought. Kraye, Bolt, Fred and Leo.

I had met Kraye: he knew me only as Sid, a despised hanger-on in the home of a retired admiral he had met at his club and had spent a weekend with.

I had met Bolt: he knew me as John Halley, a shop assistant wanting to invest a gift from an aunt.

I had met Fred: he knew my whole name, and that I worked for the agency, and that I had turned up at Seabury.

I did not know if I had met Leo. But Leo might know *me*. If he had anything to do with racing, he definitely did.

It would be all right, I thought, as long as they did not connect all the Halleys and Sids too soon. But there was my wretched hand, which Kraye had pulled out of my pocket, which Fred could have seen in the garden, and which Leo, whoever he was, might have noticed almost anywhere in the last six days, thanks to my promise to Miss Martin. Miss Martin, who worked for Bolt. A proper merry-go-round, I thought wryly.

Chico materialized out of the dusk. "It was Ping Pong, running in the first tomorrow. All aboveboard," he said. "And nothing doing anywhere, stands or course. We might as well go."

It was well after five. I agreed, and got up stiffly.

"That Fred," said Chico, casually giving me a hand, "I've been thinking. I've seen him before, I'm certain. At race meetings. He's not a regular. Doesn't work for a bookie, or anything like that. But he's about. Cheap rings, mostly."

"Let's hope he doesn't burrow," I said.

"I don't see why he should," he said seriously. "He can't possibly think you'd connect him with Andrews, or with Kraye. All you caught him doing was fixing a poster in a tree. If I were him, I'd be sleeping easy."

"I called him Fred," I said.

"Oh," said Chico glumly. "So you did."

We reached the road and started along it toward the horse box.

"Fred must be the one who does all the jobs," said Chico. "Digs the false drains, sets fire to stables, and drives tractors to pull over tankers. He's big enough for anything."

"He didn't wave the flags. He was up the tree at the time."

"Um. Yes. Who did?"

"Not Bolt," I said. "It wasn't fat enough for Bolt, even in a duffel coat. Possibly Kraye. More likely Leo, whoever he is."

"One of the workmen, or the foreman. Yes. Well, that makes two of them for overturning tankers and so on."

"It would be easier for two," I agreed.

Chico drove the horse box back to Mark's, and then, to his obvious delight, my Merc back to London.

14

Chief Inspector Cornish was pleased but trying to hide it.

"I suppose you can chalk it up to your agency," he said as if it were debatable.

"He walked slap into us, to be fair."

"And slap out again," he said dryly.

I grimaced. "You haven't met him."

"You want to leave that sort to us," he said automatically.

"Where were you, then?"

"That's a point," he admitted, smiling.

He picked up the matchbox again and looked at the bullet. "Little beauty. Good clear markings. Pity he has a revolver, though, and not an automatic. It would have been nice to have had cartridge cases as well."

"You're greedy," I said.

He looked at the aluminum ladder standing against his wall, and at the poster on his desk, and at the rush-job photographs. Two clear prints of the van showing its number plates and four of Fred in action against Chico. Not exactly posed portraits, those, but four different, characteristic and recognizable angles taken in full sunlight.

"With all this lot to go on, we'll trace him before he draws breath."

"Fine," I said. And the sooner Fred was immobilized the better, I thought. Before he did any more damage to Seabury. "You'll need a tiger net to catch him. He's a very tough baby, and he knows judo. And unless he has the sense to throw it away, he'll still have that gun."

"I'll remember," he said. "And thanks." We shook hands amicably as I left.

It was results day at Radnor's, too. As soon as I got back Dolly said Jack Copeland wanted me up in Bona Fides. I made the journey.

Jack gleamed at me over the half-moons, pleased with his department. "George's got him. Kraye. He'll tell you."

I went over to George's desk. George was fairly smirking but after he'd talked for two minutes, I allowed he'd earned it.

"On the off-chance," he said, "I borrowed a bit of smooth quartz Kraye recently handled in the Geology Museum and got Sammy to do the prints on it. Two or three different sets of fingers came out, so we photographed the lot. None of them were on the British files, but I've given them the run-around with the odd pal in Interpol and so on, just in case. And brother, have we hit pay dirt or have we."

"We have?" I prompted, grinning.

"And how. Your friend Kraye is in the ex-con library of the state of New York."

"What for?"

"Assault."

"Of a girl?" I asked.

George raised his eyebrows. "A girl's father. Kraye had beaten the girl, apparently with her permission. She didn't complain. But her father saw the bruises and raised the roof. He said he'd get Kraye on a rape charge, though it seems the girl had been perfectly willing on that count too. But it looked bad for Kraye, so he picked up a chair and smashed it over the father's head and scampered. They caught him boarding a plane for South America and hauled him back. The father's brain was damaged. There are long medical details, but what it all boils down to is that he couldn't coordinate properly afterwards. Kraye got off on the rape charge, but served four years for attacking the father.

"Three years after that he turned up in England with some money and a new name, and soon acquired a wife. The one who divorced him for cruelty. Nice chap."

"Yes indeed," I said. "What was his real name?"

"Wilbur Potter," said George sardonically. "And you'll never guess. He was a geologist by profession. He worked for a construction firm, surveying. Always moving about. Character assessment: slick, a pusher, a good talker. Cut a few corners, always had more money than his salary, threw his weight about, but nothing indictable. The assault on the father was his first brush with the law. He was thirty-four at that time."

"Messy," I said. "The whole thing."

"Very," George agreed.

"But sex violence and fraudulent take-overs aren't much related," I complained.

"You might as well say it is impossible to have boils and cancer at the same time. Something drastically wrong with the constitution, and two separate symptoms."

"I'll take your word for it," I said.

Sammy up in Missing Persons had done more than photograph Kraye's fingerprints, he had almost found Smith.

"Intersouth rang us this morning," he purred. "Smith gave them as a reference. He's applied for a driving job in Birmingham."

"Good," I said.

"We should have his address by this afternoon."

Downstairs in Racing I reached for Dolly's telephone and got through to Charing, Street and King.

"Mr. Bolt's secretary speaking," said the quiet voice.

"Is Mr. Bolt in?" I asked.

"I'm afraid not . . . er, who is that speaking, please?"

"Did you find you had a file of mine?"

"Oh. . . ." She laughed. "Yes, I picked it up in your car. I'm so sorry."

"Do you have it with you?"

"No," she said, "I didn't bring it here. I thought it might be better not to risk Mr. Bolt seeing it, as it's got Hunt Radnor Associates printed on the outside along with a red sticker saying 'Ex Records, care of Sid Halley.'"

"Yes, it would have been a disaster," I agreed with feeling.

"I left it at home. Do you want it in a hurry?"

"No, not really. As long as it's safe, that's the main thing. How would it be if I came over to fetch it the day after tomorrow—Sunday morning? We could go for a drive, perhaps, and have some lunch."

There was a tiny pause. Then she said strongly, "Yes, please. Yes."

"Have the leaflets gone out?" I asked.

"They went yesterday."

"See you on Sunday, Miss Martin."

I put down Dolly's telephone to find her looking at me quizzically. I was again squatting on the corner of her desk, the girl from the typing pool having in my absence reclaimed her chair.

"The mouse got away again, I understand," she said.

"Some mouse."

Chico came into the office. The cut on his eyebrow looked red and sore, and all the side of his face showed grayish bruising.

"Two of you," said Dolly disgustedly, "and he knocked you about like kids."

Chico took this a lot better than if she had fussed maternally over his injury.

"It took more than two Lilliputians to peg down Gulliver," he said with good humor. (They had a large library in the children's orphanage.)

"But only one David to slay Goliath."

Chico made a face at her, and I laughed.

"And how are our collywobbles today?" he asked me ironically.

"Better than your looks."

"You know why Sid's best friends won't tell him?" said Chico.

"Why?" said Dolly, seriously.

"He suffers from halley-tosis."

"Oh God," said Dolly. "Take him away, someone. Take him away. I can't stand it."

On the ground floor I sat in a padded maroon armchair in Radnor's drawing-room office and listened to him saying there were no out-of-the-ordinary reports from the patrols at Seabury.

"Fison has just been on the telephone. Everything is normal for a race day, he says. The public will start arriving very shortly. He and Thom walked all round the course just now with Captain Oxon for a thorough check. There's nothing wrong with it, that they can see."

There might be something wrong with it that they couldn't see. I was uneasy.

"I might stay down there tonight, if I can find a room," I said.

"If you do, give me a ring again at home, during the evening."

"Sure." I had disturbed his dinner, the day before, to tell him about Fred and the mirror.

"Could I have those photographs back, if you've finished with them?" I asked. "I want to check that list of initials against the racecourse workmen at Seabury."

"I'm sorry, Sid, I haven't got them."

"Are they back upstairs?"

"No, no, they aren't here at all. Lord Hagbourne has them."

"But why?" I sat up straight, disturbed.

"He came here yesterday afternoon. I'd say on balance he is almost down on our side of the fence. I didn't get the usual caution about expenses, which is a good sign. Anyway, what he wanted was to see the proofs you told him we held which show it is Kraye who is buying the shares. Photographs of share transfer certificates. He knew about them. He said you'd told him."

"Yes, I did."

"He wanted to see them. That was reasonable, and I didn't want to risk tipping him back into indecision, so I showed them to him. He asked me very courteously if he could take them to show them to the Seabury executive. They held a meeting this morning, I believe. He thought they might be roused to some effective action if they could see for themselves how big Kraye's holding is."

"What about the other photographs? The others that were in the box."

"He took them all. They were all jumbled up, and he was in a hurry. He said he'd sort them out himself later."

"He took them to Seabury?" I said uneasily.

"That's right. For the executive meeting this morning." He looked at his watch. "The meeting must be on at this moment, I should think. If you want them you can ask him for them as soon as you get there. He should have finished with them by then."

"I wish you hadn't let him take them," I said.

"It can't do any harm. Even if he lost them we'd still have the negatives. You could get another print done tomorrow, of your list."

The negatives, did he but know it, were inaccessibly tucked into a mislaid file in Finchley. I didn't confess. Instead I said, unconvinced, "All right. I suppose it won't matter. I'll get on down there, then."

I packed an overnight bag in the flat. The sun was pouring in through the windows, making the blues and greens and blond wood furniture look warm and friendly. After two years the place was at last beginning to feel like home. A home without Jenny. Happiness without Jenny. Both were possible, it seemed. I certainly felt more myself than at any time since she left.

The sun was still shining, too, at Seabury. But not on a very large crowd. The poor quality of the racing was so obvious as to be pathetic: and it was in order that such a rotten gaggle of weedy quadrupeds could stumble and scratch their way round to the winning post, I reflected philosophically, that I had tried to pit my inadequate wits against Lord Hagbourne, Captain Oxon, the Seabury executive, Kraye, Bolt, Fred, Leo, old Uncle Tom Cobley and all.

There were no mishaps all day. The horses raced nonchalantly over the tan patch at their speedy crawl, and no light flashed in their eyes as they knocked hell out of the fences on the far side. Round One to Chico and me.

As the fine weather put everyone in a good mood, a shred of Seabury's former vitality temporarily returned to the place: enough, anyway, for people to notice the dinginess of the stands and remark that it was time something was done about it. If they felt like that, I thought, a revival shouldn't be impossible.

The Senior Steward listened attentively while I passed on Miss Martin's suggestion that Seabury council should be canvassed, and surprisingly said that he would see it was promptly done.

In spite of these small headways, however, my spine wouldn't stop tingling. Lord Hagbourne didn't have the photographs.

"They are only mislaid, Sid," he said soothingly. "Don't make such a fuss. They'll turn up."

He had put them down on the table round which the meeting had been held, he said. After the official business was over, he had chatted, standing up. When he turned back to pick up the box, it was no longer there. The whole table had been cleared. The ashtrays were being emptied. The table was required for lunch. A white cloth was being spread over it.

What, I asked, had been the verdict of the meeting, anyway? Er, um, it appeared the whole subject had been shelved for a week or two: no urgency was felt. Shares changed hands slowly, very slowly. But they had agreed that Hunt Radnor could carry on for a bit.

I hesitated to go barging into the executive's private room just to look for a packet of photographs, so I asked the caterers instead. They hadn't seen it, they said, rushing round me. I tracked down the man and woman who had cleared the table after the meeting and laid it for lunch.

Any amount of doodling on bits of paper, said the waitress, but no box of photographs, and excuse me love, they're waiting for these sandwiches. She agreed to look for it, looked, and came back shaking her head. It wasn't there, as far as she could see. It was quite big, I said despairingly.

I asked Mr. Fotherton, clerk of the course; I asked Captain Oxon; I asked the secretary and anyone else I could think of who had been at the meeting. None of them knew where the photographs were. All of them, busy with their racing jobs, said much the same as Lord Hagbourne.

"Don't worry, Sid, they're bound to turn up."

But they didn't.

I stayed on the racecourse until after the security patrols changed over at six o'clock. The in-comers were the same men who had been on watch the night before, four experienced and sensible ex-policemen, all middle-aged. They entrenched themselves comfortably in the press room, which had windows facing back and front, effective central heating, and four telephones; better headquarters than usual on their night jobs, they said.

Between the last race (three thirty) and six o'clock, apart from hunting without success for the photographs and driving Lord Hagbourne round to Napoleon Close for a horrified firsthand look at the smashed-up mirror, I persuaded Captain Oxon to accompany me on a thorough nook-and-cranny checkup of all the racecourse buildings.

He came willingly enough, his stiffness of earlier in the week having been thawed, I supposed, by the comparative success of the day; but we found nothing and no one that shouldn't have been there.

I drove into Seabury and booked into the Seafront Hotel, where I had often stayed in the past. It was only half full. Formerly, on racing nights, it had been crammed. Over a brandy in the bar the manager lamented with me the state of trade.

"Race meetings used to give us a boost every three weeks nearly all the winter. Now hardly anyone comes, and I hear they didn't even ask for the January fixtures this year. I tell you, I'd like to see that place blooming again, we need it."

"Ah," I said. "Then write to the Town Council and say so."

"That wouldn't help," he said gloomily.

"You never know. It might. Do write."

"All right, Sid. Just to please you then. For old time's sake. Let's have another brandy on the house."

I had an early dinner with him and his wife and afterward went for a walk along the seashore. The night was dry and cold and the onshore breeze smelled of seaweed. The banked pebbles scrunched into trickling hollows under my shoes and the winter sand was as hard-packed as rock. Thinking about Kraye and his machinations, I had strolled quite a long way eastward, away from the racecourse, before I remembered I had said I would ring Radnor at his home during the evening.

There was nothing much to tell him. I didn't hurry, and it was nearly ten o'clock when I got back to Seabury. The modernizations didn't yet run to telephones in all the bedrooms at the hotel, so I used the kiosk outside on the promenade, because I came to it first.

It wasn't Radnor who answered, but Chico, and I knew at once from his voice that things had gone terribly wrong.

"Sid . . . ," he said. "Sid . . . look, pal, I don't know how to tell you. You'll have to have it straight. We've been trying to reach you all the evening."

"What . . . ?" I swallowed.

"Someone bombed your flat."

"*Bombed,*" I said stupidly.

"A plastic bomb. It blew the street wall right out. All the flats round yours were badly damaged, but yours . . . well, there's nothing there. Just a big hole with disgusting black sort of cobwebs. That's how they knew it was a plastic bomb. The sort the French terrorists used. . . . Sid, are you there?"

"Yes."

"I'm sorry, pal. I'm sorry. But that's not all. They've done it to the office, too." His voice was anguished. "It went off in the Racing Section. But the whole place is cracked open. It's . . . it's bloody ghastly."

"Chico."

"I know. I know. The old man's round there now, just staring at it. He made me stay here because you said you'd ring, and in case the racecourse patrols want anything. No one was badly hurt, that's the only good thing. Half a dozen people were bruised and cut, at your flats. And the office was empty, of course."

"What time . . . ?"

"The bomb in the office went off about an hour and a half ago, and the one in your flat was just after seven. The old man and I were round there with the police when they got the radio message about the office. The police seem to think that whoever did it was looking for something. The people who live underneath you heard someone moving about upstairs for about two hours shortly before the bomb went off, but they just thought it was you making more noise than usual. And it seems everything in your flat was moved into one pile in the sitting room and the bomb put in the middle. The police said it meant that they hadn't found what they were looking for and were destroying everything in case they had missed it."

"Everything . . . ," I said.

"Not a thing was left. God, Sid, I wish I didn't have to . . . but there it is. Nothing that was there exists any more."

The letters from Jenny when she loved me. The only photograph of my mother and father. The trophies I won racing. The lot. I leaned numbly against the wall.

"Sid, are you still there?"

"Yes."

"It was the same thing at the office. People across the road saw lights on and someone moving about inside, and just thought we were working late. The old man said we must assume they still haven't found what they were looking for. He wants to know what it is."

"I don't know," I said.

"You must."

"No. I don't."

"You can think on the way back."

"I'm not coming back, not tonight. It can't do any good. I think I'll go out to the racecourse again, just to make sure nothing happens there too."

"All right. I'll tell him when he calls. He said he'd be over in Cromwell Road all night, very likely."

We rang off and I went out of the kiosk into the cold night air. I thought that Radnor was right. It was important to know what it was that the bomb merchants had been looking for. I leaned against the outside of the box, thinking about it. Deliberately not thinking about the flat, the place that had begun to be home, and all that was lost. That had happened before in one way or another. The night my mother died, for instance. And I'd ridden my first winner the next day.

To look for something, you had to know it existed. If you used bombs, destroying it was more important than finding it. What did I have, which I hadn't had long (or they would have searched before) which Kraye wanted obliterated.

There was the bullet which Fred had accidentally fired into the mirror. They wouldn't find that, because it was somewhere in a police ballistics laboratory. And if they had thought I had it, they would have looked for it the night before.

There was the leaflet Bolt had sent out, but there were hundreds of those, and he wouldn't want the one I had, even if he knew I had it.

There was the letter Mervyn Brinton had rewritten for me, but if it were that it meant . . .

I went back into the telephone box, obtained Mervyn Brinton's number from directory inquiries, and rang him up.

To my relief, he answered.

"You are all right, Mr. Brinton?"

"Yes, yes. What's the matter?"

"You haven't had a call from the big man? You haven't told anyone about my visit to you, or that you know your brother's letter by heart?"

He sounded scared. "No. Nothing's happened. I wouldn't tell anyone. I never would."

"Fine," I reassured him. "That's just fine. I was only checking."

So it was not Brinton's letter.

The photographs, I thought. They had been in the office all the time until Radnor gave them to Lord Hagbourne yesterday afternoon. No one outside the agency, except Lord Hagbourne and Charles, had known they existed. Not until this morning, when Lord

Hagbourne took them to the Seabury executive meeting, and lost them.

Suppose they weren't lost, but stolen. By someone who knew Kraye, and thought he ought to have them. From the dates on all those documents Kraye would know exactly when the photographs had been taken. And where.

My scalp contracted. I must assume, I thought, that they had now connected all the Halleys and Sids.

Suddenly fearful, I rang up Aynsford. Charles himself answered, calm and sensible.

"Charles, please will you do as I ask, at once, and no questions? Grab Mrs. Cross, go out and get in the car and drive well away from the house, and ring me back at Seabury 79411. Got that? Seabury 79411."

"Yes," he said, and put down the telephone. Thank God, I thought, for a naval training. There might not be much time. The office bomb had exploded an hour and a half ago; London to Aynsford took the same.

Ten minutes later the phone began to ring. I picked up the receiver.

"They say you're in a call box," Charles said.

"That's right. Are you?"

"No, the pub down in the village. Now, what's it all about?"

I told him about the bombs, which horrified him, and about the missing photographs.

"I can't think what else it can be that they are looking for."

"But you said that they've got them."

"The negatives," I said.

"Oh. Yes. And they weren't in your flat or the office?"

"No. Quite by chance, they weren't."

"And you think if they're still looking, that they'll come to Aynsford?"

"If they are desperate enough, they might. They might think you would know where I keep things. . . . And even have a go at making you tell them. I asked you to come out quick because I didn't want to risk it. If they are going to Aynsford, they could be there at any minute now. It's horribly likely they'll think of you. They'll know I took the photos in your house."

"From the dates. Yes. Right. I'll get on to the local police and ask for a guard on the house at once."

"Charles, one of them . . . well, if he's the one with the bombs, you'll need a squad." I described Fred and his van, together with its number.

"Right." He was still calm. "Why would the photographs be so important to them? Enough to use bombs, I mean?"

"I wish I knew."

"Take care."

"Yes," I said.

I did take care. Instead of going back into the hotel, I rang it up.

The manager said, "Sid, where on earth are you, people have been trying to reach you all the evening—the police too."

"Yes, Joe, I know. It's all right. I've talked to the police in London. Now, has anyone actually called at the hotel, wanting me?"

"There's someone up in your room, yes. Your father-in-law, Admiral Roland."

"Oh really? Does he look like an admiral?"

"I suppose so." He sounded puzzled.

"A gentleman?"

"Yes, of course." Not Fred, then.

"Well, he isn't my father-in-law. I've just been talking to him in his house in Oxfordshire. You collect a couple of helpers and chuck my visitor out."

I put down the receiver sighing. A man up in my room meant everything I'd brought to Seabury would very likely be ripped to bits. That left me with just the clothes I stood in, and the car—

I fairly sprinted round to where I'd left the car. It was locked, silent and safe. No damage. I patted it thankfully, climbed in, and drove out to the racecourse.

15

All was quiet as I drove through the gates and switched off the engine. There were lights on—one shining through the windows of the press room, one outside the weighing-room door, one high up somewhere on the stands. The shadows in between were densely black. It was a clear night with no moon.

I walked across to the press room, to see if the security patrols had anything to report.

They hadn't.

All four of them were fast asleep.

Furious, I shook the nearest. His head lolled like a pendulum, but he didn't wake up. He was sitting slumped into his chair. One of them had his arms on the table and his head on his arms. One of them sat on the floor, his head on the seat of the chair and his arms hanging down. The fourth lay flat, face downward, near the opposite wall.

The stupid fools, I thought. Ex-policemen letting themselves be put to sleep like infants. It shouldn't have been possible. One of their first rules in guard work was to take their own food and drink with them and not accept sweets from strangers.

I stepped round their heavily breathing hulks and picked up one of the press telephones to ring Chico for reinforcements. The line was dead. I tried the three other instruments. No contact with the exchange on any of them.

I would have to go back and ring up from Seabury, I thought. I went out of the press room but in the light pouring out before I shut the door I saw a dim figure walking toward me from the direction of the gate.

"Who's that?" he called imperiously, and I recognized his voice. Captain Oxon.

"It's only me, Sid Halley," I shouted back. "Come and look at this."

He came on into the light, and I stood aside for him to go into the press room.

"Good heavens. What on earth's the matter with them?"

"Sleeping pills. And the telephones don't work. You haven't seen anyone about who ought not to be?"

"No. I haven't heard anything except your car. I came down to see who had come."

"How many lads are there staying overnight in the hostel? Could we use some of those to patrol the place while I ring the agency to get some more men?"

"I should think they'd love it," he said. "There are about five of them. They shouldn't be in bed yet. We'll go over and ask them, and you can use the telephone from my flat to ring your agency."

"Thanks," I said. "That's fine."

I looked round the room at the sleeping men. "I think perhaps I ought to see if any of them tried to write a message. I won't be a minute."

He waited patiently while I looked under the head and folded arms of the man at the table and under the man on the floor, and all round the one with his head on the chair seat, but none of them had even reached for a pencil. Shrugging, I looked at the remains of their supper, lying on the table. Half-eaten sandwiches on grease-proof paper, dregs of coffee in cups and thermos flasks, a couple of apple cores, some cheese sections and empty wrappings, and an un-peeled banana.

"Found anything?" asked Oxon.

I shook my head in disgust. "Not a thing. They'll have terrible headaches when they wake up, and serve them right."

"I can understand you being annoyed . . ." he began. But I was no longer really listening. Over the back of the chair occupied by the first man I had shaken was hanging a brown leather binoculars case, and on its lid were stamped three black initials: L.E.O. Leo. Leo.

"Something the matter?" asked Oxon.

"No." I smiled at him and touched the strap of the binoculars. "Are these yours?"

"Yes. The men asked if I could lend them some. For the dawn, they said."

"It was very kind of you."

"Oh. Nothing." He shrugged, moving out into the night. "You'd better make that phone call first. We'll tackle the boys afterwards."

I had absolutely no intention of walking into his flat.

"Right," I said.

We went out of the door, and I closed it behind us.

A familiar voice, loaded with satisfaction, spoke from barely a yard away. "So you've got him, Oxon. Good."

"He was coming—" began Oxon in anxious anger, knowing that "got him" was an exaggeration.

"No," I said, and turned and ran for the car.

When I was barely ten yards from it someone turned the lights on. The headlights of my own car. I stopped dead.

Behind me one of the men shouted and I heard their feet running. I wasn't directly in the beam, but silhouetted against it. I swerved off to the right, toward the gate. Three steps in that direction, and the headlights of a car turning in through it caught me straight in the eyes.

There were more shouts, much closer, from Oxon and Kraye. I turned, half-dazzled, and saw them closing in. Behind me now the incoming car rolled forward. And the engine of my Mercedes purred separately into life.

I ran for the dark. The two cars, moving, caught me again in their beams. Kraye and Oxon ran where they pointed.

I was driven across and back toward the stands like a coursed hare, the two cars behind inexorably finding me with their lights and the two men running with reaching, clutching hands. Like a nightmare game of "He," I thought wildly, with more than a child's forfeit if I were caught.

Across the parade ring, across the flat Tarmac stretch beyond it, under the rails of the unsaddling enclosure and along the inside of the door into the trainers' luncheon room and through there without stopping into the kitchen. And weaving on from there out into the members' lunch room, round acres of tables with upturned chairs, through the far door into the wide passage which cut like a tunnel along the length of the huge building, across it, and up a steep stone staircase emerging halfway up the open steps of the stands, and sideways along them as far as I could go. The pursuit was left behind.

I sank down, sitting with one leg bent to run, in the black shadow where the low wooden wall dividing the members from Tattersalls cut straight down the steps separating the stands into two halves. On top of the wall wire netting stretched up too high to climb: high enough to keep out the poorer customers from gate crashing the expensive ring.

At the bottom of the steps lay a large expanse of members' lawn stretching to another metal mesh fence, chest high, and beyond that lay the whole open expanse of racecourse. Half a mile across it to the London road to Seabury, with yet another barrier, the boundary fence, to negotiate.

It was too far. I knew I couldn't do it. Perhaps once, with two hands for vaulting, with a stomach which didn't already feel as if it were tearing into more holes inside. But not now. Although I always mended fast, it was only two weeks since I had found the short walk to Andrews' body very nearly too much; and Fred's well-aimed attentions on the previous day had not been therapeutic.

Looking at it straight: if I ran, it had to be successful. My kingdom for a horse, I thought. Any reasonable cowboy would have had Revelation hitched to the rails, ready for a flying leap into the saddle and a thundering exit. I had a hundred-and-fifty-mile-an-hour little white Mercedes, and someone else was sitting in it.

To run and be caught running would achieve nothing and be utterly pointless.

Which left just one alternative.

The security patrol hadn't been drugged for nothing. Kraye wasn't at Seabury for his health. Some more damage had been planned for this night. Might already have been done. There was just a chance, if I stayed to look, that I could find out what it was. Before they found *me*. Naturally.

If I ever have any children, they won't get me playing hide-and-seek.

Half an hour later the grim game was still in progress. My own car was now parked on the racecourse side of the stands, on the Tarmac in Tattersalls where the bookies had called that afternoon.

It was facing the stands with the headlights full on. Every inch of the steps was lit by them, and since the car had arrived there I had not been able to use that side of the building at all.

The other car was similarly parked inside the racecourse gates, its headlights shining on the fronts of the weighing room, bars, dining rooms, cloakrooms and offices.

Presuming that each car still had a watching occupant, that left only Kraye and Oxon, as far as I could guess, to run me to ground; but I became gradually sure that there were three, not two, after me in the stands. Perhaps one of the cars was empty. But which? And it would be unlikely to have its ignition key in place.

Bit by bit I covered the whole enormous block. I didn't know what I was looking for, that was the trouble. It could have been anything from a plastic bomb downward, but if past form was anything to go by, it was something which could appear accidental. Bad luck. A jinx. Open, recognizable sabotage would be ruinous to the scheme.

Without a surveyor, I couldn't be certain that part of the steps would not collapse the following day under the weight of the crowd, but I could find no trace of any structural damage at all, and there hadn't been much time: only five or six hours since the day's meeting ended.

There were no large quantities of food in the kitchen: the caterers appeared to have removed what had been left over ready to bring fresh the next day. A large double-doored refrigerator was securely locked. I discounted the possibility that Kraye could have thought of large-scale food poisoning.

All the fire extinguishers seemed to be in their places, and there were no smoldering cigarette ends near tins of paraffin. Nothing capable of spontaneous combustion. I suppose another fire, so soon after the stables, might have been too suspicious.

I went cautiously, carefully, every nerve-racking step of the way, peering round corners, easing through doors, fearing that at any moment one of them would pounce on me from behind.

They knew I was still there, because everywhere they went they turned on lights, and everywhere I went I turned them off. Opening a door from a lighted room onto a dark passage made one far too easy to spot; I turned off the lights before I opened any door. There had been three lights in the passage itself, but I had broken them early on with a broom from the kitchen.

kicking bottle tops in all directions, I was safe in the opening of a little offshoot lobby to the kitchen.

The kitchens were safest for me because there were so many good hiding places and so many exits, but it wasn't much good staying there because I had searched them already.

I was fast running out of places to look. The boiler room had given me an anxious two minutes as its only secondary exit was into a dead-end storeroom containing, as far as I could see, nothing but vast oil tanks with pipes and gauges. They were hard against the walls: nowhere to hide. The boiler itself roared, keeping the central heating going all through the night.

The weighing room was even worse, because it was big and entirely without cover. It contained nothing it shouldn't have, just tables, chairs, notices pinned on the walls, and the weighing machine itself. Beyond, in the changing room, there were rows of pegs with saddles on, the warm, banked-up coke stove in the corner, and a big wicker basket full of helmets, boots, weight cloths and other equipment left by the valets overnight. A dirty cup and saucer. A copy of *Playboy*. Several raincoats. Racing colors on pegs. A row of washed breeches hanging up to dry. It was the most occupied-looking part of the stands, the place I felt most at home in and where I wanted to go to ground, like an ostrich in familiar sand. But on the far side of the changing room lay only the washroom, another dead end.

Opening out of the weighing room on the opposite side to the changing room was the Stewards' room, where in the past like all jockeys I'd been involved in cases of objections-to-the-winner. It was a bare room: large table, chairs round it, sporting pictures, small threadbare carpet. A few of the Stewards' personal possessions lay scattered about, but there was no concealment.

A few doors here and there were locked, in spite of Oxon's having left the keys in his flat. As usual I had the bunch of lock pickers in my pocket; and with shortened breath I spent several sticky minutes letting myself into one well-secured room off the members' bar. It proved to be the liquor store: crates of spirits, champagne, wine and beer. Beer from floor to ceiling, and a porter's trolley to transport it. It was a temptation to lock myself in there, and wait for the caterers to rescue me in the morning. This was one door that Oxon would not expect to find me on the far side of.

In the liquor store I might be safe. On the other hand, if I were safe the racecourse might not be. Reluctantly I left again; but I didn't waste time locking up. With the pursuit out of sight, I risked a look upstairs. It was warm and quiet, and all the lights were on. I left them on, figuring that if the watchers in the cars saw them go out they would know too accurately where I was.

Nothing seemed to be wrong. On one side of a central lobby there was the big room where the executive held their meetings and ate their lunch. On the other side there was a sort of drawing room furnished with light armchairs, with two cloakrooms leading off it at the back. At the front, through double glass doors, it led out into a box high up on the stands. The private box for directors and distinguished guests, with a superb view over the whole course.

I didn't go out there. Sabotage in the royal box wouldn't stop a race meeting to which royalty weren't going anyway. And besides, whoever was in my car would see me opening the door.

Retreating, I went back, right through the dining-board room and out into the service room on the far side. There I found a storeroom with plates, glass and cutlery, and in the storeroom also a second exit. A small service lift down to the kitchens. It worked with ropes, like the one in the office on Cromwell Road . . . like the office lift *had* worked, before the bomb.

Kraye and Oxon were down in the kitchen. Their angry voices floated up the shaft, mingled with a softer murmuring voice which seemed to be arguing with them. Since for once I knew where they all were, I returned with some boldness to the ground again. But I was worried. There seemed to be nothing at all going wrong in the main building. If they were organizing yet more damage somewhere out on the course itself, I didn't see how I could stop it.

While I was still dithering rather aimlessly along the passage the kitchen door opened, the light flooded on, and I could hear Kraye still talking. I dived yet again for the nearest door and put it between myself and them.

I was, I discovered, in the ladies' room, where I hadn't been before, and there was no second way out. Only a double row of cubicles, all with the doors open, a range of washbasins, mirrors on the walls with a wide shelf beneath them, a few chairs, and a counter like that in the bar. Behind the counter there was a rail with coat hangers.

There were heavy steps in the passage outside. I slid instantly behind and under the counter and pressed myself into a corner. The door opened.

"He won't be in here," said Kraye. "The light's still on."

"I looked in here not five minutes ago, anyway," agreed Oxon.

The door closed behind them and their footsteps went away. I began to breathe again and my thudding heart slowed down. But for a couple of seconds only. Across the room, someone coughed.

I froze. I couldn't believe it. The room had been empty when I came in, I was certain. And neither Kraye nor Oxon had stayed. . . . I stretched my ears, tense, horrified.

Another cough. A soft, single cough.

Try as I could I could hear nothing else. No breathing. No rustle of clothing, no movement. It didn't make sense. If someone in the room knew I was behind the counter, why didn't they do something about it? If they didn't know, why were they so unnaturally quiet?

In the end, taking a conscious grip on my nerves, I slowly stood up.

The room was empty.

Almost immediately there was another cough. Now that my ears were no longer obstructed by the counter, I got a clearer idea of its direction. I swung toward it. There was no one there.

I walked across the room and stared down at the washbasin. Water was trickling from one of the taps. Even while I looked at it the tap coughed. Almost laughing with relief I stretched out my hand and turned it off.

The metal was very hot. Surprised, I turned the water on again. It came spluttering out of the tap, full of air bubbles and very hot indeed. Steaming. How stupid, I thought, turning it off again, to have the water so hot at this time of night. . . .

Christ, I thought. The boiler.

16

Kraye and Oxon's so-called methodical end-to-end search, which had just failed to find me in the ladies', was proceeding from the members' end of the stands toward Tattersalls. The boiler, like myself, was in the part they had already put behind them. I switched out the ladies'-room lights, carefully eased into the passage, and via the kitchen, the members' dining room, the gentlemen's cloaks and another short strip of passage returned to the boiler room.

Although there was no door through, I knew that on the far side of the inside wall lay to the left the weighing room and to the right the changing room, with the dividing wall between. From both those rooms, when it was quiet, as it was that night, one could quite clearly hear the boiler's muffled roar.

The light that I had switched off was on again in the boiler room. I looked round. It all looked as normal as it had before, except . . . except that away to the right there was a very small pool of water on the floor.

Boilers. We had had a lesson on them at school. Sixteen or seventeen years ago, I thought hopelessly. But I remembered very well the way the master had begun the lesson.

"The first thing to learn about boilers," he said, "is that they explode."

He was an excellent teacher: the whole class of forty boys listened from then on with avid interest. But since then the only acquaintance I'd had with boilers was down in the basement of the flats, where I sometimes drank a cup of orange tea with the caretaker. A tough ex-naval stoker, he was, and a confirmed student of racing form. Mostly we'd talked about horses, but sometimes about his job.

There were strict regulations for boilers, he'd said, and regular official inspections every three months, and he was glad of it, working alongside them every day.

The first thing to learn about boilers is that they explode.

It's no good saying I wasn't frightened, because I was. If the boiler burst it wasn't simply going to make large new entrances into the weighing room and changing room, it was going to fill every cranny near it with scalding tornadoes of steam. Not a death I looked on with much favor.

I stood with my back against the door and tried desperately to remember that long-ago lesson, and to work out what was going wrong.

It was a big steam boiler. An enormous cylinder nine feet high and five feet in diameter. Thick steel, with dark red antirust paint peeling off. Fired at the bottom not by coke, which it had been built for, but by the more modern roaring jet of burning oil. If I opened the fire door I would feel the blast of its tremendous heat.

The body of the cylinder would be filled almost to the top with water. The flame boiled the water. The resulting steam went out of the top under its own fierce pressure in a pipe which—I followed it with my eye—led into a large yellow-painted round-ended cylinder slung horizontally near the ceiling. This tank looked rather like a zeppelin. It was, if I remembered right, a calorifier. Inside it, the steampipe ran in a spiral, like an immobile spring. The tank itself was supplied from the mains with the water which was to be heated, the water going to the central heating radiators, and to the hot taps in the kitchen, the cloakrooms and the jockeys' washrooms. The scorching heat from the spiral steampipe instantly passed into the water touching it, so that the cold water entering the calorifier was made very hot in the short time before it left at the other end.

The steam, however, losing its heat in the process, gradually condensed back into water. A pipe led down the wall from the calorifier into a much smaller tank, an ordinary square one, standing on the floor. From the bottom of this, yet another pipe tracked right back across the room and up near the boiler itself to a bulbous metal contraption just higher than my head. An electric pump. It finished the circuit by pumping the condensed water up from the tank on the floor and returning it to the boiler, to be boiled, steamed and condensed all over again. Round and round, continuously.

So far, so good. But if you interfered with the circuit so that the water didn't get back into the boiler, and at the same time kept the heat full on at the bottom, all the water inside the cylinder gradually turned to steam. Steam, which was strong enough to drive a liner, or pull a twelve-coach train, but could in this case only get out at all through a narrow, closely spiraled pipe.

This type of boiler, built not for driving an engine but only for heating water, wasn't constructed to withstand enormous pressures. It was a tossup, I thought, whether when all the water had gone the fast-expanding air and steam found a weak spot to break out of before the flames burned through the bottom. In either case, the boiler would blow up.

On the outside of the boiler there was a water gauge, a foot-long vertical glass tube held in brackets. The level of water in the tube indicated the level of water in the boiler. Near the top of the gauge a black line showed what the water level ought to be. Two thirds of the way down a broad red line obviously acted as a warning. The water in the gauge was higher than the red line by half an inch.

To put it mildly, I was relieved. The boiler wasn't bulging. The explosion lay in the future, which gave me more time to work out how to prevent it. As long as it would take Oxon and Kraye to decide on a repeat search, perhaps.

I could simply have turned out the flame, but Kraye and Oxon would notice that the noise had stopped, and merely light it again. Nothing would have been gained. On the other hand, I was sure that the flame was higher than it should have been at night, because the water in the ladies' tap was nearly boiling.

Gingerly I turned the adjusting wheel on the oil line. Half a turn. A full turn. The roaring seemed just as loud. Another turn, and that time there was a definite change. Half a turn more. It was perceptibly quieter. Slowly I inched the wheel around more, until quite suddenly the roar turned to a murmur. Too far. Hastily I reversed. At the point where the murmur was again a roar, I left it.

I looked consideringly at the square tank of condensed water on the floor. It was this, overflowing, which was making the pool of water; and it was overflowing because the contents were not being pumped back into the boiler. If they've broken the pump, I thought despairingly, I'm done. I didn't know the first thing about electric pumps.

Another sentence from that faraway school lesson floated usefully through my mind. *For safety's sake, every boiler must have two sources of water.*

I chewed my lower lip, watching the water trickle down the side of the tank onto the floor. Even in the few minutes I had been there the pool had spread. One source of water was obviously knocked out. Where and what was the other?

There were dozens of pipes in the boiler room; not only oil pipes and water pipes, but all the electric cables were installed inside tubes as well. There were about six separate pipes with stopcocks on them. It seemed to me that all the water for the entire building came in through the boiler room.

Two pipes, apparently rising mains, led from the floor up the wall and into the calorifier. Both had stopcocks, which I tested. Both were safely open. There was no rising main leading directly into the boiler.

By sheer luck I was half way round the huge cylinder looking for an inlet pipe when I saw the lever-type door handle move down. I leaped for the only vestige of cover, the space between the boiler and the wall. It was scorching hot there: pretty well unbearable.

Kraye had to raise his voice to make himself heard over the roaring flame.

"You're sure it's still safe?"

"Yes, I told you, it won't blow up for three hours yet. At least three hours."

"The water's running out already," Kraye objected.

"There's a lot in there." Oxon's voice came nearer. I could feel my heart thumping and hear the pulse in my ears. "The level's not down to the caution mark on the gauge yet," he said. "It won't blow for a long time after it goes below that."

"We've got to find Halley," Kraye said. "Got to." If Oxon moved another step he would see me. "I'll work from this end; you start again from the other. Look in every cupboard. The little rat has gone to ground somewhere."

Oxon didn't answer audibly. I had a sudden glimpse of his sleeve as he turned, and I shrank back into my hiding place.

Because of the noise of the boiler I couldn't hear them go away through the door, but eventually I had to risk that they had. The heat where I stood was too appalling. Moving out into the ordinarily hot air in the middle of the room was like diving into a cold bath. And Oxon and Kraye had gone.

I slipped off my jacket and wiped the sweat off my face with my shirt sleeves. Back to the problem: water supply.

The pump *looked* all right. There were no loose wires, and it had an undisturbed, slightly greasy, slightly dirty appearance. With luck, I thought, they hadn't damaged the pump, they'd blocked the pipe where it left the tank. I took off my tie and shirt as well, and put them with my jacket on the grimy floor.

The lid of the tank came off easily enough, and the water, when I tested it, proved to be no more than uncomfortably hot. I drank some in my cupped palm. The running and the heat had made me very thirsty, and although I would have preferred it iced, no water could have been purer, or more tasteless, though I was not inclined to be fussy on that point.

I stretched my arm down into the water, kneeling beside the tank. As it was only about two feet deep, I could touch the bottom quite easily, and almost at once my searching fingers found and gripped a loose object. I pulled it out.

It was a fine mesh filter, which should no doubt have been in place over the opening of the outlet pipe.

Convinced now that the pipe was blocked from this end, I reached down again into the water. I found the edge of the outlet, and felt carefully into it. I could reach no obstruction. Bending over further, so that my shoulder was half in the water, I put two fingers as far as they would go into the outlet. I could feel nothing solid, but there did seem to be a piece of string. It was difficult to get it between two fingers firmly enough to pull as hard as was necessary, but gradually with a series of little jerks I managed to move the plug backward into the tank.

It came away finally so suddenly that I nearly overbalanced. There was a burp from the outer pipe of the tank and on the other side of the room a sharp click from the pump.

I lifted my hand out of the water to see what had blocked the pipe, and stared in amazement. It was a large mouse. I had been pulling its tail.

Accidental sabotage, I thought. The same old pattern. However unlikely it was that a mouse should dive into a tank, find the filter conveniently out of place, and get stuck just inside the outlet pipe, one would have a hard job proving that it was impossible.

I carefully put the sodden little body out of sight in the small gap between the tank and the wall. With relief I noticed that the water level was already going down slightly, which meant that the pump was working properly and the boiler would soon be more or less back to normal.

I splashed some more water out of the tank to make a larger pool should Kraye or Oxon glance in again, and replaced the lid. Putting on my shirt and jacket I followed with my eyes the various pipes in and out of the boiler. The lagged steam exit pipe to the calorifier. The vast chimney flue for the hot gasses from the burning oil. The inlet pipe from the pump. The water gauge. The oil pipe. There had to be another water inlet somewhere, partly for safety, partly to keep the steam circuit topped up.

I found it in the end running alongside and behind the inlet pipe from the pump. It was a gravity feed from a stepped series of three small unobtrusive tanks fixed high on the wall. Filters, I reckoned, so that the main's water didn't carry its mineral salts into the boiler and fur it up. The filter tanks were fed by a pipe which branched off one of the rising mains and had its own stopcock.

Reaching up, I tried to turn it clockwise. It didn't move. The main's water was cut off. With satisfaction, I turned it on again.

Finally, with the boiler once more working exactly as it should, I took a look at the water gauge. The level had already risen to nearly halfway between the red and black marks. Hoping fervently Oxon wouldn't come back for another check on it, I went over to the door and switched off the light.

There was no one in the passage. I slipped through the door, and in the last three inches before shutting it behind me stretched my hand back and put the light on again. I didn't want Kraye knowing I'd been in there.

Keeping close to the wall, I walked softly down the passage toward the Tattersalls end. If I could get clear of the stands there were other buildings out that way to give cover. The barn, cloakrooms and tote buildings in the silver ring. Beyond these lay the finishing straight, the way down to the tan patch and the bisecting road. Along that, bungalows, people and telephones.

That was when my luck ran out.

17

I was barely two steps past the door of the Tattersalls bar when it opened and the lights blazed out onto my tiptoeing figure. In the two seconds it took Oxon to realize what he was seeing I was six running paces down toward the way out.

His shouts echoed in the passage mingled with others further back, and I still thought that if Kraye too were behind me I might have a chance. But when I was within ten steps of the end another figure appeared there, hurrying, called by the noise.

I skidded nearly to a stop, sliding on one of the scattered bottle tops, and crashed through the only possible door, into the same empty bar as before. I raced across the board floor, kicking bottle tops in all directions, but I never got to the far door. It opened before I reached it, and that was the end.

Doria Kraye stood there, maliciously triumphant. She was dressed theatrically in white slender trousers and a shiny short white jacket. Her dark hair fell smoothly, her face was as flawlessly beautiful as ever, and she held rock-steady in one elegantly long-fingered hand the little .22 automatic I had last seen in a chocolate box at the bottom of her dressing case.

"The end of the line, buddy boy," she said. "You stay just where you are."

I hesitated on the brink of trying to rush her.

"Don't risk it," she said. "I'm a splendid shot. I wouldn't miss. Do you want a kneecap smashed?"

There was little I wanted less. I turned round slowly. There were three men coming forward into the long room. Kraye, Oxon and Ellis

Bolt. All three of them looked as if they had long ago got tired of the chase and were going to take it out on the quarry.

"Will you walk," said Doria behind me, "or be dragged?"

I shrugged. "Walk."

All the same, Kraye couldn't keep his hands off me. When, following Doria's instructions, I walked past him to go back out through the passage he caught hold of my jacket at the back of my neck and kicked my legs. I kicked back, which wasn't too sensible, as I presently ended up on the floor. There was nothing like little metal bottle tops for giving you a feeling of falling on little metal bottle tops, I thought, with apologies to Michael Flanders and Donald Swan.

"Get up," said Kraye. Doria stood beside him, pointing at me with the gun.

I did as he said.

"Right," said Doria. "Now, walk down the passage and go into the weighing room. And Howard, for God's sake wait till we get there, or we'll lose him again. Walk, buddy boy. Walk straight down the middle of the passage. If you try anything, I'll shoot you in the leg."

I saw no reason not to believe her. I walked down the center of the passage with her too close behind for escape, and with the two men bringing up the rear.

"Stop a minute," said Kraye, outside the boiler room.

I stopped. I didn't look round.

Kraye opened the door and looked inside. The light spilled out, adding to that already coming from the other open doors along the way.

"Well?" said Oxon.

"There's more water on the floor." He sounded pleased, and shut the door without going in for a further look. Not all of my luck had departed, it seemed.

"Move," he said. I obeyed.

The weighing room was as big and bare as ever. I stopped in the middle of it and turned round. The four of them stood in a row, looking at me, and I didn't at all like what I read in their faces.

"Go and sit there," said Doria, pointing.

I went on across the floor and sat where she said, on the chair of the weighing machine. The pointer immediately swung round the clock face to show my weight. Nine stone seven. It was, I was remotely interested to see, exactly ten pounds less than when I had last raced. Bullets would solve any jockey's weight problem, I thought.

The four of them came closer. It was some relief to find that Fred wasn't among them, but only some. Kraye was emitting the same livid fury as he had twelve days ago at Aynsford. And then, I had merely mildly insulted his wife.

"Hold his arms," he said to Oxon. Oxon was one of those thin wiry men of seemingly limitless strength. He came round behind me, clamped his fingers round my elbows and pulled them back. With concentration Kraye hit me several times in the face.

"Now," he said. "Where are they?"

"What?" I said indistinctly.

"The negatives."

"What negatives?"

He hit me again and hurt his own hand. Shaking it out and rubbing his knuckles, he said, "You know what negatives. The films you took of my papers."

"Oh, those."

"Those." He hit me again, but less hard.

"In the office," I mumbled.

He tried a slap to save his knuckles. "Office," I said.

He tried with his left hand, but it was clumsy. After that he sucked his knuckles and kept his hands to himself.

Bolt spoke for the first time, in his consciously beautiful voice. "Fred wouldn't have missed them, especially as there was no reason for them to be concealed. He's too thorough."

If Fred wouldn't have missed them, the bombs had been pure spite. I licked the inside of a split lip and thought about what I would like to do to Fred.

"Where in the office?" said Kraye.

"Desk."

"Hit him," said Kraye. "My hand hurts."

Bolt had a go, but it wasn't his sort of thing.

"Try with this," said Doria, offering Bolt the gun, but it was luckily so small he couldn't hold it effectively.

Oxon let go of my elbows, came round to the front, and looked at my face.

"If he's decided not to tell you, you won't get it out of him like that," he said.

"I told you," I said.

"Why not?" said Bolt.

"You're hurting yourselves more than him. And if you want my opinion, you won't get anything out of him at all."

"Don't be silly," said Doria scornfully. "He's so small."

Oxon laughed without mirth.

"If Fred said so, the negatives weren't at his office," asserted Bolt again. "Nor in his flat. And he didn't bring them with him. Or at least, they weren't in his luggage at the hotel."

I looked at him sideways, out of an eye which was beginning to swell. And if I hadn't been so quick to have him flung out of my hotel room, I thought sourly, he wouldn't have driven in through the racecourse gate at exactly the wrong moment. But I couldn't have foreseen it, and it was too late to help.

"They weren't in his car either," said Doria. "But this was." She put her hand into her shining white pocket and brought out my baby camera. Kraye took it from her, opened the case, and saw what was inside. The veins in his neck and temples became congested with blood. In a paroxysm of fury he threw the little black toy across the room so that it hit the wall with a disintegrating crash.

"Sixteen millimeter," he said savagely. "Fred must have missed them."

Bolt said obstinately, "Fred would find a needle in a haystack. And those films wouldn't have been hidden."

"He might have them in his pocket," suggested Doria.

"Take your coat off," Kraye said. "Stand up."

I stood up, and the base plate of the weighing machine wobbled under my feet. Oxon pulled my coat down over the back of my shoulders, gave a tug to get the sleeves off, and passed the jacket to Kraye. His own hand he thrust into my trouser pocket. In the right one, under my tie, he found the bunch of lock pickers.

"Sit down," he said. I did so, exploring with the back of my hand some of the damage to my face. It could have been worse, I thought resignedly, much worse. I would be lucky if that were all.

"What are those?" said Doria curiously, taking the jingling collection from Oxon.

Kraye snatched them from her and slung them after the camera.

"Skeleton keys," he said furiously. "What he used to unlock my cases."

"I don't see how he could," said Doria, "with that . . . that . . . *claw*." She looked down where it lay on my lap.

A nice line in taunts, I thought, but a week too late. Thanks to Miss Martin, I was at last learning to live with the claw. I left it where it was.

"Doria," said Bolt calmly, "would you be kind enough to go over to the flat and wait for Fred to ring? He may already have found what we want at Aynsford."

I turned my head and found him looking straight at me, assessingly. There was a detachment in the eyes, an unmoved quality in the rounded features; and I began to wonder whether his stolid coolness might not in the end prove even more difficult to deal with than Kraye's rage.

"Aynsford," I repeated thickly. I looked at my watch. If Fred had really taken his bombs to Aynsford, he should by now be safely in the bag. One down, four to go. Five of them altogether, not four. I hadn't thought of Doria being an active equal colleague of the others. My mistake.

"I don't want to," said Doria, staying put.

Bolt shrugged. "It doesn't matter. I see that the negatives aren't at Aynsford, because the thought of Fred looking for them there doesn't worry Halley one little bit."

The thought of what Fred might be doing at Aynsford or to Charles himself didn't worry any of them either. But more than that I didn't like the way Bolt was reasoning. In the circumstances, a clear-thinking opponent was something I could well have done without.

"We must have them," said Kraye intensely. "We must. Or be certain beyond doubt that they were destroyed." To Oxon he said, "Hold his arms again."

"No," I said, shrinking back.

"Ah, that's better. Well?"

"They were in the office." My mouth felt stiff.

"Where?"

"In Mr. Radnor's desk, I think."

He stared at me, eyes narrowed, anger half under control, weighing up whether I were telling the truth or not. He certainly couldn't go to the office and make sure.

"Were," said Bolt suddenly.

"What?" asked Kraye, impatiently.

"Were," said Bolt. "Halley said were. The negatives *were* in the office. Now that's very interesting indeed, don't you think?"

Oxon said, "I don't see why."

Bolt came close to me and peered into my face. I didn't meet his eyes, and anything he could read from my bruised features he was welcome to.

"I think he knows about the bombs," he said finally.

"How?" said Doria.

"I should think he was told at the hotel. People in London must have been trying to contact him. Yes, I think we can take it for granted he knows about the bombs."

"What difference does that make?" said Oxon.

Kraye knew. "It means he thinks he is safe saying the negatives were in the office, because we can't prove they weren't."

"They were," I insisted, showing anxiety.

Bolt pursed his full moist lips. "Just how clever is Halley?" he said.

"He was a jockey," said Oxon flatly, as if that automatically meant an I.Q. of 70.

Bolt said, "But they took him on at Hunt Radnor's."

"I told you before," said Oxon patiently, "I asked various people about that. Radnor took him on as an advisor, but never gave him anything special to do, and if that doesn't show that he wasn't capable of much, I don't know what does. Everyone knows that his job is only a face-saver. It sounds all right, but it means nothing really. Jobs are quite often given in that way to top jockeys when they retire. No one expects them to *do* much, it's just their name that's useful for a while. When their news value has gone, they get the sack."

This all-too-true summing up of affairs depressed me almost as deeply as my immediate prospects.

"Howard?" said Bolt.

"I don't know," said Kraye slowly. "He doesn't strike me as being in the least clever. Very much the opposite. I agree he did take those photographs, but I think you are quite right in believing he doesn't know why we want them destroyed."

That, too, was shatteringly correct. As far as I had been able to see, the photographs proved nothing conclusively except that Kraye had been buying Seabury shares under various names with Bolt's help. Kraye and Bolt could not be prosecuted for that. Moreover the whole of Seabury executive had seen the photographs at the meeting that morning, so their contents were no secret.

"Doria?" Bolt said.

"He's a slimy, spying little creep, but if he was clever he wouldn't be sitting where he is."

You couldn't argue with that, either. It had been fairly certain all along that Kraye was getting help from somebody working at Seabury, but even after knowing about clerk of the course Brinton's unwilling collaboration at Dunstable, I had gone on assuming that the helper at Seabury was one of the laborers. I hadn't given more than a second's flicker of thought to Oxon, because it didn't seem reasonable that it should be him. In destroying the racecourse he was working himself out of a job, and good jobs for forty-year-old ex-army captains weren't plentiful enough to be lost lightly. As he certainly wasn't mentally affected like Brinton, he wasn't being blackmailed into doing it against his will. I had thought him silly and self-important, but not a rogue. As Doria said, had I been clever enough to suspect him, I wouldn't be sitting where I was.

Bolt went on discussing me as if I weren't there, and as if the decision they would come to would have ordinary everyday consequences.

He said, "You may all be right, but I don't think so, because since Halley has been on the scene everything's gone wrong. It was he who persuaded Hagbourne to get the course put right, and he who found the mirror as soon as it was up. I took him without question for what he said he was when he came to see me—a shop assistant. You two took him for a wretched little hanger-on of no account. All that, together with the fact that he opened your locked cases and took good clear photographs on a miniature camera, adds up to just one thing to me. Professionalism. Even the way he sits there saying nothing is professional. Amateurs call you names and try to impress you with how much they know. All he has said is that the negatives were in the office. I consider we ought to forget every previous impression we have of him and think of him only as coming from Hunt Radnor."

They thought about this for five seconds. Then Kraye said, "We'll have to make sure about the negatives."

Bolt nodded. If reason hadn't told me what Kraye meant, his wife's smile would have. My skin crawled.

"How?" she said interestedly.

Kraye inspected his grazed knuckles. "You won't beat it out of him," said Oxon. "Not like that. You haven't a hope."

"Why not?" said Bolt.

Instead of replying, Oxon turned to me. "How many races did you ride with broken bones?"

I didn't answer. I couldn't remember anyway.

"That's ridiculous," said Doria scornfully. "How could he?"

"A lot of them do," said Oxon. "And I'm sure he was no exception."

"Nonsense," said Kraye.

Oxon shook his head. "Collarbones, ribs, forearms, they'll ride with cracks in any of those if they can keep the owners and trainers from finding out."

Why couldn't he shut up, I thought savagely. He was making things much much worse; as if they weren't appalling enough already.

"You mean," said Doria with sickening pleasure, "that he can stand a great deal?"

"No," I said. "No." It sounded like the plea it was. "You can only ride with cracked bones if they don't hurt."

"They must hurt," said Bolt reasonably.

"No," I said. "Not always." It was true, but they didn't believe it.

"The negatives were in the office," I said despairingly. "In the office."

"He's scared," said Doria delightedly. And that too was true.

It struck a chord with Kraye. He remembered Aynsford. "We know where he's most easily hurt," he said. "That hand."

"No," I said in real horror.

They all smiled.

My whole body flushed with uncontrollable fear. Racing injuries were one thing: they were quick, one didn't expect them, and they were part of the job.

To sit and wait and know that a part of one's self which had already proved a burden was about to be hurt as much as ever was quite something else. Instinctively I put my arm up across my face to hide from them that I was afraid, but it must have been obvious.

Kraye laughed insultingly. "So there's your brave clever Mr. Halley for you. It won't take much to get the truth."

"What a pity," said Doria.

They left her standing in front of me holding the little pistol in an unswerving pink-nailed hand while they went out and rummaged for what they needed. I judged the distance to the door, which was all of thirty feet, and wondered whether the chance of a bullet on the way wasn't preferable to what was going to happen if I stayed where I was.

Doria watched my indecision with amusement.

"Just try it, buddy boy. Just try it."

I had read that to shoot accurately with an automatic pistol took a great deal of skill and practice. It was possible that all Doria had wanted was the power feeling of owning a gun and that she couldn't aim it. On the other hand she was holding it high and with a nearly straight arm, close to where she could see along the sights. On balance, I thought her claim to be a splendid shot had too much probability to be risked.

It was a pity Doria had such a vicious soul inside her beautiful body. She looked gay and dashing in her white Courrèges clothes, smiling a smile which seemed warm and friendly and was as safe as the yawn of a python. She was the perfect mate for Kraye, I thought. Fourth, fifth, sixth time lucky, he'd found a complete complement to himself. If Kraye could do it, perhaps one day I would too . . . but I didn't know if I would even see tomorrow.

I put the back of my hand up over my eyes. My whole face hurt, swollen and stiff, and I was developing a headache. I decided that if I ever got out of this I wouldn't try any more detecting. I had made a proper mess of it.

The men came back, Oxon from the Stewards' room lugging a wooden spoke-backed chair with arms, Kraye and Bolt from the changing room with the yard-long poker from the stove and the rope the wet breeches had been hung on to dry. There were still a couple of pegs clinging to it.

Oxon put the chair down a yard or two away and Doria waved the gun a fraction to indicate I should sit in it. I didn't move.

"God," she said disappointedly, "you really are a little worm, just like at Aynsford. Scared to a standstill."

"He isn't a shop assistant," said Bolt sharply. "And don't forget it."

I didn't look at him. But for him and his rejection of Charles's usefully feeble Halley image, I might not have been faced with quite the present situation.

Oxon punched me on the shoulder. "Move," he said.

I stood up wearily and stepped off the weighing machine. They stood close round me. Kraye thrust out a hand, twisted it into my shirt, and pushed me into the chair. He, Bolt and Oxon had a fine old time tying my arms and legs to the equivalent wooden ones with the washing line. Doria watched, fascinated.

I remembered her rather unusual pleasures.

"Like to change places?" I said tiredly.

It didn't make her angry. She smiled slowly, put her gun in a pocket, and leaned down and kissed me long and hard on the mouth. I loathed it. When at length she straightened up she had a smear of my blood on her lip. She wiped it off onto her hand, and thoughtfully licked it. She looked misty-eyed and languorous, as if she had had a profound sexual experience. It made me want to vomit.

"Now," said Kraye. "Where are they?" He didn't seem to mind his wife kissing me. He understood her, of course.

I looked at the way they had tied the rope tightly round and round my left forearm, leaving the wrist bare, palm downward. A hand, I thought. What good, anyway, was a hand that didn't work.

I looked at their faces, one by one. Doria, rapt. Oxon, faintly surprised. Kraye confident, flexing his muscles. And Bolt, calculating and suspicious. None of them within a mile of relenting.

"Where are they?" Kraye repeated, lifting his arm.

"In the office," I said helplessly.

He hit my wrist with the poker. I'd hoped he might at least try to be subtle, but instead he used all his strength and with that one first blow smashed the whole shooting match to smithereens. The poker broke through the skin. The bones cracked audibly like sticks.

I didn't scream only because I couldn't get enough breath to do it. Before that moment I would have said I knew everything there was to know about pain, but it seems one can always learn. Behind my shut eyes the world turned yellow and gray, like sun shining through mist, and every inch of my skin began to sweat. There had never been anything like it. It was too much, too much. And I couldn't manage any more.

"Where are they?" said Kraye again.

"Don't," I said. "Don't do it." I could hardly speak.

Doria sighed deeply.

I opened my eyes a slit, my head lolling weakly back, too heavy to hold up. Kraye was smiling, pleased with his efforts. Oxon looked sick.

"Well?" said Kraye.

I swallowed, hesitating still.

He put the tip of the pocker on my shattered bleeding wrist and gave a violent jerk. Among other things it felt like a fizzing electric shock, up my arm into my head and down to my toes. Sweat started sticking my shirt to my chest and my trousers to my legs.

"Don't," I said. "Don't." It was a croak, a capitulation, a prayer.

"Come on, then," said Kraye, and jolted the poker again.

I told them. I told them where to go.

18

They decided it should be Bolt who went to fetch the negatives.

"What is this place?" he said. He hadn't recognized the address.

"The home of . . . a . . . girl friend."

He dispassionately watched the sweat run in trickles down my face. My mouth was dry. I was very thirsty.

"Say . . . I sent you," I said, between jagged breaths. "I . . . asked her . . . to keep them safe. . . . They . . . are with . . . several other things. . . . The package . . . you want . . . has a name on it . . . a make of film . . . Jigoro . . . Kano."

"Jigoro Kano. Right," Bolt said briskly.

"Give me . . . ," I said, "some morphine."

Bolt laughed. "After all the trouble you've caused us? Even if I had any, I wouldn't. You can sit there and sweat it out."

I moaned. Bolt smiled in satisfaction and turned away.

"I'll ring you as soon as I have the negatives," he said to Kraye. "Then we can decide what to do with Halley. I'll give it some thought on the way up." From his tone he might have been discussing the disposal of a block of worthless stocks.

"Good," said Kraye. "We'll wait for your call over in the flat."

They began to walk toward the door. Oxon and Doria hung back, Doria because she couldn't tear her fascinated, dilated eyes away from watching me, and Oxon for more practical reasons.

"Are you just going to leave him here?" he asked in surprise.

"Yes. Why not?" said Kraye. "Come on, Doria darling. The best is over."

Unwillingly she followed him, and Oxon also.

"Some water," I said. "Please."

"No," said Kraye.

They filed past him out of the door. Just before he shut it he gave me a last look compounded of triumph, contempt and satisfied cruelty. Then he switched off all the lights and went away.

I heard the sound of a car starting up and driving off. Bolt was on his way. Outside the windows the night was black. Darkness folded round me like a fourth dimension. As the silence deepened I listened to the low hum of the boiler roaring safely on the far side of the wall. At least, I thought, I don't have to worry about that as well. Small, small consolation.

The back of the chair came only as high as my shoulders and gave no support to my head. I felt deathly tired. I couldn't bear to move: every muscle in my body seemed to have a private line direct to my left wrist, and merely flexing my right foot had me panting. I wanted to lie down flat. I wanted a long cold drink. I wanted to faint. I went on sitting in the chair, wide awake, with a head that ached and weighed a ton, and an arm which wasn't worth the trouble.

I thought about Bolt going to Zanna Martin's front door, and finding that his own secretary had been helping me. I wondered for the hundredth time what he would do about that: whether he would harm her. Poor Miss Martin, whom life had already hurt too much.

Not only her, I thought. In the same file was the letter Mervyn Brinton had written out for me. If Bolt should see that, Mervyn Brinton would be needing a bodyguard for life.

I thought about the people who had borne the beatings and brutalities of the Nazis and of the Japanese and had often died without betraying their secrets. I thought about the atrocities still going on throughout the world, and the ease with which man could break man. In Algeria, they said, unbelievable things had been done. Behind the Iron Curtain, brainwashing wasn't all. In African jails, who knew?

Too young for World War Two, safe in a tolerant society, I had had no thought that I should ever come to such a test. To suffer or to talk. The dilemma that stretched back to antiquity. Thanks to Kraye, I now knew what it was like at first hand. Thanks to Kraye, I didn't understand how anyone could keep silent unto death.

I thought: I wanted to ride round Seabury Racecourse again, and to go back into the weighing room, and to sit on the scales; and I've done all those things.

I thought: a fortnight ago I couldn't let go of the past. I was clinging to too many ruins, the ruins of my marriage and my racing career and my useless hand. They were gone for good now, all of them. There was nothing left to cling to. And every tangible memory of my life had blown away with a plastic bomb. I was rootless and homeless: and liberated.

What I refused to think about was what Kraye might still do during the next few hours.

Bolt had been gone for a good long time when at last Kraye came back. It had seemed half eternity to me, but even so I was in no hurry for it to end.

Kraye put the lights on. He and Doria stood just inside the doorway, staring across at me.

"You're sure there's time?" said Doria.

Kraye nodded, looking at his watch. "If we're quick."

"Don't you think we ought to wait until Ellis rings?" she said. "He might have thought of something better."

"He's late already," said Kraye impatiently. They had clearly been arguing for some time. "He should have rung by now. If we're going to do this, we can't wait any longer."

"All right," she shrugged. "I'll go and take a look."

"Be careful. Don't go in."

"No," she said. "Don't fuss."

They both came over to where I sat. Doria looked at me with interest, and liked what she saw.

"He looks ghastly, doesn't he? Serves him right."

"Are you human?" I said.

A flicker of awareness crossed her lovely face, as if deep down she did indeed know that everything she had enjoyed that night was sinful and obscene, but she was too thoroughly addicted to turn back. "Shall I help you?" she said to Kraye, not answering me.

"No. I can manage. He's not very heavy."

She watched with a smile while her husband gripped the back of the chair I was sitting in and began to tug it across the floor toward the wall. The jerks were almost past bearing. I grew dizzy with the effort of not yelling my head off. There was no one close enough to hear me if I did. Not the few overnight stable lads fast asleep three hundred yards away. Only the Krayes, who would find it sweet.

Doria licked her lips, as if at a feast.

"Go on," said Kraye. "Hurry."

"Oh, all right," she agreed crossly, and went out through the door into the passage.

Kraye finished pulling me across the room, turned the chair round so that I was facing the wall with my knees nearly touching it and stood back, breathing deeply from the exertion.

On the other side of the wall the boiler gently roared. One could hear it more clearly at such close quarters. I knew I had no crashing explosion, no flying bricks, no killing steam to worry about. But the sands were running out fast, all the same.

Doria came back and said in a puzzled voice, "I thought you said there would be water all down the passage."

"That's right."

"Well, there isn't. Not a drop. I looked into the boiler room and it's as dry as a bone."

"It can't be. It's nearly three hours since it started overflowing. Oxon warned us it must be nearly ready to blow. You must be wrong."

"I'm not," she insisted. "The whole thing looks perfectly normal to me."

"It can't be." Kraye's voice was sharp. He went off in a hurry to see for himself, and came back even faster.

"You're right. I'll go and get Oxon. I don't know how the confounded thing works." He went straight on out of the main door, and I heard his footsteps running. There was no urgency except his own anger. I shivered.

Doria wasn't certain enough of the boiler's safety to spend any time near me, which was about the first really good thing which had happened the whole night. Nor did she find the back of my head worth speaking to: she liked to see her worms squirm. Perhaps she had even lost her appetite, now things had gone wrong. She waited uneasily near the door for Kraye to come back, fiddling with the catch.

Oxon came with him, and they were both running. They charged across the weighing room and out into the passage.

I hadn't much left anyway, I thought. A few tatters of pride, perhaps. Time to nail them to the mast.

The two men walked softly into the room and down to where I

sat. Kraye grasped the chair and swung it violently round. The weighing room was quiet, undisturbed. There was only blackness through the window. So that was that.

I looked at Kraye's face, and wished on the whole that I hadn't. It was white and rigid with fury. His eyes were two black pits.

Oxon held the mouse in his hand. "It must have been Halley," he said, as if he'd said it before. "There's no one else."

Kraye put his right hand down on my left, and systematically began to take his revenge. After three long minutes I passed out.

I clung to the dark, trying to hug it round me like a blanket, and it obstinately got thinner and thinner, lighter and lighter, noisier and noisier, more and more painful, until I could no longer deny that I was back in the world.

My eyes unstuck themselves against my will.

The weighing room was full of people. People in dark uniforms. Policemen. Policemen coming through every door. Bright yellow lights at long last shining outside the window. Policemen carefully cutting the rope away from my leaden limbs.

Kraye and Doria and Oxon looked smaller, surrounded by the dark blue men. Doria in her brave white suit instinctively and unsuccessfully tried to flirt with her captors. Oxon, disconcerted to his roots, faced the facts of life for the first time.

Kraye's fury wasn't spent. His eyes stared in hatred across the room.

He shouted, struggling in strong restraining arms, "Where did you send him? Bolt. Where did you send him?"

"Ah, Mr. Potter," I said into a sudden oasis of silence. "Mr. Wilbur Potter. Find out. But not from me."

19

Of course I ended up where I had begun, flat on my back in a hospital. But not for so long, that time. I had a pleasant sunny room with a distant view of the sea, some exceedingly pretty nurses and a whole stream of visitors. Chico came first, as soon as they would let him, on the Sunday afternoon.

He grinned down at me.

"You look bloody awful."

"Thanks very much."

"Two black eyes, a scabby lip, a purple and yellow complexion and a three-day beard. Glamorous."

"It sounds it."

"Do you want to look?" he asked, picking up a hand mirror from a chest of drawers.

I took the mirror and looked. He hadn't exaggerated. I would have faded into the background in a horror movie.

Sighing, I said, "X certificate, definitely."

He laughed, and put the mirror back. His own face still bore the marks of battle. The eyebrow was healing, but the bruise showed dark right down his cheek.

"This is a better room than you had in London," he remarked, strolling over to the window. "And it smells O.K. For a hospital, that is."

"Pack in the small talk and tell me what happened," I said.

"They told me not to tire you."

"Don't be an ass."

"Well, all right. You're a bloody rollicking nit in many ways, aren't you?"

"It depends how you look at it," I agreed peaceably.

"Oh sure, sure."

"Chico, give," I pleaded. "Come on."

"Well, there I was harmlessly snoozing away in Radnor's armchair with the telephone on one side and some rather good chicken sandwiches on the other, dreaming about a willing blonde and having a ball, when the front doorbell rang." He grinned. "I got up, stretched and went to answer it. I thought it might be you, come back after all and with nowhere to sleep. I knew it wouldn't be Radnor, unless he'd forgotten his key. And who else would be knocking on his door at two o'clock in the morning? But there was this fat geezer standing on the doorstep in his city pin-stripes, saying you'd sent him. 'Come in, then,' I said, yawning my head off. He came in, and I showed him into Radnor's sort of study place, where I'd been sitting.

"'Sid sent you?' I asked him. 'What for?' He said he understood your girl friend lived here. God, mate, don't ever try snapping your mouth shut at the top of a yawn. I nearly dislocated my jaw. Could he see her, he said. Sorry it was so late, but it was extremely important.

"'She isn't here,' I said. 'She's gone away for a few days. Can I help you?'

"'Who are you?' he said, looking me up and down.

"I said I was her brother. He took a sharpish look at the sandwiches and the book I'd been reading, which had fallen on the floor, and he could see I'd been asleep, so he seemed to think everything was O.K., and he said, 'Sid asked me to fetch something she is keeping for him. Do you think you could help me find it?'

"'Sure,' I said. 'What is it?'

"He hesitated a bit but he could see that it would look too weird if he refused to tell me, so he said, 'It's a packet of negatives. Sid said your sister had several things of his, but the packet I want has a name on it, a make of films. Jigoro Kano.'

"'Oh?' I said innocently. 'Sid sent you for a packet marked Jigoro Kano?'

"'That's right,' he said, looking round the room. 'Would it be in here?'

"'It certainly would,' I said."

Chico stopped, came over beside the bed, and sat on the edge of it, by my right toe.

"How come you know about Jigoro Kano?" he said seriously.

"He invented judo," I said. "I read it somewhere."

Chico shook his head. "He didn't really invent it. In 1882 he took all the best bits of hundreds of versions of jujitsu and put them into a formal sort of order, and called it judo."

"I was sure you would know," I said, grinning at him.

"You took a very sticky risk."

"You had to know. After all, you're an expert. And there were all those years at your club. No risk. I knew you'd know. As long as I'd got the name right, that is. Anyway, what happened next?"

Chico smiled faintly.

"I tied him into a couple of knots. Armlocks and so on. He was absolutely flabbergasted. It was really rather funny. Then I put a bit of pressure on. You know. The odd thumb screwing down onto a nerve. God, you should have heard him yell. I suppose he thought he'd wake the neighbors, but you know what London is. No one took a blind bit of notice. So then I asked him where you were, when you sent him. He didn't show very willing, I must say, so I gave him a bit more. Poetic justice, wasn't it, considering what they'd just been doing to you? I told him I could keep it up all night, I'd hardly begun. There was a whole bookful I hadn't touched on. It shook him, it shook him bad."

Chico stood up restlessly and walked about the room.

"You know?" he said wryly. "He must have had a lot to lose. He was a pretty tough cookie, I'll give him that. If I hadn't been sure that you'd sent him to me as a sort of S.O.S., I don't think I'd have had the nerve to hurt him enough to bust him."

"I'm sorry," I said.

He looked at me thoughtfully. "We both learned about it, didn't we? You on the receiving end, and me . . . I didn't like it. Doing it, I mean. I mean, the odd swipe or two and a few threats, that's usually enough, and it doesn't worry you a bit, you don't give it a second thought. But I've never hurt anyone like that before. Not seriously, on purpose, beyond bearing. He was crying, you see. . . ."

Chico turned his back to me, looking out of the window.

There was a long pause. The moral problems of being on the receiving end were not so great, I thought. It was easier on the conscience altogether.

At last Chico said, "He told me, of course. In the end."

"Yes."

"I didn't leave a mark on him, you know. Not a scratch. . . . He said you were at Seabury Racecourse. Well, I knew that was probably right, and that he wasn't trying the same sort of misdirection you had, because you'd told me yourself that you were going there. He said that you were in the weighing room and that the boiler would soon blow up. He said that he hoped it would kill you. He seemed half out of his mind with rage about you. How he should have known better than to believe you, he should have realized that you were as slippery as a snake, he'd been fooled once before. . . . He said he'd taken it for granted you were telling the truth when you broke down and changed your story about the negatives being in the office, because you . . . because you were begging for mercy and morphine and God knows what."

"Yes," I said. "I know all about that."

Chico turned away from the window, his face lightening into a near grin. "You don't say," he said.

"He wouldn't have believed it if I'd given in sooner, or less thoroughly. Kraye would have, but not him. It was very annoying."

"Annoying," said Chico. "I like that word." He paused, considering. "At what moment exactly did you think of sending Bolt to me?"

"About half an hour before they caught me," I admitted. "Go on. What happened next?"

"There was a ball of string on Radnor's writing desk, so I tied old Fatso up with that in an uncomfortable position. Then there was the dicey problem of who to ring up to get the rescue squads on the way. I mean, the Seabury police might think I was some sort of a nut, ringing up at that hour and telling such an odd sort of story. At the best, they might send a bobby or two out to have a look, and the Krayes would easily get away. And I reckoned you'd want them rounded up red-handed, so to speak. I couldn't get hold of Radnor on account of the office phones being plasticated. So, well, I rang Lord Hagbourne."

"You didn't!"

"Well, yes. He was O.K., he really was. He listened to what I told him about you and the boiler and the Krayes and so on, and then he said, 'Right,' he'd see that half the Sussex police force turned up at Seabury Racecourse as soon as possible."

"Which they did."

"Which they did," agreed Chico. "To find that my old pal Sid had dealt with the boiler himself, but was otherwise in a fairly ropey state."

"Thanks," I said. "For everything."

"Be my guest."

"Will you do me another favor?"

"Yes, what?"

"I was supposed to take someone out to lunch today. She'll be wondering why I didn't turn up. I'd have got one of the nurses to ring her, but I still don't know her telephone number."

"Are you talking about Miss Zanna Martin? The poor old duck with the disaster area of a face?"

"Yes," I said, surprised.

"Then don't worry. She wasn't expecting you. She knows you're here."

"How?"

"She turned up at Bolt's office yesterday morning, to deal with the mail apparently, and found a policeman waiting on the doorstep with a search warrant. When he had gone she put two and two together smartly and trailed over to Cromwell Road to find out what was going on. Radnor had gone down to Seabury with Lord Hagbourne, but I was there poking about in the ruins, and we sort of swapped info. She was a bit upset about you, mate, in a quiet sort of way. Anyhow, she won't be expecting you to take her out to lunch."

"Did she say anything about having one of our files?"

"Yes. I told her to hang on to it for a day or two. There frankly isn't anywhere in the office to put it."

"All the same, you go over to where she lives as soon as you get back, and collect it. It's the Brinton file. And take great care of it. The negatives Kraye wanted are inside it."

Chico stared. "You're not serious."

"Why not?"

"But everyone—Radnor, Lord Hagbourne, even Kraye and Bolt, and the police—everyone has taken it for granted that what you said first was right, that they were in the office and were blown up."

"It's lucky they weren't," I said. "Get some more prints made. We've still got to find out why they were so hellishly important. And don't tell Miss Martin they were what Kraye wanted."

The door opened and one of the pretty nurses came in.

"I'm afraid you'll have to go now," she said to Chico. She came close beside the bed and took my pulse. "Haven't you any sense?" she exclaimed, looking at him angrily. "A few quiet minutes was what we said. Don't talk too much, and don't let Mr. Halley talk at all."

"You try giving *him* orders," said Chico cheerfully, "and see where it gets you."

"Miss Martin's address," I began.

"No," said the nurse severely. "No more talking."

I told Chico the address.

"See what I mean?" he said to the nurse. She looked down at me and laughed. A nice girl behind the starch.

Chico went across the room and opened the door.

"So long, then, Sid. Oh, by the way, I brought this for you to read. I thought you might be interested."

He pulled a glossy booklet folded lengthwise out of an inner pocket and threw it over onto the bed. It fell just out of my reach, and the nurse picked it up to give it me. Then suddenly she held on to it tight.

"Oh no," she said. "You can't give him that!"

"Why not?" said Chico. "What do you think he is, a baby?"

He went out and shut the door. The nurse clung to the booklet, looking very troubled. I held out my hand for it.

"Come on."

"I think I ought to ask the doctors. . . ."

"In that case," I said, "I can guess what it is. Knowing Chico. So be a dear and hand it over. It's quite all right."

She gave it to me hesitantly, waiting to see my reaction when I caught sight of the bold words on the cover: *Artificial Limbs. The Modern Development.*

I laughed. "He's a realist," I said. "You wouldn't expect him to bring fairy stories."

20

When Radnor came the next day he looked tired, dispirited and ten years older. The military jauntiness had gone from his bearing, there were deep lines around his eyes and mouth, and his voice was lifeless.

For some moments he stared in obvious distress at the white-wrapped arm which stopped abruptly four inches below the elbow.

"I'm sorry about the office," I said.

"For God's sake—"

"Can it be rebuilt? How bad is it?"

"Sid—"

"Are the outside walls still solid, or is the whole place a write-off?"

"I'm too old," he said, giving in, "to start again."

"It's only bricks and mortar that are damaged. You haven't got to start again. The agency is you, not the building. Everyone can work for you just as easily somewhere else."

He sat down in an armchair, rested his head back, and closed his eyes.

"I'm tired," he said.

"I don't suppose you've had much sleep since it happened."

"I am seventy-one," he said flatly.

I was utterly astounded. Until that day I would have put him in the late fifties.

"You can't be."

"Time passes," he said. "Seventy-one."

"If I hadn't suggested going after Kraye it wouldn't have happened," I said with remorse. "I'm so sorry . . . so sorry. . . ."

He opened his eyes. "It wasn't your fault. If it was anyone's it was my own. You wouldn't have let Hagbourne take those photographs to Seabury, if it had been left to you. I know you didn't like it, that I'd given them to him. Letting the photographs go to Seabury was the direct cause of the bombs, and it was my mistake, not yours."

"You couldn't possibly tell," I protested.

"I should have known better, after all these years. I think . . . perhaps I may not see so clearly . . . consequences, things like that." His voice died to a low, miserable murmur. "Because I gave the photographs to Hagbourne, you lost your hand."

"No," I said decisively. "It's ridiculous to start blaming yourself for that. For heaven's sake snap out of it. No one in the agency can afford to have you in this frame of mind. What are Dolly and Jack Copeland and Sammy and Chico and all the others to do if you don't pick up the pieces?"

He didn't answer.

"My hand was useless, anyway," I said. "And if I'd been willing to give in to Kraye I needn't have lost it. It had nothing whatever to do with you."

He stood up.

"You told Kraye a lot of lies," he said.

"That's right."

"But you wouldn't lie to me."

"Naturally not."

"I don't believe you."

"Concentrate on it. It'll come in time."

"You don't show much respect for your elders."

"Not when they behave like bloody fools," I agreed dryly.

He blew down his nostrils, smoldering inwardly. But all he said was, "And you? Will you still work for me?"

"It depends on you. I might kill us all next time."

"I'll take the risk."

"All right then. Yes. But we haven't finished this time, yet. Did Chico get the negatives?"

"Yes. He had two sets of prints done this morning. One for him, and he gave me one to bring to you. He said you'd want them, but I didn't think—"

"But you did bring them?" I urged.

"Yes, they're outside in my car. Are you sure—?"

"For heaven's sake," I said in exasperation. "I can hardly wait."

By the following day I had acquired several more pillows, a bedside telephone and a reputation for being a difficult patient.

The agency restarted work that morning, squeezing into Radnor's own small house. Dolly rang to say it was absolute hell, there was only one telephone instead of thirty, the blitz spirit was fortunately in operation, not to worry about a thing, there was a new word going round the office, it was Halley-lujah, and good-bye, someone else's turn now.

Chico rang a little later from a call box.

"Sammy found that driver, Smith," he said. "He went to see him in Birmingham yesterday. Now that Kraye's in jug Smith is willing to turn Queen's evidence. He agreed that he did take two hundred and fifty quid, just for getting out of his cab, unclipping the chains when the tanker had gone over, and sitting on the side of the road moaning and putting on an act. Nice easy money."

"Good," I said.

"But that's not all. The peach of it is he still has the money, most of it, in a tin box, saving it for a deposit on a house. That's what tempted him, apparently, needing money for a house. Anyway, Kraye paid him the second installment in tenners, from one of the blocks you photographed in his case. Smith still has one of the actual tenners in the pictures. He agreed to part with that for evidence, but I can't see anyone making him give the rest back, can you?"

"Not exactly!"

"So we've got Kraye nicely tied up on malicious damage."

"That's terrific," I said. "What are they holding him on now?"

"Gross bodily harm. And the others for aiding and abetting."

"Consecutive sentences, I trust."

"You'll be lucky."

I sighed. "All the same, he still owns twenty-three per cent of Seabury's shares."

"So he does," agreed Chico gloomily.

"How bad exactly is the office?" I asked.

"They're surveying it still. The outside walls look all right, it's just a case of making sure. The inside was pretty well gutted."

"We could have a better layout," I said. "And a lift."

"So we could," he said happily. "And I'll tell you something else which might interest you."

"What?"

"The house next door is up for sale."

I was asleep when Charles came in the afternoon, and he watched me wake up, which was a pity. The first few seconds of consciousness were always the worst: I had the usual hellish time, and when I opened my eyes, there he was.

"Good God, Sid," he said in alarm. "Don't they give you anything?"

I nodded, getting a firmer grip on things.

"But with modern drugs, surely . . . I'm going to complain."

"No."

"But Sid—"

"They do what they can, I promise you. Don't look so upset. It'll get better in a few days. Just now it's a bore, that's all. Tell me about Fred."

Fred had already been at the house when the police guard arrived at Aynsford. Four policemen had gone there, and it took all four to hold him, with Charles going back and helping as well.

"Did he do much damage?" I asked. "Before the police got there?"

"He was very methodical, and very quick. He had been right through my desk, and all the wardroom. Every envelope, folder and notebook had been ripped apart, and the debris was all in a heap, ready to be destroyed. He'd started on the dining room when the police arrived. He was very violent. And they found a box of plastic explosive lying on the hall table, and some more out in the van." He paused. "What made you think he would come?"

"They knew I took the photographs at Aynsford, but how would they know I got them developed in London? I was afraid they might think I'd had them done locally, and that they'd think you'd know where the negatives were, as it was you who inveigled Kraye down there in the first place."

He smiled mischievously. "Will you come to Aynsford for a few days when you get out of here?"

"I've heard that somewhere before," I said. "No thanks."

"No more Krayes," he promised. "Just a rest."

"I'd like to, but there won't be time. The agency is in a dicky state. And I've just been doing to my boss what you did to me at Aynsford."

"What's that?"

"Kicking him out of depression into action."

His smile twisted in amusement.

"Do you know how old he is?" I said.

"About seventy, why?"

I was surprised. "I'd no idea he was that age, until he told me yesterday."

Charles squinted at the tip of his cigar. He said, "You always thought I asked him to give you a job, didn't you? And guaranteed your wages."

I made a face at him, embarrassed.

"You may care to know it wasn't like that at all. I didn't know him personally, only by name. He sought me out one day in the club and asked me if I thought you'd be any good at working with him. I said yes, I thought you would. Given time."

"I don't believe it."

He smiled. "I told him you played a fair game of chess. Also that you had become a jockey simply through circumstances, because you were small and your mother died, and that you could probably succeed at something else just as easily. He said that from what he'd seen of you racing you were the sort of chap he needed. He told me then how old he was. That's all. Nothing else. Just how old he was. But we both understood what he was saying."

"I nearly threw it away," I said. "If it hadn't been for you—"

"Oh yes," he said wryly. "You have a lot to thank me for. A lot."

Before he went I asked him to look at the photographs, but he studied them one by one and handed them back shaking his head.

Chief Inspector Cornish rang up to tell me Fred was not only in the bag but sewn up.

"The bullets match all right. He drew the same gun on the men who arrested him, but one of them fortunately threw a vase at him and knocked it out of his hand before he could shoot."

"He was a fool to keep that gun after he had shot Andrews."

"Stupid. Crooks often are, or we'd never catch them. And he didn't mention his little murder to Kraye and the others, so they can't be pinched as accessories to that. Pity. But it's quite clear he kept it quiet. The Sussex force said that Kraye went berserk when he found out. Apparently he mostly regretted not having known about your stomach while he had you in his clutches."

"Thank God he didn't!" I exclaimed with feeling.

Cornish's chuckle came down the wire. "Fred was supposed to look for Brinton's letter at your agency himself, but he wanted to go to a football match up north or something, and sent Andrews instead. He said he didn't think there'd be a trap, or anything subtle like that. Just an errand, about on Andrews' level. He said he only lent him the gun for a lark, he didn't mean Andrews to use it, didn't think he'd be so silly. But then Andrews went back to him scared stiff and said he'd shot you, so Fred says he suggested a country ramble in Epping Forest and the gun went off by accident. I ask you, try that on a jury! Fred says he didn't tell Kraye because he was afraid of him."

"What! Fred afraid?"

"Kraye seems to have made an adverse impression on him."

"Yes, he's apt to do that," I said.

I read Chico's booklet from cover to cover. One had to thank the thalidomide children, it appeared, for the speed-up of modern techniques. As soon as my arm had properly healed I could have a versatile gas-powered tool-hand with a swiveling wrist, activated by small pistons and controlled by valves, and operated by my shoulder muscles. The main snag to that, as far as I could gather, was that one always had to carry the small gas cylinders about, strapped on, like a permanent skin diver.

Much more promising, almost fantastic, was the latest invention of British and Russian scientists, the myo-electric arm. This worked entirely by harnessing the tiny electric currents generated in one's own remaining muscles, and the booklet cheerfully said it was easiest to fit on someone whose amputation was recent. The less one had lost of a limb, the better were one's chances of success. That put me straight in the guinea seats.

Finally, said the booklet with a justifiable flourish of trumpets, at St. Thomas' Hospital they had invented a miraculous new myo-electric hand which could do practically everything a real one could except grow nails.

I missed my real hand, there was no denying it. Even in its deformed state it had had its uses, and I suppose that any loss of so integral a part of oneself must prove a radical disturbance. My unconscious mind did its best to reject the facts: I dreamed each night that I was whole, riding races, tying knots, clapping—anything which required two hands. I awoke to the frustrating stump.

The doctors agreed to inquire from St. Thomas' how soon I could go there.

On Wednesday morning I rang up my accountant and asked when he had a free day. Owing to an unexpected cancellation of plans, he said, he would be free on Friday. I explained where I was and roughly what had happened. He said that he would come to see me, he didn't mind the journey, a breath of sea air would do him good.

As I put the telephone down my door opened and Lord Hagbourne and Mr. Fotherton came tentatively through it. I was sitting on the edge of the bed in a dark blue dressing gown, my feet in slippers, my arm in a cradle inside a sling, chin freshly shaved, hair brushed, and the marks of Kraye's fists fading from my face. My visitors were clearly relieved at these encouraging signs of revival, and relaxed comfortably into the armchairs.

"You're getting on well, then, Sid?" said Lord Hagbourne.

"Yes, thank you."

"Good, good."

"How did the meeting go?" I asked. "On Saturday?"

Both of them seemed faintly surprised at the question.

"Well, you did hold it, didn't you?" I said anxiously.

"Why, yes," said Fotherton. "We did. There was a moderately good gate, thanks to the fine weather." He was a thin, dry man with a long face molded into drooping lines of melancholy, and on that morning he kept smoothing three fingers down his cheek as if he were nervous.

Lord Hagbourne said, "It wasn't only your security men who were drugged. The stable lads all woke up feeling muzzy, and the old man who was supposed to look after the boiler was asleep on the floor in the canteen. Oxon had given them all a glass of beer. Naturally, your men trusted him."

I sighed. One couldn't blame them too much. I might have drunk with him myself.

"We had the inspector in yesterday to go over the boiler thoroughly," said Lord Hagbourne. "It was nearly due for its regular check anyway. They said it was too old to stand much interference with its normal working, and that it was just as well it hadn't been put to the test. Also that they thought that it wouldn't have taken as long as three hours to blow up. Oxon was only guessing."

"Charming," I said.

"I sounded out Seabury council," said Lord Hagbourne. "They're putting the racecourse down on their agenda for next month. Apparently a friend of yours, the manager of the Seafront Hotel, has started a petition in the town urging the council to take an interest in the racecourse on the grounds that it gives a seaside town prestige and free advertising and is good for trade."

"That's wonderful," I said, very pleased.

Fotherton cleared his throat, looked hesitantly at Lord Hagbourne, and then at me.

"It has been discussed . . . ," he began. "It has been decided to ask you if you . . . er . . . would be interested in taking on . . . in becoming clerk of the course at Seabury."

"Me?" I exclaimed, my mouth falling open in astonishment.

"It's getting too much for me, being clerk of two courses," he said, admitting it a year too late.

"You saved the place on the brink of the grave," said Lord Hagbourne with rare decisiveness. "We all know it's an unusual step to offer a clerkship to a professional jockey so soon after he's retired, but Seabury executive are unanimous. They want you to finish the job."

They were doing me an exceptional honor. I thanked them, and hesitated, and asked if I could think it over.

"Of course, think it over," said Lord Hagbourne. "But say yes."

I asked them then to have a look at the box of photographs, which they did. They both scrutinized each print carefully, one by one, but they could suggest nothing at the end.

Miss Martin came to see me the next afternoon, carrying some enormous, sweet-smelling bronze chrysanthemums. A transformed Miss Martin, in a smart dark-green tweed suit and shoes chosen for looks more than sturdy walking. Her hair had been restyled so that it was shorter and curved in a bouncy curl onto her cheek. She had even tried a little lipstick and powder, and had tidied her eyebrows into a shapely line. The scars were just as visible, the facial muscles as wasted as ever, but Miss Martin had come to terms with them at last.

"How super you look," I said truthfully.

She was embarrassed, but very pleased. "I've got a new job. I had an interview yesterday, and they didn't even seem to notice my face. Or at least they didn't say anything. In a bigger office, this time. A good bit more than I've earned before, too."

"How splendid," I congratulated her sincerely.

"I feel new," she said.

"I too."

"I'm glad we met." She smiled, saying it lightly. "Did you get that file back all right? Your young Mr. Barnes came to fetch it."

"Yes, thank you."

"Was it important?"

"Why?"

"He seemed very odd when I gave it to him. I thought he was going to tell me something about it. He kept starting to, and then he didn't."

I would have words with Chico, I thought.

"It was only an ordinary file," I said. "Nothing to tell."

On the off-chance, I got her to look at the photographs. Apart from commenting on the many examples of her own typing, and expressing surprise that anybody should have bothered to photograph such ordinary papers, she had nothing to say.

She rose to go, pulling on her gloves. She still automatically leaned forward slightly, so that the curl swung down over her cheek.

"Good-bye, Mr. Halley. And thank you for changing everything for me. I'll never forget how much I owe you."

"We didn't have that lunch," I said.

"No." She smiled, not needing me any more. "Never mind. Some other time." She shook hands. "Good-bye."

She went serenely out of the door.

"Good-bye, Miss Martin," I said to the empty room. "Good-bye, good-bye, good-bye." I sighed sardonically at myself, and went to sleep.

Noel Wayne came loaded on Friday morning with a bulging briefcase of papers. He had been my accountant ever since I began earning big money at eighteen, and he probably knew more about me than anyone else on earth. Nearly sixty, bald except for a gray fringe over the ears, he was a small, round man with alert black eyes and a slow-moving mills-of-God mind. It was his advice more than my knowledge which had turned my earnings into a modest fortune via the stock markets, and I seldom did anything of any importance financially without consulting him first.

"What's up?" he said, coming straight to the point as soon as he had taken off his overcoat and scarf.

I walked over to the window and looked out. The weather had broken. It was drizzling, and a fine mist lay over the distant sea.

"I've been offered a job," I said. "Clerk of the course at Seabury."

"No!" he said, as astonished as I had been. "Are you going to accept?"

"It's tempting," I said. "And safe."

He chuckled behind me. "Good. So you'll take it."

"A week ago I definitely decided not to do any more detecting."

"Ah."

"So I want to know what you think about me buying a partnership in Radnor's agency."

He checked.

"I didn't think you even liked the place."

"That was a month ago. I've changed since then. And I won't be changing back. The agency is what I want."

"But has Radnor *offered* a partnership?"

"No. I think he might have eventually, but not since someone let a bomb off in the office. He's hardly likely to ask me to buy a half share of the ruins. And he blames himself for this." I pointed to the sling.

"With reason?"

"No," I said rather gloomily. "I took a risk which didn't come off."

"Which was?"

"Well, if you need it spelled out, that Kraye would only hit hard enough to hurt, not to damage beyond repair."

"I see." He said it calmly, but he looked horrified. "And do you intend to take similar risks in future?"

"Only if necessary."

"You always said the agency didn't do much crime work," he protested.

"It will from now on, if I have anything to do with it. Crooks make too much misery in the world." I thought of the poor Dunstable Brinton. "And listen, the house next door is for sale. We could knock the two into one. Radnor's is bursting at the seams. The agency has expanded a lot even in the two years I've been there. There seems more and more demand for his sort of service. Then the head of Bona Fides, that's one of the departments, is a natural to expand as an employment consultant on the management level. He has a gift for it. And insurance—Radnor's always neglected that. We don't have an insurance investigation department. I'd like to start one. Suspect insurance claims, you know. There's a lot of work in that."

"You're sure Radnor will agree, if you suggest a partnership?"

"He may kick me out. I'd risk it though. What do you think?"

"I think you've gone back to how you used to be," he said thoughtfully. "Which is good. Nothing but good. But . . . well, tell me what you really think about that." He nodded at my chopped-off arm. "None of your flippant lies, either. The truth."

I looked at him and didn't answer.

"It's only a week since it happened," he said, "and as you still look the color of a grubby sheet I suppose it's hardly fair to ask. But I want to know."

I swallowed. There were some truths which really couldn't be told. I said instead, "It's gone. Gone, like a lot of other things I used to have. I'll live without it."

"Live, or exist?"

"Oh live, definitely. Live." I reached for the booklet Chico had brought, and flicked it at him. "Look."

He glanced at the cover and I saw the faint shock in his face. He didn't have Chico's astringent brutality. He looked up and saw me smiling.

"All right," he said soberly. "Yes. Invest your money in yourself."

"In the agency," I said.

"That's what I mean," he said. "In the agency. In yourself."

He said he'd need to see the agency's books before a definite figure could be reached, but we spent an hour discussing the maximum he thought I should prudently offer Radnor, what return I could hope for in salary and dividends, and what I should best sell to raise the sum once it was agreed.

When we had finished I trotted out once more the infuriating photographs.

"Look them over, will you?" I said. "I've shown them to everyone else without result. These photographs were the direct cause of the bombs in my flat and the office, and of me losing my hand, and I can't see why. It's driving me ruddy well mad."

"The police . . . ," he suggested.

"The police are only interested in the one photograph of a ten-pound note. They looked at the others, said they could see nothing significant, and gave them back to Chico. But Kraye couldn't have been worried about that bank note, it was ten thousand to one we'd come across it again. No, it's something else. Something not obviously criminal, something Kraye was prepared to go to any lengths to obliterate immediately. Look at the time factor. Oxon only pinched the photographs just before lunch, down at Seabury. Kraye lived in London. Say Oxon rang him and told him to come and look: Oxon couldn't leave Seabury, it was a race day. Kraye had to go to Seabury himself. Well, he went down and looked at the photographs and saw . . . what? What? My flat was being searched by five o'clock."

Noel nodded in agreement. "Kraye was desperate. Therefore there was something to be desperate about." He took the photographs and studied them one by one.

Half an hour later he looked up and stared blankly out the window at the wet, gray skies. For several minutes he stayed completely still, as if in a state of suspended animation: it was his way of concentrated thinking. Finally he stirred and sighed. He moved his short neck as if it were stiff, and lifted the top photograph off the pile.

"This must be the one," he said.

I nearly snatched it out of his hand.

"But it's only the summary of the share transfers," I said in disappointment. It was the sheet headed S.R., Seabury Racecourse, which listed in summary form all Kraye's purchases of Seabury shares. The only noticeable factor in what had seemed to me merely a useful at-a-glance view of his total holding, was that it had been typed on a different typewriter, and not by Miss Martin. This hardly seemed enough reason for Kraye's hysteria.

"Look at it carefully," said Noel. "The three left-hand columns you can disregard, because I agree they are simply a tabulation of the share transfers, and I can't see any discrepancies."

"There aren't," I said. "I checked that."

"How about the last column, the small one on the right?"

"The banks?"

"The banks."

"What about them?" I said.

"How many different ones are there?"

I looked down the long list, counting. "Five. Barclays, Piccadilly. Westminster, Birmingham. British Linen Bank, Glasgow. Lloyds, Doncaster. National Provincial, Liverpool."

"Five bank accounts, in five different towns. Perfectly respectable. A very sensible arrangement in many ways. He can move round the country and always have easy access to his money. I myself have accounts in three different banks: it avoids muddling my clients' affairs with my own."

"I know all that. I didn't see any significance in his having several accounts. I still don't."

"Hm," said Noel. "I think it's very likely that he has been evading income tax."

"Is that all?" I said disgustedly.

Noel looked at me in amusement, pursing his lips. "You don't understand in the least, I see."

"Well, for heaven's sake, you wouldn't expect a man like Kraye to pay up every penny he was liable for like a good little citizen."

"You wouldn't," agreed Noel, grinning broadly.

"I'll agree he might be worried. After all, they sent Al Capone to jug in the end for tax evasion. But over here, what's the maximum sentence?"

"He'd only get a year, at the most," he said, "but—"

"And he would have been sure to get off with a fine. Which he won't do now, after attacking me. Even so, for that he'll only get three or four years, I should think, and less for the malicious damage. He'll be out and operating again far too soon. Bolt, I suppose, will be struck off, or whatever it is with stockbrokers."

"Stop talking," he said, "and listen. While it's quite normal to have more than one bank account, an inspector of taxes, having agreed to your tax liability, may ask you to sign a document stating that you have disclosed to him *all* your bank accounts. If you fail to mention one or two, it constitutes a fraud, and if you are discovered you can then be prosecuted. So, suppose Kraye has signed such a document, omitting one or two or even three of the five accounts? And then he finds a photograph in existence of his most private papers, listing all five accounts as undeniably his?"

"But no one would have noticed," I protested.

"Quite. Probably not. But to him it must have seemed glaringly dangerous. Guilty people constantly fear their guilt will be visible to others. They're vibratingly sensitive to anything which can give them away. I see quite a lot of it in my job."

"Even so, bombs are pretty drastic."

"It would entirely depend on the sum involved," he said primly.

"Huh?"

"The maximum fine for income tax evasion is twice the tax you didn't pay. If, for example, you amassed ten thousand pounds but declared only two, you could be fined a sum equal to twice the tax on eight thousand pounds. With surtax and so on, you might be left with almost nothing. A nasty setback."

"To put it mildly," I said in awe.

"I wonder," Noel said thoughtfully, putting the tips of his fingers together, "just how much undeclared loot Kraye has got stacked away in his five bank accounts?"

"It must be a lot," I said, "for bombs."

"Quite so."

There was a long silence. Finally I said, "One isn't required either legally or morally to report people to the Inland Revenue."

He shook his head.

"But we could make a note of those five banks, just in case?"

"If you like," he agreed.

"Then I think I might let Kraye have the negatives and the new sets of prints," I said. "Without telling him I know why he wants them."

Noel looked at me inquiringly, but didn't speak.

I grinned faintly. "On condition that he makes a free, complete and outright gift to Seabury Racecourse Company of his twenty-three per cent holding."